Return to Valhalla

Oct. 2012

Return to Valhalla

by
mike whicker

a Walküre imprint

This is a work of historical fiction

ISBN: 978-0-9844160-6-6

printed in the United States of America

FOREWORD

It is elementary for intelligence professionals to *"find, know and never lose the enemy"* (our creed). In conflict, time is a variable where hindsight leaves more to regret than it does to favor. It is the role of intelligence to execute before the attack and, should time be unforgiving, to be as cunning and intolerant as the enemy faced.

In his Erika Lehmann World War II spy trilogy that ends with *Return to Valhalla,* Mike Whicker superbly recognizes several assets the intelligence community relied on during WWII. Through portraying intelligence collection from all sides of the conflict, Whicker establishes the fact that there were no definitive enemy lines. Imagery intelligence through the study of aerial photographs identified the target. Weapons intelligence prepared them for what they would face. Communications intelligence through Morse code intercept pointed them in the right direction. Counterintelligence operations told them how to keep sensitive information out of enemy hands. Clandestine operations and espionage led the chase and the extensive use of broadcast propaganda at times led them astray.

Whicker accurately exposes the significant roles of both military and civilian intelligence agencies in their infantile, yet profound beginnings. The astute depth of his research combined with his unparalleled ability to coalesce fiction with history keeps you on the edge of your seat throughout the trilogy. Through the American OSS, the British SOE, and the German Abwehr, Whicker makes the reader intimate with the realities of the battlefield; opening eyes to the fact that intelligence drives operations.

Entrapped by both the lure of history and realities of the battlefield, *Return to Valhalla* stimulates the reader's emotions and mind for an adventure not easily forgotten. Only through the plot Mike Whicker provides can the reader begin to realize they were missing a crucial piece of the puzzle the entire time. It is then that hindsight pays a visit.

— Patrick Hulin
Human Intelligence Collector/Interrogator
4 tours – Operation Iraqi Freedom
Interrogation Instructor
U.S. Army Military Intelligence Headquarters,
Fort Huachuca, Arizona

— Savannah Hulin
Military Intelligence Analyst
3 tours – Operation Iraqi Freedom
Military Intelligence Instructor,
U.S. Army Military Intelligence HQ,
Fort Huachuca, Arizona

Für

Josh & Erin
Aya & Paul
Zach & Abby
Van & Pat
Kel & Tim

World War II Acronyms and Organizations

American
- **OSS** – Office of Strategic Services (WW II forerunner of the CIA)

British
- **BSC** – British Security Coordination
- **FANY** – First Aid Nursing Yeomanry
- *Intrepid* – codename for William Stephenson, head of the WW2 SIS
- **MI-6, MI-9** – British military intelligence organizations within the SIS
- **RAF** – Royal Air Force
- **SIS** – Secret Intelligence Service (oversaw all sectors of British Secret Service)
- **SOE** – Special Operations Executive, a super secret organization commissioned by Winston Churchill to insert agents behind German lines to disrupt and sabotage enemy operations
- **STS** – Special Training School, secret camps in England, Scotland and Canada where SOE agents were trained
- **WAAF** – Women's Auxiliary Air Force

German
- **Abwehr** – Abwehrabteilung, German military intelligence
- **BND** – post-WW2 German intelligence organization, equivalent to America's CIA
- **Gestapo** – the Geheime Staatspolizei, secret police
- **Heer** – German army
- **Kriegsmarine** – German navy
- **Kripo** – civilian police
- **Leibstandarte-SS** – (LSSAH) elite of the SS and Hitler's personal bodyguards
- **Luftwaffe** – German air force
- **OKW** – Oberkomando der Wehrmacht, high command of the German military
- **RSHA** – Reich Main Security Office, established by Heinrich Himmler to coordinate efforts among the SS, SD, Gestapo and Kripo
- **SD** – Sicherheitsdienst, intelligence branch of the SS, separate from Abwehr
- **SS** – Schutzstaffel, a para-military organization
- **Totenkopf-SS** – "Death's Head" division of the SS, responsible for the concentration camps
- **Waffen SS** – the front line fighting divisions of the SS
- **Wehrmacht** – German military (includes army, navy, air force)
- **Volkssturm** – a German civilian organization that performed various duties on the German homefront in support of the military

German Military, SS, and Gestapo Ranks and American Equivalent

(ranks referenced in *Return to Valhalla*)

Military (starting at highest rank referred to)
- **Oberst** – colonel, army or air force
- **Korvettenkapitän** – lieutenant commander, navy
- **Oberleutnant** – first lieutenant, army or air force
- **Oberleutnant zur See** – ensign, navy
- **Oberstabsführerin** – women's auxiliary rank equal to a first lieutenant
- **Oberscharführer** – sergeant first class, army or air force
- **Unterfeldwebel** – sergeant, army or air force
- **Oberschutze** – private first class, army or air force

SS
- **Gruppenführer** – lieutenant general
- **Oberführer** – major general
- **Obersturmbannführer** – lieutenant colonel
- **Sturmbannführer** – major
- **Hauptsturmführer** – captain
- **Untersturmbannführer** – second lieutenant
- **Oberscharführer** – sergeant major
- **Scharführer** – staff sergeant

Gestapo (approximate equivalents)
- **Kriminalrat** – major
- **Kriminalkommissar** – captain
- **Kriminalsekretät** – lieutenant

Abwehr
- **Sonderführer** – meaning "special leader," a rank within Abwehr usually given to that organization's spies

Prologue

The Fruit Girl

1938—June
Sicily—Messina

Giovanni Bagarella avoided routines. Wise for a man in his position, he knew. Even at the Buono Mangia Café on the Piazza Duomo his visits were scheduled to *avoid* being on schedule. But his brother-in-law owned Buono Mangia, and occasional sightings of Bagarella enjoying an espresso was good for the café's business, and what helped his brother-in-law's café helped his brother-in-law's wife—Bagarella's sister. And after all, the Buono Mangia served the best espresso in Messina, so Bagarella made sporadic, out-of-the-blue appearances.

But always with his bodyguards. As capo bastone of the Messina La Cosa Nostra, the bodyguards were practical.

His duties as underboss, second in power only to the capo de tutti capi, granted Bagarella many enemies. Satisfying the wishes of the boss of bosses was his job, which on occasion meant eliminating whoever the supreme capo felt needed eliminating—no questions asked. In his younger days, Bagarella had worked hands-on in the murders. Now life was simpler; he had only to give the orders.

Today, the late-morning sea breeze made it perfect for enjoying his coffee alfresco, so Bagarella sat at one of the round, wrought-iron tables in front of the café. This way, those going in or out, or walking by, could more easily pay homage to the capo bastone. One of his bodyguards sat next to him, another stood nearby, and the third walked back and forth along the block patrolling, all armed with double-barreled shotguns. As Bagarella sipped his espresso, he joked with the bodyguard sitting beside him about people on the street. Bagarella pointed to a young woman across the narrow cobblestone avenue selling fruit from a basket to people coming out of a small hotel.

"There is a woman for you, Tomasino," Bagarella said to the bodyguard. "A ripe fruit just right for your picking. And maybe ripe for me, too." Bagarella laughed with the guard. Almost as if the girl heard the conversation, or perhaps the loud laughter, she looked over at the two men and offered a very slight smile, then turned away and resumed hawking her fruit.

A "Buongiorno, Don Bagarella," came from an old man leaving the café. Bagarella nodded to acknowledge the old man's reverence but did not return the greeting. The old man picked up his pace and quickly walked away. Best to pay respects and not linger, the old man knew. One did not risk interfering with the capo bastone's conversation or his enjoyment of the coffee. Others who passed by his table offered similar greetings—respectful but hasty. No one wanted the feared underboss showing them undue interest.

Bagarella sipped coffee and returned his attention to the fruit girl who was now farther down the street. He waved over the standing bodyguard and pointed to the girl. "Salvatore, go tell her I want to buy some fruit." The guard left to fetch the girl and returned with her in short order, she eager to make a sale and stepping quickly. She was barefoot and wore a light brown peasant dress.

"Ciao, kind sir," she greeted pleasantly. "I have apples, grapes and pears. All are very good. None of my fruit has worms or moths."

"I'm sure of that," Bagarella said tongue-in-cheek. "But first you'll sit with us for coffee."

"Thank you, but I don't have the time. I must sell."

The underboss looked at Tomasino, who immediately stood and pulled out a chair for the young woman next to Bagarella. She looked at him and at Bagarella whose friendly expression had now disappeared. She hesitated, but the handsome young bodyguard's smile seemed to reassure her. She sat and placed her basket on her lap. Tomasino, attempting chivalry, reached for the basket.

"No, that's my fruit!" The girl seemed ready to fight for her basket of apples, grapes and pears.

Bagarella thought the girl's reaction amusing and burst out laughing. "Tomasino, what's wrong with you? Trying to steal this young woman's fruit. You'll need confession." He laughed again. With a wave of his hand, he signaled Tomasino to sit back down.

Bagarella gazed at the girl. "Apparently you don't know who I am, young lady. You must not be from around here."

"I'm from Calabria."

"Calabria? You don't have that look." Unlike the dark hair and eyes of most southern Italians, the girl's hair was reddish-brown and eyes green. "What's your name?"

"Tars."

"Tars? Is that a nickname?"

The girl nodded.

"What does your father do in Calabria?"

"He's a coffin maker."

Bagarella looked at Tomasino and laughed loudly. "Maybe we can give him some business, Tomasino!"

The young woman spoke. "I'm sure you can, and in a different way than you think." With that she drew her hands from inside the basket, sprang to her feet and with her right hand buried a stiletto in Bagarella's throat. Blood geysered onto her arm and dress. With her left hand she simultaneously pointed a revolver at Tomasino's chest and pulled the trigger. The bullet knocked the bodyguard off his chair and onto the sidewalk.

Salvatore, the standing bodyguard, swung his shotgun from his shoulder and was raising it to fire at the girl when from across the street a loud rifle crack came from a second-floor hotel window. Salvatore's shotgun discharged into the sidewalk as the bullet spun him around and back into the café's plate-glass window, shattering it. Patrons inside screamed and shouted but they knew what to do. Street killings happened on occasion in Sicily. Those inside the café, including Bagarella's brother-in-law, made a beeline for the back door and high-tailed it down the alley.

By this time, the patrolling bodyguard who had been at the far end of the block when the first shot sounded, sprinted toward the café shotgun in hand. The girl saw him coming and ran into the now empty café to give him the impression she was fleeing, then surprised him by stepping back out of the doorway and firing the five remaining rounds. The fast-moving bodyguard, still a quarter of a block away, was a difficult target for the girl's revolver, but one of the bullets winged the man's hip and he stumbled to the sidewalk. He started to rise, but that brief pause allowed the hotel sniper to get a bead and a bullet exploded the man's head.

The shooting was over.

Bodies, blood, gun smoke, and broken glass glinting in the bright Mediterranean sun now served as sidewalk décor for the Buono Mangia Café. With stiletto in hand, the fruit girl checked Salvatore, whose upper body dangled inside the café window frame while his legs hung outside. He was dead. She walked over to Bagarella, stepping bare-footed into the pool of blood that ran a stream toward the street. With his jugular severed, the underboss had bled out in seconds.

"So, Capo Bastone," she spoke to the dead man, "you begin your journey to Hell with eyes bulging and tongue hanging out. Have a pleasant trip, you pig."

The girl heard a cough behind her and turned quickly. The noise came from Tomasino. She walked over and knelt beside him. The bullet from her revolver had penetrated a lung and nipped his spinal cord; he struggled for breath and could not move.

The fruit girl smiled at him and stroked his hair. "Don't be afraid. I'm here now."

Tomasino gasped in another short breath and looked at her. "Help . . . me."

She leaned over, kissed him, and stuck the stiletto under his rib cage and into his heart while their lips touched. A faint but growing louder police siren could be heard as a man sprinted out of the hotel carrying a long musical instrument case. He rushed over and pulled at the girl's arm.

"Let's go!"

He guided her toward a waiting car, her right arm and much of her dress now dark red. As she ran, her bare feet left bloody footprints on cobblestones. But before she had allowed the man to pull her away, she made sure to grab her fruit.

Part 1

"Since knowledge is but sorrow's spy, it is not safe to know."

— William Davenant
English poet/playwright
1606 - 1668

Chapter 1

The Package

Canada—near the northern shore of Lake Ontario
Thursday, 02 December 1943

A spruce branch clawed at the window as if aching from the cold and seeking refuge from the stiff winter wind. Colonel Humphrey Naylor, his back to the window and the suffering evergreen, sat at his desk eating the fried Spam sandwich he had ordered brought to him so he could continue working. No time to eat in the camp canteen. After one bite, he heard a knock.

"Come in."

A man in a Canadian Army uniform opened the door and entered.

"Sorry to interrupt your lunch, Colonel, but your orders were to notify you immediately when the package arrived."

"So it's here then?"

"Yes, Colonel. It's in number four. The escorts are there as well."

"Tell them I'm on my way, Captain."

"Yes, sir."

As the captain left, Naylor took one more bite of the sandwich then rose and grabbed his long coat from a rack in a corner of his spartan office. Special Training School 103, also known as Camp X, offered no frills and few comforts. Hastily built in 1941, most of the buildings, including the one housing the commandant's office, were simple, wood structures personnel referred to as "doghouses" because of the thin walls that challenged the oil space heaters to keep room temperature bearable during the stout Canadian winters. Naylor walked out into wind that immediately took notice of his hat, doing everything in its power to swat it off his head. The colonel held the hat tight as he trudged through ankle-high snow past the water tower on his way to Building 4. Although still qualifying for doghouse status because of its lean construction, Building 4 was not small. A large T-shaped building, 4 included several offices and rooms of various sizes

1

for a mixture of purposes. When Naylor stepped through the doorway, the captain, two men in business suits, and two uniformed Royal Canadian Mounties were waiting. Naylor immediately noticed the disheveled uniforms of both Mounties, unusual for the always dashing RCMPs. One had a tightly packed piece of cotton extruding from his left nostril—evidence of a fresh bloody nose; the other, a goose egg on his forehead. The Canadian Army captain introduced the men in suits.

"Colonel Naylor, this is Mr. Carr of the American OSS, and this is Mr. Thomas of the British SOE."

"Gentlemen," Naylor said as he shook hands. Although both men wore suits, the OSS man, Carr, was clearly the better dressed. Perhaps in his early to mid-40s, Carr could easily be taken for a lawyer or successful businessman. Thomas, probably a few years younger than Carr, was a tall, dark-haired man with a long, jagged scar under his left eye. He impressed Naylor as having the look of a pub brawler given a cheap suit as a disguise. Naylor looked again at the roughed-up Mounties.

"I see perhaps you had a problem in transit," Naylor commented.

Thomas frowned. "I warned them not to talk to her," he said in a Scots accent. "Sometimes things can be said that are taken in a different way."

Naylor walked over to a metal door—one of the few metal doors in the camp—and slid back a small steel plate the size of a wallet that allowed a view into the other room. Inside a young, blonde woman in a straitjacket sat on a wooden chair facing the door—her head hanging down and her hair a mess. She heard the plate slide, raised her head, and locked eyes with Naylor. She gazed at him with a look that made Naylor feel as if he were the one being scrutinized, not her. He took a moment to look her over then slid the metal plate closed.

"She doesn't look as if she'll be causing us much trouble tonight," Naylor joked. "We'll leave her in the jacket until she comes around and decides to mind her manners."

Carr, the American, laughed as one might at a truly ridiculous statement. "Colonel Naylor, that straitjacket isn't going to hold her,"

Carr cautioned. "If she feels the agreement isn't being kept, she'll burn down this camp and take everyone with it."

It was Naylor's turn to laugh. "Really now, Mr. Carr. A slight exaggeration, wouldn't you say?"

Carr glanced at Thomas.

"She's highly trained, Colonel," said Thomas, "and she has absolutely no fear of dying. You'll do well to keep up your guard."

"You noticed the Mounties," Carr added. "She did that while in handcuffs. One of them got impatient when she refused to respond to a question and uttered what she apparently considered an insult. That little episode was small potatoes for her; they're lucky to be walking. She'll be the cruelest person you've ever dealt with when she feels it's time."

"Feels it's time? What do you mean?" Naylor asked.

"We didn't deliver one package, Colonel; we delivered two," Carr stated flatly. "There are two people in that straitjacket. When the one sitting there now decides the other is needed, you'll know it."

Chapter 2

Operation Trekker

England—High Wycombe (30 miles west of London)
Three weeks later; Thursday, 23 December 1943

A large man of late-middle-age wearing a British Army uniform stepped through a side door to the conference room. Eight other men, all wearing military uniforms except one, and a woman in civilian dress sat at a conference table. When the general entered, they stood.

"Sit down, gentlemen," said Major General William Sanders, ignoring the secretary. "I certainly hope at least one of you has some good news for a change." Impatience in the general's tone was unmistakable; he looked quickly from man to man.

One spoke—a major.

"General Sanders, we found a Women's Land Army nurse working at a military hospital in Southampton. She's very close to the right height. The hair color is a shade darker but we can fix that, of course."

"What color are the eyes?" Sanders asked, impatiently rapping a fountain pen on the dark oak table, a habit he had developed over the past month.

A slight pause while the major adjusted himself in his chair. "Brown . . . just brown I'm afraid, General."

"Goddammit!" Sanders roared and threw down the pen so hard it bounced off the table and onto the floor. "You know the eyes have to be brown and green!" The general looked at a young lieutenant—his aide.

Thinking the general's look signified his help was needed, the aide clarified, "Hazel."

"I know it's called *hazel*, goddammit!" Sanders frowned at the lieutenant, then turned to the major. "Hazel! Yes, we can change hair color but we can't change the bloody eyes, Major!"

4

Sanders stood and moved behind his chair, his hands behind his back. It seemed a good move to the others because the general lowered his voice. "Gentlemen, we've had a month to find a woman. Surely there's a WAAF, a FANY, or some woman in the whole of England who is 5'8", blonde with hazel eyes, and resembles this woman in the face." The general referred to photographs lying on the table with the words OPERATION TREKKER stamped in a corner, photographs all the men in the room had numerous copies of and had studied for hours. There was no need to look them over now.

One of two colonels in the room, Colonel Trinder, spoke up. "General, we've found women within the military and the SIS who fit the bill in various ways but always something is missing. When the eyes match, then it's something else that disqualifies them: they're too short or can't pass for the age—something. I say we use Eileen Nearne. Nearne and Violette Szabo are the most qualified. Nearne has already completed parachute school at Ringway and is at Lord Montague's estate at Beaulieu in the final stages of training as we speak."

The other colonel interjected, "We were told this look-alike we're trying to find doesn't have to be trained to drop."

"I realize that," Trinder shot back. "I'm just saying Nearne has already completed much of the training."

"Szabo looks more like the woman in the photo than Nearne," the other colonel argued.

"Szabo is too short," Trinder replied, then looked back at the general. "Nearne is the correct height. Her eyes aren't the right color, General, but I feel the SIS is making too much of the eye-color requirement. Surely eye color can't make that much difference for this assignment."

The general now spoke calmly. "I might agree with you, Colonel; unfortunately it doesn't matter what we *feel*. The assignment for you men and your staffs is to find a woman with facial characteristics that resemble those of the woman in the photographs; one who is the right height—or very close to it—with blonde hair, hazel eyes, middle-twenties looking with no distinguishing marks other than a knife-wound scar on the inside of her upper right arm and a gunshot-wound scar on the outer left arm. Eye color is a requirement where there are no options. That was made very clear in my meetings with the Admiralty. Yes, we can work with a bit of variety on some of the other requirements: hair color can be adjusted; moles can be removed, the scars can be taken care of quickly with a fillet knife, but there is nothing we can do about eye color. It has to be the same."

The only man in the room wearing a business suit spoke up. He was a member of the Special Operations Executive or SOE, a branch of the SIS—the British Secret Intelligence Service. "General Sanders is right. The eyes have to match. The Jerries will check the eyes straight away. And Nearne will serve a better purpose if she's on the team that trains *Trekker.*"

The general put an end to the discussion—such banter and differences of opinions over the past month's numerous meetings had grown exasperating.

"How many times will we go over this? Neither Nearne or Szabo, nor anyone else this task force has suggested has been acceptable to the Admiralty or the SOE. I don't want to hear any more about Nearne or Szabo. Nearne will be useful as a trainer, I agree, but neither fits the bill to be *Trekker.* I receive orders, too, gentlemen. I was ordered to assemble a task force to find a suitable candidate. You're that task force and you haven't found one. I was forced to go before the First Lord of the Admiralty and ask for an extension. I'm not asking the First Lord for another extension, gentlemen. Your time is running out. I'm giving you until New Year's Eve to find me *Trekker.* That's one week from now. Happy Christmas to you."

The general stalked out through the door he had entered; the others rose and began filing out through a different door. Last to leave were the young lieutenant and the secretary. When the others were out of earshot, she looked up at him and rolled her eyes.

"He becomes more difficult by the hour," she complained, referring to the general.

The lieutenant nodded. "That he does. Bad for you that you got assigned as his personal secretary."

Once outside the conference room, the two walked to the secretary's desk, located just outside the general's office in a large room with many secretaries busy with that day's mountain of wartime paperwork.

"Are we still on for the USO dance tomorrow night, Misty?" the lieutenant asked.

"I'm looking forward to it." She smiled.

"Pick you up at eight o'clock?"

"I'll be ready, Robert."

Chapter 3

The Yanks Waste No Time

England—Fortune Green (7 miles north of London)
Next day; Friday, 24 December 1943

"Thank heaven it's December, Robert. If it were summer it would swelter in here so a body couldn't bear it," Misty Hutchinson said as she and Robert Braxton fought their way through a tight crowd of British and American soldiers with their dates. Or just soldiers if they had no date. Many dances were segregated by rank—some solely for officers, others for enlisted personnel, but at tonight's Christmas Eve dance the two groups rubbed shoulders.

"What did you say?" Braxton shouted. The crowd and shrill band made it nearly impossible to hear.

Misty turned and shouted, "Never mind!" The two walked beneath a *Merry Christmas to Our Troops* banner suspended from the ceiling.

Tonight's dance was sponsored by the American USO and held at what was originally designed to be a military-vehicle parts warehouse but had been abandoned in the fall of 1940 when Hermann Göring switched tactics from bombing RAF bases in more remote parts of England to sending his Luftwaffe over London. Because the drive from High Wycombe took longer than expected, the couple arrived late to find an overflow crowd occupying every table and packing the dance floor. Lieutenant Robert Braxton and Misty Hutchinson, the aide and the personal secretary to General Sanders, finally found a place to stand near a water cooler.

"I'll get us a drink," Braxton half-shouted. "Will ale do?"

Misty nodded and the lieutenant left to elbow his way through the throng. The band finished its song and immediately struck up a fast-paced version of Harry James' *Concerto for Trumpet*. Not missing a beat, the dance crowd whirled in the smoky room. As Misty waited for her date to return, an American G.I. approached and asked her for a dance. The women of England knew it was bad form to turn down a

8

soldier who asked for a dance, especially an American so far from home. A dance was assured if an American asked an English girl. Misty led the G.I. onto the dance floor. Many young American servicemen were skilled swing dancers, often much better than their British counterparts. Misty was twirled until she grew dizzy and laughed.

"Let me catch my breath."

"Okay, baby," said the G.I. He slowed down and took the opportunity to hug her in a tight embrace and place his hands quite low on her hips.

Misty moved his hands up. "You're a naughty one, you are."

He moved his hands back down and she again moved them up. Besides their affinity for dancing, English women knew the Americans had other interests. They were well-known for that, too. After moving the G.I.'s hands a third time only to feel them soon again on her buttocks, Misty gave up and there his hands stayed until the song ended.

"Thank you, ma'am," the bold soldier said politely and smiled. Misty had to grin and shake her head as she left the dance floor. *"Yanks!"*

Holding two paper cups, Braxton waited at their space near the water cooler. The crowd had prevented him from spotting her on the dance floor.

"There you are," he said and handed her a cup of ale.

"An American private asked me to dance."

"The Yanks don't waste any time, do they, love?"

"Certainly not." She thought of the G.I.'s hands.

"You look a bit flushed, Misty. Want to take a stroll outside?"

"That would be lovely."

They quickly finished the small drinks and retrieved their coats from a rack near the front doors before stepping out into the brisk night air. The former warehouse had no windows—perfect for the blackout. The heavy night clouds cast the area in near-total darkness—the only light came from the weak headlamps of an occasional car pulling into the parking area, its beams reduced to an anemic amber glow by the mandated headlamp blackout shrouds required of all vehicles traveling at night.

"Ah, the cold feels lovely," Misty commented, "and the fresh air."

"And we can hear ourselves think," quipped Braxton as he placed his arm around her shoulder.

Misty pulled a pack of cigarettes from her coat pocket and placed one between her lips. With his free hand, Robert found his lighter and held the flame for her. She handed the cigarette to him, then repeated the process with another for her. A few minutes of treasured silence followed, which they both enjoyed after the tumult of the overcrowded warehouse and the past hectic weeks. Misty finally broke the silence.

"What if they don't find someone for Operation Trekker? What will they do?"

The lieutenant hesitated. "I don't know."

"The general is becoming quite out of sorts about the entire affair."

"I do know that much."

"The other day," Misty continued, "he went into a rant because the coffee Celeste brought him had no sugar. The office ran out of this month's allotment of sugar the previous day. You should have seen him. It was awful. He had Celeste in tears."

Braxton shook his head. "That's certainly not right, and it's unlike him, but I know what you mean. He's gotten so testy that the other officers avoid him at all costs unless he summons them; then they enter his office looking like men marching to the gallows. Since he had to go before the First Lord and ask for more time, all else has been put on hold. He's never had to deal with the Admiralty before; the general has always worked with the Imperial General Staff. I think he feels he has to deliver for the sake of the Army's honor when the Royal Navy was given charge of this Trekker business. We're spending all our time trying to find someone who looks like the woman in the photo—everything else be damned. There's so much I should be doing instead."

"I hope someone is found soon. What are the chances do you think?"

"At first I didn't think it would be that difficult, but I was certainly wrong, wasn't I? Now it's not looking good."

They finished the cigarettes and returned to the dance, but a group of soldiers had laid claim to their standing spot near the water cooler. Misty needed the ladies room, which was near the front doors. While waiting for his date, Braxton struck up a conversation with another British lieutenant standing nearby, also holding two drinks.

"Yours must be in the loo, as well," said Braxton.

The other man grinned. "If it's as crowded in there as in the men's we'll be waiting here for a fortnight. Women can't take care of business as quickly as us gents."

Braxton laughed. The man said he was assigned to the 22nd Dragoons and lucky enough to have garnered a brief Christmas leave. Robert told him he was assigned to General Sanders's staff. They stopped at that; any more discussion concerning current duties was prohibited. As they talked, four London policemen entered the nearby doors.

"Must be some trouble," Braxton commented to the Dragoon lieutenant.

"They're probably on tart patrol."

Sure enough, one policeman pointed to a woman drinking with a soldier, letting his partners know he had spotted someone. He walked over to the woman, took her by the arm, and tried to lead her away. She resisted, but he became more forceful and, half dragging, escorted her out the door. The other policemen fanned out to walk the room.

"It's the same girls who seem to work all the dances," said the Dragoon lieutenant. "The bobbies know them all."

The Dragoon lieutenant's date finally emerged from the ladies room. He handed her back her drink and turned to Braxton. "Cheerio, and good luck."

"Cheerio, and good luck to you."

As the couple walked away, Braxton returned his attention to the police and their work but now could see only one of the bobbies in the tight crowd and that one quickly disappeared into the mass. A moment later, Misty walked out of the ladies room with a strange look on her face, almost a look of shock. She returned to his side and said nothing.

"What's the matter, love?"

She didn't answer.

Braxton said, "What do you say we move away from the loo?" He started to lead her away.

"Don't move."

"What do you mean—don't move?"

"Just stand here for a moment, Robert."

"What's the matter, Misty? Did something happen in there?"

"Just wait here for a minute. Watch that door." She nodded toward the door to the ladies room.

"Why?"

Again she didn't answer. In a moment a woman walked out of the door and back into the crowd. Braxton looked at Misty who remained focused on the door. A second woman emerged and joined two other women standing nearby.

"Really, Misty, what's gotten into you?"

As soon as he said that, a third woman, the woman in General Sanders's photographs, walked out of the ladies room.

Chapter 4

The Woman in the Loo

England—Fortune Green
Same evening; Christmas Eve, 1943

Lieutenant Robert Braxton stood drop-jawed as the woman pictured in the Operation Trekker photographs approached.

"My god," he said to Misty. "It's either her or her twin sister."

"Hazel," said Misty.

"What?"

"She stood next to me at the lavatory. I could see her eyes in the mirror. I'm almost certain they're hazel."

As the woman drew near, she noticed the British lieutenant and the woman next to him staring at her but she ignored them and walked on.

Misty reacted before the woman disappeared into the crowd. "Stop her, Robert."

Robert stepped quickly to catch the woman, Misty on his heels.

"Miss!" he said loudly and touched her arm. She stopped, turned, said nothing.

"I, uh . . ." He didn't know quite what to say as the woman gazed at him.

Misty whispered, "She even looks the height." With the din of background noise Robert failed to hear her. Still not sure of the best way to proceed, Robert tried small talk.

"Umm . . . this is Misty Hutchinson; I'm Lieutenant Robert Braxton."

"So?" She looked at them suspiciously.

"May I ask your name, Miss?"

"What's it to you, you British bastard?" The woman's Irish brogue was strong and unmistakable.

Her salty response set him back. "You . . . you're Irish?"

"Fook yuh! Leave me alone. I don't do it with Brits, only Yanks." She looked at Misty. "And I don't do it with the ladies neither, darlin'."

13

At that moment one of the policemen emerged from the crowd. Having been in the ladies room when the police arrived, the woman was unaware of their presence but now spotted the bobby out of the corner of her eye and bolted for the door.

"Stop!" the policeman shouted and took off after her. Robert and Misty stood frozen for a moment, then chased after the policeman.

Outside, the woman tried to run through two policemen stationed just outside the doors. She almost succeeded in getting past them in the dark, but the policeman chasing her with Robert and Misty on his heels emerged from the building just in time to shed light on the area from the open doors. They watched a burly policeman tackle the woman rugby-style. On the ground, the woman kneed the policeman between the legs. He grunted loudly and let go of her, but by then his partner and the policeman who had spotted her inside were there to seize her.

"Let me go, you kooksuckers!" the woman shouted. The men dragged her to her feet. One of the policemen shone his flashlight on her face and immediately recognized her.

"Oh, it's you, Maeve," said the policeman. "I thought we might run into you tonight."

"Let me go, Harold," the woman said. "It's Christmas."

"Sorry, Maeve."

"Then you can kiss my arse, Harold."

The policeman chuckled, and then he and the other bobby held her arms tight as they escorted her to a waiting paddy wagon where the woman escorted out earlier already sat inside. The man she had kneed was now up and walking slowly toward the wagon.

"Irish bitch." Robert and Misty heard the man remark to his partners.

The doors to the building again opened and another woman, a short redhead, was led out by two policemen who had remained inside. "We think that's it, Harold," one of them bellowed.

"Alright, then, load her up and we're off," Harold ordered.

As one of the policemen closed and locked the paddy wagon door, Robert approached the bobby who seemed in charge—Harold.

"Excuse me, Officer. I'm Lieutenant Braxton, aide de camp to General Sanders. May I ask about the blonde woman in the wagon?"

"Maeve? What do you want to know?"

"Who is she, exactly, and where will you take her?"

"She's one of the trollops who normally works Piccadilly Circus, but we usually run into Maeve at these military dances, 'specially if the Yanks attend. The girls like the Yanks because they're liberal with their money."

"And where are you taking her?"

"She'll spend the night at the Strumpet Inn, Lieutenant. That's the cell at the Camden Town clink we reserve for the whores and dollywops."

Chapter 5

Low Women

London—Camden Town
Same evening

Shortly before midnight, Robert Braxton parked his 1935 Sunbeam in front of the Camden Town jail. He and Misty had followed the paddy wagon to the police station in this north London neighborhood and watched the wagon disappear through a gate to the gaol's rear door where its human cargo would be unloaded.

Camden Town was but a 15-minute drive from Fortune Green, and the closest jail to both Fortune Green and other military installations outside London's north end. The jail's staff were well accustomed to British military policemen dropping off drunken or brawling soldiers for a night until they could be moved to a military brig the next day, and also accustomed to London civilian police delivering women who consistently appeared at social functions frequented by military men with money in their pockets—women willing to do more than simply dance and chat with a homesick soldier or sailor.

Braxton and Misty entered through the front door and asked a policeman to direct them to the booking desk.

"Through those doors, all the way to the end of the hall."

When they reached the desk, Braxton read the sergeant's name above his badge. "Sergeant Ruggles, I'm Lieutenant Braxton and this is Misty Hutchinson. We're assigned to General Sanders's staff at High Wycombe. I believe some officers just brought in three women taken from a military social function at Fortune Green tonight."

"They're not processed, Lieutenant. I don't yet know who they are. What's your interest in them?"

"I'd like some information about one of the women. I believe her name is Maeve."

"Maeve Shanahan?"

"I don't know the last name."

"Is she Irish? Do you know that?"

"Yes, Sergeant, apparently she is."

"She's a handful, that one. One of the Piccadilly Circus tarts. What else you want to know?"

"Anything you can tell me, anything at all."

"We don't waste much time writing the biographies of the prostitutes brought in here, Lieutenant."

"I'd like to speak with her, Sergeant."

The sergeant paused and looked quizzically at Braxton. "A general sent you here to parley with Maeve Shanahan?"

"No, General Sanders knows nothing about this. Not yet, anyway. But I have my reasons for wanting to talk to her. It could be important, but I'll be honest and tell you it will probably come to nothing."

"Very well, Lieutenant. You'll have to wait till we get her processed. Have a seat over there."

"Fletcher here will take you back now, Lieutenant," said Ruggles a half hour later. "Only one allowed back there," he added when both Braxton and Misty rose from the bench.

Misty said, "I'll wait here."

Braxton nodded, then followed the man Ruggles had summoned. They checked through a guarded metal door and walked past several small holding cells occupied by men, all of whom rose to stare at the military man as he passed down the narrow corridor.

"We keep the floozies in here," Fletcher told Braxton when they reached a door at the end of the hall. "We have to keep them where the men can't see them—too much noise otherwise."

Once through the door, Braxton expected to see more barred cells, but the area was simply a windowless holding room with two benches and half-dozen mattresses on the floor. Separating him and Fletcher from the five women inside was a rope stretched across the room a few feet from the doorway. Upon their entrance, all of the women except one immediately approached the rope.

"Don't touch the rope! Don't touch the rope!" Fletcher barked at the women. "Maeve Shanahan, you have a visitor!"

The blonde that Braxton immediately recognized was lying on one of the mattresses when the men entered, and that's where she stayed. The other women were curious about Braxton.

"Well, aren't you the handsome one, and a general to boot," said one of the women. Braxton thought he recognized her as the brunette, the first to be arrested at the Christmas dance.

"I'm a lieutenant, Miss," Braxton corrected.

"General, lieutenant, they're all the same. Aren't they, dearie?" She directed the question to another woman standing alongside who looked to be about 50 years old.

"All the same when it comes to shagging, that's for sure," joked the older prostitute. Both women laughed and the older one reached over the rope to touch Braxton's arm. Fletcher reacted quickly, grabbing her hand and issuing a warning.

"Don't touch the rope or reach over the rope! You know the rules, Darlene." Fletcher wanted to get this Army lieutenant's business over with and again shouted, "Maeve, come over here!"

The blonde on the mattress looked up, inspected Braxton, then rolled over turning her back to the men.

Fifteen minutes later Maeve Shanahan sat handcuffed to a wooden chair in a small room used to file outdated paperwork and store raincoats and other peripherals of police work. When she refused to cooperate in the holding room, Braxton returned to the booking desk and asked Sergeant Ruggles for a place to speak to her privately. Ruggles ordered Fletcher to move her to the storage room. The handcuffs were added not because they feared the woman might attempt escape (after all, she would be released in the morning after paying her one guinea fine), but merely to ensure she stayed put and give the lieutenant a better chance of keeping her attention. Because Maeve was no longer in the confinement area, Misty was allowed to accompany Braxton.

When the lieutenant and the general's secretary entered the room, they saw Maeve rummaging through a desk drawer she could reach with her free hand. She stopped snooping and watched Braxton and Misty sit down in the chairs Fletcher had placed in the room for them.

"Aye, the merry couple from the dance. Who are you people and what do you want?" Her hair was in disarray. Makeup was a war casualty in England, its ingredients either rationed or not available at all. Her only makeup was the beet juice used to color her lips.

"I'm Lieutenant Robert Braxton and this is Misty Hutchinson. We're both on General Sanders's staff at High Wycombe. We'd like to talk to you . . . Maeve. Do I have that correct? Your name is Maeve Shanahan?"

She looked back and forth from Braxton to Misty. "You've gone to all this trouble yet aren't sure of me name? If you're still looking for a shagging, Lieutenant, you'll have to pay me fine and give me five quid . . . seven quid if the lady is involved."

"I thought you didn't do business with British men or women," Misty countered. She knew the woman was toying with them, or attempting to shock her, so Misty made it a point to let her know she was not succeeding. Misty smiled and added, "That's what you told us at the dance."

"I'll make an exception, darlin', if you get me out of here now."

Braxton interrupted the verbal duel. "Maeve, I want to have an Army photographer come here and take some photographs of you. Do you have any objections?"

"Photographs? Why?"

"I can't tell you that."

"Then piss off."

"Your eyes are hazel—is that correct?" Misty interjected.

"Eyes? What do you care? You must both be wankers."

"Do you have syphilis?" Misty asked.

"If I do you'll be the first to find out."

Braxton again verbally stepped between the women. "Maeve, I want you to listen to me carefully. This is wartime, you've committed a crime, and your options are limited—in fact, you have no options. I can have you charged with soliciting a British officer. The penalties for that are much stiffer than the one-guinea public-nuisance fine the London police levy on you when they pick you up at a dance."

Braxton turned to Misty. "Miss Hutchinson, would you please get to a telephone and wake Corporal Eckley? Ask him to report here as soon as possible."

"Right away, Lieutenant."

As Misty turned and left the room, Maeve asked, "Who's this Eckley, another British wanker who's off his nut?"

"He's General Sanders's staff photographer."

"What are your plans after you get the photographs, Robert?" Misty asked as they stood outside near the police station entrance waiting for the photographer. "Are you really going to the general with this?"

Braxton shook his head. "I don't quite know what to do, Misty. Sanders is likely to have me thrown in the loon basket."

"You need to get her checked out medically. If she's infected we can drop the entire idea before going to the general."

"Right. Except I don't have the authority to order that. It would take orders from at least a colonel. Another problem is she'll be released in a few hours. If something were to come of this, imagine trying to find a woman like that once she's out and about."

"You can charge her with soliciting an officer, like you mentioned. That will keep her here."

"So you think we should pursue this?"

Misty hesitated, and then said, "No."

Chapter 6

Misty Knows

England—High Wycombe
Six days later; Thursday, 30 December 1943

As he had done the previous week, Major General William Sanders sat down to an early morning meeting with the same eight men and woman.

"Have a seat, gentlemen. As you know, I go before the First Lord tomorrow with our final recommendation for Trekker. I've been told there may be some good news from the SOE." Sanders directed his attention to the only man not in uniform. "Is that correct, Mr. Thomas?"

"Somewhat good news, General," said Thomas, the SOE man on the committee. The rugged-looking Thomas was the same Mr. Thomas who had accompanied the woman in the photographs to Camp X in Canada a few weeks earlier. "The SOE has decided that two candidates this committee previously rejected should be recommended to the Admiralty."

Thomas opened a folder, rose, and handed two photographs to the general. "Neither of the candidates offers everything we're looking for; but as you know, General, training has to begin."

Sanders looked at the photographs, then passed them to the other men who in turn looked them over and passed them on.

"Even though both candidates were initially rejected," Thomas continued, "we've reconsidered given the difficulties this committee has faced."

The general frowned and glared at Thomas, irked that the man's tone indicated Operation Trekker was being salvaged by the SOE. Sanders took this as a negative reflection on himself, even a slap in the face. "I'll be the one who decides if I recommend these women to the First Lord, Mr. Thomas. And my decision will be based on the consensus of this committee, not made by the SOE. Is that clear?"

"Of course, General," Thomas said with what Sanders judged to be a smirk.

Sanders waited for all the men to examine the photographs. Lieutenant Braxton, the lowest-ranking officer in the room, was handed the pictures last. In the days since last weekend, he had said nothing to the general about Maeve Shanahan. Braxton looked at the photos and recognized them as women previously discussed. In Braxton's opinion, both only slightly resembled the woman in the Trekker photographs. Misty Hutchinson looked at him for some sign of his thoughts, but Braxton remained pokerfaced as he put the photos down on the table.

Thomas spoke again. "We've discussed these women at length and everyone here has portfolios on them. Just briefly, they're both acceptable as far as height, age, and hair color. The eye color of both is light brown, not exactly right but close enough we hope. One is the secretary at Scotland Yard Colonel Trinder submitted for consideration early on, and the other works in a Downing Street bakery. I submitted her. She's the better choice of the two, in my opinion. We would all prefer a WAAF or a FANY, but women civilian volunteers are in SOE training as we speak and many are working out nicely. Violette Szabo, one of our top SOE operatives and one this committee briefly considered but rejected because of height, worked behind a department store perfume counter when we recruited her."

Sanders felt himself backed into a corner, did not like it, and let Thomas know.

"Thomas, if the bloody SOE found a bakery girl they want to use they should have gone directly to the Admiralty and saved us all a lot of fucking time. Now I have to go before the First Lord and recommend two women who have been previously passed over." Sanders addressed the others: "Let's make this short. Does anyone have any compelling reasons why I should not submit our recommendation of these women to the First Lord tomorrow?"

The men in turn said, "No, General."

"Very well, that will be all." Sanders pushed his chair back, stood, and left the room.

As the other men filed out, Braxton waited for Misty to collect the photos and paperwork from the conference table. Misty, who had not been handed the photographs during the meeting, looked at them as they walked out of the room together. When they reached her desk, she sat and looked up at Braxton.

"I know what you're thinking, Robert," she said. "And I'm sure you still have the photos in your satchel."

Braxton nodded. Misty hesitated for a moment, then pressed a buzzer on the box atop her desk. In a moment, the general's impatient voice came over the intercom.

"What is it, Miss Hutchinson?"

"Lieutenant Braxton is asking for a moment of your time, General."

"What about, goddammit?"

"I'm sure it's important, General."

"Christ! . . . Alright, send him in."

Braxton entered the general's office and closed the door.

"What is it, Lieutenant? Out with it," Sanders barked as Braxton stood before his desk. "Sit down, dammit."

Braxton sat and opened his satchel. "I have some photographs, General." He extracted a folder and handed it to Sanders. The general opened it and looked over the photos.

"Why are you showing me these, Braxton? I know what this woman looks like. I see her bloody face in my sleep."

"Those are not the Operation Trekker photographs, General. Those photographs were taken Saturday last of a woman at the Camden Town jail."

Sanders looked at Braxton, then back at the photos. He opened a desk drawer and pulled out the folder containing the Operation Trekker photographs and compared them.

"I hope you're telling me this woman *works* at the jail."

"No, sir."

"Continue."

"Last Saturday, Miss Hutchinson and I attended the Fortune Green Christmas Dance for military personnel. At the dance, that woman was arrested for being a public nuisance."

"Public nuisance? How?"

"She's a prostitute. I'm told she normally works Piccadilly Circus and frequents military social events. She targets Americans for the most part."

Sanders stared at Braxton for a long moment then pressed his intercom buzzer. Misty answered.

"Yes, General."

"Step into my office, Miss Hutchinson." When Misty came through the door, he ordered her to sit and then held up one of the lieutenant's photographs.

"You and the lieutenant came across this woman at Fortune Green?"

"Yes, General."

"Did either of you approach her?"

Braxton spoke for both of them. "We talked to her, General—at the dance and again at the jail."

"And?"

"We mentioned nothing of Trekker, of course. I ordered Corporal Eckley to report to the jail and take those photographs. After that, we left."

"What do you think of this, Miss Hutchinson?"

The question floored Misty. The general had never asked her opinion before.

"I . . . she certainly resembles the person in the Trekker photographs, General."

"Resembles?" Sanders looked closely at the black-and-white photographs. "She could be her bloody twin. Would you agree?"

"Yes, General Sanders."

Braxton had expected a harangue—either for waiting so long to inform Sanders, or simply for laying information on his desk about a woman arrested for prostitution.

"General Sanders," Braxton interjected, "Miss Hutchinson recommended that I not inform you of this. She has nothing to do with it." He thought if a stinging rebuke were forthcoming it should be directed at him.

Surprisingly, so far the general's famous fury had not surfaced. He ignored Braxton's defense of Misty.

"I assume her height is acceptable, and eye color, or you would not be here now. Is that right, Lieutenant?"

"Yes, sir."

"And you hesitated to come to me because of the woman's circumstances," said Sanders.

"Yes, sir."

"So why now?"

"I don't think the women you'll recommend to the Admiralty tomorrow look enough like the subject in the Trekker photographs to fool anyone, certainly not anyone who has seen the subject in person or studied photographs. This woman Miss Hutchinson and I stumbled across in Fortune Green is a ringer. You yourself, General, thought I had handed you the Trekker photographs. If you study the photos of both women carefully, you can notice a slight dissimilarity with the ears. But a woman's hair normally covers the ears, and you see the ears only because the hair of both women was pulled back for the sake of the photos."

"And you, Miss Hutchinson?"

"If the main objective to Operation Trekker is to find a woman who can physically pass herself off as the woman in the Trekker photographs, then Lieutenant Braxton has found her, General."

"What is her name?"

"Maeve Shanahan," Braxton answered. "She's Irish."

"Irish?"

"Yes, sir."

"Where is this woman now?"

"She was due to be released Sunday morning if she could pay her fine. I thought it might be extremely difficult to find her later—after her release—so I charged her with soliciting an officer. She's still in the Camden Town jail."

Misty looked at Braxton, surprised.

"Has the woman had a medical examination?" Sanders asked.

"No, sir," answered Braxton. "I don't have the authority to order one."

25

"Lieutenant, go fetch this woman from Camden Town and bring her here. Miss Hutchinson, type up the necessary orders for us to assume custody and I'll sign them. Lieutenant, take her to my physician, Major Elliott. I'll call the good doctor and tell him this woman is to undergo a full examination, including a check for venereal diseases, and that I need the results by the end of the day." Sanders paused and Braxton thought he noticed a slight twinkle in the general's eye.

"Wouldn't that put those cocky SOE bastards in their place?" Sanders said aloud to himself as he again looked over the photos from the Camden Town jail. He did not expect or want an answer. "Having an Irish Piccadilly tart as the Trekker." He looked up from the photos. "Thomas made a point of telling us today that the SOE is having success with civilian recruits, didn't he? Maybe we've found him one." The general seemed to almost chuckle. "Lieutenant," he continued, "if this woman passes the physical examination, no one is to be told about her occupation. Not until after I go before the First Lord. Understood?"

"Yes, sir."

"That goes for you, too, Miss Hutchinson. If this . . . Maeve Shanahan . . . passes the medical exam, she's not a prostitute. She's a librarian."

Braxton spoke up. "General, I'm not quite sure what her cooperation level will be."

"You let me worry about that, Lieutenant. You have your orders. Get her to Major Elliott straight away, then bring the examination results to me before day's end."

Chapter 7

Eileen Nearne

London—Camden Town Jail
Same day; Thursday, 30 December 1943

"What, you're not hungry, Maeve?"

The guard took the tray of untouched food from the slot in the cell bars. Maeve Shanahan had been moved from the room normally used to separate female from male inmates and now sat on a cot inside a solitary cell in another part of the jail normally reserved for counsel/inmate conversations. On Sunday morning, Maeve had succeeded in getting her fine paid and was being processed for release when word came that the lieutenant who visited her at the jail Saturday night had filed a grievance of solicitation against her—a crime that carried a significant penalty including jail time. So Maeve was taken back to lockup and on Monday appeared before a magistrate who ordered her held until trial after the New Year. She had never spent more than a night in jail but had now been here five days—an ordeal for Maeve who was claustrophobic and became extremely jittery after just a few hours behind bars. Her hair a mess, her clothes now dirty and wrinkled, and with red blotches on her face brought about by nerves, Maeve looked the worse for wear.

"Does it look like I'm hungry? Has Harold come on yet? I told you I want to talk to Harold."

"He's here but he's busy. You'll have to wait. It's not that you don't have time to wait, is it, Maeve?" The guard chuckled.

"Fook you, ya wanker."

The guard laughed and left with the tray.

Maeve's appetite had deserted her and she had not slept well since Saturday—some nights not at all. Deathly afraid of an extended prison stay, thoughts of suicide had crossed her mind. With no money (to pay her original fine she had to call on the kindness of her elderly landlady who thought Maeve worked as a seamstress), her fate would lie in the hands of an overworked court-appointed solicitor who likely would invest little effort in defending an Irish prostitute in a wartime London court against charges leveled by a British Army officer. Her right hand began to tremble; she stood and began pacing her cell to expend some nervous energy just before the door across the corridor opened. Officer Harold Judson, the policeman who arrested her at the dance, stepped through the door followed by two uniformed Royal Military Policemen.

"Visitors for you, Maeve," said Judson.

Maeve looked at the RMPs. "What's this, Harold?"

"Good news and bad news, Maeve," Judson said as he inserted a key in the cell door. "Good news is you get to leave this place. Bad news is you're going with these gentlemen."

"Why? Going where? You said I would be here until me trial." Maeve certainly welcomed leaving the jail, but was confused.

Judson opened the cell door but did not answer her questions.

"Let's go," ordered one of the RMPs.

Maeve offered no resistance. For her, even a short time to be taken somewhere, probably to appear before a military judge she imagined, would be a welcomed respite from the cramped, windowless cell. Judson and the RMPs escorted Maeve to the booking desk where she saw the lieutenant from Saturday night.

"What's he doing here, Harold?" Maeve asked Judson without rancor. She was not angry at the lieutenant, only surprised.

"You're going with him, Maeve. The lieutenant has the paperwork for you to be turned over to him."

Braxton greeted her pleasantly. "Hello, Maeve. We meet again." He was stunned at her sorry appearance. The attractive woman of Saturday was now scruffy and unsightly. Braxton was especially concerned about the inflamed blemishes on her face, but he kept up his cheerful front. "Let's get you out of here. What do you say? Jolly good, I would imagine."

The RMPs loaded Maeve into the back of a military paddy wagon where they joined her. The lieutenant sat up front with the driver and so was unavailable for her questions. The drive took an hour during which time she learned nothing. The RMPs sitting with her knew only that their assignment was to accompany a lieutenant and escort a prisoner. Maeve Shanahan arrived at the military hospital at High Wycombe not knowing why she was there.

Near eight o'clock that evening, wearing only a hospital gown, Maeve was roughly deposited in a chair by yet another RMP. The man closed the hospital room door behind him and she was now alone for the first time since leaving her cell at Camden Town. Maeve's patience had fled about halfway through a grueling six hours of being stripped, scrubbed clean by a team of three Army nurses, fingerprinted, and then enduring a marathon of physical examinations including numerous blood draws and detailed measurements of every body part (in addition to her bust, waist, and hip measurements, one man measured her feet to determine shoe size). All this with steadfast refusals to tell her anything when she asked what was happening to her. When Maeve's frustration got the best of her and she jerked a stethoscope from a doctor's ears, the RMPs were called in and they made it quite evident that her reaction was unacceptable. Her left arm still ached from being handled roughly by an RMP when later she refused to cooperate with a nurse drawing blood for the third time.

After ten minutes of being left alone, Maeve heard the door open and watched a woman carrying a package wrapped in brown paper enter and close the door behind her. She was a pretty brunette, but her feminine features were overshadowed by an intimidating mien. About Maeve's height and age, she wore civilian clothes and looked fit and confident. She smiled at Maeve, approached, and stuck out her right hand.

"Surely you're Maeve. My name is Eileen."

Maeve did not shake the woman's hand. "What's happening to me?" she demanded.

The woman in turn ignored Maeve's question. Her hand was still outstretched. "You must shake my hand, Maeve."

Maeve looked at her. The woman smiled pleasantly, but her dark, serious eyes seemed to lock onto Maeve's and tighten a grip. Maeve slowly took her hand. The woman shook it and without letting go laid the package on the bed beside them.

"I brought you some clothes; I'm sure they'll fit nicely." Still holding Maeve's right hand, the woman sat on the bed. Maeve tried to reclaim her hand but the woman tightened her hold with a grip like a man's. She laid Maeve's hand in her lap and patted it with her other hand.

"How are you feeling, Maeve?"

"What's happening to me?"

"How are you feeling, Maeve?"

Maeve hesitated. The woman continued smiling and gazing into her eyes.

"I'm tired and sore."

"Yes, of course. That's to be expected."

"Will you please tell me why I'm here?"

The woman said nothing, raised Maeve's hand from her lap, spread the fingers and turned Maeve's hand over several times, inspecting it closely.

"Let's get you dressed, shall we?" She finally released Maeve's hand, tore open the package, unfolded the clothes (a pair of khaki slacks, a white button-down shirt with collar, black ankle boots, white socks, underpants and a brassiere) and laid them out on the bed. "I'll return shortly."

She left the room and Maeve dressed quickly. It was no surprise that everything fit, even the shoes, considering all the measuring and inspecting she had endured that day.

When the woman returned, she escorted Maeve out of the room where an RMP stood waiting in the hall. "We won't need your help any further," she told the RMP. "I'll take her."

Maeve followed the woman down two flights of stairs and out of the hospital to a waiting car. The woman who had said her name was Eileen dismissed the driver—another military policeman. "I'll drive, Corporal. You can return to your other duties. Thank you."

Eileen opened the front passenger door for Maeve.

"No guards?" Maeve asked sardonically as she got into the car. "Until now I've been watched over like one of those American gangsters. Aren't you afraid I'll pull me escape and light off into the bushes?"

The woman smiled, closed the door, and calmly walked around to the driver's side.

No one escaped from Eileen Nearne.

Chapter 8

O'Rourke

England—High Wycombe
Same day; Thursday, 30 December 1943

"They've just arrived, General," the voice of Misty Hutchinson announced from the desk speaker.

Sanders pushed the button. "Have the RMP watch over the one and send Nearne in first."

"There's not an RMP with them, General."

"What? Why no guard?"

After a delay, the intercom voice said, *"Eileen says a guard was not necessary."*

"Well, one is necessary now. Is there an RMP in the office?"

"No, sir."

"Dammit," Sanders mumbled privately then again pressed the button. "Is Reddington at his desk?" Lieutenant Reddington was a sturdy, former university cricket player.

"Yes he is, General."

"Tell Reddington to take charge of the woman and to not let her out of his sight while I talk to Nearne, then send her in."

"Yes, sir."

A moment later, Eileen Nearne entered Sanders' office. Lieutenant Braxton sat in a chair beside the general's desk.

"Sit down, Nearne. Why are there no guards?"

"Unnecessary, General," she said as she sat.

Sanders stared at her. He was aware of Nearne's qualifications and decided not to waste time scolding her for a breach of protocol.

"Well, speak up," Sanders ordered. "What do you think?"

"Other than being nearly twenty pounds lighter than the subject in the Trekker photographs, she's certainly a solid match physically," Nearne began. "I'm sure we can put weight on her."

Sanders went on, "I read the examination report. The tests for venereal diseases were negative, and it seems she is relatively healthy other than her blood is anemic. Elliott noted in the report that improving her diet and a few vitamin injections will take care of that. Give me your initial impressions. You'll be involved in her training. Do you think she's physically able to perform the mission?"

"Impossible to say, General," Nearne answered. "We won't know until she's been at the camp for awhile—if that's what indeed comes of this."

"What about her demeanor and character?" Sanders asked.

"She has a lively mouth on her, so perhaps she has spunk but that doesn't mean she has heart. As for her character, that's highly questionable. Most likely she's of low character—certainly of low morals. I must spend training time with her to give you a better opinion of her trustworthiness."

"She's certainly of low character, no question there. And I say that not only because of her line of work. Less than an hour ago I received a report from SIS Belfast. I showed it to Lieutenant Braxton; you can read it later. Let's get her in here." Sanders pressed his intercom button. "Miss Hutchinson, ask Lieutenant Reddington to bring the woman into my office." A moment later the lieutenant escorted Maeve in, and on Sanders' instructions placed her in a chair facing his desk.

"Thank you, Lieutenant. That will be all."

"Yes, sir." Reddington closed the door behind him.

Maeve looked at Braxton, then at Eileen, then at the general.

"What is that red shit on her face?" Sanders asked Braxton as if Maeve couldn't hear. "I didn't see anything about that in the doctor's report."

Braxton answered, "Major Elliott says they are hives, most likely caused by nerves. Her skin was clear last Saturday, General, as you can see from the photos. The doctor believes the anxiety of several days in jail brought them on. He says they normally disappear quickly when circumstances change."

Sanders mumbled a profanity under his breath then exclaimed, "What else will I have to bloody well deal with?"

Finally, Sanders addressed Maeve, not bothering to introduce himself.

33

"You're a sorry one, aren't you?"

Maeve didn't reply.

"Nothing to say?" continued Sanders. "You call yourself Maeve Shanahan. *'Shanahan'*—you must like that name for some reason."

"That's me name, Captain." Maeve knew he was a general from the name on his door and the nameplate sitting on his desk.

Braxton interjected, "She knows who you are, General Sanders."

"How do you like jail, Miss *Shanahan?*" Sanders emphasized her last name.

"It's grand."

"Yes, quite, I can see it is by looking at your face. I'm happy you like it because you'll be enjoying living in one for many years to come. When Lieutenant Braxton told me about you, and said you were Irish, I was immediately curious about what brought an Irish whore to London. I'm sure there are well enough opportunities to ply your trade in the Emerald Isle. So the first thing I did was send copies of your photographs Lieutenant Braxton had taken last Saturday and your fingerprints to our security office in Belfast. It's a short flight so they arrived straight away." Sanders paused for a reaction. Maeve remained pokerfaced. Sanders continued, "It didn't take long for the Belfast office to identify you and wire me the report. You weren't a prostitute back home, were you?"

Maeve continued her silence.

"And you now call yourself Maeve Shanahan because it would be unwise to use your real name, isn't that also correct?" The general didn't expect an answer. "You now call yourself Maeve Shanahan because Maeve O'Rourke is wanted for questioning in a Belfast bank robbery—a British bank. Both your father and your brother are well-known members of Óglaigh na hÉireann. Your father was a friend and confidant of Michael Collins until they split when Collins advocated a treaty with the Crown and your father joined the anti-treaty faction. Your brother is well-known as an explosives expert who went underground after being identified as the leading suspect in a bombing that seriously injured a British official in Lisburn, south of Belfast. Stop me if any of what I'm saying is off the mark, Miss O'Rourke."

Sanders paused and checked the report in front of him. "And it was only after your father's arrest for his Irish Republican Army activities, your brother's disappearance, and you yourself being placed on a Most Wanted list in Ireland that you turned up in London. How am I doing so far, Miss O'Rourke?"

"Don't talk about me family," Maeve said with an icy stare.

"Tell me, Miss O'Rourke, how does your father like jail? I hope he thinks it's as grand as you do because he's there to stay. He was 56 years old when arrested two years ago for breaking three of his IRA comrades out of a Newtownabbey jail. He was sentenced to twenty years, so that will probably do it for him. My money is on him dying in prison. I'm sure that causes quite a hardship on your dear mother. Or has she, like her cherished daughter, now turned to whoring to support herself?"

Maeve sprang from her chair and started over the general's desk trying to get at him, knocking several desk items to the floor. "I'll kill you, you English shite!"

Braxton and Eileen Nearne reacted quickly, stopping Maeve before she reached Sanders. Nearne dragged her from the desk and took her to the floor. Maeve did not fight Nearne's hold and started sobbing.

"Get her out of here!" Sanders shouted as he stood.

Nearne dragged Maeve to her feet and escorted her out. When the women were gone, Sanders looked at Braxton.

"Good work, Lieutenant. I think she's bloody well what they're looking for. Put the files of those two recommendations from that SOE horse's arse Thomas back in the 'Rejected' file. I go before the First Lord tomorrow at fourteen-hundred. Get the Irishwoman's signature on the papers sometime before then."

Two hours later, Lieutenant Braxton and Eileen Nearne walked into a small brig on the far edge of the High Wycombe military compound. The wooden structure consisted of a tiny office and three narrow cells. Maeve O'Rourke was tonight the brig's only guest. Braxton and Nearne identified themselves and showed the duty sergeant their papers.

Braxton turned to Nearne. "I'll go first."

The sergeant unlocked the door to the cell area and Braxton stepped in. Maeve sat on a cot in the first cell.

"It's you." The disdain in Maeve's voice was obvious.

"Maeve, I'm going to fill you in on why you're here," said Braxton. "I know you want to know, of course, and I'm sorry I could tell you nothing until this point. I needed permission from General Sanders."

"And now you have that permission." Maeve said it as a statement, not a question.

"First, I want you to look at something. It might answer a few questions." Braxton opened a folder and handed three photographs through the bars. The end of the cot where Maeve sat was close enough to the bars that she could take the photos without standing. Braxton said nothing as Maeve looked them over.

"So what did she do?" Maeve thought the photos, a frontal facial photo and two profile photos, were mug shots.

"Does she look like anyone you know, Maeve?"

"No, never laid me eyes on her."

"Except when you look in a mirror."

"So she looks a wee bit like me, so what?" Maeve handed the photographs back to Braxton.

"A *wee bit* like you? When I handed General Sanders the photographs of you that Corporal Eckley took last Saturday at the Camden Town jail, the general at first thought I handed him these photographs."

Maeve, still thinking the photographs were police mug shots, took a moment to think.

"Well, I guess that pretty much says it, doesn't it, as to why I'm here. When you came across me at Fortune Green you thought I was this criminal. Only later did you find out I wasn't her. What a stroke of luck for you when you found out about me. I'm sure it would have been a grand embarrassment for you and your general to go to all this trouble and expense over just a low woman."

"I'm afraid you're wrong on all accounts, Maeve. A month before I met you, a task force was formed to find a woman who can pass herself off as the woman in those photographs. You're by far the best candidate we've come across."

"Pass meself off as her? Why?"

"You'll be told that when the need arises."

"If she's not a criminal, who is she?"

"She's a criminal, you were right in deducing that, but not in the sense you imagine. Will you cooperate?"

"Work for the Brits? Never."

"Think of it as working for your family, Maeve. If the mission is successful, General Sanders is willing to offer you a deal. The general has been assured by the powers-that-be that your father will receive a pardon, and charges dropped against you and your fugitive brother. You'd like to see your father released, I'm sure."

Maeve did not answer.

"Of course, we can leave things as they are: your father spending what will most likely be the rest of his life in prison, and your brother arrested and sentenced to a lengthy term when he's caught—and he'll be caught sooner or later. And, of course, you'll be tried for the bank robbery and receive a very long sentence yourself. That is unless you're innocent of the charge. Are you innocent, Maeve?"

Maeve sat unresponsive.

"The mission is of a military nature, and I will warn you that it is not without risk. If the enemy discovers you're a fraud, it could lead to the worst for you."

"The enemy? I assume that means *your* enemy. The Germans?"

"Yes, and that's all I can tell you now."

"I have no quarrel with them. The Nazis can take over your fooking island for all I care."

Braxton thought his blood would boil. He lost his only sister in the Blitz. "Very well, it's out of your mouth, isn't it? Then we'll leave you and your family to stew in your own shit. It's what you deserve." He walked out and slammed the door behind him.

Back in the office, Eileen Nearne heard the door slam and saw Braxton's red face. "I can see it didn't go well. What happened, Lieutenant?"

"The bitch can rot. Let's go."

"The plan called for me to talk to her, too. I'm assuming she refused the offer; if that's the case I need to hear it from her so I can include that in my report." Nearne nodded at the sergeant then walked into the cell area. Maeve was now standing with her back to the bars.

"You need to eat, Maeve," Nearne said when she saw the untouched tray of food. "I'm told you didn't eat well at Camden Town. You need to keep your strength about you."

Maeve turned and faced Eileen. "What for? I'm not working for the English."

"I'll be among those training you, Maeve. And, yes, you will indeed work for England. You won't allow your father to die in prison and your brother to end up there with him—that is if your brother isn't shot trying to flee when he's located. And then there's your mother. She has no means of support without your father and brother. It's my guess that you've been sending most of your money to your mother. That's why you couldn't turn out one guinea to pay your fine at Camden Town and were forced to call on your landlady. With you in jail, what will become of your mum? So let's not be silly. Of course you'll take the offer. Now, eat your supper, dear. We must add a bit of weight to you."

Chapter 9

"Hello, Maeve"

Canada – Camp X (SOE Special Training School 103), near Whitby, Ontario
Three weeks later; January 1944

Without a chair, Maeve O'Rourke stood. In fact, the room had no furnishings at all: no desk, no table, not even a window. Eileen Nearne had placed her in the room, said she would return shortly, then disappeared. That was an hour ago, maybe longer. Maeve wasn't sure because there was also no clock.

Nearne was right that day at the High Wycombe brig. Maeve had to cooperate if there were any chance doing so could save her family. To Maeve it was blackmail, pure and simple, and she knew she had no guarantee the English would keep their word. She worried about that. After she did their bidding they could cast her back into jail and no one would hear of any agreement. And who would care? Nobody would take up her banner and set things right. It would be her word against theirs, and in an English court she knew who would be believed. Surely it wouldn't be a prostitute with family loyalties to the Irish Republican Army. As far as the English were concerned, she was a criminal from a family of criminals.

Maeve did not want to be a criminal; at least she hadn't intended it so. The Crown bank she robbed in Belfast had illegally confiscated her father's life savings—ordered to do so by the Black and Tans. The note she handed the bank teller demanded only the amount once in her father's account and surely not a large sum. Yes, she turned to prostitution after fleeing to London, but no one would hire an Irishwoman. She had applied for every menial task, including scrubbing toilets at a train depot, but was scorned and turned away as soon as the person hiring heard her accent. In the end, selling her body to American G.I.s was the only way she could avoid more serious crimes like theft to support herself and her mother back home who had no income with her husband in prison and son a fugitive. Unlike theft, to Maeve's way of thinking, with prostitution men chose to part from their money.

But prostitution had changed her, she knew. The health risks of having intercourse with random strangers had forced her to stop caring about her physical well-being. Selling her body had hardened her heart and made her harsh, yet Maeve often thought growing callous might not be such a bad thing considering the world as it was today. Regardless, she knew the Maeve O'Rourke of just a few years ago, the never-missing-a-Sunday-Mass maid with lofty ideals and hopes for a loving husband and children was gone. Yet Maeve blamed no one for her descent. Looking back, she felt she should have gone to Holland or one of the Scandinavian countries. Perhaps she could have picked up enough of the language to communicate sufficiently with parents and find a job as a nanny—babies care little about what language you speak. But she crossed the Rubicon that night an American private offered her a cigarette as she stood at a sidewalk newspaper kiosk looking over the headlines. He treated her to coffee, then shocked her when out of the blue he offered her two American dollars and a pack of cigarettes for oral sex. Everyone has choices to make, and she made hers that night. No, she would not blame the English or Yanks for her choice.

The past three weeks were a blur. After she signed the papers Eileen Nearne and Lieutenant Braxton set in front of her in the High Wycombe brig, she was hustled off to an SOE assessment compound in Cranleigh, Surrey, about an hour south of London. There she underwent yet another physical examination, plus three days of psychological tests. Apparently the military psychologists found her sane enough, or perhaps they had found her crazy and wanted a lunatic—she wasn't sure which and they didn't say. It was at Cranleigh that she met a man identifying himself as an associate of Eileen Nearne and calling himself Mr. Thomas. But unlike Nearne, Thomas displayed an impatient and surly attitude toward her. Maeve decided quickly she did not like Mr. Thomas.

During her three days at Cranleigh, the hives on Maeve's face began clearing and more photographs were taken, including many of her body from different angles (she was allowed her underpants and bra). Eileen Nearne briefed her on a few particulars of the assignment, but seldom answered any of Maeve's questions, so much remained in the dark. Maeve knew she was there because of her close resemblance to the woman in the photographs Braxton had shown her at the High Wycombe brig. She learned it would be her job to pass herself off as this woman, and to do so she would have to do a great deal of traveling. To where, Nearne wouldn't say. Maeve was given the codename *Trekker* because of the traveling aspect of the mission.

After Cranleigh, Maeve had no idea where Eileen Nearne took her next, but was happy to hear Mr. Thomas would not be going with them. Thomas, she was told, had other responsibilities. This drive—about two hours—Maeve and Nearne spent in the back of a windowless military van. When the vehicle stopped and the rear door opened, Maeve stepped out onto the grounds of a lavish estate surrounded by forest. She asked where she was, and not surprisingly Nearne did not answer.

After arriving at the secluded estate, Maeve spent two weeks laboring through an elaborate regimen combining physical exercise, instruction in outdoor survival, and lessons in rudimentary French—all conducted by the ever-present Nearne. Some of the physical activities Maeve completed satisfactorily, with others she struggled. Nearne stayed constantly at her side, even at meals where she insisted Maeve eat second servings of the rare beef and fruit chosen for her. *You must add some solid pounds, Maeve.* Nearne ignored Maeve's insistence she could eat no more, not allowing her to leave the table until Maeve had satisfied her overseer by stuffing her face. Twice Maeve vomited from a belly too full of rare meat. The SOE agent was a severe taskmaster and suffered no complaints. Other times Nearne gave effort to be friendly. "Call me 'Didi,'" Nearne told Maeve one day. On one occasion Nearne did relent and answered one of Maeve's questions. When Maeve asked her how she knew French so well, Nearne said her family moved to France when she was little and lived there until the war broke out in 1939 when they returned to England.

Three days ago, Maeve and Nearne rode again in the van and this time were taken to a Royal Air Force airfield. They boarded an RAF Transport Command Group 45 Liberator modified with extra fuel tanks and a few metal chairs bolted to the floor that looked terribly out of place amid the empty crates—the two women the only passengers. Not until they were airborne did Nearne finally tell Maeve they were flying to Canada.

The flight went poorly for Maeve, to say the least. She had never flown before and during takeoff her right hand shook badly. She closed her eyes but that was no help. Nearne saw the shaking and held her hand, but that didn't help either. When the plane reached cruising altitude, Maeve thought she had gained control of herself until they encountered turbulence a couple of hours into the flight. Maeve began perspiring, her heart raced, and she felt she was going out of her mind. She unfastened her seat harness; her thought was to run. Having nowhere to run *to* didn't matter. Nearne quickly undid her own harness, sprang up, hovered over Maeve and held her in her seat. Nearne produced a tablet from a pocket and told Maeve to swallow it. Quite willing, Maeve spent the next six hours of the 23-hour flight asleep. When she awoke, Nearne handed her a canteen containing a drink that kept her groggy for the rest of the flight. *I'll never fly again!* Maeve told Nearne after they landed. She didn't know they had landed outside St. John's, Newfoundland, and would have to get right back on another plane for the final leg to Ontario. When Maeve found this out, she asked for a canteen refill.

The door opening suddenly jolted Maeve from her ruminations. Eileen Nearne stepped in followed by a soldier carrying two wooden chairs. He set the chairs down by the door and left without speaking. Nearne arranged the chairs facing each other in the middle of the room, about six feet apart.

"Sit here, Maeve," said Nearne as she put her hand on the chair that had its back to the door. "She's being brought here now. There was a bit of trouble yesterday, but I'll have them remove her handcuffs while you two meet. I'm absolutely certain you're in no danger, Maeve. I have her word and I believe her. I think she's eager to meet you. She is eager for this mission, and someone who looks so much like her as you do is a critical part. She knows that and she will not harm you."

"You make her out to be a monster."

Nearne ignored the comment. "Remember what we've discussed. You must learn everything you can about her—not just her history but little nuances. But don't concern yourself with that today. Just talk a bit and try to establish some rapport. And as we discussed, do what she asks and don't lie to her, Maeve. She'll know it and won't trust you. She has to trust you. Any questions?"

"You're asking me if I have any questions? That's certainly a brilliant surprise."

Eileen "Didi" Nearne smiled. "I'm glad you're not frightened or apprehensive."

"I didn't say I wasn't, now did I?"

Eileen Nearne had been gone about ten minutes when Maeve heard the door open. Her chair faced away from the door and Maeve did not turn around. She could hear what she knew were handcuffs being unlocked and removed because she had experienced that herself and, of course, Nearne had said the cuffs would be removed.

Maeve had decided before the door opened to not turn around. She would try to stay on equal terms with her look-alike and not show fear or too much curiosity (although she felt both).

The door closed. In a moment, Maeve sensed someone standing directly behind her . . . just standing silently . . . and close. Maeve stiffened. *What is she doing? She's standing there looking down me back!* After a nerve-racking minute that seemed an eternity, she heard the voice behind her.

"Hello, Maeve."

Chapter 10

Maeve Meets Her Double

Canada—Camp X
Same day; January 1944

The woman walked around Maeve and sat in the facing chair. Putting aside the hair—hers was shorter than Maeve's and lighter blonde—it was as if Maeve gazed into a mirror. The woman wore khaki slacks and shirt issued by the SOE, the same as Maeve. For at least two minutes they sat silent, staring at each another. Finally, the woman spoke.

"I'm Erika. I'm glad to meet you. Turn your head to the side, please." She spoke in a British accent. Maeve hesitated, but turned her head, revealing her profile, and then turned back to face her. "I think from the side our noses may be a tad different. Yours is prettier. But the difference seems slight, and I don't notice it when you look directly at me."

"You're British?"

The woman stared at Maeve for a moment. "They haven't told you about me?"

"No, nothing."

"Nothing?"

"I was shown your photographs and told I must pass meself off as you. They said I would travel a great deal."

"That's all you know?"

"That's all. I didn't know your name until you told me."

"I see. Well, to answer your question, no, I am not British. Would you prefer another accent? How about American?"

— "I think our noses are different." She now sounded like a New Yorker.

— "Our beaks ain't the same." (Southern slang)

— "I think our noses miss the mark." (American Midwest)

— "You're Celtic, Maeve. How about, 'Our noses are a wee bit off,'" she said in an Irish accent. "Which accent should I use?"

"How about your real one?"

"You might not like it."

"You'll have to give me the chance to decide, now won't you? I was told I have to find out everything about you."

"Ich komme aus Deutschland."

Maeve's eyes widened. She did not speak German but she understood the woman was telling her she comes from Germany. "You're . . . German . . . a Nazi?"

"Nazi? Is that a guess or an assumption, Maeve? If it's an assumption, it's a broad one. Not all Germans belong to the Nazi Party. In fact, most don't."

"So . . . you're not a Nazi?"

The woman never changed expression. "Is there something about me that leads you to believe I'm a Nazi?"

"No. I just thought. . . ." Maeve hesitated.

"Thought what?"

"Are you a Nazi or aren't you?"

"Stand up, please."

"Stand up? Why?"

"Because I asked you to, and I hope that's sufficient reason. If you ask me to stand, I will."

Maeve remained in her chair. If she did not jump at the woman's requests, maybe she would be accepted as an equal. "What have they told you about me?"

"You're an Irish prostitute, living in London, and you're doing this to save your family who has heavy ties to the Óglaigh na hÉireann. Fascinating. Lucky day for the British when they found someone who looks so much like me and who carries your baggage. Now stand up, please."

"What if I don't want to?"

"You'll do many things you don't want to do, might as well get used to it."

"Fook you."

"Another thing they told me is that you have quite the tongue on you," she said. "You must learn to control it." The woman rose, gently took Maeve's hands and lifted them to prompt her to stand.

45

"Okay, there you are," Maeve said, trying to remain bold. "I'm standing."

The woman sat back down. "Take off your clothes."

"What?"

"Take off your clothes, Maeve. It's a simple enough request. I'm sure in your occupation you hear that request quite often."

"If I ask you to take off *your* clothes, will you do it?"

"Yes."

"I normally get paid to take off me clothes. It will cost you."

The woman played along. "Until the British issue us money, you'll have to trust me for it."

"No credit."

Suddenly, the woman's friendly eyes corrupted to the icy stare of a raptor. "Do it now. We have only a short while together today."

The woman's quick metamorphosis frightened Maeve and she remembered Eileen Nearne's advice: *Do what she asks.* It now seemed a warning. Maeve had done a fairly good job of hiding it, but this woman terrified her. She began removing her clothes and laying them over the chair.

"What now?" Maeve asked when she was down to her brassiere and underpants.

"Take off everything, please."

Maeve paused and gazed at her, but then removed her underwear without comment. The woman looked her up and down quickly but thoroughly then told Maeve to turn around. Maeve turned and could feel the woman's eyes scanning her.

"Thank you, Maeve. Please get dressed now."

"That's it? You don't want me to stand on me head? One of me regulars likes that." Maeve quipped nervously. "You didn't take yours off."

"You didn't ask me to." The hazel eyes were once again pleasant.

Maeve started dressing. "I don't speak German. Did they tell you that?"

"I'll teach you a few phrases that will get you by if needed."

"A few phrases will get me by in Germany? I'm thinking I'm going to Germany, aren't I?"

"No, not to Germany."

"Not to Germany? Where then?"

"Several countries, but Germany is not one of them."

"France then," Maeve stated.

"No, not France."

Maeve sat down. "Not to Germany and not to France. Where on earth would I have to pass meself off as you, a German, if not Germany? And why have I been given lessons in French if I'm not going to France?" Her frustration was surfacing. "When will someone tell me what the fook I'm supposed to do, and where I'll have to do it?"

"I'll tell you anything you want to know, Maeve. Starting tomorrow, so will the SOE woman who brought you here. Your briefings will begin in the morning. One place you'll go is to the United States."

"To the United States?"

"Yes. I hope you're excited. You've never been to America, have you?"

"No."

"Well, then of course you're excited. A wonderful country. You'll love it."

"What will I do in America?"

"Pose as me, of course."

"I mean exactly."

"There's more to it than we have time for now. You'll begin your training tomorrow. I wrote down some basic things you'll need to know about me. The SOE woman, Eileen, has that file. She'll give it to you today and you can read it tonight in preparation for your briefing tomorrow. After that we will spend a great deal of time together, you and I. During those days, you may ask questions and I'll tell you anything that comes to mind that I think you might need to know."

The door opened noisily and Eileen Nearne and two guards walked in. Without being told, the woman stood and held out her hands for one of the guards to handcuff. Maeve remained seated.

"It was nice meeting you, Maeve." She leaned down and kissed Maeve's cheek. "I'll see you tomorrow," she said as the guards led her away. As they reached the door, the woman stopped as if she had forgotten something, turned to Maeve, and said, "Oh, by the way, you were right, Maeve. Ich gehöre der Nationalsozialistischen Deutschen Arbeiterpartei an. I *am* a Nazi, and you'll need to become one, as well. On behalf of the Führer, welcome to the Party."

Chapter 11

Maeve Meets Her Roommate

Canada—Camp X
Same day; January 1944

"What did she mean, I'll need to become a Nazi?" Maeve asked Eileen Nearne as the two women walked a path across the Camp X compound under the frost dance of stars. The path, shoveled through two feet of snow, was too narrow to allow side-by-side walking, so Maeve followed Nearne. Well past nightfall, each woman carried a flashlight. Maeve also carried a folder Nearne had given her. "She just means since I'll be posing as her, they'll think I'm a Nazi. That's what she means, right Eileen?"

"I wish you'd call me Didi."

"Alright then, Didi. That's what she means, right?"

"We'll talk about that later." The women could see their breath in flashlight beams, but the night was serene and Nearne did not have to raise her voice or turn her head for Maeve to hear. "First things first. We need to get you squared away in your quarters. You'll billet in the barracks that houses the security personnel. You'll have a room separate from the men, of course, although it's small and you have a roommate."

"A roommate? Erika, I suppose."

"No, not yet. A few problems with Erika have Mr. Thomas convinced the brig should be her home for now. We hope to have you and Erika bunking together before long. The woman you'll share your cubby-hole with for now is named Tarsitano—Tars for short. She'll go through training with you. Get to know her. It's important you get off on the right foot; you'll need to get on with each other."

"Why?"

"She'll be your bodyguard during your assignment."

"She'll be with me?"

"Yes, dear. It would be rather hard for her to look out for you if she wasn't with you, wouldn't you say?"

"Who is she? Tarsitano . . . is that a code name?"

"No, that's her real name. She's Italian but her English is excellent. Growing up she had a South African nanny, and in her early teens she lived with an aunt in the United States for three years before returning to Italy."

"Italian. Well, at least she isn't British . . . no offense, Didi. Of course, you lived most of your life in France. That's why you're different from wankers like Mr. Thomas and that general at High Wycombe."

"Thomas is a Scot."

"Same island."

Nearne smiled in the dark.

The barracks that housed security personnel sat behind a row of evergreens, hunched by their heavy burdens of snow, north of the administration building. Nearne led Maeve up three wooden steps beneath large, sinister-looking icicles clinging to the eave—a waterfall frozen in time. Inside, the women walked through a room with ten bunkbeds and about half that many men, one wearing only a towel.

"Hello, gentlemen," Nearne said as they passed through. A couple of the men returned the greeting, all of them stared at Maeve.

"Well, well—it's Erika," one of the men commented. "I see Thomas has released you from the hoosegow again. How long will it be for this time?" A couple of the men chuckled.

"This isn't Erika, Rodney. This is Maeve."

"What do you mean it's not Erika?" It was obvious to the Mountie he was looking at Erika.

Maeve spoke up. "You heard her, you wanoge. I'm not Erika."

At the rear of the men's bunkroom, a short hallway accessed two small rooms. Once in the hall, Nearne turned to Maeve.

"*Wanoge?*"

"That's a wanker and an eejit all in one."

Nearne knocked on one of the doors but did not wait for it to be answered. She turned the knob and led Maeve inside. Maeve knew immediately that Nearne had used the correct word in describing the room—*cubbyhole.* She had been in bigger single-inmate jail cells. One bunk-bed, one wooden chair, and a small dresser with two drawers filled the tiny space. On the side wall: two shelves and a small clock; on the far wall a tiny window. One ceiling bulb supplied the light. The room also contained a woman who sat on the lower bunk. Nearne closed the door and made introductions.

"Maeve, this is Tars. Tars, this is Maeve."

Maeve said hello. The woman on the bed stared at her but did not return the greeting.

"I'll have your things brought over shortly," Nearne told Maeve. "The loo with shower room is off of the men's bunkroom. When you're using it turn the sign on the door over to tell the men you're in there. Take a few minutes tonight to look over that folder I gave you, and I'll see you both at six in the morning, in our meeting room—Tars knows where it is. We'll start off with a meeting with Mr. Thomas, then eat a quick breakfast and begin training. Good night, ladies."

Suddenly the exhaustion from the flights, the long drive from the landing strip to the camp, and the tense meeting with her look-alike overtook Maeve and her only thought was of sleep. She did not care that her roommate seemed unfriendly. She assumed her bunk was up top since Tars sat on the bottom one. Ignoring Nearne's instructions to look through the folder, Maeve climbed the ladder and collapsed on the mattress fully clothed, too tired to get under the blankets.

Not long into the night, Maeve woke shivering. When her eyes opened she looked directly into a set of moonlit eyes.

"Ahhh!!!" she screamed and sat up, her heart racing from the start. Tars stood beside her bunk staring at her in the moonshine beaming through the window, her head just barely above the edge of Maeve's upper bunk. "Grab me teats and call me Lucy! What's wrong with you? Are you mad?"

Tars did not reply or change expression. Maeve jumped off the bed and pulled the light chain. The two looked each other up and down. Tars wore a white T-shirt and navy-blue shorts. Nearne had said Tars was Italian, but the woman's reddish-brown hair and green eyes looked more Irish or Scot. She was not tall—at least four or five inches below Maeve's 5'8"—and her slight frame was a surprise.

"Why were you standing there watching me sleep?" Maeve did not try to hide her displeasure.

"I was waiting for you to wake up," Tars said matter-of-factly.

"Why?"

"I want to know if you like peaches."

"What? If I like peaches? Why in God's name do you want to know that?"

"Well, do you?"

"Why is that important? If you have some fooking peaches they can wait till the mornin'."

"I don't have any. They don't have them here."

Maeve stood looking at her and thinking: *This is my bodyguard? A skinny lunatic?*

Now too wound up to sleep, Maeve sat down in the chair and opened the folder Eileen Nearne had given her. Tars got into bed.

"Are you leaving that light on?" Tars asked.

"Yes, I'm leaving the light on!" Maeve's patience had left her and her nerves were shot. "I can't read in the dark, now can I?"

"You never answered my question."

"No, I don't like fooking peaches! I hate peaches! Now leave me alone." Maeve liked peaches.

Tars took some time to contemplate Maeve's answer then turned over and faced the wall. Maeve ignored her and opened the folder. Inside she found several typed pages each with a red TOP SECRET stamped near the top. She began reading.

- Erika Marie Lehmann
- Birth: 16 December 1917, Oberschopfheim, Germany
- Father: Karl Wolfgang Lehmann, German
- Mother: Louise Gwendolyn Minton, British
- Religion: Roman Catholic

Maeve read for about an hour until she felt the need for more sleep. She dropped the folder onto the desk, rose, took off her clothes, turned off the light, and climbed the ladder.

Chapter 12

Mr. Thomas

Canada—Camp X
Next day; January 1944

"How did you and Tars get on last night?" Eileen Nearne asked Maeve. The two women stood together in a Camp X meeting room. Tars and Erika Lehmann talked with Mr. Thomas on the other side of the room. It was 6:20 a.m.

"She's as crazy as a drunken monkey," Maeve answered.

"She has her spells," Nearne explained. "But most of the time her mind is put together."

"Most of the time? That's grand. How did she end up here? And she's supposed to be me bodyguard? She doesn't look like she could fight her way out of a haystack."

"What she lacks in physical power she makes up for in tenacity. And she's certainly not untested when it comes to mixing it up. Tars was an assassin for a criminal organization in Calabria, Italy, called the 'Ndrangheta."

"An assassin?"

"Does that shock you?"

"I'm beginning to learn that nothing you people do should shock me." Maeve refused to show it, but it did unnerve her and left her to think Tars could prove her biggest danger. "What surprises me is that you people would take in a lunatic."

"Despite her problems, Tars will be totally focused on protecting you. It's something about the way she thinks. Someday you might find yourself very glad she's with you. And Erika needs someone like her as well."

"Erika?"

"Your assignment is only the start of the mission. When you've completed your task, Tars will join Erika for the rest of the mission."

"And what is that?"

"You'll be told today everything about your assignment, but as for the rest—the part you're not involved in—it's best you don't know, dear. We've been honest with you about the possible danger if things go amiss. If things get muddled and you find yourself under enemy interrogation, you can't tell what you don't know. Did you read the folder I gave you last night?"

"Yes."

"You have to get to know Erika very well."

"How will I do that when she's locked up most of the time?"

"That will end. Erika will make sure of that. She wants this mission to go forward, and knows for that to happen you and she have to spend time together. On her own accord she'll stop doing the things that have caused her confinement." From across the room, Mr. Thomas signaled Nearne. "Looks as if he's ready to start. Let's find a seat."

All four women found seats together.

Thomas stood. A highly trained commando formerly assigned to the British 1st Airlanding Brigade and recruited into the SOE in the spring of 1943, Thomas was a veteran of both combat action in North Africa and clandestine activities in Sicily. He was a hard—sometimes seemingly cruel—taskmaster when assigned training duties. But being a tough instructor was certainly not a negative quality in the SOE creed. His patriotism was unquestioned, his experience and skills impressive, and these qualities ensured him a place among the SOE's top agents.

(While conducting undercover activities in Sicily shortly before the Allied invasion of that island, Thomas heard tales of a young, female assassin who had eliminated several high-ranking mafia chieftains. Thomas was intrigued—he knew such a woman could come in very handy. He learned the woman worked for the 'Ndrangheta—a criminal organization based in Calabria and blood enemy to the rival La Cosa Nostra which had placed a huge price on her head after a number of its bosses ended up with their throats slit. While Thomas was undercover his hands were tied, but later, after the Allies took Sicily, he returned with an SOE team to find Tars and spirit her out of the country. His actions surely saved her life although his reasons for doing so were anything but humanitarian.)

"Everyone here is already familiar with Maeve's mission except Maeve," Thomas began. "That's why we're here this morning, to go over things with her. First, let's discuss codenames. Erika's is *Lorelei*— her German Abwehr codename. Normally, we would issue a new codename but in this circumstance we have reason to not do that, but I can't stress too strongly that none of us are to let it slip to others here at Camp X that Erika is a German agent. It's not that we don't trust the instructors and other agents training here; they all have sufficient clearance or they wouldn't be here. But knowing she is a German agent could very well stir up trouble among many of the men who have lost friends and colleagues to the enemy and we have no time to deal with that."

Thomas stopped for a moment to let the instructions sink in. "As for other codenames, Tarsitano is *Lady* and Maeve is *Trekker*. Commit those names to memory, but we will not use them here at Camp X. Codenames for this mission will be used only for radio transmissions. Here we will use first names only, or as in Tarsitano's case an abbreviation: Erika, Tars, Maeve. Eileen's codename is no concern to you at the present; she's here to help with your training. Call her Didi, her nickname, from here on out. Any questions about name protocol?"

No one had a question.

"Good." Thomas turned his attention first to Erika. "We have to get something worked out right now, Erika." His voice was loud and impatient. "We need more and better cooperation from you. I need you out of the brig. Maeve needs you out of the brig. Bloodying guards and instructors when you have a mind to isn't going to get you out of the brig. Am I getting through?"

Erika looked at Maeve. She knew spending time with her would be critical to the mission. She turned back to Thomas. "There isn't going to be any more trouble from me."

"I have your word?"

"You have my word it won't start with me."

Thomas gazed at Erika for a moment and then addressed Tars. "You're well aware that during Maeve's part of the mission, your job is to protect her and ensure nothing interferes with her accomplishing her task. When Maeve has completed her assignment, you'll join Erika for the remainder of the mission."

Tars acknowledged with a nod.

"Maeve, you know you're here because of your uncanny resemblance to Erika. Your task here at Camp X is to learn as much as you can about her and try to mimic her in every way possible. That means going through training with Erika—she's physically fit so you must become as fit as possible. I see you've gained some weight since I last saw you in England. We'll monitor your weight and get you as close to Erika's weight as we can. You need to *become* Erika, even *think* like her. It's the only tool you'll have to keep yourself safe and allow the best opportunity to succeed. Since your phase of the mission must begin no later than mid-April, you have eleven weeks to become Erika."

Thomas waited through another of his patented pauses before continuing. "Now, Maeve, to your task once the mission begins. You already know from the dossier Didi gave you that Erika is a German Abwehr agent. The Abwehr is the intelligence-gathering apparatus of the German military. It's the German version of our MI-6 or the American OSS. Have you heard of them?"

"I've heard of MI-6," Maeve replied.

"Good. The mission requires Erika's return to Germany. There's no need to discuss particulars of her mission once she's in Germany; you're not going there so that doesn't concern you. The only thing you need to know is her assignment will take place there. It must appear that Erika returns to her homeland from the United States, where she was last sent by the Abwehr. For her to suddenly appear in Europe without a trail from America would arouse great suspicions on the part of the Germans. But because of the time required for training with our European team, Erika will not have time to make that journey herself. That's where you come in, Maeve. Your job will be to pose as Erika and travel from the States to mainland Europe in a manner that a fleeing enemy agent would be forced to make the journey. In April, after we set you on your way, Erika will return to Great Britain to finish training with the remaining members of the team who are there training as we speak. By the time you reach your destination in

Europe, Erika's training will be complete and she'll be there waiting for you. It's at that time you and she will secretly switch places and your assignment will be over. Your final destination will most likely be a neutral city in Portugal or Spain. We'll have people there waiting to spirit you out and return you to England."

"I'd like to be taken back to Belfast when I'm finished."

"You'll be required to undergo debriefing in England. After that, it's up to you where you end up. You'll accumulate nursing yeomanry pay from here on out until your assignment is complete and will be paid in a lump sum after your final debriefing. It won't be a great deal of money but certainly enough to allow you to return to Ireland and help support your mother for awhile."

"Me ma will need money before then."

"That's no concern of mine; you get nothing until you complete your assignment. And you need to get rid of that idiotic Irish brogue and begin talking like a civilized human being."

Thomas' insulting remark about her speech and especially his heartlessness to her mother's plight enraged Maeve. "You can suck my arse, you fooking Scot. Your people haven't been treated much better by the English than mine. I'm surprised you're sucking English kooks."

Infuriated, Thomas briskly walked over to Maeve, grabbed her roughly and lifted her from her chair. "You listen to me, you Irish tramp...."

Tars sprang from her seat and jumped on Thomas' back. The commando easily flipped Tars off and she thudded to the floor. On her feet quickly, Tars grabbed a chair and had begun the motion of swinging it at Thomas' head when Erika stopped her and pulled her away. Tars struggled but had no hope of breaking away from the larger, much stronger German. Didi Nearne stood but there was nothing for her to do.

"Let's calm down." Erika's accent and syntax were American. She had decided to use American speech from here on for Maeve's sake. "No more trouble—we just talked about that. That should apply to us all, including you, Mr. Thomas."

Thomas delayed for a tense moment then released his grip as he angrily shoved Maeve away. Erika released Tars.

Maeve wanted assurances. "As soon as my part is finished, that's when me father will be released from prison and the charges against me brother dropped. That's the agreement."

"If you do what you're told," Thomas answered gruffly, "and your part of the mission is successful." Erika Lehmann watched Thomas closely as he answered Maeve's question.

Thomas now turned his attention to his attacker, glaring at Tars. "As for you, I have every head doctor who's evaluated you telling me you belong in the bughouse. I can easily arrange that."

Tars had taken off a shoe and stared at her foot. "Can I get a pair of gray socks? I don't like white socks."

Eileen Nearne reminded Thomas, "You did assign her to protect Maeve, you know."

Chapter 13

Wild Bill and *Intrepid*

Canada—Camp X
Two weeks later; Friday, 04 February 1944

The assemblage settled into their chairs in the conference room adjacent to the camp commandant's office. The commandant of Camp X, Colonel Humphrey Naylor, relinquished his head chair to a higher-ranking officer, Major General William J. Donovan. Although Naylor was an officer in the Canadian Armed Forces and Donovan an American, this etiquette was standard.

William "Wild Bill" Donovan was a close advisor to President Roosevelt and he headed the Office of Strategic Services. In fact, it was Donovan who deserved most of the credit for forming the OSS shortly after Pearl Harbor. The organization's commission encompassed the gathering of intelligence, sabotage, and counterespionage efforts for the United States.

Next to Donovan and occupying an equal place of importance at the table was another Bill—William Stephenson. Donovan's British counterpart, Stephenson had been appointed by Churchill to head the British Security Coordination agency. As the name implied, the BSC oversaw and coordinated all of the various agencies that made up the British Secret Service including MI-6 and the ultra secret SOE. But unlike Donovan, whose name and position were well known around Washington and among the press, Stephenson was such a shadowy figure that few outside the upper reaches of the British intelligence community and the top echelons of British government knew him by his real name. Most knew only that out there somewhere was a phantom in charge of British spying, sabotage, and dirty tricks with the codename *Intrepid.* Indeed Stephenson was not even headquartered in England. His workplace was room 3553 at 630 Fifth Avenue in New York City, with the BSC offices spread throughout two floors of Rockefeller Center.

Joining Donovan, Stephenson, and Colonel Naylor were Leroy Carr, Al Hodge, Victor Knight, and a British MI-6 psychiatrist. Carr and Hodge both worked for the OSS with Carr heading up the counterespionage section. Hodge was Carr's assistant. The two men had pursued Erika Lehmann in the United States and had conducted numerous interrogations since her capture last fall. They knew the German spy better than anyone else in the room. It would be their job to supervise any parts of the SOE's Operation Trekker mission taking place in the United States.

Victor Knight, aka Mr. Thomas, was an SOE agent and Stephenson was his boss. Even though the Americans had captured Erika Lehmann, in a deal between Donovan and Stephenson given the green light by Roosevelt and Churchill, the German spy would be on loan to the SOE for this one mission and then returned to the OSS if she survived. *Intrepid* had placed Knight in charge of mission training and the mission itself once it began in Europe. Knight wondered if Stephenson could be *Intrepid,* but knew he might never find out. When Stephenson showed up at top-secret meetings, he always claimed he was there as a liaison who reported to *Intrepid.* Some within the British Secret Service had suspicions that Stephenson was the ghost himself, but Knight had yet to meet anyone in the SOE who could say for certain that the man across the table was not simply a subordinate who reported to the phantom.

There were no introductions. Stephenson started things off. "Major Sims, we'll hear from you first. We assume you're prepared with your findings?" Major James Sims was the MI-6 psychiatrist.

"Yes, sir." Unlike Knight, Sims had never laid eyes on the man asking the question. And it never occurred to the British doctor that he might now share the same room with his spectral boss. He had seen photographs of Donovan in various newspapers, so Sims simply assumed the man sitting next to the famous "Wild Bill" held authority, and Sims had been with MI-6 long enough to know not to ask questions about identification in these situations.

"Let's hear what you have," said Stephenson.

"Two of the women, the ones called Maeve and Tars, have been evaluated by me and another doctor. I've had sessions with both women over the course of the past ten days here at the camp, and they were seen by Captain Barrow in England. The woman called Erika, only I have evaluated as far as I know." Sims was an experienced MI-6 analyst and realized the names he was given might not be real so he added the "called" before the names when identifying them.

Sims had been charged with overseeing the women's mental appraisals, and to assess them properly it was necessary he know their backgrounds. Along with the other men in the room, Sims was one of the very few who knew Erika Lehmann was a German Abwehr operative, that Tars had labored as an assassin for the Calabria 'Ndrangheta criminal organization, and that Maeve was an IRA bank robber turned prostitute. Sims was told no particulars of the mission other than it was important and dangerous, and that his job was to appraise the trustworthiness and emotional strength of these women.

"Let's begin with Maeve," Stephenson decided. "As you know, Major, the main thing we're interested in is, in your opinion, can we trust these women to not betray their mission once out in the field?"

"Maeve displayed an extremely defensive attitude during our sessions, which made assessment difficult," Sims reported. "I wouldn't go so far as to classify it as paranoia, but she has a very low opinion of anyone British, and I think it highly unlikely that she'll let that curtain drop to the point where she allows herself to trust any Englishman."

"Can *we* trust *her*, Major?" asked Stephenson. "That's what's important."

"She has a very strong emotional bond with family. She's here to help her family and for that reason I think she can be trusted to at least attempt to do what's asked of her. However, to expand on that I feel she doesn't realize the dangers that can go along with wartime clandestine missions and I can't say how she'll react if things go badly. Maeve suffers from a significant case of claustrophobia and if she's captured and confined she might crack."

Donovan asked, "What's your opinion of her pluck?"

"If my feet were held to the fire, General, and I was forced to offer an opinion on her resolve, I'd say it's fairly sturdy. Her moral character is questionable, of course, but I think Maeve is rather strong emotionally."

"Let's move on to Tars for now," said Stephenson.

"Tars was the easiest to evaluate. You're dealing with a psychopath."

Donovan said, "Keep going, Major."

"Murder causes Tars absolutely no guilt, remorse, or shame. When ordered to kill somebody by her 'Ndrangheta bosses, she had no more second thoughts than a baker would have if asked to bake a cake."

"Can Tars be trusted to remain loyal to the mission once she's in the field and unsupervised?" Donovan asked.

"I can't say, General." Sims paused. "There's no evidence that she was not loyal to her 'Ndrangheta handlers. I think if she feels loyalty to either you—her overseers, the mission, or perhaps to the other women, she'll stick with the plan. But I could be wrong."

"You're not giving us a lot with that statement, Major," said Stephenson.

"I'm sorry, sir. Psychopaths are unpredictable."

The men glanced around at one another.

"Sir," Victor Knight said to Stephenson. "Might I ask a question?"

"Yes."

Knight looked at Major Sims. "What is the story with Tars as far as her mind fading in and out? She'll seem to be fine one minute, perhaps even for days, then suddenly she loses touch. One minute I'll be talking to her about an important aspect of training and she seems to be totally focused then out of the blue she'll ask me some bonkers question like what color of apples do I like. Do I like red, green, or yellow?"

Sims answered quickly, "When I asked her about her life as a child, she asked me when was the last time I ate fried peppers. That's a personality disorder. Tars doesn't quite know how to relate to other human beings and inserting a peculiar question like that into a conversation doesn't seem odd to her. I wouldn't be too concerned with that. She's not actually losing touch with reality. It's her psychotic disorder that makes her unpredictable that is the concern."

"Any more questions about Tars?" Donovan looked around the table. "Alright, Major, what about the German?" Donovan had a lot at

63

stake here. Erika Lehmann was a highly capable undercover operative who spoke four languages fluently, including Russian. The OSS planned to use her considerable skills after the war, since Donovan and almost everyone else in Washington believed their current ally Russia would be anything but that after the Axis surrender. "We've all read the reports from Agents Carr and Hodge; they've questioned her and spent more time with her than anyone. So what's your take on her?"

Sims's face turned red and he was silent.

"Major, let's have it," ordered Donovan.

Sims composed himself. "She's a dedicated Nazi, that's a certainty. I've evaluated other captured German agents in England. A few remained loyal and chose the gallows; most couldn't wait to become turncoats to save their hides. But even the Nazis I've assessed who remained loyal to the end could do little more than expound clichéd phrases they had read in Nazi-run newspapers or had drilled into them when they were Hitler Youth. They didn't know any more about true Nazism than a Liverpool lorry driver. Erika, on the other hand, has her own ideas of what makes a good Nazi. Of course, I don't know anything about this mission or her role in it but a critical element in evaluating subjects is to get to their *real* reasons for accepting a dangerous mission—a mission that puts their lives at risk. Erika referred to an unnamed *enemy* in Germany, and she's taking part in this because she expects to confront this enemy. Her motive is revenge."

Leroy Carr looked at Al Hodge and then at Donovan. None of them spoke. They knew that while Lehmann was in the United States on a secret Abwehr mission, Heinrich Himmler had sent an assassin to find and kill her, a plot that failed when she turned the tables and killed the assassin. And they knew she felt certain Himmler had ordered her father's murder last summer while she was still in America. That plot had succeeded. When she found out her father was dead, Erika allowed herself to be captured and struck a deal to lead an SOE mission back in Germany to eliminate certain important members of Himmler's Gestapo and SS. For Erika Lehmann, this was a revenge mission. For the Allies, it was a way to disrupt Himmler's machine of terror.

Sims continued, "I know you want to know about her trustworthiness. In my opinion, and this is strictly just my opinion, gentlemen, if the mission includes a chance for her to get to this enemy, I'd say you can trust her because that's her entire focus. But I also feel that if she thinks she's been double-crossed, she'll kill every member of the mission team who gets in her way."

"Are you telling us besides being an enthusiastic Nazi she's a psychopath, too?" asked Knight.

"No, absolutely not. That's what is most curious, and what makes my report on her difficult. Erika is totally sane, and the most charming and intelligent woman I've ever met."

Chapter 14

Elite Instructor

Canada—Camp X
Four days later; Tuesday, 08 February 1944

"You're leaning in too far again," Erika told Maeve. "That will be used against you. You want to force your opponent to lean." Erika was instructing Maeve in unarmed hand-to-hand combat in the Camp X PT (physical training) room.

"Why do they keep it so hot in here?" asked a frustrated, perspiring Maeve. "At night in our room I freeze me teats off but in here it's hotter than the devil's oven."

"Never mind that," replied Erika in her American accent.

Now at the end of her second week at the camp, Maeve was struggling with both the obstacle course and this aspect of training. Normally trained in hand-to-hand by Mr. Thomas or an SOE instructor during group sessions with other agents, Maeve had confided to Erika her distress at the way things were progressing with her training. She seemed to be making little headway, especially with the fight training and the obstacle course, so Erika had recently begun giving Maeve personal instruction during their free time.

"Keep your feet wide and underneath you," Erika instructed. "Grab my arm with both hands, turn and stick your fanny into me and instead of trying to pull my entire weight over your back, pull me over your hip."

Maeve did it slowly and Erika let herself be tossed to the mat.

"Better," said Erika as she rose to her feet. "Do it again."

Maeve knew she had an imposing trainer in Erika. Though Didi Nearne was a skilled fighter who helped in fight training, Maeve had watched Erika make short work of Didi in full-speed fighting competitions. Erika had even embarrassed male trainees who made the mistake of underestimating her because of her gender.

During regularly scheduled group training, Tars trained with them. Hand-to-hand was not Tars' strong suit either, and fellow trainees encountered few problems taking down the slight-built Italian; the other agents, however, soon began trying to avoid getting paired with Tars because of her propensity to bite her opponents after she was down. Usually it was an arm or leg that ended up tattooed with Tars' bite pattern, but earlier that week after one of the men easily wrestled Tars to the mat, her face ended up between the man's legs. His howl was ear shattering and he limped for two days. Now some of the other men laughingly referred to the unfortunate fellow as "Agent Swollen Bag."

Erika made Maeve throw her to the mat again and again until it was time to report to the gun range. The two women donned their coats and walked the short distance to the range, perspiration stinging Maeve's face in the cold air. But she was glad the fight training and the early morning obstacle course with its running, jumping over hurdles, climbing fences and other exhausting physical tasks were over for the day. On the gun range Maeve enjoyed more success. She was not unfamiliar with guns, as she had grown up around them and even bagged a few rabbits with a .22 rifle while hunting with her brother when they were teenagers. She had never before fired a handgun, which was the focus of the SOE training, but her scores were improving daily. (When Tars asked what she had used to rob the bank in Belfast, Maeve explained that she waved an unloaded pistol.)

As the two women neared the range they could see others were already there. Tars, Didi, and two male agents stood waiting. They spotted Mr. Thomas and the gun range supervisor walking up another path. Maeve commented to Erika: "For the past few days Tars has seemed less crazy."

"I was with her here for nearly a month before you arrived," Erika responded. "Much of the time she seems fine. I don't know what causes her spells. I don't think anyone knows, including Tars."

When everyone had reached the firing tables, Thomas growled, "Take your positions!" Maeve was always placed between Erika and Tars. The supervisor distributed empty weapons from a metal suitcase he had brought with him. Each agent was given one weapon; the makes and calibers varied. Maeve and Erika were given 7.65 caliber Berretta *Brevettata* model semi-automatics. That model handgun was standard issue in the Italian Air Force and also a popular choice among German Wehrmacht officers. But they practiced with this particular gun because it was Erika's handgun of choice, the Abwehr knew this, and so it was the gun Maeve would be issued when her assignment began. Although Tars had displayed her greatest expertise in training with knives, wielding a dagger like a surgeon his scalpel, she was familiar and comfortable with a wide range of handguns and gave her approval of the Italian-made Beretta and requested the same. Occasionally, Erika and Tars also practiced with an odd-looking pistol called a Welrod, a 9mm handgun surprisingly quiet when fired, but neither woman was given a Welrod today.

The range supervisor first placed targets at 25 feet and then handed each shooter two clips and four boxes of shells in the appropriate calibers. "Load clips!" he barked. When all had their clips loaded they laid them on the firing tables. The next command was "Seat clips!" whereupon everyone took the loaded clips in hand and tapped the backside against the table, seating the cartridges against the clip housing. This procedure was drilled constantly because it cut down on the possibility of a bullet jamming in the weapon. After the tapping of the clips, the supervisor inspected them to ensure that the agents had seated them properly.

At Camp X, ear protection was not used when shooting took place outside. The supervisor positioned himself behind the two male agents and yelled, "Fire at will!"

The two male agents began firing simultaneously under the supervisor's watchful eye. Mr. Thomas and Didi were there to observe the women. Thomas always required the three women in his charge to take turns so he and Didi could observe each individually and offer advice. Tars went first. She slid the handgun's slide to chamber a round, aimed using both hands in the approved method Thomas insisted on, and squeezed off the eight rounds in the clip. Two rounds were within the two-inch bulls-eye, three within the next circle, two within the third circle, and one in the fourth. Good shooting, but Thomas, ever the demanding teacher, chose to temper any praise.

"Not bad, but you did better yesterday on your first go."

Maeve shot next. She raised her gun, took a moment to steady it, then pulled the trigger until the clip emptied and the slide stayed open. She did not fire as quickly as Tars, but she managed to put one hole on the edge of the bulls-eye, one in the second circle, and the rest scattered helter skelter in the outer circles. All eight rounds hit somewhere on the target—very acceptable shooting for a beginner and Didi congratulated Maeve on her consistent improvement, but here again Thomas looked for something negative.

"You're still all over the place, Maeve, and you're taking too long to fire. If someone is shooting back at you, I doubt they'll stand there waiting patiently for you to take aim."

Next came Erika. Thomas did not waste his time watching her, knowing the outcome. He moved back behind Tars and ordered her to get ready.

Erika lifted her Beretta and with rapid fire emptied the clip, shredding the black bulls-eye.

Chapter 15

Maeve spricht Deutsch

Canada—Camp X
Next day; Wednesday, 09 February 1944

"Are you perfect in everything?" Maeve asked.

Erika looked at her. "What do you mean?" They stood side-by-side with Tars under the running water of the gang shower in the men's barracks—the low-pressure water trickling from the shower heads.

"You toss around Didi and many of the men during fight training," said Maeve as she soaped her front. "Only Mr. Thomas can take you down and he has to be at his best to do it. You run the obstacle course like a stag, and on the gun range you seldom place a hole outside the bulls-eye. I feel as if they've given me an impossible task—to pass meself off as you."

"You're doing fine, Maeve. Your shooting is very acceptable for a beginner and getting better every day, and you've done very good learning Morse code and practicing the key pad. Turn around." Having no washcloths, Erika lathered her hands and soaped Maeve's back. "I'm not perfect. Not even close. I've made many mistakes in my life."

"What mistakes?"

"Too many to talk about. Let's leave it at that if you don't mind. And don't worry about matching me in fighting and shooting. If your assignment goes according to plan, you won't need to do those things."

Erika turned and Maeve washed her back. Although they were the same height and their facial resemblance remarkable, their bodies differed. Maeve was soft and feminine, her breasts larger, arms shorter, and shoulders narrower. The German's body reminded Maeve of a sculpture of the Roman goddess Diana, the huntress, she had seen in a London museum. Diana's sculpted marble body was beautiful but with a feral, dangerous quality not unlike that of a panther with muscles taut, ready to spring.

When Maeve finished washing Erika, both women turned toward Tars who immediately told them no one was touching her back. They rinsed, dried, donned robes and left the shower room, turning over the chained sign on the door so the men would know they had finished. They walked through the men's bunkroom untroubled by crude jokes or flirting, the proud Mounties always professional. A few days earlier, feeling sheepish about the insult she directed at the Mountie on her first day at Camp X, Maeve apologized to the man. In fact, if any suggestive dialogue or behavior took place between the women and the men it came from Maeve. And now, as they left the shower, Maeve purposely left her robe untied, allowing the men an eyeful.

"What are you doing?" Erika asked.

"Giving the lads a gander," Maeve answered.

"Don't do things like that unless it aids your mission," was Erika's advice. "And you're forgetting again to practice your American accent."

The three women now bunked together. Didi Nearne had moved Maeve and Tars into a larger room, big enough to also accommodate Erika after Mr. Thomas released the German from the brig two days after Maeve's arrival. Now back in their room after the evening shower, Erika and Tars dressed. Maeve remained in her robe.

"Let's get started," Erika said to Maeve. The two sat down at a small table while Tars sat on her bunk, lit a cigarette, and opened a satchel containing several maps. It had been discovered that Tars had an amazing memory. She could remember conversations verbatim that took place years ago and even the exact dates they occurred. She could quote long passages of books not read since her school days, including numerous chapters of the Old Testament. So Mr. Thomas gave Tars the job of memorizing maps of regions that would come into play during the mission.

"First, let's go over the German phrases we've been working on, Maeve. What will you say if someone speaks to you in German?"

Maeve took a moment to think. "Es ist nicht klug, deutsch zu sprechen. Sprechen Sie Englisch."

"And what are you saying?"

"It's not wise to speak German. Speak English."

"Good. You don't have to know what they said, just use that phrase if someone speaks German to you. Since you won't be in Germany and will be posing as me, the person will think you understand what they said but you want them to speak English for discretion's sake since I would be on the run and trying to avoid the authorities. But you need to work on pronunciation. *Nicht* is not pronounced 'nicked' it's 'nitch', no hard *k* sound. Say it again."

Maeve repeated the phrase several times, and they practiced a few other phrases Erika thought might give the impression that Maeve spoke German if the need arose. Everyone hoped that need would not present itself. At any rate, it was the best they could do; Maeve could not be expected to become fluent in a foreign language in eleven weeks. She did not possess Tars' photographic memory, but she had a good one and remembering the phrases was not the problem—it was her Irish accent, though she was actually doing better mimicking a German accent than an American one. English was a language she normally spoke and German was not, so it was easier for her to parrot Erika's pronunciation of German words—words Maeve had never spoken—than try to change the way she pronounced English words she had spoken her entire life. Maeve's struggles with the American accent concerned Erika.

Besides language, a critical aspect of Maeve's assignment was to be convincing—to be Erika—in other ways. This included knowing extensive biographical information on Erika and her family, names of close friends, and knowledge of Erika's likes, dislikes, and personal philosophy including religious beliefs and political ideology. Like Erika, Maeve was a Roman Catholic so here at least was one area not requiring extensive work.

"I thought Nazis didn't believe in God," Maeve had remarked when she learned Erika was Catholic.

"More propaganda," Erika had replied.

The reason for all this preparation was the likelihood that somewhere along Maeve's journey she would be intercepted and questioned by someone working on behalf of the Abwehr. The ocean crossing would have to be by freighter. Flying was out of the question.

A German spy on the lam somehow managing to trick the enemy military into a plane ride was a scenario too ridiculous—no bogus excuse for being able to pull that off would ever be accepted by her overseers in Germany. And credentials for transatlantic flights aboard the commercial Pan-Am Clipper were checked too thoroughly. Of course, the SOE or OSS could manufacture false credentials, but offering Abwehr some fantasy about how those credentials were gained was far too risky. No, Maeve aka Erika and Tars would have to cross on a sea-going cargo freighter, preferably one registered in a neutral country, because that's what Erika would do. Phony credentials would not be necessary on a foreign freighter, only enough money to bribe the ship's captain.

But it was because of the freighter crossing that Abwehr would have to be contacted. Freighters were high-priority targets and easy prey for the *Unterseeboote.* It could not be left to chance that Maeve's ship might end up in the crosshairs of a patrolling U-boat's telescope. The U-boats would have to be warned and called off. Abwehr would have to be given the name and flag of the freighter.

So, with the Abwehr notified that one of its prized agents was attempting to make her way back to Europe, Maeve could expect someone to ask questions somewhere along the journey—either before the ship sailed from the Western Hemisphere, or immediately upon arrival on the European mainland. What troubled Erika most was the possibility that a U-boat would be assigned to intercept and board the freighter mid-ocean to verify the Abwehr agent's identity, in which case Maeve's inability to speak German would surely betray her. If an ocean boarding by a U-boat crew were imminent it would be Maeve's duty to use her *L pill,* a lethal cyanide capsule, and end her life to avoid capture.

If capture was imminent and Maeve hesitated to commit suicide, Tars had orders to kill her before ending her own life. Concerning Maeve, Tars had two assignments: first, protect Maeve in any circumstance that warranted it and help her elude capture if possible; second, eliminate Maeve if capture became unavoidable. If Maeve were captured and underwent Gestapo interrogation she would surely crack—everyone cracked sooner or later once the Gestapo got hold of them. If Maeve was not alive to divulge information about the limited aspects of the mission it was necessary for her to know, perhaps the mission could be salvaged. Mr. Thomas had briefed Tars and Erika on these protocols in meetings before Maeve arrived at Camp X. To avoid frightening Maeve, Thomas would only *suggest* that she use her *L* pill to circumvent capture—an option available to her. But she would never be told about Tars' second duty if she hesitated to use the cyanide. Maeve would know only of Tars' first duty—to protect her.

Erika knew Tars' killing skills were why the SOE overlooked her mental peculiarities. They needed Tars' abilities on this mission. The SOE knew that if ordered to do so, the 'Ndrangheta assassin would harbor no qualms about pulling a trigger or burying a knife in someone's flesh. And it was because of those abilities that Erika needed Tars to join her after Maeve reached Europe. Only then would the real mission begin. Maeve's assignment was a diversion—a necessary and important diversion, but a diversion nevertheless. Another very important facet of Tars' resume that influenced the SOE to ignore her aberrant behavior was the fact she was Italian. This could not be underestimated. The cover story would be that while in America, Erika met another patriot from an Axis country who sought to return to Europe to fight the Allies. This cover for Tars was perfect; easy to prove, and something the Germans would readily accept. The Abwehr watchdogs could run a background check on Tars and prove to themselves she was who she claimed to be without the SOE being forced to supply counterfeit paperwork or plant false records.

"Any questions about your German phrases?" Erika asked Maeve after forty minutes of repetition.

"No, but why is Didi still giving me classes in French if I'm not going to France?"

"I speak French, you're me, so it can't hurt. Any questions about French? Is there anything you want to say in French? I can help you."

"How do you say 'Thomas is a wanker'?"

"Quit saying 'wanker,' Maeve. Americans don't use that word."

Chapter 16

Scars

Canada—Camp X
Later that month; Thursday, 24 February 1944

The Canadian Army doctor and army nurse had waited inside the first-aid hut at Camp X for nearly an hour. During that time an enlisted man had rolled in a gurney. On the gurney was a set of surgical instruments.

"Someone injured in an accident, it seems," commented the doctor to the nurse.

"What is this place, Major?" asked the nurse. "Who are these people?"

"I have no idea, Lieutenant."

As they speculated, the door suddenly opened and three women walked in.

"Hello," one of the women said. "My name is Didi. I won't introduce these two. I'm sure you understand." Nearne then thanked them for coming, as if they had a choice.

The two other women looked like sisters, perhaps twins, although one looked heartier.

"We need a slight bit of surgery performed, doctor," Nearne said.

Erika removed her coat and shirt. She rolled up the sleeves of her T-shirt and held out her arms. On the inside of her right bicep was a thin scar about two inches long; on the outside of her left arm a longer scar, thick and ugly, stretched from the front of the bicep to the back of her arm.

"We need these scars duplicated exactly on this woman." Nearne motioned to the other twin.

"You're joking," the doctor said incredulously.

Didi's somber stare and the anxious look on the slighter twin's face assured him the request was not a joke.

[that evening]

"I'm sorry that had to be done, Maeve," said Erika. "But it was necessary. You realize that, of course."

Maeve nodded. Back in their room after evening mess, the women sat at the room's small table ready to begin that night's personal instruction. Both of Maeve's upper arms were heavily bandaged.

"Tell me again," Erika said. "Where did you receive those wounds and what caused them?"

"The scar on my right arm I got at Quenzsee during knife training."

"What is Quenzsee?" Erika asked.

"The training camp for Abwehr agents outside Berlin. The scar on my left arm is from a gunshot wound I received in Cincinnati." Maeve winced. The Novocain had worn off.

"And where is Cincinnati?" (Actually the wound was suffered a few miles south of Cincinnati, in Kentucky, but Abwehr would not know that and Erika was keeping things as simple as possible.)

"Ohio. It's one of the states in the United States."

"That's right, but don't say 'it's one of the states' unless you're asked specifically for that information by someone not from the United States. To volunteer that information is a dead giveaway that you're not an American. Americans assume everyone in the world knows Ohio is a state. And why were you in Cincinnati?"

"To make contact with a friend of my father's who could help me."

"That's good, Maeve. We'll talk more about Cincinnati and the friend after we cover all the basics. Now let's continue where we left off last night with your biographical information. Simple things first. Never underestimate the easy details by thinking deeper information is more important. More spies have blown their cover making errors about what should, for them, be easy facts about their cover biography than with mistakes about the more in-depth details. Start with when and where you were born and your parents' and grandparents' names."

"I was born on December 16th, 1917 . . ."

Erika interrupted. "Stop right there. How would a German say the date?"

Maeve began again. "I was born on 16 December 1917 in Oberschopfheim, a small village in Baden, Germany. My father, Karl Wolfgang Lehmann, was German; my mother, Louise Gwendolyn Minton, was British; my grandfather on my father's side . . ."

This time Tars interrupted Maeve from her bunk. "If the bastards around here would let me keep one of the knives we use in training, I could have given you those scars, but the shitheads make me give them back every day."

Chapter 17

Reunion

England—Ringway Airport outside Manchester
Six weeks later; Wednesday, 05 April 1944

"How was your flight from Canada, Victor?"

SOE Colonel Ralph Winnecke faced Victor Knight across a desk in an office at the back of hangar 3C. For SOE agents who would be dropped behind enemy lines, the parachute training phase of their preparation was conducted mostly at Ringway. Among other duties, Winnecke ran the parachute school and was one of the SOE's resident experts on the Abwehrabteilung, or Abwehr, German Military Intelligence. The two men had just shaken hands and sat down.

"Long, and we flew through a bloody lightning storm over Ireland that rattled teeth."

Winnecke chuckled. "Good thing you were over land and you're well experienced with a parachute."

"Shall I bring her in?"

"By all means."

"She knows me only as Mr. Thomas," Knight said as he rose to fetch Erika Lehmann waiting outside the colonel's office.

"Of course. And we'll have no introductions. I don't intend to hand a German Abwehr operative my name."

With Maeve's training nearly completed at Camp X, the final, and most critical phase of Erika's training would begin soon. Most of that training would take place in Scotland. With this brief lull in the schedule before Maeve's assignment started, *Intrepid* ordered Knight to take Erika to England where a few preliminaries to her final preparation would be gotten out of the way. This would save important time. The stay would be brief; in three days they would return to Camp X where Erika would help get Maeve's leg of the mission underway in the United States.

Among other interviews, interrogations, and briefings scheduled for Erika on this trip was this meeting with Winnecke, the

SOE Abwehr expert. Knight opened the office door and signaled her to come in. Winnecke, well aware of the German spy's reputation, was eager to meet with her.

"Ah, Sonderführer Lehmann, the infamous *Lorelei,*" Winnecke said as he motioned for her to take a seat (*Sonderführer* was Erika's Abwehr rank). As Winnecke had instructed, no introductions were offered. There was no name on his office door or nameplate on his desk and he was not in uniform. "Did Mr. Thomas tell you that you're practically a legend in our tight-knit little Secret Service family?" Erika stared at him. "No? Well, we know quite a lot about you, Fräulein Lehmann. Of course we are well briefed by the Americans on your latest escapade in their country—posing as an American and managing to get a job at one of their shipyards where you managed to steal information on a new metal alloy the Yanks are developing, along with other top-secret information.

"But we can trace your Abwehr career further back than that. There was your infiltration of the American Embassy in Portugal back in 1940—again posing as an American and managing to break into the embassy safe. Jolly good work—for you, of course. Not for our side I'm afraid.

"And, of course, your efforts haven't been directed solely at the Yanks. You've also graced our island with your attention. A couple of years ago you kidnapped one of our MI-9 French Resistance experts who was also a leading cryptographer—Henry Wiltshire. I know Henry—good bloke—or should I say 'knew' Henry? What's happened to him, by the way? I hope the old boy wasn't turned over to the Gestapo. And how did you manage to get Henry out of England? U-boat?"

"I'll not discuss anything that doesn't relate to the coming mission," Erika stated flatly. "General Donovan promised me I would not be expected to answer non-mission-related questions, and Mr. Knight (she looked at Thomas) agreed. I made it very clear to everyone that I will not betray my country. I'm taking part in this to eradicate vermin that are poisoning Germany."

"How do you know my name?" the surprised Knight demanded.

"Oh, I know a lot about you, too. Don't forget that Abwehr and the SIS play the same game, Victor. I've seen your photograph and I know of your exploits in North Africa with the First Airlanding Brigade and your later work in Sicily for the SOE." Winnecke and Thomas looked at each other. Erika turned back to Winnecke. "But I'll answer your question about Henry's welfare. No, he was not turned over to the Gestapo. I made sure of that. He was questioned by our Abwehr people and he'll sit out the war in a prisoner of war camp with other captured Brits and Americans. No harm will come to him if he doesn't try to escape. I know where you're going with this. You want to know if Henry talked, and if he did, what he divulged. I will not answer that. It's not related to this mission. Now, next set of subtle questions, please . . . Major Winnecke. Or have you made colonel by now?"

After a two-hour interview where he gleaned none of the insights into the inner workings of the German intelligence community he had hoped for, Ralph Winnecke called an end to the fruitless parley with Erika Lehmann. Victor Knight led her out to the car where the RMP driver waited.

"Where to now?" Erika asked Knight after they slid into the back seat.

"York. It's a short jaunt, only a couple of hours. Two men from our Edinburgh section have come down to meet you. We'll spend the night there before returning to London tomorrow."

"When will I see my grandparents? You promised a visit."

"In a couple of days—before we return to Camp X. That is if all goes well. The interview just now wasn't very good form on your part. Your attitude could very well be considered hostile. You're supposed to be cooperating."

"Not when it comes to answering questions it was agreed I wouldn't be asked. I could consider that hostile on the SOE's part, or at least consider it as tainting our deal. And if I'm not allowed to see my grandparents I *will* take that as breaking the agreement. My participation in the mission will end, and you'll have to hand me back to the Americans. They can toss me into prison or execute me as they choose, but only after I explain to them that the British reneged over such a simple matter as letting me see my grandparents, which was promised me."

[two days later—07 April; Saint Cecilia's Abbey, Isle of Wight]
A Benedictine nun in full habit led an elderly couple through a labyrinth of stone hallways to the abbey's small chapel. "Please have a seat in here, Sir Louis and Lady Minton," the nun instructed. "They will bring your guest in directly. Here you will not be disturbed."

"Thank you Sister Catherine," said Louis Minton. He knew the nun's name only because she had introduced herself when he and his wife arrived a few minutes ago. Neither had ever been inside this remote abbey until today. They sat down in the second of three pews.

"Why this place, Louis? Why so far from London?"

"I don't know, Marie."

Since last autumn they had waited for the promised visit with their granddaughter. Louis Minton, a former foreign ministry official, was a man with connections and he had made inquiries to the Imperial General Staff trying to find out when this visit might occur. His questions went unanswered until this morning when a short, balding man who introduced himself as Mr. Brown appeared on their London doorstep unannounced, ready to take them on this rendezvous. After a two-hour train ride to Portsmouth and a boat ride aboard a Royal Navy launch, now they were on the Isle of Wight.

"Will I recognize her?" Marie asked. She had not seen their granddaughter since before the war broke out in 1939. Her husband had seen Erika recently—the previous fall, when he had gone to America to visit her. At the time, she was being held prisoner in the stockade at Fort Knox, Kentucky.

"Yes, of course, my dear. Erika looks the same."

It had been a great shock when they learned their granddaughter was a German spy. Of course they knew their son-in-law, Erika's father, was German. Their daughter met him in Berlin when Louis was assigned to the British embassy there before the Great War. They also knew that Karl Lehmann worked for Joseph

Goebbels' Propaganda Ministry; this was no secret. And naturally Erika was a German citizen having been born in that country. But a *spy!* At first they did not believe it. Only after Louis arrived at Fort Knox after being informed of his granddaughter's predicament by an American woman who befriended Erika were the English grandparents forced to accept the fact that their granddaughter was indeed a Nazi secret agent.

"I'm quite nervous, Louis."

"Don't be nervous, Marie. We'll have only a few minutes, and it's unlikely we'll be left alone with her. Remember we talked about not wasting our time dwelling on her past activities for the Germans. There's nothing she can tell us about that or her upcoming mission. At least we know she's now working for our side and that's certainly a relief. Let's see if we can help her in any way. That will be the best use of our time and we'll. . . ."

The conversation was interrupted when the chapel door opened. Mr. Brown led Erika in followed by an RMP. When Erika saw her grandparents she rushed over. They stood to greet her.

"Grandmum!" Erika hugged Marie tightly and kissed her cheek. "I love you." While still hugging her grandmother with one arm she reached out and drew her grandfather in. "Granddad."

Chapter 18

Off to America

Canada—Ontario
One week later; Thursday, 13 April 1944

Maeve took a sip of the barbiturate-laced water from her canteen as the Lockheed Electra taxied to the runway. She had hoped her nerve-shattering dread of flying had left her by now, or at least decreased, given the amount of time she had spent inside airplanes over the past three months, but no; the plane was not yet in the air and Maeve was shaking. She looked outside. A half-rain, half-snow Canadian spring drizzle ran down the window and wetted the wing. Inside, Erika Lehmann sat next to her at the window. Tars sat directly behind Erika. No guards were on hand; the only other passengers were Leroy Carr and Al Hodge who sat beside each other a few rows forward on the other side of the aisle.

When the Electra reached the runway it stopped momentarily; engines grew louder and the aircraft jerked into motion. Maeve gasped loudly, took a big swig, and tightened her grip on the armrests.

"Calm down, Maeve," Erika said as the plane picked up speed. "This flight won't be long—nothing like the flights across the Atlantic."

When the nose of the Electra rose and the wheels left the ground, Maeve panicked and shouted, "Holy Mary!"

"There she goes," Tars said from behind. "Didi told us she'd do this. Erika, have the co-pilot fuck her. That will take her mind off it."

Maeve took another drink, and then another, until Erika took the canteen from her. "You have to go easy on that stuff, Maeve. When we land you have to be able to walk. I don't want to have to carry you off the airplane."

The flight from the airfield north of Camp X to Fort Dix, New Jersey, lasted two and a half hours. After landing, Maeve worked her way to the hatch before the plane finished taxiing and stepped off first. By the time Leroy Carr, the last one off, stood on the ground a small Army bus had pulled up. They were taken to the fort's administration building where Carr went inside while everyone else waited. During the wait, a curious Army corporal—the bus driver—kept looking in his rearview mirror at the two blondes he figured had to be twin sisters—even their hairdos matched. (Three days ago, Didi Nearne took Maeve and Erika to a hairdresser in Toronto who dyed Maeve's hair to match Erika's shade of blonde exactly, and then cut and styled both women's hair to match.)

Twenty minutes later Carr returned to the bus and handed the corporal some paperwork. Carr signaled to Erika and the two of them got off. Maeve, Tars, and Al Hodge stayed on.

Erika and Carr watched the bus pull away. "How long will it take them to reach New York City?" Erika asked.

"About two hours, maybe a bit more," Carr answered.

An Army Jeep and driver waited for them nearby, but Erika asked if they could walk back to the airplane. Carr thanked the private and told him he wouldn't be needed.

"It will be good for Maeve to be with Tars without me around," Erika remarked as they began the long walk. "They'll have to get comfortable working together, just the two of them."

"That's right. I could have left them at the compound in Canada until you get to New York and then brought them down. But I thought it was time to get them on their own. This trip will give Al a chance to see how they handle themselves without guards and without the secure environment of the camp. They're not here to sightsee; they're here for further training. Some important parts of their preparation can't be simulated at Camp X; we need a city."

"I'm sure part of the training will be to have them followed, and it will be their job to elude the tail in a strange city."

Carr looked at Erika.

"Standard Abwehr training," she added. "I was taken to Dresden, a city I had never visited, and tailed."

Carr smiled. "And you eluded the tail, of course."

"If I hadn't, I wouldn't be here now. Maybe I would have been wise to have failed and returned to my previous life. Perhaps I would be a teacher now—of languages or music."

"Do you regret how your life has worked out?"

"Wishing things had turned out differently serves no purpose. Does it?"

"No, I guess not."

They reached the refueled Electra that sat silent with engines off. The Army pilot and co-pilot were having coffee inside a nearby Quonset hut. When they spotted their two passengers through the window, they walked out to the plane.

"We're ready any time you are, Major," Carr said to the pilot.

"Then let's board and get underway," said the pilot. "The plane is ready."

Carr asked, "What time can we expect to land?"

"Normally it's a three-hour flight, but it looks like we'll have a headwind to deal with. Better figure about three and a half hours." The pilot looked at his wristwatch. "We'll have you in Cincinnati around suppertime."

Chapter 19

Tars Improvises

New York City
Next day; Friday, 14 April 1944

"Come on, get your worthless Irish ass out of bed!" Tars shook Maeve from her sleep at just past five o'clock in the morning. "Hodge is knocking on the door."

Not opening her eyes, Maeve grumbled sleepily and turned away. "Tell him to get fooked."

Another knock. Tars cursed and went to the door. Al Hodge stood in the hotel hallway.

"We're coming. Don't get your balls in a ringer, Al. That's what you Americans say, right?"

Hodge stepped inside. "I told you two to be ready by five." He saw that Tars was dressed in the clothes he had issued for today. "What's the problem? Where's Maeve?" Hodge could not see the beds from where he stood. Suddenly a sleepy-eyed Maeve walked into view—totally naked—on her way to the bathroom.

"Holy. . . ." Hodge turned away.

"What's the matter?" Tars asked. "First time you've seen rib bumpers and a man holster?"

"You're a real genteel lady, Tarsitano. That's why we gave you that codename—*Lady*. Get her dressed and meet me in the lobby in fifteen minutes. Be sure you both have the money I issued you last night."

Thirty minutes later Maeve and Tars stepped off the elevator into the lobby of the Waldorf=Astoria. A fuming Al Hodge was waiting.

"That was a long fifteen minutes. I hope you two realize that for the mission to proceed you have to complete the training here to my satisfaction. If for any reason I think you're not up to the task, all deals are off."

Tars said, "I don't care what you or your OSS buddy thinks."

Hodge frowned, looked around quickly, and warned in a low voice, "Never mention the OSS in public. Someone might overhear."

Maeve, now fully awake, had her family at stake. "We'll pass the requirements, won't we Tars?"

Tars shrugged. "I doubt it; you can't get your butt out of bed in the morning."

Al Hodge shook his head and felt disaster loomed with these two.

"This is quite the place," Maeve commented in the American accent she had practiced. "Your . . . (she stopped herself as she almost said 'OSS'). Your *company* must have a great deal of money."

"When we need a hotel we choose carefully," Hodge said, leading them toward the hotel entrance. "There are reasons we're here. This hotel was built by a wealthy American family—the Astors. Lady Astor, who lives in the penthouse, has for years been a supporter of women's rights and causes. This hotel is known as a place where unescorted women can come and go safely. Because of that, no one will be nosy about two unescorted women staying here, as might be the case at some other hotels. Besides, some rooms here aren't as expensive as you'd think for a hotel like this. You two are in one of those rooms."

"Thanks, Al," said Tars, "for letting us know you're an avaro."

Hodge responded, "I'm sure that's Italian for something vulgar."

"Cheapskate."

"That's almost flattering coming from you."

"Screw you, Al."

"That's more like what I expected."

Maeve broke in. "Can we talk about why we had to drag out of bed at such an unholy hour?" The doorman opened the door and they walked into brisk air under a still dark sky.

"You're going on a walking tour of Lower Manhattan," Hodge answered as they began strolling Park Avenue. Under a streetlight, he handed them a map with a wending red line representing a walk of many miles. "Walk this route exactly. It will take you through SoHo, the Bowery, and Times Square. I've figured in more than enough time to complete the walk without being rushed. You can stop when you need to rest, you can walk in and out of buildings, shops, and cafes along the way, but when you leave them, continue the route. Be on guard for a tail. Your assignment is to spot the tail and give me an accurate description of the person tailing you. That's all. It's not your job today to elude—that will come later. Simply be able to give me a description, and tell me where along the route you were followed. You might be followed just once or multiple times by different persons. Any questions?"

Maeve and Tars looked at each other. No questions.

Hodge continued, "Be back here by nine o'clock tonight—no later. If you are one minute late, you fail. Do you understand?"

The women nodded.

"You have money for lunch and dinner and will have plenty of time to stop and eat along the way. Don't lose the map. Have a great day, ladies."

Hodge turned and walked back toward the hotel. Maeve called after him, "What about breakfast?"

"Don't worry. I'll enjoy it," Hodge called back.

Tars mumbled to Maeve, "They're all a bunch of *bastardi.*"

"How are we supposed to know if we're being followed? There must be thousands of people walking the streets." Maeve made the comment as she and Tars ate lunch inside a SoHo delicatessen. Now noon, they had walked for over six hours, stopping when they chose to at various points along the way. "I wish Erika were with us, she'd know if we were being followed."

"I can tell if we're being followed," Tars crowed.

"So we haven't been followed?"

"I'm not sure." Tars bit into her cod sandwich.

"What do you mean? You just said you would know."

Tars swallowed. "I know what I said. When I worked for the 'Ndrangheta, I was the one doing the following, except for a couple of times when I think I was followed."

"You *think* you were followed? What did you do?"

88

Tars looked at Maeve like she had just asked a silly question. "I killed them, of course." She took a drink of Pepsi-Cola.

"Have you noticed the guy in the gray jacket?" Maeve asked Tars as they stood on the corner of 7th Avenue and West 43rd Street just after nightfall. The city lay under a wartime brown-out. Less burdensome than a blackout, every other streetlight was still lit, but the enormous neon advertising signs of Times Square surrounding the two women were dark—the signs ordered turned off in 1942 when the U.S. Navy determined that German U-boats offshore used the bright backdrop of the city to silhouette merchant vessels on a dark sea, making them easy targets.

"No, why? Is someone following us?" Tars knew not to turn around.

"I think so. I noticed him after we left that restaurant where we ate dinner. And aren't you the one who said you could tell when you're being followed? What should we do?"

"Start walking and don't turn around."

"Me feet are ahowlin'."

"That's because you're fat. Nearne makes you eat too much. And your Irish brogue is creeping back. You're supposed to use that American accent you've been practicing."

"I'm not fat. I still don't weigh as much as Erika and she's anything but fat. I'm just tired. I've walked me arse ... my ass off."

Tars took control. "When we get to the next storefront, we'll stop and look through the window. We'll be able to tell then if he's following us. You said he has a gray jacket?"

"Yeah, and a floppy hat."

They soon came upon a seedy theater. Two women, obviously prostitutes stood at the doorway smoking. The building had no windows but numerous signs. Tars stopped. The prostitutes finished their cigarettes, dropped the butts on the sidewalk and disappeared inside.

"This looks like your kind of place, Maeve."

"Bite my arse ... butt."

"Alright, shut up and listen," Tars spoke quickly. "We'll pretend to read the signs. Look for him out of the corner of your eye like we worked on at the camp. Remember what Didi told you: when he gets near, turn and smile at him. If he's not tailing you he'll think you're flirting and come over because he thinks he might get lucky. And like she said, if he *is* tailing us he'll ignore you and walk by and dawdle somewhere up the street until we start walking again."

When the man neared, Maeve turned, looked at him and smiled. He glanced at her briefly and continued on.

"Let's go," Tars whispered when the man was just a few steps past.

"Wait. We haven't given him time to get ahead and stop."

Tars ignored her and took off after the man, walking quickly. Maeve followed. Tars spotted a rusty piece of pipe in a heap of debris on the trash-strewn sidewalk, picked it up, ran up behind the man and bashed him over the head. He grunted and fell on his face. He was still conscious when Tars hit him again, this time on his back. The man yelled in pain, turned over, and reached into his back pocket.

"Here's my wallet! Take the money!" he said in a panic while grimacing from the blows.

Maeve grabbed Tars and pulled her away. "What are you doing?!!"

Tars struggled to break away, shouting "Let me go!" but the stronger Maeve held on.

"We've got to get out of here!" Maeve said loudly.

Tars dropped the pipe, snatched the man's wallet from his hand, and the two women ran, cutting through a series of alleys.

"That guy wasn't following us," Maeve said when they stopped running. "He thought we were robbing him."

"You don't know that. That might be standard procedure for a tail—to act like he's innocent if confronted."

"Well, that's grand. If he was a tail, what are we going to tell Hodge when the man reports what you did? We were told to just supply a description."

"That's why I took his wallet. What better way to supply information on someone? We'll give the wallet to Hodge. Sometimes you have to improvise. Those OSS and SOE butt-lickers know that."

"Grand." Maeve shot Tars a look of disapproval.

"Americans don't say 'grand' when they mean 'great' or 'fantastic.' You're slipping again."

It was just after 8:30 p.m. when Al Hodge answered the knock on his hotel room door.

"Well, you're not late. Good work, ladies. Come in."

Maeve and Tars walked in.

"Have a seat," Hodge offered as he closed the door. "How'd it go?"

"Fine," Maeve said while chewing a large wad of gum. She sat in one of the Windsor chairs. Tars picked the divan.

"Did you complete the entire route?"

"Yes," Maeve answered.

"Good. Were you followed?"

Maeve hesitated and looked at Tars.

Tars answered. "Yeah, a 31-year-old guy in a gray jacket and floppy hat."

"Where along the route?"

"Times Square."

"Times Square, gray jacket and floppy hat." Hodge verified the information.

"Here's his wallet." Tars handed it to him.

"So that's how you knew his exact age. How did you get his wallet?"

"I improvised."

"Elaborate."

"There was a struggle. We got the best of him and I took his wallet to give to you."

Hodge looked at her. "Okay, ladies. That's all for today. Get some sleep and meet me in the lobby tomorrow morning at nine. I'll let you sleep in a little tomorrow and give you time to eat breakfast."

When the two women were out in the hallway, Tars smirked, "Ha! I told you he was a tail."

"Still, we weren't supposed to attack him."

"Like I said, sometimes you have to improvise."

[Cincinnati—early the next morning]

When his phone rang at 7:30 a.m. Leroy Carr was shaving. He grabbed a towel and wiped shaving cream from his face before walking out of his hotel bathroom to answer.

"Hello."

"Leroy, it's Al. I'm calling from a pay phone down the street from the hotel. If you don't want to talk on your hotel phone, call me back from another phone. I'll give you this number."

"Go ahead, Al. You know what you can say and what you can't."

"Yesterday I sent Maeve and Tars out for the day on the no-tail assignment."

"Right. How'd they do?" Carr knew there would be no one assigned to tail the women on no-tail day. The goal was to see if the women reported correctly that no one had tailed them, or if they incorrectly thought they had been followed at some point.

"They waylaid an innocent civilian in Times Square about seven-thirty last night. They thought the guy was following them. Tars stole his wallet. I called the police, gave them the guy's name, and asked if there had been a report of an assault. Sure enough. I went down to the police station, used my U.S. marshal I.D. and requested a copy of the report. Tars snuck up behind the guy and hit him over the head with a pipe. The guy told the police 'the shorter of the two women,' so it was Tars."

"Damn! What did Maeve do?"

"Tars clubbed the guy again—in the back after he was down. Maeve—the report said the 'taller woman'—pulled her away. Tars then took the guy's wallet and they ran off."

"Do we have to worry about the police?"

"No. The cops asked me if I had any information but I told them another marshal in our office found the guy's wallet and we were curious if there had been any trouble. I told them it was standard U.S

marshal procedure to inquire about foul play when a wallet is found with no money. I had taken the money out to make it look like a robbery."

"Good thinking."

"I was surprised to find money in it. I figured those two pirates would take the money before handing me the wallet."

"What do the women have to say for themselves?"

"For now, I'm letting them believe the guy was a tail, so they went to their room last night feeling pretty cocky—especially Tarsitano."

"Good work, Al." Carr thought for a moment. "Just sit on this for now. Go ahead and proceed with the schedule. We can't afford trouble like this but there's too much at stake to put the skids on things over one screw-up. Let's see how they do today when they're actually tailed. Was E Street able to get us Marienne Schenk?" (on E Street in Washington D.C. was where OSS headquarters was located.)

"She checked into a hotel on Fifth Avenue yesterday."

"Good. Schenk's the best shadow in the business, and those two won't be expecting a woman. If they can spot Marienne and lose her we'll finally have something positive to report. Call me tonight and let me know how it went—doesn't matter how late."

"Okay. But I wouldn't get my hopes up that they'll spot Marienne, let alone lose her. How's it going in Cincinnati with you-know-who?"

"She spent most of yesterday out on her own. She won't tell me where she went, of course. I think she plans to contact her man today."

"I know you trust her not to disappear, but that has to be frustrating giving her carte blanche with no way to keep tabs on her."

"It's frustrating not to know exactly what she's doing and whose she seeing, but trying to tail Lehmann would be laughable, especially when she's expecting it. She'd spot the tail and lose it faster than you can wind your watch. Besides, having a certain amount of free rein is part of her deal with Donovan and *Intrepid.* You and I just have to consider it a phase of the training—a test. If we can't count on her to not disappear here in the States we're sure as hell not going to be able to count on her to not disappear in Europe—her home turf. We'll just have to keep our fingers crossed. If she did disappear we'd have our work cut out finding her, unlike with Maeve and Tars who we'd probably round up before the day was out. But you're right, I think Erika will keep her part of the deal. She wants this mission too badly. Anything else?"

"Maeve is still struggling with the American accent. She'll sound okay for a sentence or two then slip and her brogue comes out."

"Perfect," Carr said sarcastically. "I was hoping when she got to New York and was surrounded by Americans it might be easier for her. We're going to have our work cut out for us keeping this mission from being scrubbed, Al, let alone holding any hope it succeeds."

Chapter 20

Adalwulf

Cincinnati, Ohio
That evening; Saturday, 15 April 1944

On the screen of the RKO Century Theater, Tallulah Bankhead argued with Walter Slezak. The characters they portrayed sat adrift in a lifeboat far out to sea with other survivors after a German U-boat torpedoed their ship. The Americans in the lifeboat had just learned that Slezak's character was the captain of that U-boat, also destroyed in the confrontation. They had pulled him from the water thinking he was another of their equally unfortunate shipmates. Now that the truth was known, the Americans were debating what to do with the U-boat captain—let him remain in the lifeboat, or toss him back into the drink.

Adalwulf von Krause sat in his reserved balcony box as he did every Saturday evening regardless which movie happened to be on the marquee. Many times he quickly became bored with American movies; he considered most Hollywood films frivolous if not idiotic, and he rarely stayed for the second feature. But tonight he enjoyed Alfred Hitchcock's *Lifeboat*. To Krause, the Nazi U-boat Kapitän was winning the ideological debate. *What the Kapitän told the Americans made sense; why could they not understand?*

It had taken many twists and turns of fate for Krause to end up in a Cincinnati movie theater. Before the war, he had for awhile conducted banking business in the United States on behalf of his native Germany, and had been asked to remain in this country after the onset of the war to oversee Reich financial interests in the Americas—the behest on behalf of the Führer himself. He was now in the States surreptitiously, ordered by the powers back home to apply for American citizenship before the war. Adalwulf von Krause, to anyone curious, was simply a retired banker.

Krause glanced at the seat to his right—where *she* had sat. He could not remember what movie had played that autumn evening, yet he remembered the night he met her as his best occasion in years: the theater, dinner, the long chat in his study, her playing the piano—a most fond memory. She was beautiful, intelligent, refined and gracious—without a doubt the perfect Aryan woman. He held no designs or desires for her physically. No, he was more than twice her age and now free from the carnal urges men suffer from so severely in their younger years. For Krause, a Prussian aristocrat, she was the fascinating daughter of an old friend and a kindred spirit who, for a time, restored to him vigor and purpose.

When she asked for his help, with great delight he responded. To help was his duty to the Fatherland and to her father, a friend and brother of the Ring. Nevertheless, he worried. The help he had arranged for her she had not employed. She had yet to call on his associate in New York who could give her what she needed—a way home. As the months passed, Krause could only hope the worst had not befallen her.

When *Lifeboat* ended, Krause stayed for the newsreels. In the Pacific, U.S. carrier-based planes had recently begun an attack on the Mariana Islands. In Europe, film footage from the air showed Hamburg ablaze after the Americans dropped 3,000 tons of bombs on the beleaguered city—excruciating for Krause to watch. After the newsreels, Krause knew a Three Stooges short would follow—the Americans seemed to insist on such inane lunacy. This time the Stooges were construction workers. After Larry inadvertently lit Moe's pants afire with a blowtorch and scorched his buttocks, Moe retaliated by bonking Larry over the head with a heavy monkey-wrench. Then Moe turned his attention to Curly (who had done nothing), poked him in the eyes and slapped his face with a handsaw. The audience on the theater floor roared with laughter. Krause rose to leave.

As he walked through the theater lobby, the manager called Krause's name and hustled over. "I was asked to give you this envelope before you left, Mr. von Krause." Just as the man handed Krause the envelope, one of the concession counter girls yelled for her manager's help. It was intermission, the lobby was crowded with moviegoers ready for their popcorn, Cracker Jacks, candy and soda and the persnickety cash register had decided to give her trouble.

"An envelope?" Krause was surprised. "Who . . .?" But the manager darted away to address the emergency before Krause could finish his question. He tore open the end of the sealed envelope and extracted a card.

Dearest Adalwulf, I'll be waiting for you at the restaurant where we last dined. I have missed your company and I hope to see you there.

Karl's daughter

Krause stepped briskly toward the concession counter and hurriedly worked his way through the crowd. One teenager shouted, "Hey, old man, no cutting in line!"

"Telephone for a taxi immediately," Krause ordered the manager.

He waited impatiently in front of the RKO for the cab that took twenty minutes to arrive. *A taxi would never take this long to arrive in Berlin.* Finally, the yellow car pulled up to the curb.

"Netherlands Hotel," he told the driver as he slid into the back seat. Once the cab pulled away, Krause again looked at the note. He was elated at the prospect of seeing and talking with Erika again, but what had happened? Why was she still here? If things had gone as he'd planned for her, she would have been back in Germany months ago. What went wrong? The note proved she was free so that was a relief. The worst, as Krause had sometimes feared for her, had not happened. He was filled with anticipation at seeing her again and lost patience with the driver whom he thought a slowpoke.

"Driver, you are taking too long. We should have been there by now."

"Buddy, look out the window. That's traffic you're lookin' at."

"A twenty dollar tip for you if you have me there in five minutes."

The driver laughed. "Twenty dollars? Yeah, right." For him that amount was half a week's wages.

In the rearview mirror, the driver watched Krause pull his wallet from the inside breast pocket of his expensive three-piece suit. He quickly yanked out a $20 bill and dropped it on the passenger seat beside the driver.

Suddenly the taxi picked up speed and began weaving through traffic.

The upper crust dined at The Palms in the Netherlands Hotel, and Adalwulf von Krause was a regular. To The Palms he had taken Karl's daughter on the night they met—the night she appeared out of the blue at the RKO Century.

The majordomo greeted Krause. "Ah, Mr. von Krause. Wonderful to see you. Only one dining tonight?" The man knew Krause almost always dined alone but asked for politeness sake.

"I'm meeting a young woman, but I'm not sure if she has arrived." Krause knew she would be cautious. Suddenly he felt a gentle hand on his arm and there she was, standing next to him. Erika wrapped her arm around his and smiled.

"Ah, and here she is," said the majordomo. "Perfect timing."

They followed the man to Krause's preferred table, she on his arm and dressed elegantly as one would expect of a chic woman dining at the finest restaurant in the city. Her thin white evening gown fit her like a second skin and accented her curves; the white, fur-trimmed wrap covered her shoulders but did not hide her cleavage the dress offered—just the right amount to draw the eye and please both men and women, but not so much as to be tawdry. Her hair and makeup perfect. Krause remained standing while the majordomo pulled a chair for Erika.

"May I take your wrap, madam?"

"Yes, please." She handed him the wrap; he bowed and left to return to his station.

"Adalwulf, I'm so happy to see you," Erika said as they settled into their chairs.

"And I am happy to see you, my dear. But tell me what has happened. I was most surprised to receive your note tonight. I would have thought you would be in . . ." Krause stopped before he said *Germany* and looked around at the other diners nearby. ". . . at home by now."

"Many delays, my dear Adalwulf. I'll tell you all about it later, after dinner."

Krause understood. The discussion was not one to conduct with other ears nearby.

Erika reached over the table, put her hand on his and smiled. For a long moment they sat silent, simply enjoying the reunion.

She was first to break the silence. "I see you still attend the theater."

"Yes, old habits are hard to break, it seems. Your hair is lovely, my dear. Shorter I believe." He did not bother to comment on the color. During their dealings last fall her hair changed color often. Krause knew she had good reason to adjust her appearance.

"Yes, it is shorter. How is your grandson?"

Krause frowned. "Wilmar is much the same, I'm afraid. He still is extremely skillful at finding trouble—most of it his own doing, I'm sure. Just last month some ruffian thrashed him outside a squalid tavern in Over the Rhine. He spent the night in hospital." He left out the article before *hospital* as a German might do.

"That's unfortunate. I'm sorry." Erika's own experience with Willy assured her he surely deserved every blow. Last fall she had attacked Willy herself. She changed the subject. "And you, Adalwulf. Your health? You've been well?"

"Yes, quite well. For an old man I have no complaints." He noticed her right hand. "I see you still have the Ring."

"Of course," she said as the waiter arrived to take their orders.

They lingered over dinner, sipping a fine Rhône wine with the rack of lamb, and they enjoyed talking of small matters. For dessert, Krause ordered raspberry-almond tart and Amaretto.

When it came time to leave the table, Erika said, "I have a room here in the hotel where we can talk."

◊ ◊ ◊

[same evening—New York City]

Maeve and Tars sat at a table in a Bowery dive talking to a woman they met there. The Blue Balls Tavern, along with most of its clientele, smelled of strong drink, cigarette smoke, and grease. Today was their second day of training in New York City. The assignment today was to again look for someone following them, but instead of simply spotting the tail and supplying a description, Al Hodge told them they must lose the tail this time. So far they felt they had not been followed, but three hours still remained before they were to report back to Hodge at the hotel.

"So what's your name again?" Maeve asked the woman sitting with them. She was forced to raise her voice to be heard above the jukebox and loud cursing of the patrons. Whiskey sours sat in front of all three women. Maeve was on her fourth round, Tars her third.

"Marienne," she answered and took a sip of her second drink. She had walked into the bar after Maeve and Tars.

"Are you married?" Maeve asked in her native Irish accent. The last whiskey sour had shooed away her faux American accent.

"Yeah. My husband is a Marine. Just enlisted a month ago. He's in basic at Parris Island."

"Aye, and you're here to be naughty." Maeve laughed and leaned over on Tars.

"Maeve knows all about being naughty," said Tars. "Don't you, Maeve?" Tars turned up her drink and finished it.

"I do sure!" Maeve killed her drink as well.

"Bartender!" Tars shouted. "Bring us another round, ya bald-headed sonuvabitch!"

More loud laughter from the three women ensued, and hoots from some men at the bar. When the bartender delivered three more whiskey sours he told the women that these drinks were compliments of a man at the bar.

"Well, send him over," Maeve slurred. "And bring us all a shot on the side." As the bartender started away, Maeve called after him. "And wash your apron, why don't you. It looks like you wiped your arse with it!"

In a moment a burly man with a dark moustache walked over carrying the three shots of whiskey. He set down the drinks and looked at Maeve. "Spud told me you invited me over." Maeve burst out laughing at the name *Spud,* but the man thought she laughed at *him.*

"What's so funny, you drunk bitch?"

Maeve stopped laughing. "Don't get your gonads in a twist, Mister. That name you said is funny. What did you think I was laughing at?"

"How much for a wall job?" The man was apparently familiar with prostitutes and assumed three lone women in a dive bar must be on the job. And he knew *wall job* was a common term referring to the preferred position among such women, who thought if they stood during sex they were less likely to become pregnant. Therefore, most transactions were completed with the girl standing and leaning against a wall. This position also expedited the contract by negating the need to find a bed.

"How much ya got?" Maeve giggled as she looked at Tars and Marienne.

"We'll call it even for those drinks." The man grabbed Maeve's arm and roughly jerked her from the chair.

Chapter 21

The Shadow

Cincinnati
Same evening; Saturday, 15 April 1944

Erika Lehmann led Adalwulf von Krause into a room on the 7th floor of the Netherlands Hotel. She would not spend the night, renting the room solely for a secure place to talk. Now on her second day in Cincinnati, Erika spent yesterday watching Krause's home and shadowing him on his morning walk and later errands. Today she followed him to the movie theater (expecting to do so knowing it was his Saturday routine), left the note with the manager then made her way through town to wait in a shop across from the hotel—the shop giving her a vantage point to spot any irregularities with his arrival. She trusted Krause, but given their earlier collaboration it was possible he could be under surveillance without his knowledge. Last fall she had worked hard with her planning to keep Krause clear of suspicion, and she was happy for Krause when after two days of following him she saw her efforts had succeeded. And it was for Krause's sake that Erika refused to tell Leroy Carr where she was going or whom she was contacting while in Cincinnati. Carr knew only that she would be making the necessary arrangements for Maeve.

"Have a seat, dear Adalwulf, please," Erika said as she closed the door.

He chose a wooden chair, sat, stood his expensive teak walking cane with its snarling, solid silver wolf's head handle between his legs and rested his hands on it. Erika sat on the edge of the bed.

"Sollen wir Deutsch sprechen?" She asked him if he wished to speak in German.

"Ja, wunderbar."

The rest of the conversation was in their native tongue.

"Many things have happened to cause my delay since we last saw each other, Adalwulf," Erika began. "I cannot speak of them; I know you understand."

"Of course, my dear." Krause knew she was an Abwehr agent and limited on what she could divulge.

"Adalwulf, I met an Italian patriot, a woman, who also needs safe passage back to Europe. I can vouch for her. She can help our war efforts if she can escape with me. There were other delays, but I eventually resolved the problems and am now ready to proceed with our plan. Because of the long delay, and because of the Italian, I felt I should come see you again and assure you of my well-being and let you know I'm now ready to return home."

"Very good. I will contact my comrade in New York and inform him our original plans were delayed but all is now ready to proceed. And I will tell him a woman will be accompanying you."

"Thank you, Adalwulf. Please tell your associate certain things that will identify me. Of course, I have the Ring." She held out her right hand. Krause had given her a reproduction of an ancient Viking ring called the Valhringr, or Ring of the Slain, now worn by a small brotherhood including Adalwulf, his friend in New York, and Erika's father before he died. Adalwulf's New York friend owned an ocean freighter company.

"That will be very important," Krause said. "When he sees the Ring, he will wholeheartedly offer his help with any additional requests you might have."

"If your associate is prudent, and I hope he is, after I call on him he will telephone you that I have arrived and will give you a description of me for verification. This is my natural hair color. I don't think you've seen it before."

"It's the color of your mother's hair." Krause had first met Erika's parents in the early 1920s.

"Yes, and it's the color I will have when I get to New York. Tell him to look for my scars. I'm sure you noticed this one." She pointed to the considerable scar on her left bicep. Krause had noticed the scar immediately when she removed her wrap at dinner, but the proper gentleman would never comment to a woman about such a thing. "I have another, not so obvious, on my other arm." She showed him the smaller scar on the inside of her upper right arm. "So all those things should rest his mind that I'm the person you sent to him."

"Yes, I'm sure."

"I know you haven't given your friend in New York my real name or told him anything about me." She paused for his reply.

"Of course not, my dear."

"I will use the name Maeve and speak with an Irish accent, Adalwulf. This will give me a good cover."

"Maeve." Krause repeated.

"Yes. For identification to your associate: Maeve, Irish accent, blonde, and the scars."

"Very well. I will not forget."

"And, of course, the Ring."

"Yes, the Ring. That is very important."

"That should be enough. Most men will not ask about eye color, but if he does, my eyes are greenish-brown."

Krause nodded. "I'm sure we have plenty to identify you, and I'm confident you will not have a problem."

"Thank you, Adalwulf." Erika knew things should now be set up sufficiently for Maeve to stand in for her in New York, and for Tars to go along. Deceiving Adalwulf was absolutely necessary for the mission's sake, and the deception would protect him. She rose, walked over to Krause and kissed him on the cheek. "Let's go somewhere and have a drink, my darling. I dread the thought of parting from you. Do you have the time?"

Krause stood. *What man,* he thought, *could refuse such a magnificent creature?* "For you my dear I have all the time in the world."

Erika smiled. "When we leave the room, Adalwulf, let's not forget to speak English," she said in German and laughed pleasantly.

Krause smiled and thought himself a very lucky man.

[Cincinnati—the next morning]

For the second day in a row, Leroy Carr received an early-morning phone call from New York. This one came even earlier, rousing him from sleep. He sat up on the edge of the bed and reached for the telephone.

"Yes?" His voice was scratchy.

"Leroy. It's Al. We've got trouble."

Carr stood. "What is it?"

"Yesterday Marienne followed the two brigands. Their job was to spot any tail and lose it."

"What happened?"

"Well, first off, they not only didn't recognize Marienne as a tail, they actually ended up inviting her to sit at their table at some sleazy bar in the Bowery."

"Geez Louise."

"Hold on, you ain't heard nothing yet. Maeve and Tars both got shitfaced and Tars sliced up some guy in the bar with a knife."

"What??!!!"

"To make a long story short, Marienne told me Maeve invited some low-life over to their table, one thing led to another, and Tars went after the guy."

"Where did Tars get a knife, for Christ's sake?"

"Marienne said one of their stops earlier that day was at a sporting goods store. I issued them too much goddamn money."

"How bad off is the guy?"

"According to Marienne, one of his arms was sliced pretty badly and Tars stuck him once in his left leg. She said Tars was going to kill the guy. When he went down, Tars straddled him and was about to sink the knife in his chest when Marienne jumped her and grabbed the knife. As it is, Marienne doesn't think any of the wounds are life-threatening."

"Jesus . . . where are those two now?"

"They're in their room. Marienne hustled them out of the place and down some alleys. She's watching them. I told her not to let those knuckleheads out of the room. It sounds like Tars is having one of her episodes. Marienne told me this morning that last night when they got to the room Tars asked her if she likes biscuits."

"Call Fort Dix and get those two on an airplane this morning and bring them to Cincinnati!" Carr was trying not to shout but failed. "I want their asses here this afternoon!"

"Should I bring Marienne?"

Carr lowered his voice. "No. We've wasted enough of her time. We pulled her away from her other duties at Catoctin and she needs to get back. Call me as soon as you land. If I'm not in my room, leave a message at the desk. Time for a serious powwow before those two hooligans blow this entire operation."

"Okay, Leroy. See you later today."

Instead of hanging up, Carr pounded the disconnect button three times in quick succession to reach the hotel desk. "Room 414, please." In a moment, the phone at the other end rang.

"Hello."

"Erika, things aren't going well in New York. Meet me downstairs for breakfast in twenty minutes."

"I'm sure Tars thought she was protecting Maeve," Erika commented after Carr told her about the knifing incident in the Bowery tavern. "That's her job." Carr had briefed Erika on Tars' and Maeve's first two days in New York as they sat in the hotel restaurant awaiting their breakfast orders.

"We can't have things like this happening during training, Erika. I have to include all of this in my reports. Unless we see vast improvement quickly from those two we're flirting with the entire mission being axed. It happened once before. I know you remember Thomas telling us about a similar mission planned over a year ago, before you or I were involved. That one got scrubbed."

"You said Maeve and Tars will be here this afternoon?"

"Right. I'm going to lay it on the line. They have to shape up immediately."

"Will they spend the night here?"

"Yep. They'll fly back to New York with Al tomorrow morning. Why?"

"I'm not sure what time I'll get back tonight," Erika said. "But I'd like to talk to them after I get back to the hotel."

The waitress delivered breakfast: Carr's eggs over easy, hash browns and toast; Erika's double helping of scrambled eggs, hash browns and biscuits and gravy. Due to rationing, ham, bacon, and sausage were seldom available. Carr made small talk while the waitress poured coffee.

"You eat like a lumberjack," he commented.

"I've always been hungry at breakfast, even as a child."

"One more problem," Carr said after the waitress walked away. "Al told me Maeve's still having problems mastering an American accent."

"I was worried about that. She'll never get it in the short time she has now. I set it up so she can use her Irish accent with the man she meets in New York—when she poses as me. Yesterday, I told my contact here that I'll be using an Irish alias and an Irish accent for a cover."

Carr looked at her. "That's good thinking, Erika, but you should have cleared that with me."

"I knew you wouldn't mind."

"How'd things go yesterday, by the way?"

She smiled and changed the subject. "Is my other Ring ready?" She gobbled a large forkful of hash browns.

Carr reached into his suit jacket pocket, pulled out a small box and handed it to her. She opened it and removed a silver Ring with a black stone and two engravings. She compared it to the Ring on her right ring finger.

As she examined it, Carr assured, "It's an exact duplicate."

"It looks fine." She returned the Ring to its box and put it in her pocket.

"Al has Maeve's Ring. Why do you need another one?" Carr asked.

"I want you to promise me something, Leroy," she said, ignoring his question.

"What?"

"In Germany, our name for a suicide mission is a *Himmelfahrtskommando*. It's obvious that Mr. Thomas considers this operation one of those. If he thought Tars and I had any chance of returning to England, he would have devised an escape route for us through the Balkans—it's much safer than the route through the Low Countries he's spent very little time discussing. Partisans in the

Balkans have networks for protecting and helping downed Allied airmen escape that are much more stable than the Dutch whose resistance cells are constantly being compromised." She looked at Carr. "Unless all that has changed since I left Germany the summer before last."

"No. The Balkans is still the best option."

"The odds of Tars and me surviving are one thing," she continued, "but Maeve has a decent chance of making it if things go according to plan—her part in this ends as soon as she lands in Europe. But whether she makes it or not, if she stays true to the mission I want you to promise me you'll make sure the promises made to Maeve are kept—the promises to release her father from prison and to drop the charges against her brother."

"Is there some reason you think the British aren't planning to keep their end of the deal?"

"Just promise me."

Carr studied her for a moment. "I promise."

"Okay. Thank you. And don't worry about Tars and Maeve getting their act together. I'll have a talk with them tonight."

Leroy Carr was sure of that.

Chapter 22

Elizabeth

Cincinnati
Next day; Sunday, 16 April 1944

Elizabeth Ault's job required odd work hours. As an investigative reporter for the city's leading newspaper, *The Cincinnati Observer,* she worked with a 10:00 p.m. deadline so she usually reported to the newsroom in the early afternoon. Now just past lunch, she had just walked into the building and stood at the newspaper's mailroom window waiting for the mailroom girl to hand her any messages delivered that day.

"Here they are, Elizabeth."

"Thanks, Donna. How's Kelli doing?" Kelli, the mailroom girl Donna temporarily replaced was pregnant and had been out for several weeks.

"She's fine. The baby's due sometime near the end of the month."

"If you talk to her, give her my best," Elizabeth said as she flipped through the messages.

"Will do."

Two of the messages were postcards: one from the Red Cross asking the recipient if he/she had given blood this month, the other a note from a local Army recruiter thanking Elizabeth for writing a recent article about a local soldier killed in March during the fighting to take Monte Cassino. The soldier left behind a wife and three young children. There were also two envelopes—on one her name was typed, on the other handwritten. As Elizabeth climbed the stairs to the newsroom, she opened the handwritten envelope first.

My dearest Elizabeth, can you meet me in Fountain Square this evening at 8:00? I'd very much enjoy seeing you again. Please come alone. With all my love and affection, Erika.

Halfway up the staircase, Elizabeth stopped in her tracks. *It can't be! Erika is in England, or on her mission by now.*

[same afternoon—Lunken Airfield, Cincinnati]
Leroy Carr was waiting when the C-47 landed (that morning at Fort Dix, Al Hodge had settled for the Army cargo plane when told an Electra would not be available until later in the day). When the plane finished taxiing and the pilot cut the engines, Carr crossed the tarmac and stood beside the plane as the propellers stopped turning. When the hatch opened, a crewman jumped down and placed a step-box under the door. Al Hodge sent Tars out then signaled to Carr, who climbed aboard to help remove a drugged and groggy Maeve.

[that evening—Fountain Square, downtown Cincinnati]
Elizabeth gazed up at the bronze lady with outstretched arms 40 feet overhead, then down at her wristwatch. It was 8:10. She had found a dry spot on the ledge of the great fountain and had been sitting there since shortly after 7:00 watching people strolling to and from the square, the Sunday downtown pedestrian traffic meager compared to any other evening of the week.

"Elizabeth!"

The voice came from behind and was just loud enough to hear over the water falling from the bronze lady's hands. Elizabeth turned and there was Erika smiling at her from the other side of the fountain pool. Both women started around the pool, but both stepped to their right which took them away from each other. They both stopped and started back to their left at the same time, which kept the comical game of circling the fountain going. Both women burst out laughing. "Stay right there!" Erika shouted over the water. Elizabeth paused to see which way Erika walked then stepped toward her. When they finally reached each other they embraced.

"Let's move away from the fountain so we can talk," Erika suggested. They moved to one of the benches farther out in the square. "When I was here last fall, the city leaders were considering turning off the fountain for the duration."

110

"It's an ongoing debate," said Elizabeth. "Some people feel it should be turned off to save electricity. Others argue it should stay on as a morale booster and feel turning it off would be giving in to the enemy. But let's delay the small talk, lady. I spoke with your grandfather in London just last week. He told me he recently met with you in England. How is it you're back here?"

"I can't talk about why I'm here. I'm sure you understand. But yes, I met with Granddad and Grandmum. They look well. And you look well. You've recovered fully, I hope?"

Last fall, Erika Lehmann had saved Elizabeth's life and spared the life of her police detective husband after Elizabeth was shot by a sheriff's deputy in Kentucky who mistook her for Erika. The German spy could have escaped the manhunt by shooting Elizabeth's husband and fleeing; instead, she allowed herself to be captured while she tended to Elizabeth's wound, then later gave her blood when a suitable blood type was not available in the small, rural hospital.

"It was about February before I felt fully healed, but because of you I'm alive to talk about it."

"How's Frank?" Frank was Elizabeth's husband.

"Frank must be pretty healthy. He got me pregnant."

"What?" Erika laughed and looked at Elizabeth's belly. "Let me see."

"I'm not showing yet. I just found out a couple of weeks ago."

"Let me feel. I can always tell if it's a boy or a girl. I'm never wrong."

Elizabeth laughed. "I'm not going to open my blouse here in Fountain Square."

"Just lift it up." Erika reached over and began pulling at Elizabeth's blouse where it tucked into her slacks.

"Stop that!" Elizabeth said while laughing and attempting to push away Erika's hands.

Erika succeeded in getting enough of Elizabeth's stomach exposed to place a hand on her skin. "It's a boy."

"A boy, huh? Okay, I'll hold you to that. My mother is predicting a girl."

"Nope. A boy. Definitely a boy."

"May I tuck my blouse in now, or do you want me to do a striptease in the fountain?" Erika released the blouse and Elizabeth began tucking. "I see you're using your American accent."

"When in Rome . . .," Erika said.

"Blonde hair now?"

"It's my own."

"And I see your grandfather gave you the Ring."

"Yes." Erika looked at the Ring on her right hand. After Elizabeth had been shot, Erika had slipped the Ring on the unconscious Elizabeth's finger when she knew she was going to be captured. Elizabeth had in turn given it to Erika's grandfather to return to her in England, which he had done at Saint Cecilia Abbey. As fate would have it, the return of the Ring was fortuitous for the upcoming mission. It was used to make a copy for Maeve who would need it for identification. Erika took from a pocket the spare Ring Leroy Carr gave her that morning.

"I want you to have this, Elizabeth. It will remind you of the bond between us."

"Erika, how could I ever forget all that happened between you and me?"

"Still, I want you to have it." She placed the Ring in Elizabeth's hand. "But I have to ask you not to wear it until the war is over. Did you tell Frank we were meeting tonight?" Erika knew the answer. Elizabeth's protective husband would never let his pregnant wife rendezvous with a German spy unattended, even if their past history had established a mutual regard.

"No. Every time you come into my life it seems it causes me to lie to my husband, or at least keep things from him."

"I realize that, and I'm sorry. But if Frank sees the Ring he'll want to know how you got it back. So I'll have to ask you to hide it securely, perhaps in a bank lockbox, until the war ends. Then it won't matter, regardless of the war's outcome." Erika had also thought of Adalwulf von Krause who had given her a Ring for identification purposes. Adalwulf dined at the Netherlands Hotel restaurant regularly, and she knew Elizabeth and Frank Ault dined there occasionally. It was not impossible that they cross paths. That possibility was remote, but Erika had seen stranger things happen during missions and knew there was no such thing as a too-careful spy. It would be disastrous for Adalwulf to see the Ring and ask Elizabeth about it. It might expose Adalwulf, who secretly worked for Germany, to questioning by Elizabeth's detective husband whose own curiosity would be piqued as to how Adalwulf knew about the Ring. "Will you promise me you won't wear it until after the war?"

"I promise. I have a lockbox at the newspaper. Every reporter has one. I'll keep it there."

"Good. When the war is over, I'll try and visit you again someday."

"Promise me you'll be careful, Erika. I want you to survive the war."

Erika smiled and kissed Elizabeth on the cheek. "And I want to see that baby. Since it's a boy he'll probably look just like Frank."

"Oh, God, I hope not."

Both women laughed.

[late that night—The Palace Hotel]
Vigorous knocking at their hotel door woke both Maeve and Tars.

"What time is it?" asked a sleepy Maeve. "Who can that be?"

"It's after midnight," Tars said as she sat up on the edge of her bed. "It's probably Carr. He must have remembered something else to bitch at us about." Because she slept in her underpants and a T-shirt, Tars went to the door in lieu of the naked Maeve.

After arriving in Cincinnati that afternoon, Maeve was given until that evening to shake off her drug-induced stupor. Then the two women were subjected to a long meeting with Leroy Carr, who for two hours julienned them for their conduct in New York City.

"Go away, asshole!" Tars shouted when she reached the door.

"It's me . . . Erika."

Relieved it was not one of the OSS men, Tars unlocked the door. As she undid the chain, the door smashed into her chest and propelled her backward and onto the floor. Before Tars knew what was happening, Erika was on her. She grabbed Tars' T-shirt, lifted her to her feet then flung her onto the dresser, knocking most objects on it to the floor. Tars sprang at Erika but was sent sprawling over Maeve when Erika violently backhanded her, the blood from Tars' nose spraying the bedsheets covering the shocked Maeve.

"I've been told you two had some problems in New York," Erika said as she pulled a switchblade from a pocket, snapped it open, and stuck the blade into the wooden dresser. Tars by that time was standing and glaring at her attacker.

"There you are, Tars," said Erika. "You like knives. You can keep this one if you can stick it in me."

Tars seemed to like the offer. She smiled, said "Okey-dokey," then rushed over, pulled the knife out of the dresser top, and went after Erika. Tars was expert with a knife but she'd seen Erika train at Camp X and knew she'd have to use caution. She feigned a thrust to try to get Erika to commit but the German wasn't fooled, so Tars moved forward while slashing through the air at 45-degree angles from high to low seeking to make contact even if Erika ducked. Instead of ducking, Erika spun and kicked Tars in the left side, crumpling her. Erika moved in quickly, grabbed the hand gripping the knife, and elbowed Tars hard in the stomach just below her ribs. With the wind knocked out of her, Tars fell to her knees and Erika twisted the knife from her hand. Maeve sat wide-eyed in bed, holding the covers tight to her chin as if they might protect her.

From the end of the bed, Erika pulled the covers off Maeve, grabbed her ankles and dragged her off the bed. Maeve thudded to the floor. With no clothes to grasp, Erika yanked her to her feet by her hair. Maeve grimaced from the pain but did not cry out. Erika slammed her face first into the wall and pinned her there with one hand while holding the knife in the other. Maeve felt the point of the knife being guided down her back, hard enough to hurt but not so hard as to break skin and draw blood.

"What do you think of this, Maeve?" Erika said seductively, her mouth at Maeve's ear so Maeve could feel her breath. "Do you like this?"

"Fook you, Erika," Maeve answered.

"No? Don't like it?" Erika pressed the knife harder. "Why not? Some people think this is fun." Erika slowly moved the point across Maeve's buttocks. "I think I like doing it."

"Let me go! You're as crazy as Tars."

Erika again grabbed Maeve's hair, jerked her around so they faced each other, and slammed her back into the wall. "Don't move." Erika went over to the still kneeling and gasping Tars, dragged her roughly to her feet and slammed her into the wall beside Maeve. Tars, with blood running from her nose, tried to bite Erika's right hand but Erika took her left hand, placed it on Tars' forehead and jammed the back of her head into the wall.

Erika said calmly, "Maeve, darling, it's not 'fook.'" Then she addressed both women. "And as your friend, I'd be very happy to see some improvement from you both right away."

Chapter 23

Laura

Annapolis, Maryland—Middleton Tavern
Three days later; Wednesday, 19 April 1944

Established in 1750, the Middleton Tavern had served many a patron a drink or two, including George Washington, Thomas Jefferson, Benjamin Franklin (a loyal customer when in the area) and many members of the Continental Congress.

Now, on this clear spring evening in 1944, the historic tavern hosted the famous head of the OSS, "Wild Bill" Donovan; the OSS head of counterintelligence, Leroy Carr; William Stephenson whose codename was *Intrepid;* a gruff and abrasive but dedicated and loyal SOE commando (Victor Knight, aka Mr. Thomas); and an enigmatic Nazi spy no one could figure out. Other than Donovan, no one in the room knew Stephenson was the mysterious *Intrepid* who controlled all branches of the British Secret Service. Donovan had introduced Stephenson as *Mr. Jones,* there on behalf of *Intrepid.*

"My opinion about the earlier discussion, gentlemen," Erika was saying, "is that despite the problems in New York I'm confident Maeve has a good chance of succeeding." (Maeve and Tars were back in New York City with Al Hodge repeating the stalker training that had caused so much trouble a few days ago.)

The only man in the room Erika did not know responded first.

"What's your reasoning, Fräulein?" asked Mr. Jones, who had for the past hour referred to Erika as *Fräulein.*

"Maeve has fortitude, Mr. Jones," Erika answered. "You might call it *heart.* Fortitude and courage will many times compensate for a world of other shortcomings. She has a crushing motive—saving her family. And she's intelligent. It's true that she's struggled with an American accent, as Mr. Carr said earlier, but I've taken steps to solve that problem. Mr. Carr briefed you on that a few minutes ago. Mr. Thomas personally supervised Maeve's Morse code transmission training and she passed all the tests. She's done an excellent job learning my background information, and she's doing well with the German phrases I've taught her. And she's become very proficient with information about the Party. In fact, Maeve has taken it upon herself to read books on her own accord and has impressed me with her knowledge about the Reich."

"We've already agreed your part of the mission will go forward," said Jones, ignoring Erika's praise of her double. "But there are other alternatives to using Maeve." He turned to Donovan. "General, I don't consider Maeve O'Rourke worth the risk, and the Italian lunatic is totally unpredictable. We've invested too much in this mission's European leg to have it torn asunder before it starts."

"So you're for the alternative," Donovan responded, "cancelling Maeve's participation and having Erika contact Abwehr from here in the States and return on a U-boat."

Erika broke in. "That is a last-resort option that has several problems, as all of you know. I do not have my Enigma code sheets. They've been in FBI hands since the Evansville incident. If I contact Abwehr in any code other than Enigma, the High Command will consider sending a U-boat a bad risk and likely deny the request. The alternative—to recover those codes—will require you to send a request to the FBI, which I know you don't want to do. This would be a signal to the FBI that you know something they don't—mainly that I survived Evansville. And, if my superiors convince Admiral Dönitz to send a U-boat, as soon as I return to Europe I'll be under suspicion. Abwehr is aware I lost my codes and transmitter because I was forced to send them a message in simple American teletype code using a newspaper radio teletype in Cincinnati and an American HAM radio transmitter in Kentucky. I would not have risked that if I still had my codes and German transmitter. So I will have to invent some fantasy about how I suddenly reacquired my codes and transmitter. The Abwehr is far from stupid, Mr. Jones."

Erika looked at Leroy Carr and Mr. Thomas. "And, needless to say, if I'm on a U-boat I cannot be in Scotland training with the insertion team." She redirected to Jones and Donovan. "Maeve is the best option."

"I agree," Carr announced to the group.

"And I second that," said Thomas. "The training time in Scotland is critical."

Donovan called an end to the meeting. "This is a British mission so the final decision will rest with Mr. Jones who has authority from *Intrepid* to decide. Mr. Jones and I will discuss this. If you'll excuse us, I'd like to speak to Mr. Jones."

Carr, Thomas, and Erika rose to leave.

"Leroy, what time will Ruth and Kay arrive?" Donovan asked.

"Eight o'clock, General." Carr looked at his watch. "They should be here shortly."

"Okay, I'll meet you downstairs."

"Mr. Thomas," said Jones. "If you'll wait for me at the car, I'll be down shortly."

"Yes, sir."

Carr, Thomas, and Erika Lehmann walked downstairs to the tavern's nearly full dining room. Thomas left to wait for Mr. Jones as instructed. Carr picked out a table. As he and Erika took their seats, the bizarreness of the situation was not lost on the OSS man: Here he was ready to meet his wife for dinner with an enemy spy at the table. But Bill Donovan had suggested the dinner, telling Carr it was to the OSS's advantage to begin absorbing Erika into the fold now if she were to survive the war and later join forces with them.

Apparently the same notion occurred to Erika.

"This is strange, Leroy. I wouldn't think you've discussed me with your wife. What are you going to tell her?"

"I'll introduce you as an OSS secretary. That's standard procedure with female operatives when they're included in social situations."

Erika changed the subject. "What is your take on the meeting?"

"I'm expecting the mission to proceed as planned. Our window of time to get started is closing fast. I don't think General Donovan and Mr. Jones, even with his doubts, will jump ship now." Carr paused when a woman walked in and began looking around the room. "There she is." Carr stood and waved so his wife would see him; she smiled and headed their way.

Erika commented, "She looks much younger than you."

Carr chuckled.

Kay Carr reached the table and husband and wife exchanged a brief hug. Carr held her chair as she sat. Leroy Carr's wife was a stunning brunette and a surprise to Erika.

"Kay, this is Laura Wilson, one of Bill's secretaries he brought along to record the minutes of the meeting. Laura, this is my wife, Kay."

The two women nodded and smiled. Erika looked at Leroy and almost laughed: *Laura Wilson?*

"Hi, Laura," said Kay pleasantly.

"Nice to meet you, Kay."

Leroy asked his wife, "Where's Ruth?"

"She'll be here shortly. Where's Bill?"

"He's still upstairs. He'll be down in a few minutes."

Erika said, "Gee, I get to meet Mr. Carr's wife and General Donovan's wife on the same night. The other girls in the office will be absolutely green with envy."

A waitress appeared and drink orders taken. Leroy ordered his regular gin and tonic, Kay a Zinfandel, and Erika a brandy.

"Brandy," Kay commented. "That's a bit different."

"I think brandy is an acquired taste," Erika responded. "It was around my home growing up. My father would let me have a sip on holidays."

"So where are you from, Laura?" Kay knew it would be bad form to ask an OSS employee, even a secretary, a question about what she did at work.

"Cincinnati, originally." Erika knew the best way to divert questions about her was to start asking questions of her own. "I hope you don't mind me asking, but how did you and Mr. Carr meet?"

Kay smiled. "I don't mind. I met Leroy in Montana when I got a job as a legal assistant at the firm where he worked as an attorney. I'm originally from Illinois, but my family moved to Montana when I was a child."

Erika looked at Leroy. "I didn't know you were from Montana, Mr. Carr."

"I was born in Maryland." The OSS counterintelligence chief was uneasy with the back-and-forth questioning between his wife and a German spy. He tried to end it by picking up a menu. "What do you want to order, ladies?"

Erika was enjoying the conversation with Kay Carr and ignored her husband. "Working for the general, I don't see Mr. Carr that often during the day. Do you have children?"

"No, not yet," Kay answered. "Are you married?"

"Same answer. Not yet."

"Anyone important in your life right now?"

"Oh, I don't know," Erika said. "I doubt anyone has a serious interest in me right now."

"That's hard to believe," Kay responded. "I should think you'd have young officers lined up."

Erika laughed. "Thank you for the compliment. Maybe someday."

Kay Carr and Erika Lehmann looked at each other. Kay already suspected Laura was no secretary. She knew something of her husband's work, and his comment that Laura was there to "record the minutes" surprised her. Kay had been married to Leroy Carr long enough to know that few meetings between her husband and Wild Bill Donovan were of the type where minutes were kept. And the woman across from her did not look like a secretary. To Kay, she looked more like a female Ringling Brothers lion tamer.

In married life, secrets are many times hard to keep no matter how hard partners try. Kay knew her husband had for the past year been on the trail of a mysterious and elusive woman. She remembered telephone calls to their home, some late at night, where she heard her husband say words like "Lorelei" and "Cincinnati" to whomever was on the other end. Words her husband did not realize she unintentionally overheard as she walked by, or as she lay in bed, her husband thinking the phone had not awakened her. Laura said she came from Cincinnati. Leroy had spent several weeks in Cincinnati last fall, and recently returned there just last week.

Her husband would never know it, but Kay Carr felt strongly that her husband had found the mysterious and elusive woman.

Chapter 24

Back Home on E Street

Washington, D.C.
Next day; Thursday, 20 April 1944

It was late morning when Al Hodge called from New York.

"Leroy, it's me. I just got back to the hotel and the desk clerk gave me your message. When did you get back to E Street?"

"After the meeting in Annapolis yesterday we drove back to D.C. I actually got to sleep in my own bed last night."

"Must be nice. What's up? How'd the meeting go?"

"Things are a 'go' as planned," said Carr.

"No surprises there. It would be tough to make changes now."

"How are Maeve and Tars after Erika paid them that little visit in Cincy?"

"They're okay. Maeve wasn't hurt, just pissed off for a day or so but it's behind her now. I think Erika purposely took it easy on her, not wanting to mess up her double. Tars wasn't mad. Violence is such a part of her life she apparently doesn't think twice about it. Her nose wasn't broken after all; she took the bandage off this morning. She's got a shiner and a goose egg; apparently Erika slammed the back of her head into the wall, but she's okay. You knew that would happen after you told Erika the mission was in danger of being scrubbed because of those two, didn't you?"

"I had a hunch. Tars has a black eye?"

"Yeah, the right one."

"We need to come up with a cover story for that," Carr said. "How'd they do this time with the stalker repeat?"

"They're still not great at it, Leroy, but they did better. Marienne wore a wig and changed her overall appearance so they wouldn't recognize her. She had to make the tail a little more obvious to give them a chance to spot her, but at least this time they finally did."

"So you got Marienne back from Catoctin?"

"Yeah, I had her come in for the day."

"Did Maeve and Tars elude her?"

"Are you kiddin'? Tars was Tars. When they spotted the tail they ducked into an alley. But instead of trying to lose Marienne, Tars hid and tried to brain her with a trashcan lid. Marienne expected it, of course, and fended her off."

"I guess we can at least count ourselves lucky she didn't try to knife Marienne."

"I made sure she didn't have a knife on her before she left the hotel. I frisked her. She had an ice pick wrapped in a washrag stuffed in a pocket and two steak knives she stole from the hotel restaurant stuffed down her socks."

"Holy Toledo."

"And so she couldn't buy a knife while out on the streets I didn't give them any money this time—told them they'd have to wait to eat when they got back to the hotel. I told Marienne that during the tail if she saw them go in any place that might sell knives to call me immediately in case Tars decided to steal one."

"Okay, Al. Good work as usual. I'll see you in New York later today."

"So when does it all start? It must be soon if you think we need to invent a cover story for Tars' shiner."

"Tars will be happy. She'll get her knives and a gun soon. We're going to have Maeve make her phone call tomorrow morning."

Chapter 25

Maeve Makes the Telephone Call

New York City
Next day; Friday, 21 April 1944

At 9:00 a.m., Erika Lehmann, Leroy Carr, Al Hodge, Tars and Maeve huddled around the telephone in Leroy Carr's hotel room at the Waldorf=Astoria. A speaker connected to the phone would allow everyone to hear the voice on the other end while Maeve spoke into the hand receiver.

Carr gave the signal. "Okay, Maeve, make the call. Just remember what we've talked about a dozen times, and don't be nervous."

"And speak in your normal voice," Erika added. "Don't forget he's been told I'll be using an Irish accent as a cover."

The paper Erika gave her with the telephone number lay on the table by the phone. Maeve picked up the receiver and dialed the hotel switchboard. "Yes, operator, Belmont 27932, please."

Erika was not concerned about the OSS agents in the room. She had revealed to no one Adalwulf von Krause's name, not even to Maeve. Maeve had only to mention "our mutual friend in Cincinnati." That would be enough and anything more would draw suspicion. And even though hearing the phone number would give Carr what he needed to identify the New York contact, Erika knew the OSS would do nothing concerning him. If he were arrested, Adalwulf would find out and alert Abwehr. She had made sure both the Americans and the British were aware that the Abwehr would be notified if this New York contact were detained or questioned. The entire mission would be blown.

Everyone listened to the phone ring four times and then heard the click of the receiver being picked up.

"Hello."

"Hello," Maeve said. "This is Karl's daughter. I believe a mutual friend in Cincinnati notified you I'd call."

There was a moment of silence at the other end.

"I assume you are now ready?"

"Yes."

"And there are two of you?"

"Yes."

Another pause.

"Be standing under the large American flag in the Grand Central Station terminal at eight o'clock tonight. Don't be late. Be prepared to begin your journey—you leave tonight. Bring no more than one suitcase each that you can easily carry. Do you understand everything?"

"Grand Central Station, under the flag, eight o'clock. We'll be ready."

The man at the other end clicked off without another word. Maeve returned the receiver to the cradle.

"The wanker forgot to say good-bye," Maeve pointed out. "And he didn't tell me how to identify him." Erika had instructed her not to ask any questions.

"Someone will approach you," said Erika. "That man you spoke to might not be the one who meets you, but whoever it is will have your description and know about Tars. And he'll look for your Ring."

Maeve looked at the Ring on her right hand. "Why Grand Central Station? That's the train station, isn't it? Why do we need a train?"

"You don't," Carr answered. "Grand Central Station makes sense. He's having you go there so you won't draw attention. Waiting around in Central Park or in Times Square with suitcases would look out of place."

Erika nodded. "Yes, and he won't take you to the place you'll leave from until he feels comfortable you are who you say you are."

Erika spent the rest of the morning and afternoon in her room with Maeve reviewing personal history, German phrases, and information on Abwehr and other Third Reich agencies.

"Who's this?" Erika had for the past fifteen minutes quizzed Maeve with photographs.

"Reinhard Heydrich," Maeve answered. "In charge of the SD until he was assassinated in Prague in '42."

"This?"

"Admiral Wilhelm Canaris, head of Abwehr."

"Okay. Enough of that." Erika returned the stack of photographs to a satchel. "Any last-minute questions?"

"Do you think Tars will be okay?"

"Yes," Erika reassured her. "Tars will be focused on protecting you. Her history in Italy indicates when she starts an assignment she stays single-minded and finishes it."

"If things go terribly wrong, do you think I should use my pill?"

Erika answered frankly. "You don't want to undergo questioning by the Gestapo, Maeve. Death would be better. They will kill you anyway—after long torture. I know the Gestapo." Erika changed the subject. "What is *Gestapo* an abbreviation of?"

"Geheime Staatspolizei—the 'secret state police.'"

"And the SS?"

"Schutzstaffel—the 'protection squadron.' What time is it?"

"Where's your wristwatch?"

"In my suitcase."

"Be sure you wear it tonight." Erika looked at her watch. "It's a quarter after four."

At the same time in Leroy Carr's room, he and Al Hodge were going over last-minute details with Tars.

"Tars, we're all aware of your last-resort option when it comes to Maeve," Carr was referring to her orders to prevent Maeve's capture at all costs, even if that meant she eliminate Maeve. "But we want to avoid that. Your first and foremost duty is to protect Maeve. You're perfectly clear about that?"

"Yes. Protect first. Kill her if I have to."

"I'd prefer you phrase it: 'I'll do everything in my power to avoid the last option.'"

"I always obey my orders. I will protect her and not kill her if I don't have to."

Hodge asked, "I'm curious, Tars. Do you like Maeve?"

"I like her and won't kill her until I think it's time."

◊ ◊ ◊

After a hastily-eaten dinner, everyone was once again in Carr's room. Erika briefed Maeve and Tars about what to expect at Grand Central Station.

"You might be made to wait well past the appointed time," said Erika. "Whoever is there to meet you might want to observe you for awhile before approaching. That's common; don't be concerned if someone doesn't approach at eight o'clock."

Carr added, "If no one approaches you and it gets very late, call the phone number you called this morning. You have it with you, right?" Maeve nodded and Carr kept on. "Do not call here or anywhere else. If you're being watched and they see you make two phone calls they will be spooked and the jig will be up."

Erika responded to Carr's statement. "And the man is an amateur so it's impossible to say what might scare him off. It could be anything. This man is not a trained agent. He's a businessman who owns a freighter company. Keep in mind he is not the enemy. He has voluntarily agreed to help you, but he'll be cautious, and, being an amateur, his actions will be unpredictable."

Hodge added his instructions: "If no meeting takes place and you cannot get the man on the phone, do not come back here. If you're followed here—and you two have trouble recognizing a tail as we all know—eyebrows will raise when they see you walk into the Waldorf. Find a fleabag hotel and call us. A fleabag won't have a phone in the room but most have one in the hallway. No one will see you call from there unless they're standing in the hallway, and it's unlikely even an amateur will be dumb enough to follow you into the hotel."

Carr added one last reminder: "Always keep your codenames straight, Maeve. When you're communicating with us, you're *Trekker*. When communicating with the Germans, you're *Lorelei*—Erika's Abwehr codename. Any questions, either of you?"

Maeve shook her head. Tars thought for a moment and asked in all seriousness, "Why don't penguins freeze their assholes when they sit on the South Pole?"

Carr looked pained, as if he had a headache. "Let's check your suitcases and weapons again."

[7:40 p.m.]
Maeve and Tars walked into Grand Central Station and immediately saw the giant American flag hanging from the high ceiling of the enormous train terminal. Al Hodge had dropped them at a taxi stand six blocks away where they got into a taxi to come here. Both women wore rugged, gray slacks. Maeve had on a light gray, short-sleeved shirt; Tars' shirt was navy blue and long-sleeved.

They crossed the terminal, stopped under the flag, put their suitcases on the floor and waited.

Part 2

"My feelings as a Christian point me to my Lord and Savior as a fighter. It points me to the man who once in loneliness, surrounded by a few followers, recognized the Jews for what they were and summoned men to fight against them."

— Adolf Hitler,
12 April 1922 speech
at Munich's Hofbräuhaus

Chapter 26

The *Raven*

New York City
Friday, 21 April 1944

"No one yet?" Tars asked. Maeve sat on her suitcase and Tars had just returned from the restroom. It was 45 minutes past the appointed rendezvous time.

"No," Maeve answered. "Do you think I should call the telephone number?"

"Maybe."

"Maybe? Is that a yes or no?"

Tars shrugged.

Maeve stood. "I'm going to call. You stay here in case someone comes." Maeve had taken only a few steps when she saw a man looking at her and approaching. She stopped. He kept eye contact and continued toward her. He was blond, probably mid-30s, and wore a gray suit. Tars also noticed him.

"Move back here with me," said Maeve's protector. Tars had a hand in a pocket.

Maeve walked back to stand next to Tars. When the man reached them he stopped and looked at Maeve.

"Who are you?" he asked.

"Karl's daughter."

He looked Tars over but did not address her. "Come with me."

The women picked up their suitcases and followed him out of the terminal to a shiny black Cadillac waiting at the curb.

"Put your suitcases down," he instructed. "You get in here," he said to Maeve as he opened the rear door. He then opened the front passenger door for Tars. "You here."

The women got in. Next to Maeve in the back seat sat an older, finely dressed man. The younger man opened the trunk, loaded the suitcases, walked around and got in behind the wheel. Ambient light from street lights, buildings, and other car headlights lit the inside of the car well enough to see faces clearly.

"May I see your right hand, Miss?" the man beside Maeve asked. She extended her hand. He used a small flashlight to inspect the Ring as the driver pulled out onto East 42nd Street. Maeve noticed he wore an identical Ring on his right hand. "And forgive me but I must ask to see your arms." Erika had suggested that Maeve be issued a short-sleeved shirt for that reason. She pulled up her sleeves and showed the man her scars. He seemed satisfied and clicked off the flashlight.

"My associate in Cincinnati who sent you to me told me you're using the name 'Maeve' and an Irish accent."

"Yes, that's right."

"And this woman is the Italian he spoke of, of course." Tars watched out the window.

"Yes," Maeve answered.

The man seemed to relax. "What did my friend tell you about me?"

"Nothing. Only that I can trust you."

He smiled. "I am happy to help a fellow countryman and wearer of the Ring. My name is Emil." He nodded toward the driver. "This is my son, Kurt." Kurt was in the midst of a left turn but said hello when he heard his father introduce him. Emil addressed Tars in the front seat, raising his voice slightly.

"So, young lady, I understand you are an Italian patriot and a supporter of Germany and Italy's mutual efforts."

"Do you have any juice?" Tars asked.

Emil stared at her for a moment, confused. Kurt also glanced over.

"No," Emil finally answered. "I'm afraid I have to say we didn't bring juice."

"Well, fuck you then," Tars said and turned back to the window. Maeve winced. Both men looked at Tars, shocked.

"Excuse my friend," said Maeve. "The past several weeks have been nerve-racking for her . . . trying to get out of this country. So much waiting."

Emil nodded. "I understand. The waiting is now over. You'll be on your way tonight."

"What's our route?" (Erika had told Maeve she could ask that question if the information was not offered: A spy trying to flee an enemy country would naturally want to know.)

"I assumed you'd want to be on your way as soon as possible. After your call this morning I looked over the schedule. I have a ship delivering plumbing materials and welding equipment to Haiti leaving tonight. It was scheduled to sail at seven o'clock this evening but I held it for you. You'll sail at midnight. The captain and crew know nothing true about you, of course. To explain the departure delay, I told the captain a doctor friend of mine called on me for a favor. I explained that you two are missionary nurses being sent to Haiti for medical relief work, and that free passage on one of my ships will save the charity money. No one will suspect otherwise."

"Thank you, Emil. Tars, did you hear that?"

"I heard. That's a good story."

Emil continued. "In Haiti you'll dock in Cap-Haitien, a city on the northern coast. Your voyage to Haiti will take just under five days; you should arrive in Cap-Haitien during the afternoon on Wednesday. I'm afraid you must manage a two-day layover in that country. The vessel you'll sail on tonight is not the one taking you to Europe. That ship docks in Cap-Haitien next Friday morning and will sail for Barcelona later that day."

With her photographic memory, Tars had become a map whiz at Camp X. She spoke up from the front seat, "Maeve and I thought it might be Lisbon. But I like Barcelona better. It's much closer to Vichy France—less than two hundred kilometers. Once we're in France, we're safe."

Maeve was impressed. Tars had worded it nicely, giving no hint that she wasn't who the men believed her to be. Despite her struggles in social situations, Tars' life as a professional killer in Sicily had forced her to be an apt pupil of subterfuge—a requirement of survival.

Maeve noticed that Kurt made many turns during the drive and often checked in the rearview mirror. Erika had told her: *He'll drive around for quite some time, Maeve, before you get to where you're going; expect an amateur to be very paranoid about being followed.*

"I have money for you," Emil said as he pulled two envelopes from an inside pocket of his suit jacket. He offered her one.

"Thank you, Emil, but we have plenty of money," said Maeve. "Money that I brought with me from Germany." (She did, in fact, have plenty of money issued by Al Hodge.)

"But I suspect it is not in Haitian gourdes, the currency of that country. Please take this. In here you'll find the equivalent of 200 American dollars. Half of that amount will easily pay for two days lodging and food for both of you in Haiti. The rest can be used for any incidentals you might need, or if you discover you need some equipment."

Maeve thought she might have blundered by turning down the money, and did her best to cover her error. "I had planned to exchange dollars for local currency along the way, but this is appreciated, Emil. It will save me that task." She accepted the envelope.

"Also in that envelope are the names and addresses of two hotels in Cap-Haitien. I'm afraid the lodgings in that country are certainly not up to American or European standards, but the establishments listed are the best that city has to offer."

The car turned south onto 12th Avenue, and Maeve thought they might finally be nearing their destination when she saw the Hudson River on her right and they began passing numerous piers and large, docked ships. Emil handed her the second envelope.

"Unlike the ship you'll sail on tonight, I do not own the vessel that will take you across the Atlantic. It's a freighter of South American registry—Venezuela—with home port Caracas. This envelope contains money for the captain. Remember his name—*Gonzales.* I know him well; my company and the company he works for have conducted a great deal of business together over the years. He can be trusted. I would not put you on a ship unless I trusted the captain. Still, since he doesn't work for me I think it wise to add some incentive for his cooperation. That second envelope contains 500 Swiss francs; give it to him when you board."

"Very well."

"That concludes our business." He seemed relieved and offered chat. "My friend in Cincinnati tells me you have actually spoken with our Führer."

"Yes, many times."

"Fascinating. Tell me about him."

"He's a great man, and he has always been quite cordial to me. My father and the Führer have been friends since the early twenties." (Erika instructed Maeve that if she spoke of Karl Lehmann to speak as if he still lived. Erika had not told Adalwulf of her father's death. She had learned of his death from her British grandfather, and if she returned to Germany with that knowledge the Abwehr would want to know how she found out while in America.)

The chat was cut short when Emil's son pulled the car over and stopped at Pier 67.

"Here we are. Kurt will take you aboard and introduce you to the captain," Emil said. "His name is Finney. He will make sure you're shown to your quarters. He works for me and will be at your disposal. Just remember you are nurses; Captain Finney and his crew know nothing of your or my true loyalties. Is there anything else I can do for you?"

Maeve replied as Erika would, "No, dear Emil. Thank you so much. Perhaps someday we'll meet again." She leaned over and kissed him on the cheek as Erika might.

He smiled. "You are charming, my dear. *Gute Reise.*"

Maeve did not know the German term was the equivalent of *bon voyage,* but guessed it was a farewell. *"Auf Wiedersehen,* Emil. *Danke schön!"* She opened the car door and stepped out quickly. Tars and Kurt were already out of the car.

Kurt retrieved their bags from the trunk and apparently planned to carry them aboard, but Maeve took her suitcase from him. *Never let anyone carry your suitcase,* Erika had told her. *You're me, and I would never allow that, even if there were nothing in it to hide.* Tars took her suitcase as well.

On the pier in front of them was a docked freighter with the word *Raven* on the bow. Kurt led the women out onto the pier and up the gangway.

◊ ◊ ◊

Erika Lehmann and Leroy Carr stood in the shadows between two of the scores of cargo containers stacked high on the dock adjacent to Pier 67 and with binoculars watched Maeve and Tars board the *Raven*. Although an unseen Al Hodge had been at Grand Central Station and watched the women leave with a man, it had not been necessary to follow the car. Adalwulf had told Erika the name of the shipping company his associate owned and it was a simple matter of Leroy Carr using his phony U.S. marshal identification to check with the Port Authority to find out which piers the company utilized. From that information, they knew Maeve and Tars would leave from one of three piers—65, 66, or 67. They split the difference and concealed themselves near Pier 66, and were waiting when they saw a car stop at Pier 67 and the women get out.

Although it was impossible that they would be heard across the distance separating them from the idling car, Carr still spoke sotto voce. "*Raven*. Open sea freighters have to file detailed logs. I'll call the Port Authority in the morning and find out if it's taking them all the way across and to what European city, or if not, where it's going."

Kurt bade farewell after introducing Maeve and Tars to the captain, who ordered his boatswain to show the women to their quarters. Their cabin, located near the stern, was not much larger than the cubbyhole Maeve shared with Tars her first few days at Camp X. But it would do. The level of accommodations during the mission was the least of their concerns.

Tugs pushed the *Raven* away from Pier 67 at 11:30 p.m. Since the cargo was loaded and the crew ready, Captain Finney saw no need to wait any longer once the nurses he had been ordered to hold the ship for were aboard.

The only females aboard the *Raven* stood at the starboard rail as the ship left the mouth of the Hudson and entered the Upper Bay. The *Raven* passed Ellis Island on her starboard. Lights from the numerous buildings on the island could be seen as well as lights from Jersey City.

Like New York City, surrounding cities and towns were not under a full blackout; in the brown-out about a third of the lights of peacetime still shone.

After Ellis Island, in a few minutes Maeve spotted another, smaller island. It took a moment for the shadow of a very tall lady holding a torch over her head to register.

"Look, Tars, it's the Statue of Liberty!"

Tars looked for a moment. "She's giving a Hitler salute."

"No she's not!" Maeve said, incredulous.

The lady grew larger as the *Raven* passed nearby. As the ship kept moving, at one point the small sliver of the waning moon moved over and sat on Liberty's shoulder.

"Look at that, Tars!" Maeve said excitedly. "She's holding up the moon." The women paused to watch the moon move away. "I want to come back to this country someday—maybe bring me family here to live."

Tars stayed silent, but doubted the Irishwoman would ever see America again.

They remained on deck as the *Raven* sailed through the Lower Bay and into the black Atlantic.

Chapter 27

Yankee Clipper

Waldorf=Astoria
Next day; Saturday, 22 April 1944

Leroy Carr had been on his hotel room telephone with the New York City Port Authority; Al Hodge and Erika watched him hang up.

"They're going to Haiti," Carr announced, "but not Port-au-Prince. A place called Cap-Haitien. According to the freight company's log, it's scheduled to arrive there Wednesday." Hodge opened a map while Carr continued. "That ship's captain is not licensed for trans-Atlantic crossings, so they must be changing freighters in Haiti."

"Here it is," said Hodge, pointing at the map. "Cap-Haitien. It's on the northern coast."

"You were right, Erika . . . about the Caribbean."

"That was a guess based on it wouldn't be wise for anyone involved in smuggling a fugitive enemy spy back to Europe to use a ship with a United States registry—at least not for the ocean crossing. The ship they transfer to in Haiti will most likely be registered in Scandinavia, South America, or some African country not involved in the war. Also, Abwehr has a strong network of contacts in the Caribbean. It's likely Maeve will be tested there."

"You're sure Abwehr will know about Haiti, and when they're arriving?" Carr asked. "That guy who owns the freighter company is an amateur when it comes to all of this."

"Abwehr will know." Erika knew the shipping company owner here in New York was an amateur, but Adalwulf von Krause in Cincinnati was not. Adalwulf had ways of notifying Abwehr through the Bolivar network, a string of Reich communication relay stations in Central and South America. As far as Adalwulf knew, the real Erika Lehmann was on his New York friend's ship, and Adalwulf would make sure his friend kept him abreast of the journey. Adalwulf, in turn, would provide Abwehr with the details of her escape, thinking

Abwehr would be there to help if she ran into trouble. It would be Adalwulf's way of protecting her.

"Looks like I'll be shuffling off to Haiti," Hodge said. The scenario of a possible transfer to another freighter for the ocean crossing had been discussed at length the past few weeks. With no way for Maeve and Tars to contact them, the OSS would have to be on scene at the port of transfer to find out the name of the ship taking them across the ocean—and its destination port.

"We'll have the Army fly you down this afternoon," said Carr. "Get you on scene a few days before the freighter arrives so you can check things out and get your bearings."

"You must be very careful," Erika said to Hodge. "Abwehr people will be there and be watching closely."

Carr replied, "This kind of thing is Al's specialty."

"Shall I go with him?" Erika asked Carr.

"No. Thomas is already in Scotland working with the insertion team, and the Brits are getting antsy. The agreement with the SOE was that the OSS would deliver you to Thomas as soon as we got *Trekker* on her way. I need to get you to Scotland. We'll leave today so I can get back to E Street before that freighter arrives in Haiti Wednesday."

The wheels went up on the Army Electra with Al Hodge aboard at mid-afternoon. According to the Army Air Corps pilot, after a refueling stop at the Naval Air Station near Jacksonville, Florida, the plane would touch down in Cap-Haitien around 11:00 p.m. Haitian time. Flying with him was an OSS radio operator/code expert who brought along a short-wave transmitter, and an Army private Hodge shanghaied from the Fort Dix motor pool who had no clue why he was on the airplane.

Leroy Carr canceled his order for an Army transport flight to the United Kingdom after he learned a commercial flight aboard a Pan Am Clipper was leaving New York Harbor for Foynes, Ireland, at five o'clock that afternoon. The only Army C-47 available on such short notice lacked extra fuel tanks and would need to refuel in Newfoundland and Iceland. On the other hand, the Pan Am flying boats, after a quick refueling at Botwood, Newfoundland, remained in the air the rest of the way across the Atlantic, ignoring the several-hundred-mile navigational detour to Reykjavik. Carr called his secretary at the E Street Complex and instructed her to go through channels and have a British Liberator waiting in Foynes to fly them to Edinburgh. Using a Clipper to cross, then the military plane from Foynes would cut as much as half a day off the journey.

The Boeing B-314 Yankee Clipper with an American OSS agent and a German spy among its 72 passengers skipped across the water of the LaGuardia seaplane marina and rose into the sky at 5:20 that afternoon. Erika sat next to a window, Carr in the seat beside her.

"This is a bit different from your military C-47s or Liberators we've flown on, Leroy," Erika commented as the enormous, four-engine seaplane lumbered into the air. The Yankee Clipper was a flying hotel with every comfort imaginable: luxurious staterooms with beds, dressers, and desks; dressing rooms; separate men's and women's restrooms; and a dining room where passengers were served the finest, four-course meals.

"Isn't that the truth," Carr agreed. The difference was stark when comparing the lavish Clipper to the noisy, cold ride on a Gooney Bird or Liberator. "These planes were taken over by the U.S. military when the war broke out. That's why the crew and attendants wear Naval-type uniforms; most are civilians but now technically work for the government. Many of these Clippers have been converted to cargo planes but some still fly passengers."

"It looks full. Did our luck get us the last two seats or did Leroy Carr have something to do with it?"

"Government priority in wartime. I bumped a couple of war correspondents from the flight. They'll have to catch the next one—probably next week. I think the Clippers are crossing weekly right now."

New York City disappeared quickly as the Yankee Clipper climbed into a cloudy, gun-metal sky.

"Good-bye, America," Erika murmured to the window.

Carr overheard. "You'll be back."

"Will I?" It was a question not expecting an answer. "I wonder how Maeve is doing at sea. Seeing how she struggles when flying, I hope she isn't having problems with seasickness, too."

"Al gave her some seasickness pills. Hopefully they'll have calm seas along the way."

[same time—200 miles off the North Carolina coast]

Rain smacked the porthole glass, and anything that could tip over or roll was on the floor doing so in Maeve and Tars' tiny cabin. An hour ago the *Raven* sailed into a vigorous spring storm that had moved in from farther out at sea, and for that hour the freighter had creaked and groaned, rolled and listed. At one point a 15-foot swell lifted the bow out of the water, then slapped it back down into the sea with such force the main deck from mid-ship forward submerged before bobbing back up.

And for this past hour, Tars had leaned off her bunk with her face over a small trash can. The *Raven* rolled 11 degrees to port. Items that had fallen from shelves when the ship encountered the storm fled from the starboard bulkhead where they had rolled just a moment ago and rolled back to port. And once again Tars vomited.

"Can I get you something else?" Maeve asked. When Tars first got sick, Maeve had given her a seasickness pill. Maeve had so far not needed the pills, and the medication wasn't working for Tars.

"Why aren't you sick?" Tars asked weakly.

"I don't know. I feel grand."

Chapter 28

The Nurses

The Bahamas Chain
Three days later; Tuesday, 25 April 1944

Luckily for Tars, after the Saturday storm the seas had been kind. She had eaten little during the voyage and, although nausea remained her sailing companion, the seasickness pills seemed to help on the calmer seas. Maeve on the other hand was living it up. Unlike flying, sailing had no negative effect on her. In fact, the opposite was true: The sea calmed her nerves. For the past few days she had eaten like one of the *Raven's* hardy deckhands and had even volunteered in the galley, helping the cook—a crusty old sea dog the crew called Grumpy Joe. Grumpy Joe had quite a colorful lexicon of vulgar words and obscene references Maeve could easily match. Most of the crew had a hard time getting along with Grumpy Joe, but the pretty young woman's help in his galley and her salty vocabulary endeared her to the old cook.

Now, at lunch time, Maeve stood at the rail with a plate of food, Tars beside her not eating. Men finished with chow were back at work on the forward deck making certain ropes and chains holding cargo in place were secure. In the distance, yet another island came into view. All morning Maeve, and even Tars, had marveled at the pristine waters of the Bahamas—shades of fluorescent green and blue so clear they could see sharks swimming yards under the surface.

"'Tarsitano' – that's your last name, right?" Maeve asked as she ate and Tars stood against the rail.

"That's right."

"What's your first name?"

"I don't tell anybody my first name."

"Why?"

"I just don't." Tars looked at Maeve. "How can you stuff your face like that?" Any remnants of the black eye Erika had given Tars in Cincinnati had by now disappeared. No one had asked her about it so the cover story of her abrupt turn into a cabinet door Maeve thoughtlessly left open had not been needed.

"It's good and I'm hungry."

"You're not acting like a nurse."

"Why?" Maeve challenged. "Because I'm eating?"

"No, because you flirt with the crew, and cuss and talk dirty with that cranky old bastard in the kitchen."

"It's called the *galley*." Maeve scooped another big spoonful of beans into her mouth.

Above the women, in the wheelhouse, Captain Shirl Finney finished checking navigational charts with his executive officer and looked out at the deck to make sure his deck crew kept busy. He spied the two women at the rail.

Finney did not care much for having women on board—the old seafaring superstition that women at sea brought bad luck. The smaller one had been no trouble, but the taller blonde stirred up the men with her flirting. Finney didn't like that and had spoken to her about it. He would be glad when the ship docked tomorrow and the women were gone.

Suddenly a machinist's mate burst into the wheelhouse. "Captain! We've got an injured man in the engine room! Guthrie was replacing a seal on the port shaft; the pry bar jammed and caught his arm on the ricochet. It looks pretty bad."

Finney turned to his executive officer. "Take charge of this. Get the corpsman down there." He paused for a moment and looked back out at the deck. "And tell those nurses I want them to help. Let them earn their keep."

[near Mallaig, western Scotland]

With a five-hour time difference, while Tars watched Maeve eat lunch on the deck of the *Raven,* Erika Lehmann had just sat down for a late-afternoon meeting in what before the war had been a hunting lodge in the rugged countryside of Inverness-shire between Loch Morar and

Loch Nevis. The lodge was now a secret SOE training camp—STS 23. Leroy Carr sat beside her. They were alone in the room.

Sunday, after the Liberator flight from Ireland, they had landed at an airfield outside Edinburgh. At the Edinburgh airfield they were met by a female SOE agent who introduced herself as Amanda McBride. McBride took them to an SOE office in the city where Erika was interrogated for three hours. Directly after the questioning, McBride and an Army sergeant drove Erika and Carr to Mallaig on the western coast. There, McBride transferred them to another vehicle, this one with an SOE driver, for the journey to STS 23. They had arrived late last night.

"I leave for Washington as soon as this meeting is over, Erika," Carr said. "I'm running a day behind schedule. I thought I would be flying back yesterday."

"Kay will be glad when you get home—you're away a great deal."

"Thomas will keep me informed about how things are going here. That's part of the deal. And I'll be back at some point before you leave on the mission."

"I'm eager to finally meet the people Mr. Thomas has selected to be on the insertion team. That's why we're at this meeting, if I understood Amanda correctly."

"That's right. They're all supposed to be here. That's why I stuck around another day. I want to see who they are."

"Are you flying back on a Clipper?"

"Afraid not. It's a long-range Gooney Bird going back."

"Be sure to wear your long skivvies."

The door opened and in walked Mr. Thomas followed by five men and two women. All looked to be in their late 20s or early 30s. All wore the gray, standard-issue SOE training fatigues like those Erika wore at Camp X. One of the women was Amanda McBride.

"Seven? Surely not all these people are on the insertion team," Erika remarked to Carr. "With Thomas and me that makes *nine.*"

Thomas walked to the front of the room and stood. Everyone else found a seat.

"Let's get the introductions out of the way," Thomas began. "First, I'd like to introduce Mr. Carr, a representative of the United States government and an important supporter of this mission." It wasn't necessary for Carr to stand or further identify himself. Everyone in the room assumed the only man in a suit was the OSS agent charged with delivering the German.

"For the rest of you," Thomas continued, "stand when I call your name. We'll get this one out of the way first because I realize it doesn't sit well with some of you to work with the enemy. Nevertheless, you were made aware before progressing this far into your training that this mission requires you to work alongside an Abwehr agent." Thomas looked at Erika. "Stand up." Erika rose. "This is Erika Lehmann. There's no need for me to repeat details about her; you've studied her history." Some of the agents gazed at her poker-faced, others with looks ranging from displeased to hostile. Thomas again directed his attention to Erika. "Sit down."

Thomas called names and others stood. The introductions were for Erika's benefit. Everyone else had trained together for several weeks.

"Gerald Cuthbert," said Thomas, and a short, wiry man stood. "Cuthbert came to the SOE from the 38th Welsh Infantry. He's a sharpshooter and small arms expert."

"John Mayne." An imposing man, Mayne was tall—over six-feet—wide-shouldered, and appeared well-muscled despite his long-sleeved shirt. "John served with me in North Africa and Crete with the First Airlanding Brigade; hand-to-hand combat and silent killing are his forte."

"Michael Doulton. He was with Scotland Yard before the war: an expert handgun marksman and an explosives expert." Doulton was not as tall or as powerful looking as Mayne, but the former detective looked fit and sturdy.

"Archie Hope. He came to the SOE from the 10th Armored Division: communications and hand-to-hand expert." Hope had a large burn scar on the right side of his face.

"James Granville. A Dragoon explosives man—also skilled with a knife. He's been with the SOE since '42. Speaks French and German."

145

Granville was the youngest looking of the men. A freckled-face redhead, he did not look the part.

Thomas finally came to the women.

"You've met Amanda McBride. She speaks fluent French and will be inserted into France and remain there undercover to handle communications and the enciphering and deciphering of our transmissions to and from Baker Street." Erika knew about Baker Street; she had worked as a secretary at MI-9 during her mission in London in 1942. MI-9 was located at Wilton Park, but her secretarial position required her to on occasion type low-level clearance (less than top-secret) communiqués delivered by courier to the SOE headquarters on Baker Street. The OSS had taken up residence in Sherlock Holmes territory, occupying six large buildings under the cover name Inter-Services Research Bureau.

"Stephanie Fischer." A brunette about Erika's size stood. "Fischer was born in Germany and speaks fluent German." Thomas stopped there. Unlike what he did for the others, Thomas did not say what Stephanie Fischer did before joining the SOE. Erika immediately wondered why.

Thomas once again focused on Erika. "Everyone on the insertion team has total authority to put a bullet in your head if at any time during the mission they think you might be betraying them or simply not fulfilling your duties to the team. Do you understand?"

"This is too many people," Erika said, ignoring Thomas's remark. "Half this number would be much better."

John Mayne, Thomas's Airlanding Brigade comrade, spoke up. "Why don't you keep your mouth shut? You're lucky you're not a dead Nazi already."

"You might be the first to die," Erika said to Mayne. "Maybe I'll take care of that during training."

Mayne laughed and rose to his feet. "We can decide that right now."

"John." Thomas held up his hand, signaling Mayne to back off, and then looked at Erika. "I'll decide who's on the team, not you."

"In some of your introductions," Erika continued, "you mentioned if a person speaks French or German, and you said one man speaks both. Am I right in assuming if you didn't mention a language that person speaks neither?"

"If they speak one of the languages, I mentioned it."

Erika shot back quickly. "It's obvious the SOE considers this an abeyance mission, but we don't have to give ourselves obstacles that will get everyone killed before any of the objectives are reached." In the dark world of clandestine operations, the word *abeyance* was used to denote a risky, dangerous mission with minimal chance of success; agents assigned to abeyance missions were those judged to be expendable. "You once told me that everyone on the team would speak fluent French or German or both. Now I find out that besides you and me, only two speak French, and two German. You're out of your mind if you think this mission has a chance. How will the rest of these people maintain a cover?"

"This is the team and you'll do what you're told."

Erika looked at Leroy Carr.

[same time—aboard the *Raven*]
The ship's injured machinist's mate, Guthrie, lay on a table in a small room used as a makeshift sickbay when the infrequent need arose. Next to him stood the corpsman, the only man aboard who knew first aid. Guthrie's arm was badly injured and the corpsman whose duty it fell on to doctor the injured man was nervous.

"I'm glad you're here," the corpsman said to nurses Maeve and Tars. "I don't know shit about something this bad. What do you think?"

Standing several feet away from the injured man, the women looked at the corpsman and then at each other.

"I think he'll probably die," Tars answered. A groaning Guthrie looked up. "What???"

"You haven't looked at his arm yet," said the puzzled corpsman.

"Oh, I forgot," Tars responded. But neither she nor Maeve approached the table.

The corpsman stared at the nurses. "Will you look at it for Christ's sake?"

Maeve and Tars slowly stepped toward the injured man.

"I'm not sure if it's broke or not," the corpsman commented as the women looked at the injury. "But looks like there's a piece of metal in the cut." The man's right forearm was bruised and bloody, the blood running from an ugly and deep six-inch-long gash.

Tars leaned over to inspect closer and shrugged. She reached into her pocket, withdrew a switchblade, flipped it open and cut the embedded, dime-sized piece of metal out of the howling man's arm.

"We best clean it for germs," Maeve suggested. She spotted a bottle of iodine in the open cabinet and walked over to fetch it. She unscrewed the cap and poured the entire bottle over the wound. Guthrie shot off the table with an ear-splitting scream.

"What if it's broke?" the corpsman asked the nurses.

Guthrie answered before the women could speak: "It's not broke! It's not broke! See, I can move my wrist okay!" He demonstrated. "Just let me out of here, goddammit."

The corpsman was just happy to be off the hook. "Shut up, Guthrie—you pussy. You can't leave till they stitch you up."

Chapter 29

Wardrobe Help from Mr. Thomas

SOE Special Training School 23—western Scotland
Next day; Wednesday, 26 April 1944

Erika Lehmann did not quarter with the other team members. Mr. Thomas assigned her to what was for all purposes a makeshift jail cell. A small, one-room trailer on wheels with windows boarded over and a padlock on the outside of the door would be her home at STS 23.

Leroy Carr left to return to Washington the previous evening. Now, early morning, Thomas paid a visit.

"No one at this camp knows my real name except you and John Mayne who served under me in the First Airlanding Brigade. I want to keep it that way, understand? Even the other team members know me only as Mr. Thomas. Are we clear?"

"That's fine," Erika replied. As Thomas talked, she began donning the clothes he brought for her that morning. After slipping into the fatigue pants, she took off her bra.

"What are you doing?" Thomas blurted out in reaction to her casual exhibitionism.

"I don't wear a bra during training, especially for hand-to-hand. Not enough support and something extra for the opponent to grab. I've had it happen. It's easier to knock a hand away from a grip on a shirt than from both the shirt and what's underneath." She looked at him. "Why? Am I shocking you?"

Thomas ignored the question and continued. "This will be your quarters while we're here. You won't billet with the rest of the team. I don't fully trust you yet, and this is for your protection as well. You saw how some of the team reacted to you yesterday."

"Thanks for the concern for my welfare," Erika said tongue-in-cheek. "But to be honest, I prefer to remain here. I don't want to get friendly with the team. My guess is they're all going to die." As she talked, she bound her breasts tight against her chest using a long, six-inch-wide cloth she had cut from a bed sheet at Camp X and brought to

149

Scotland with her. Erika had discovered early in her training days at Quenzsee—the German spy and saboteur training school near Brandenburg—that a brassiere was a hindrance during hard physical training and especially while fighting. Binding offered better support and lessened the pain of blows.

"I'm not going to stand here and tell you we'll all make it," Thomas responded. "You're too smart and experienced for that. But there's a chance some of us might come back."

"Without knowing the specifics of the mission plan, it's hard for me to share your optimism since half the agents you want to insert don't speak the local language." Erika stepped toward him. "I'm going to take a half-breath and I want you to pull this tight." She handed Thomas the ends of the cloth that was now wrapped in several layers around her breasts. She took in a half-breath and nodded. Thomas pulled the ends of the material.

"Do you need someone to help every time you wear this thing?"

"No. I can do it, but you were handy. Pull once more, this time after I take a full breath." She sucked in as much air as her lungs would hold and Thomas pulled again. "Tighter." The strong commando pulled harder. "Too tight," she reacted. "Loosen just a bit, not much." Thomas backed it off slightly. "Right there."

"Shall I tie it off?" asked Thomas.

She shook her head. "Can't have a knot, that's asking for a broken rib." Erika took the ends from him, crossed the material, and tucked it securely into the harness under her left arm; she then picked up the shirt Thomas had brought and put it on. "What's on the training menu today?"

"A bit of everything. The others have been here or at various camps for several weeks. We need to catch you up and our time is limited. If she doesn't get herself killed along the way, *Trekker* should arrive in Europe in about two weeks and you must be there to change places with her. Two weeks isn't much time, but I've seen you train at Camp X. The physical part won't be a worry for you. Your being here has as much to do with the team's readiness as yours. To them you're an unknown factor. It's important that they're convinced you're qualified."

150

"The only thing concerning me is the mission profile. When will I hear that?"

"Soon." Thomas started to leave. "This door will remain unlocked during the day but you'll be locked in at night. The others have already eaten. You won't get breakfast today, and none of us will have midday mess while we're here—too much to do in the limited time we have to waste time in the middle of the day eating. Starting tomorrow your breakfast will be delivered here at 0500. Be out of bed and dressed by that time if you want to eat because training begins at 0530 every morning. I'll let you take one meal a day with the team as long as no problems arise. That will be suppers and we'll see how that goes—any problems, your fault or not, and I'll have you eating all your meals here."

"Just go ahead and do that now. I'd rather not eat with the others."

"Not your decision. You'll supper with the team until I tell you otherwise. That meal is at 1800 hours, then we'll hold evening meetings that will end at 2100 hours. After that, you'll be escorted back here and locked down for the night. Be in front of the main lodge in fifteen minutes ready for a day outside."

Chapter 30

The Fort Dix PFC

Port of Cap-Haitien, Haiti
Same day; Wednesday, 26 April 1944

With the *Raven* scheduled to arrive in Haiti that afternoon, Maeve and Tars had packed their suitcases that morning. Just after lunch, when the coast came into view, they returned to their cabin for a double-check. The first thing Tars did was make sure Maeve had chambered a round in her Beretta and that the safety was on.

"After we land, make sure you're never out of my sight," Tars insisted as she handed the gun back to Maeve. "When you need to piss, I want to be there."

Maeve nodded. "Erika thinks someone from Abwehr will be there to question me. I'm more than a wee bit nervous about that."

As she had done for Maeve, Tars pulled back the slide on her gun to chamber a round and clicked on the safety. "You'll do fine. Don't worry about it."

Both women would carry their handguns in slim holsters that fit inside the back of their slacks. Too warm in this part of the Caribbean to wear jackets without drawing suspicion, they concealed the weapons with loose-fitting shirts left untucked. Besides her identical Beretta, Tars equipped herself with an assortment of knives: a switchblade in her right front pants pocket; a smaller, folding knife in the left; and a slim dagger with a four-inch blade sheathed and strapped to her right leg just above her sock. Maeve carried one folding knife in a pants pocket.

"Give me some of that Haitian money," Tars ordered. Maeve divided what Emil had given her; Tars wadded the bills and stuck them in her left pants pocket. "Okay, got everything?"

"Yes," said Maeve as she clicked shut the locks on her suitcase.

"Let's take our bags and be on deck when we dock," said Tars. "I can't wait to get off this tub."

152

When they reached the deck, the *Raven* had just entered the U-shaped Bay of Cap-Haitien. Distant mountains, some lush and green, others brown and barren from deforestation, rose up to the west and south of the bay. To the east, plains. A tug soon appeared as escort, and when the *Raven* neared the Cap-Haitien cargo docks and cut her engines, the tug moved in to push the freighter into position to tie up. The deck crew hustled to throw monkey fists to men on the dock so heavy lines could be dragged from the deck.

"Everybody is blacker than a crow in a coal mine," Maeve commented as they watched dockworkers on the Cap-Haitien pier scurry to tie up the ship. "Where are the white people?"

"I think all the people here are Negroes," said Tars. "Didn't you know that?"

Maeve shrugged, unwilling to admit she did not.

With lines secured, the crew raised a gangway and tied it off at the rail. No one was allowed to leave or board the *Raven* without the captain's okay. Finally, Finney appeared on deck and handed Maeve a note.

"The doctor you're supposed to meet had this radioed to me this morning," Finney said. "You can disembark now." The captain walked away, relieved to be rid of the women.

Maeve read the message. "Al's here." She handed it to Tars.

Sorry I could not get away to meet you but duties at the hospital have stranded me there. I am sending one of my associates to meet you. Dr. Albert Hodge.

"He sent this because he can't take the chance of meeting us now in case someone is watching," Tars said.

"Who's he sending?"

"How should I know?"

They descended the gangway onto the concrete pier where a large group of Haitian men and boys quickly surrounded them seeking to carry their bags, hoping for tips. Remembering Erika's advice to allow no one to carry their suitcases, they each kept a tight grip and fended off several men reluctant to take *No* for an answer and who tried to wrest the bags from their hands.

"We don't understand a word you're saying!" Tars shouted to the throng even though she knew they would not understand her either. The *Raven* and her crew had made previous trips to Haiti. The corpsman had told them most people here spoke Creole even though French was the official language. Finally, when the Haitians hoping for a gratuity realized they wasted their time, they faded away and headed toward the pier where the next ship was scheduled to arrive.

Maeve and Tars stepped over several railroad tracks and emerged on a dusty street. To the left and right they saw colorfully painted, but shoddily built huts where locals sat out front selling a variety of items from fruits and vegetables to cooking pans, articles of clothing, and live animals. Women walked by balancing large buckets and baskets on their heads. A teenage boy leaned against an abandoned car missing engine and tires, smoking a cigarette with one hand and holding a shotgun with the other.

"There's no one here to meet us. What do we do now?" Maeve asked Tars. "Emil gave us a list of hotels, but Erika told us to never stay at a hotel someone recommends. So where do we go?"

Tars had no answer.

Despite the women's initial impressions at the dock, a few white faces emerged in the sea of black ones. A white man sped by on the back of a motorbike driven by a black man, the driver constantly honking the horn to warn pedestrians out of the way. A white priest in black robes walked along the opposite side of the bustling street.

Another foreign face a half-block away went unnoticed. A Latin man in a white summer suit and matching Panama hat observed the women from a nearby alley, concealed behind a vendor's stand selling chickens and a goat.

As Maeve and Tars stood looking around, a black man drove up on a rickety and paint-worn three-wheeled scooter. "Taxi?" he asked. He wore short pants and a multi-colored shirt like many of the Haitian men on the street.

"No, thank you," Maeve answered. "Someone is supposed to meet us."

"You're Maeve and Tars, right?" he asked in an American accent.

"Yes," Maeve answered.

"Mr. Hodge sent me. Get on, please."

The two women looked at each other and picked up their bags. The seat behind the driver faced backwards and was wide enough for two. They climbed on and held their suitcases in their laps. When the driver started away, the old machine belched a cloud of blue smoke.

"Who are you?" Maeve asked the man after he had driven about a block. She wasn't forced to shout. The scooter's underpowered engine was not loud.

"I'm Private First Class Kevin Wells. I work in the Fort Dix motor pool. I don't know what the hell I'm doin' here—forgive my French, ma'am—except Mr. Hodge showed up the other day at the motor pool, looked around, spotted me, and the next thing I know I'm in the captain's office being told I'm going someplace with Mr. Hodge. So here I am. Mr. Hodge paid a man to borrow this motorcycle, gave me these clothes, showed me your pictures and told me where to meet you. He wants you to tell me the name of your next boat and when it leaves. That's my orders. He said don't write it down because we're probably being followed and if they see you writing and giving it to me it won't look good."

Since the women faced backwards, spotting a tail was easy. A block away, a black Mercedes-Benz looked terribly out of place, moving slowly down a street where locals walked, rode burros, or pedaled old bicycles. The only motorized vehicles besides the dust-covered Mercedes were taxi-scooters and rusty old pick-up trucks with beds full of either produce or animals.

Tars of the photographic memory gave PFC Wells the information he asked for. "We weren't told the name of the ship. We know it leaves Friday afternoon for Barcelona, Spain; it's registered in Venezuela and sails out of Caracas. The captain's name is Gonzales."

Because of the color of his skin, Wells had been offered only two choices by his Army recruiter when he signed up: He could learn to be a cook or a mechanic. The Army never bothered to investigate the sharpness of his mind. Wells easily committed the information to memory and repeated it quickly. "Leaves Friday afternoon for

155

Barcelona, Spain, registered in Venezuela, sails out of Caracas, Captain Gonzales."

"That's it. That's what we know," said Tars.

"I imagine that will suit Mr. Hodge," Wells added. He braked hard when a naked boy darted out into the dirt street. The frightened mother chased down the child, slapped his rear, and pulled him by the arm off the street.

"Where are you taking us?" Maeve asked.

"Mr. Hodge told me to take you to the hotel. Other white folks stay there and Mr. Hodge is there, too. But he told me to tell you if you see him act like you don't know him. He said that was real important. If he needs to talk to you before you leave, he'll find a way that's safe. He said it would not be safe for you to look for him." After a few more blocks, Wells pulled over and stopped in front of the Hotel du Roi Christophe. "This is it," he said. "Mr. Hodge said it's important you hand me a coin, doesn't matter how much."

The women alit with their bags. Maeve's Haitian money was all bills, so she handed Wells an American quarter. He took it, wished the women luck, then drove away. As they walked into the Hotel du Roi Christophe, the black Mercedes drove by then pulled over and stopped farther down the block.

Chapter 31

On the Mat

STS 23, western Scotland
Same day; Wednesday, 26 April 1944

Archie Hope slammed Amanda McBride to the mat and twisted her
arm much harder than necessary. She grimaced; Hope laughed and
twisted harder. No one tried to stop him from inflicting the
unnecessary pain.

Unlike in standard training where hand-to-hand was expected
to be vigorous but unnecessary injury avoided, at STS 23 hand-to-
hand was full, no-holds-barred combat. If an opponent ended up
injured, even seriously injured, so be it—that was part of the bargain.
Agents knew not to give or expect any quarter during fight training,
and no allowances were made for gender. SOE women were expected
to fight any man Thomas pitted them against. He had told the women,
*"If it comes down to it, the Jerries won't stop what they're doing and find
a woman to fight you because they think it would be unfair for you to
fight a man."*

The team had trained for nearly six hours. As at Camp X, the day
started with an obstacle course where climbing fences and passing
over, under, or through barriers was the focus. None of the team
members had trouble with this aspect of training, as all were fit and
sufficiently agile—the key attributes needed for scaling and ducking
under. Erika Lehmann clearly had the best time of all the agents, but
Thomas insisted that his old comrade, John Mayne, had tied her even
though all knew Erika had beaten him by several seconds. Thomas
ordered a second competition between just those two; Erika, now
familiar with the course, ran it even faster and stood at the finish line
smiling at Mayne when he crossed.

After obstacle training, came a 3-mile run. Here again the
women shined, with Amanda McBride finishing first.

Now they turned to fight training, held indoors in the Physical
Training room—a large area in the lodge where, before the war,

157

hunters assembled to fraternize in the evenings. After an hour of fundamentals and technique review, hand-to-hand would end each day with a full-speed competition. As might be expected, in this facet of training the men dominated.

Rules were simple—there were none, other than the first fighter off his or her feet lost. Thomas called a name and that agent stepped to the center of the mat and stood ready for challenges by any team member. The last fighter standing earned an extra pint of ale that night, along with the satisfaction and pride of winning. Thomas had called James Granville first. Archie Hope challenged him and won by taking him to the mat. Amanda McBride challenged Hope, and now she was down and had a sore arm to boot.

Gerald Cuthbert, the Welsh infantryman, was next to challenge Hope. Cuthbert gave Hope all he wanted, but Hope finally landed a punch to Cuthbert's jaw hard enough to stun, and that gave Hope the opportunity to finish him by getting him off balance and tripping him to the mat.

Erika had watched Hope carefully and now raised her hand. When Thomas nodded, she stepped onto the mat and immediately sprinted toward Hope and dove into his ankles. By rule, going to the floor lost her the match, but the tactic succeeded in knocking Hope off his feet. He landed on top of Erika and put out his hands to break his fall. She grabbed his left hand, wedged it tight to her shoulder and rolled over it, breaking two fingers and separating another at the knuckle. Hope yelped and grabbed his hand. When he stood, all could see the mangled fingers. A bone jutted through the skin of one, and the dislocated finger lay flat against the back of his hand. As Hope stood there thinking the match was over and looking in horror at his hand, Erika jumped up off the mat and from behind kicked him in a kidney. Hope grunted and dropped to his knees. Erika leaned over and placed the gasping man in a headlock then looked up at Thomas.

"Should I break his neck?"

"Do what you think best," Thomas replied.

She looked at the others. "How about a vote?"

No one spoke. John Mayne smiled. Erika released her grip, placed a hand on Hope's face and shoved him over.

"Get off the mat, Archie," Thomas ordered the injured man. "Report to the FANY." Thomas had brought to STS 23 a member of the First Aid Nursing Yeomanry to minister to any injuries. "Next challenge!"

"She lost," Michael Doulton reminded Thomas. "She was first to go to the mat."

"Doulton, does it look to you as if she lost?" Thomas said sarcastically. "Why don't you ask Archie if he won? Next challenge!"

Doulton and Hope had established a friendship at the camp and Doulton raised his hand. A strong man, the Scotland Yard sleuth made the mistake many strong men make when fighting a smaller opponent—relying too much on that strength. After trying in vain to grab Erika (which she eluded), or land a haymaker (which she ducked), Doulton's training day ended, along with his participation in the mission, when Erika sent him to his knees by kneeing his groin, then dropping her full weight onto his ankle with her knee, rupturing his Achilles tendon. Thomas had to summon men to carry Doulton out.

Ignoring her sore arm, Amanda McBride raised her hand next. Although enthusiastic, agile, and unafraid of her formidable opponent, McBride found herself lying on the mat in a matter of seconds. Embarrassed but unhurt, she rose and trotted off.

Only Stephanie Fischer and John Mayne remained. Not bothering to raise her hand and wait for Thomas's nod, Fischer stepped onto the mat and immediately went on the attack. For a moment Erika thought she had underestimated the quick and strong Fischer when the woman almost succeeded in toppling her, but finally, after a longer than expected fight, Erika got an arm between the woman's legs, lifted her wrestling-style, and pounded her to the mat, unharmed except for having her wind knocked out. After four opponents, Erika was perspiring and breathing heavily.

Thomas looked at Mayne. "John, you're up, and the last of the day."

Mayne fixed his eyes on Erika. "The Nazi and I will see each other on the mat tomorrow. I want her fresh."

◊ ◊ ◊

At six o'clock, the remaining members of the SOE team sat at a long table in the former hunting lodge's dining room, trays of hearty but simple food before them. Mr. Thomas sat at the head, John Mayne to his immediate right. All were grouped together at the table except Erika, who had separated herself from the others by leaving open chairs between her and the closest person to her, Stephanie Fischer.

Michael Doulton and Archie Hope were not at the table. Both had been sent to a hospital in Mallaig, the closest town. There was no hope that their injuries would heal in the two weeks before the mission began. They were out of the mix and would be reassigned after recuperation.

Few words had been spoken as the group ate until Gerald Cuthbert spoke up. "It doesn't sit well with me to share table with a Nazi." He said it to Thomas, but loud enough for all to hear.

There was a moment of silence until Stephanie Fischer spoke. "Leave her alone."

"I see you Huns stick together," Cuthbert shot back. "That's another bad stroke for my digestion—two Huns at the table."

"Go screw yourself," Fischer shot back.

Erika ignored everyone and finished her meal quickly. "I'd like to be taken to my quarters now."

"Fine." Thomas signaled a guard standing near the door. "Meetings start in forty minutes; I'll have someone fetch you when it's time." Erika rose and walked out with the guard. The others also finished eating quickly and in short order only Thomas and Mayne remained at the table.

"Well, Victor," said Mayne when they were alone, "that was certainly a delightful meal."

"And in record time," Victor Knight aka Mr. Thomas added. "John, tomorrow, when you fight Erika you can't damage her—you understand that, I'm sure. The mission hasn't a prayer without her."

"I know that, Victor. And I always hate to admit when you're right, old chum, but you probably are in this case. She's a tough one, I'll give her that. Archie Hope is no easy opponent in hand-to-hand and she could have killed him. And she's dead on with that Beretta of hers. Do you think Cuthbert is going to be a problem?"

"He won't be here long enough to be a problem."

"Why do you say that?"

"After fight training today, it's obvious to me what Lehmann is doing. She told us yesterday she thinks there are too many on the team, and those who don't speak French or German will be a liability. She's eliminating those people from the team. She got rid of two today—Hope and Doulton speak only English. But you notice both women she fought came away uninjured. That wasn't luck, and it's not because of some bond Erika feels with other women. She'd be quite happy to eliminate a woman as quickly as a man. The women were at the table tonight because McBride speaks French and Fischer speaks German."

"You actually think she's forming the team to her own liking?" Mayne asked.

"We'll find out for sure tomorrow. Cuthbert doesn't speak French or German but she didn't fight him today. Granville didn't come up against her today, but Jimmy speaks both French and German so I'll wager he remains healthy. Cuthbert will be the next one she puts off the team, and she'll do it soon knowing I'll need time to adjust the mission for the agents left."

"If what you say is true, Victor, it strikes me that we'll have no hope of controlling her in the field if we can't control her now."

"I've known since I first met her at the Army base in America that we'll have no control over her in the field. You don't control someone like her, what you have to do is convince her that it suits her purpose to work toward the mission's goal. Some Gestapo will end up dead—the ones involved with her father's death—and that's what we're after even if they aren't the names on our list. Add to that any others that you and I or other team members can pick off along the way and we'll count the mission a success." Thomas finished his coffee. "I'm going to be hard on her while we're here, and tomorrow you can teach her a lesson on the mat. Bloody her up a bit, John, but nothing that won't heal in a few days."

John Mayne nodded.

Chapter 32

Herr Gutiérrez

Cap-Haitien, Haiti
Same day; Wednesday, 26 April 1944

Most Americans and Europeans would consider the Hotel du Roi Christophe beneath acceptable standards of hotel quality: guest rooms with no plumbing, a shared toilet and shower at the end of the hall, beds and furnishings barely utilitarian, aesthetics not fretted over during design. Even so, rooms and latrines were kept clean, and the small hotel offered a restaurant many guests considered one of the better in Cap-Haitien.

After suffering through check-in with a desk clerk who barely spoke English, Maeve and Tars found themselves in a guest room on the top floor of the two-storey hotel.

Maeve laid her suitcase on the only bed in the room. "I need a smoke."

Tars looked at the bed. "If I have to sleep in that bed with you, you're going to have to wear some clothes."

"I can't sleep with clothes on unless I'm totally exhausted."

"You'll have to try for the next two nights."

Neither woman had yet opened her suitcase when the knock sounded. They looked at each other. Maeve whispered, "I wonder if that's Al or the guy who followed us."

Tars said, "I'll get it. You stay there."

Tars went to the door, opening it only partially. A man wearing a white suit who looked to be Latin stood in the hallway.

"Hello," he said. "I've been expecting you and I'm here to help. May I enter?" His Spanish accent was strong, but he spoke English well.

Tars opened the door the rest of the way and signaled the man to enter. When he stepped through and Tars closed the door, both Maeve and Tars drew their guns.

"Take off your jacket," Maeve ordered. The man removed the jacket, revealing a shoulder holster with a small revolver. Tars plucked the gun from the holster, frisked him, and checked the jacket he had dropped to the floor. She found no other weapons. All of this, from the brandishing of their weapons to the frisking, Erika had drilled into them at Camp X. *(Don't be trusting and friendly with him, Maeve, when you first meet. Yes, his duty will be to verify that you are me, but after that he knows his job is to aid you. Don't be timid. Make sure he knows you're the boss.)*

After Tars finished shaking him down, the man said to Maeve, "I've heard amazing stories of the *Lorelei* and it's my honor to meet you. I'm at your service, Sonderführer." He raised his right hand. "Heil Hitler." The man knew only the code name and *Lorelei's* Abwehr rank.

Maeve returned the salute. "Heil Hitler. Introduce yourself."

"My name is Ricardo Gutiérrez. I was born in Argentina, and I'm proud to say I've been a supporter of our Führer ever since he came to power in 1933. I've traveled three times to the Fatherland and once I actually shook the Führer's hand in a reception line. In 1937, I was asked to head the Reich's Bolivar Network station in Uruguay. I accepted, of course, and have lived there since. When your associates at Abwehr recently found out you had eluded the American authorities and sought to return to the Fatherland, they contacted me and requested that I assist you. After your friend in Seeseenhatee (he butchered 'Cincinnati') relayed to Berlin the details of your arrival in this country, I was notified by your superiors at Abwehr and I flew here to be at your disposal."

Maeve holstered her handgun; Tars kept hers trained on Gutiérrez. "Put away your gun," Maeve ordered Tars. *(When the two of you are with the Abwehr contact,* Erika had told Tars, *Maeve has to be seen as in charge. He will expect me to be in charge, and I would be.)*

Tars lowered her gun but kept it in her hand.

"Gracias!" Gutiérrez picked up his jacket.

"Give him back his gun," Maeve told Tars.

Tars handed his weapon back and Gutiérrez returned it to his shoulder holster.

"There is no need for you to stay in this hotel," he said. "I understand you are here for two nights. I've set up a headquarters with a transmitter for you in a nearby village, and I brought one of our radiomen with me. There you will stay in a home with servants who will care for your needs. My car is waiting. Shall we leave?"

"Very well," said Maeve. *(If he wants to move you to a different location, go with him. In a circumstance like this, moving you to a more secure location is standard Abwehr procedure, and it will look suspicious if you hesitate.)*

The women collected their suitcases. Maeve said, "Lead the way, Señor Gutiérrez."

"I prefer Herr Gutiérrez in friendly company."

"Sehr gut, Herr Gutiérrez."

"Danke, Sonderführer. I'm afraid you'll find my German lacking. I'm trying to learn more."

"I'm not concerned with that. It's best we avoid speaking German from here on out."

"Of course, Sonderführer. And should I address you as *Lorelei* or Sonderführer?"

"Sonderführer will do when we're in close company. Otherwise, I'm using the name 'Maeve Shanahan'—an Irish cover. That's why I'm using an Irish accent."

"Maeve Shanahan. That is very good. But we would expect nothing less from *Lorelei."*

Tars was impressed by Maeve's handling of Gutiérrez. They left down the stairs and through the lobby. The Mercedes was now parked directly in front of the hotel. The driver, a young man who also looked Latin, leaned against the car. He quickly loaded the women's bags in the trunk, then opened both passenger doors.

"Perhaps you would like to sit here," Gutiérrez said to Tars, motioning to the front. Tars got in. Gutiérrez and Maeve got in the back, the seating arrangements ending up the same as during the ride in New York with Emil.

"Let's go, Javier," Gutiérrez said to the driver. The man started the car and pulled out into the street. "This is my aide, Javier Espino," he said to Maeve. "He has been with me for three years. I'm afraid he doesn't speak English or German, but I can promise you his devotion to our cause is as strong as ours."

"As strong as ours? I'll hold you to that promise, Herr Gutiérrez. Do you have a cigarette?"

He looked sheepish and apologized. "I'm sorry, I have only cigars."

"That will do."

"Javier, dos cigarros, por favor."

Javier opened the glove box in front of Tars and handed back two cigars.

"Cuban," Gutiérrez said. "Top quality." He leaned forward and said to Tars, "Would you like one?" Tars shook her head no.

Gutiérrez took a cigar guillotine and a lighter from a jacket pocket and snipped the end of the cigars. He handed one to Maeve and held the lighter for her. She put the cigar to the flame and puffed until well-lit. He did the same.

"So tell me about your friend in the front seat," Gutiérrez said after his cigar produced sufficient smoke. "I was told she's Italian. She doesn't look Italian."

"Her name is Tars. And not every Italian has dark hair and eyes, Herr Gutiérrez. I'll remind you that in his youth, Mussolini's hair was the same color as hers."

"Of course, Sonderführer. I meant no offense to your friend."

"How far to this place you're taking me?" Maeve asked him. "I want to radio Abwehr soon."

"Plaine du Nord is only sixteen kilometers from here, but because of the poor road conditions in this country it will take us some time."

Maeve soon found out why. Once the Mercedes left Cap-Haitien, the dusty city roads became a gauntlet of deep, muddy potholes, downed trees, small streams to ford, and other obstructions that forced Javier to slow the car to a crawl. She hoped Al Hodge would not find it necessary to get in touch with her and Tars. Maeve knew Hodge could not follow them; it would be impossible to go undetected on these all but abandoned roads. Maeve puffed on her cigar and blew the smoke out the open window.

The journey took a kidney-jolting hour and a half. During the drive, Gutiérrez seemed interested only in small talk. He did not test Maeve to confirm she was *Lorelei,* and she did not offer proof. *(If he doesn't test you right away, don't offer evidence. He'll get around to it.)*

The car crested a hill and a small town appeared in the valley. "Más adelante, señor," said Javier.

"Ah, Plaine du Nord. We've finally arrived," Gutiérrez announced. "I rented a plantation house on the outskirts of town. We'll have it to ourselves. The family will stay at a hotel in Cap-Haitien for the next two days, but the servants have remained. This is a poor country, Sonderführer, as you have seen. This home has the nicest accommodations available in this area, and I hope they will be satisfactory. There is an indoor toilet."

"Lavish lodgings are of no concern to me, Herr Gutiérrez. Security is."

"Of course. And for that reason I picked this out-of-the-way place."

Maeve looked at her watch. It was just after six o'clock. The car passed through what seemed a small-scale version of Cap-Haitien: colorful but flimsy huts; palm trees, people on burros; men lingering in small groups; women carrying burdens on their heads; goats and chickens wandering freely; merchants selling fruits, vegetables, and other goods; and small children running about—some naked, like the boy in Cap-Haitien.

When they reached the far edge of town, Gutiérrez announced, "We're almost there. The plantation is just a mile from the town." They drove for another ten minutes down a narrow road through thick forest before finally arriving. The Mercedes stopped at a wooden gate in a fence made of spiny cactus. Javier honked the horn and a man carrying a sawed-off, double-barreled shotgun ran out of the house and opened the gate. They drove in and parked in front of a large, two-storey concrete house with a red tile roof. To Maeve, it looked like a mansion compared to the one-room, straw-roofed huts they had passed. The gatekeeper hustled to the car and opened the doors for the women. Javier turned off the engine and everyone got out.

"Javier will bring your bags," Gutiérrez said. "Let me show you inside."

"Thank you, but we'll carry our bags," Maeve said.

"Of course."

Gutiérrez led them up three steps onto a covered porch then held the door. Maeve and Tars stepped into a small foyer. He showed them into a large room where two men immediately aimed shotguns at them. Javier stationed himself behind Tars and held a pistol to her head.

"Raise your hands!" Gutiérrez ordered. Maeve and Tars did. Two more men appeared from an adjacent room. "Take their guns," Gutiérrez told the men in Spanish. "They're holstered behind their backs. Then frisk them." The men followed orders and found the knives. Gutiérrez motioned to some chairs and the men who did the frisking forced Maeve and Tars to sit. The men with guns kept them trained. Javier stationed himself behind Tars with his Luger pointed at the back of her head.

"I wondered when you would get around to this," Maeve said. "I was beginning to think you incompetent." Maeve rolled up her sleeves. Gutiérrez approached, looked at the scars, and then at Maeve's eyes, checking the color carefully. He motioned for one of the men to place a chair where he could sit a few feet from her. Another man handed him a folder. Inside were two sheets of paper and several photographs. One was an Abwehr mug shot of Erika taken at Quenzsee, the only name on it *Lorelei*. Gutiérrez took out the photo and looked back and forth several times from the photo to Maeve. He returned that photo to the folder and took out the others.

"I have some photographs and a list of five questions sent to me by Ulrich von der Osten. You know him, I'm sure."

"Of course. Major von der Osten is my handler at Abwehr."

"He knows you well?"

"I don't know how well. You'd have to ask him that question."

"He knows things about your training others wouldn't know. Would you agree with that?"

"Yes. I would think that's accurate." Maeve felt an unsettling in her stomach.

Gutiérrez held up one of the photos. "Who is this?"

"Ernst Kaltenbrunner."

"What is his position?"

"Head of the RSHA and president of Interpol. He replaced a friend of mine, Reinhard Heydrich, after Heydrich's death."

"What is the RSHA?"

"It's an agency ultimately overseen by Reichsführer Himmler that combines three agencies: the Sicherheitspolizei, the Gestapo, and the Kripo."

"What is 'Gestapo' an abbreviation of?"

"Geheime Staatspolizei. Do you want a translation?"

Gutiérrez looked at her. "That won't be necessary. And this?" He held up another photo.

"Baldur von Schirach, head of the Hitler Youth."

Gutiérrez held up six more photographs. The first five she identified; one was a photo of Klara Hitler, Adolf Hitler's mother. But the last face was one Erika had not shown her at Camp X. "May I see that one more closely?" she asked. He handed it to her. *(Keep your nerve, Maeve. He may try to trick you.)*

"I don't recognize this man," she admitted.

"Surely you know who he is."

Maeve looked again and handed the photo back. "No. I don't recognize him."

"Interesting," said Gutiérrez. "Now to the five questions sent by the major."

Gutiérrez read from the sheet. "Who was the chief instructor of English at Quenzsee during your training sessions?"

"Ernest Kappe."

"What is the significance of the dagger emblems some agents have embroidered on their Quenzsee training uniforms?"

"Each dagger represents a mission completed successfully."

"Describe the room you slept in when at Quenzsee."

"A small cell on the second floor of the women's barracks: a bed, small desk with a chair, one window, and a picture of the Führer on the wall."

"What gift did Major von der Osten present you upon your initial graduation from Quenzsee in 1939?"

Maeve hesitated. Her stomach now churned. Erika had told her she graduated from the spy school in 1938, but mentioned nothing about a gift. Maeve imagined the incorrect date was an attempt to rattle her, but had Erika forgotten some obscure but important detail such as a gift? Gutiérrez stared at her and waited for an answer. *(If you don't know an answer, just become me, Maeve.)*

"My initial graduation was in 1938, Herr Gutiérrez. And I remember no gift. That would be highly inappropriate, and I doubt Major von der Osten is in the business of handing out gifts to recruits. If he offered me a gift, I'm sure I refused it."

"One last question. What event interrupted your parents' honeymoon?"

Maeve tried to smile as she thought Erika might. "Very good, Herr Gutiérrez. My parents were on their honeymoon in the Italian Alps in 1914 when Archduke Ferdinand was assassinated. The answer to your question is the outbreak of the First War."

Gutiérrez closed the folder and stood. "Thank you, Sonderführer. You realize this was necessary, and I was simply following orders."

"I would worry if this had not been done, Herr Gutiérrez." Maeve forced herself to offer a calm front but felt inside as if she were going to be sick.

"Now," Gutiérrez continued as he switched his focus to Tars. "We shall discuss your friend. Berlin is concerned about her and not convinced she should leave this place alive. I need additional information. What can either of you tell me that will reassure Berlin?"

Maeve had to act quickly. "Mir reicht's jetzt!" she said loudly and stood. "That means 'I've had enough' for those of you who don't speak German but claim to support our cause. I think these are *your* thoughts, *Señor* Gutiérrez, not Berlin's (she emphasized *Señor,* taking away his preferred *Herr*). The powers at Abwehr know me well enough to understand I could never be duped into bringing back a double agent or infiltrator. Tars' background information has already been sent to Berlin by my friend in Cincinnati. Abwehr will check that information thoroughly. If any doubts remain, they will be addressed when we reach Barcelona. Shall we use the transmitter now and verify this protocol, and also verify whether these concerns you speak of are Berlin's, as you claim, or yours? And need I remind you how the High Command deals with operatives who take matters into their own hands without clearance? Especially if their actions turn out to be wrong."

Gutiérrez's blush could be seen despite his brown face. "I apologize, Sonderführer. My aim is simply to be cautious. That transmission won't be necessary." He stood. "We are at your service. Heil Hitler!" The other men stretched out their right arms and repeated the salute.

"Heil Hitler!" Maeve raised and then dropped her arm. "Now, it's been a long day. Please direct me to the room with the toilet."

"Of course. Just down that hall." Gutiérrez pointed. Maeve left the room and, when out of the men's sight, broke into a run. She found the room, slammed the door behind her, and vomited into the toilet. A minute had not passed before Maeve heard shouting. She wiped her face with a tissue and quickly returned to find Tars standing behind a kneeling Javier, holding her dagger at his throat. The men with guns again had them trained on Tars.

"I ordered her weapons returned and she attacked Javier!" Gutiérrez shouted to Maeve.

"Put away the guns!" Maeve ordered. The men looked at Gutiérrez who nodded. They lowered their weapons. "Tars! Let him go, now!"

"I'm going to open up this sonuvabitch like a ripe melon!"

"Take the knife from his throat, now! Those are orders!"

Tars slowly released Javier and stepped back. A red line of blood could be seen on his neck where she had applied pressure with the razor-sharp dagger.

"I suggest we all need rest, Herr Gutiérrez." Maeve said, restoring his preferred title in a show of reconciliation. "Please show us to our quarters. I prefer to transmit at 0400—less clutter in the airwaves. Please have someone wake me at 0300 to allow me time to prepare."

"Yes, Sonderführer." Gutiérrez returned Maeve's gun and knife, then led the way to a room on the second floor with two beds and a box fan not spinning because of no electricity. Still daylight, electricity was supplied by a generator never turned on before dark.

"Tell me, Herr Gutiérrez," said Maeve. "Who is the man in the last photograph?"

"He's a German baker whose shop is down the street from my office in Montevideo. I'm a regular customer."

Tars stowed the luggage in a corner and closed the door.

"Don't you want dinner?" Tars asked. "I'm hungry. Maybe they have a cherry pie."

Maeve didn't answer and collapsed on one of the beds fully clothed.

Chapter 33

A Late Night

OSS Headquarters—Washington, D.C.
Next day; Thursday, 27 April 1944

Tuesday night Leroy Carr slept at 8,000 feet over the Atlantic, arriving back in D.C. late yesterday afternoon. He had not yet been home, having to settle for a quick phone call to Kay to let her know he was back. Last night he slept in his office. It wasn't the first time. He kept the folding camp bed stored in a maintenance closet down the hall. Carr wanted to be at E Street when Al Hodge's transmission came in, and he knew that might be very late or even middle of the night. At midnight, Carr realized he was there for the long haul and set up the camp bed. He gave orders to be awakened as soon as Al began transmitting.

Hodge made contact at 3:20 a.m. and the lengthy message took nearly an hour to decode. Now, at 9 a.m., Carr sat down in Bill Donovan's office.

"Maeve and Tars made it to Haiti, Bill. Arrived yesterday afternoon. As planned, Al sent the colored private from the Fort Dix motor pool to meet them posing as a Haitian taxi driver. He dropped them at the hotel but they were there just a few minutes when the Abwehr operative showed up. Al said the motor pool private did a helluva good job and asked me to relay that to his captain."

"Do we know who the Abwehr operative is?" Donovan asked.

"Al relayed that he got a photo of the guy. It's from a distance, so we'll have to wait and see if we have a decent facial shot. And he got the license plate of his car. I checked it out and the car is registered to a large banking firm in the Dominican Republic. But to answer your question, no, we don't know who he is—not yet. Al said he looks Latin and that's all we know right now. I doubt if he works for the Dominican bank; he'd have to be pretty dumb to use a company car from a place where he works. More likely a second or third party secured the car for him and he drove it across the island into Haiti.

When Al gets back with the film, we'll develop it and see if we can tag him."

"You said they were at the hotel for only a few minutes?"

"Yeah. They left with the enemy agent. Al followed them but had to end the tail when they left town and got on some lonely country road where there was no way he wouldn't be spotted. He said they left Cap-Haitien heading southwest."

"What's in that direction?"

"The maps show a few villages and small towns here and there. No big towns or cities. I'm guessing he won't take them too far—hard to get around in that country. After we got Al's message, I woke up one of our topography guys at home and had him come in and go over the maps. He told me it gets pretty wild heading that direction from Cap-Haitien: mountains and forests that are half jungle. He said that's Voodoo country."

"Voodoo country! Well, they ought to love that wacky Italian—probably elect her president."

Despite the weightiness of the situation, Carr had to laugh. "Good news is we got the main information we needed—the name of the ship taking them across and its destination. The women didn't know the name of the ship, but from the information they gave the Fort Dix mechanic we figured it out. They told him it was a freighter registered in Venezuela, home port Caracas, the captain's name is Gonzales, and the cargo is headed to Barcelona. I had that information radioed to our people in Caracas. I heard back an hour ago. The name of the freighter is the *Bahia de Cata*. It left Caracas Monday evening and is scheduled to dock in Cap-Haitien tomorrow morning, unload and load cargo then leave Haiti for Barcelona late tomorrow afternoon. According to the International Maritime Log, the freighter company that owns the ship recorded an estimated time of arrival in Barcelona as Friday, May 12th—two weeks from tomorrow."

Donovan wrote down the information. "Okay. I'll pass this information on to *Intrepid*. Barcelona is a stroke of luck for the Brits—they can establish a clearer ETA when the ship passes through the Strait of Gibraltar. We just have to hope those women get out of Haiti. Do you think O'Rourke can convince them she's Lehmann?"

"I don't know, Bill. We can only cross our fingers. We'll know tomorrow. Al will be in position somewhere around the dock to see if they board that freighter."

Chapter 34

Valkyrie

Special Training School 23—western Scotland
Same day; Thursday, 27 April 1944

Mr. Thomas changed the routine on this second training day at STS 23. Yesterday saw no firearms practice, so that was today's first order of business. In the first firing phase, agents used handguns of their choice. Erika fired her Beretta *Brevettata*. Other guns used by team members varied from .32 caliber up to the powerful Colt .45 semi-automatics preferred by John Mayne and Mr. Thomas. There were no poor shots among the team; everyone consistently made holes in the black bulls-eyes at 25 feet or placed their rounds very close. The best marksmen among the group were Thomas and Mayne, Erika Lehmann and Stephanie Fischer. Stephanie preferred the German-made Walther PPK and seldom missed the black.

During the second phase of target practice, everyone fired the same type of handgun—a Welrod. Erika had trained with this pistol at Camp X, and the other agents had also become familiar with it at STS 23 prior to her arrival. Designed by the SOE and known as the *assassin's pistol*, the bizarre-looking Welrod looked less like a handgun and more like a short plumbing pipe or piece of metal tubing with a handle. It had several disadvantages, including a weight over twice that of Erika's Beretta or Stephanie's PPK, and even though the Welrod's clip held six rounds it was not semi-automatic—the shooter had to manually load each round into the firing chamber by pulling back the bolt-action hammer. But the Welrod could prove to be an important weapon for several reasons: it was accurate up to 50 yards, its powerful 9mm rounds delivered significant stopping power, and, most importantly (and the reason it was designed), the gun was practically silent when fired—its report no louder than the snapping of a finger. What's more, the Welrod's muzzle sported a cutaway design that allowed it to be held in direct contact with the target. A shooter could press the gun tight against a head or chest and fire without worry of backfire, as might be a concern with a conventional weapon.

Here again, everyone on the team displayed high-quality marksmanship. Erika watched Stephanie place four of six rounds in the black at 25 feet, and three of six at 35 feet with the errant three no farther than two inches from the bulls-eye.

The obstacle course came next. Mr. Thomas apparently felt it not challenging enough the previous day as the height of several barriers had been raised. The last outdoor chore—the 3-mile run—was again won by the marathon runner, Amanda McBride.

Since the team did not eat lunch at STS 23, at noon the agents gathered in the PT room for hand-to-hand practice. During the first hour, Mr. Thomas demonstrated new techniques and agents practiced familiar fundamentals. Erika sought out Stephanie Fischer. Erika had been impressed with both women on the team, and especially with Stephanie's hand-to-hand skills when they had fought yesterday.

"Where are you from?" Erika asked as the two practiced blocking blows from a club.

"I was born in Uttrichshausen, but my family moved to Berlin when I was ten," said Stephanie.

"Where did you learn to fight?"

"Same place you did. Quenzsee."

Erika stopped and stared at her as Mr. Thomas barked it was time for the competitions.

"Be careful when you fight John Mayne," Stephanie warned as they walked over to return the practice club to the rack. "He's the best in hand-to-hand I've ever seen and he won't hesitate to be vicious. He could have put us all out of action by now if he had a mind to. Go to the mat quickly."

"Would you do that?"

"No, I don't think I would."

When the group was assembled around the mat, Thomas announced a change in the competition rules. Today, instead of open challenges, he would decide who fought whom.

"Granville and Lehmann," said Thomas.

Erika and the red-haired Dragoon explosives man stepped onto the mat. When Thomas signaled the match to begin, Granville stepped toward Erika and was greeted by a spinning backhand to the side of his head that seemed half-hearted. He shook it off quickly, grabbed Erika and flipped her to the mat, ending the match. Everyone looked around at the others, surprised the fight ended so quickly.

John Mayne, standing next to Thomas, remarked, "She threw the fight."

"Of course she did. Jimmy speaks French *and* German. Just testing my theory, old chap."

No one was more surprised at the quick outcome than James Granville. He reached down, grabbed Erika's hand to help her up and said, "Why did you do that?"

"Do what?"

Thomas shouted, "Lehmann stay there! Granville off! Mayne!"

John Mayne removed his shirt, revealing arms and torso of rippling muscles, bulging veins, and shoulders and a back covered in whip scars. As he stepped onto the mat, Erika could see what looked like healed cigarette burns dotting his stomach.

"Gestapo?" Erika asked.

"I've had the pleasure of being in their company."

"Yet you're still alive. Very fortunate for you."

"Are you going to allow me to win like you did Jimmy?"

"No. You're an asshole." Erika spun and as hard as she could, delivered a round-house kick to Mayne's side. The force of the blow surprised Mayne, but he kept his feet. For Erika, it felt as if she'd kicked an anvil and she backed away limping.

"Try the other side," said Mayne. Instead, she braced herself for his attack. As Mayne moved forward, Erika again spun and with all her might delivered a back-handed punch that missed the intended jaw and struck full force on his nose. Still, Mayne seemed indestructible and impervious to pain. The thought flashed through Erika's mind that she again fought Axel Ryker, the brutish Gestapo killer Heinrich Himmler sent to America last year to murder her. She realized her only chance against Mayne was to use her quickness to stay out of his grasp and try to move in occasionally to deliver a blow in hope that would eventually wear him down.

A small trickle of blood appeared under Mayne's nose, which he ignored. Erika kept her distance, circling. She darted in and tried to kick Mayne between his legs, but he reacted surprisingly fast for a muscle-bound man and turned sideways. Her kick landed on the side of his hip, and Mayne managed to grab her pants leg. She tried to kick away but couldn't break out of his vise-like clutch. He grabbed the front of her shirt and released her pants. She tore at the shirt and dropped to the mat. As she rolled quickly away, Mayne was left holding only the shirt. He threw it off the mat and came after her.

When Erika sprang to her feet, Mayne attempted to punch her in the stomach. She saw it coming and tried to spin out of the way, but the punch landed on the side of her left breast. The binding cloth only partially lessened the pain of the heavy blow and it knocked out her wind. Mayne grabbed her left arm and twisted it at the wrist. Erika dropped to her knees but Mayne pulled her back to her feet and twisted the arm behind her back. Holding onto the twisted arm, he put his other arm between her legs, lifted her off the mat, turned her sideways and, instead of driving her to the mat and ending the fight, knelt on one knee and dropped her on his other leg. He lowered her head to the mat, stood, and, keeping her suspended upside-down, placed his foot under her chin and applied pressure.

Enjoying Mayne's brutality, Gerald Cuthbert felt like joking. "Look, a Hun with her legs in the air. If they all do that I'll enjoy my time in Germany. Maybe I'll become a father in the Fatherland."

As he laughed at his own joke, Stephanie Fischer, standing next to Cuthbert, turned and delivered a violent elbow strike to his jaw, knocking him cold. His head hit the wooden floor with a thud. Mr. Thomas observed but said nothing, letting Cuthbert lie where he fell.

On the mat, Mayne used his boot to scrape the side of Erika's face, bloodying her ear. "Had enough?" he asked her.

"No. Do it again."

Mayne lowered himself to the mat, turning Erika's body so she faced down. He straddled her right leg and twisted her left, stopping just short of dislocating her hip.

"Now?"

Erika grimaced in pain and sweated profusely, but she refused to cry out. "Is that the best you can do, fuckhead?"

Mayne used his free hand to reach into a pants pocket and drew out a straight razor. He flipped it open and ran the blade across her back, opening about three inches of skin. The cut was not deep, but blood appeared. "Now? Or should I fillet you like a perch?"

"Give me a matching one on my stomach."

Mayne released her leg, stood, and offered her a hand up. She slapped it away. Mayne walked off the mat.

"Fischer and McBride up next," Thomas yelled. Erika was still down on the mat. "Off the mat, Lehmann, we have another match and no time to waste on you." Erika slowly stood and limped off.

John Mayne returned to stand next to Thomas. "We better hope all Nazis aren't as tough as that one or it's going to be a very long war."

Thomas grinned. "Aye. It's not every day a woman bloodies the nose of John Mayne. And did I notice a limp as you walked off the mat?"

"Those kicks felt like a sledgehammer; I'm already tightening up. I've never been kicked that hard by a man. But I'm not talking about that. I don't think there's anything I could have done to break her short of killing her. I shouldn't have scraped her face with my boot, and I shouldn't have cut her. To treat a Valkyrie like that is disrespectful."

Thomas looked at his old comrade. "A Valkyrie? You've certainly promoted her quickly from the first meeting the other day.'"

"I've killed a lot of Nazis without a second thought and been glad about it, but when I walked off the mat just now I felt guilty—like I'd done something wrong. I won't fight her again. And get rid of Cuthbert. If you don't, I'll get rid of him on the mat tomorrow."

"John, Valkyrie or not, let's not forget she's an unrepentant Nazi and our enemy."

"She's a fallen Valkyrie, but a Valkyrie just the same."

Chapter 35

Voodoo Drums

Plaine du Nord, Haiti
Same day; Thursday, 27 April 1944

Moonlight cast macabre shadows of trees and ghoulish silhouettes of the forest canopy behind the plantation veranda where Maeve and Tars sat sipping Haitian rum drinks brought by one of the house servants. Where the house staff had been last night when Gutiérrez interrogated Maeve remained a mystery, but after the 4:00 a.m. transmission, the women returned to bed and had later risen to find the servants busy preparing a breakfast of fruit, fried eggs, and bread.

Gutiérrez had offered his radioman for the transmission, but Maeve insisted she key the message knowing that's what Erika would do. The radioman used an Enigma machine to encode the message in the newest Enigma code called *Shark,* then established contact with Gutiérrez's Montevideo Bolivar relay station. After that, Maeve sat down at the key pad. Her message was not long: She identified herself as *Lorelei,* sent information about the freighter that would carry her and Tars to Europe, and signed off. Montevideo would relay the message to Berlin.

The relaxed tone of this day stood in stark contrast to the tense atmosphere of the night before. Now that Gutiérrez and his men were confident they were in the presence of *Lorelei,* the women were treated like celebrities, especially Maeve. Two men asked for a photo with Maeve and for her autograph, but both Maeve and Gutiérrez nixed those requests telling the men such things would be a gross breach of security for an Abwehr agent undercover. After lunch, Maeve told Gutiérrez that she and Tars wanted to go for a walk. At first he balked, but finally relented when Maeve agreed to bodyguards. The women walked around Plaine du Nord for two hours followed closely by three men with shotguns.

"What did you think of the goat meat?" Maeve asked Tars. Dinner two hours ago had been goat meat over rice covered in red gravy with beans on the side.

"Lots of bones, but not bad."

Maeve nodded. "Pretty good I thought."

"I'm not looking forward to getting on another ship tomorrow," said Tars.

"Maybe it will be easier for you. The seasickness might not bother you this time since you've already been on a ship."

"Yeah, right. You mean like flying was easier for you on those flights to Fort Dix and Cincinnati because you'd already been on a plane?"

"I see your point."

The generator had been turned on when darkness fell, and a weak bulb in a table lamp at the far end of the veranda supplied a small amount of light. Maeve lit a cigarette from a pack given her by one of Gutiérrez's men and offered one to Tars.

As the women smoked and sipped their rum, the faint beat of Voodoo drums rose from somewhere in the forest.

Chapter 36

"We'll Toast the Führer"

STS 23—western Scotland
Next day; Friday, 28 April 1944

"You left an impression on John Mayne," Mr. Thomas said to Erika. Since she was not allowed to breakfast with the team, he had come to her quarters with information he received early that morning about Maeve and Tars. But before he got to that, he spoke about Mayne. "John and I billet together. This morning he had a bruise the size of the King's crown on his side and one nearly as big on his hip from your encounter on the mat yesterday."

"He kicked my ass," she said. Her left ear was partly covered by a bandage, and Thomas saw the dressing over the cut on her back as he helped tighten the breast binding.

"All the same, he felt guilty for cutting you and refuses to fight you again. He considers you a Valkyrie." Erika made no comment. "I'm sure you noticed the absence of Gerald Cuthbert at last night's meal. It was John who insisted on his removal. I knew it was just a matter of time until you'd eliminate Cuthbert, like you intentionally eliminated Hope and Doulton, so I went along with John's request to save us some time. Now that they're gone, I trust the remaining team meets your approval. I don't want you making any more decisions about who remains on the team and taking things into your own hands. We clear on that?"

Erika realized she had underestimated his insight and saw no reason to deny she had taken out Hope and Doulton on purpose. "If Cuthbert is gone, that leaves six, which is still one or two more than we should take in. But at least those left speak one of the languages— all except Mayne. But a man that fierce can be useful. We just have to be careful to keep him out of situations where his inability to communicate with locals will betray him—and any team members with him."

"I have news about *Trekker*," said Thomas. "Your lady friends arrived in Haiti Wednesday and are scheduled to leave later today for Barcelona."

"Barcelona?"

"Have you been there?"

"Yes."

"How familiar with it are you?"

"Only slightly familiar. I once spent ten days in Spain on holiday before the war. I visited Madrid, Zaragoza, and Barcelona. I spent three days in Barcelona. When will they arrive?"

"Two weeks from today; at least that's their ETA. Tomorrow, *Intrepid* will send two agents to Barcelona to reconnoiter and report back to us. You and I will leave here two days ahead of *Trekker*'s arrival so we can do some investigating of our own. We have no room for mistakes when it comes to the switch, and surely your Abwehr people will be on the dock in Barcelona when the ship arrives."

"Yes, they will be there. And so we have twelve more days to adjust our final mission plans for the team," Erika stated.

"Aye. That's a few more training days than we would have had if the freighter docked in Lisbon. We can certainly put those days to good use."

Erika finished buttoning her shirt. "What's the story on Stephanie Fischer?"

"How do you mean?"

"She's German, and she told me she trained at Quenzsee. How did she end up with the SOE?"

"Stephanie was the first one to come to my mind when we began looking for *Trekker*. She's your size, speaks German, even trained at Quenzsee, as she told you. But her eyes are dark brown and her facial resemblance isn't close enough to pass as you. She and her sister will be important to us."

"Her sister?"

"The sister is still in Germany. She's Gestapo. Be on the obstacle course in ten minutes." Thomas left, not answering Erika's question about how Stephanie Fischer had come to the SOE, and leaving her with several more questions about the sister.

183

◊ ◊ ◊

[that afternoon—Cap-Haitien]

Cap-Haitien had three piers but only one that served cargo ships. The inadequate facility made it necessary for ships to unload and load cargo quickly in order to free the dock for ships waiting at anchor in the bay. In Cap-Haitien, seldom did a freighter's crew have the luxury of unloading, spending a night aboard to rest, and then loading the next day, splitting up the back-breaking chores.

Now tied up to the cargo pier was the *Bahia de Cata,* a Panamax freighter—the largest size that could traverse the Panama Canal. The 75,000 tonne *Bahia de Cata* dwarfed freighters the size of the 20,000-tonne *Raven.* As the *Bahia de Cata's* tired crew finished loading the last of the cargo bound for Spain, a black Mercedes-Benz pulled up and stopped near the dock.

"The *Bahia de Cata,*" said Ricardo Gutiérrez. "This is it." Not knowing the name of the ship, yesterday Gutiérrez wired his people in Montevideo. They did the same thing as Leroy Carr—used Maeve's information to check the International Maritime Log for the ship's name. He then instructed his subordinates in Uruguay to radio the information to Berlin, despite Maeve assuring him Berlin would surely check the maritime log as he had done. Gutiérrez was a man who covered his bases.

"Is there anything more I can do for you, Sonderführer?" he asked. Maeve sat beside him in the back seat; Tars was again in the front next to Javier. Javier had tried to avoid Tars after the incident Wednesday evening; for her part, Tars seemed to think nothing out of the ordinary had happened.

"No, Herr Gutiérrez," Maeve said. "Thank you."

"I hope you will report to Berlin that I fulfilled my duties faithfully and efficiently."

"Yes. I will."

"Thank you, Sonderführer. It has been my honor and my privilege to serve you and to serve the Führer."

Everyone got out of the car. Javier went to retrieve the suitcases from the trunk.

"Good luck, Sonderführer," Gutiérrez said to Maeve in parting. "I hope to someday see you again—perhaps in Berlin after the war where we'll toast the Führer and our victory."

"I look forward to that, Herr Gutiérrez."

Chapter 37

The *Bahia de Cata*

Atlantic Ocean
Four days later; Tuesday, 02 May 1944

"At least we don't have to play nurse on this ship," said Maeve. She and Tars were busy swabbing the deck. Now in their fourth day at sea and far from land, they had found gazing out at the endless ocean had finally ended its fascination. Yesterday, to pass the time they picked up mops and went to work.

Tars remarked, "Speak for yourself. I enjoyed digging that piece of metal out of that guy's arm and stitching him up."

"I don't doubt that. You probably enjoyed all the screamin'."

"I might become a nurse after the war."

"In that case, I'll try me best not to get sick or hurt."

So far, their days aboard the *Bahia de Cata* had proved uneventful. The seas had been relatively calm, and Tars' susceptibility to seasickness had not been a major issue. Mornings, upon first awakening, she felt queasy and stayed away from breakfast, but after taking a seasickness pill her stomach would settle and she could keep down lunch and dinner if she ate lightly. This daily morning nausea had prompted Maeve to tease Tars that maybe she was pregnant.

"I'll never let some guy stick his thing in me," Tars had responded, then pulled out and held up her knife. "If they try it, I stick this in *them.*"

When they boarded in Cap-Haitien, Maeve had handed over to Captain Gonzales the envelope of money Emil had given her. Gonzales ordered one of his men to show the women to their cabin and that's the last interaction they had so far had with the ship's captain. Except for Gonzales, most of the men spoke little or no English. Maeve gave up on her attempts to flirt, so despite some occasional leering, the crewmen had left the women alone. At chow, Maeve and Tars were allowed to go to the front of the line, then ate by themselves in their cabin or on deck, usually sitting on tool lockers near the stern where they now mopped.

"So why don't you tell anyone your first name?" Maeve asked.

"It's none of your business why; I just don't. Quit asking."

"I want to know your first name."

"Why?"

"Because we're friends."

"We're not friends!" Tars seemed indignant. "I don't have friends. Never had a friend and don't want one."

"Why?"

"Shut up!"

"What do you think Erika's doing right now?" Maeve couldn't stop asking questions.

"God! You're a pain in my ass! How should I know what Erika's doing? Probably breaking somebody's skull or shoving their balls up to their throat."

[same day—an island in Loch Morar, Scotland]

Less than two miles south of STS 23 lay Loch Morar. With a depth of over 1,000 feet, it was the deepest freshwater body in the British Isles—deeper even than Loch Ness. That morning, the team was driven to the loch where they loaded into two john-boats and putted a short distance out to a heavily forested island. Mr. Thomas had brought them to this remote, wild place for three days of wilderness-survival training. They would have to hunt, fish, or forage for food and build their own shelter. Team members were allowed to bring their handguns and knife. Thomas issued everyone a canteen with a detachable tin cup they could use for cooking, and a small survival kit some would take with them on the actual mission. The kit was a sock that fit into a pocket; inside were matches, fishing line with a hook stuck into a cork, a small bottle of water-purification tablets, two candy bars, and a few rudimentary first-aid items such as iodine swabs and bandages. Each team member was given a waterproof naval pea jacket, but nothing else to ward off the elements including no blankets or tents.

Everyone had eaten one of their candy bars for lunch then spent the afternoon shopping for dinner. The island was a riot of spring green, but the wild blackberries and gooseberries, abundant in summer, were not yet on hand. The menu for the next three days would be whittled down to meat or fish. With her Beretta, Erika picked off a hare hiding under a bush. Amanda McBride proved quite an angler, bringing back to camp two large salmon. The men were equally successful and a feast now roasted over a campfire. Stephanie Fischer shot a swimming duck, but had gotten drenched to her waist retrieving it from the water and now shivered by the fire.

The sky was clear with no rain forecast for that night so they did not waste time building shelters that day. This first night their roof was the stars. If clouds moved in tomorrow, each team member would be responsible for building his or her own shelter.

The team was now set. Inserted into Hitler's Fortress Europe would be three men: Mr. Thomas, John Mayne, and James Granville. And three women: Erika, Stephanie Fischer, and Amanda McBride. Each had unique skills and separate responsibilities and, although she would still opt for a smaller team, Erika felt better about the group now than she had on her first day at STS 23. She leaned over the campfire and cut flesh from the rabbit, duck and salmon roasting on flat rocks and offered some to Stephanie and Amanda. Perhaps not intentionally, but as sometimes happens, the group had segregated by gender. The three men sat on one side of the fire and the women on the other.

"Warming up?" McBride asked Fischer.

"Yeah, my pants are finally drying."

"Eat extra," Erika told the women. "More than you want. We'll need the extra fuel tonight to stay warm." The women ate in silence for a few minutes until Erika turned to the French-speaking Amanda McBride.

"Amanda, je veux pratiquer l'allemand avec Stephanie pour un moment." She was telling her she wanted to practice German with Stephanie for a moment. Her real reason was to enable a private conversation.

"Bien," said Amanda.

Erika switched to German and addressed Stephanie. "Mr. Thomas told me you have a sister in the Geheime Staatspolizei."

"That's right—Kathryn," Stephanie answered, also in German.

"And she'll be working with us?"

"Ja."

"Where is your sister headquartered?"

"Her home base is Berlin, but she often travels throughout the Reich, including many of the occupied countries. She's an officer."

"Your sister is an officer in the Gestapo?"

"Kathryn is a Kriminalkommissar in the Enemies Section."

Erika knew women officers were scarce within the Gestapo. Most women in the organization served as interrogators—the infamous Gestapo Frauen, many of whom were misfits or even criminals before the war. For a woman to reach the rank of Kriminalkommissar, equal to a captain in the military, was very rare.

"You said you trained at Quenzsee," Erika stated.

"Yes. You have quite the reputation there, especially among the women trainees *Lorelei* is quite the legend."

"How is it you're with the SOE?"

"I won't answer that, Erika. Not now. My reason for being here isn't revenge, as yours is. I have my reason, and Kathryn has hers for helping if we need her. But it's not what you might think; we are not traitors. We fight for our country."

Chapter 38

U-621

Mid-Atlantic Ocean
Two days later; Thursday, 04 May 1944

Kapitänleutnant Jürgen Rauch was below when one of his lookouts on the conning tower spotted a possible smoke plume. Rauch ascended the ladder, took the binoculars from the lookout, and focused on the horizon where the crewman had pointed. Yes, it did indeed look like a curl of exhaust from a vessel. Rauch called down to the control room and issued orders to submerge. As the two lookouts scampered down the ladder, Rauch took one last look through the binoculars then followed the lookouts below as the sea sprayed over the deck of *U-621*.

On the deck of the *Bahia de Cata,* deckhand Manny Vega had spent the past hour greasing the boom fittings on the port deck crane. The last few nights had been chilly this far out and he was enjoying his work in the warm afternoon sun. Vega looked forward to returning to Barcelona. When the *Bahia de Cata* spent three days there for repairs last winter he had met Alita. She had since written him wonderful letters. In just a week or so he would see Alita again. Vega wondered if she would be on the dock when his ship arrived. He hoped so.

Through the periscope of *U-621*, Kapitän Rauch had identified the ship as a large freighter 20 minutes ago, but was just now able to make out the flag. He telescoped in until he got a good view of the yellow, blue, and red ensign.

"Venezuela," Rauch announced to the other men in the control room. The freighter was fair game. Although technically a neutral country, the Venezuelan government severed diplomatic ties with Germany after Pearl Harbor and now furnished the Allies with vast oil supplies. Standard Kriegsmarine protocol for a U-boat or any German warship encountering a Venezuelan merchant vessel was to board, seize the manifest and search the ship. If cargo was deemed valuable to the German war effort, the ship would be commandeered and escorted to the nearest Axis-controlled port. If cargo of little value was aboard, Rauch would order the U-boat's deck gun be used to sink the ship. No need to waste one of the limited number of torpedoes on a ship that couldn't return fire. Rauch ordered the engines slowed in order to let the freighter approach, then he would turn *U-621* around and surface on her port side.

Manny Vega had climbed to the top of the crane's boom when he first noticed the frothing of the water. *Too much disturbance to be anything but a whale,* Vega thought. He froze when he saw the conning tower break the surface. Finally, he started shouting but apparently someone in the wheelhouse had also seen the submarine because men were already running up on deck. Vega heard the captain's order over the intercom to don life jackets and the same men who had just run onto the deck turned and scurried off in various directions creating a scene of chaos. As Vega climbed down off the boom he saw the two women who had boarded in Cap-Haitien step out and look over the port rail.

After surfacing and maneuvering *U-621* closer to the freighter, Rauch had the ship's loudspeaker brought to the conning tower from below. A bulky device that barely fit through the hatch, the voice amplifier could shatter the eardrums of anyone directly in front of the speaker. Rauch took the microphone while a crewman pointed the speaker toward the freighter. Rauch announced in German: *"This is Kapitänleutnant Rauch of the German Navy. These orders are for your captain. Fail to obey and your ship will be sunk. Stop all engines. You will be boarded and you and all hands are ordered to be on deck and unarmed. Any man found armed or below deck will be shot. Drop your sea ladder and prepare to be boarded. Sound once with your ship's horn if you understand these orders."*

The freighter's horn did not sound and the ship stayed under power. "Bring me the recordings and the machine," Rauch ordered the first-watch officer standing beside him. The man disappeared down the ladder and returned in a moment with a leather case and a device to play audio wire. "Load the Spanish wire first," Rauch told the Oberleutnant zur See. Even though the ship flew a Venezuelan flag, he knew the captain and crew might be of various nationalities. The leather case held audio-wire messages in English, French, Russian, Spanish, Portuguese, Greek, Italian, and three Scandinavian languages. Once the officer loaded the Spanish wire on the machine, Rauch held it to the microphone. A message with the same demands he had announced in German now played in Spanish.

In a moment, the freighter sounded its horn and its engines stopped.

Maeve and Tars had run back to their cabin without speaking. Maeve reached into a pocket and took out her *L* pill. As she stood looking at it, Tars decided not to use hers; she would shoot herself. What was now happening was the worst-case scenario and one that had been discussed at Camp X. If a German warship commandeered the ship and found Maeve, nothing good could follow. If the U-boat's captain knew *Lorelei* were aboard, he might take her onto the submarine for her protection. But there Maeve would quickly be discovered as a fraud since her German was limited to a few terms and phrases. And if the captain were not aware of *Lorelei*, women so out of place would be immediately suspected of being spies, or at the very least fugitives, and handed over to the Gestapo as soon as the sub returned to port.

"We'll stay here in the cabin," said Tars.

"Everyone else is going to the deck. That must be what that message said."

"You're worried about that when we're both going to die in a few minutes? Better to stay here. Give me your gun. We'll keep the door closed. When they come through the door, I'll shoot as many as I can then shoot myself. When I start shooting, you bite down on that pill." Tars did not know how many Germans would come through the door, but she knew that if Maeve lost her nerve and did not bite the capsule, before she ran out of ammunition she would have to shoot Maeve before killing herself.

A large rubber dinghy with eight Unterseebootmen paddling furiously over mid-ocean waves reached the freighter's sea ladder that had been dropped over the side and tied to the rail. The Germans ascended the ladder, drew their machine pistols and ordered the freighter's crew to back away to the far rail. Captain Gonzales stepped forward but communication was impossible and the Germans motioned with their weapons for him to step back. Two of the Germans kept the crew covered and the other six split up into pairs and began searching the ship. It would take several hours to thoroughly search such a large vessel, but they started with the crew quarters and in about 30 minutes Maeve and Tars heard men speaking German making their way down the corridor outside their cabin. They heard doors being opened and slammed. Tars stood against the wall beside the door where she wouldn't be seen until someone stepped in. She held her pistol about chest high and gripped Maeve's gun in her other hand to use when hers ran out of bullets. With tears in her eyes, Maeve placed the glass cyanide capsule in her mouth, crossed herself, and prayed out loud, "Forgiving Father, have mercy on Tars and me, and on the men who will die with us."

When Maeve could hear the men just outside their door, she used her tongue to roll the glass capsule into place between her back teeth. The door handle turned and the door flew open. Tars readied herself to start squeezing off rounds, but before the German stepped in, he spotted Maeve and froze. He called out something in German and his partner ran out of the next cabin and looked over his fellow crewman's shoulder. They stood there for a moment looking at her. Suddenly, through the open porthole, another announcement in German blared from the submarine. The two men looked at each other. The message was repeated and they turned and ran away.

On the conning tower of *U-621*, Kapitän Rauch lowered the microphone and watched his eight crewmen hustling off the freighter's deck and down the sea ladder. Earlier, after identifying the freighter's name through the periscope, before surfacing he followed Kriegsmarine protocol concerning engagement with a vessel flying a neutral flag: He ordered a coded message sent to Kriegsmarine Command with the ship's name and flag, and stating his intentions to board and search the ship to learn if he should seize or sink it. He again looked at the decoded message that had been sent back in reply:

Take no action against Bahia de Cata / Do not board or impede / Stay all current orders and escort ship to Strait of Gibraltar / Radio for further orders if an Allied vessel approaches Bahia de Cata

Rauch had never before received such an order. *Escort a Venezuelan freighter?* The first-watch officer standing next to Rauch heard him mutter, "What in Neptune's name is on that ship?"

Providence had come to rescue Maeve and Tars in the form of Erika's Abwehr handler, Ulrich von der Osten. Erika had been right in speculating that if a German warship came across Maeve's ship it would likely take her aboard, and that had been the original plan once Berlin learned *Lorelei* had eluded the Americans and was attempting to return. But last week when von der Osten (charged with returning *Lorelei* safely to Berlin) expressed concern about the recent spike in U-boat losses in the Atlantic, discussions started. Today, when Kriegsmarine Command received the transmission from *U-621* and Abwehr was notified that a U-boat had indeed come across the ship carrying the returning agent, von der Osten hastily interceded. Arriving in Barcelona would require passage through the British-held Strait of Gibraltar, a dangerous place for German submarines. Since the start of the war, the Allies had sunk nine U-boats and damaged ten attempting to pass through the Strait. Adding to the danger, the Abwehr outpost in Tangiers had learned the British had recently sown the Strait with mines at depths that would allow surface ships to pass but make it extremely dangerous for submarines. Allied subs would be allowed through on the surface; German U-boats would not receive that kindness. A Venezuelan freighter, however, need not worry about submarine mines or attack from an Allied warship in the Atlantic or Mediterranean. Von der Osten argued that *Lorelei* was Abwehr's best agent and she would be safer left on the freighter. Grand Admiral Dönitz agreed to von der Osten's request. *Lorelei* would remain on the freighter and *U-621* would be assigned to escort and defend the freighter before breaking off at the Strait.

Chapter 39

Operation Kriemhild

SOE Special Training School 23—western Scotland
Next day; Friday, 05 May 1944

The team had returned from Loch Morar that afternoon. Survival training had not proved difficult for any of the highly trained agents. Last night a stiff wind kicked up on the loch and a light rain fell for awhile, but earlier that day everyone had constructed crude lean-tos of branches and foliage and slept through the night protected from the worst of the elements.

Time was running out. Months ago at Camp X, Mr. Thomas had received orders from *Intrepid* that the mission had to be underway in Europe no later than mid-May. For that reason, Maeve had been sent off in late-April so she could make her way to Europe, posing as Erika, and arrive by mid-May to make the switch. Thomas assumed this May deadline had much to do with what everyone, including the Germans, knew was coming: the Allied land invasion of France. With *Trekker* due to arrive in Spain a week from today, Thomas' first mission priority (of many priorities) was to ensure the switching of Maeve and Erika went off without a hitch—a swap that would have to be carried out literally under the eyes of the Abwehr.

And other problems presented themselves.

Although *Trekker's* ship was scheduled to arrive in Barcelona next Friday, there were no guarantees. The progress of a ship across the Atlantic, especially a slow one such as a freighter, always depended on a number of factors: headwinds or tailwinds, rough weather and high seas, and the exact route, which was not known to the SOE. Freighter captains often avoided the shortest course because German U-boats patrolled the popular sea routes. *Bahia de Cata* might arrive a day or two late or day early if aided by tailwinds and calm seas. Sending an Allied ship or airplane to track the ship was too risky since the Germans might do the same. With no way of pinpointing the day the freighter would dock in Barcelona until it reached the Strait of

Gibraltar, Thomas decided he and Erika would depart STS 23 on Tuesday.

After three days of eating only rabbit, fish, and duck, at dinner that evening the potatoes, beans, and bread disappeared first. It was a pleasant meal for Erika. Open hostility directed at her before had ended. Although some of the agents still did not fully trust her (including Mr. Thomas), they had learned that she was a formidable member of the team—one who could assuredly keep up her end. *(If she doesn't betray us.)* Every team member realized the mission's dangers, and knew the odds that all of them would someday see home again were low. But they also knew that without Erika, those chances dropped much lower.

During dinner, Thomas announced he would go over mission responsibilities at that evening's meeting. No one was happier to hear that than Erika. Until now, Thomas had discussed only bits and pieces of the mission—the parts directly related to her training. He had met with Erika in her quarters on several occasions to ask questions about what to expect in Germany during certain situations, and he listened to her input, but she had yet to hear the plan in full.

Now the team was assembled in the meeting room.

"This mission has been given the codename Operation Kriemhild," Thomas began. "That name was chosen by *Intrepid* several months ago but kept secret, even from you. In case you're curious why that name, I was told Kriemhild is a character from a famous German epic: Kriemhild was a woman who sought revenge when her hero was murdered.

"As you are all aware, the goal of our mission is to eliminate certain important members of the Gestapo, SS, and SD to throw a spanner in Himmler's machine and create confusion and delays right before the invasion of France. We don't know the exact date of the invasion, or where it will take place, but we know it's not far off—even the Jerries know that. Erika and I will leave here on Tuesday. For the rest of you, after I'm gone John Mayne will handle the final days of training next week and make sure everyone receives the proper documents and clothing. This meeting tonight is for the team as a whole, so I won't go into all the details of everyone's job. As you all know and have heard said many times, 'What you don't know can't be tortured out of you.' Still, everyone needs to know the mission sequence and who's responsible for what part of the general plan."

Thomas started with Amanda McBride.

"We all know that Amanda is an expert cryptographer and shortwave transmission specialist. She'll serve as the communication link between team members, and between the team and Baker Street. Because her transmitter is crucial to her mission, we won't risk damage by dropping her and it in by parachute. Rather, a Lysander will fly her into France during a moon period. The full moon this month is May 8th—Monday—and the moon period will end on the 15th. Amanda will be flown to a secret French Resistance airfield— really just a large pasture in a forest but it gets the job done—during the early-morning hours of the 14th. That's a Sunday morning and we're hoping any Jerries in the area will be sleeping off their Saturday night beer. Many of our agents have gone into and out of France by Lysander and we expect no problems with Amanda's insertion. Where she'll land isn't something the rest of you need to know. Eileen Nearne has been in France for three weeks working with the French Resistance on another assignment. She'll be at the landing pasture along with members of the Resistance to meet Amanda and help her get situated. Didi will watch Amanda's back and move her often to keep the Jerries off balance as they monitor the airwaves."

This was the first time Erika had heard Eileen Nearne's name mentioned since leaving Camp X.

"Jimmy is on the actual assassination team along with me, John, Erika, and Stephanie. Because Jimmy speaks French and German he'll start off in France. He'll leave one night before Amanda and be dropped in. From there he'll make his way to Berlin to meet up with me. I would prefer to operate out of Frankfurt or Munich, but it's a sure bet Abwehr will take Erika to Berlin so we have to start off there. Amanda knows we'll eventually move around to other cities because not all of the enemies we target are in Berlin.

"Stephanie Fischer will be flown to Sweden in the afternoon of the 13th then taken by launch to Denmark after dark that night. She spent a great deal of time in Denmark before the war and is familiar with much of that country including Copenhagen and Odense. From there it's off to Berlin for her as well. We're hoping three days allow more than enough time for both Stephanie and Jimmy to get to Berlin even with the train delays now common in Germany thanks to our and the Americans bombing of the tracks here and there. So we're aiming at all of us being in Berlin by the 16th. Erika will be in Berlin two or three days before the rest of us; I'm betting Abwehr will have her on a plane within an hour after her arrival on the mainland." Thomas didn't mention Barcelona. Other than himself, the only person in the room who knew of Operation Trekker was Erika. Thomas had not discussed Trekker even with John Mayne.

"None of us traveling by land in Germany will carry transmitters, of course. They'd be impossible to hide during even a cursory search at a train station. The Gestapo picks out travelers at random for searches, sometimes searching up to half of the passengers even if their papers are in order. We also can't carry weapons or a significant amount of money; you'll be issued enough money in currencies of the countries you'll travel in to cover what's required for train tickets and normal living expenses on your way to Berlin. No one will have a weapon on them when they're inserted except Amanda—she doesn't have to travel by train. But as far as the rest of us, the Nazis outlawed ordinary citizens owning handguns years ago and if they find a gun on you during a routine train depot search you'll be awarded a free ride to the nearest Gestapo interrogation chamber. Jimmy and Stephanie, you'll be unarmed and invisible to Baker Street—off the radar, as we say—until you find me in Berlin."

The last member of the team was John Mayne. "Because John doesn't speak German, he'll be dropped just outside Berlin. It's risky, but John's accustomed to that. I'll be there to meet him, and by then I'll have found a discreet place for him to lie low. John will bring a brief-case transmitter powerful enough to reach Amanda—that's all the power we need. It's not easy to drop in with a transmitter and keep it in one piece, but John has done it before. Amanda will have the main transmitter, one capable of contacting Baker Street. Also dropped with John will be our weapons, more money, and other supplies the killing team will need. John will be responsible for relaying our communications to Amanda, and be ready to support us with muscle or backup as needed."

Thomas looked around the room. "Besides letting you know tonight when and where you'll be inserted, and how you'll get your weapons, I doubt if I've told you anything you didn't already know. Everyone here has been aware of the objectives of this mission since early on, and we are all under orders to avoid capture at any cost. Everyone will be issued an *L* pill to use if it comes to that. Are there any questions of a general nature? As I said, I won't go into specifics about anyone's individual assignment. I'll do that during one-on-one meetings this weekend."

James Granville, the explosives expert, asked, "So John's bringing the fireworks?"

"That's right," Thomas answered. "Dropped with John will be a container with the explosives, the Welrods, each agent's other handgun of choice, ammo, knives, and a few other things such as more German currency and additional forged papers for everyone in case an identity needs to be discarded."

"Is there an estimated timeline for this mission?" Amanda asked.

"No. If the invasion begins soon and goes well, maybe we'll all meet for a Christmas dinner in London to cheer the end of the war. Then again, we may be away much longer. If things go badly, it will be every man for himself. We've discussed various escape plans and John will go over them with you again in detail after Erika and I leave on Tuesday. Anything else?"

There were no more questions. "Then I suggest we adjourn to our billets. I'm sure a bed will be welcome after three nights in the bush. Get a good sleep; we're back to work tomorrow. We've a great deal to get done in the few days ahead."

Chapter 40

Back on Deck

Atlantic Ocean
Two days later; Sunday, 07 May 1044

Placing the *L* pill in her mouth last Thursday believing she must bite down in a matter of minutes had shaken Maeve badly. One quick bite and her life would be over. She would never see another day. She would never again see her family. Sleep since then had been difficult, and when she did drop off, nightmares stole any rest. Now she was fidgety and distracted during the day, and Friday she had refused to go on deck after Tars told her that morning the U-boat was still out there. *"What if they change their minds and decide to board again?"*

Tars had assured her that if they were going to do that they would have already, but Maeve wasn't sold. Now three days after the close encounter with the U-boat crewmen at their cabin door, Maeve still had not been back on deck, leaving their cabin only for food and to use the toilet or shower and then returning straightaway.

Tars tried again to convince Maeve to go on deck.

"What would Erika do, Maeve?" asked Tars. "Those are her people and if she were really here she wouldn't worry about letting them see her. That submarine is following this old tub for one reason: the captain thinks *Lorelei* is on it. If they didn't know that when they came aboard the other day; they know it now. Those Germans at our door saw you, and you know they told their captain there was a blonde woman aboard. Abwehr thinks Erika is on this ship; you told them that yourself in your transmission from Haiti so that sub captain has to know that by now. It probably looks suspicious that you haven't been back on deck. They're probably wondering where you are. You better get out there and let them see you or they might come aboard again just to make sure you're not sick or something."

That last part convinced Maeve and she reluctantly trailed Tars out onto the deck. "It switches sides a couple of times each day," Tars said as they walked. The submarine cruised on the surface about 500 yards off starboard and Tars led Maeve to the rail. The U-boat was much farther away than when it had surfaced to board on Thursday, but Maeve could still make out men on the conning tower holding binoculars and looking toward the *Bahia de Cata.*

"I wonder how Mr. Thomas plans to make the switch between me and Erika in Barcelona," Maeve said. "Erika told us her Abwehr people will be at the dock waiting for us, and the switch is one thing we couldn't work on at Camp X."

"Don't worry about it. They'll make plans to deal with that. When the SOE people show up, we'll just do as they say."

[one hour later—Abwehr Headquarters, Tirpitz-Ufer 72, Berlin]
Doktor Erich Pfeiffer, chief of naval intelligence for the Abwehr, walked into Oberführer Walter Schellenberg's office after being shown in by Schellenberg's secretary.

"We received another transmission from *U-621*, Oberführer," Pfeiffer reported.

"Have a seat, Doktor."

"Thank you." Pfeiffer sat, produced a paper from his briefcase and handed it to Schellenberg. "The message was received and decoded about 30 minutes ago. The U-boat Kapitän reported seeing her on the deck of the freighter." Abwehr was aware that *Lorelei's* hair was now blonde, her natural color, since receiving the transmission from Ricardo Gutiérrez after he returned to Uruguay.

"Good." Schellenberg seemed relieved. Tars had been right. The Abwehr had grown concerned when Erika had not been seen on deck, and Schellenberg had reluctantly considered asking Kriegsmarine Command to order Rauch to have his men board again to make sure there wasn't a problem. "I didn't want the U-boat crew boarding again and tip our hand to that freighter captain that a woman aboard was the reason his ship is being escorted. He might decide to try to curry favor with the Engländer in Gibraltar and radio that information ahead." Schellenberg did not need to remind Pfeiffer, who well knew that the British let freighters from neutral countries pass through the Strait, but not until the freighters docked and underwent inspection. If the British learned that a U-boat had escorted the freighter because of a woman aboard, they would surely take her off in Gibraltar for identification and questioning, and he knew the British had records and an MI-9 personnel photo of *Lorelei* when, using the name *Margaret Harrison,* she infiltrated that organization two years ago.

"All our plans are in place concerning Lehmann?" Schellenberg asked.

"Yes, Oberführer. Ulrich von der Osten and his men left this morning."

[that evening—STS 23, western Scotland]

Mr. Thomas had spent two hours in Erika's quarters going over details of what he expected of her once the mission began and showing her photographs of Gestapo and SS/SD personnel he considered worthy targets.

Erika laid down the photographs. "You realize avenging my father is my first priority," she reminded Thomas. "I've been clear about that from the start. I was willing to be turned over to the American FBI and be hanged as a spy if that were not part of this mission. Both your superiors and the American OSS head, General Donovan, agreed to my stipulation."

"We've been through all that a dozen times," Thomas said impatiently. "You can avenge your father; that bargain will be kept. But all the trouble we've gone through to put this mission in place wasn't done just so you can cut the throats of a few low-ranking Gestapo lackeys. Eliminating a few churls isn't going to create confusion in Himmler's ranks. We need to get rid of some of the bigger fish—people with clout."

"I don't know all those men," she said, referring to the photos. "But the ones I recognize do have some level of authority; some much more than others. Do you know their locations?"

"We know the location they work out of but many of them move around—mostly in Germany, France, or Czechoslovakia, but they could be anywhere in Axis-occupied territory."

Erika thought for a moment. "Ah, Stephanie's sister, the Gestapo Kriminalkommissar. That's where she can help you, of course."

"That's right."

Erika remained very curious about the Fischer sisters. "How did someone trained at Quenzsee end up with the SOE?"

"The Germans didn't know she's Jewish," Thomas answered. "When they found out, Stephanie escaped and made her way to England to take up the fight for her people. By the way, I've always been curious as to how you'll find out which men killed your father."

"I will find a way. I always do when it's something I want badly enough, Mr. Thomas. Or I guess I can call you Victor since no one is with us. The plans we discussed about the switch: Have you decided?" One night while the others sat around the campfire on the island in Loch Morar, Thomas and Erika took a walk. They discussed the advantages of Erika switching with Maeve in Gibraltar when the ship would dock for inspection. Erika concurred this was the better course. Yes, Abwehr had its spies in the Strait and they would be watching the ship, but in British-controlled Gibraltar they would have to be few, far off, and lying low, unlike in neutral Barcelona where the docks would swarm with Abwehr when the freighter arrived.

"Aye. We'll make the switch in Gibraltar. You and I will leave here on Monday instead of Tuesday."

"Good. The sooner we make the switch the better. I don't feel good about the fact we can't keep that freighter under surveillance."

Chapter 41

Fishermen

Atlantic Ocean—75 miles west of Gibraltar
Four days later; Thursday, 11 May 1944

The *Bahia de Cata's* captain, Sofronio Gonzales, had taken that day's first watch and was in the wheelhouse at dawn when he saw the German U-boat suddenly disappear. "Gracias a Dios," Gonzales had muttered to himself, thanking God. He had hoped that when they neared Gibraltar he might finally see the last of the submarine that had tracked his ship for a week. Any captain whose ship crossed the Atlantic would be foolish not to learn all he could about the U-boats, and Gonzales knew that, even though his ship was slow, German submarines were even slower when submerged. Only on the surface could a U-boat maintain the *Bahia de Cata's* average sailing speed of 14 knots. When the submarine dropped back and submerged he knew he was at last rid of it. It had taken a lot of talking and creativity for him to explain the presence of the German submarine to his nervous crew—reasons Gonzales fabricated because he had no idea why the U-boat was out there, or why the Germans had suddenly boarded last week then mysteriously left his ship in a hurry.

About an hour after the submarine disappeared, a watchman spotted a Spanish fishing trawler off the port bow. Gonzales sounded the ship's horn to warn the fishermen to clear the way, but the boat kept making its way toward the *Bahia de Cata.* Four fishermen stood on the boat's deck waving frantically, as if in need of assistance, so Gonzales ordered the engines slowed and sent one of the helmsmen down to see what the problem was. The helmsman went to the deck, leaned over the rail, and spoke to the fishermen who had pulled their boat to within a few feet of the freighter. He ran back to the wheelhouse and told Gonzales one of the men had a message for him.

"Let him board," Gonzales ordered half-heartedly. *What now?*

The sea ladder was dropped, and one of the fishermen climbed aboard and was escorted to the wheelhouse where he handed

Gonzales an envelope containing two solid gold eight Escudos coins worth a small fortune and a note in Spanish:

Greetings Captain Gonzales: I've asked these kind fishermen to deliver this note. My daughter, Lorelei, is on your ship. Because I know you sail to Barcelona, I've hired these fishermen to meet you and bring her to Cádiz where I wait to take her home to Switzerland. If you will please have your men help her off with her possessions I will be most indebted. Thank you for caring for my daughter during her journey, and please accept these coins as a token of my gratitude. Yves Moix

Gonzales didn't know which of the two women was *Lorelei* and he didn't care. Even though the note said nothing about a second woman, they had boarded together and he assumed they would leave together. He knew Cádiz was only a short way up the Spanish coast and Gonzales considered this a stroke of luck. Within the past hour the U-boat had disappeared; he would now be rid of his passengers, and he had gotten rich. It was the start of a very good day.

"Vinicio," Gonzales addressed the helmsman, "tell the women to gather their things quickly. They're leaving the ship." Gonzales reconsidered, remembering that the women would not understand Vinicio's Spanish. "Never mind, I'll do it myself."

Gonzales went to the women's cabin and knocked. Because breakfast was in 15 minutes, they were up and dressed. He handed them the note and translated. "Please gather your things," he said. "I'll wait for you in the corridor."

"This makes sense," Tars said after the captain stepped out and closed the door. "Trying to make the switch in Barcelona would be hard. The place will be crawling with Nazis. Let's hurry and get off this rust bucket. You should be happy. Your part is over; now you can go back to Ireland and rob more banks."

They quickly threw their things into the suitcases and followed Gonzales out on deck. He ordered a crewman to lower the luggage to the fishing trawler. Waves kept bumping the trawler against the enormous freighter's hull, but the fishermen held the sea ladder steady as Tars and then Maeve climbed down. When they were safely on the trawler's deck, the *Bahia de Cata* crew raised the sea ladder while one of the Spanish fishermen used a long pole to push the trawler away from the colossal freighter. Maeve and Tars heard the trawler's engine fire and it started away.

"Your people below," said one of the fishermen in broken English as he motioned toward a hatch. He led them over to it and pointed for them to descend the steps.

"I wonder if Erika is here or if Mr. Thomas is taking us to meet her," Maeve whispered as she followed Tars down.

"I don't know," answered Tars. "It could be either."

When they reached the bottom of the steps, two men dressed as fishermen stood in the small room cluttered with commercial fishing equipment. Neither was Mr. Thomas. Surprised to see a second woman, the men gave Tars a quick once over then focused their attention on Maeve.

"Welcome, Sonderführer Lehmann," one of them said in German. He showed them his Abwehr identification. "I am Agent Kluesner; this is Agent Scheu." The other man held up his identification. "We're here to take you to Major von der Osten who waits for you on the coast. The major made these arrangements to get you off the cargo vessel now so you would not have to deal with possible questioning from the Engländer in Gibraltar. We have an airplane waiting. I'm pleased to tell you that you'll be dining in Berlin tonight among friends. I'm sure this is very good news after so much time among the enemy. Ja?" Kluesner smiled.

Other than the *Willkommen, Sonderführer Lehmann,* Maeve didn't understand a word.

Chapter 42

In the Strait

Tarifa, Spain
Same day; Thursday, 11 May 1944

The town of Tarifa, in Andalucia, held the distinction of being the southernmost point in continental Europe. A Spanish coastal town facing Morocco, Tarifa sat at the narrowest point across the Strait of Gibraltar. Here the British had established a check station where freighters wishing to traverse the strait in either direction had to dock for mandatory inspection. The British recorded the ship's manifest and searched ship and cargo. If none of the cargo was found to be on the list of prohibited or suspicious items, the ship was allowed to pass. This hunt through a ship and its stowage could take anywhere from a couple of hours to a full day, depending on the size of the freighter and the extent of its consignment.

Given the high probability that the Abwehr would be surveilling the check-station dock, Mr. Thomas, Erika Lehmann, Leroy Carr and Al Hodge waited in disguise as tugs pushed the *Bahia de Cata* against the Tarifa British naval pier. Thomas had decided at STS 23 that attempting the switch in Barcelona was too risky, especially since a safer alternative offered itself. Last weekend, when Carr learned the SOE would make the switch in the Strait, the OSS counterintelligence chief opted to be on hand for the switch instead of returning to Scotland to see the mission off as originally planned. Carr and Hodge had arrived in Tarifa early yesterday morning, two days after Thomas and Erika. After huddling for several hours yesterday to discuss the plan to switch Erika and Maeve, the four agents had been ready since yesterday evening—the earliest estimated time the freighter might arrive.

The plan was simple. Dressed in British Port Authority uniforms, the four would join the legitimate Port Authority search crew going aboard. That Erika was a woman presented no problem: women were often part of the search crews, and there were two other women on the ten-member search team now ready to board the Venezuelan freighter. The disguised Erika would not draw attention if Abwehr watched from afar. Erika, wearing a brunette wig and dark eyeglasses under her white, short-visored Port Authority cap, would switch clothes, wig, and glasses with Maeve in her cabin. Maeve, now taking Erika's place as a Port Authority inspector, would simply walk off the ship with the others; Erika would stay aboard with Tars and sail to Barcelona to be greeted by Abwehr.

When the search crew stepped off the gangway and onto the deck of the *Bahia de Cata,* Captain Gonzales met them with manifest in hand as per standard protocol. Mr. Thomas discreetly told the captain he was aware of the women aboard and assured him there was no problem: He and three of his Port Authority comrades simply wished to talk to them. It was then they learned about the U-boat and the Spanish fishing trawler.

Erika slammed the car door after entering the back seat beside Mr. Thomas. Al Hodge took the wheel with Leroy Carr beside him in the front. Erika ripped off her cap, wig, and glasses and threw them against the back of the seat in front of her.

"I saw this coming!" she half-shouted. "Not tracking that damn freighter was a mistake!"

Thomas shouted back. "You know as well as anyone we couldn't do that and risk being seen by your goddamn Jerry friends!" He was just as angry as Erika. "This changes everything."

"No shit!" Erika responded angrily. "That's what the Americans would say to that, right Leroy and Al?"

From the front, Carr tried to get things under control. "Let's calm down and put our heads together. We won't get anywhere insulting each other."

Silence reigned for a moment as Hodge started the car and drove off.

Erika was still livid. "Do we have a map of Spain in this fucking car?"

"Glove box, Leroy," Al Hodge said as he drove. Carr found the map and handed it over his shoulder to Erika.

"This can't be Abwehr," Erika said as she opened the map. "They wouldn't have to resort to some sneaky plan involving Spanish fishermen to reacquire me. If the Abwehr wanted me off the freighter before Barcelona, they could have had the U-boat take me off days ago." The others waited as she took a couple of minutes to study the map and gather her thoughts.

"It's possible the fishing boat crew is in league with someone in Germany," she said. "There are many Spanish Nationalists grateful to us since we bailed their asses out of the fire during their Civil War in '36. But it's just as possible the fishermen were misled and simply dupes with no idea what they were doing. But none of that matters as far as we're concerned.

"This has Himmler's name stamped on it," she continued. "He must have found out I was returning. He knows, or at least assumes, that since I'm still alive I know he sent one of his assassins to America to kill me, and he can't allow me to return to Berlin and report him. Now the Gestapo has Maeve and Tars."

Leroy Carr spoke from the front. "You told me once that Abwehr doesn't cooperate with Himmler. How did the Gestapo find out about your return?"

"I don't know," Erika answered. "But Himmler has his tentacles spread wide: He has direct access to nearly all levels of German government, and in the few areas where he doesn't hold authority he uses moles and informants—either willing ones or those he blackmails." She thought for a moment. "The U-boat! The freighter captain said the U-boat escorted his ship for a week. That's how Himmler found out I was on that freighter." (She didn't say 'Maeve'— everyone in the car knew the Germans thought Erika was aboard the *Bahia de Cata*.) "Himmler is privy to German naval transmissions. U-boat captains radio Kriegsmarine Command for orders when they come across a neutral freighter. The Kriegsmarine knew the name of the freighter I was on and assigned the U-boat to guard it. Himmler found out about the freighter a week ago."

She paused for a moment to think. "That freighter captain told us the fishing trawler showed up this morning about an hour after the U-boat disappeared. Himmler knew the U-boat captain would blow that fishing boat into toothpicks. But he also knew that the sub couldn't follow the freighter through the Strait. When the U-boat captain radioed Command that he was pulling back, the Gestapo was ready."

"Do you have any thoughts about where they'll be taken?" Thomas asked.

"There will be Gestapo on the fishing trawler. They'll probably let the fishermen get them to wherever it is on the coast they're going then they'll kill Maeve and Tars and most likely the fishing crew. Himmler never leaves witnesses or loose ends."

Carr said, "That freighter captain said the note from the fishermen mentioned taking them to Cádiz, so we know that's *not* where they'll be taken."

"Of course Cádiz is not the true location," Erika commented as she and Thomas looked over the map and saw Cádiz just a short distance up the Spanish coast. "But that has to be the direction. The only other place the trawler could go is into the Strait or south to the African coast. German agents can operate much more easily in Spain than in Morocco."

Thomas said, "If all this is as you say, I'm sure the Gestapo flew in. Al, take us to the commander's office. There's a squadron of Spitfires and Hurricanes in Gibraltar. I'll ask the commander here to notify the RAF squadron commander in Gibraltar and send up some planes to reconnoiter that area of the coast, looking for any aircraft on the ground. Then we'll head that way; it's not far from here. If we don't get there in time to save the women, maybe we can eliminate some Gestapo."

"There's something we haven't discussed," Carr noted. "That Tars does her job."

Erika had already considered it. *If Tars has done her job, either some Gestapo agents are dead and she and Maeve have escaped, or if escape had not been possible then Tars has killed Maeve and then herself.*

Chapter 43

8 Prinz Albrechtstrasse

Berlin—Headquarters of the SS and Gestapo, 8 Prinz Albrechtstrasse
Same day; Thursday, 11 May 1944

Heinrich Himmler had just finished reading a report from SS-
Obersturmbannführer Adolf Eichmann detailing the number of
Hungarian Jews shipped by train to Auschwitz-Birkenau since the
beginning of the month. As Himmler closed the folder, Ursula Ziegler,
his secretary, buzzed to tell him Heinrich Müller had arrived.

"Show him in," Himmler ordered. Müller was Himmler's Gestapo
chief, but despite their shared first name and the fact they controlled
the vast European Gestapo network, they had little in common.
Himmler did not trust Müller, but then the Reichsführer trusted no
one.

"What is it, Müller? I have a lot of work."

"I have a report from this morning's operation in Spain." He
immediately had Himmler's attention.

"Already? Let's have it. Is she dead?" It was now that Himmler
noticed Müller's face—an extraordinarily pale face.

"Gerber reports that when the fishing boat made it back to
shore, Scheu and Kluesner were dead and *Lorelei* was not on board."

The normally poker-faced Himmler suddenly had a look
somewhere between shock and rage. He jumped to his feet and
screamed the German equivalent of, "Fuck everything, Müller!" as if he
were confused as to what to say. Müller sank back into his chair not
knowing how to act in response to the peculiar retort. He had endured
withering salvos from Himmler before, but with this he didn't know if
Himmler blamed him or had simply blown a gasket at the world in
general.

"What the fuck happened?!" Himmler shouted.

"Gerber waited on shore for Scheu and Kluesner to return with
Lehmann," Müller explained quickly. "When the boat arrived, the

Spanish fishermen were in quite a state of fright and confusion as one might expect. Apparently there was another woman with Lehmann."

"Another woman? Who?"

"We don't know, Reichsführer. The fishing boat captain told Gerber they were underway when suddenly they heard gunshots from below; then this other woman ran up on deck and held a gun to the captain's head and demanded he take them directly to the nearest shore. He was forced to guide the boat as close to land as possible without grounding, then the woman and Lehmann jumped off and swam a short distance to the shore. The trawler captain told Gerber the last he saw of them they were running into the forest. With the women gone, he went below, found Scheu and Kluesner dead, then sailed to where he had agreed to meet Gerber farther up the coast."

Himmler said, "Scheu and Kluesner were new agents—Gestapo for less than a year. That's why I chose them. She's been away nearly two years. She couldn't have recognized them. We gave them Abwehr identification. Lehmann is trying to return to Germany and to Abwehr; why would she kill two men who she had to think Abwehr had sent to help her?"

"I agree, Reichsführer. It makes no sense. Lehmann and the other woman were in such a hurry to flee they left their possessions behind. Gerber and his men searched their luggage and found nothing out of the ordinary—only clothes and a few female items."

Himmler walked to the window and gazed out at the traffic on Prinz Albrechtstrasse for a long minute.

Finally, Müller asked for guidance. "Gerber has detained the Spanish fishermen and awaits further orders, Reichsführer."

Himmler surprised Müller by responding calmly: "Tell Gerber to have the Spaniards show him where Lehmann went ashore, then have him eliminate the crew and take the boat out and sink it. Find Lehmann and this other woman, Müller, and make sure they never reach Germany. Am I being perfectly clear?"

Müller stood. "Jawohl, Reichsführer."

213

Return to Valhalla

Part 3

"You have performed a military feat which will become part of history. You have given me back my friend Mussolini!"

— Adolf Hitler,
congratulating Otto Skorzeny for his daring rescue
mission of the captured Italian dictator, 1943

Chapter 44

Hasty Revision

Gibraltar, Spain
Thursday, 11 May 1944

Mr. Thomas, Erika, Leroy Carr and Al Hodge had just disembarked the American-made RAF Catalina flying boat and now stood on the pier. The moon lit the crest of the waves as the Catalina powered away to return to its squadron's dock in Algeciras on the other side of the bay. Instead of returning to Tarifa, the group had decided to fly to Gibraltar after spending the afternoon and early evening flying over the coastal region of southwestern Spain.

They had accepted the fact that Maeve and Tars were dead. An hour before the Catalina picked them up in Tarifa, three RAF Hurricanes were dispatched from the 544th Fighter Squadron in Algeciras to reconnoiter the route the fishing trawler likely headed after removing the women from the freighter. When one of the pilots reported a burning and sinking trawler two miles off the coast southwest of Barbate, then spotted a john-boat with three Caucasian men skipping across the waves heading away from the trawler, it was evident that the Gestapo had done its work. Maeve, Tars, and most likely all of the Spanish fishermen now rested at the bottom of the sea. Operation Kriemhild was in danger of ending before it started.

"Let's hope we did the right thing not blowing that john-boat out of the water," Leroy Carr said. When the Hurricane pilot radioed for instructions, Thomas ordered him to back off. In charge now that he and Erika had reached mainland Europe, Thomas had changed his mind from earlier and decided to ignore the john-boat after Erika told them a Gestapo leader doubtless waited on shore.

"It would have gained us nothing other than eliminating three Gestapo lackeys and tip our hand if more Gestapo waited on shore as Erika suspects," Thomas replied.

The four watched a British submarine sweeper, its running lights on, enter the bay after a day patrolling the strait. It passed a similar vessel heading out on night patrol.

"What's the latest guess on when that freighter will arrive in Barcelona?" Erika asked Thomas.

"Since it was a half day behind schedule arriving in Tarifa this morning, it won't make it to Barcelona tomorrow as expected. It left Tarifa at noon today. It's a two-day voyage to Barcelona at freighter speed, so it should be around late-morning Saturday when it docks."

"Himmler has to be very careful no one at Abwehr or the High Command discovers what he did today," Erika said. "Abwehr will be in Barcelona expecting me and another woman to walk off that freighter. When we don't, they'll question that freighter captain. Abwehr might assume I arranged for the fishermen to meet the freighter. It would not be unlike me to do something like that simply as a precaution."

"You don't think Abwehr will suspect foul play from Himmler or think the British found out about you and moved in to capture you?" Al Hodge asked.

"Abwehr knows nothing about Himmler's plots against my father and me; it's possible they might at first suspect the British, but they'll realize the British could have captured me in Tarifa without going to all that trouble. As I said, my guess is that Admiral Canaris and Ulrich von der Osten, my handler, will come to the conclusion that I arranged the fishing boat. I'll admit to that in Berlin. I'll get a scolding from Canaris but that's all that will come of it."

Carr asked, "So you think the mission can proceed?"

"As long as I can convince the Admiral that I sneaked off the freighter on my own. Best plan now is for me to make my way to Vichy France and contact von der Osten. He'll extract me from there."

"How will you explain the loss of Tars to the Abwehr?" Carr asked her.

"I don't know yet. I'll have to think of something."

Thomas broke in. "We can drop you into Vichy so you don't have to bother crossing Spain."

Erika nodded. "Stephanie will have to take Tars' place in Germany. You'll have to call off her other duties and assign her to me. Agreed?"

"Agreed," answered Thomas.

"I'll need you to figure out a way to get her to Berlin sooner than the sixteenth."

"That will be difficult."

Erika gave Thomas a glassy stare, though he missed it in the darkness of the pier. "Get her to Berlin by Monday; that's only one day sooner. I'm sure such a renowned commando from the First Airlanding Brigade can find a way."

"That will put her in Berlin before me. How will she find you?"

"Tell her to go to the Lili Marlene Café on the Voightstrasse Monday evening. Ask for Carla; she owns the café. I can trust Carla and I'll leave further instructions with her. Tell Stephanie to identify herself as *Early's friend.* If the café has suffered bomb damage and is not open, tell Stephanie to meet me at the Brandenburg Gate at nine o'clock that night. But the café is safer and the first choice."

Thomas was ready to be flexible. He was just glad he was not hearing a litany of reasons from Leroy Carr why Operation Kriemhild should be scuttled. The SOE man knew the OSS hoped the Russian-speaking *Lorelei* survived this mission and the war. After Operation Kriemhild, their agreement required the SOE to return *Lorelei* to the Americans, for whom she would be an invaluable asset spying on the Russians in post-war Europe. "Very well. I'll find a way to get Fischer to Berlin by Monday." Thomas withdrew a pen and small tablet from his suit jacket and wrote down Erika's instructions for Stephanie. "Carla . . . Lili Marlene Café . . . Early . . . I remember that's a name you sometimes used in America."

"That's right. It's a childhood nickname, and it will assure Carla the message is from me and that Stephanie can be trusted."

"Alright," Thomas said as he put the tablet back in his pocket. "And if the café is closed, you'll meet her at the Brandenburg Gate at nine."

"Yes, but the café if it's open. As for our rendezvous plans later in the week—yours and mine—I see no reason to change those. I'll bring Stephanie with me."

Everyone gazed out at the bay for a moment until Thomas broke the silence.

"It's unfortunate that Operation Trekker ended badly. I'll make sure Maeve's mother gets the back pay she has coming from Camp X. I know Maeve was concerned about that. And I'll send a message through channels to *Intrepid* asking him to consider keeping the rest of the bargain with her—the part concerning her father and brother. Since she didn't complete her mission, that decision lies with *Intrepid*, but I'll recommend it."

It was a decent gesture coming from the brusque commando, but no one commented about it or about the two women. Erika had grown fond of Maeve, but war often allows little time to mourn.

Chapter 45

The Witch

Southwest Spain
Same day; Thursday, 11 May 1944

Getting the jump on the Germans on the fishing trawler had not been difficult. They believed Maeve was Erika and assumed she would be happy to be back in German hands. Tars simply pulled her gun and fired, leaving the men no time to unholster theirs. The two women escaped with their weapons and the Swiss francs Al Hodge had issued them. While Tars went on deck and held her gun to the fishing boat captain's head, Maeve stuffed the money into her pockets. They left everything else behind.

After ordering the captain to guide the trawler to the nearest shore, they jumped off and swam the short distance to land. The rest of the day was spent double-timing it as best they could to put distance between themselves and the beach, slowing to a walk when needing a break, staying in the trees and avoiding open meadows and glades. Though in excellent physical shape after months of training at Camp X, after a day spent constantly on the move both women were hungry and fatigued.

Just before dark, they entered a mountain range. The half-moon supplied enough light to keep them moving, but darkness and rough terrain slowed their pace considerably. Earlier, the sun and a warm spring breeze dried their clothes, but now in the darkness and at higher altitude the air had grown chilly.

"What are we going to do when Erika finds out you killed two of her Abwehr people?" Maeve asked fretfully. Neither woman had any way of knowing the men Tars shot were Gestapo sent to kill Erika.

"You've asked me that three times. What else could I do? Maybe I could have told them we needed a manicure and to please drop us off at the nearest salon. You don't speak German; it would have taken those guys about 5 minutes to figure out you weren't Erika. My number-one duty is make sure you're not captured. I did my job."

"How will Erika explain it to Abwehr? They'll think she killed them."

"I don't know, Maeve. I couldn't think about that. I had to do my assignment. She'll think of something. Right now we need to think about our next move. Sooner or later we're bound to come across a village or town or at least a farm."

"Erika will find us," Maeve said confidently. "After that freighter gets to Barcelona and she sees we're not on it she'll come looking for us." The women also could not know that Mr. Thomas had changed the switch point to Tarifa and that he and Erika already knew about their disappearance and believed them dead.

Tars explained, "When we're not on that freighter in Barcelona that will mess up their plans for the switch. But Erika and that prick Thomas will think of some way to pull it off. Then Erika will be in Abwehr's hands and won't be able to look for us. Thomas doesn't actually need you there. It might even make things easier for him because now he won't need to hide you. What we have to do is lie low and not get you captured until we can contact the SOE so they can send someone to get us. We need to find a transmitter, and even if we do it's not going to be sitting out waiting for us to use it. It'll be guarded. We need a plan."

"Do you think the Germans are after us?"

"They will be if those two guys on the fishing boat weren't alone. Any of their buddies waiting on shore would force that fishing boat captain to show them where we jumped off. I would have killed those fishermen but the local police would get involved if Spaniards came up dead. Then we'd be running from Germans *and* the Spanish police. As it is now, the Germans aren't going to report their dead guys to the police because they're not supposed to be operating in a neutral country in the first place."

As the women trudged up another hill, they heard the faint sound of music. When they came to the crest, they saw an encampment in the valley below. Several wagons surrounded a large campfire. People milled about: some ate near the fire, a man played a stringed instrument, a few women danced.

"Look!" Maeve exclaimed cheerfully.

"Keep your voice down," Tars ordered. "And get down." She grabbed Maeve's arm and pulled her down to squat behind a boulder. "Those are Roma," Tars whispered.

"What's that?"

"Gypsies."

"So what? Maybe they'll help us—at least give us something to eat."

"And they're just as likely to slit our throats or capture us and sell us as prostitutes, especially you. They'd get a lot of money for a blonde. I know about Gypsies; there are a lot of them in Italy. Thieving and whoring is what they do. It's their way of life. They even whore out their own daughters."

"But you're not sure they'll try that, right? I say we go down there. I'm tired, cold, and starving. We have guns."

"So do they."

"I say we take the chance. We're lost in the bush in a strange country. Maybe we can offer them money to take us to a town or someplace we can catch a train to a big city. It's easier to melt in and lie low in a big city—that's why I went to London."

Tars knew all about hiding; she had done it for nearly two years after La Cosa Nostra put a price on her head. Maeve was right about the city, and Tars realized a city would offer the best chance of locating a transmitter. "Okay, but be ready to shoot your way out. You have a round chambered?"

Maeve checked her gun. "Yes."

"Now we have to hope we can make them understand us. They're not going to speak English. When we get down there they'll draw their guns. Don't start shooting then; just hold up your hands. We'll need time to see if we can get their help. If it comes time to pull out our guns just follow my lead."

The Gypsies camped beside a stream about two hundred yards away at the bottom of the slope. The women made their way down. When Maeve and Tars walked out of the woods, the Gypsy women scattered and, as Tars had predicted, the men drew guns. Several held rifles; the others pistols. When Maeve and Tars held up their hands, two men rushed up from behind and held the muzzle of their rifles against the women's backs. A man near the fire began shouting.

"He's hollering in Italian," Tars told Maeve.

"That's grand. You can speak to them."

"I can speak to them, but that won't change their minds about us just because I speak Italian. This bunch probably fled here because the Nazis are rounding up Gypsies in Italy and shipping them off to concentration camps."

The man doing the shouting seemed to become more agitated because the women spoke a strange tongue he didn't understand. Some of the Roma women, who had run off when they saw Maeve and Tars walk out of the forest, now returned and stood behind the men. One woman approached, felt Maeve's hair, and said something to the men.

"Just what I thought," said Tars. "She told them you'd fetch a good price."

"Why don't you talk to them? Tell them we have money."

"Let me handle this. If I tell them about the money they'll search us right away and find our guns. I'm going to tell them we want to talk to their leader."

"Vogliamo parlare con il vecchio," Tars said loudly.

The shouting man stared at Tars for a moment; then, ignoring her request, he ordered a search. Their guns were found and taken, along with the knives both women carried in their pants pockets and Maeve's money, still damp from her earlier swim. Their *L* pills were also found. As the searcher looked curiously at the capsules, Tars told him they were candy and urged him to try one, but he put them in the bag with the other items. The only jewelry either woman wore was the Ring Erika had given Maeve for identification. The searcher took it off her finger. With guns at their backs and hands in the air, Maeve and Tars could do nothing.

During the search, a man climbed down from the wagon nearest the fire to observe. When the search ended, he stepped forward and spoke to the others. One man bowed and hustled off.

"Who's that?" Maeve asked Tars nervously. "What's he saying?"

"That's the leader . . . the Gypsy king. He told the other man to bring the witch."

"The witch?"

"The clan witch. Gypsies believe in magic and fortune telling."

Soon a hunchbacked woman limped toward the group near the fire. The withered old woman, decrepit and stooped, wore a black robe and shawl. A large wart stood out on her long, crooked nose and a white eye lacked iris and pupil. Around her neck hung several emblems on silver chains, and on each finger she wore a ring.

The Gypsy king spoke to the crone, who then walked up to Maeve and placed a hand over Maeve's heart. After a moment in a trance-like state the old woman said in Italian, "Sell this one." Then she limped to Tars. As soon as she touched Tars' chest the crone backed away as if she had touched an electrified fence.

"What is it?" the king asked the witch.

"This one is not safe. She has been touched by Cain. Kill her."

Chapter 46

Gypsy King

Seville, Spain
Same day; Thursday, 11 May 1944

Conrad Gerber sat on the veranda of the Barcelo Renacimiento Hotel in Seville drinking schnapps. He had chosen Seville as headquarters for his mission to eliminate Erika Lehmann—an assignment given him personally by Heinrich Himmler. Gerber was thankful for the assignment. Last summer, on Himmler's orders, he had eliminated Karl Lehmann and he was as eager as Himmler to tie up loose ends. And Gerber knew that Lehmann's Abwehr daughter was the most dangerous loose end.

Two other men sat with Gerber.

"Tomorrow morning, at first light," Gerber told them, "I want our plane in the air scouring every area she might have reached on foot. Understood?" Darkness had forced him to call off that day's search. Earlier, he ordered the Spanish fishermen to show him where the woman went ashore, then he had the fishermen killed and their boat sunk. The Spaniards had mentioned a second woman. Gerber had no idea who that could be but it didn't matter.

"Of course, Kriminalsekretär," responded the highest ranking of the two men, an SS Oberscharführer. Gerber had brought along members of both the Gestapo and the Totenkopf-SS (Death's Head) division. Gerber's rank of Kriminalsekretär made him the equal of a Wehrmacht lieutenant. Himmler had bestowed the promotion after Gerber eliminated Karl Lehmann. Even though the reason for the promotion had to be kept secret, it had been a proud moment for Gerber. That mission had not been an easy one. Killing someone was not difficult, but numerous precautions were necessary with Lehmann, a trusted old friend of the Führer. Attention to detail was essential in order that the Führer never suspect foul play. After much planning, Gerber pulled it off by making Karl Lehmann's death look like a sailing accident.

"The Abwehr woman must not under any circumstances set foot on German soil," Gerber stressed. "Do what is necessary. And this second woman the fishermen spoke of, eliminate her, of course."

"Of course, Kriminalsekretär."

[same time—Gypsy camp]

The Gypsy king nodded his permission for the witch's decrees to be carried out. The man holding the rifle at Tars' back roughly grabbed her hair with his free hand and guided her into the forest to be shot. Another man pushed Maeve toward one of the wagons to be tied up and then sold at the soonest opportunity.

"Take your hands off me, you kooksucker!" Maeve yelled. The man didn't understand but slapped her across the face for her belligerence. The king warned him not to damage valuable property. Maeve managed to break away and run toward the forest but other men stood in her way and she was quickly corralled. The king ordered the men to tie her and carry her to the wagon. They bound her wrists then forced her to her knees. As they started to tie her ankles, Maeve heard Tars shouting.

"Ehi, guarda qui, figil di puttana!" *("Hey, look over here, motherfuckers!")* Tars stood at the edge of the clearing. The man who took her into the woods was on his knees and appeared to be bleeding. Tars knelt behind him for cover and held the man's rifle to the back of his head. The Gypsy who searched the women had checked only their pockets, missing the dagger Tars kept taped to her ankle. She added in Italian, "Untie her and let her go or I'll blow this motherfucker's brains out then shoot as many of you as I can!"

Tars switched to English. "Maeve, as soon as they untie you, grab our weapons and money and a couple of their rifles then come over here by me!" Maeve by this time was on her feet.

The king told Tars he would cut Maeve loose and walked over to her, but instead he placed his knife to her throat. "Ora è tempo per voi di decidere," he said to Tars *("Now it's time for you to decide")*.

Maeve didn't understand the Italian but the knife at her throat told her what was going on. "He's bluffing, Tars."

227

Tars thought the situation over. "No he's not, Maeve. He won't think twice about sacrificing this guy unless he was his firstborn son— his heir. Looks like I didn't get that lucky. When I throw down this gun they'll shoot me immediately, but you'll be okay. They know they can make a lot of money selling you. They can't understand me so listen carefully. After they sell you, wait your chance to escape from whoever buys you. You can pull that off. Then contact the SOE if you can find a transmitter. If you can't, try to make your way to Portugal and the American or British embassy in Lisbon."

"Don't do it, Tars!"

Tars threw down the rifle. The hostage, whom Tars had only nicked with her dagger so she wouldn't have to drag a severely wounded man back to the camp, quickly scrambled away.

"Shoot her!" The king ordered. The men raised rifles and took aim.

"Stop!" the witch shouted from the back of a wagon. "The curse! The curse will be on us!" She had walked over to inspect the articles confiscated from Maeve and Tars and had just found Maeve's Ring. "One of them wears the Ring of the Slain!" The witch hobbled over as fast as she could to where the king stood with his knife at Maeve's throat. "It's this one! She wears the Ring of the Slain!" The crone was frantic.

"What are you talking about, old woman?" the king asked. "What curse?"

"It is anathema to remove the Ring of the Slain from the finger of one who wears it. It must be given back. Take your knife from her."

Other men stood talking and worrying about the witch's warnings. The king withdrew his knife from Maeve's throat. "Give back the Ring," he said. "Then we'll sell her."

"No, wearers of the Ring are warriors for the god of the North. To interfere with her fate will bring the daughters of the sky down upon us."

"The daughters of the sky? What are you babbling about, hag?"

"The daughters of the god of the North with swords drawn ride the clouds on warrior steeds. They know all those who wear the Ring."

The Gypsy king had long ago tired of the crone's croakings of doom; she had plagued him for years, but his people believed so he dared not ignore her prophecies.

"What about that one?" he pointed at Tars.

The witch turned toward Tars and took a minute to think. She remembered the foreboding she felt when she touched this one's breast. "That must be the dragon sent in woman's form to guard the Ring. That is why she can talk to the Wearer of the Ring and to us; a dragon in human form knows all languages. If you try to kill it, you'll release the abomination."

Chapter 47

Ring of the Slain

Seville, Spain
Next day; Friday, 12 May 1944

At mid-morning, Conrad Gerber and his radioman sat in Gerber's hotel room radioing his flight crew. The plane had been airborne for two hours combing a wide area east of the point where the trawler captain told Gerber the two women went ashore.

"Any signs of them?" Gerber asked into the microphone.

"Sir, there's a small range of mountains and east of that some plains where we spotted a few farms. We saw nothing in the mountains other than a Gypsy caravan traveling east through a mountain pass. There are no towns or villages in this area. The closest towns according to our map are Tarifa to the south and Algeciras to the east."

Gerber studied his map. "Is there anywhere to land so you can check those farms?" The airplane carried two motorcycles, and each could carry two men.

"I'll ask the pilot." The radio went silent until the radioman returned. *"He thinks there are sections of the plains that might be suitable."*

"Search the farms and the Gypsy caravan when it comes down out of the mountains. Keller speaks Spanish. Tell Keller to use the story that you're working with the Spanish government to find a criminal. If you don't find *Lorelei,* ask the farmers and Gypsies if they've seen a blonde woman in the area, perhaps traveling with another woman. Give them some money to help their memories."

"Yes, sir."

[same time—Gypsy caravan]
Maeve and Tars sat facing backwards at the rear of the third covered wagon of the ten-wagon caravan, their legs dangling over the edge as the wagon jolted over the rutted trail. Hanging pots and pans clanked.

Two young boys and their mother also rode in the wagon. The mother sat near the front sewing; the father sat up front on the buckboard driving the team of two mules. For the past hour, the boys had taken great delight in sneaking up behind Tars and pulling her hair. One of the boys, a five-year-old, had just pulled it again.

Tars turned as he scrambled out of reach. "I'll brain you with one of these pans, you little fuckhead!" she shouted in Italian. As the child giggled, Tars reached for one of the tin pans and held it on her lap.

"You can't hit a little kid with that pan, Tars," Maeve told her. "They're just playing. They think you're a dragon." Tars had explained to Maeve what the old crone said the night before.

"I'll show the little bastards a dragon if they don't leave me alone."

Last night, things changed dramatically after the witch explained who the visitors were. The adults avoided Tars like the plague, thinking a nefarious beast had entered their camp. Only the children took delight in having a dragon among them. Maeve, on the other hand, had been treated with great deference.

And their bellies were full.

When Maeve said she was hungry, Tars translated, and the Gypsies brought her that evening's rabbit stew. They did not bring a bowl for Tars, being unsure if a dragon ate human food. But Maeve assured them that a dragon *does* eat stew when in human form. A woman brought a bowl for Tars, but unwilling to approach a dragon, she set it by the campfire and scurried away. Tars had to go get it. Both women ate like starved jackals: four full bowls for Maeve, three for Tars. Breakfast today had been coffee, unleavened biscuits, fish, and wild onions.

"Hey, if you're me personal dragon," said Maeve, "you have to do me bidding. You have to tell me your first name."

"Screw you," Tars replied.

"I can see you're in a grand mood."

The caravan continued on. The little boy again sneaked up behind Tars but she saw him out of the corner of her eye, turned quickly, and whacked him over the head with the pan. The child's eyes crossed and he fell backward, dazed.

"There's one for ya, you little cocksucker!" said Tars. His mother shrieked and scrambled over boxes to drag the boy to safety. She gathered her other son and moved them to the front next to her, irked that Baval, the king, had assigned the dragon to her husband's wagon.

After knocking the kid cuckoo, Tars felt better. "Hey, that Nazi Ring Erika gave you sure saved our bacon. I'm a dragon and they think you're some kind of Joan of Arc or something."

"The Ring has nothing to do with the Nazis." (Erika had taught Maeve about the tenets of the Ring in case Adalwulf's friend in New York questioned her). "The Ring of the Slain is a Viking ring."

"Viking? I guess that's why the witch talked about the 'god of the North.'"

"That's right. 'God of the North' is Odin, the Viking god. The 'daughters of the sky' you told me the witch talked about have to be the Valkyries—Odin's daughters who escort brave warriors to Valhalla when they die."

"Valhalla? What's that?"

"Sort of the Viking heaven." Maeve held up her hand to show Tars the silver Ring. "The Ring has to be worn on the right hand. The black stone means invisibility—black gives off no light."

"Invisible from what?"

"Your thoughts and intentions remain invisible to your enemies." Maeve pointed to one of the two engravings flanking the black stone. "This is Gungnir, the spear of Odin. This one is Hrungnir's Heart; it honors those who fall bravely in battle."

"So why was the witch so worried that they took your Ring? Why didn't one of them just put it on and get the magic or whatever they think is in the Ring?"

"Anyone who steals the Ring from a worthy wearer will be cursed. I'm not worthy, but the Gypsies don't know that."

"You sound as if you believe in that mumbo jumbo."

Maeve hesitated. "I want to believe . . . that I'm worthy. But I know I'm not. I'm not brave like you or Erika."

"You did a good job in Haiti during that questioning."

"And I threw up me guts afterwards." Maeve changed the subject. "How are we going to get out of here?"

"I told you; we need to find a transmitter."

"What about going to Portugal like you said last night?"

"I just mentioned that as a last resort. Portugal is another country where we don't speak the language and will stick out like a sore thumb. Much better to find a transmitter, and the sooner the better. Then if we find one, we'll have to figure out a way to convince whoever controls it to let us use it. That will be the hard part. Almost all transmitters nowadays are in the hands of the military, and the few that aren't are guarded by the military. Even the military of a so-called neutral country like Spain isn't going to let two broads on the run waltz in and use a transmitter."

Just then a low-flying airplane soared over the caravan.

"That's the third time we've seen that same plane," Maeve commented.

"Pretty much answers your question about if the Germans are looking for us," replied Tars.

"Pretty much."

"They can't land in these mountains, but we'll have to do something before we get to the flats."

Chapter 48

The Junkers

Seville, Spain
Later that day—Friday, 12 May 1944

The airplane allocated to Conrad Gerber for his mission to Spain was a Junkers Ju 52. A tri-motor aircraft, the Ju 52 could accommodate Gerber's equipment and twelve-man team (now ten with the loss of Scheu and Kluesner). The two Zündapp KS 750 motorcycles crowded the plane, but they were necessary for ground transport. The Gestapo chose the Junkers for this mission because, even though German-made, the airplane would not draw unwanted attention in Spain. Ju 52s had been purchased by several European countries as commercial passenger aircraft or cargo transports since the mid-1930s. Francisco Franco's government had purchased many from Germany since the civil war and it was not unusual to catch sight of one in the Spanish sky.

On Gerber's earlier orders, the Junkers had landed on the plain east of the small mountain range and four men dispatched on the motorcycles to check area farms. After dropping off the ground crew, the plane resumed its flyovers of the area. That was three hours ago and since then Gerber, monitoring the operation from his hotel room in Seville, had received several updates from the Junkers' radioman, each time over a different frequency for security. Now it was time for another update. Static crackled from the radio in front of Gerber.

"The men on the ground report that all farms and ranches in the target region have been searched and locals asked if they've seen any unfamiliar women in the area. No sign of her, sir. We await your orders. Should we broaden the search area? There are more farms farther out."

For the past hour, Gerber had thought a great deal about the Gypsy caravan his men had reported seeing in the mountains heading east, away from the coast.

"How is your fuel?" Gerber asked.

"Getting low. The pilot estimates less than two hours of flying time remains."

"Is the Gypsy caravan still in the mountains?"

"Yes, sir."

"What is your estimate on when the Gypsies might reach open ground?"

"Difficult to say. We flew over the caravan again about thirty minutes ago. It still has a way to go and moving very slowly."

"Those wagons cannot cross untraveled terrain; they have to stay on a trail. Find where the trail comes out of the mountains and radio the coordinates to the men on the ground. Instruct them to station themselves there—where the trail leaves the high ground. When the Gypsies get there, detain them until I arrive. Bring the plane back to Seville for refueling and I'll be waiting for you at the airfield."

"Yes, sir."

The Junkers' cruising speed was 100 miles per hour—nearly the exact distance for the return to Seville. In just over an hour the plane was on the ground and refueling. Gerber climbed aboard and soon the wheels were off the ground. He left his radioman at the hotel in case he might need to relay a message to Berlin. Gerber looked at his wristwatch as the airplane climbed over Seville.

"It's just past 1800 hours," he said to the navigator who was also the co-pilot. "What will be the landing situation if it's growing dark when we get to the location?"

"Last night it wasn't completely dark here until 2030. Light will not be a problem, Kriminalsekretär. We'll be there in one hour."

Using the coordinates radioed to them, the German ground team located the spot where the trail left the mountains. Concealed, they waited nearly an hour before hearing the sound of wagons.

"Remember," the SS Oberscharführer in charge told the three other men, "first we talk to them and offer money for their cooperation. Gypsies cannot be trusted. If the woman is with them and has given them money for protection, the Gypsies will betray her for more money. If they don't cooperate, then we use force. Understood?"

The others nodded or said, "Jawohl."

The first wagon appeared around a bend. The Germans held back until all ten wagons were down from the mountain then broke out of the trees and motorcycled to the lead wagon. They flagged it down and asked to speak to the leader; Keller, the German who spoke Spanish, did the talking. Keller quickly found out the Gypsy leader did not speak Spanish, but the clan had been in Spain for more than a year and a few of the Gypsy men had learned enough Spanish for rudimentary communication with locals. Baval summoned one of those men.

"Greetings, friends," Keller said again once the communication problem had been resolved. "We seek a woman with blonde hair. Did you happen to see such a woman during your travels since yesterday? She may be in the company of another woman."

Baval waited for the translation. "No. No such woman."

Keller looked at the Oberscharführer, who flashed a wad of money. "We'll gladly pay you for any information you can supply us," Keller told the king.

Baval nodded and the Oberscharführer handed him the money. "We've seen no blonde woman," he repeated and handed the money to his interpreter, a man with a rifle at his side.

Goddamn Gypsies, the Oberscharführer thought, *they'll take the money anyway.* He drew his Schmeisser machine pistol and the other Germans did the same. In German he shouted, "Tell him to drop his rifle!" Keller translated the German into Spanish, and then the Gypsy with the rifle translated the command into Italian. Baval took a moment then signaled his interpreter to drop his gun. The German barked more orders. "I want everyone in this caravan out of the wagons and standing where we can see them—men, women, and children. NOW! Anyone armed will be shot." The other Germans spread out down the line of wagons.

"Be warned," Baval told the sergeant. "You're not in Italy where you can bring your tanks and dogs and as many men as you need to take away my people."

After the translation, the SS man fired his machine pistol—a compact machine gun—at Baval's feet. Baval didn't flinch and stood his ground glaring at the German. An ugly old woman with a white eye hobbled over to Baval and said something to him in Carpathian Romani. Baval looked at her then gave the order for his people to hop out of the wagons. The Germans lined everyone up, looked to make sure no one held a gun, then two of the Germans searched the wagons while the others held the Gypsies at gunpoint. When the search ended, a German shouted from the last wagon, "She is not in any of the wagons, Oberscharführer!"

"Keller! Tell this . . . *king* . . . to have all the women remove their scarves."

[30 minutes later]

The Junkers co-pilot first spotted the Gypsy caravan and yelled back to Gerber, who went to the window on the other side of the fuselage and looked out. The wagons were still near the base of the mountains where the trail fed out of the high country but the caravan was now moving.

"My orders were to keep them there until I arrived!" shouted Gerber. "Get them on the portables." Portable hand-held walkie-talkies had a limited range; usually, the ground crew had to be in sight of the plane to communicate. The radioman did his job and handed the portable to Gerber.

"Who is this?" Gerber shouted.

"Keller."

Gerber recognized the voice. "Keller! Why is the caravan moving? I gave orders to hold it until I arrived."

"The woman was not with the Gypsies, sir, and they have not seen her. The Oberscharführer decided to let them proceed."

Gerber was furious his orders had been ignored, and growing ever more disconsolate that the woman had not been found. After no sign of her at the farms, he felt certain she had to be with the Gypsies. "Where are you Keller, and where is that SS fuck who is supposed to be in charge down there?"

"We're where you ordered us to be, sir. We're waiting for you at the bottom of the trail."

"I'll be there as soon as we land, Keller. Tell that Totenkopf motherfucker I'm going to fry his ass. Don't anyone move until I get there! Understood?"

"Understood."

By the time the Junkers pilot circled twice to determine the best landing spot, 20 minutes had passed before the plane set down. The pilot taxied as close to the base of the mountain pass as he could, which, because of scrub oaks, high grass, and rough terrain was about a thousand yards from where the German ground crew stopped the caravan. Taking a walkie-talkie with him, Gerber got off the plane with the two remaining Gestapo agents, leaving the civilian pilots aboard. They had no experience in combat or covert operations and would just be in the way if any trouble on the ground presented itself, and Gerber could not afford to lose the pilots. When the plane returned to Berlin, the pilots would be eliminated.

The Gypsy caravan had not gotten far; in fact, it was between the Junkers and the foot of the mountain, but angling away. Though Gerber wanted to search the caravan himself, he had only the two men so he waited. The slow-moving wagons would be easy to catch after he assembled the rest of the team. Gerber and his two men jogged through knee-high grass toward the base of the trail where the ground crew waited. As they neared, Gerber called out but heard no reply.

"Look!" one of his men yelled. Thirty yards up the forest trail three naked men—Gerber's ground crew—were tied to trees. They ran up the trail to find all the men dead, their throats slit. One man was missing.

"Where's Keller? Look for Keller and the motorcycles! The woman is with the Gypsies!" Gerber exclaimed frantically. "I knew it!"

His men quickly searched the immediate area—no Keller and no motorcycles. "We have to catch that caravan! Back to the plane!" On board was an array of heavier weapons including a Maschinengewehr

34 machine gun and rifle-launched grenades. Despite being down to three men including himself, Gerber knew that with those weapons he would have a huge advantage over single-shot Gypsy rifles.

As Gerber and his men began running back to the Junkers, he saw the Gypsy caravan change course and now angle toward the airplane. Suddenly something was thrown out of the rear wagon— something that looked like a body.

"What the hell?" Gerber exclaimed. He ordered his men to continue on toward the plane, then stopped and tried to reach Keller on the walkie-talkie. No answer. Gerber saw two Gypsies jump off the wagon and run toward the Junkers. The distance made it difficult to tell, but they looked like two female Gypsies.

Gerber began running and screaming "Get to the plane!" to his men who were now well ahead of him. He saw the Gypsy women jump into the plane's open fuselage door. As his men neared the aircraft a shot rang out and one of Gerber's men fell. More shots followed. The caravan had stopped and two Gypsies in the rear wagon were firing on them. More Gypsies with rifles jumped from other wagons and started firing. Gerber had only his sidearm; he drew it and returned fire but he was twice as far from the Gypsies as his men and at this distance it would be a miracle to shoot true with a handgun. The remaining Gestapo agent knelt and fired his Schmeisser, but the jerking machine pistol was also an inaccurate weapon at any distance beyond 50 yards.

The left-wing engine of the Junkers fired and coughed the white smoke common from the 12-cylinder BMW engine. Gerber looked on in horror. "That's her! Fire on the plane! At the engines!" he screamed ahead to his man. The remaining agent turned his gun toward the airplane and opened up but after a short burst a Gypsy bullet felled him. Then the Gypsies turned their attention to Gerber. He was far enough away that even the excellent Gypsy marksmen would have to get lucky to pick him off, but their fire forced Gerber to jump into a shallow ditch for cover. He heard the right-wing engine come to life. Gerber raised his head; the Gypsies opened up and he ducked back down. When he heard the nose engine of the tri-motor airplane fire he raised himself enough to empty his clip in vain at the airplane, ignoring Gypsy fire.

Out of bullets, Gerber ducked down again but peeked up enough to watch the Junkers start moving, swinging its tail his direction. It slowly picked up speed across the wide plain then lifted off. He expected the Gypsies to come after him, but they jumped back on the wagons and the caravan headed away. As the plane gained altitude, it suddenly banked and headed back toward Gerber. He rose to his feet and climbed out of the ditch. *Let them shoot me,* he thought. He was a dead man anyway once Himmler learned that not only had the 12-man team he dispatched to eliminate *Lorelei* failed to accomplish that mission, she had hijacked and escaped on their airplane.

As the Junkers flew toward him it dropped altitude and, as it passed overhead, the blonde woman stood in the open fuselage doorway, her Gypsy robes now gone. The plane passed by so close he could see her holding up a walkie-talkie. Gerber put his walkie-talkie to his ear and heard: *"Thank ye kindly for the ride, ya kooksucker!"* Gerber didn't understand the English, but he understood the finger she held up.

As the Gypsy caravan rumbled away, Baval felt satisfied he had avenged members of his clan and the other clans he ruled. Overpowering the four men had not been difficult. Three had been taken down as they walked down the line of women looking for the Wearer of the Ring. When the dragon stabbed one, distracting the others, Baval threw the knife he kept up his sleeve as did others of the skilled knife-throwers in the clan. Three Germans were wounded; the one who spoke Spanish dropped his weapon and raised his hands. Baval slit the throats of the first three and later ordered the fourth killed in retribution for his people in Italy the Germans had taken away never to be heard from again. And now the clan possessed clothes and weapons taken from the Germans. And though the motorcycles were very difficult to load onto the wagons, they would garner fine prices.

◊ ◊ ◊

Maeve closed the airplane door. Clearly she had conquered her dread of flying, never before so happy to be on an airplane. She walked to the front of the plane where Tars kept her Beretta trained on the pilots.

"Where do we go now?" Maeve asked Tars.

"I don't know yet," answered Tars. "Find out if these guys speak English." So far, their guns had done a fine job of communicating with the pilots.

"Sprechen Sie Englisch?" Maeve asked.

The pilot shook his head. "Nein."

The co-pilot said, "Ja, a little, not so good."

"Map!" Tars shouted at the co-pilot. He didn't understand. "Landkarte, shit-for-brains, *Landkarte.*" Tars knew the German word for *map* having studied so many from Germany. The co-pilot pointed to a drawer under a small table built into the fuselage behind the cockpit. Maeve opened it and took out several maps.

"Why do you think the Gestapo is after Erika?" Maeve asked Tars. After the Gypsies killed the three Germans, Maeve and Tars looked at their identification. They convinced Baval to keep Keller alive so he could answer the walkie-talkie call from the airplane they expected would come. Keller was taken onto a wagon and forced to give the misinformation about the ground team waiting at the base of the trail, then the Gypsies killed him.

Tars knew the answer to Maeve's question. As part of the kill team, she knew Erika's father had been murdered by the Gestapo and Himmler would not want her returning to Germany. But since that information was not important to Maeve's part of the mission, she had not been briefed.

"Don't talk about that now," Tars said. "This guy might understand some of what you say. We haven't searched these guys or the cockpit yet for guns, so keep 'em covered while I look over these maps."

Chapter 49

The Hauptsturmführer

Mediterranean Sea—90 miles southwest of the island of Ibiza
Next day; Saturday, 13 May 1944

In the midnight blackness, the German Schnellboot raced unseen over the dark Mediterranean toward the stern of the *Bahia de Cata*. The speedy, steel-hulled S-boots were the German version of the plywood American PT boats, but were slightly longer, faster, and with a longer range. On deck was a five-man team sent by the Abwehr to retrieve *Lorelei*. The team leader, Major Ulrich von der Osten, *Lorelei's* Abwehr handler, would remain on the S-boot. Four other men would board the freighter: three Abwehr agents and a 27-year-old Waffen-SS Hauptsturmführer (captain) named Kai Faust who was a member of Otto Skorzeny's Leibstandarte-SS-Adolf Hitler elite commando unit. Faust had been on Skorzeny's team that rescued Mussolini from the mountaintop prison at Gran Sasso the previous fall.

For security reasons, von der Osten wanted to take *Lorelei* off the Venezuelan freighter before it arrived in Barcelona, and he sent his request to Skorzeny asking to use Faust because Faust was a stellar special operations commando. That was the official reason. Von der Osten had another motive to ask for Faust, one he didn't put in the request. He knew Kai Faust was in love with Erika Lehmann, and knew the elite commando would do everything in his power to ensure her safe return.

Von der Osten had decided not to alert the freighter and slow it for boarding. There was no need with Faust on the team. It would be Faust's job to get onboard and then drop the sea ladder for the other three men.

When the S-boot had maneuvered close enough to the stern, Kai Faust shot a roped grappling hook out of a launcher. The moon allowed just enough light to see the hook arch over the rail, Faust drew the rope in until the hook caught on one of the bars, then swung out to the freighter's hull. Von der Osten and the other men watched Faust quickly climb up the side of the ship, jump over the rail, and disappear into the darkness on the blacked-out ship's deck.

[same time—Spanish plains 70 miles south of Cordoba]
Maeve and Tars sat just outside the door of the Ju 52 eating German Army rations found on the airplane. Even though they were miles out on the uninhabited plain, they opted against a campfire and instead used flashlights when necessary—the flashlights another find on the well-equipped plane. The two German pilots sat on the ground a few yards away also eating. A one-foot rope bound the right ankle of one man to the left of the other and they had been ordered not to touch it. Tars never took her eyes off them.

"I don't think those guys are Gestapo or SS," Tars said about the pilots. "They're scared shitless and don't seem to know what's going on. I think they're just a couple of guys who can fly an airplane."

"I think so as well," Maeve agreed, "and that's grand for us."

The women had yet to decide where they should fly to, so instead of cruising around Spain all night and using up the plane's fuel, they had flown northeast for an hour until twilight waned then had the pilots set down on this barren plain south of Cordoba. They hoped they would soon know where to go. They had sent the SOE a message.

Hijacking the German plane had not only facilitated their escape, it had solved the problem of finding a transmitter. The plane's German transmitter took some study—the dials and markings different from the British and American transmitters used during training at Camp X, but eventually Maeve figured it out. In a special SOE code created just for her, and on the shortwave band and frequency Mr. Thomas had instructed her to use, Maeve keyed in the message.

Green moon / In Spain / Trekker and Lady / have airplane /
awaiting instructions / Red moon

Moon colors merely signaled the beginning and end of the message. As insurance, Maeve keyed the message three times, waiting about ten minutes between transmissions. That was two hours ago and they stayed close to the plane's open door so any incoming signals could be heard.

"You better try and get some sleep," Tars said. "Sleep in the plane, close to the transmitter."

"What about you?"

"One of us has to keep an eye on these guys. It's about six hours till daybreak, I'll wake you up in three hours and we'll switch."

◊ ◊ ◊

By 3:00 a.m. Walter Schellenberg had received the phone call at his home and was back at his office sitting across from Doktor Pfeiffer, the Abwehr chief of naval intelligence. An hour earlier Ulrich von der Osten notified headquarters that *Lorelei* was not on the Venezuelan freighter, and he relayed the details of why she was not aboard according to the freighter captain.

"I agree, Herr Oberführer," Pfeiffer responded. "Highly unlikely the Engländer or Amis are behind this. If they knew she was on board the freighter, they would have used their warships in the area to stop and board the ship. A scheme involving local Spanish fishermen would not be necessary. Or they could have waited and taken her off during the inspection in the Strait."

"Whatever is happening," said Schellenberg, "we have a Level 4 operative with whereabouts unknown."

Abwehr classified its spies in levels of abilities and accomplishments. Those who just recently graduated from training at Quenzsee were classified Level 1 until they successfully completed a mission when they would move to Level 2, where most stayed for their careers. Only the elite moved up to Level 3, which required more than simply completing another mission. To qualify as a Level 3 operative, one had to demonstrate special skills and abilities over time. Level 3 agents were the cream, the elite. As for Level 4, a classification practically impossible to ascend to within Abwehr, only three operatives had risen that high since the start of the war. Two of those three were men and one of them was dead. Level 4s were given the most important missions, which usually also meant the most dangerous, and life expectancy was short. *Lorelei* was currently one of only two Abwehr Level 4 operatives, and the only woman ever accorded that classification.

"Is it possible she acted on her own as a precaution?" Pfeiffer asked. "Perhaps she was concerned about the British inspection in the Strait."

"Possible," Schellenberg answered. "Level 4s don't live long if not cautious. It's too late to search the area of the Spanish coast where she might have been taken. That was two days ago. She'll be far away by now. She'll contact us, or if stories others tell me about her are true, she'll walk in off the street later today and ask my secretary to lunch."

[3:30 a.m.—coast of Denmark]

Mr. Thomas moved up Stephanie Fischer's STS 23 departure one day to allow adequate time for her to make it to Berlin for her rendezvous with Erika Monday night. On Friday afternoon, an RAF Hudson aircraft delivered her to an airfield outside Göteborg in neutral Sweden. Arrangements had been made to drive her south along the coast to a safehouse where she waited for nightfall then boarded a small launch for the eight-mile cross of the Öresund Strait to Denmark.

Now, under cover of darkness, Fischer jumped off the launch into knee-high water and waded the few yards to a desolate, rocky shore 20 miles north of Copenhagen.

[7:30 a.m.—Spanish plain]

The sun had been up more than hour and Maeve and Tars still had received no reply from the SOE. Maeve had sent the message again at four o'clock, then repeated it at five.

"What's happening?" Maeve worried. "Why haven't they contacted us and told us what to do?" They sat in the doorway of the Junkers.

"I don't know," Tars replied. "Maybe your transmissions aren't getting through. Are you sure you're using that German radio right?"

245

"I'm sure. I can tell the messages are going out because of the whispers." At Camp X, Maeve had been taught to listen for *whispers*— radioman jargon for the sounds made by a wireless transmitter shortly before it began broadcasting and during the intervals between keystrokes.

"Well, we can't sit around here all day," said Tars. "Now that the sun's up, the plane can be seen. If another plane flies over and sees it sitting out here in the middle of nowhere, they'll probably think we're in trouble and radio someone to come help us. Then we're screwed."

"The plane has over a half tank of petrol," said Maeve. "I wonder if it could fly us to Ireland?"

"I'm not going to Ireland. I need to get to Erika. My assignment's not over." Tars thought for a moment. "See if you can find out from the guy who speaks a little English how far we can fly with the fuel on board. England is closer than Ireland. If it can get us to England, we can kill two birds with one stone. You'll be safe, and the SOE can get me to Thomas and Erika."

Maeve jumped down and walked over to the pilots who still sat on the ground a few yards from the plane. It took some doing, but Maeve eventually got the questions across to the co-pilot.

"He says the plane can fly a thousand kilometers on a full tank," Maeve came back to report. "He guesses the fuel remaining will take us about six hundred kilometers. How far is all that in miles and how far is it to England?"

Being from Italy, Tars knew the metric system and in addition to possessing a photographic memory, her mind made mathematical calculations like a slide rule. "Six hundred kilometers is three-hundred and seventy-two miles—that's how far we can fly on the fuel he says we have." She opened a map and measured distances. "The south coast of England is just over nine-hundred miles from here—too far."

Maeve's heart sank. Tars kept looking at the map.

"But the south coast of England is only about five hundred and fifty miles from the northern coast of Spain. If this plane can fly a thousand kilometers on a full tank, that's six-hundred and twenty miles. If we can refuel somewhere on the northern Spanish coast we should be able to make it."

"What are we waiting for? We have plenty of money to pay for the petrol. Let's go."

"Just a minute," cautioned Tars. "We're in a German airplane. The Brits are liable to send up planes to shoot us down when we get close to the English coast."

"I'll keep radioing as we fly and tell them about the plane. Surely the messages have to start getting through."

"We better hope they do."

Chapter 50

Surprising News

Gibraltar, Spain
Same day; Saturday, 13 May 1944

After the debacle in Tarifa, Mr. Thomas moved the operation to Gibraltar. The British airbase there would serve better as headquarters to plan and facilitate Erika's drop into Vichy France. Thomas, Erika, and the two OSS men had met for two hours that morning to discuss those plans, talked more at lunch, and now, in the mid-afternoon, again huddled in a conference room on the RAF base when a courier knocked and entered the room to deliver a packet to Thomas.

"This must be the report from Barcelona," Thomas said after the courier left. The SOE had dispatched two agents to Barcelona several days before Thomas and Erika left STS 23 in Scotland. Originally, the agents' assignment involved reconnoitering the Barcelona docks and supplying logistical information to Thomas. In the end, that work proved unnecessary once Thomas changed the switch venue to Tarifa. But Thomas had instructed the two agents to remain in Barcelona and discreetly observe and photograph the Abwehr agents there to gather *Lorelei* off the freighter when it arrived. Facial photos, even taken from afar, might later prove useful for identification purposes. Thomas opened the large envelope and took a moment to read.

"Well, fancy that," Thomas said. "It looks like the Abwehr had the same idea we did—to get the women off the freighter before Barcelona. Our men in Barcelona were watching the docks this morning when the freighter pulled in. Abwehr was not on the pier waiting for it; it seems they were actually on the ship and got off when it docked. Obviously they boarded somewhere between Tarifa and Barcelona."

"Abwehr won't know what happened to Maeve—or in other words what happened to me—other than what that freighter captain can tell them," Erika said. "They'll know only that some Spaniards on a fishing boat took them. They won't know the boat was later sunk. Abwehr will assume I'm alive."

"They'll mount a search," Carr remarked.

"Yes, unless Admiral Canaris concludes I got off ahead of time on my own," Erika added. "In that case he knows I'll contact him."

Thomas took three 8" x 10" black-and-white photos from the envelope and scrutinized them with a magnifying glass included in the envelope. "Our men took some photographs in Barcelona this morning. They mention in the report that one man was waiting on the dock. I recognize him. It's your handler von der Osten," he said to Erika. "But I don't know the other four—the ones who walked off the freighter. Do you recognize any of them?" He handed the photos and magnifying glass to Erika. "It seems one is dressed differently than the others."

She looked over the photos obviously taken from a distance, yet the faces were discernible with the glass. She recognized von der Osten. Three of the other men wore the standard Abwehr night fatigues. She didn't recognize any of them and would not have told Thomas if she did. That was not part of the deal; from the start Erika had told the Brits and Americans she would not betray Abwehr. One man wore what looked to be SS commando mission garb she had seen at Quenzsee. She used the glass to look closer at his face.

The three men in the room noticed Erika's face go ashen.

"It appears you recognize someone," guessed Thomas.

Erika handed the photos and glass over to the OSS men. "No. I don't know any of them other than von der Osten, as you already pointed out."

Another knock came at the conference room door and an RAF captain entered. "Mr. Thomas, may I see you for a moment."

"Yes, come in, Captain."

"Out here if you don't mind, sir."

Thomas got up and left the room. In the hall, the captain handed him a sealed envelope labeled *Top Secret — For Your Eyes Only.* Thomas thanked the officer and the man walked away. He opened the package and read the message. He stood thinking for a long moment, then walked back into the room and closed the door.

"This is quite a surprise," Thomas said as he sat down. "It seems *Trekker* and *Lady* might not be dead after all."

"What?!" said Carr. It was as much an exclamation as a question.

"Baker Street received several transmissions last night from Spain, starting at midnight—supposedly from *Trekker.*"

Erika glanced at the wall clock. "Midnight—that's 15 hours ago. Why weren't you notified immediately? What took so long?"

Thomas explained: "Yesterday I sent a message to Baker Street that we believed the women dead. That led Baker Street to assume these transmissions were German tricks, that the Gestapo tortured information and the transmission code out of *Trekker* before they killed her then used it to supply misinformation to lead us on a wild goose chase or to flush us out. Baker Street followed protocol and filed the transmissions under *Suspicious,* which means they take no action until it's verified."

"So the transmissions are now verified?" asked Al Hodge.

"No, not yet," Thomas replied. "But they have received subsequent transmissions, so *Intrepid* ordered them to forward the information to me merely as a heads-up. Baker Street is working to either verify or debunk the transmissions. Until that happens, I'm ordered to sit tight on this and proceed with our new plan to drop Erika into Vichy."

Erika said, "Do you have the exact wording of the transmissions in that envelope? If you do, let me see."

Thomas refused. "I can't do that. It's marked for my eyes only."

Erika understood and switched gears. "Did the *Trekker* transmissions give a location other than just Spain? Can you paraphrase what the latest transmission said? The one you said came in an hour ago."

"All I can tell you is that if the latest transmission is actually from *Trekker,* it seems she and *Lady* have commandeered a German airplane and are flying to England."

Chapter 51

Jugs

In the air over the Bay of Biscay
Same day; Saturday, 13 May 1944

At the same time Mr. Thomas, Erika, Carr and Hodge were learning Maeve and Tars might still be alive, the Junkers Ju 52 was an hour north of Gijón—about 100 miles out over the Bay of Biscay. Getting the German pilots to understand where to fly had not been difficult. Tars held her gun to the pilot's head and pointed to England on a map. Likewise, the refueling at the airfield in Gijón, a city on Spain's north coast, had proved easy. Despite the language barrier (neither the women nor the pilots spoke Spanish) Maeve had only to point to the fuel receptacles on the wings and flash money. In 30 minutes the plane was refueled. Their luck seemed to be holding. As soon as they returned to the air, Maeve sent a transmission to the SOE that they had taken off from Gijón and were headed to England; she repeated the same message 30 minutes later.

"I hope that transmission gets through," said Tars.

"I'll keep sending it every half hour."

"And let's hope that co-pilot didn't lie about how far this plane can fly on a tank of gas."

"I don't think he's lying," said Maeve. "If we run out and crash into the sea, he goes down with us, and I don't think he's ready for that. I think both of them realize being held in England till the end of the war is a great deal more lovely than being a carcass in Davey Jones Locker."

"Go ahead and send the message again," Tars said.

"Okay."

[same time—Gibraltar]
When Mr. Thomas told the group Maeve and Tars were presumably flying to England in a stolen German airplane, a lull in the

conversation occurred. Even Erika was momentarily speechless. Finally, Al Hodge asked the obvious.

"How in heaven's name did they get a German airplane?" Of course it was a question to which no one had the answer.

Thomas replied, "Obviously, that's one of the things that leads Baker Street to assume these transmissions are misinformation by the Germans."

Carr asked, "You said the SOE is attempting to corroborate the transmissions. How are they going about doing that?"

"*Intrepid* has asked the Americans to scramble two fighter planes from a squadron based near Plymouth—that squadron is the southernmost in England and closer to the Bay of Biscay than the Spitfire squadron outside Southampton. The American fighters will find the plane—if it exists—and escort it back to Plymouth. This phantom plane won't come within range of our radar for three or four hours, but a transmission has been sent ordering *Trekker* to relay their coordinates. If the last transmission is accurate and to be believed, the women's plane is still a long way from England, but with the American fighters' flying speed and a little luck, they should have it in sight in a couple of hours."

[same time—aboard the Junkers]

Maeve and Tars were elated to finally receive a transmission from the SOE. *Contact, at last!* The transmission asked for their location and Tars was going over the maps. They had asked the co-pilot for the coordinates, but Tars didn't trust him so she checked them herself.

She told Maeve, "Look at the altitude thing-am-a-jig and the speedometer and we'll send that information, too." Maeve leaned over the pilot's shoulder and read the altimeter and flight-speed indicator.

"Looks like 2000 meters altitude," said Maeve, "and 160 kilometers an hour. You'll have to do the arithmetic if you want feet and miles."

"Okay," Tars said instantly. "Figuring that speed and with the time since we took off from Gijón we're a hundred miles north of the Spanish coast. It looks like he was telling the truth about the coordinates: 45.3 north, minus 5.02 west. The SOE can use that and our speed to figure out our path and about when we'll enter their radar so they'll know it's us and not shoot us down."

Maeve took the paper and began encoding.

[30 minutes later—Luftflotte 3 airfield; outside Brest, France]
Luftwaffe fighter pilot Maximilian von Hoch taxied his ME 109 out to the runway; his wing man, Ebbe Kieffer followed behind. Von Hoch had been ordered to intercept an aircraft that radar picked up flying north across the Bay of Biscay. The presence of the aircraft was not the concern; many planes flew north and south over the Bay. What concerned von Hoch's commander was several encoded transmissions the plane had apparently sent. Ground radiomen had been unable to decipher the code, but after triangulating the source of the transmissions, it was determined they came from a moving point over the Bay, the locations coinciding with radar coordinates of the mystery aircraft. So the commander ordered von Hoch and his wing man to find the plane and investigate. Von Hoch heard his wing man's voice in his earphone.

"How far out is it, Major?"

"The latest radar report places it three-hundred kilometers south of here and heading this way, Ebbe." Von Hoch had already done the calculations, given the mystery plane's speed reported by the radar room and the ME 109's cruising speed of 600 kilometers an hour. "If it doesn't change course, we should have it in sight in 15 or 20 minutes."

[same time—American Fighter Squadron outside Plymouth, England]
Lieutenant Billy Fiske lowered himself into the seat of his P-47 Thunderbolt and fastened the strap on his flight helmet. He left the goggles up; he thought they restricted his view and usually avoided wearing them. He had been the only pilot in the barracks when Captain Mel Howell walked in a half hour ago to find a wing man. Billy had shipped over from the States just ten days ago and this was only

his third mission. The first two were uneventful bomber escorts to the French coastal area around the Pas de Calais. This would be his first mission as wing-man. He knew the captain preferred a more experienced pilot to cover his back on a two-plane mission, but today Billy was his only choice and the young pilot was determined to do a good job. With his cockpit canopy still open, Billy heard the captain's Thunderbolt fire up in front of him. Billy pulled out the choke and pressed the ignition button. The 2500-horsepower Pratt & Whitney turbo-supercharged engine grumbled then roared to life.

Billy had not had much of an opportunity to talk to his captain in the few days since he joined Squadron 173, but no one had ever accused him of being shy. As they taxied he offered chat.

"Captain, did you know both of our planes were built in my home town?"

"No, Lieutenant, I didn't know that. You're from Indiana, right?"

"Right. Evansville. There's a big Jug factory there." (*Jug* was one of the nicknames Thunderbolt pilots affectionately assigned their fighters.)

"Is that right?"

"My mom works at the plant. She puts rivets in the tail section. She's a *bona fide* Rosie-the-Riveter. My mom probably worked on our Bolts."

"Okay. Write your mom that I said thanks for a great job."

"I will."

"The plane we're ordered to find and escort isn't on our radar yet, Lieutenant. The radar boys will let us know when they pick it up. I want you on my right wing flying south, and on my left on our way back—in other words I'm between you and the French coast both ways. Should be a routine mission. Let's go."

"Yes, sir."

◊ ◊ ◊

[same time—Gibraltar]

Mr. Thomas adjourned the meeting and left with Leroy Carr for the base communication center to keep abreast of the American Army Air

Corps' efforts to find the airplane supposedly containing Maeve and Tars. Al Hodge and Erika delayed for a moment while Hodge took another look at the photographs from the Barcelona dock.

"So the only one you recognize is your handler, von der Osten?" Hodge asked. The SOE and OSS had files on Ulrich von der Osten dating back to 1938, long before Erika entered the picture.

"The others must be new to Abwehr since I left Germany for America," she answered. "That's a while ago—August of '42."

Hodge commented on what everyone had noticed. "That's a little odd that the one is dressed differently. The uniform shows no rank, but that's par for the course for clandestine operations. If there's any unit insignia on the uniform the photos were taken from too far away to see it, but we can have E Street identify the uniform. I'm sure the Brits can, too."

Erika knew he was right; they would identify the dissimilar uniform quickly. "That's an SS commando night-mission uniform. They must have boarded the freighter at night." She stopped there. She wasn't going to tell Hodge that Kai Faust was her husband.

Chapter 52

Flugzeuge!

Over the Bay of Biscay
Same day; Saturday, 13 May 1944

Radar range for both the Germans and British was approximately 175 miles depending on atmospheric and solar conditions. The Luftwaffe radar command post at Brest was 150 miles south of the British post at Plymouth, hence when Luftwaffe pilots Maximilian von Hoch and his wing man Ebbe Kieffer took off they were already 150 miles closer to the mystery airplane, had its radar position, and could receive updates while in the air.

"That must be it, Ebbe," said von Hoch about the dot ahead that just came out of a cloud. "You pass underneath; I'll go over."

Ebbe came back, *"Jawohl, Major."*

◊ ◊ ◊

On board the Junkers, the pilot was first to spot the rapidly approaching aircraft.

"Flugzeuge!" he yelled.

Maeve and Tars stood and looked over the pilots' shoulders as the two planes ahead split up and rocketed over and under the Junkers so fast they blurred.

"Messerschmitts!" the pilot hollered and smiled.

"Oh, shit!" said Tars.

"Oh, fook!" said Maeve.

◊ ◊ ◊

Von Hoch and Kieffer turned and quickly caught up with the cargo plane then slowed when parallel with its wings. Von Hoch radioed his base.

"We've got an unarmed Junkers Ju 52. I'll make contact. Aus."

256

"Klar," was radioed back.

Von Hoch maneuvered closer to the Junkers so the pilot could see him clearly. He held up his thumb and two fingers, signifying the pilot to dial his radio to 300 kHz.

◊ ◊ ◊

"He vants to talk on three-hundert band," the co-pilot said.

"Fuck him," said Tars. "Keep flying. We're in a German plane. He won't shoot us down."

"He will when he sees we're flying to England!" Maeve argued.

"Unbuckle!" Tars ordered the co-pilot and held her gun on him, careful that the gun could not be seen from outside the window. When he released his lap harness she grabbed his shirt collar, pulled him out of his seat and moved him to the radio. By this time, Tars had a detailed map of the Bay in her head. "Tell him you're delivering German radio parts to Brest. And don't try to get cute and think you can say something in German to give us away. She understands enough German to know if you're screwing us over. Understand?" Tars doubted Maeve knew enough, but she figured the co-pilot didn't know that.

"Ja, Ja. I zink I understand."

"You better understand if you want to see the sun tomorrow." She held her gun to his head.

Maeve asked, "What are we going to do when they see we aren't going to Brest?"

"I don't know, but this will give us a little time to think. Because of the shape of the Bay, Brest is almost due north. They won't know we're not going there until we pass it. We'll have to think of something by then, so get to thinking."

◊ ◊ ◊

"One of the pilots reports they are delivering radio parts to Brest." Von Hoch was again on the radio with Luftflotte 3. "Should I ask about the coded transmissions? Aus."

"Standby. The Oberst is right here." After a moment's pause the base radioman came back. *"He says 'negative.' Escort the airplane and order it to land here at Luftflotte 3 instead of the commercial airfield. The Oberst said the coded transmissions will be addressed when the crew is in our hands. Aus."*

"Klar."

◊ ◊ ◊

The P-47s were 100 miles south of Plymouth when the message came through.

"Okay, Billy," radioed Captain Howell. "Our radar boys picked it up. Coordinates are 47.83 north and minus 5.07 south. It's just south of Brest and heading our way. Follow me and let's put the pedal to the metal, Lieutenant."

"Yes, sir, Captain."

Howell and Billy Fiske went to full throttle. The Thunderbolts, flying low at 400 feet above the waves to evade German radar, screamed over the English Channel at 375 miles per hour.

◊ ◊ ◊

Ebbe Kieffer, flying off the Junkers' left wing, spotted the planes first.

"Seven o'clock low, Major. Traveling too fast to be anything but fighters."

Von Hoch shot out in front of the Junkers to get a look. The planes Ebbe referred to were climbing toward them but still too far away to identify. "Can't be ours, Ebbe. We would have been notified. Peel off."

Both Messerschmitts turned their wings vertical, peeled away from the Junkers and dove toward the planes.

"American, Ebbe," von Hoch said when the distance closed. "I'll take the one on our right."

Both Germans fired a burst from their 13mm machine guns, forcing the Americans to angle away. Still having the advantage of altitude, Ebbe sighted in and fired his 20mm cannon, barely missing

Billy who did a 360-degree vertical roll and dove back toward the sea to escape the direct line of fire. Captain Howell, determined to gain altitude, yanked his stick back and went into a steep vertical climb, turning his wing toward the Messerschmitt to give its pilot a smaller target. When Howell leveled off, von Hoch succeeded in getting on his tail and fired another burst. Billy saw his captain in trouble and, gunning his Thunderbolt for all it was worth, rocketed skyward, ignoring Ebbe's tracers flashing past his canopy. Billy briefly got von Hoch in his sights and let loose with a burst from his eight 12.7mm machine guns, but Von Hoch quickly peeled away. Howell immediately nosedived and came up perpendicular with Ebbe's plane and managed to send a round through the Messerschmitt's vertical stabilizer but the damage wasn't enough to affect the durable ME 109's performance. Von Hoch, with Billy still in pursuit, rolled hard to his left, which aimed his plane directly at the nose of the Junkers.

◊ ◊ ◊

On board the Junkers, the pilots shouted frantically, unsure what to do. Should they descend, ascend, or keep current altitude? Should they change course? When they saw the Messerschmitt turn and head directly at their nose like a bullet aimed between the eyes, they panicked and dove—the wrong thing to do. At the same instant, Von Hoch dove, which set the two planes on another collision course. Von Hoch jerked the stick back with all his might.

Maeve and Tars stood wide-eyed, holding on to whatever was handy, watching the dogfight from behind the pilots. Tracer bullets flashed their deadly stream all about them. They watched the German fighter heading directly toward them. At the last moment, the fighter pulled up just enough and screamed over the Junkers, missing it by mere feet. The 350 mile-an-hour draft from the fighter shook the Junkers till it seemed it would burst apart. Then the American plane on the Messerschmitt's tail thundered past, also violently shaking the Junkers. Tars lost her grip and was thrown back.

Howell and Ebbe now fought it out about a mile ahead of the Junkers. Suddenly a smoke trail could be seen coming from the

German plane. Inside the Junkers, Maeve shouted, "The Americans got one of them!" Tars had regained her feet and was trying to get back to the front as the Junkers shook and rattled. "I love those Yanks!" Maeve cheered.

◊ ◊ ◊

Howell saw the smoke trail, sensed the kill, and fired a long burst. The occasional tracer rounds told him he struck the German again. The Messerschmitt began its death spiral toward the sea.

Von Hoch did not see Ebbe go down but when the second American fighter joined in his pursuit he assumed the worst. A German ace, von Hoch had fought two planes together before, even three on one occasion. He pushed the stick, turned his plane upside down and dove. As the Americans responded to the maneuver, von Hoch pulled back and went vertical, bringing him in line with one of the Americans. His aim was true and the American's right tail wing shredded off in pieces. Howell's plane went into an uncontrollable yaw. Billy got behind von Hoch and opened up.

If the Junkers' pilot had stayed his course all would have been fine for his plane, but he panicked and suddenly veered sharply to his right, taking the Junkers directly into the line of fire. It was impossible to tell if the Junkers was hit by von Hoch's fire at Howell, or Billy's fire at Von Hoch, but the Junkers' left-wing engine burst into flames and part of the same wing's aileron sliced off.

While von Hoch concentrated on Howell's plane, one of Billy's rounds went into his right wing, destroying that machine gun. Von Hoch saw he had damaged the one American enough to knock him out of the battle, so he turned his attention to the one shooting at him. The German ace used his rudder to "put on the brake" and did a barrel roll. The maneuver fooled the inexperienced Billy whose plane shot past von Hoch, enabling the German to soar up behind him. Von Hoch fired his cannon, shattering Billy's canopy and sending glass slivers into his face. The rush of wind nearly knocked Billy out and he was forced to cut speed. His face bleeding, Billy saw the Messerschmitt flash by and circle to return for the kill. Instead, the German pilot pulled up beside

Billy, now flying at 80 miles an hour with his canopy mostly gone. The German looked at him, nodded his head to acknowledge a fellow warrior, and made no effort to finish Billy off.

Billy descended to try to find the remains of his captain's plane. After slowly flying wider and wider circles, he saw floating debris and a short distance away the captain, who had managed to bail out, afloat in his life jacket. Billy flew over Howell, rocked his wings to let him know he had been seen, then radioed Squadron 173 command with his downed captain's position.

Ebbe, wounded and unable to bail, had not been as lucky as Captain Howell. Ebbe's wife and three young children in Rüdesheim would never see their husband and father again.

◊ ◊ ◊

Certainly the civilian Junkers' pilots could be accused of failing to keep their heads in a combat arena, but they could not be rightly accused of being incompetent pilots. They had flown Ju 52s for years and knew the aircraft well. When the left-wing engine was hit and ablaze they shut it off, knowing the tri-motor plane could fly on two engines. Cutting fuel to the burning engine did not extinguish the fire, but lessened it to a great degree. More vexing was the damaged aileron that made the airplane extremely hard to control. The pilots knew they must head toward the French coast, which luckily was only 30 miles away.

◊ ◊ ◊

Von Hoch wanted to look for Ebbe but the war-hardened pilot knew his first duty was to stay with the crippled Junkers and learn its fate. As he watched the Junkers turn toward the coast, he radioed the plane but received no answer. In 15 minutes the coast came into sight and the Junkers started descending rapidly. Von Hoch could tell the pilot struggled to control the aircraft. From above, he watched the plane fly over the beach, over a few copses of trees, and crash-land in a pasture that was too small and too rough. The landing gear collapsed after hitting a ditch and the plane slid on its belly into a thicket of trees where both wings sheared off. With nowhere to land, von Hoch descended and flew over for a closer look. He saw no one on the ground, but the body of the plane, although dented and the cockpit windows smashed, looked in one piece and was not burning. Losing the smoking left wing to the trees was fortunate, von Hoch surmised. He noted the Junkers' location then flew back out to sea to look for Ebbe.

◊ ◊ ◊

Billy had placed his captain's welfare over that of the mission, a decision he knew would cost him a major league chewing out from the colonel, but he didn't care. He was just relieved the captain had survived. Billy lost track of the Junkers and assumed it had crashed into the ocean. He saw the Messerschmitt whose pilot had let him live combing the area and knew he was looking for his partner. Billy had been told by other pilots in the squadron that most German fighter pilots would not fire on a downed enemy pilot. The last he saw of the Messerschmitt was when it disappeared farther out to sea, widening its fruitless search. Luckily for the captain, a speedy Royal Navy gun boat patrolling the southern Channel wasn't far away. The bleeding young pilot kept his captain in view until the gun boat plucked him from the water, then he nursed the Thunderbolt his mom might have worked on back to England.

Chapter 53

The Barn

French forest near Crozon
Same day; Saturday, 13 May 1944

After the Junkers was shot up and everyone aboard realized a crash landing inevitable, Maeve and Tars strapped themselves into seats. The Junkers had several windows along the fuselage and the women could see the coast come into view. Both were glad it seemed they might avoid landing in the water, but at the same time they knew a ground landing would be perilous.

Other than being jarred to the bone, after the plane came to rest in the trees both women had escaped pretty much unscathed. The pilots weren't as lucky. They were alive, but tree branches that shattered the cockpit windows continued inside to injure the men. Both sustained numerous abrasions and the pilot's left arm was fractured. But they could walk, and after all four spent a few minutes sitting in their seats regaining their senses, everyone got off the airplane. The men stood looking nervously at the two armed women, worried about what was on their minds.

"I'm going to kill these guys so they can't report anything about us," Tars decided. The co-pilot who spoke some English understood enough and pleaded for their lives, mentioning wives, children, and in the pilot's case, grandchildren back home.

"No, Tars," said Maeve. "You can't kill them in cold blood."

"Of course I can."

"No!" Maeve aimed her gun at Tars.

Tars looked at her, amused. "You don't have the balls."

Maeve dropped her gun. "Please, Tars."

"I ought to shoot you for aiming that gun at me." Tars stared at the men for a moment, then holstered her gun. "I don't want to listen to you cry and bitch. But I'm telling you right now you're making a big fucking mistake."

Maeve quickly ordered the pilots to disappear before Tars changed her mind; they most happily obeyed and let out into the forest. After the men vanished into the trees, Maeve and Tars went inside the wrecked plane and tried to use the transmitter but the outside antenna had been snapped off during landing. They got nothing but static and knew transmitting would be futile and a waste of valuable time. Knowing the Germans had the crash location and would be there soon, they needed to put distance between themselves and the plane. They grabbed one of the rucksacks full of German Army rations, two Schmeisser machine pistols and ammo, and fled into the forest in a different direction from the pilots. For the second time in two days, Maeve and Tars found themselves on the run in the wilds of a strange country.

[three hours later]

"At least we're not in the mountains this time," Maeve commented. They had stopped briefly to eat.

Tars looked up at dark, boiling clouds that appeared an hour ago and followed them from the coast. "It looks like rain. We need to find a place to sleep," she said.

"Where do you think that might be?"

"I don't know," Tars answered. "Maybe we can find a rock overhang or something—just some place out of the rain."

Both needed sleep badly. The previous night they were forced to take shifts to guard the pilots and had gotten little rest. Tars slept for three hours. Maeve was so wound up from the events of the day it took her a long time to drop off and slept less than two.

They ate quickly, again checked the menacing sky, and took off through the forest. After two more hours of walking, and jogging when the terrain allowed, they had come across no rock ledges. As daylight waned they came to the edge of the forest. In the valley sat a farmhouse about a mile away with several outbuildings and a barn. Thunder clapped and the women felt sprinkles.

"Thor struck his hammer and released the rain," said Maeve.

Tars looked at her like she was crazy. "What are you talking about?"

"Nothing. Just something Erika told me."

"It looks like it's going to piss and pour, and we won't get any sleep in the rain," Tars reasoned. "We'll wait here in the trees until dark, then we'll sneak down there. That closest storage shed is pretty far from the house, so is the barn. We'll sleep in one of those tonight."

[southern England]

As Maeve and Tars waited for darkness to fall over France, so did James Granville. In a hangar at an airfield outside Tangmere in southern England, he listened to last-minute instructions from John Mayne. Later that night, an American B-24 Liberator would drop Jimmy outside Tiercé, France, 40 miles southeast of Le Mans.

[France]

Maeve and Tars waited another hour despite the rain that began falling in earnest just after nightfall. Soaked, they left the safety of the trees to head down a gentle hill to the nearest outbuilding—the structure farthest from the farmhouse. Clicking on a flashlight for the briefest of time, Tars busted the lock. Farm tools and equipment were stacked all the way to the shed's low ceiling, and they could hardly squeeze through the door.

"Better try the barn," Maeve said.

They trudged through mud toward the barn, barely able to see but not wanting to use the flashlights in open ground. Halfway there lightning flashed, which lit their way but also made them visible to anyone by chance looking their direction.

"Damn!" Tars remarked about the illumination.

"Do you think someone saw us?" Maeve asked.

"That farmhouse is quite a ways off. Probably not but keep your fingers crossed."

The sliding barn door was closed but not locked. They went inside, joining two stabled mules and a horse. Once inside and with the door closed they used the flashlights to look around. The hay loft overhead offered an easy decision for the sleep-deprived women.

"Look, horse blankets," said Maeve.

The women grabbed blankets, climbed the ladder to the loft and fell into the straw.

[2:00 a.m.—France, 200 miles east-southeast of the barn]
Staying low to evade German radar forced the B-24 to fly through the worst of the thunderstorm, but the plane had taken off as scheduled. The RAF weatherman reported to John Mayne that the system headed northeast, and that the odds were decent that the Liberator would emerge from the storm before reaching the designated drop area near Tiercé. That was enough for Mayne to make his decision, and the weatherman proved right this time. The plane had entered calmer skies twenty minutes ago, and the French countryside lay quiet in the half moon. Mayne sat beside Granville near the open hatch.

"The Resistance cell in the area has been notified and will be waiting for you," Mayne shouted over the engines and noise of wind. "As soon as they get you to a transmitter, send the signal that you're on the ground and squared away. That will be your last communication until you join us in Berlin."

"Got it, John," Jimmy shouted back. He had been schooled on this protocol a hundred times but knew it was Mayne's duty to repeat it last minute. He would transmit one word—*Proper*. This would tell Baker Street he was now on the ground in France.

When the pilot turned on the red jump light, which meant the drop zone neared, both men stood and moved to the hatch. Mayne attached the deployment strap to Jimmy's ripcord. The jump would be brief. The less time spent under a chute the better. Time spent drifting helplessly to earth was time spent as a sitting duck. Jimmy would jump at only 700 feet with a parachute designed to bring him down quickly. He had spent two years in France as a teenager; his return would be a jolting one.

The light switched to green. Mayne patted Jimmy solidly on the shoulder and he stepped into the French sky. The Liberator pilot throttled up and banked for home. Jimmy's parachute deployed nicely but on the way down a wind gust blew him off course of the open field and toward a copse of trees. The gusts kept up, bobbing him up and down and putting slack in his chute cords. Trying to avoid the trees, Jimmy pulled on the cords and one became wound around his neck as he fell into the trees. The parachute canopy snagged in the upper branches and the cord became a hangman's noose, snapping Jimmy's neck, his feet less than a yard from the ground.

[two hours later—in the air, 30 miles north of Marseille, France]
The red light was on and Erika stood ready at the hatch. Mr. Thomas stood behind her and checked her parachute one last time.

Thomas did not yet know Jimmy Granville was dead. He had, however, been notified just before the Halifax took off from Gibraltar a few hours ago that the plane supposedly bearing Maeve and Tars had dropped off the radar screen over the Bay of Biscay, and that one of the American fighter pilots sent to intercept the plane had reported seeing it on fire. Thomas kept that information to himself, not telling Erika or the OSS men.

The revised plan concerning Erika had been kept as simple as possible; Thomas knew the simpler the plan the better—fewer details meant fewer things could go wrong. Erika would be dropped into Vichy France, just north of Marseille. She would quickly make her way to Marseille and contact Abwehr, telling them she had sneaked across the Spanish/French border on foot the previous day then hitched rides to Marseille. Her people would pick her up there and take her to Berlin.

The rest of the original plan remained the same with the exception of Stephanie Fischer's mission. Stephanie would replace Tars. Sunday night, Thomas and Amanda McBride would be delivered to France—Amanda landed by a Lysander from England; Thomas, leaving from Gibraltar, would parachute into a different location. Jimmy Granville should already be on the ground in France (Thomas thought), and Stephanie Fischer had landed by boat on the Danish coast yesterday. John Mayne would be the last to leave England.

Thomas wanted to be in Berlin before Mayne arrived so he would be there to meet him; Thomas would send word through Amanda McBride stationed in France letting Mayne know when to depart.

When all members of the Berlin team had arrived, they would meet up and proceed with the mission.

The green light came on and Erika stepped out of the Halifax.

Chapter 54

Moon Plane

Near Sablé-sur-Sarthe, about 40 miles southwest of Le Mans, France
Next day; Sunday, 14 May 1944

If a parachute drop was not an option, the airplane used to insert SOE agents into occupied France was the British Lysander. Nicknamed the "moon plane," the Lysander's unique specifications allowed it stealth after dark. Painted flat-black for night service, the single-engine Lysander flew more quietly than larger, more powerful aircraft. These moon planes flew under radar and could land and take off in pastures as small as 150 yards in length. Drawbacks included slow airspeed and the capacity to seat only one passenger with gear, but for the purposes of transporting a single agent the relatively short distance from England to rural France the Lysanders worked exceedingly well.

Eileen Nearne waited in the trees with three members of a local French Resistance cell. The torches that served as runway lights had been set afire 20 minutes ago. *What is keeping them?* Nearne asked herself silently, not wanting to alarm the nervous Frenchmen. *Torches lit this long are dangerous.* Finally she heard an aircraft engine and saw the silhouette of a small plane pass overhead, visible only as a shadow against the half moon. The aircraft circled and dropped down over the trees and into the pasture. As soon as the landing gear touched ground the pilot cut the engine and coasted to an abrupt stop just feet from the edge of the pasture.

Nearne and one of the Frenchmen ran to the plane; the other men dashed to extinguish the torches then took on lookout duty.

The pilot opened the cockpit canopy but remained in his seat. A young woman seated behind him rose and reached behind her seat for her gear.

"Will you need the torches relit for takeoff?" Nearne asked the pilot.

"No way," he answered. "Leave the damn things out. I can see the outline of the treetops in the moonlight. Just turn me around."

Nearne and the Frenchman helped the woman get her gear to the ground. "I'm Didi Nearne."

The young woman offered her hand. "I'm Amanda McBride. Do you need my codename?"

"No. Let's get out of here."

The three Frenchmen picked up the tail of the light aircraft and swiveled it around so the plane faced the open pasture. As they and the two women disappeared into the trees, the pilot revved the Lysander's engine, released the brake, and bumped across the pasture picking up speed. Soon airborne, the moon plane's wheels softly brushed the treetops as it soared into the night.

[another location in France – later that morning]

When Tars awoke in the hayloft, her face was covered by the horse blanket and something was pressed against her left eye. She flipped down the blanket and found it was Maeve's right nipple. The other breast was pressed to her cheek. Tars kicked off the blanket and sat up in a start.

"What the . . . ?" She started to curse, but stopped until she checked the barn floor below. No one was there. Maeve was naked and still fast asleep. Tars shook her. "Wake up, idiot!"

Maeve stirred. Tars shook more vigorously.

"Wake up!"

Maeve opened one eye and grumbled, "What?"

"You had your tits in my face! What's wrong with you? Why are you naked?" Last night when they collapsed in the hay, both were clothed.

Maeve took a moment to clear cobwebs. "I woke up in the middle of the night to take me pee and couldn't go back to sleep in wet clothes."

"And you needed a place to rest your tits and chose my face?"

"I must have rolled over."

"No shit. Get dressed. We have to get out of here before the farmer shows up."

[three hours later—Abwehr Headquarters in Berlin]

"Von der Osten picked up Lehmann an hour ago, Oberführer, and they're already in the air," Pfeiffer reported. "She should be sitting here in your office by the late afternoon."

Walter Schellenberg stood at a window looking down on a small group of boys running through a vacant lot across the Tirpitz-Ufer chasing each other with sticks. Automobile traffic was steady on the busy boulevard; the civilian vehicles that had pulled over to let a line of canvas-covered military trucks pass were again moving.

Just after six o'clock that morning, Erika Lehmann called Abwehr headquarters from Marseille. Von der Osten, still in Barcelona with his Abwehr team, was notified and left for the French city immediately.

"Von der Osten reports there was only Lehmann in Marseille," said Schellenberg. "Do we know what happened to the other woman who was supposed to be with her?"

"Not yet, Oberführer. We'll find that out when Lehmann arrives. What about Kai Faust? He was dismissed and sent back to his SS unit yesterday. He thinks she's still missing and von der Osten fears Faust may create a problem. Should we notify Skorzeny that we have her and ask him to call off Faust?"

"No," Schellenberg decided. "Faust believing she's still missing might work to our advantage. Let him go about his business looking for her. Lehmann has an end game and there is more to this than meets the eye."

[late afternoon—Luftflotte 3 airfield, outside Brest, France]

The Luftwaffe sergeant hung up the telephone. He had just received a call from the colonel that a Leibstandarte-SS-Adolf Hitler captain who was a member of the Skorzeny squadron would be there in a moment to question the Junkers pilots. The sergeant had never met one of Skorzeny's men, but he knew of their reputation. The LSSAH was made up of the cream of the crop within the Schutzstaffel, and Skorzeny's men were the cream of the Leibstandarte. Every German knew of Skorzeny and his squadron of crack commandos. Newsreels of their daring rescue of Mussolini last fall had been shown in all the movie houses. The sergeant was making sure his uniform was in order when a tall, strikingly handsome young man walked through the door.

"I'm Hauptsturmführer Faust of the SS Adolf Hitler," the man said while reading the sergeant's name badge. "I see you are Unterfeldwebel Deicken. Your Oberst granted me permission to talk to the Junkers pilots you are holding here."

"Jawohl, Hauptsturmführer," the sergeant replied. "The Oberst just called. I will say it is an honor to meet one of Otto Skorzeny's men. Heil Hitler."

"Heil Hitler."

"This way, Hauptsturmführer." Deicken led Kai Faust through a doorway and down a corridor. As they walked, the sergeant quickly briefed Faust on the Junkers pilots' story.

Less than a half hour ago, Faust landed his Focke-Wulf Fw 190 fighter at Luftflotte 3. Yesterday, after the Abwehr dismissed him in Barcelona, Faust called his boss, Otto Skorzeny, told him Erika was missing, and requested permission to search for her himself. Only eight years older than Faust but more of a father figure than a superior officer to his close knit group of commandos, Skorzeny granted Faust's request. Moreover, Skorzeny, who was fond of Erika himself, added that Faust should contact him if his help was needed.

Earlier that morning, as Faust flew over the Spanish coastal area near where the Venezuelan freighter captain said the fishing trawler took Erika off the ship, he received a call to return to the nearest Luftwaffe airfield in Vichy. The call indicated a possible lead as to Erika's whereabouts. When Faust landed, he was told two civilian German Junkers pilots had been picked up south of Brest, questioned, and were being detained at a Luftwaffe airfield nearby.

Deicken stopped outside a door and opened it for Faust. There was no brig at Luftflotte 3, and no need for one where the Junkers pilots were concerned. They were most happy to be in the hands of the Luftwaffe instead of the Gestapo, and were sitting in a small office drinking coffee with a private who had drawn the easy duty of chaperoning them. Both pilots sported numerous facial abrasions and a sling held one pilot's arm. When the sergeant and Faust entered, the private leapt to his feet. The civilian pilots, not sure what to do, followed the private's lead and stood. The pilots saw the SS rune symbols that resembled two lightning bolts on Faust's uniform and immediately became edgy. Deicken ordered the private out of the room, then followed him out and closed the door behind him.

"Sit, please," Faust said pleasantly. They sat and Faust took the chair the private had occupied. "You have no reason to fear me. Just tell me everything about the last two days."

The men nodded and told Faust about the Gypsy caravan, the women's hijacking of their airplane, the demand to be flown to England, the dogfight, and the crash landing.

"A few questions," Faust said after they finished. "Who hired you? The man's name."

"Gerber," the pilot answered. "Conrad Gerber of the Gestapo."

"Who was with Gerber on your plane?"

"Other Gestapo and some SS. The Totenkopf."

Faust worried: *Why were the Gestapo and Death's Head in Spain pursuing his wife?*

"I'm Leibstandarte-SS, not Totenkopf," Faust assured them. "Again, you need not worry about me if you tell the truth and omit nothing. The sergeant briefed me, but not thoroughly. Tell me about the women."

The pilot again spoke for the two. "Two women. One, a blonde, spoke English and German. The other, smaller with brown hair, spoke only English to us."

Faust produced a small photograph from his tunic pocket. "Is she one of the women?" In the photo, Faust and Erika hugged and smiled for the camera.

"Yes, that is her. That is the blonde woman." The pilot handed the photo to his co-pilot. He agreed the woman on board the Junkers was the woman in the picture.

"You're absolutely sure?" Faust wanted to confirm. Both men took a second look. Both again said, "Ja."

Faust continued. "Tell me about the other woman."

"Not a good one," said the co-pilot. "She wanted to kill us after we landed the aircraft."

"Why didn't she?"

"The other woman, the woman in your photograph, stopped her."

"Tell me about the last you saw of the women."

"After landing, the blonde woman told us to flee into the forest. We did so and that's the last we saw of them."

Chapter 55

Wera's Old Friend

If ever a government presented a labyrinth of fractured loyalties, suspicions, and distrust between factions of power it was the Nazi Party under Adolf Hitler. From those at the zenith of power such as Heinrich Himmler, Hermann Göring, Martin Bormann, and Joseph Goebbels, to mid-level and low-level Nazi officials, trust was non-existent. Mutual respect occurred rarely, and if voiced at all usually represented a facade in deference to power. Hitler wanted it this way. He knew men in power wary of one another lowered the possibility of plots against the ultimate ruler.

Even within organizations, splinter groups attempted to elbow one another out of the way in order to gain power or the Führer's favor. In the Gestapo and SS, both organizations under Himmler, friction between blocs existed. The Waffen-SS and the Leibstandarte-SS-Adolf Hitler generally despised both the Gestapo and Totenkopf-SS—the Death's Head regiment that controlled the concentration camps. Though the Totenkopf found few problems with the Gestapo, it held no esteem for the Waffen and grew jealous of the Leibstandarte and its reputation among the German people and even many Party leaders as the premier unit within the SS.

But no greater ill will and hostility existed within the top echelon of Reich overseers than that between Heinrich Himmler and Abwehr chief Wilhelm Canaris. And while other powerful men in Hitler's Reich kept secret their mistrusts and low opinions of fellow high officials, neither Himmler nor Canaris attempted to hide the hatred each held for the other and conflicts were common. Despite the benefits that cooperation between Canaris' Abwehrabteilung, the military intelligence branch of the Wehrmacht, and Himmler's Sicherheitsdienst (SD), the intelligence-gathering branch of the SS, could offer Germany, the two leaders refused to cooperate and many times operated in direct conflict. Himmler had gone to Hitler numerous times voicing complaints and offering suspicions about Canaris, but for much of the war Hitler refused Himmler's requests to subjugate the Abwehr and place it under Himmler's SS/SD/Gestapo umbrella. Hitler knew such a move would enrage the Wehrmacht High Command, a situation the savvy politician Hitler avoided unless it suited his purpose. The Führer deemed that Himmler wielded enough power and his rivalry with Canaris offered balance. This was the way in the Third Reich.

But eventually Himmler succeeded in convincing Hitler of Canaris' involvement in intrigues against the Nazi party and in February of 1944, Canaris was cashiered and replaced by Walter Schellenberg, who had served as chief of counter-intelligence for the SD, and as Himmler's personal aide. Himmler had gotten his wish.   — the author

Berlin—Abwehr Headquarters on the Tirpitz-Ufer
Same day; Sunday, 14 May 1944

Wera Schwarte screamed when Ulrich von der Osten led Erika into her office. "Erika!" Schwarte yelled and rushed from behind her desk.

"Wera," Erika returned the greeting as the two women embraced. Wera Schwarte had been Wilhelm Canaris' personal secretary when the admiral ran the Abwehr. Now she worked for SS Oberführer Walter Schellenberg. Over the years, Wera and Erika had grown close.

"It's been almost two years," Schwarte said teary-eyed. "When we didn't hear from you for so long we thought you were dead."

"Well, I'm here now, my wonderful Wera." Erika kissed her cheek.

"There have been many changes, Erika," Wera said, then lowered her voice, "and not all for the better. You're aware Admiral Canaris has been replaced?"

"Yes. Major von der Osten informed me in Marseille."

A loud, irritating buzz sounded from the intercom box on Wera Schwarte's desk and the voice of Walter Schellenberg boomed out, *"Frau Schwarte, send Lehmann in as soon as she arrives."* When Schellenberg received no answer, he said, *"Frau Schwarte . . . are you there?"*

The secretary, sobbing with joy and not at her desk, could not answer. Von der Osten walked over and pressed the intercom button. "Sir, this is von der Osten. Lehmann is here."

"She's here? Then why isn't she in my office? Where's my secretary?"

"She and Lehmann are saying hello."

"Well, if they don't mind and can manage to pull themselves apart, may I see Lehmann now?" Schellenberg said sarcastically. *"That's if it's agreeable with them, of course."*

When Erika sat down opposite Walter Schellenberg, she noticed that the office had changed little from her memory of it two years ago when Wilhelm Canaris sat in the chair now occupied by Schellenberg. The dark paneling and woodwork still infused a constant dimness in the room. The brown leather couch still sat along a wall. The model of the light cruiser *Dresden* had not moved, nor had the trio of bronze monkeys that were a gift from the Japanese symbolizing the cardinal virtues of any good spy—see all, hear all, say nothing. The *Dresden* and monkeys sat on a table under an enormous wall map of Europe. The single change Erika noticed was the painting of Adolf Hitler hanging behind Schellenberg's desk. No images of Hitler decorated the office when Canaris occupied Schellenberg's seat.

For a moment, the new Abwehr chief and Erika simply stared at each other across his desk. Erika sat thinking that Reinhard Heydrich finally got his wish. Years ago, the late Heydrich tried to recruit her into his SD, but she had spurned Heydrich for the Abwehr. Now, under Schellenberg, who had been Heydrich's second in command at the SD and a former aide to Himmler, the Abwehr was controlled by Himmler and his SD puppeteers.

Finally Schellenberg broke the silence.

"Welcome back."

"Thank you."

"Have you heard about your father?"

"Yes. What can you tell me?"

"He died in a boating accident," Schellenberg offered.

Erika said nothing.

"Stephanie Fischer is already in Berlin," said Schellenberg. "She has kept us abreast of the SOE plot and the plans to send a team to Berlin. She'll meet you at the Lili Marlene tomorrow night as agreed."

Erika was shocked but hid it. "How do you know about her?" If Stephanie told Schellenberg that Erika believed Himmler ordered her father's murder and returned for revenge, Erika would be dead before the day was out.

"She's one of us," he answered. "Admiral Canaris planted her in the SOE eighteen months ago. Your Mr. Thomas thinks she is a Jew who fled to take up the fight against Germany. Stephanie Fischer has no more Jewish blood than you."

"And the other plant?" She now knew Stephanie's sister must be another Canaris double agent infiltrating the Gestapo.

"What other plant?" Schellenberg looked perplexed.

He doesn't know about Stephanie's sister in the Gestapo! Erika quickly covered up with a lie. "Before I left Germany two years ago, I thought the admiral was considering planting an agent in the American OSS, like he planted Stephanie in the British SOE."

Schellenberg shook his head. "I've come across no records of that, and the admiral mentioned nothing about a plant in the OSS. He's been entirely cooperative since stepping down."

Not as cooperative as you think, she thought. "He must have decided against the OSS plant. How is the admiral?"

"He's fine and resting at home. Keep your meeting tomorrow night with Fischer. I instructed her to be at your disposal, and I understand from her that Victor Knight has issued her the same orders—she's to work with you. That works out nicely for our purposes. Fischer filled us in on how the British convinced you to join this doomed assassination mission. Clever on your part striking a deal for your freedom and a half-million Swiss francs."

Erika again realized Stephanie had covered for her! "The capitalists think money will turn anyone," she said.

"Now tell me when Knight and the others plan to arrive. I want them captured alive for interrogation."

"I won't know until Knight notifies me."

"Very well. Meet Fischer tomorrow night and both of you report back here together at 0900 Tuesday morning. What happened to the Italian supposedly returning with you?"

"All that was a façade by the SOE. They found a lookalike for me and sent her across on a freighter to make it look like I was returning from America—the freighter Major von der Osten and his men boarded searching for me. The Italian was sent along as a bodyguard with orders to eliminate the lookalike if capture by the Gestapo seemed imminent. The last I heard, the women had hijacked a Gestapo plane and were returning to England." Erika hoped Maeve and Tars had made it.

Schellenberg did not react and she knew then that he asked the question simply to test her forthrightness. Erika kept her composure and smiled.

"I can see you already knew. How?" she asked.

"Originally we were fooled. We thought you were on the freighter. But when I learned the pilots of the hijacked plane were ordered to fly to England, then I knew it couldn't be you."

"I see you called Kai Faust," she said.

"Von der Osten's request. How did you find out?"

"The SOE took photographs at the Barcelona dock. Can you tell me where he is now?"

"I'll venture that Skorzeny is allowing him to search for you, or to be more precise, he's searching for your lookalike who was on the freighter."

"Do we know if the hijacked plane made it to England?" She knew he would have received the report from Himmler if that information was known.

"It was shot down and crash landed in the French countryside near Brest. Your lookalike and the Italian are fugitives in France, but they'll be in Gestapo hands shortly—we have a lead."

[Quimper, France]

The Gestapo was waiting for Maeve and Tars when they emerged from the barn. Tars had no time to react with a gun. Maeve pulled her *L* pill from a pocket. As she was about to place it in her mouth, Tars knocked it from her hand. Tars wasn't sure why she did it; she knew she shouldn't have. Tars cursed herself for not allowing Maeve to kill herself and for allowing them to be captured. And she cursed the elements. *It must have been that damn lightning strike when we were in the open last night.* She supposed correctly. Locals had been warned by Gestapo in the area to report the sighting of any unfamiliar women, and the French farmer, a collaborator, had spotted them when the lightning illuminated the meadow. He dispatched a son to find and alert the nearest Germans.

After the arrest, Maeve and Tars were driven to Quimper, a town 50 miles south of the farm and the location of the nearest Gestapo sub-station. They were separated and spent the afternoon being interrogated. So far, both had stuck to their story about being Axis supporters seeking to find their way into German hands. The story might have worked given Maeve O'Rourke's allegiance to the Irish IRA (easily verified through Belfast police records) and that organization's anti-British activities. And Tars was Italian, also easily verifiable, but the Quimper Gestapo realized they must be the hijackers of the downed Junkers that, according to warnings circulated by the Luftwaffe in Brest, had been ordered to fly to England, not Germany.

Since the questioning had so far proved fruitless, it was time for the next phase of interrogation. Maeve and Tars were brought to the same room.

Chapter 56

Frau Zweig

Quimper, France
Same day; Sunday, 14 May 1944

"So, are you ready to cooperate?" Gestapo Frau Irmhild Zweig asked. Zweig stood next to Maeve, riding crop in hand. The naked Maeve stood with her hands bound to an overhead post. Tars was tied into a chair and hanging upside down, suspended from a meat hook so she could watch what was about to happen to Maeve.

"Fook you," Maeve said.

Zweig moved behind Maeve and with all her might snapped the riding crop across her buttocks. Maeve did not want to cry out and give the sadistic woman her satisfaction, but she couldn't help it. The strike left a red mark and welts appeared immediately.

"You better hope I never get out of this chair, you fat pile of shit," Tars shouted.

"You won't!" said Zweig. "I can assure you of that. Just wait patiently; you have much more to see. And now with your threat, I think my blow torch will work nicely for you when I finish with your friend." Zweig drew back and delivered a second blow to Maeve's buttocks just before another Gestapo agent opened the door.

"Frau Zweig," the man said. "Kriminalsekretär Schrolucke orders the interrogation halted for the moment. Untie the women and have that one get dressed, but keep them here."

"Why?" Zweig asked, clearly disappointed.

"SS is here inquiring about the women. Do as you're told."

In the front office, Kai Faust stood before a seated Marten Schrolucke, head of the Quimper Gestapo sub-station.

"So, you say you have come to identify the women?" Schrolucke asked.

"That is correct," answered Faust.

"May I ask why the SS has an interest in them?"

"The blonde might be a person of interest to the SS."

"May I see your paperwork, Hauptsturmführer?"

"I bring no paperwork, Kriminalsekretär. I reported here immediately from Luftflotte 3, where they told me as I was leaving that a report came in that the women from the downed Junkers were in your custody. Just let me see the blonde. If she is not the woman I'm seeking, I'll be on my way."

"This is irregular, Hauptsturmführer, but very well." Schrolucke had no desire to get on the bad side of the SS, especially a Skorzeny commando, and he saw no down-side to allowing the request. If the SS Adolf Hitler captain could identify one of the women it would save him the time. "The women are being readied. I'll take you back in a moment."

"Why do they have to be readied?" Faust asked brusquely.

"The second phase of interrogation has begun, but I ordered it suspended. It will be just a moment."

Faust knew what the second phase of Gestapo interrogation entailed and immediately walked toward the door that led to the interrogation room in the back of the building. Schrolucke rose from his chair and voiced his objections. "I will lead you back when the suspects are prepared, Hauptsturmführer. Please wait here."

Faust ignored him and went through the door.

Tars had been cut loose, and Maeve was buttoning her shirt when a man entered followed by Schrolucke. The man was a handsome German officer wearing an SS uniform. When he looked at Maeve his eyes lit up. Maeve simply looked back. Frau Zweig stood to the side, also inspecting the SS officer.

Faust turned to Schrolucke. "You'll release these women into my custody, Herr Schrolucke."

"I will not!" replied Schrolucke sternly. "You haven't the paperwork. What right do you have to make such a request?"

"This woman," Faust said, motioning to Maeve, "is a Level 4 Abwehr operative. I need no paperwork to take charge of her and ensure she returns safely to Berlin."

"A *what?*" Schrolucke asked incredulously.

"I repeat: She is a Level 4 Abwehr operative. Release her immediately. If you doubt, wire the OKW in Berlin. Tell them you have *Lorelei,* her codename, in custody."

"What is her real name?"

"That's classified and none of your concern. Wire the OKW."

"How do I know she is who you claim?"

"Ask her."

Before Schrolucke could ask, Maeve said, "Ich bin *Lorelei.*" She hadn't understood most of the conversation, but she recognized a few key words such as *Abwehr, Lorelei,* and *frag,* which meant *ask.* She replied with the phrase Erika taught her to say when asked to identify herself.

"Why didn't you tell us this from the start?"

Maeve didn't understand so she said in German, "I will say no more." Erika had told her to use the phrase if she were questioned in German and didn't understand.

Schrolucke left to send the wire with Faust going with him to make sure he actually sent it. Frau Zweig remained to watch the prisoners.

After 15 minutes, the wired response from the OKW in Berlin was on Schrolucke's desk. Faust sat across from him as the Gestapo leader read:

Start.
Questioning of Lorelei is forbidden.
If detained, release immediately.
On foreign soil follow orders of Lorelei if your help is requested.
Further questions—contact OKW.
End.

Now worried about repercussions from subjecting an Abwehr agent to torture, Schrolucke made an effort to cover his tracks.

"How was I to know?" he asked Faust. "And still I have no proof the woman is this *Lorelei,* other than your word—and hers. I must be assured. "

"Are you telling me you think I'm lying?" Faust asked with a frown.

"Nein, of course not, Herr Hauptsturmführer. It's just that. . . ." Before Schrolucke finished his sentence, two gun-shots rang out from the back. Faust and Schrolucke ran to the interrogation room and found Tars standing over Frau Zweig. Two other men, Gestapo agents on duty that evening, also ran to the doorway. Tars had sneaked up behind the Gestapo Frau and taken her holstered handgun.

Faust quickly overpowered Tars and took the gun.

"I warned the bitch she better hope I never got out of that chair," Tars said. Schrolucke knelt to check Zweig.

"She's dead," Schrolucke said shocked, then looked at Tars. "Shoot her!" he ordered his men.

Faust outdrew the Gestapo agents and ordered Schrolucke and his men against the wall. "Take their weapons," he instructed Maeve and Tars. Neither woman understood his words but knew what to do. They stripped the men of their weapons and for good measure Tars hit the two assistants over the head with one of the handguns; Maeve kneed Schrolucke in the groin. When finished, the women backed out of the room, Faust locked the men inside, and all three ran outside.

"Get in," Faust ordered and they leapt into the open Kübelwagen[1] on loan from Luftflotte 3. Sitting was painful for Maeve so she leaned to one side. Faust started the vehicle and roared off.

"Killing the Gestapo Frau was foolish and unnecessary," Faust yelled in German to Tars, seated behind him and understanding not a word. "Schrolucke had already received OKW orders to release you." When Tars failed to respond, Faust looked at Maeve beside him but he said nothing to her.

Tars tested Faust with a question in English about the weather. When he did not reply, she turned to Maeve. "He doesn't speak English so listen to me. We've got to get away from this guy. He's SS. I stashed one of the Gestapo creep's guns under my shirt. I'll shoot this guy in the back of the head and we'll make a break for it."

Still driving with one hand, Faust swiveled in his seat and punched Tars in the jaw, knocking her cold and taking the gun. His move was lightning fast; Tars never saw it coming.

---

[1] A small, open-top military vehicle; the German equivalent to the American Jeep.

"Your friend's idea is a bad one," Faust said to Maeve in English. "The Gestapo would pick you up within hours and you would again be back in a place like the one you just left."

"You do speak English," said Maeve.

"My wife taught me."

Faust slammed on the brakes and stopped the vehicle. He drew Maeve to him and kissed her passionately. She had no idea what was happening but returned the kiss.

"Who are you?" he questioned, "and why are you posing as the person we both know you're not?" When he first saw her, he thought there was something different about her, but he knew people's looks changed to at least some degree in two years. Until now he thought she might be practicing some ruse, acting to not recognize him for the sake of the other woman. But the kiss confirmed the truth: She was not Erika.

"I can't tell you."

"Where is the woman you're impersonating?"

"I don't know," Maeve replied. "Where are you taking us?"

"Berlin."

Faust put the Kübelwagen back in gear. Since his Focke-Wulf fighter was a single-seat aircraft, he would need to call on Otto Skorzeny.

Chapter 57

Lili Marlene

Berlin
Next day; Monday, 15 May 1944

Since Abwehr operatives would never have a taxi drop them at the site of a clandestine rendezvous, Stephanie Fischer ordered the cab to pull over three blocks away. She paid the driver and stepped out into a hearty spring rain. As she turned to walk along the Frankfurter Allee, she tilted her head to allow rain to drain from the brim of her gray leather beret and down her trench coat.

At the intersection of the Voightstrasse, Stephanie turned left and walked another half block to the Lili Marlene Café, unaware of the shadow watching her from an alley up the street. Inside the small café, the crowd filled most of the tables or milled around the bar. Stephanie removed her coat, hung it alongside others on a coat rack, and took a small table in a corner. Several nefarious-looking men stared at her from the bar. On initial impression, the Lili Marlene seemed to Stephanie a lair for cutthroats. A young girl approached.

"A drink?" the waitress asked.

"I'm hoping to speak with Carla."

"She's behind the bar."

"Tell her a friend of Early's is here, please."

The girl walked to the bar, spoke to a blonde, and pointed at Stephanie. The blonde stopped pouring a drink and joined in the staring at the stranger. She said something to a man rolling dice with other men at the end of the bar. He cursed, but obeyed the woman and took her place as bartender. She walked over to Stephanie's table. The blue-eyed, wiry-framed Carla appeared fit and confident.

"May I help you?"

"You're Carla?"

"Ja. Who are you?"

"My name is Stephanie. Early sent me."

Carla sat down. "Early was here this afternoon. You are to wait here until she arrives. She doesn't know what time that might be."

"Very well. Is that all of her message?"

"If it was not, I would have told you the rest."

"I didn't mean to question your instructions."

"Let me be frank," Carla said sternly. "Early is a friend of many of those around you, including me. She is safe here. Anyone seeking to harm her in any way will never walk out of here. You need to understand that."

"Is that a threat?"

"Yes."

Stephanie smiled. "Early has dedicated friends."

Carla waved the waitress back to the table. "The Fräulein is our guest tonight," she told the girl, assuming Stephanie was single since she wore no wedding ring. "Her drinks are on the house. Bring her a Berliner and a Green Fairy."

"That's generous of you," said Stephanie. "May I ask how long you've known Early?"

"Several years, since before the war. And you?"

"Only a short while—a few months."

A rugged-looking man walked over and glared at Stephanie. "Is there a problem, Carla?"

"No," she said impatiently. "If there's a problem I will tell you there's a problem. Go away, Helmut."

He immediately backed off and returned to the bar. The waitress delivered a large beer and a dram of a bright green drink.

Stephanie picked up the small drink. "So this is the Green Fairy," she said. "I've never tried one." She knew about the infamous Green Fairy, a hallucinogenic drink made from absinthe.

"Very popular in Paris and here in Berlin," Carla commented.

"If you don't mind, I'll wait to sample it until after I meet with Early." Stephanie set down the green drink and instead took a swig of beer. At that moment Erika walked in. Carla rose and she and Erika kissed each other's cheeks. Several men walked over to greet Erika. She kissed them then approached Stephanie and did the same. The kissing elevated Stephanie to the status of a Lili Marlene regular, and the attitude toward her immediately brightened.

"I like your hat," Erika told Stephanie. "Let's step outside." She turned to Carla. "Carla, we'll be back in a few minutes." Stephanie grabbed her coat and the two stepped out. The Lili Marlene's canvas awning gave them a place to stand out of the rain.

"You arrived quickly," Stephanie said. "Carla had me believing I might wait hours."

"I was just down the street."

"Observing me enter alone and checking to see if I was followed. I would do the same."

"That's right," said Erika. "I'm glad the café is still open. I wasn't sure it would be with all the bombing reports we hear in America and England. The bomb damage is not nearly as severe as Allied newspapers and movie newsreels report."

Stephanie agreed. "Yes. I expected much more damage, also."

"Do you like the café?"

"Lovely. Carla threatened to draw and quarter me if I betray you."

Erika laughed. "And she would. Just watch out if her eyes turn gray; they do that only when she's really angry. Actually, she's wonderful. If she becomes a friend, she's as true a friend as you'll ever know."

"Do you know everyone in there?"

"No. There are new faces; it's been two years. But still there are several regulars from before. We could talk in there without concern but the fresh air is nice. I love the rain. When I was a child, my father told me the splashing rain drops were dancing fairies."

Stephanie knew Erika had returned to avenge her father's murder. Thomas had briefed the team in Scotland. "And you were very close to your father."

Erika did not comment. "Did you have any trouble getting to Berlin?" she asked instead.

"No. Everything went smoothly. A train from Copenhagen to Hamburg, then another to Berlin. I arrived early this morning."

"Yes, I imagine it was easy for an Abwehr agent. I see now why you would not discuss in Scotland what brought you to the SOE. Clever—posing as a Jewess who fled. Thomas seems to have no suspicions. Of course your sister can't pose as a Jew with the Gestapo. How did you get around that?"

"The Gestapo doesn't know we're sisters. I went through Quenzsee with the last name Hauschild and all my records are under that name, and Fischer is such a common name there is no reason to make a connection. The Abwehr was very creative when it came to editing our background information."

"You and your sister play a dangerous game."

"Especially Kathryn."

"When did you find out Canaris was replaced, Stephanie?"

"Yesterday. When I arrived in Berlin and reported to headquarters. I thought all along I was sending my reports to the admiral."

Erika put her to a test. "I'm afraid I made a huge mistake. I mentioned your sister, Kathryn, to Schellenberg."

"No! Goddamn you! They'll kill her! Why did you do it? I covered your ass! I have to get to Kathryn!" Stephanie started away in a panic. Erika grabbed her arm. "Let go!" Stephanie shouted as she jerked her arm away.

"I didn't mention Kathryn. I needed to know about you and her. Now I know. And I know you covered for me. Thank you."

"You scared the shit out of me," Stephanie said angrily.

"Let's go inside and have a drink."

"Screw that. I don't feel like it now."

Erika let her cool down, and in a moment she did, realizing Erika's suspicions would be her own if positions were reversed.

"So," Stephanie said finally, still annoyed. "Where do we go from here?"

"Operation Kriemhild is a disaster and Knight and the others haven't even arrived yet. Schellenberg wants the SOE team captured alive. We'll know more after we meet with him tomorrow. You and I must go along with the capture, but we need to figure a way that they end up in Otto Skorzeny's hands and not Schellenberg's. Schellenberg will turn them over to the Gestapo and they'll be tortured, which might reveal your sister. Even the toughest of men can crack under Gestapo interrogation. If Skorzeny has them they'll undergo intense interrogation but not the torture the Gestapo is quite skilled at devising. When Skorzeny finishes with them he'll turn them over to the Luftwaffe and they'll be placed in a Luft-Stalag as prisoners of war with Red Cross protection."

"Prisoners of war? They won't be in uniform when they're captured."

"We'll bring British uniforms to dress them in. Abwehr uses enemy uniforms for infiltration assignments. I can steal what we need."

"So you know Otto Skorzeny?"

Erika nodded.

Stephanie asked: "Then what is your plan for avenging your father?"

"If you decide to join me, it will be just the two of us with your sister supplying us inside information. If caught, we'll die. I don't have to tell you that. But for me, I will die with no regrets if I've first made the men pay who killed my father. But if you want out, you can say so now or at any time. You can take my place in Abwehr. Schellenberg will promote you. You're qualified."

"So. My choice is a promotion or likely death hunting down some Gestapo lowlifes?"

"I would say that's an accurate assessment. If you're still considering joining in with me, you should speak with your sister before deciding. She has the same option; she is free to decline."

"I'll speak with Kathryn. Neither of us would be sorry to see a few of Himmler's miscreants dispatched, but I make no promises."

Her answer pleased Erika. Stephanie committing immediately would be foolhardy, and the mission would require everyone involved to be both prudent and cautious. "Good decision," Erika said.

"How are we going to capture John Mayne alive?" Stephanie wondered.

"I don't know. Brute force won't work with him. We'll need subterfuge and a sound plan. Did you hear any news about the others, Granville and McBride, before you left?"

"No. Thomas moved my departure up a day so I could meet you tonight. Both were still at STS 23 when I left. Granville was scheduled to leave shortly after me that same day and McBride the next day. By the way, Mayne told me I was being sent out a day early because of a change in my assignment. Now my duty is to replace someone who was to assist you. Who was he and what happened to him?"

"It was a woman," Erika answered, "an Italian. We're not sure what happened, but things didn't go according to plan. That's all I know."

Erika wondered about the fate of Maeve and Tars. The last she had heard, Schellenberg said they were fugitives in France.

The rain intensified and its drumming on the canvas awning made conversation difficult, but the important issues had been discussed.

"What do you say now about that drink?" Erika asked.

"Alright," Stephanie relented. "But just one. We can't be out late. We meet with Schellenberg in the morning."

Chapter 58

Wie heißen Sie?

Berlin
Next day; Tuesday, 16 May 1944

Stephanie's plan for one quick drink with Erika at the Lili Marlene didn't go as designed. Whether it was the impish workings of the Green Fairy, or the fact that both women were finally home after a long time abroad among the enemy where every word and action demanded vigilance to avoid the hangman's noose, or a combination of the two, for whatever reason or reasons Erika Lehmann and Stephanie Fischer let their hair down.

After several hours of drinking, the two ended up on the street in front of the café riding piggy-back on hulking men who considered it a worthy idea to bet on races while carrying the women on their backs. After a series of races, the crowd went back inside to argue about which team won. The well-inebriated Stephanie sent one drunk crashing over a table when he insisted that Erika's team won. The just-as-drunk Erika laughed when another man picked up Stephanie from behind and tried to throw her out the door, only to be waylaid by Carla who smashed a full bottle of gin over his head. When Carla demanded the half-conscious man and his team pay for the liquor, a brawl ensued, spilling into the street. Both Erika and Stephanie waded into the fight. Someone from the apartment building across the street called the police.

At seven o'clock in the morning, after a few hours behind bars, Erika sobered up enough to give the jailor a phone number to call. Major von der Osten appeared in front of their cell an hour later and had both women released. Now, at nine o'clock, Erika and Stephanie sat across from a glaring Walter Schellenberg. Von der Osten stood near the door, behind the women.

"Ihr zwei Schwachköpfe sehen beschissen aus," Schellenberg said from behind his desk. ("*You two nitwits look like shit.*") Both women's clothes were disheveled and in some places ripped, their hair a mess, and both looked out of bloodshot eyes. "I have in front of me a Level 4 and a Level 3 Abwehr operative. You don't look the part. You look like circus clowns that have been shot out of cannons. You're a disgrace! What do you have to say for yourselves?"

Neither woman answered.

Schellenberg continued his rebuke. "I think I'll have the major here return you to that jail. That's a good place for you." He then concentrated on Erika. "This is the example you set for Fischer! I guess she now knows what it is to be a Level 4 operative. You take her to an establishment of suspect reputation and get her drunk and arrested."

Stephanie attempted to interject. "It wasn't her fault. . . ."

"Shut up! I'll get to you in a minute, Fischer. Lehmann, this morning I had Frau Schwarte order a report on that café. The place is a den of thieves. Why did you go there?"

"The owner is my friend."

"Your friend! Well, how foolish of me. That settles the matter. As for you, Fischer, I'm demoting you to Level 2 for making a public spectacle of yourself."

"That's not fair to her, Oberführer," said Erika.

"*Fair?* By the gods, you're right. Major, please take a note: I must be more *fair.* And by the way, Lehmann, you're now Level 3. Now get out of my sight, both of you. Clean yourselves up and report back here in two hours in uniform prepared for inspection. That's all. Dismissed!"

Nursing roaring headaches, both women rose gingerly. Von der Osten opened the door to let them out, then walked over and sat down.

"You really plan to demote them a grade?"

"No," Schellenberg admitted. "But don't tell them. Any news of the women Faust escaped with in France?"

"My assumption is he will bring them to Berlin—to Skorzeny. The aircraft Faust flew to France was a single-seat fighter, so he will have to contact Skorzeny to dispatch a larger plane to pick them up."

◊ ◊ ◊

[30 minutes later]

The Heinkel He 111 set down at Tempelhof—or rather splashed down into landing strip puddles, reminders of last night's rain—shortly before 10 a.m. Otto Skorzeny had ordered the Heinkel pilots (men in his commando unit, comrades of Kai Faust) to return to Tempelhof, the commercial airport, instead of landing at the military airfield outside Potsdam to avoid questions about the flight log that Skorzeny had altered. When the plane taxied to a stop, Skorzeny went aboard. Once inside, he saw, in order: Kai Faust getting out of his seat; Kai's wife, Erika Lehmann, sitting and staring at him; and another woman with a black eye and a swollen nose, bound, gagged, and tied into her seat at the rear of the plane.

◊ ◊ ◊

When the plane came to a stop, Maeve remained in her seat because the handsome SS man who had kissed her told her not to move until he said. Her rear was still sore, but the padded airplane seats made sitting bearable. When the fuselage door opened, she watched a tall, dark-haired man in an SS uniform come aboard. He sported a pencil moustache and a long scar on the left side of his face.

◊ ◊ ◊

Tars saw the tall man board as the SS man who had taken them from the Gestapo in France approached and began untying her. He had knocked her out in the Kübelwagen. When she regained her senses, she tried to hit him over the head with a spanner she found on the floorboard under the seat, but he reacted quickly and knocked her out again. When she awoke the second time—on an airplane taxiing for takeoff—she found herself bound. After she called him a vulgar name shortly after takeoff the SS man stuffed a handkerchief in her mouth and secured it with tape from a cockpit emergency kit.

◊ ◊ ◊

Skorzeny looked again at Maeve. When Faust called late last night, he told Skorzeny's aide only that a plane was needed to bring two women to Berlin and it was important it be done discreetly. When Skorzeny was informed of the request, he assumed one of the women was Erika, whom he had permitted Faust to search for. And when the commando chief boarded and first saw the blonde, he was sure it was her. But Erika knew him well and when this woman didn't react to his presence he asked Faust: "Kai, who is this woman?"

"I don't know, Obersturmbannführer." Skorzeny encouraged his men to call him *Otto,* but Kai Faust couldn't bring himself to do so. He respected Skorzeny to such a degree that he found referring to him by his first name awkward. Faust always called him by rank or *sir.* "Obviously her mission requires impersonating Erika."

"Yes," Skorzeny agreed. "I'd say that's quite obvious." He looked at Maeve. "Wie heißen Sie?"

Maeve understood *"What's your name?"* The phrase was one of the first Erika taught her at Camp X. "Lorelei," she replied.

Skorzeny chuckled and moved down the aisle toward Tars, still partially tied into the rear seat. Faust ripped the tape from her face.

"Stronzo!" the pain forced Tars to exclaim in Italian. Then she yelled in English, "You asshole! Let me put tape across your mouth and rip it off!" She looked at Skorzeny as he approached. "Who's this? One of your SS butt-buddies? I bet you guys love showering together."

Incensed at the insult directed at Skorzeny, Faust roughly jerked Tars head back by her hair and stuffed the handkerchief back in her mouth. Skorzeny put a hand on Faust's arm.

"Take out the gag, Kai," he directed.

Faust pulled the handkerchief out of Tars' mouth.

Skorzeny had heard Tars' Italian exclamation when Faust pulled the tape. "This man standing beside me," Skorzeny said in Italian, "you should bless for saving you from the Gestapo. And be assured you have no hope of overpowering him or escaping as long as he's in charge of you. Judging from your appearance, I think you might agree. The gag will remain out if you control your tongue. Otherwise, I'll let him muffle you and bind you like a mummy. Which option is your choice?"

Tars glared at Skorzeny but kept her mouth shut, knowing she could not fulfill her orders to shield Maeve while trussed up like a Christmas goose. She nodded.

"Very well," Otto Skorzeny said.

Chapter 59

Reichsführer-SS

Berlin—8 Prinz Albrechtstrasse
Same day; Tuesday, 16 May 1944

Late Sunday night, Heinrich Himmler received the report from the Quimper Gestapo. It told only the basics: the Quimper agents captured *Lorelei* and the mystery woman, but the unknown woman killed an interrogator and they escaped, aided by one of Skorzeny's men.

"I have the report on Skorzeny's man, Herr Reichsführer." Heinrich Müller laid the folder on Himmler's desk.

"Skorzeny," Himmler said with a frown. "I get a gas bubble every time I hear that name." Although Skorzeny was SS, Himmler exerted no power over him. But not for lack of trying. Skorzeny was not only Leibstandarte Adolf Hitler, but also a favorite of the Führer who denied every request Himmler had made to take control of the famous commando and his men. "Go ahead, Müller."

"Schrolucke, our Kriminalsekretär in Quimper, reports the man was a Hauptsturmführer named Faust. We ran a check: Johan Faust, usually referred to by his middle name, Kai, has been Leibstandarte since 1938. He was a member of the Führer's personal security detachment until, with the Führer's permission, recruited by Skorzeny in May 1943. This Faust was on the team that rescued Mussolini from Gran Sasso last fall."

"What else?"

"Nothing else, Reichsführer."

"I don't understand Skorzeny's interest in Lehmann. What about this other woman? Did Schrolucke get anything out of her before Skorzeny's man stepped in?"

"No, Reichsführer. Schrolucke reports that the second phase of interrogation had just begun when Skorzeny's man arrived."

Himmler's secretary buzzed to inform him that the man they had been waiting for had now arrived and was being held in an interrogation room.

Himmler rose from his chair. "Let's go, Müller."

Conrad Gerber sat in an interrogation chamber in the bowels of 8 Prinz Albrechtstrasse. After the two women hijacked his airplane, Gerber decided to shoot himself but couldn't pull the trigger. Instead, he started walking, not caring where he ended up knowing Heinrich Himmler had plenty of underlings who would not share his hesitation to pull the trigger of a gun held to his head. He finally found himself in a village with a telephone and contacted headquarters. *Better to die in Berlin where my wife can bury me than to end things as a rotting carcass and carrion for buzzards in some god-forsaken Spanish backwater.*

Gerber had waited in the chamber but a few minutes when the door opened and in walked Himmler followed by Müller. Gerber was shocked. It was almost unheard of for Himmler to descend to the dungeon-like interrogation area. He nervously rose to his feet, came to attention, and gave a Heil Hitler.

"Sit down, swine!" Himmler yelled. "You dare still consider yourself Gestapo and salute the Führer? You were given a dozen men to eliminate one woman. Not only are your men dead and the woman still alive, she escaped in your airplane! You're a fucking clown, Gerber."

Gerber sat down quickly and told Himmler what he already knew. "There was a second woman, Herr Reichsführer."

"Well that explains it." Himmler turned to Müller. "Müller, there were *two women!* How stupid of us. We should have given Gerber two dozen men!"

"I am prepared to die," Gerber said meekly.

"Shut up, idiot! Don't speak except to answer my questions." Himmler glared at Gerber and came to the point. "Did you at least manage to eliminate the Spanish fishermen, or did you hire them to take you tuna fishing?"

"The fishermen are dead, Reichsführer!" Gerber answered forcefully.

"One more question before I turn you over to Müller's Frauen: Did you get a look at this second woman?"

"No, Reichsführer. But Lehmann stood in the doorway of the Junkers as it flew by very near to where I stood. I assure you the blonde woman was Lehmann."

"I didn't ask you about Lehmann, goddamn you. Müller will send in a Frau to administer Phase 1 interrogation, Gerber," Himmler stated. "If I think you told us everything, it will not progress to Phase 2 and I might consider returning you to your duties. Do you understand?"

Gerber couldn't believe what he was hearing. Himmler was telling him he would undergo a long and grueling interrogation but if he told everything he knew the questioning would not progress to torture. The chance that he might live floored him; he had felt certain he would be dead by the end of the day. He again stood. "Yes, Reichsführer! Thank you, Reichsführer! I assure you I will tell everything, and. . . ."

"Sit down!"

Gerber again collapsed into his chair. Himmler and Müller left the room.

"I assume this is a deception to get Gerber to open up quickly," Müller said as they walked down the corridor. "After we have what we need he will be canceled."

"No," said Himmler. "Gerber stays alive for now. I have other plans for him."

The Reichsführer-SS reasoned that Karl Lehmann's killer would serve a better purpose as a sacrificial goat on a tether—bait to lure the lioness to action. When the lioness came for the goat, Himmler would be waiting.

Chapter 60

In Uniform

Berlin
Same day; Tuesday, 16 May 1944

Erika had taken a room at the Kempinski Hotel when she arrived in Berlin. Stephanie arrived a day later and had a room waiting at the Four Seasons, a room she had yet to enter having spent her first Berlin night in jail with Erika. But with the short time Schellenberg had given them before reporting back, they decided to forego a trip to their hotels. Instead, they cleaned up in a small locker room in the basement of Abwehr headquarters. When they entered, a naked man passed before them on his way from the shower. They began preparing their uniforms, starting by shining their shoes. The uniforms had been stored at headquarters when the women left Germany on undercover assignments. When the man finished dressing and left, the women took turns in the single shower.

There were no official Abwehr uniforms. Spies refrain from advertising that they are spies. But the Abwehr was a branch of the military and its agents and administrators subject to military law and regulations. In certain circumstances uniforms were necessary and required. Agents above the second level were given the Abwehr rank of Sonderführer (Special Leader) and issued uniforms of one of the military branches. Level 3 and 4 operatives held military officer rank. It was all quite official for the sake of cover; if inquiries were made to the OKW, the report would confirm an agent's military status. Stephanie Fischer held the rank of a Luftwaffe Women's Auxiliary Oberstabsführerin (First Lieutenant); Erika's uniform indicated she was a Kriegsmarine Korvettenkapitän (Lieutenant-Commander).

"So why the uniforms?" Stephanie asked. "Just to piss us off?"

"Sure. He knows we're hung over and he wants to make things difficult with an inspection. He's taking delight in making us pay for last night."

"I feel a little better after the shower but I still have a headache."

"Me too."

"I guess this is the last day I'll wear this rank," Stephanie said as she buttoned her shirt. A drop in military rank accompanied any demotion within Abwehr. "What do you think about the demotion?"

"I wouldn't worry too much about that." Erika looked in the mirror and began tying her necktie. "Maybe he's just bluffing; but if he's serious it won't change anything as far as assignments."

When finished dressing, each woman turned so the other could inspect the back of her tunic for lint; then they headed for the stairs and Walter Schellenberg.

When Wera notified Schellenberg that the two agents had reported back he cleared them to enter. Alone in his office, he offered no comment about their uniforms and there was no inspection; instead, Schellenberg ordered them to sit and shifted directly to business.

"Lehmann, I assume you informed Fischer of our plan to capture the SOE team."

"Yes, Oberführer."

"Fischer, you should know these men even better than Lehmann, you trained with them longer. You'll be on the capture team."

"Yes, sir."

He turned again to Erika. "Lehmann, how will Victor Knight find you?"

"I told him I would book a room at the Kempinski Hotel. After he arrives he will leave a message for me at the desk under the name of Dieter Scherer with a phone number of a public place and the time for me to call."

"Very well. You and Fischer work with Major von der Osten to devise a capture plan, and I'll assign the necessary personnel when the strategy is finalized. The three of you will begin meeting this afternoon, with von der Osten in charge. Understood?"

Both women nodded.

"Oh, I almost forgot. There is one other small matter that might interest you, Lehmann," Schellenberg said sardonically. "Your double and her Italian bodyguard are here in Berlin."

Erika sat stunned and speechless.

Schellenberg continued. "They were captured by the Gestapo in France but someone you know who thought the double was you rescued them and delivered them to Berlin this morning."

Erika knew he referred to Kai but remained silent.

Schellenberg continued. "When your friend didn't find you on that freighter he went searching, as I thought he might. By the way, your double's bodyguard killed a Gestapo Frau. We learned the name of the bodyguard from our man who met them in Haiti. We ran her background and some interesting details were uncovered. The agent I sent to Calabria reports that the people down there who know her say she's a lunatic."

Erika shrugged. "But apparently she's in control enough to hijack a Gestapo airplane right from under their nose."

"What's the double's name?"

"The SOE gave her a cover name of Maeve Shanahan for the freighter journey, but her real name is Maeve O'Rourke." Erika could not take the chance of telling a lie while playing cat and mouse with Schellenberg until she uncovered how much he knew. She would stick to the truth if the truth mattered little.

"Who is she? A civilian or someone the British found in the military?"

"She's an Irish prostitute."

"A prostitute?" Schellenberg thought it implausible.

Erika nodded. "She told me a British officer in the group assigned to find a lookalike for me stumbled upon her at a military dance. Maeve was there looking for a customer. Where are the women?"

"They're being held in a Schutzhaus on the Bendlerstrasse."

Chapter 61

Photographs

Berlin
Same day; Tuesday, 16 May 1944

"I'll ask you again to tell me anything you know about Erika Lehmann, the woman you impersonate," Kai Faust said to Maeve. He had brought the women to this apartment—an SS Schutzhaus, or safehouse—directly from the airport. Skorzeny had just left. Faust, Maeve and Tars sat in a bedroom with boarded-over windows.

"Don't tell that SS crud anything, Maeve," said Tars. "Don't be suckered by that shit about how he wants to protect Erika. He's lying. His saving us from the Gestapo is probably a set up to fool us into trusting him. They're probably working together."

Faust summoned a safehouse guard and ordered him to take Tars to another room. The guard jerked Tars to her feet and pulled her toward the door.

"I'm not leaving her, asshole," she said to Faust, then repeated to Maeve as the guard dragged her out of the room: "Don't tell him anything, Maeve! Keep your nerve!"

When Tars was gone, Faust took out the photo of him and Erika and a piece of paper. He had tried to avoid this, but now felt he had no choice. Time was critical. If these women held any clue to Erika's whereabouts he wanted to find out now, and he felt the look-alike would be more likely to reveal it. He handed the photo and paper to Maeve.

"Erika is my wife," Faust said. "This photo is from our honeymoon."

Maeve looked at him and then at the photo capturing him and Erika in an embrace, smiling at the camera. She opened the folded paper, a marriage certificate attesting to the union between Johan Kai Faust and Erika Marie Lehmann. At the bottom, she recognized Erika's handwriting—handwriting Maeve had practiced at Camp X. The new bride had signed her new name: *Erika Marie Faust.*

"We were forced to hide our marriage from most, for reasons I will not tell you." He reached into a pocket and brought out another photograph and handed it to Maeve. It showed Erika holding a baby. "We have a daughter."

Flabbergasted and wide-eyed, Maeve stared at the photos and marriage license.

"Will you help me find my wife and the mother of my child?" Faust asked.

Maeve looked at Faust, then back at the photos, then back at him. She believed the photographs, she believed the signature, and she believed Faust. "The only thing I know is the reason for my involvement was so Erika could return to Germany without suspicion. My job was to pose as her to make it look like she escaped from America, and we were to switch places in Barcelona. Everything went wrong when the men on the fishing boat took Tars and me off the freighter. That's all I know. I don't know where she is."

Kai Faust stood and walked out the door.

Twenty minutes after Kai Faust left, the safehouse telephone rang. The Waffen-SS staff sergeant in charge picked up the receiver. "Hallo."

"Who is speaking?" the voice on the other end asked.

"Scharführer Haas."

"Scharführer, this is Oberführer Schellenberg."

"Yes, Oberführer!" The sergeant stood rigid, proud to be on the telephone with such a high official.

"Two Abwehr agents are on their way there to pick up the women dropped off a few hours ago. They will have identification and the appropriate paperwork. Release the women into their custody."

"Yes, Oberführer."

[same time]

When Kai Faust left the safehouse he drove directly to the building at 72 Tirpitz-Ufer—Abwehr headquarters. After asking at the security desk to see Schellenberg, he was escorted to Wera Schwarte. It was an unusual request coming from an individual not affiliated with Abwehr, especially from a captain, a relatively low rank considering Wera had seen colonels forced to wait hours for an audience with the head of the spy agency. Wera was surprised when Schellenberg gave his permission for the captain to enter his office right away.

"Have a seat, Hauptsturmführer," Schellenberg said. "It's nice to meet you."

Faust sat down. "Thank you, Oberführer Schellenberg. And thank you for seeing me."

"I thought you might come calling today."

The comment surprised Faust. "May I ask why you thought that, sir?"

"I learned you landed in Berlin this morning with the imposter."

That didn't answer Faust's question, but he moved on. "You knew about the imposter all along, Herr Oberführer?"

"Not at first. Very clever by the SOE. How closely does she resemble Erika?"

"She could be a twin sister."

"Amazing," Schellenberg said. Then he addressed the question he knew Faust was there to ask. "Yes, Erika is in Berlin." Schellenberg knew of the past relationship between the two. Von der Osten told him when he requested Faust be brought in on the freighter rescue mission (although neither man knew of the marriage).

"Where is she, Herr Oberführer?"

"She and another agent are on their way to pick up the imposter and the other woman. I'm taking them into Abwehr custody. If you hurry you might catch up to them."

Faust rose, quickly thanked Schellenberg, and walked rapidly out of his office.

◊ ◊ ◊

Scharführer Haas stood drop-jawed, gawking at one of the women who had come to collect the detainees. First, he was surprised they were women. Oberführer Schellenberg had not said the Abwehr people would be females. Second, one of the Abwehr women resembled one of the detainees so closely that for a second Haas thought the woman had escaped and for some strange reason decided to return.

"May we see the women we are here for, Scharführer?" Erika asked.

Stephanie Fischer remained in the apartment's living room while Haas showed Erika to the bedroom.

◊ ◊ ◊

When possible, Kai Faust wove around cars and buses as he drove back to the SS safehouse; but heavy, late-afternoon traffic slowed him several times and made him curse. Skorzeny and Faust had no choice but to place the women in the safehouse; there was no place else to take them other than a Gestapo holding facility. Faust knew Schellenberg, as SS, would find out about the women but he didn't think it would be this quickly.

◊ ◊ ◊

Tars had been taken back to the bedroom where Maeve was being held to allow the guards easier supervision. The women sat alone on the bed.

"I told that SS guy what I knew, which wasn't much," Maeve said to Tars.

"What??? Why did you do that?"

"That guy and Erika are married."

"What???" Tars exclaimed again in disbelief. "Bullshit. He played you for a fool, Maeve."

"No he didn't. He showed me photographs and their marriage license. It was signed by Erika. I know her handwriting, Tars. I spent days practicing it. They have a daughter."

"No! It's all a trick."

The bedroom door opened. Erika stood in the doorway looking at them.

◊ ◊ ◊

Faust skidded to a stop in front of the apartment building, ran up the stairs, and pounded on the safehouse door. SS Scharführer Haas opened the door.

"Are the Abwehr people here?" Faust half-shouted as he stormed inside.

"Oberführer Schellenberg called and ordered me to turn them over to them, Hauptsturmführer." Haas was confused and uneasy about the hubbub.

"I know that! That's not what I asked! Are the Abwehr people here?"

"No, sir. They left with the detainees just a few minutes ago."

Chapter 62

Kai's Apartment

Berlin
Same day; Tuesday, 16 May 1944

After Kai Faust missed Erika at the SS safehouse, he raced back to Abwehr headquarters. She was not there and neither was Schellenberg. Wera Schwarte would not tell him where Erika was, but Kai suspected that if she had not brought her double and the Italian back to Abwehr headquarters, then they were together elsewhere. Faust knew the SS was not the only organization with safehouses.

He told Frau Schwarte he would wait for the Oberführer's return and was shown to a room across the hall. The afternoon passed without Schellenberg returning, and at five o'clock security asked Faust to leave. After five, non-Abwehr personnel were not allowed in the building unless their presence had been requested by Schellenberg or a high-ranking Abwehr official.

After he left Abwehr headquarters, Faust tried to reach Skorzeny but the commando chief was attending a reception and dinner with some OKW bigwigs. Next, he drove by the apartment building near the Tiergarten where Erika's father had lived and where she used to stay when in Berlin. He knew someone else lived there now, but he drove by anyway. He didn't stop, knowing she would not be there and wondering why he'd gone there in the first place. Finally, Faust stopped for dinner at a small restaurant near the Olympic Stadium that was Erika's favorite in Berlin. He lingered there over dinner thinking about his next step. Tomorrow, he would report to Skorzeny and request more time to search for her, and he would make a pest out of himself at Abwehr until he got his audience with Schellenberg.

By the time Faust left the restaurant darkness had fallen. He drove to an apartment building in Spandau, a district in western Berlin, parked his car and climbed the stairs to his third-floor apartment. When he unlocked the door and stepped inside, he turned on a light and dropped his car keys on the table.

"Hello, Kai."

His wife was sitting on the sofa.

Part 4

1938

"I guess I was never the girl next door."

— Erika Lehmann

Chapter 63

New Recruit

1938—May
Tegel, Germany

"Next! . . . Name!" hollered the quartermaster of the Tegel paramilitary academy. He stood behind a counter in the supply room issuing clothing to a group of new recruits. Tegel served as the first stop in an arduous journey for those recruited for possible service as field operatives in the military intelligence arm of the Wehrmacht—the Abwehrabteilung. If recruits successfully completed the five-week indoctrination and training at Tegel, they progressed to the next phase: extensive training at the main academy, Quenzsee, that lasted for months. The quartermaster knew that even if they endured Tegel, few of the 14 men and 3 women in his line would graduate from Quenzsee. It was not uncommon for an entire group to wash out, with no one lasting to the end.

The quartermaster showed his displeasure by yelling again, and louder, when he felt the woman now at the front of the line responded too slowly. "Name! Goddammit!"

"Erika Lehmann."

"Middle name, too! Haven't you been paying attention, Dummkopf?"

"Marie."

The man looked at his list and made a check mark by her name. "Shoe size!"

"Seven and a half."

Without checking size, the quartermaster grabbed a pair that turned out to be size eight and slammed them on the counter. He quickly looked her over and pulled an assortment of clothing from nearby shelves, not particularly concerned if they fit. "There! Go! . . . Next! . . . Name!"

The plebes waited outside until everyone in the group was outfitted, then a Tegel instructor marched them single file to another building where they underwent a second physical examination that day and answered the same family and medical background questions they had answered again and again in the days leading up to their arrival at Tegel. After the examination, Erika was directed to the next room.

"Name?" asked a middle-aged woman sitting behind a small desk and wearing a Volkssturm uniform. Not given time to dress, Erika stood in her underwear holding both the clothes she had been wearing and the ones just issued.

"Erika Marie Lehmann."

"Age?" The woman's eyes remained focused on the checklists in front of her; she rarely looked up.

"Twenty."

"Have you passed the racial purity regulations?"

"Yes." Erika knew that information had to be in the paperwork the woman held.

"Are you training with the Abwehr group or the Schutzstaffel group?" Tegel and Quenzsee trained personnel for both the Abwehr and the SS.

"Abwehr."

"Your sponsor's name?" Volunteers were not accepted at Tegel or Quenzsee. Only applicants who had been recruited by a person or persons of position and responsibility within the Reich were considered, and a sponsor who could be held accountable for the commendation was required.

"Ulrich von der Osten of the Abwehr."

"Were you employed or at university before coming here?"

"Both. Until last week, I worked at the Seehaus in Berlin translating foreign radio broadcasts. I went to university in the United States for one year, and since returning to Germany I've taken courses at the Charité and at Friedrich Wilhelms Universität."

"Are you fluent in any foreign languages?"

"English, French, and Russian."

The woman looked up. "I'm not asking if you speak *some* of a foreign language. Only the ones in which you are fluent."

"English, French, and Russian."

The woman stared at her, doubting, then opened and checked Erika's file and found she had successfully passed the tests in those languages.

"Isn't all my information there?" Erika asked pleasantly, not wanting to annoy, but wondering why she was being asked information surely in her file.

"Are you trying for my job?"

"No."

"Thank you. I have a son at university and two daughters in Gymnasium. They need my money."

When Erika laughed, the woman smiled—the first smile Erika had seen that day.

"Get dressed in the brown fatigues you were issued and wait outside. A group leader will march you and the other women to your quarters."

"Thank you."

Not waiting for Erika to dress, the woman called in the next plebe. A handsome young man about Erika's age walked in. She hadn't noticed him in her group before, but seeing him in his underwear left an impression. He looked lean and hard and well-muscled. Their eyes locked for an instant then she looked away and began putting on her fatigues.

"Name?" the Volkssturm Frau asked.

"Johan Kai Faust."

"Age?"

"Twenty-one."

"Have you passed the racial purity regulations?"

"Yes."

"Are you training with the Abwehr group or the Schutzstaffel group?"

"Schutzstaffel."

"Your sponsor's name?"

"Adolf Hitler."

The woman thumbed through his file and found that he was recommended for the Führer's personal bodyguard detachment of the

Leibstandarte—the Begleitkommando. These men accompanied Adolf Hitler and only he could sponsor an applicant.

"Were you employed or at university before coming here?"

As she questioned him, the young man glanced sideways and watched the blonde walk out the door. "I was an infantryman in the Heer before joining the SS last autumn."

"Are you fluent in any foreign languages?"

"No."

Chapter 64

Quenzsee

One month later; June 1938
Brandenburg, Germany

The primary German training academy for the art of espionage and the science of sabotage was located at Quenzsee in Brandenburg, not far from Berlin. The buildings were part of a lavish old estate that included a lake, a large park, and beautiful gardens. A high fence topped with barbed wire encircled the grounds, belying the serene setting. Machinegun-toting guards patrolled both sides of the fence, a leashed and muzzled German shepherd attack dog at their side.

The motto at Quenzsee was *Fetch the Devil from Hell*. The goal of the school: to train agents to carry out that mission. Although members of other organizations such as elite military commandos and certain members of the SS spent training time at Quenzsee to hone skills such as hand-to-hand fighting and radio communications, the overriding purpose of Quenzsee was to train prospects to be Abwehr intelligence-gathering operatives or saboteurs who could carry out missions behind enemy lines.

The espionage section at Quenzsee taught trainees international Morse code and the use of shortwave transmitters (later they would learn how to build their own transmitters at a school in Potsdam). Trainees became well-versed in microphotography of documents and the coding and decoding of messages, along with knowledge of the chemistry of secret inks. They learned burglary skills including gaining access through locked doors and windows without leaving evidence of entry, lock picking, and safe cracking. For specific countries, satisfactory language skills entailed much more than just proper speech. Regional dialects, mannerisms, and idioms demanded constant practice; syntax, grammar, and accents had to be flawless. Would-be agents attended classes on the country to be infiltrated. Knowledge of the target country's history and geography was meticulously tested: skill in map-making demanded.

Quenzsee's second branch, the sabotage section, instructed trainees in the use of explosives and fire bombs (advanced candidates learned how to create bombs from ordinary materials available in hardware or agricultural stores).

All trainees fired an assortment of pistols and rifles for at least one hour each day with pistol marksmanship especially stressed. Before they left the school, agents could devise homemade silencers from readily available materials. Effective use of blackmail was an important course. Hand-to-hand combat was practiced every day, and silent killing methods studied.

Even though prospective agents were carefully selected and screened, given the extremely high standards of excellence Wilhelm Canaris and his Quenzsee overseers demanded, few would ever see duty as an *asset*—the Abwehr euphemism for secret agent. The few hard-working elites who made it through to graduation demonstrated exceptional aptitude and grit.

Erika Lehmann arrived at Quenzsee a week ago and now stood at the firing range with two other women and seven men in her Anlernengruppe—a group of plebe recruits. Among the group were none of the recruits she mustered in with at Tegel. Some in her initial group who failed to pass the Tegel standards were still there or already home; some who had been bumped up to Quenzsee like Erika had been assigned to other Anlernengruppen. Erika had just fired her first clip of the day. Her muscles sore from strenuous physical training, along with bruises from fight training, amplified the uncomfortable kick of the Luger.

"Goddammit, Lehmann, you have to do better than that!" Sonderführer Patrick, their drill instructor, shouted at the back of her head. Patrick (probably an alias, Erika imagined) was a former Heer sergeant and now a Level 3 Abwehr operative. "You're all over the target. If your groupings don't get tighter you're not going to be here very long." He directed similar comments at the other Abwehr trainees. The two SS men practicing with her group were excellent marksmen, and Patrick, who disliked the SS, said nothing about their shooting.

After the group spent just over an hour at the range, Patrick marched them to the physical-training building for instruction in hand-to-hand combat. Erika dreaded this part of the day. Her energy level was low from lack of sleep and she was not a good fighter. She performed well on the daily, early-morning obstacle course; her quickness and agility helped her there. And despite Patrick's complaints at the firing range, her marksmanship had improved since she first arrived. Erika excelled at the evening swimming tests in the Quenzsee lake (just last year she won the first place swimming medal at the Party Day Aryan Maids Games in Nuremberg). But in hand-to-hand she struggled.

Once inside, Patrick lined them up to observe demonstrations of fight techniques they would work on that day. Another group was there to share the training time. Two Quenzsee instructors took to the giant mat that covered nearly the entire floor of the barn-sized building and showed the trainees the first drill—how to apply a chokehold that would render an opponent unconscious but not kill. After the demonstration, trainees were ordered to pair up on the mat and the instructors spread out to observe and coach.

Erika and one of the women in her group paired up to practice the moves. When the time allotted for practice in slow motion ended, instructors signaled the recruits to go full speed. Her partner fended off Erika's initial attempt to get in position for the hold; Patrick saw and rushed over.

"Lehmann! Why are you not better at this?" he shouted so loudly all could hear. "You have the ability! You're fast and strong, you swim like a goddamn porpoise and your tits aren't that big! Only women with big tits have an excuse for being poor fighters; their tits get in the way! You don't have big tits so don't try and use them for an excuse, goddammit! Now pick it up or I'm going to run you until you puke and die! Pair up with someone else!"

Her partner walked away to find another, and Patrick went looking for someone else to harangue. A man from the other group approached.

"I almost didn't recognize you with your clothes on," he said. "The last time I saw you, you were in your underwear."

She studied him and finally recognized him as the young man from Tegel. "I train in hand-to-hand with the other woman," Erika said.

"So I frighten you?"

"No one frightens me. But if anyone did, it wouldn't be you."

"Then we'll begin?"

Erika did not answer or return his smile.

He continued, "First of all, when behind an opponent attack the kidneys. Unless you have a weapon to strike them over the head, a blow to the kidneys is the only thing that will disable an opponent from the back. And before you can get in position for the chokehold, you must make your opponent wary of something else. One way is to feign a blow you previously landed. Even if it didn't cause damage or pain, if you've landed it your opponent will expect it again. So you can use it to your advantage."

For the next several minutes, Kai Faust demonstrated various blows and showed Erika how to realistically feign them so that she could close in and apply a headlock or chokehold. When they went full speed, Erika finally landed a kick to the side of his leg and got close enough to get her arm around his neck. But he flipped her off and slammed her to the mat, his body on top of hers. Their lips nearly touching, he grinned and said, "That instructor was right. You are strong."

"But he also said my breasts aren't big. Does that disappoint you?"

He chuckled and felt tempted to kiss her despite the inappropriate setting. She recognized his desire and parted her lips slightly to invite him, then kneed him in the groin.

Chapter 65

The Lake

Two months later; August 1938
Quenzsee

Each day recruits reported to the lake for one hour of mandatory swimming, scheduled immediately after dinner so recruits were forced to swim with full stomachs. Weekly tests determined skill levels in stamina, speed, and the length of time a recruit could remain underwater. After daily swimming practice, recruits reported to the mess hall for the required relaxation event: usually a speech by someone of note, either in person or on film. Speeches by the Führer were shown at least twice weekly. After the relaxation event, recruits were allotted two hours of free time until curfew when they were to be in their barracks for bed check.

Erika Lehmann surpassed everyone in swimming at Quenzsee, instructors as well as fellow plebes. Swimming relaxed her, and most evenings she returned to the lake during her free time, as she did this evening. She changed into a Quenzsee-issued swimsuit inside the boathouse and dove from the small pier into the water. And as was also the case most evenings, Kai Faust soon appeared at the lake, knowing he would find Erika here.

He always sought her out when their groups trained together. Since the SS contingent at Quenzsee did not study to be spies, Kai had no access to her during her various classroom and laboratory sessions. Generally, their groups came together for the morning obstacle course and the afternoon fight training. It was quite obvious he was pursuing her, and on the rare occasions when they were not being watched by a Quenzsee instructor he had tried to kiss her. Once or twice she had allowed it, other times not.

Erika admitted to herself that she was attracted to him physically, but at present her interest in a relationship was zero. The grueling training schedule at Quenzsee gave her little time to think about anything but the next drill, test or manual to read. When her head hit the pillow at night, she fell asleep within minutes with no dreams of romance.

Kai had been of great help to her the past two months. He was a skilled and fierce fighter, and because of his extra tutelage in hand-to-hand, Erika now easily bested the other women in full-speed bouts (in July, two more women joined her group), and she was beginning to hold her own with some of the men.

Kai walked out of the boathouse in swimming trunks, dove in, and began swimming toward Erika who had left the water on the opposite shore. She watched him swim. She had offered him tips to improve his swimming but so far her coaching yielded only minor results. He was an acceptable swimmer, not outstanding, but the SS were not required to pass the swimming tests given the Abwehr prospects. Kai swam now only because that was the fastest way to reach her on the far shore. Walking around the lake through the high reeds and cattails would take more time, and he knew if he remained in his fatigues and circled the lake she would let him get near then take back to the water just to disappoint him.

True to form, when Faust got within 20 yards of where she stood, Erika walked back into the lake and submerged. He stopped and treaded water, spinning to see where she surfaced. But Erika remained underwater for such a long time he grew concerned and ducked his head to find her. The water was clear enough to see her on the bottom, only 10 feet down. She gripped a rock to stay submerged and watch him. As soon as he saw her, she pushed off the bottom and rocketed toward him. When she broke the surface she laughed.

"When you swim you splash like a Panzer fording a stream," she said.

He reached out for her, but she easily eluded him and kept her distance, teasing. "What is it you want?" She pivoted in the water and headed toward the boathouse pier, backstroking so she could watch him and laugh at his futile attempts to catch her. When Kai finally made it back across the lake, Erika had been out of the water for several minutes and sat on the pier dangling her feet in the water.

As he neared, he looked past her and asked, "Why is your drill master here?"

When she turned to look, Patrick was nowhere to be seen, but then she felt a strong grip on her ankle and was yanked back into the lake. He had her now and drew her to him. They stood on the sandy bottom chest high in the water. His arms and shoulders were as hard as the rock she had gripped at the bottom of the lake. She felt tempted to let him have his way.

"It's getting dark," she said, "and I have a great deal of reading assigned."

He kissed her neck. It took all of her willpower to refuse him. "Let me go, Kai."

His hands held her waist and he left them there, refusing to release her. "Tomorrow is my last day here," he said. "Then I have three days furlough. I found out that if Abwehr recruits pass their tests this week they'll be granted an evening leave Saturday night. Is that true?"

He was right. The first leave since her group arrived in June would be granted this weekend for recruits in good standing.

"It's for only a few hours," she said. "Anyone earning leave has to be back by midnight."

"Will you join me for dinner? But before you answer, you should know I'll happily stand in this water all night with my hands on you until you say *yes.*"

"I don't have a dress with me here appropriate for a dinner out."

"It doesn't matter. I believe your leave will begin at six o'clock that evening?" He had done his research.

"Yes."

[one hour later]

Erika was on the mess hall telephone—the only telephone at Quenzsee available to recruits—listening to it ring on the other end. A man picked up.

"Hallo. Lili Marlene Café," he shouted over background noise.

"Carla, please," Erika said.

"She's busy!"

"Is this Philo?"

"Ja. Who's this?"

"Early."

"Ah, Early. Hold on, I'll get her."

In a moment, Carla came on. "Early?"

"Hallo, Carla. I need a favor."

"What is it?"

"I need a dress for a dinner date."

"What do you mean you need a dress? Where are you?"

"I'm about an hour from Berlin at an estate west of Brandenburg an der Havel. I didn't bring any dresses and I can't go out and get one right now."

"Why not? What are you doing there?"

"That's not important, Carla. Can you help me with a dress? I need it for Saturday evening. Nothing formal, just a cotton summer dress will be fine. Can you ask someone to bring it to me?"

"How slutty do you want to look?"

"Not slutty."

"Do you like the man?" Carla asked.

"Yes."

"Leave it to me. You're about a size eight, right?"

"I've gained weight. Make it a ten."

"I'll have Philo bring it to you. I'll put him back on the phone and you can tell him where to deliver it."

Chapter 66

The Führer's Bodyguard

Later that week; August 1938
Genthin, Germany

"How did you find this restaurant?" Erika asked as Kai parked his 1938 Horch Sport Cabriolet. The restaurant was in Genthin, a small town about 20 minutes east of the Quenzsee estate.

"A comrade in my detachment grew up near here and assured me this is a good place. I know a very good restaurant in Potsdam and several in Berlin I would like to take you to, but since we have only a few hours I didn't want to waste half our time driving." He stepped out and came around to open her door. Rain had been forecast for the area, but so far none had fallen.

Once inside, they were shown to a table. The small restaurant was charming rather than elegant, and all but two of the eight tables were occupied. Kai helped Erika remove her coat. Despite the August warmth, she had worn her thin, Quenzsee-issued rain slicker because of the forecast. He laid her jacket over a spare chair and pulled another out for her.

Erika's body was changing. The soft arms and legs of two months ago had grown toned and firm. And despite the vigorous daily exercise, she ate heartily at Quenzsee and had gained weight. She now wished she had told Carla to send a size 12. The red and white cotton summer dress felt tight and revealed more cleavage than Erika would have chosen. She wasn't surprised when she noticed Kai looking at her chest. He noticed her noticing him and looked up quickly, a bit sheepish that she caught him staring. He cleared his throat and looked for something to say.

"Wine?" he asked quickly.

"That would be nice."

He opened the wine list, but knew nothing about wines and admitted it. "You should decide. I'll pick the wrong one." He handed her the list. "Your dress is beautiful."

She smiled. It was just a polka-dot summer dress. "Thank you. You look dashing." He wore his SS parade dress uniform. "You didn't tell me you were an officer. Twenty-one is young for an Untersturmführer."

"Don't be too impressed; I didn't earn it. I was an enlisted man in the Heer but was offered the lieutenant rank to join the SS. Many others have gotten the same offer."

"You surprised me the other day at the lake when you told me your training was finished," Erika commented. "I don't know why, but I assumed SS training lasted as long as ours."

"I wish it did. I'd still see you every day. Most of our training takes place elsewhere. Our Quenzsee program is only eight-weeks. I asked my group leader and he told me the Quenzsee training program for Abwehr lasts a lot longer."

"Yes. And after Quenzsee I'll have a series of practice missions to complete that take several months."

"What determines how long you'll be at Quenzsee?"

"Test scores—in both physical training and classroom instruction."

"The long program at Quenzsee then the practice missions, and add to that the time you've already spent at Tegel—that's a lot of training time."

"And all this is just the initial program that determines if they want to accept me," Erika added. "If accepted, I'm not sure the training ever ends. I'll be sent back to Quenzsee for advanced training and eventually to Potsdam for shortwave transmission school." A waitress approached. "I'll get a red," she told Kai, then ordered a bottle of Spätburgunder. Before the waitress walked away, she left menus.

"My comrade who told me about this place says the Rouladen is very good."

"Ah, that's my father's favorite dish."

"What does your father do?"

"He works at the Ministry of Enlightenment."

Kai was impatient to learn more about her. "Tell me about yourself, Erika. What got you involved with Abwehr?"

"I think my recruitment had a lot to do with the fact I speak Russian, English, and French. I was working at the Seehaus translating foreign radio broadcasts when I was approached."

"How did you learn all those languages?"

"My mother was British and spoke French, so I learned English and French from her. I learned Russian while working at the Seehaus. It seems I have a knack for languages and can pick them up fairly quickly. I know this is very unscientific, but I've always thought my musical background—being able to read music—aids me with languages."

"Interesting. First time I've heard that. So what do your parents think of your move from the Seehaus to Abwehr?"

"My father was not happy when I told him my decision. My mother died last year in America, an auto accident. We lived there for four years. My father served as press secretary to our ambassador in Washington."

"I'm sorry about your mother."

"And your family?" she asked.

"My father was a German hero killed in the Great War. My mother lives in Cologne where I grew up. I have a brother in the Kriegsmarine. Do you have brothers or sisters?"

"No."

The waitress returned with the wine and to take their orders. Erika ordered a Schnitzel, Kai the Rouladen.

"So you are to be one of our Führer's bodyguards," she said as he poured two glasses of the wine.

"Yes. I have actually spoken with the Führer," he said proudly. "He insists on meeting beforehand any man who will undergo training for his personal guard. I met him at the Berghof in Bavaria. Three of us being considered for the Führer's detail were taken there. Our conversation was very brief. He had read the report containing the military service information about my father and told me he fought in some of the same battles. He shook my hand and that was the end of it. The meeting lasted perhaps two minutes."

"That's exciting." Erika didn't tell Kai that her father was a trusted friend of the Führer and that she had visited Adolf Hitler many times, or that she was on friendly terms with Eva Braun. She wondered if Kai knew of Eva. Most Germans had never heard of her, but if he had been to the Berghof perhaps he knew who she was. "Do you know a woman named Eva Braun?"

Kai shook his head. "No. I don't recall the name. Who is she?"

"A friend of mine. Once you are assigned to the Führer I'm sure you'll eventually meet her."

Kai nodded then asked her opinion about a current event much in the news of late. "Do you think the Jews are trying to start a war?"

"I don't know," she answered. "Certainly they are according to the newspapers. My father thinks the Anschluss of Austria last spring will go a long way toward ensuring peace, but he feels problems in Czechoslovakia need to be addressed. Germans living there are treated badly. But Father is confident the Führer will find a solution, and that should end talk of a possible war."

When their dinner arrived, further talk of politics ceased. They ate slowly and spoke of pleasant things. It turned out that Kai could be quite funny and he made Erika laugh several times. By the time the waitress delivered the strudel, they had been at the restaurant well over two hours.

"I know of a beer hall that's on the way back to Quenzsee; it's in Rossdorf. We have the time. Would you like to stop there?"

"I would love that."

After dessert, as Kai paid for their meal, another customer walked up to their table.

"Untersturmführer," the man said. He held an ink pen and piece of paper. "It is an honor. My son recently turned ten years old and is now in the Hitler Youth. Would you mind signing an autograph for him? I know it will thrill him to have the autograph of an SS officer. His name is Stefan."

Kai took the paper and pen, wrote a brief note to the boy and signed it.

"Thank you, Untersturmführer."

"My best wishes to your son," Kai replied.

As the man walked away, Erika teased, "I didn't realize I shared dinner with a movie star." She thought she noticed him blush slightly.

"That is the first time that has happened to me."

"It won't be the last, I'm sure. A suave young officer who will be one of the Führer's personal escorts—you'll have to fend off the Fräuleins with a stick, their hearts aflutter."

"Suave? Now you're making fun of me."

She smiled.

On the way to the tavern in Rossdorf, as twilight waned, Kai pulled over to put down the convertible top. While he worked, Erika walked down to a shallow brook a few yards from the road, removed her shoes and waded in ankle deep. When he finished he walked down to join her.

"You're always in the water," he said from the edge of the stream. "I think you're part mermaid or the Lorelei who bewitches men and lures them to their doom."

"The Lorelei. I like that." She walked out of the water and put her arms around his neck. "Maybe you're right. You might be doomed."

The kiss lasted ten minutes. The forecasted rain never fell and they spent the rest of their time together by the brook, never making it to the beer hall in Rossdorf.

Chapter 67

Christmas with the Führer

1938—Christmas Eve
On the Obersalzberg near Berchtesgaden, Germany

By the third week of October, Erika had successfully completed her initial Abwehr training sessions at Tegel and Quenzsee. As she was being processed out of Quenzsee she was given orders to report to Admiral Wilhelm Canaris in Berlin. At that meeting, Canaris, whom Erika had never met, sized her up and after a long interview told her if she satisfactorily completed a series of test missions he would consider her for operative status within the Abwehr. Before the month was out, she was in Nuremberg on the first of those trial missions.

Now in December, Erika was enjoying a two-week Christmas furlough and had gone home to her father's Berlin apartment to spend Christmas with him. Two days ago, one of Hitler's adjutants called Karl Lehmann at the Propaganda Ministry to extend the Führer's invitation to Christmas on the Obersalzberg. Yesterday afternoon, father and daughter were flown to Munich where they spent the night. It was in Munich that Erika had lived with her parents when she and her mother returned from England in the late-1920s, and yesterday Erika enjoyed a brief reunion with Ilse Dorsch, a childhood friend. Ilse dined with Erika and her father, and later that evening the two women enjoyed a walk through the Christmas markets near the Marienplatz.

This morning an SS sergeant picked up the Lehmanns and drove them to Hitler's mountain retreat near Berchtesgaden. The 100-mile journey from Munich, only a two-hour summer drive, took five hours on snow-packed Alpine roads. When they reached the SS guard shack at the base of the Kehlstein mountain, the guard checked their identification against his list of invited guests. In winter, no automobile could ascend the treacherous, icy mountain road to the newly completed Kehlsteinhaus, a gift from the Party to the Fuhrer for his 50th birthday. Although Hitler's personal residence, the Berghof, sat lower on the mountain than the Kehlsteinhaus where tonight's

Christmas festivities would take place, the entire mountain was considered the Führer's home.

An SS guard escorted Erika and her father to a tank-tracked personnel carrier that would take them to the top. The vehicle had been modified for the Führer's guests with padded seats and an extra door, but it was still a tracked military vehicle and the ride would be interesting, and certainly less than smooth. Many among the Reich elite had already arrived, including Herman Göring and family who arrived yesterday, and early today Joseph and Magda Goebbels with their children. An SS officer accompanied each transport of important guests from the guard shack to the mountaintop chateau, and after the Lehmanns were seated in the snow vehicle, the SS officer who had drawn the duty this time walked out of an adjacent building and got in the front by the driver. The officer was Kai Faust.

Erika had not seen Kai since their dinner in August. He had sent letters, which she answered, although some not always promptly. In September, he had been accepted into Adolf Hitler's personal escort detachment, the SS-Begleitkommando des Führers.

When Faust took his seat, he picked up the clipboard with the names of the special guests: Reichsleiter Karl Lehmann and daughter. He turned to acknowledge and welcome them.

"Welcome to the Obersalzberg, Reichsleiter Lehmann and Fräulein Leh . . ." He stopped mid-sentence when he saw Erika.

"Hello, Kai," she said.

Karl Lehmann looked up from the papers he had started to read—work brought along from Berlin. "You two know each other?"

"We met at Quenzsee," she said.

Karl looked at Faust for a moment over the top of his reading glasses then returned to the papers.

"Hello, Fräulein Lehmann. Welcome to the Führer's home." Faust kept his return greeting formal. Karl Lehmann's title of Reichsleiter demanded respect and formality, especially from an SS officer. *Reichsleiter* was an extremely high rank within the Party, usually reserved only for those who had stayed by the Führer's side during the early, difficult years. When he had read *Karl Lehmann* on the clipboard, the name had not sparked a connection to Erika. *Lehmann* was not an uncommon surname in Germany.

Kai was caught off guard. He knew only the very elite of the Reich would receive an invitation to Christmas with the Führer. Erika had mentioned her father worked for the Ministry of Enlightenment, but so did a thousand others. That her father was a Reichsleiter and apparently either a friend or confidant of the Führer was quite a surprise. He wanted to talk to Erika but knew that holding an informal conversation with a Reichsleiter's daughter in his presence would be bad form and a breach of etiquette coming from a young lieutenant he didn't know. For the rest of the slow, jostling drive up the mountain, Kai sat facing forward and remained silent. When the vehicle finally arrived at the Kehlsteinhaus, Kai and the driver got out and opened doors. Karl Lehmann and his daughter were met by an adjutant and escorted up the steps. The young lieutenant and the driver got back into the personnel carrier and started back down the mountain.

Father and daughter were shown to their rooms, but before Erika had time to hang up her clothes there came a knock on her door.

"Erika! They told me you and your father had arrived." Eva Braun and Erika embraced and kissed cheeks.

Erika first met Eva during the Berlin Olympics in 1936, introduced by Eva's sister Gretl and Eva's best friend, Herta Schneider.

"Look at you!" Eva exclaimed. "How fit you look."

"I've had a lot of exercise lately."

Eva laughed. "I've heard some of the SS guards talk of Quenzsee. Apparently it's tough. How did it go?"

"Oh, it went fine. I met one of the Führer's guards there. He rode up the mountain with us."

"No! What's his name?"

"Kai Faust."

"*Faust.* He sounds deliciously devilish. I don't recall the name, but I would probably recognize him."

"He's an Untersturmführer."

"Ah, an officer. Handsome, I'm sure. Has he taken you to bed?"

Erika laughed. "Eva, you're impossible."

"That doesn't answer my question."

"No," Erika grinned. "We're just friends."

"Oh, I see. Just friends." Eva rolled her eyes. "The last time one of my friends told me that, it turned out she was pregnant at the time and didn't know it."

Erika was not unacquainted with lovemaking. There was the boy in America from her high school years, and the fellow translator at the Seehaus who taught her Russian. Then there was Wera Schwarte's son, Georg, who was now in the Kriegsmarine and currently at submarine school. But she had told Eva the truth about Kai Faust. After their dinner date last summer, they kissed and fondled—nothing more.

Eva continued, "The Beisammensein (social hour) is at seven; dinner at eight. Did you bring a gown? I had various sizes brought in for the ladies just in case."

"I brought one," answered Erika. "Tell me if it's suitable." In addition to a valise, she brought a dress bag. She unzipped it and took out the gown.

"Beautiful," Eva commented on the pale green evening gown. "You'll be the loveliest woman tonight."

"I doubt that," Erika said. Eva Braun was a beauty in her own right.

"Gretl and Wera are in Berchtesgaden shopping but will be back for the evening festivities, of course. I'll leave you for now. Some of the preparations the staff is making I must oversee, and I know you want to spend time with your father. I'm so happy you're here. Give me a kiss, my darling, and I'll see you this evening."

Karl Lehmann stood outside on a terrace missing his wife. Louise Lehmann had died in an automobile accident the year before in Washington, D.C. Not a day had passed since her death that he didn't long for her. The couple met before the Great War when His Majesty George V appointed Louise's father attaché for the British consul in Berlin. Karl was a young German soldier assigned to the British embassy as one of the drivers for the various diplomats and their family members. One day Louise, the beautiful daughter of the British attaché, needed a ride around Berlin. Karl drew the assignment.

"Your mother loved Christmas, Liebchen," he told Erika. "And she loved the mountains and the snow. I think because London sees little snow." The Alpine panorama stretching before them made it seem the entire planet must be white. In the far distance, a few of the highest baroque towers of Salzburg, Austria, could be seen. Below them the Ach River, flowing too fast to freeze, continued its impatient journey to the Danube.

Karl and Louise Lehmann's daughter had proved to be a handful growing up, and the trouble she occasionally caused and the bad decisions she sometimes made had at times set father and daughter in conflict. All the same, Erika had always been a loving daughter, never disrespectful despite her propensity to sometimes yield to her wild side. Since Louise's death, father and daughter had grown closer.

"I can see why Mama enjoyed winter here," Erika responded. "This has to be one of the most beautiful places on earth during Christmastime." Though the temperature was below freezing, father and daughter were not uncomfortable. The wind was slight and both were well bundled.

On her first day of furlough in Berlin, Erika had answered her father's myriad questions about her past months in the Abwehr training program. And although she still had to complete two more practice missions, it looked like she was well on her way to satisfying the stringent requirements for consideration as an Abwehr operative.

Karl left his daydreaming and turned to current family matters. "You know how I feel about your involvement with Abwehr, Liebchen. I expressed my reservations when you came to me about it last spring."

"I know, Father." She put her arms around his waist.

"I'm just relieved there is no war; that is my only consolation."

[that evening]

While the children enjoyed the entertainment of clowns and magicians in another part of the chateau, the adults assembled in the reception area. When Erika entered, the large room already overflowed with the high and mighty of the Third Reich engaged in casual chat, laughing and drinking. Spruce branch swags festooned the walls along with several wreaths. A 12-foot-tall Christmas tree made bright with holly berries and burning candles dominated one corner. Uniformed SS circulated with drink platters, the vivid red and black swastika armbands adding a splash of color to their snow-white tunics.

Erika did not know everyone in this milieu of top Nazis, and she didn't see Hitler or Eva. But she recognized Hermann and Emmy Göring, and Joseph and Magda Goebbels. She spotted Rudolf Hess standing alongside Martin Bormann. Heinrich and Margarete Himmler chatted with Reinhard Heydrich and his wife Lina. Heydrich, a notorious philanderer, had made sexual advances toward Erika and last spring had attempted to recruit her into his SD, the intelligence gathering arm of the SS, but she disappointed him by entering Abwehr training instead. Baldur von Schirach, head of the Hitler Youth, and his wife Henriette stood near the fireplace talking to Heinrich Hoffman, the Führer's photographer. When Erika saw Hoffman, she thought of the story Eva told her of how she met Adolf Hitler.

It was 1929. Eva was 17 years old and worked in Hoffman's Munich photography shop as his assistant and model. One day Hitler walked into the shop to discuss business with Hoffman. Forty-one years old at the time, Hitler took notice of Hoffman's young, pretty assistant and his occasional visits to the shop suddenly became frequent, with Hitler choosing to come there instead of summoning Hoffman to Party headquarters as he could have easily done. Eva told Erika that the future Führer acted shy around her, but that he eventually worked up the nerve to ask her if she would like to take a walk.

"Erika!" The voice jarred her from her thoughts. She turned to see Herta Schneider and Gretl Braun weaving through the crowd. Erika started toward them.

"You look dazzling," Herta said.

Erika embraced and exchanged kisses with both women. "So do both of you. It's so wonderful to see you. Where's Eva?"

"Oh, who knows?" answered Gretl, Eva's sister. "She has to play the hostess. The Führer is in one of his studies talking to some foreign diplomat. Eva's probably stuck entertaining the man's wife. She should be down shortly. But tell us all about what you've been doing. Eva told us you might get on with Canaris' people. Why do you want to do that? Isn't that dangerous?"

"Nothing is definite, Gretl. I haven't completed the program and have been offered nothing. And Father tells me he can arrange for me to back out if I change my mind. We'll have to wait and see."

Herta, Eva's longtime best friend, changed the subject. "Eva told us you have a love interest among the Führer's bodyguards."

"What?" Erika laughed. "I never said that."

"Which one is he? Is he one of the men serving drinks?"

"No. And I told Eva only that I met him last summer. That's all."

Herta and Gretl exchanged grins, and Herta said to Gretl, "But she knew immediately he was not in the room among this crowd." She turned back to Erika. "Okay, Erika, whatever you say."

When an adjutant announced dinner, the crowd moved to the banquet hall. The number of guests demanded two long tables: Hitler sat at the head of one, Deputy Führer Hess at the other. Erika sat next to her father, who, as an old friend of the Führer, was seated at Hitler's table. On Erika's other side was Margarete Himmler with her Reichsführer husband next to her.

Both Karl Lehmann and Heinrich Himmler had been at Adolf Hitler's side since the early days. Both had accompanied Hitler to innumerable beer hall speeches in the early 1920s and both took part in the failed Beer Hall Putsch in 1923. The animosity between the two also went back as far. For whatever reason, the two men hadn't gotten on well since the day they met, and their relationship grew icier over the years. Erika knew her father detested Himmler. He considered the SS chieftain a schemer whose personal ambition overshadowed his devotion to Germany. On Himmler's part, for years he suspected that Karl Lehmann used every opportunity to undermine him with the Führer, and it galled Himmler when at times the Führer listened to

Lehmann's advice over that of higher officials such as himself. So the mutual loathing festered over the years. Himmler had been elated when Lehmann was sent to America in 1933. From there he couldn't bend the Führer's ear, but now he was back. And Lehmann's polyglot daughter turning down a personal invitation from Heydrich to join the SD and then turning right around and joining Abwehr was another slap in the face. Along with Karl Lehmann, Himmler considered Wilhelm Canaris another enemy among a long list of enemies—real or imagined.

But in public, Karl Lehmann and Heinrich Himmler remained professional if circumstances forced interaction. Tonight they simply ignored each another. Erika was glad she and Margarete offered a buffer between them.

Dinner was pleasant, the table conversation relaxed, the roasted goose excellent. Hitler told a story about a Christmas in Austria when he was a boy. Erika had read magazine articles claiming the Führer was a vegetarian, but even though she didn't see him sample the goose, at the end of the meal he voiced his approval of the liver dumpling.

Erika sat too far from Eva Braun to converse during dinner, but after dessert talk and the brandy, Hitler rose (it was bad form for anyone to leave the table while the Führer still sat). When other guests began leaving their chairs, Eva came over to Erika.

"Follow me," Eva said. "I have your Christmas present."

"Tonight?" Erika was surprised. "Christmas is tomorrow."

Eva led Erika up some stairs to the smallest of the chateau's three studies. Eva opened the door and said, "Merry Christmas." Erika waited for her to lead the way, but Eva waved her in. "I'm not going in. You'll see the present just inside."

When Erika stepped in, Eva closed the door behind her. Kai Faust stood in the room looking confused.

"Erika."

"Kai, what are you doing here?" She thought her reaction might seem rude, so she added, "How nice to see you."

"My commander ordered me to report to the chateau on the request of Fräulein Braun, and when I got up here I was shown to this room. I've been here two hours."

A knock sounded and Erika answered the door. A kitchen girl pushed a cart into the room. On it sat a silver bucket containing an iced bottle of champagne, beside it a bowl of caviar and round crackers. An SS waiter followed the girl in and took care of popping the cork. The girl curtsied, the SS man clicked his heels, and they left without speaking.

Kai Faust was a bit overwhelmed.

"Well," Erika said. "Imagine this. Here we are."

Chapter 68

A Knock at the Door

1939—January
Stuttgart, Germany

After successfully completing the Abwehr's long and grueling preliminary training program that had taken her to Tegel and Quenzsee, Erika entered the second phase: training missions where her aptitude would be assessed.

In late October, she was ordered to Nuremberg on the first of these missions. Her assignment: to burglarize the office of a doctor, his name chosen at random from the telephone directory. Erika was expected to accomplish this without leaving any trace of the illegal entry—no broken window glass, no damaged door lock. That night Abwehr supervisors waited in a car down the street for her to return with a sample of the doctor's letterhead to prove her success. Checks with local police were made the next day to ensure Erika's entry had been discreet. If someone from the doctor's office called the police the next morning about an apparent break-in (even if nothing of value were missing) her mission would be judged a failure. No such police report was made.

Erika was now on her second ersatz mission, this one in Stuttgart. Her assignment was to follow a local government official for two weeks and record the man's daily routine (like the doctor, this man was chosen randomly by her Abwehr supervisors). With the assignment almost over, Erika doubted the man's wife knew of the young woman whose apartment he visited twice weekly.

Erika and Kai had not seen each other since Christmas, and then only briefly. They enjoyed their time together in the Kehlsteinhaus study—Erika's gift from Eva—but the rendezvous was painfully brief. After an hour and a half of conversation over the champagne, Kai had to report back to his station. A long good-bye kiss was the extent of their intimacy.

Now, after a four-month tour of duty accompanying Hitler and his entourage, it was Kai's turn for furlough. He spent a day visiting his mother in Cologne then drove to Stuttgart to be with Erika.

"So tell me all about guarding the Führer," Erika said to him. This was their first evening together. Kai had arrived from Cologne too late for dinner, so they talked over coffee in a café. "How many men protect him?"

"There are twenty of us in the core unit always assigned to him," Kai answered. "But of course more men join us if the circumstances warrant, such as a parade or public appearance. Obersturmführer Bruno Gesche is our commander. Do you know him?"

"Yes, I've met Gesche. My father introduced us. I think it was last winter."

"To put it mildly, I was surprised to see you on the Obersalzberg for the Christmas dinner. Why didn't you tell me your father is a Reichsleiter and a friend of the Führer when we were together last summer at Quenzsee?"

"I don't know. It's not a secret. I suppose I didn't think about it at the time."

Kai took a drink of coffee. "How do you like Stuttgart?"

"I like it. I've been here many times. A cousin and his family live here. Unfortunately, I can't visit them. My orders prevent me from contacting anyone I know locally while I'm on these assignments."

"Can you tell me anything about what it is they're having you do?"

Erika thought for a moment and decided she wouldn't be sinning too badly by telling one of the Führer's personal guards about a mere practice exercise. "I've been following a local official for nearly two weeks, recording where he goes and his daily routine. I have two days left."

"I suppose the aim is that he doesn't become aware of being followed?"

"Yes."

"Is it hard to remain undetected?"

"With this man, no. He has no reason to be wary of being followed and that makes all the difference. It's much more challenging to shadow someone who's looking out for it."

"Where do you go after this?"

"Dresden for two weeks. My role will be reversed. My orders will be to walk or ride around that city by taxi at different times of the day and night and elude Abwehr people who will at times follow me. I must spot the tail and elude. The hardest part is I won't be told when I can expect to be followed, and they allow no room for error. If just once I fail to spot a tail and dodge it, I have to start the two weeks over. If I fail a second time, I'm out of the program."

"You trained for all this at Quenzsee?"

"Just in the classroom."

"Interesting. I've never had any of that type of training—to evade people, I mean."

"And why would you need it? You just have to be prepared to shoot them or beat them up, and you'll do that wonderfully," Erika teased and smiled.

"I'm not sure that's a compliment, but if it is, thanks . . . I think."

The café was only a block from her hotel. When it came time to leave he walked her back.

"Where are you staying?" she asked as they passed a clothing store with a large Star of David painted on the window—a legal requirement for any Jewish business owner. Someone had used chalk to write on the door, *Kauft nicht bei Juden (Don't buy from Jews)*. The owner, one of a rapidly dwindling number of Jews still in business after Kristallnacht two months ago, was prohibited by law from removing the graffiti.

"I have a room at the Graf Zeppelin," Kai answered.

"Will I see you tomorrow evening?"

Her question disappointed him. He hoped their evening together would be extended in her hotel room. "Yes. May I take you to dinner? Since you're more acquainted with this city, maybe you can suggest a place."

"There's a very nice restaurant just outside the city that I've been to in the past."

"That's where we'll go."

When they reached her hotel, they ignored the elevator and walked up two flights of stairs. Erika opened her door and turned to kiss him good night. He grabbed her, kissed her passionately, and attempted to guide her inside as they kissed, hoping she'd accept him into her room. She pulled away.

"No. I'll see you tomorrow."

Again Kai drew her to him and kissed her. She returned his affection, but after a few minutes she pushed away.

"Good night, Kai." She smiled and closed the door, leaving him standing in the hall.

Kai Faust returned to his hotel frustrated. His feelings for Erika were strong, and not just in a physical way. There was something very different about her. Maybe it was her confidence, maybe it was the way she delightfully went about teasing him. She was beautiful and talented, but not haughty or self-absorbed. And she was tough and disciplined; he admired that in a woman. Perhaps it was all those things and more. He needed a cold shower and took one. Two hours later he lay awake in bed thinking about Erika when someone knocked. He pulled on a bathrobe and went to the door. In the hall, Erika stood gazing at him like a predator stalking its prey.

Chapter 69

Becoming *Lorelei*

1939—June
Berlin

In the basement of the Schulungszentrum der Heere, an army training facility in Berlin, smoke wafted from the bore of Kai Faust's SS-issued Walther, the clip just emptied into the heart of the silhouette target eight meters away. Erika raised her Beretta and did the same, every bullet an instant kill.

At times Kai marveled at her improvement in the year since Quenzsee. Not only was Erika now his equal on the target range, she had become a handful when, in their free time, he instructed her in hand-to-hand. Faust ranked among the elite close-quarter combatants in the SS and she had improved to the point he had to fight her in earnest. He would always best her, but it now took work. The last-summer Quenzsee days of him toying with her on the mat were over.

Both maintained demanding schedules and their time together since Stuttgart in January had been limited. He would be in whatever city the Führer was in, she usually someplace else on additional training missions or at Quenzsee for advanced training. They stole an infrequent day together when possible, and if providence was kind, a weekend when they would spend their time walking, enjoying a dinner, occasionally training together, and making love.

He had yet to understand her and thought perhaps he never might. At times she seemed to alter herself and become dissimilar Erikas. Like that first night in Stuttgart when she rebuffed him at her door, then appeared at his hotel and shocked him with the intensity and aggression of her lovemaking.

"Is that Beretta an Abwehr-issued handgun?" Kai asked her.

"No. I bought it. I like it better than the Mauser they issue."

"They let you choose which gun you carry?"

"Yes. As long as the gun is easily concealed and I pass the firing tests with it."

"I doubt you'll pass," he teased. "Better practice more often."

She glanced at him, shoved another clip in the Beretta, and unloaded eight rounds into the forehead of his target.

"Oops," she said. "You're right. I must practice more; I missed my target completely."

Kai grinned. "The beautiful Abwehr spy—always proving a point."

Even though Erika had yet to be assigned a real mission, her successful completion of the initial Abwehr training program and an offer of a job from Wilhelm Canaris made her an official member of the Abwehr, her rank Level 1. She had been sworn in after she finished her last practice mission in April.

"What's next for you?" he asked. "Last night you mentioned a furlough. Any plans?"

"I'll be free for two months, from mid-July to mid-September. Maybe I'll spend some time in Paris. After that, I report to Potsdam for communication training."

Kai regretted he would have no free time while she was off. "I'll be on duty during that time."

"That's too bad. Paris in summer is wonderful," she said as she loaded another clip. "I have my codename."

"Oh? What is it?"

"*Lorelei.*"

"That's a fitting one for you. The Rhine River siren that lures men to their doom."

"You suggested it. Don't you remember?"

Kai looked at her.

"Last summer," she continued. "When I was standing in the water of that brook."

Now it came to him. "Yes. I remember. So I'm to credit for your codename. I like that. How did that happen?"

"They assigned me another name, but I requested *Lorelei.* Since no one else had that codename they agreed."

"Will you lure me to my doom, *Lorelei?*"

"We'll wait and see."

Part 5

1944

Walter Schellenberg in a post-war interview,

"The only difficulty with Himmler was that he was of a sneaky nature. I never knew whether I would be promoted or imprisoned the next day."

Chapter 70

Róta

Berlin
Tuesday, 16 May 1944

When Gestapo Kriminalkommissar Kathryn Fischer stepped into her apartment the phone was ringing.

"Hello."

"Is Róta there, please?" a female voice asked.

"I'm sorry," Kathryn said. "You have the wrong number."

"Pease accept my apology."

Kathryn hung up and left her apartment. *Róta* was her Abwehr codename. For security, discussions never took place on her apartment telephone. There were two public telephone booths within two blocks of her flat—in opposite directions. Today was the 16th so Fischer walked to the phone used on even-numbered dates. In five minutes the phone rang.

"This is *Róta.*"

"Did your roses arrive?"

"No. Violets were sent by mistake."

The mutual confirmation was complete.

"Hello, Kati."

"Steph! I knew it was you!"

"Meet me in the Tiergarten in one hour. Wait in front of the zoo's main entrance. I'll use the Schatten protocol. You use the Umleitung protocol."

"Understood," Kathryn said, and hung up. She last saw her sister a year and a half ago, just before Canaris sent Stephanie on her mission as a plant within the SOE. Kathryn started out immediately on a zigzag route to the Tiergarten. Her protocol meant she must use an unpredictable route to the rendezvous point making many detours along the way. Stephanie's protocol would place her at the rendezvous point first, where she would remain hidden until she felt confident no one had followed Kathryn.

The Tiergarten, Berlin's expansive public park, was a 15-minute walk away if Kathryn used a direct route. But because of the protocol she started in the opposite direction and meandered around the city alternating walking with bus-riding. In 55 minutes, she stood in front of the Berlin zoo's main entrance. Two old men sitting on a bench looked at her and rose and walked away. Kathryn was not in uniform; Gestapo rarely wore uniforms in Germany, only in occupied countries. But she knew why the men left. Her black-leather trench coat, issued to all Gestapo officers, had become a symbol of terror. And even though a law-abiding German should in principle have no reason to feel uneasy around any government agent, trifling offenses lacking proof had delivered many good Germans into Gestapo hands. Since Canaris sent her undercover inside the Gestapo nearly two years ago, Kathryn had grown accustomed to being feared by the innocent.

After about 20 minutes, she saw her sister approach. Stephanie wore her Luftwaffe Oberstabsführerin uniform. Both sisters were joyful to see each other but dared not express that joy in public.

"Greetings, Oberstabsführerin," said Kathryn.

"Hello, Kriminalkommissar. I have a car."

They walked two blocks, using their training to make sure they weren't being followed. Often they would abruptly stop and engage in frivolous conversation so one could face backward and observe the path they had just walked. Several times they stopped to look in shop windows—another opportunity to scan the streets around them.

Finally, Stephanie pointed to a black Volkswagen parked at the curb. "Here we are."

They got in and Stephanie started the VW and pulled out into traffic. After a few turns and several glances in the rearview mirror they felt safe and could at last smile.

"Where did you get the car?" Kathryn asked. "Abwehr I assume."

Stephanie nodded. "Untraceable plates."

"When did you get back to Berlin?"

"Just yesterday morning. What really happened to Canaris?" Stephanie asked.

"Himmler finally convinced the Führer the admiral couldn't be trusted. That's all I know. What's going on?"

"I know you've heard of *Lorelei?*"

"Has anyone who went through Quenzsee not heard of *Lorelei?*"

"Her name is Erika Lehmann. The three of us need to meet—you, me, and Erika."

[same time—Kai Faust's apartment]

Kai began the day in France with the two women he rescued from the Gestapo. After the flight to bring them to Berlin, and after learning his wife was in town, he spent the rest of the day looking for her, missing Erika by mere minutes at the SS safehouse. Frustrated, Kai finally returned to his dark Berlin apartment where, after he flipped on a light, he found her sitting on his sofa. She did not give him time to return her *Hello.*

"How is Ada?" Erika asked. They had named their child Adelaide.

"She's healthy and speaking quite well for her age."

Erika nodded sadly. Ada was only a year old when she last saw her. "She just had her third birthday."

"Three days ago," he said. "I missed it searching for her mother. I have a few recent photos—from only a month ago."

"I saw them." Erika had already prowled through the drawers. She rose from the sofa, walked over to Kai, helped him out of his tunic, and began unbuttoning his shirt.

◊ ◊ ◊

Water cascaded down their bodies as they kissed. Before the shower, they made love for three hours. Erika shut off the faucet and led Kai out. She reached for a towel and began drying him.

"I need your help, Kai."

Chapter 71

A Note from Eva

Berlin
Next day; Wednesday, 17 May 1944

After spending the night as husband and wife, Erika left for her hotel and Kai reported to his squadron.

Their marriage had been preceded by a foolish moment of passion on their part when they failed to take precautions and she became pregnant. That happened in the early fall of 1940, not long after her first Abwehr mission in Portugal. The SS encouraged its members to impregnate German women out of wedlock in order to swell the Aryan population, but Himmler's policy dictated that those babies be sent to a Lebensborn, a cluster of SS-run orphanages that reared the children according to Himmler's design of parenting. Refusing to even consider sending her child to one of Himmler's baby mills, yet knowing the war would prevent her from remaining in Germany with her daughter, Erika finally acquiesced to one of Kai's numerous marriage proposals—but only if he agreed to keep the marriage and their daughter secret. They married quietly in Greece in March 1941. During her ninth month, Erika sequestered herself in Switzerland to await the birth. Adelaide Louise Faust was born in Zurich on the 13th of May 1941. Two weeks later, Erika's espionage skills served her well when, posing as a nurse, she entered the hospital's records room and stole her own and the baby's files. No written records of their child's existence remained.

After learning of her father's death and knowing it was murder ordered by Himmler, Erika knew even more certainly that making off with the hospital records had been wise. She would certainly not put it past Himmler to threaten her daughter if he thought it served his purposes.

Erika knew Kai was in love with her. For her part, she cared for Kai very much, and respected him, but didn't think she loved him as a wife should love her husband. Sometimes she felt guilty for that. She had, however, remained faithful to him in her personal life. Her only sexual encounters outside their marriage had been undertaken to further a mission.

Entering the hotel lobby, she stopped first at the desk.

"Good morning. Do I have any messages?" she asked the desk clerk.

"Ah, good morning, Miss Drexler. I will check."

She had registered under the name Anne Drexler. *Annie Drexler* was a friend from her college days in America. Erika dropped the *i* from *Annie,* and Drexler was a good German surname.

"Yes, two messages." He handed them to her.

"Thank you."

The man nodded and wished her a good day. As she walked away, she opened the first message. It was handwritten.

Greetings from Dieter Scherer. I can be reached at 8:00 tonight at Nordpol 8160. Call from your hotel.

Victor Knight—Mr. Thomas—had made it to Berlin.

The second message was from Eva Braun. Yesterday, Erika learned that Adolf Hitler was in Munich. Erika had her reasons for wanting to go to Munich, but she knew Schellenberg would not allow it with all that was going on at the present—not unless the summons came from someone who could not be turned down. So Erika contacted Eva and asked her for a *Führerruft*—an official summons on behalf of the Führer. Eva's message, sent by wire, was typed.

I am so happy! I can't wait to see you. Adolf is also in Munich and he wants to see you as well. If you will report to Bormann at the Reichstag tomorrow morning he will see that you are taken to the airport and have a plane waiting. I will ask one of the Führer's adjutants to meet your plane in Munich. I will see you tomorrow, my darling! Eva

◊ ◊ ◊

[two hours later]

Schellenberg turned to Stephanie Fischer. "Fischer, be with Lehmann when she makes the telephone call. Knight instructed her to call from her hotel. That means the rendezvous point is probably nearby and he will likely give her the minimal amount of time to get there."

Erika, Stephanie, and Major Ulrich von der Osten had assembled in Schellenberg's office after Erika called to let them know about Victor Knight's message. Schellenberg looked at Erika.

"Lehmann, von der Osten will be with you when you make the call. After the call, when you know the rendezvous point, tell him so we can monitor the location."

"The utmost care will be necessary, Oberführer. Knight is very good and will be wary. The SOE has a file and photograph of the major. Knight will recognize him if he sees him."

"I realize that, Sonderführer; so does the major. He will have another agent serve as observer, and Knight will not be followed when the meeting ends. We need only the information about when and where the other agents will arrive."

"I spoke with Kai Faust yesterday and he agreed to help us. He thinks his participation will not be a concern to Skorzeny since we'll be capturing the enemy." Schellenberg had agreed to Erika's request to use Kai, and the SS general had no qualms about using SS for Abwehr missions. Things had indeed changed. Erika knew Canaris would never have allowed it. Maybe this was a change that would work in her favor.

"Who's Kai?" Stephanie asked. No one answered.

"I have something else, Oberführer," Erika stated.

"What is it?"

"The Führer has summoned me to Munich."

"When?"

"Tomorrow."

[8:00 p.m.]

Erika dialed and heard the phone at the other end pick up after one ring.

"Hallo." It was Victor Knight speaking German. It took only the one word for Erika to recognize his Scottish accent poking through, an accent he claimed he didn't have when speaking German.

"Hallo."

"What is the name of the island we spent three days on?"

Erika had to think. "You never told us the name. It was an island in Loch Morar."

"What did you add to our dinner the first night on the island?"

Again, Erika pondered. "Rabbit."

Knight was satisfied. *"Did Fischer make it?"*

"Yes. She's here with me now."

"The Altenkeller beer hall on the Kurfürstendamm three blocks west of your hotel. If you walk quickly you can be there in fifteen minutes. If you are not there twenty minutes from now, I will be gone. Any questions?"

Already he's made a mistake, Erika thought. *A native German would use the shortened Ku'Damm to refer to the boulevard.* "No questions."

Click.

Erika turned to Major von der Osten and the Abwehr agent standing beside him brought along for surveillance. "A café four blocks east on the Ku'Damm," she said. "Major, your man here must use every precaution to remain undetected."

"He will not enter the café," said von der Osten, "only monitor from outside and at a distance."

"Let's go, Stephanie," said Erika. "We have fifteen minutes."

Von der Osten turned to the agent. "Go with them to the lobby, but let them leave on their own. You can proceed to the location five minutes after they have left the hotel. Walk at a normal pace."

"Yes, sir."

A bellman loaded down with luggage waited in the lobby for the elevator door to open. When it did, two women stepped out and walked toward the hotel entrance. Stepping into the elevator while focusing on his burden, the bellman almost tripped over a man lying unconscious on the floor. He dropped the bags and ran for help.

On the street, Erika told Stephanie, "I had no choice. Knight trains agents on ways to spot surveillance. He won't be inside when we arrive. He'll be outside and unseen, looking for someone like that guy."

"As soon as you knocked him out I knew you must have given von der Osten the wrong meeting place, and now I see we're walking in the opposite direction."

"Of course."

"And tomorrow you'll go to Munich and leave me here to listen to Schellenberg's tirade."

Erika smiled. "What are friends for?"

The public area of the Altenkeller was in the building's basement. Erika and Stephanie found a table and sat down to wait. The place was fairly busy; a man stood in a corner playing an accordion; a Beer Fräulein walked up and Erika placed the order.

"Two Berliners and a pack of cigarettes, please." The Beer Fräulein had cigarettes with her, laid a pack on the table, and left to fetch the beers.

"I didn't know you smoked," said Stephanie. "You didn't smoke at the Lili Marlene."

"Thomas smokes. It will relax him if we smoke with him. And it would look odd to offer him a cigarette if I don't smoke." Erika pulled several cigarettes from the pack and disposed of them so the pack looked used. She lit one and pushed the pack and matches across the table to Stephanie.

"I don't remember learning that at Quenzsee," Stephanie said.

"It's merely something I do."

Stephanie lit a cigarette as the waitress delivered the beers. "How long do you think we'll be waiting?"

Erika glanced over Stephanie's shoulder. "He just walked in."

Thomas saw them, took a moment to scan the room, then walked over and sat down. Greetings were bypassed.

"When did you arrive?" asked Stephanie.

"Last night," answered Knight. They spoke German and kept their voices low but did not whisper. Customer banter and the accordion ensured no one would overhear them.

"Did you have any trouble getting to Berlin?"

"Nothing of concern. One tense moment at the Frankfurt train depot. The ticket clerk took a long time looking over my papers, much longer than he had taken with the people in line ahead of me, but he finally waved me through. There was another check on the train, this one by Gestapo, but I think he was in a hurry to finish and get back to the bar in the restaurant car. He didn't look at my papers as thoroughly as the ticket clerk. And you?"

"No problems," Stephanie answered. "Smoke?"

Knight took a cigarette from the pack and saw the waitress approaching. "What beer is that?" he asked the women.

"Berliner," Erika said.

Knight ordered the same. After the waitress walked off he looked at Erika. "I see your jump must have gone well." The last time he saw her was on the plane before she parachuted north of Marseille.

"It went fine," she said. "Why didn't you tell us Admiral Canaris had been replaced? It happened three months ago. I know the SOE had to know."

"Yes, we knew. *Intrepid* decided not to tell you based on the fact that if you were returning in the manner we wanted the Germans to believe—as we set up with Operation Trekker—you would not know about the change until you returned. *Intrepid* felt it important to keep your responses as authentic as possible."

"That was a bad decision. Better to brief us. It would have been disastrous if Schellenberg had somehow learned about Kathryn Fischer before our arrival. All of us would be dead."

"We had no reason to believe Schellenberg knew about Kathryn. And we knew you certainly wouldn't reveal it. And Schellenberg taking over for Canaris works out nicely for us. Schellenberg ranks high on our list of possible targets. We now won't have to spend time hunting him down. We know where he is."

Knight had played roulette with her and Stephanie's lives. Erika dropped it and moved on. "Any news of Maeve and Tars?" she asked. "Did they make it to England?" She played her role. When Erika last saw Knight, the only news of Maeve and Tars she was aware of was the women had hijacked a plane and were attempting to fly to England. Now she wanted to find out what Knight knew.

"Disappointing news there, I'm afraid. Our last report was their plane was shot down. No word since then." Knight was not hiding anything this time; the only information the SOE had on the women's fate was the report by the young American pilot that the Junkers was hit during the dogfight, caught fire, and was seen descending rapidly. Knight assumed the women were dead. "Amanda McBride arrived in France okay, but I have more bad news. Granville is dead. According to the report from the French Resistance on hand to meet him, he was blown into trees. A chute cord became wound around his neck and that was that. We can't let this affect our work; we'll just have to pick up the slack."

"That's unfortunate," Erika commented. She certainly was not going to tell him Tars was in Berlin and could be brought back into the SOE mission picture. "So with the loss of Granville and Tars we're down from the original six to just four if Mayne makes it here. Let's hope he does or we won't have any weapons other than handguns. When will he arrive?" Erika deflected her question about Mayne's arrival, the real subject of her interest, with her false concern about the weapons.

"I sent a message to Amanda McBride this afternoon to relay to Baker Street. John will depart soon."

"Soon?"

"I will meet him and get him and the weapons stowed away in a safe place, then I'll contact you. We'll hold a strategy meeting at that time to discuss how we cover Granville's duties. Stephanie already knows she's taking over for Tars."

"Do you need our help transporting the weapons?" Erika asked.

"No. John and I can handle that. No sense in getting you two involved when it's not necessary."

Erika had to be careful. The easiest capture would be when Mayne parachuted in. But she knew Knight did not trust her totally, and it would draw suspicion if she appeared too eager to be present when Mayne dropped in—his most vulnerable moment. She took a drink of beer and made eye contact with Stephanie. When Knight reached for his cigarette burning in the ash-tray she shook her head ever so slightly to let Stephanie know the subject had to be dropped.

Capturing the two British commandos and getting them into Otto Skorzeny's hands, instead of Schellenberg's, was the only way to save their lives. It would be more difficult, but the capture would now have to wait until Knight summoned them to the meeting with John Mayne.

Chapter 72

Lunch with the Führer

Munich
Next day; Thursday, 18 May 1944

Four men of the Leibstandarte-SS Adolf Hitler were already stationed at the restaurant when Erika arrived. They were members of the Begleitkommando des Führers, Hitler's personal bodyguards and the unit Kai Faust was assigned to until 1943 when Otto Skorzeny received Hitler's permission to recruit Kai into the special commando squadron he was assembling at Hitler's request.

The Osteria, Hitler's favorite restaurant, drew him there often when in Munich. Surprisingly, the restaurant remained open to the public when Hitler dined there. That decision was certainly not the Begleitkommando's. It was well known among the public that the Führer enjoyed the restaurant and in 1938 it had been the venue of a foiled assassination plot by an Englishman working for the Russians. But the Führer declined the SS request that the restaurant close during his visits. He said doing so would look cowardly and supercilious—something de Gaulle or Stalin would do. So the SS built a windowless room inside the restaurant and lined the walls with steel plating.

Erika showed her OKW identification to the SS guard outside the restaurant and informed him of her invitation to lunch with the Führer. The guard had already been informed the Führer expected a guest. He opened the door and another SS man led her to a seat at the Führer's table in a corner of the small, fortified room within the restaurant.

"Thank you," she said. The SS man said nothing and returned to his post near the restaurant's front door.

Erika had arrived from Berlin two hours ago. Driven to the Führer's apartment on Prinzregentenstrasse, she enjoyed a brief reunion with Eva. Hitler was not there, but at work in his office at the Führerbau. Eva told Erika the Führer wanted to talk to her and his only time available that day was at lunch. Eva had another luncheon to attend with the wives of several Party Gauleiters in town for a meeting with Hitler, so she and Eva made plans to meet again later, before Erika's return to Berlin that evening.

Erika could not see out into the restaurant beyond the sealed room but she heard the commotion as Hitler's SS entourage arrived. The door to the Führer's room opened and Adolf Hitler walked in. Two SS bodyguards attempted to follow him in but he ordered them to wait outside the special room. Erika stood.

"Mein Führer."

"Hello, Tschapperl." Hitler had referred to her with that nickname ever since she was a little girl. It was a Viennese diminutive meaning *little thing.* "Please, sit."

The owner of the Osteria, his wife, a teenage boy, and two waiters were escorted in by the SS to take the food orders of the Führer and his guest. The owner beamed—his restaurant was the Führer's favorite and everyone in Munich knew it.

"Mein Führer," the owner said too loudly. "It is wonderful to see you again."

Hitler stood because of the man's wife. "Thank you, Herr Hahn." Hitler took the woman's hand and bowed slightly, a formal German greeting from a man to a woman. "Frau Hahn, so nice to see you."

Erika thought the woman might faint.

"Mein Führer," said Herr Hahn. "May I introduce our nephew, Harald, my brother's son from Düsseldorf. He leaves for Heer infantry training in two weeks and came to visit us before he leaves. When we found out you were coming today he begged to meet you."

Hitler shook the boy's hand, wished him well, and sat down. "I'm sure you remember Karl Lehmann, Herr Hahn. He and I ate here on several occasions."

"Of course, mein Führer."

"This is his daughter, Erika."

Hitler let Hahn and his wife make a fuss over meeting Erika for a minute until he decided it was time to move on. "What would you like, Tschapperl?" When the Führer dined at the Osteria, menus lay unopened. Whatever the Führer or his guests desired would be attended to, even if it meant the restaurant staff had to rush out to find something necessary to the meal.

"Something with fish, Herr Hahn," Erika said. Because of wartime food shortages, fish was much more readily available than beef or pork, so she took mercy on the owner, not wanting to cause him embarrassment in front of Hitler by ordering something he might not have available.

"We have two wonderful fish dishes today, Fräulein Lehmann. A braised tuna over pasta and a sea bream sautéed in wine and herbs."

"Sea bream, thank you."

Hitler's favorite food was pasta and the key reason he frequented the Osteria. The head chef was Italian and pasta dishes the restaurant's specialty. Hitler ordered baked rigatoni in a meatless marinara. Unlike Erika, his not ordering meat had nothing to do with courtesy on Hitler's part; he seldom ate meat.

Herr Hahn knew Hitler was a teetotaler but didn't mind if those around him partook, so he suggested a glass of Riesling with Erika's fish. She nodded. Hitler told them that would be all for now—a clear signal for everyone to depart. The owner and his wife walked out immensely relieved that the food orders would not be a problem. The waiters hadn't said a peep. The SS closed the door.

"You must know by now about your father, Tschapperl," Hitler said. "You have now lost both your father and mother." He seemed sincerely sorry.

"Yes, mein Führer."

"Someone in my position has few he can consider true friends, but Karl was a true friend. I owe many debts to your father. How can I help you? Don't be hesitant. Would you like some time off from your duties?" Hitler asked.

"Yes, I think I would, mein Führer. Perhaps not right away, but a furlough would be welcome." Erika's desire for time off wasn't fueled by a want for holiday. It would be time used to hunt her father's killers.

"I've read the report from Schellenberg about how you escaped from the Engländer. Very clever, Tschapperl. These men are the ones who captured you?"

"I fell into American hands first then was turned over to the British."

Hitler nodded. "I'll inform Schellenberg that you are to receive as much time off as you wish at the time of your choosing."

"Thank you, mein Führer. Oberführer Schellenberg briefed me about my father's accident . . . a boating accident I was told."

"Yes. I ordered Himmler to conduct a full inquiry."

Erika looked into Hitler's fluorescent blue eyes and believed he didn't know the truth. It was as she expected. Himmler would not be breathing if Hitler knew he had ordered her father's murder. To eliminate a Reichsleiter, especially one who was a trusted friend of the Führer, Himmler would need unquestionable proof of betrayal and Hitler's approval. He had neither in this case.

"Your father received a state funeral, of course," Hitler assured, "with full military honors."

Erika nodded as the room door opened. The two silent waiters walked in with the meals. Herr Hahn knew to deliver the food quickly to the ever busy Führer. Hahn stood behind the waiters watching, ensuring they did everything perfectly.

"Anything else, mein Führer?" Hahn asked. "Shall I post a waiter here to handle any needs?"

"No. That will be all."

Hahn snapped his fingers at the waiters and followed them out.

At one time during her capture and time at Camp X, Erika had considered telling Hitler everything when she returned to Germany: how Himmler sent an assassin to America to murder her and how he failed at that only to succeed in disrupting a mission important to Germany. And she wanted to tell Hitler her father's death was not an accident, but ordered by Himmler. But one didn't go to Hitler without proof, and she had none. Axel Ryker, the hitman sent to America, was dead and his body never recovered as far as Erika knew. Himmler could easily cover up Ryker's involvement by manipulating a few records if any existed at all, and there would surely be no SS records of a plot against her father. Himmler was no fool. If she went to Hitler, it would be her word against Himmler's with nothing more she could offer.

"Fräulein Braun I'm sure was very glad to see you," said Hitler as he gazed at the food in front of him. They had yet to take a bite and Erika realized he waited for her, another old German custom when a man ate with a woman. Hitler esteemed the old customs and thought it important to German life that they be maintained.

"And I was very glad to see her, mein Führer. We spent only a few minutes together this morning; my plane didn't arrive until ten o'clock. But we have plans to see each other this afternoon." She cut into her fish and took a bite.

Adolf Hitler picked up his fork.

[one and a half hours later]
The taxi dropped Erika in front of a house on Peter Vischerstrasse in the Pasing district of Munich. Her knock was answered promptly; Ilse Dorsch expected her.

"Erika!"

"Hello, Ilse." Friends since childhood, the women embraced and kissed. "How have you been?"

"As good as can be expected with this war. We've had no bombing since February, but everyone says it's just a matter of time before more American bombers darken the sky. I was surprised but happy to get your call yesterday. Things are well with you?"

"Fine."

"She's in the living room."

Erika followed Ilse to the living room where a blonde, three-year-old girl sat playing with a baby doll. The child looked up when the women entered.

"Look, Mutti," the child said to Ilse, holding up the doll.

"I'm sorry, Erika. She thinks I'm her mother."

"I understand, Ilse," Erika said forlornly. "What else could she think?" Her daughter was one year old the last time Erika saw her. Even though Kai visited the child when possible, Ilse was unaware the two were married. And she knew nothing about Erika's involvement with Abwehr. Ilse believed Erika was an OKW secretary assigned to various foreign embassies and that, along with the war, kept her out of the country for extended periods. Erika walked over to the child and knelt beside her. "Hello, Ada. Is that your baby?"

The child looked at the stranger and held up the doll to show her.

"May I hold you?" Erika reached out her arms. The child hesitated for a moment then reached out. Erika gathered her into her arms, kissed her cheek, and hugged her as if she hoped to never let go.

[same time—Berlin]
Maeve and Tars sat on a couch in the Abwehr safehouse where Erika deposited them two days ago. They hadn't seen Erika since. A safehouse guard had brought them into the living room and ordered them to wait on the couch, but he hadn't told them why.

Maeve looked at Tars who stared blankly at the ceiling. During the travels and trials of Operation Trekker, Tars had held herself together mentally, not revealing the lapses from reality that had at times surfaced at Camp X. But after they arrived in Berlin, Tars started acting peculiar again. Yesterday, she asked one of the guards if the potato on her plate was born in Madagascar. Maeve wondered if perhaps this was just the way it was with Tars: A mission was her only reality.

A bell rang and a guard answered the door. A woman stepped in, showed the guard her identification then walked over to Maeve and Tars.

"I remember you," Maeve said. "You were with Erika when she brought us here."

"Let's go," said Stephanie Fischer.

(With Erika out of town, Stephanie had endured alone Schellenberg's wrath over Erika's attack on the surveillance operative the previous night. Stephanie again covered for Erika by telling Schellenberg Erika knocked out the agent because she felt Knight was too skilled to not spot the surveillance. After haranguing Stephanie for half an hour he ordered her to fetch Maeve and Tars from the Abwehr safehouse and bring them to his office.)

"Where are you taking us?" Maeve asked. "Where's Erika?"

Stephanie didn't answer. A guard handcuffed Maeve's hands behind her back. When he attempted to do the same to Tars, she broke away, grabbed a lamp from a nearby table and tried to brain him with it. Stephanie punched Tars in the face and sent her sprawling, the lamp crashing to the floor. After Tars was handcuffed, Stephanie placed hoods over both women's heads.

Thirty minutes later, the hoods were jerked roughly off their heads and Maeve and Tars found themselves sitting in a large office across the desk from a dark-haired man. On one wall hung a large map; on a table beneath the map sat a model ship and a small statue of three monkeys. Both women were still cuffed. Stephanie Fischer and a guard stood nearby. The dark-haired man kept staring at Maeve. Her resemblance to Erika amazed him.

The women had undergone only preliminary questioning at the safehouse. Schellenberg had them brought to headquarters where they would now undergo a thorough grilling that might take days. Before he turned them over to his Abwehr interrogators he wanted a look at them.

"So you're the Irish prostitute," Schellenberg said to Maeve. Stephanie translated. Maeve did not answer and Schellenberg seemed unconcerned about a response. He looked at Tars. "You're the assassin from Calabria. We've put together quite a file on you." Again Stephanie repeated his words in English.

Tars had been staring at the monkeys.

"Those monkeys don't have dicks," she said to Schellenberg. After the translation, Schellenberg stared at Tars for a moment. The Abwehr report from Calabria stated that some locals who personally knew the Mafia killer talked of mental unsteadiness.

"Maybe they're female monkeys," he replied, then waited for Stephanie.

Tars laughed and shook her head. "No tits, dumb-ass."

Stephanie translated precisely.

Chapter 73

The Cabin

A forest outside Falkensee, Germany
Next day; Friday, 19 May 1944

Just west of Berlin, near Falkensee, a secluded cabin sat hidden in the forest. Karl Lehmann had purchased the property shortly after he brought his daughter back to Germany. It allowed him an occasional escape from the frantic pace of the city and the pressures of work. Fishing in a nearby small lake relaxed him.

At noon, Erika and Stephanie and Kathryn Fischer sat in the cabin's only room. In a corner stood a bunk bed, in another a pot-bellied stove; a small table and the wooden chairs the women sat on completed the spartan furnishings.

"I'm glad we can meet like this during the day," said Erika. "This place is almost impossible to find after dark. Kathryn, I'm glad you didn't have trouble getting away from Prinz Albrechtstrasse." Kathryn was a couple of inches shorter than her sister, but Erika could see the family resemblance.

"During the day I often come and go on investigations," Kathryn replied. "No one will wonder about my whereabouts."

Stephanie said, "Kathryn and I decided we will listen to what you have to say, Erika. We have our reasons for hating the Gestapo as you do. But the plan has to be sound—neither one of us wants to sacrifice our lives needlessly by jumping in with a strategy doomed to fail and accomplish nothing. That's why we're here today—to talk about a plan—to listen to you and offer suggestions of our own. We promise nothing other than that we will not betray you. If what we hear today does not satisfy us, we will keep your secret and this meeting never happened."

"That's very fair," Erika responded.

"Of course," Stephanie went on, "if we could prove either that Himmler sent an agent to America to kill you or that he was involved

363

in your father's death, you could go to the Führer." She turned to her sister, "Kati?"

Kathryn responded, "Eliminating an Abwehr operative without solid proof of treason, and then to go even further and eliminate the agent's father—a Reichsleiter and the Führer's trusted friend and advisor—would be suicide for Himmler. He's too canny to leave a paper trail on something like this. There will be no records; I guarantee you that."

"So we have no hope of proving any of this to the Führer?" Stephanie assumed.

Kathryn thought for a moment. "Not directly with written records referencing the plots. None of those will exist. But we could perhaps put together circumstantial evidence concerning the plot against her father. A scheme against someone like Karl Lehmann would have to be meticulously planned. It would be imperative to know Reichsleiter Lehmann's movements and routines. In the Enemies Section, I have access to all logs. Erika, if I know exact dates and locations of your father's travels and stays in the days leading up to his *accident* I might be able to piece together a list of any Gestapo personnel who were tracking him."

"Circumstantial evidence won't be enough to take to the Führer," Erika decided quickly, but it would be enough for her. "If you can put together a list of those names, Kathryn, that's the first step. But let's take one mission at a time, shall we? First comes the SOE capture mission. Stephanie and I have no choice but to be a part of it, but we must not let Knight and Mayne fall into Gestapo hands. We wouldn't need to worry about that if Admiral Canaris still ran things— he'd never turn Abwehr captives over to the Gestapo, but Schellenberg will. As I already discussed with Stephanie, even the toughest of men can crack under Gestapo interrogation. If they crack, the Gestapo will know why I returned to Germany, and they'll find out about you, Kathryn, and that you and Stephanie are sisters. All three of us will be arrested. We have to make sure Knight and Mayne end up in a Luft-Stalag as prisoners of war to save their lives as well as to protect our covers. Let's talk about that first."

[four hours later—Berlin]

Walter Schellenberg was out of his office when Erika and Stephanie returned from their secret meeting with Kathryn. Since Wera Schwarte expected him back that afternoon, the women waited. Finally, at 4:30, Wera stepped across the hall to the waiting room and told them Schellenberg had returned.

"So. What business is at hand today?" Schellenberg asked after the women sat down. "Have you heard from Victor Knight?"

"Not yet," Erika answered. "But we think we have the best plan to capture him and his partner alive so you can interrogate them."

"And that is?"

"We need to split them up. The best chance of doing that is if they both think they will be meeting me. We need your permission to use Maeve O'Rourke and Tarsitano. John Mayne, the SOE agent Knight is waiting for, has never met Maeve. She fooled your man in Haiti into believing she was me for two days and I feel certain she can fool Mayne for a few minutes—that's all we need."

"A bizarre request, Sonderführer. Asking me to trust two enemy agents to help capture the men who trained and sent them here."

"Mayne didn't train either one; he was stationed at the SOE training camp in Scotland while Maeve and Tarsitano trained in Canada. Again, he's never met them. And neither woman feels any particular bond with the English. Maeve despises them—I'm sure your investigators have uncovered her IRA ties. She agreed to be part of the SOE mission only because of a deal offered her concerning her family."

"What does von der Osten think of this?"

Stephanie answered. "We haven't spoken to the major about this yet. Erika and I first discussed this idea at lunch this afternoon. I trained for several months with those men, Oberführer. They are formidable and they have worked together for years. I agree with Erika. If you want them taken alive we need to separate them."

Erika summarized the plan: "Stephanie, Maeve, and Kai will take charge of capturing Mayne. Kai speaks English—not without a German accent, but Maeve can tell Mayne that Kai belongs to a Nazi resistance group. Stephanie will assure Mayne he can be trusted. I'll take

Tarsitano with me to capture Knight. He thinks she died when the Junkers went down, but when he learns she survived and made it to Berlin he'll be glad she can resume her duties in the SOE mission."

"I think your Mr. Mayne will be exceedingly suspicious of a new German face suddenly added to the mix." Schellenberg said, referring to Kai Faust.

"Maeve, who Mayne will believe is me, will tell him Kai is her old flame. They can pull it off, and they have to sell it for only a few minutes—until Mayne drops his guard."

"I'll consider it and let you know," Schellenberg replied. "To allow the Irishwoman's participation, that is."

"And Tarsitano?"

"Impossible. I told you our people in Calabria sent an extensive report on Tarsitano. You were never made aware the woman is a Jew?" Schellenberg sneered.

Erika hesitated. "No."

"She's already on her way to Dachau." He grinned and added, "Good-bye, Jew."

Chapter 74

New Assignment for Gerber

Berlin
Same day; Friday, 19 May 1944

"It took me a long time to locate her file because I didn't have a complete name," said Kathryn Fischer. Maeve was not the only one who did not know Tars' first name; it seemed no one did, including Erika. "Yes, your comrade is Jewish. She left Berlin about four hours ago and is being taken to the camp at Dachau, not far from Munich. It's about a seven-hour drive in a military truck." Now early evening, Kathryn stood talking to Erika and Stephanie outside a Berlin tram station where a hasty meeting had been called. Stephanie contacted her sister for information after they learned Tars had been taken away by the Gestapo.

"So she's being taken by truck, not train?" Erika asked.

"Yes, in a truck along with a few dissidents who have been held at Prinz Albrechtstrasse for several days," Kathryn responded. "There aren't enough Jews left in Berlin to warrant using trains to transport them. Most of the Jew relocation trains are now in the east transporting Hungarian Jews to camps in Poland."

"Is there any truth to British propaganda about mass killings, Kathryn?" her sister asked.

"I would say *no.* It would be insane, even for Himmler. All information concerning those camps is handled by an Obersturmbannführer named Eichmann, and the only records he puts on file are the transportation logs, work orders, and lawful executions. I've heard rumors of many dying in the camps in Poland but the deaths are attributed to diseases that can sweep through a camp. As far as records I've seen personally, the only executions are those permitted under the Geneva Convention: spies, saboteurs, and traitors."

"Hopefully they won't find out about Tars' role in the SOE assassination plot," said Erika. "Right now, Schellenberg thinks she was merely an escort for Maeve who had no plans to enter Germany."

"I wonder if Mr. Thomas—Knight—knew Tars is a Jew," remarked Stephanie.

"I don't know," Erika rejoined. "But it would not have made any difference. Knight thought he was sending a Jew back to Germany when he sent you, Stephanie."

Stephanie addressed her sister. "Why Dachau? There are camps closer to Berlin."

"Dachau is where most dissidents and political prisoners start out," Kathryn responded. "Sometimes they later transfer women political prisoners to Ravensbrück, an all-female camp. But since your Tarsitano is a foreigner they regard her as a foreign enemy, not just as a Jew. So Dachau sounds typical."

[same time—SS/Gestapo Headquarters, 8 Prinz Albrechtstrasse]

"I don't believe this, Schellenberg!" Heinrich Himmler ranted from behind his desk. "Lehmann arrived in Berlin Sunday and I just find out this afternoon? How can that happen?"

"I don't know, Reichsführer," Schellenberg answered. "I sent the reports through normal channels. In this case they went to the Enemies Section." Schellenberg had no idea why Himmler was so interested in Erika Lehmann. "Had I been aware her arrival in Berlin was of particular interest to you, I would have contacted you personally, I assure you."

Himmler fumed. No one knew about his plots against the Lehmanns other than Heinrich Müller and the killers. He realized Schellenberg had no reason to think the Abwehr's *Lorelei* was of special interest to him and he wanted to keep it that way. Still he was livid that the report took five days to reach his desk.

"This is unacceptable, Schellenberg," Himmler growled. "Five days for a report to go a few blocks? Ridiculous!"

"I agree, Reichsführer. I'll make inquiries at Abwehr. If the delay was caused at our end I will address the problem immediately."

"Where is she now?"

"Lehmann?"

"No. Your grandmother. Yes, Lehmann, the person we've been discussing, goddammit!"

"She was in my office this afternoon. We spoke of the planned capture of two SOE agents."

"Fill me in on that."

Schellenberg spent a few minutes briefing Himmler on the planned capture, including Erika's request to use her double. When he finished, Himmler sat thinking.

"Call Lehmann into your office first thing tomorrow," Himmler instructed. "Agree to her request to use the double, but leave my name out of it. Do not mention me to Lehmann at all, nor this conversation. Is that clear?"

"Yes, Reichsführer."

"Then tell her you will assign a man to her capture team."

"A man? Who?"

"His name is Conrad Gerber—I doubt you know him. He's Gestapo and works mostly on special projects. He'll keep an eye on Lehmann for us."

"Very well, Reichsführer."

"Again, don't mention my name, Schellenberg. All this is your idea as far as Lehmann is to know."

After Schellenberg departed, Himmler ordered Conrad Gerber brought up from the bowels of the building where he had been held and interrogated for the past three days. When the guards deposited Gerber in the chair across from Himmler, he looked disheveled and exhausted. Himmler ordered the guards out.

"Gerber, your interrogation is over. I have an assignment for you."

Gerber perked up. "Thank you, Reichsführer Himmler."

"I'll give you an assignment you can handle this time, Gerber. It's quite obvious you can't find anyone—you proved that in Spain. But apparently you can eliminate them; you handled that satisfactorily with *Lorelei's* father so we'll keep you in your area of expertise. I found

369

Lorelei for you, so all you have to do is cancel her. Do you think you can accomplish that, Gerber? . . . you idiot."

"Yes, Reichsführer."

"Walter Schellenberg will assign you to an Abwehr team as an extra hand on an upcoming capture mission. *Lorelei* is in charge of the team. Her double, the woman who made an ass out of you in Spain will also be on the team. Do you think the double will recognize you?"

"No, sir. She saw me only from the airplane as it quickly flew by. The plane was at least a hundred feet in the air and I was wearing a hat. No. I'm confident neither the double nor her accomplice will recognize me. "

"There is only the blonde woman—the double, Gerber. Her accomplice is a Jew who is now on her way to Dachau."

"A Jew?" Gerber was aghast.

"That's right, Gerber. And by the way, the double is an Irish prostitute. You were outwitted by a Jew and a whore. Makes you feel proud, I'm sure."

Gerber looked as if he would vomit. "A Jew!"

"Pay close attention, Gerber. You have the same mission as in Spain: cancel *Lorelei.* You have an opportunity here to redeem yourself. It should not be hard to make it look like she was killed by the British agents targeted for capture. This is a perfect opportunity Gerber. You can't ask for better scapegoats than the British agents."

Gerber sprang to his feet. "I will not fail, Reichsführer!"

"Do not discuss your orders from me with Schellenberg or anyone at Abwehr. I told Schellenberg I want you along to keep an eye on *Lorelei,* nothing more. Now, Gruppenführer Müller expects you in his office where he'll brief you further. Dismissed."

"Thank you, sir!"

Himmler watched Gerber walk out. He doubted Gerber would pull it off. Lehmann would most likely kill Gerber the instant he tipped his hand. And that would be fine. Nothing ventured, nothing gained. Gerber deserved to die because of his bungling, but if by some stroke of luck Gerber succeeded the Lehmann problem was solved, and Gerber could always be eliminated later.

Chapter 75

New Team Member

Berlin
Next day; Saturday, 20 May 1944

Erika and Kai had just finished breakfast and were leaving her hotel for another meeting with Walter Schellenberg.

She had heard nothing from Victor Knight since the beer hall meeting Wednesday. Thursday saw her in Munich. Friday had been taken up with an early morning meeting at Abwehr headquarters with Ulrich von der Osten, followed by the clandestine midday rendezvous at the cabin with the Fischer sisters, and after that the late-afternoon meeting in Schellenberg's office where she learned about Tars. A second secret summit with the Fischer sisters at the tram station capped off the long day of meetings.

When Erika finally returned to her hotel last night, a message from Abwehr waited for her at the desk, ordering her to report to Schellenberg at eight o'clock this morning. As she and Kai walked through the lobby she stopped at the desk. There was a message from Dieter Scherer.

"It's from the SOE mission chief," she told Kai as she read the brief message. "He wants to make contact this afternoon."

Forty minutes later, Wera Schwarte escorted Erika and Kai into Schellenberg's office. Kai had not received the order to report, but since he was approved to serve on the capture team Schellenberg gave Wera instructions to send him in also. When they entered, Erika saw Ulrich von der Osten standing as he always preferred to do, and a slightly-overweight man with a round face and broad, sweaty forehead who looked as if he hadn't slept in days sitting across from Schellenberg. Erika did not recognize him. Less than a minute later, Stephanie Fischer entered.

371

"Good," said Schellenberg. "We are all here. First, let me introduce everyone to Kriminalsekretär Conrad Gerber of the Gestapo. He has been briefed and he knows who all of you are so we can skip further formalities. The Kriminalsekretär will aid you with the capture mission. As you know, the Gestapo controls vast resources, and if any of those resources can be of benefit to the mission, Kriminalsekretär Gerber will provide them. I want the Kriminalsekretär included in all planning sessions and he is to be on hand when the capture goes down. Any questions?"

No one spoke. Schellenberg directed his attention to Erika. "Now, regarding your request to use the Irishwoman in the mission: I'm open to anything that might facilitate capturing the men alive. That is a priority. There will be much they can tell us. As you suggested, the woman's remarkable resemblance to you might help in separating the SOE agents. Therefore, I have decided to grant that request. It will be your responsibility to ensure her cooperation and make sure she doesn't escape. If she were to escape, I'll hold you accountable, Lehmann. Do I make myself clear?"

Erika glared at Schellenberg.

"I repeat: do I make myself clear?"

"Yes, you are clear," Erika finally answered begrudgingly. She was already fuming that the Gestapo was being included, and the uncalled-for threat about Maeve set her off. "I find it hard to believe you feel an amateur could possibly escape us. She has no money or resources, and other than a few words and phrases she doesn't speak German. If she ran off, she wouldn't remain at large for more than a few hours. If you have someone else you feel is better qualified to handle this assignment, I suggest you use him."

(Gerber couldn't believe what he was hearing—*a subordinate castigate a superior in the Third Reich!*)

"Sonderführer, you very well know there is no one else we can use," Schellenberg snapped back. "You are Victor Knight's contact. It was not my objective to insult you, Sonderführer, but neither do I intend to allow your insolence. Make no mistake: You will pay the price if the Irishwoman escapes or somehow sabotages this mission. Now if there is nothing else, I have work to do. You might find this hard to believe, but the Abwehr has responsibilities other than catering to the famous *Lorelei.* Continue your strategy meetings with Major von der Osten and be sure to notify Kriminalsekretär Gerber of those meetings so he can attend."

Erika wasn't finished. "If I'm answerable for Maeve O'Rourke, I want custody and control. I decide where she stays."

"I've already instructed Frau Schwarte to prepare the paperwork to place her in your charge. I don't give a damn where she stays. That's your predicament." Schellenberg knew he was off the hook; his orders to grant her request concerning O'Rourke came from Himmler. Himmler could blame no one but himself if things went badly. "Last thing, Major von der Osten informed me before you arrived this morning that your next strategy meeting with him will occur after Victor Knight has contacted you. Have you heard anything from Knight?"

Erika had received the message from Knight on her way out of the hotel that morning.

"No," she answered. "Nothing yet."

Kai volunteered to drive Erika and Stephanie to pick up Maeve, but before they got into his car he pulled Erika aside.

"I need to talk to you privately," he said.

Stephanie overheard. "I'll get in."

When Stephanie was inside the car, Kai spoke to Erika on the street. "When I was searching for you in France, I questioned the pilots of the airplane the women hijacked. They were not military pilots, merely civilians hired by the Gestapo. When I asked them who was in charge, they told me a Gestapo Kriminalsekretär named Conrad Gerber."

Normally a professional skilled at hiding her reactions, Erika paled.

Kai continued, "And why didn't you tell Schellenberg you received contact from the SOE agent this morning? I need answers, Erika. I can't protect you if I don't know whom I'm protecting you from."

She wasn't prepared to tell him the whole truth about her father's death and her motive in returning to Germany. "I'm just annoyed at how things have changed. Now we have the Gestapo looking over our shoulder. That's why I lied to Schellenberg. Wera is right, things have certainly changed for the worse since Canaris was removed."

The Abwehr safehouse holding Maeve was a block off the Unter den Linden not far from the Brandenburg Gate. At Erika's request, Kai waited outside while she and Stephanie fetched Maeve.

Erika showed her identification and the release papers to the guard who answered the door. Wera had called ahead and Erika and Stephanie were expected.

"This way," the guard said and led them back.

"Is she ready?" Erika asked him.

"She's dressed for the day, but we don't tell detainees anything about their status. She does not know she's being released. She has a few injuries. When the Gestapo picked up the Jew yesterday, there was a struggle and she had to be subdued."

When he unlocked and opened the door, Maeve was sitting on the floor by the bed. Erika saw a cut across Maeve's nose and a bruise on her forehead. When Maeve saw Erika and Stephanie she jumped to her feet.

"Erika! They took Tars! Three men came and kicked her and beat her horribly and took her away. We have to find her!" she shouted with the guard standing at the door.

"It's too late for Tars, Maeve. She's a Jew. Forget about her." Even though Erika spoke English, she carefully constructed her response to Maeve on the off chance the guard understood the language.

"*What?* You're crazy!!!" Maeve went into a rage, picked up a chair and started swinging it, not caring who she hit. Erika reacted quickly before the guard could step in. She separated Maeve from the chair and took her to the floor.

"We'll handle this," Stephanie told the guard. "She's no longer your responsibility. That will be all, thank you." Stephanie guided the man out and closed the door behind him.

"Keep your mouth shut, Maeve," Erika whispered sternly. "You can't blurt things out; you never know who might understand English. We're going to try and save Tars if she's still alive, but don't say anything about her around anyone unless I tell you in advance they can be trusted. And say nothing about her to the man who will be driving us. You've met him—the SS captain who saved you and Tars in France."

"Your husband?" Maeve said quietly.

Erika frowned and looked back at Stephanie, who apparently didn't overhear. "How do you know that?"

"He told me."

"Keep your mouth shut about that, too. Understand?"

Maeve nodded. "How are we going to save Tars? And what do you mean, 'if she's still alive'?"

"Keep your voice down, dammit. We'll talk about that later. Just go along with everything I say and do when others are around. Got it?" Maeve nodded again. Erika pulled her to her feet. "Now grab your things . . . quickly."

"I have no things. They took my bag."

"Doesn't matter. You're staying with me. I'll get you what you need. The guard said you had injuries. Anything other than what I see on your face?"

"My shoulder hurts. The bastards twisted my arm till I thought it would snap off, but I'm okay. I didn't even holler this time when they did it. Fook them, the fookin' wankers."

"Alright, alright. Let's get out of here."

Chapter 76

Maeve's Advice for the Prime Minister

Berlin
Same day; Saturday, 20 May 1944

Stephanie, Kathryn, and Maeve sat quietly in Erika's hotel suite living room while Erika spoke on the bedroom telephone to Victor Knight. Once again, the message left at the hotel desk provided Erika a number and time to call, nothing more. Kai was not at the hotel—too risky in case Knight was watching. Erika hung up and joined the others.

"Where do we meet him?" Stephanie asked in English. Both Fischer sisters spoke English and they all agreed to use that language for Maeve's sake when no one else could possibly overhear.

"In ten minutes we're to start walking west on the Ku'Damm and keep walking. I told him Kathryn and *Trekker* are here with me."

"He might have been surprised that Stephanie and I have already contacted each other," Kathryn noted.

"He didn't comment, of course—not over a hotel phone with a switchboard operator. But since you're part of his mission plans I doubt he was overly surprised. But there was a definite pause when I said *Trekker*." Erika couldn't help but grin. "I know that had to be a stunner. He wants all of us to meet with him."

Maeve was totally in the dark and piped up. "Who were you talking to?"

"Victor Knight," Erika answered.

"Who's that?"

Erika remembered that Maeve did not know Knight's real name and knew nothing about this phase of the original mission. "Mister Thomas. His real name is Victor Knight."

"Mister Thomas? What's that wanker doing here?"

"It's a long story and not important right now," said Erika. "Stephanie or I will fill you in later."

"I'm not working with that horse's arse any longer! I did what I agreed to do to help me family! By God I did a lot more than I agreed to: Tars and I had our teats in a wringer four or five times along the way—stuff happened that Thomas sure as shite never talked about or prepared us for. He should be in England keeping up his end and having Da let out of that prison and the charges against me brother dropped!"

"Calm down, Maeve."

"I don't want to calm down, Erika. Did you tell him about Tars? The only way I'll work with Thomas is if he helps us save Tars."

"No, Maeve. I didn't tell him about Tars. Not on the telephone. I told you we will try to save Tars. You need to calm down and listen. First, if you ever have to speak on a telephone, be very careful about what you say especially if it goes through a switchboard. And when we're in public don't speak at all if anyone can possibly overhear you. Even if they don't understand English, a German is going to be alarmed to hear someone speak it. If they're a good citizen they will consider it their duty to alert the authorities, which will be the Kripo—the civilian police—or the Gestapo."

Erika turned to Stephanie and Kathryn. "About Maeve and Tars, we'll tell Knight the truth—that they survived the plane crash, were picked up and brought to Berlin where the Gestapo found out Tars is a Jew and took her away. But for now we don't mention Kai Faust. Are we agreed?"

Everyone nodded.

"We better get moving."

Erika found herself in a quandary regarding her husband. The truth was she simply did not know the man very well. Other than a brief few days together after their hasty and secret wedding, the war had kept them from living as husband and wife. Kai wasn't even around for the birth of their daughter. During the weeks Erika stayed in Switzerland awaiting Ada's arrival, Kai tried to arrange time off but in the end was able to visit her just twice, and one of those visits was for three hours. Only once could he spend the night.

Erika knew Kai loved her, but she couldn't count on that love assuring his sanction of her plan to avenge her father, not without providing solid proof of Gestapo involvement. Kai was glad to be part of the capture team—the enemy was involved. But in the matter of her father, she would have to convince Kai to work against his countrymen. Kai was a patriot, and even though she knew he detested the Gestapo, with no hard proof that her father's death was anything other than an accident she felt he might not support her. Kai would never betray her; she knew that. Rather, he would probably try and talk her out of it or try to convince her to wait. It would muddle even further a scheme already vastly more complicated than her original plan and seeming to grow more complicated every day. One surprise had followed closely on the heels of another starting on the day Maeve and Tars were taken off the Venezuelan freighter. With her husband an unknown factor, Erika felt her best course was to avoid adding another stumbling block to a path already cluttered with them. So she had decided to not tell Kai how her father really died or of her plans for vengeance.

When the women stepped out of the hotel, a warm, clear afternoon greeted them. The Ku'Damm was a boulevard known for its department stores, boutiques and cafes. Before the war, American tourists referred to the area as the "Fifth Avenue of Berlin." So far the Ku'Damm had escaped significant bomb damage. In fact, after walking five blocks, the four women had not noticed any destruction.

They crossed at another corner and Stephanie said, "A man is following us on the other side of the street. He's a half block behind us. That's got to be Knight."

Right," Erika confirmed. "He began tailing us two blocks ago. Don't turn around and look, Maeve."

"I'm not going to turn around. I remember the training. The wanker tailing us taught it to me."

As they progressed, the street grew busier with walkers coming and going. "We'll speak only German now," Erika said in German, then softly added in English, "Maeve, we're going to switch to German. Too many people about now to chance being overheard speaking English. Remember what I said in the hotel: Knight will question you about how you got here. Tell the truth but don't mention Kai Faust. Just say the Abwehr picked you up in France. Okay?"

Maeve nodded.

Victor Knight had picked up his pace and was now even with them across the street. At the next intersection, as the women waited to cross, Erika said, "Do you want to have a little fun with Herr Knight?"

"How?" asked Kathryn.

"Let's scatter in different directions. I'll take Maeve and head back toward the hotel. Stephanie, you keep going straight. Kathryn, head that way." Erika pointed down the intersecting street. The sisters smiled and took off. Erika turned Maeve around and they headed back the way they had come.

It took only a moment for Knight to see what was happening. He jogged across the street and caught up to Erika and Maeve.

"Very funny," Knight said in German.

"You didn't need to follow us to see if we were being followed," Erika said. "We would never let anyone follow us to a meeting with you."

"I'm sure of that," he said. "Just a by-the-book precaution, Erika. Sometimes there's nothing wrong with following the book." He turned to Maeve. "Hallo, Maeve." He realized she would not understand much more than the greeting.

"Hallo," Maeve returned.

Stephanie saw Knight catch up to Erika and whistled loudly at Kathryn. In a moment the group was together.

Knight nodded a greeting to Stephanie and looked at Kathryn. "And you are Kathryn. I can see the resemblance to your sister. Nice to finally meet you."

"Hallo, Herr Knight," Kathryn said.

"Let's walk, shall we?" he said and they continued back toward the hotel. "As you can imagine, I was surprised when Erika told me Maeve was here. I'm quite curious to hear that story. Since Maeve is with us does anyone know a place other than Erika's hotel room where we can safely speak English?"

"I have an auto from the Abwehr motor pool," said Stephanie, "but five people are too many for a KDF Wagen."

"We can use mine," Kathryn offered. "It's Gestapo, what we call a 'dark cover' vehicle. It does not have Gestapo license plates and won't draw attention."

They continued to walk, saying little of importance, until within two blocks of Erika's hotel. Knight stopped them there and they waited on the corner while Kathryn walked ahead. Ten minutes later she pulled up in a black Mercedes. Erika suggested Knight sit in front, where typically a man in a car with four women would sit. In the back seat, Erika sat behind Kathryn, Stephanie directly behind Knight and Maeve in the middle.

Knight switched to English as Kathryn pulled out into the Ku'Damm traffic. "Fill me in on your odyssey, Maeve. The last news I received came from the Americans. Their report indicated your plane was shot down and probably lost at sea."

Maeve related the story, sticking to the truth but leaving Kai Faust's name out as Erika had directed.

"Too bad for Tars," Knight said when Maeve finished. He mentioned nothing about trying to locate her.

"We're going after her, right?" asked Maeve.

"Tars is an unfortunate casualty of war," Knight said. "We can't risk the mission trying to extract someone from a concentration camp."

Erika put her hand on Maeve's leg to gain her attention. When Maeve looked at her, Erika shook her head, signaling her to drop the subject.

"Is me father released from prison and the charges against me brother dropped?" Maeve asked. "I did my part; that's our deal."

"When I thought you were lost, Maeve, I sent a communiqué to my superiors asking that your back pay for the months at Camp X be sent to your mother. I know that will be done if it hasn't already. As for the rest, you didn't exactly fulfill the mission as we outlined it. You ending up in Berlin was definitely not part of our plans. You don't speak German and your presence here gives us additional problems to deal with. The decision to honor the rest of our agreement will be made by the head of British Intelligence."

Maeve quickly sat forward in her seat and put a knife to Knight's neck. "I'll slice your throat you British shite. I kept me part and then some. You better make sure the deal is kept or I'll kill you *and* your dog."

Erika had watched Maeve reach for her knife and could have stopped her, but she doubted Maeve would harm Knight—not today at least. It was a gamble not stopping Maeve, but then Knight had gambled with their lives by not telling them about Canaris' removal so turnabout seemed fair play.

"You're going to cut my throat, Maeve?" Knight chuckled. "What a terrible mess in Kathryn's car." In a flash, he grabbed Maeve's knife hand and twisted it till the knife dropped into the front seat. He folded the knife and handed it back to Maeve.

She sat back. "You better keep that deal. You gave me your word and said you spoke for the British government. If the deal isn't kept then you're all nothing but lyin' shites."

Now Knight was growing angry. "We're liars are we? Have you forgotten what you did for a living when we took you off the street? Watch what you say if you know what's good for you."

"Watch what I say? Why? What are you going to do? I'm not scared of you or any other British bastard. You can tell that Churchill that Maeve O'Rourke says he can stick one of his cigars up his fat arse."

Stephanie broke in. "Okay, now that we have Maeve's advice for the prime minister, can we get down to business?"

"I second that," said Erika. "When will John Mayne arrive with the weapons?"

"Soon."

"You keep saying *soon*, Herr Knight. What does *soon* mean?"

"His drop this deep into Germany is risky. We need the perfect moon and weather, and his plane will have to fly in with a bombing mission. One enemy plane by itself this deep into Germany will stick out. One plane among a skyful will not draw extra attention."

"So why are we meeting? These meetings are risky as well."

"When I left the note at your hotel I had no intentions of meeting today. I wanted to simply check in by telephone to see if anything of concern had presented itself since our first meeting. But when you told me Maeve was with you I decided on our walk. I'm quite curious as to something about Maeve."

"What is that?" Erika asked.

Knight removed his hat, quickly pulled a derringer from it and turned and aimed it at Erika. "Why is Maeve, an inexperienced civilian who can't speak any foreign languages but succeeded in eliminating several Gestapo agents in Spain, hijacking a German airplane, and eluding more Gestapo in France, not locked up or dead?"

Knight's suspicion was justified, but he had placed himself in a precarious position with the dangerous women in the car. Stephanie began inching her hand toward the gun under her blouse. Kathryn was prepared to crash the car and throw Knight into the windshield.

Erika looked him in the eye. "Maeve *was* locked up. I convinced Schellenberg to release her into my custody. I told him she could help Stephanie and me distract you. Schellenberg wants you captured or dead, and we could have easily already taken care of either. We're all armed. Turns out I was right about Maeve. She did help us. Because of her you called this impromptu meeting. Stephanie could have easily knocked you out or put a bullet in the back of your head as soon as we got in the car. If we had intended to carry out Schellenberg's orders you'd already be dead or unconscious and on your way to a Gestapo dungeon. It's time for you to decide if you're going to trust us. Just know that your mission has no chance if you don't. Pull the trigger or put the gun away."

[that evening]

Erika, Maeve, and the Fischer sisters sat around a table in the Lili Marlene. They had just arrived.

"That was remarkable, Erika," said Stephanie (in German). "What you did with Knight. I thought for a moment I'd have to shoot him."

The Fischer sisters now knew why the Abwehr's *Lorelei* had achieved her iconic reputation within the close-knit German clandestine community. Telling Knight about his planned capture but not that it was to take place only after John Mayne arrived was a calm and clever response to Knight's suspicions about Maeve. Erika's quick thinking not only defused a tense situation, but turned things to their advantage. Knight's trust in them had increased because of her resourcefulness. A waitress approached.

"Wir wollen vier dunkle Biere, bitte," Maeve said to the waitress who nodded and walked away. Erika and the sisters stared at Maeve in surprise. She had correctly ordered dark beers for them all. Maeve saw them staring and whispered in English, "One of you has to pay. I'm broke. The Gestapo took my money in France."

Erika glanced around then leaned forward and warned very quietly, "That was good Maeve, but be careful. It's easy to slip up. Now, no more English—not in here. We'll fill you in on anything important after we leave. "

The German women knew that language mistakes made by a peacetime tourist would be ignored or considered funny by Berliners. But during wartime those same syntactical slips would draw suspicion and most likely earn a call to the authorities. Even among Erika's friends at the Lili Marlene their secret must remain guarded. No one in the café, not even the regulars Erika knew from the old days, had any inkling that spies sat among them.

When the waitress delivered their beers, Erika asked about Carla and was told she was in a backroom with the gamblers. "If she's not back there on Saturday nights a fight always breaks out," the waitress added. "Should I tell her you're here?"

"No," Erika replied and paid for the drinks. "Leave her to her business. If I don't see her before I'm ready to leave I'll go back and say hello."

When the waitress walked off, Stephanie said, "Our Bier Fräulein does a good job of promoting her talent." Maeve didn't understand, but Erika and Kathryn smiled knowing it was a joke referring to the abundant cleavage exposed by the buxom woman's low-cut blouse. Stephanie added, "Erika, I'm glad your friend, Carla, is in the back and doesn't know we're here. The last thing I want tonight is a visit from the Green Fairy."

Kathryn got down to business. "Knight said that Mayne's arrival will coincide with a bombing raid. When I got back to Prinz

Albrechtstrasse this afternoon I did some checking. Nearly all Allied nighttime bombing raids into Germany the past six months have occurred when the moon is in its quarter-to-half or half-to-quarter phases. None has come during a new or full moon. The next moon phase that fits within that pattern starts the twenty-seventh; that's a week from now. Could it be that long before Mayne arrives? I was under the impression the SOE was in a hurry to get started. And the mission can't proceed until Mayne arrives with the weapons. Correct?"

"That's right," said Stephanie. "For the mission Knight trained us for in Scotland we at least need the Welrods."

"Welrods? What's that?" Kathryn asked.

"Silent handguns the SOE developed."

"If that time-table holds true," Erika mentioned, "it gives me more than enough time to try and save Tars if she's still alive."

Unable to be a part of the conversation, Maeve occupied her time sending flirtatious smiles to men at the bar who looked her way. Some were obviously intrigued by the table of four women who had to be two sets of sisters—the brunettes showed a familial resemblance and the blondes surely had to be twins. When Maeve heard the name *Tars* mentioned her ears perked up and she turned to listen, hoping she could make out something of what was being said.

"Is saving this person important?" Kathryn asked.

"She's skilled with a knife and a very good marksman," Erika responded. "Her history shows that once she starts a mission she's relentless, never stopping until it's finished. She can help me with my plans."

"It's going to be more difficult, Erika," Kathryn stated. "Since she was mentioned in the meeting with Knight today, I checked on her status when I went in to review the bombing reports. Your Tarsitano is still alive but she left Dachau this morning and is being transferred to a camp in Poland, near Krakow. As far as what I can do to help, I can get you the paperwork for her release, but I can't help you get through the numerous check stations you'll have to drive through along the way. The Wehrmacht controls them. You'll have to drive through Czechoslovakia and into Poland and will be stopped many times."

"Helping me with the release papers will not expose you?" Erika asked.

"I'll have to pilfer them," Kathryn answered. "No one will know who took them, but eventually they'll figure out someone did and mount an investigation."

"You say this camp is near Krakow?"

"Yes, just west of Krakow," Kathryn confirmed. "Near a small town called Auschwitz."

Chapter 77

Suse

A small farm west of Ulm, Germany
Two days later; Monday, 22 May 1944

"Hello, Suse."

"Erika! Grüß Dich!" greeted the young woman who answered the door. "Come in." The women hugged and Susanna Hohner closed the door behind Erika. "You can imagine my surprise when you called yesterday. It's been so long."

"I think about three years," Erika acknowledged.

"We have much catching up to do."

"Yes. I'm sorry the reason for my call was to ask a favor, Suse. I would have called sooner but I returned to Germany only a few days ago."

"I understand. With the war I know your duties must be overwhelming." Suse knew Erika held the Kriegsmarine rank of Korvettenkapitän but knew nothing of her Abwehr ties. "I have enough coffee to make us a small pot. Let's go into the kitchen and we can talk while I make it. I told Mother you called; she sends her best. She's staying in Blaubeuren for a few days tending to Aunt Trude after her surgery." Both of Suse's brothers were away serving in the Heer.

Erika and Suse had met and become friends in 1937 when both worked at the Seehaus in Berlin translating foreign radio broadcasts. Both women spoke fluent English and French and many times found themselves sitting side-by-side at receivers tuned to those broadcasts.

Over coffee they chatted for 20 minutes then Suse said, "I'm sure you want to see the Stork." She led Erika outside to the barn. When she slid open the door, among the farm implements and stacks of animal feedbags sat a small, single-engine airplane with its fabric wings folded back. Erika recognized the Fieseler Fi 156 Storch (German for "Stork"). The small aircraft accommodated a pilot and two passengers who sat in tandem.

"I have to admit I was surprised you still have it, Suse."

"I haven't flown it in eight months—too hard to get fuel."

"Fuel won't be a problem. Is it in working order?"

"Uncle Horst is coming by this afternoon and we'll check everything."

"So we can leave in the morning?" Erika asked.

"Yes. As long as you can get us fuel. We need to fill up before we take off, and I checked my maps: Krakow is 725 air kilometers from here. We'll have to stop once along the way to refuel, and then once again on the return flight."

As a teenager in the 1930s, Suse had become a fan of the German aviatrix Elli Beinhorn and the American Amelia Earhart. While working at the Seehaus she took flying lessons in her spare time. In 1939, Suse and her uncle went in together to buy the used Storch at a very good price because it needed some mechanical work. Uncle Horst, a mechanic by trade, didn't pilot the plane but enjoyed going up as Suse's passenger.

Erika knew Kathryn Fischer was right when she warned of the difficulty a drive to Poland would present. Although driving would have allowed Erika to take along Stephanie, who volunteered to help rescue Tars, without the proper checkpoint paperwork she would be stopped and questioned at each of the numerous Wehrmacht check stations along the way. Because the Storch had room for only three including the pilot, Stephanie could not come along as backup. Still, the Storch offered a much better alternative than attempting to reach Poland by automobile.

"Suse, I want to warn you again there might be some danger in this." Since Kathryn had supplied Erika with the paperwork to gain Tars' release, she didn't foresee any problems at the camp, but still Erika wanted her friend aware of the risk and had warned her when she called from Berlin yesterday. Perhaps a Russian fighter plane might cross their flight path and take an interest in them. The Russians knew the German military used *Storche* as scout planes.

"I look forward to flying again, Erika. I'm dying of boredom."

Chapter 78

The Stork

Near Ulm
Next day; Tuesday, 23 May 1944

Just after dawn, Erika, Suse, and Uncle Horst pushed the Storch out of the barn. With a fuselage and wings made of canvas, rolling the little airplane out of the barn was not difficult. Suse and her uncle had given the plane a thorough inspection the previous afternoon, along with standard maintenance including an oil change, spark plug check, and firing the engine several times to blow out any carbon build-up. Then, taking along gasoline cans, Erika accompanied Uncle Horst into Ulm and used her OKW credentials to purchase the rationed fuel. The uncle spent the night with his niece and Erika at the farmhouse so he could help with the early morning takeoff.

Erika and Uncle Horst folded the wings into position while Suse climbed into the cockpit, fired up the engine, and started her preflight instrument check. A log of all civilian flights had to be called in to the closest government-registered airfield before takeoff, even if that takeoff would be from a farm pasture. There was no reason for Erika to think the flight log of a farmer's small plane would make its way to Abwehr or the Gestapo in Berlin, but Erika had Suse wait until the last minute anyway, placing the call to the Ulm aerodrome that morning just before they walked out to the barn.

When Suse was satisfied with her instrument check and the response of the flaps, ailerons, elevator, stabilizer and rudder to her controls, she signaled Erika she was ready. Wearing her naval uniform, Erika climbed into the seat behind her. Suse waved to her uncle and taxied out into the pasture. A Storch worked nicely for open field takeoffs and landings because it needed minimal distance, only 200 feet for takeoff and 65 feet to land. Drawbacks included the aircraft's 10-gallon fuel capacity giving it a range of only 250 miles before refueling became necessary, and a cruising speed of only 95 miles per hour (not engineered for speed, the Storch could fly as slow as 35 miles per hour without stalling). Because of the small fuel tank and slow air speed, the flight to southwest Poland would take around six hours.

The Storch lifted off and gained altitude slowly, giving Erika the impression of gliding instead of the sensation of muscling into the sky that passengers on most planes feel. Suse banked eastward, soaring over Ulm and passing directly over the Ulmer Münster, the tallest church steeple in the world.

"I see no bomb damage at all, Suse," Erika commented. She spoke loudly but did not have to shout over the low-powered engine.

"We've had no bombing so far," Suse replied. Here again, Erika recalled the newspaper and radio reports in England and America that gave the impression that German cities were already mountains of rubble.

Suse climbed the plane to 3000 feet and for the duration of the flight Erika assumed the duty of navigator, using the mapping skills taught her at Quenzsee. The first leg of the journey proved uneventful save for a pocket of air turbulence near the Czech border that bounced the light plane around like a fanned feather and expended extra fuel when Suse was forced to increase power to maintain control. They landed on fumes at a civil airfield south of Prague where Erika's uniform staved off any questions about the need for fuel.

With Erika supplying the headings, two hours after taking off from Prague they entered Polish airspace and began seeing a series of military outposts. Soon they flew by a massive conglomeration of camps and sub-camps near the Polish town of Oświecim, a name many Germans found hard to pronounce so on most German maps the name was customarily spelled *Auschwitz.*

They flew on and radioed the airfield west of Krakow built by the Wehrmacht to serve the area's numerous military encampments. After receiving permission to land, Suse set the Storch down and taxied up to an area of fuel trucks, again not a minute too soon with the fuel gauge needle pointing to the red line. She cut the engine and both women climbed out.

"Let's find someone in charge, Suse, and I'll make sure the plane gets refueled while I'm gone." The plan was for Suse to stay with the airplane while Erika went about her business. Erika hoped things went quickly at the camp so she could return with Tars in time to fly back that afternoon. Because of night-time flying restrictions over Germany for non-military aircraft, they needed to take off from Poland six hours before dark or they would be forced to spend the night in Krakow.

They found a Heer private wandering around amidst the fuel trucks. He directed them to a small building down the tarmac. Erika showed her papers to a sergeant and explained their needs: fuel and a driver to take her to the Konzentrationslager. The sergeant brought over an officer who checked Erika's papers, found them in order, and instructed the sergeant to comply.

In 15 minutes Suse was talking to a refueling crew and Erika was riding in a Kübelwagen driven by a Heer lance corporal on her way to Auschwitz.

Chapter 79

Arbeit Macht Frei

Auschwitz Concentration Camp
Same day; Tuesday, 23 May 1944

At a guard shack outside the main gate, Erika showed an SS soldier the prisoner release papers Kathryn Fischer had pilfered at 8 Prinz Albrechtstrasse. The Heer driver waited outside the gate as a guard escorted Erika under an iron sign with the words *Arbeit Macht Frei.* Most of the Konzentrationslager used the phrase to greet arriving detainees and *Work Makes Free* assured them that if they worked hard they would eventually regain their freedom. Erika had never agreed with the wholesale confinement of civilians. She knew the Americans concentrated their Japanese-Americans, but for her, only proven enemies should be kept under lock and key. *Such a thing is one of the many unfortunate offshoots of war,* she thought as she followed the guard under the sign. *Hopefully it will be over soon.*

The guard led her to the main administration building where a Totenkopf-SS major took her papers and looked them over. "It's very rare that an inmate leaves the camp, Korvettenkapitän," stated the major.

"But I was told it does happen occasionally, Sturmbannführer," she countered. "And everything is in the paperwork. The prisoner is wanted for interrogation in Berlin. That's all I know. I'm here on orders."

He grunted and said, "I will find out to what block this prisoner is assigned." He disappeared with the paperwork down a corridor. Gone for quite a while, he finally returned and led Erika outside. He looked around for someone handy and spotted a Totenkopf sergeant he recognized among men gathering near the train tracks that entered the camp through its enormous main gate.

"Eder!" the major shouted. When the sergeant looked his way, he waved him over. "Schnell!"

"Scharführer Eder," he said brusquely, "the Korvettenkapitän is here to take into custody a prisoner wanted for questioning in Berlin." The major looked at a paper. "Its number is D14735. It's in cell block 24. Turn it over to the Korvettenkapitän and get back here as quickly as possible so you can be on hand when the train arrives."

"Yes, Herr Sturmbannführer!" the man shouted as he stood at attention and raised his right hand. "Heil Hitler!"

"Yes, of course," said the major. "Heil Hitler. Now get moving and get back here for the next train."

"Yes, Sturmbannführer!"

The major turned and up the steps he went, eager to return to his office.

"We will use that, Korvettenkapitän." Eder motioned to a nearby motorcycle with a sidecar. "Block 24 is too far to walk." He got on and started it. Erika got in the sidecar.

"Tell me about the camp, Scharführer," said Erika. *The rumors and enemy propaganda will finally be put to rest by seeing things first hand,* she thought. But the Death's Head sergeant seemed to think she asked about his situation.

"It's much better than the Russian Front, Korvettenkapitän. Of course there is the human waste we are forced to deal with each day, but other than that it is good duty."

"But the camp. Tell me about the camp."

He responded by taking on the role of tour guide, pleased that his superior had singled him out for a duty. "This section is where we house the Gypsies," he said as they putted past a long row of barracks. "Across the way we keep the homosexuals. Other sections contain Slavs and other vermin. Several blocks house Russian prisoners of war. And then there are the Jews."

"So what are the duties of the prisoners? Where do they work?" she asked as they drove past a long stretch of barbed-wire fences. "I don't see many of them about." Occasionally they passed a few gaunt inmates in striped clothing that resembled pajamas.

"They are ordered to stay in the barracks if not at roll call or assigned to a task. The ones selected as suitable for work are marched or transported where needed. For instance, we sent a few dozen to a ball-bearing factory in Pilsen yesterday."

"So most that remain here are too old or young or too infirm to work?"

"No. Everyone in these barracks serves a purpose for the Reich or they leave in the smoke."

Erika looked at him. "Meaning what?"

"The smoke." He pointed to two tall smokestacks barely visible in the distance. She had spotted the stacks as Suse flew by earlier but assumed they were from a power plant. No smoke had issued from the stacks then, and none rose now. The Totenkopf sergeant grinned. "Our saying here is: 'Wave good-bye to the Jews only when they leave in the smoke.' May I ask what will happen to this Jew you have come for?"

Erika ignored the question. His comment about the smoke filled her head. At last they reached Block 24 where Eder pulled over and stopped.

"Please wait here, Korvettenkapitän. I will find it and be right back." He returned in ten minutes. "It's been assigned to Research Block 10. I know a shortcut." Like the major, Eder used the non-human pronoun to refer to prisoners. He started the motorcycle and cut through a series of barracks and sped by a succession of gallows.

"Stop!!!" Erika shouted.

Alarmed, Eder put on the brakes. Erika left the sidecar and slowly walked toward a gallows. A little girl, who could not have been older than three—Ada's age—slowly swayed in the breeze, hanged by the neck. On the gallows next to the child was a doll, also hanged. On the ground lay a dead woman. Erika stared, speechless.

"Oh," said Eder, "I see now what drew your attention. Yes, quite the commotion this morning. The child was a Polish Jew caught stealing a ration of bread. One of the guards hanged the child's doll hoping that would teach her a lesson, but the girl's crying created such a scene that other prisoners began assembling and we hanged the child as a warning to them. The woman is the mother. She charged forward trying to save the child and a guard was forced to shoot her. The Jews—what can you say? Still they think they should run things."

Erika couldn't take her eyes off the little girl. Now blue in death, the child's sweet, angelic face seemed serene; her open, innocent eyes looked up, focused on Heaven.

"Don't be concerned, Korvettenkapitän," Eder added. "Despite being short-handed, we are very organized here. We leave the bodies on display for a time to make an impression on any prisoners not yet convinced to mind the rules, but we'll have the Jewish kapos clean this up tomorrow. If it were winter we could leave the display longer, but now that the days are getting warmer we have to take that into account. We must continue on. I have my orders to meet the next train."

In shock, Erika barely heard Eder. He repeated his request to move on and like a sleepwalker, Erika returned to the sidecar. When she regained her senses, her first thought was to kill Eder on the spot, but she realized if she did she would never get Tars out, and she thought of Suse. If Erika didn't make it out of the camp after killing Eder, Suse would not leave without her and would soon be taken into custody at the airfield.

In a few minutes Eder stopped in front of Block 10. This time Erika followed him in despite his appeal for her to wait outside.

The Block 10 and Block 11 buildings were much larger than the prisoner barracks. Once inside the main Block 10 structure, Eder explained the reason they were there to a female SS guard who led them back to a large laboratory where a man in a white lab coat and two women dressed as nurses busied themselves with work. In the middle of the room sat a large, galvanized-steel tank full of ice water. A groaning and shivering young man sat in the water, submerged to his neck. On a bench along a wall sat four naked women, one of them Tars. She sported numerous bruises on her face and body, her head was shaved, and she looked noticeably thinner than just the week before, the last time Erika saw her. When Tars looked at Erika, Erika shook her head to warn Tars not to show any sign of recognition. The man in a lab coat walked over and addressed Eder.

"What is this about, Scharführer?" he asked.

"Doktor Rausch, the Korvettenkapitän is here to pick up a prisoner wanted for questioning in Berlin."

"What is all this?" Erika asked.

Rausch explained matter-of-factly. "We are conducting experiments for the Luftwaffe. Too many downed pilots and crews have been lost to hypothermia in icy waters—men who could have been saved. Here we see how low a subject's body temperature can be lowered before it reaches the point of no return. We are now testing different ways of warming the subject. We tried immersion in warm water but test results indicate that method is too much of a shock to the system and most don't survive. We're now testing a slower warming, using body heat from the women. After the subject is taken from the water, the women will attempt to warm him with their bodies. So far we are getting better results this way. Which prisoner are you here for?"

Eder looked at his paper. "D14735, Herr Doktor."

Rausch gave his permission. "Go ahead and call it out, Scharführer."

"D14735!" Eder shouted out. "D14735! Stand up!"

The other three frightened women each checked their tattoos, but not Tars. Erika could tell Eder was growing angry and feared he might take out that anger on the women.

"That's the woman, Scharführer." Erika pointed at Tars. "I was shown a Kripo photograph before I left Berlin."

Eder stomped over and jerked Tars to her feet. "Why didn't you stand up, swine?"

Tars didn't understand the German and said in English, "You Death Head fucks are big brave men with your dogs and machine guns against naked women, aren't you? You better hope we never meet outside this shit-hole."

Eder didn't understand what she said but he could tell she had a surly attitude. His face became a mask of rage and Erika stepped quickly between the two. "My orders are to deliver her able-bodied enough for questioning, Scharführer." She turned to Tars and slapped her across the face. "You won't be so arrogant after the Gestapo has you for a few days. Now get dressed!" She spoke in German for Eder's sake knowing Tars would understand the purpose of her slap. She shoved Tars toward the mound of clothes on the floor the women had been forced to remove.

Rausch grew impatient to end the drama and return to his work. "Korvettenkapitän, if you're taking her then please do so and stop wasting my time." He turned to a nurse. "Frau Lescher, call for a replacement. The test requires four women. Tell them to send one quickly . . . we'll be removing this one from the tank soon." The young man in the ice water had stopped shivering and was now unconscious. The other nurse held a board under his chin to prevent him from drowning.

"Let's go," Erika said. It had taken Tars only a few seconds to slip on her prison pants and shirt. There was no underwear or shoes to bother with.

Since Eder refused to allow Tars to ride behind him, Erika took the second motorcycle seat and they put Tars in the side car. Concerned about time, the sergeant sped back to the main gate. The train had arrived and Eder cursed. As he pulled to a stop another sergeant shouted, "Eder, where have you been? This one's loaded." After Eder explained the duty that had made him late, the other sergeant walked over to look at Tars. "So, one Jew leaves and two thousand arrive." Then he turned to Eder. "We're meeting tonight at the Tawerna Rogu for Weber's birthday. Now hurry—they're about to open the doors."

The train had stopped with some cars inside the gate and some still outside; the camp entrance was totally blocked.

"How do I get out with my prisoner?" she asked Eder.

"It's too late. As we empty the forward cars the train will move forward. You and your Jew will have to wait until the train is empty." Eder hustled off, glad to be rid of the Korvettenkapitän and her Jew.

For the next two hours Erika had no choice but to witness the nightmare unfold. The area became a hellish panorama of barking attack dogs, shouting and cursing guards, and families being pulled apart—husbands from wives, parents from their children. SS officers stood on the platform ordering the unfortunate human cargo to move to the right or to the left.

"What are they doing?" Erika asked Tars.

"A thumb to the right sends them into processing. That's what I got. A thumb to the left sends them to the gas chambers. The elderly and many of the children go directly to the gas. Anyone who looks like they cannot work or be a suitable guinea pig for medical experiments won't see the end of the day."

Erika felt unsteady. It had to be a dream—a nightmare. One of the guards noticed Tars in her camp clothing, eyed her suspiciously, and walked over. "What are you doing up here, Jew?" He had drawn his pistol.

Erika shoved him away and shouted, "This is my prisoner! Your superiors know my orders are to take her to Berlin! We're waiting to leave! Get away!"

Another guard on the platform kept shouting, "Zwillinge! Zwillinge!"

"Why does that one keep shouting for twins?" Erika asked Tars.

Tars pointed to an officer on the platform. "That one uses them for experiments. They say he's a doctor." Tars pointed to an SS captain.

Erika thought she recognized him and took a hard look. "Mengele."

"Yeah, that's his name. The mothers talk about him and he comes by with candy for the children—the sick bastard. Do you know him?"

Erika had met Josef Mengele at an opera attended by the Führer two years ago, before leaving on her assignment in America. But she didn't answer Tars' question. She didn't hear it. Erika stood there stupefied by the truth.

Chapter 80

Hunting the Beast

Krakow, Poland
Same day; Tuesday, 23 May 1944

Suse milled about the Storch and checked her wristwatch. Now late afternoon and too late to make Ulm before dark, she wondered what kept Erika. Flying a civilian aircraft over Germany at night was extremely dangerous. Besides breaking wartime regulations which could land her in jail, everyone knew the enemy sometimes used small aircraft to insert enemy agents behind the lines. The newspapers warned German citizens to be alert for any suspicious aircraft flying at night and notify the authorities immediately if one was spotted. Her civilian Storch displayed no German markings—no German cross or swastika on its wings or tail—and might be shot out of a nighttime sky.

Finally, she saw a Kübelwagen leave the road beside the airfield. It crossed the runway, drove directly toward the Storch and stopped. Erika sat in the back seat beside a woman with a shaved head who wore a long raincoat.

"Get in, Suse," said Erika.

Suse climbed into the seat beside the Heer driver.

"Where are we going, Erika?" Suse asked.

"It's too late to fly back tonight, correct?"

"Yes. We needed to leave at least two hours ago; three would have been better."

"The driver will drop us at a hotel in Krakow. We'll fly out first thing in the morning."

With the nicer hotels filled with officers and important German civilians who in some way aided area military operations, anyone who owned a building with beds and an indoor toilet or two was now a hotel magnate regardless of the quality of other amenities, or lack of them.

The only hotel the Heer driver could find with vacancies tonight had been a grungy tenement before the war, but the large influx of German military personnel meant the slum lord could earn much more profit from prostitutes who had descended on Krakow from far and wide looking for a bed to ply their trade with German soldiers, than from the poor Polish families living in his cramped, shabby rooms before the invasion. With no other options for accommodations, Erika gave Suse the money to pay for the room then she hustled Tars up the backstairs. Erika had found the raincoat that covered Tars' camp clothing in the Kübelwagen's bumper-mounted supply box, but still there was her shaved head and the need to not draw undue attention.

"Suse, this is Tars," Erika said once they were all in the room. She had not introduced them in the presence of the Heer driver who believed Tars to be a prisoner. "Suse, we need to find Tars some clothing. Since I should probably stay with her, do you mind?"

"No, of course not. What should I get?"

Erika handed her more money. The Heer driver had told her all Polish businesses had been ordered to accept Reichsmarks. "It doesn't matter, something simple—and shoes and a hat—whatever you can find. As we drove in, I saw a small clothing shop in the next block that looked to be open."

Tars told Suse her sizes and they determined her hat size to be about the same as Suse's.

"I'll be back as soon as I can."

"When you get back we'll find something to eat," said Erika.

After Suse left, for a long time no one said anything, Tars weak and exhausted, Erika in a twilight zone, her mind fighting to not believe the horrors of that day. At last Erika broke the silence.

"Tell me about Dachau."

"Mostly political prisoners, I think. I was there only one day but other inmates told me most die from suicide or disease. I can believe that. The number of suicides at these hell-holes has to be very high. I saw several at the camp here rush the fences knowing they would be gunned down . . . and that's what they wanted. And the food . . . no wonder disease takes many. My last meal was a bowl of something claimed to be soup. It looked like dishwater and had tiny worms swimming around in it. People eat the worms and leave the broth. The worms are the only nutrition.

"They brought me here on a train, in some type of freight or cattle car packed so full of standing people that when some fainted they couldn't even fall down. The small children and babies had to be held overhead by their parents or be crushed. There was no water. The train stopped several times to pick up more people but they wouldn't let us out for toilet, people shitting and pissing themselves, vomiting on each other. When we got here, most in my car got the left thumb and were marched straight to the gas. Three of the women who went to the gas were heavily pregnant."

Erika stood at the window, looking out.

"So what's the plan?" Tars asked. "Where is Maeve?"

Still gazing out the window, Erika did not answer.

"Erika, are you there? What do we do now?"

Soon after midnight a dozen Totenkopf camp guards spilled out of the Tawerna Rogu tavern. Having celebrated a comrade's birthday, many were unsteady on their feet.

"Now it's back to the Jews!" one of them slurred. "The Jews miss us! Back to the Jews, one and all!"

Most laughed. One said, "I say we go back in for one more drink."

One of the more sober guards reminded the others that another train was due just after dawn. Two men ignored him and went back inside the tavern. The rest began splitting up and heading their separate ways trying to remember where they had parked their vehicles.

The intoxicated Wenzel Eder and Oswin Stegall thought they remembered and started staggering down the street. They had walked less than a block when a female voice called to them from an alley.

"Hey, over here, boys."

The men stopped, looked down the dark alley and saw nothing.

"Who's there?" Eder slurred.

"An old friend."

Eder looked at Stegall.

"What do you mean, a friend? Who are you?"

"Who do you want me to be?"

Both men laughed. Eder turned to Stegall. "It has to be Edyta. She's the only whore around here who speaks German." Edyta was a foul-mouthed Polish prostitute who frequented the Tawerna Rogu. Many of the guards had hired her in the past.

Stegall yelled into the dark alley, "Is that you, Edyta?"

"Yes. It's Edyta."

Eder and Stegall started into the alley. "It will have to be a quick one, Edyta," Eder said. As they walked they began unzipping their pants. "Where are you, goddamn you. We can't see you."

The voice speaking German had been Erika's, but the woman who stepped out into the weak light from an overhead window was Tars. The men couldn't see her face shadowed by a floppy peasant cap.

"Edyta! You've lost weight." Both men pushed their pants and underwear down around their knees. "There they are, ready for you. Now get busy, tramp."

The woman took off her cap, revealing her shaved head. "I'm not Edyta. I'm D14735."

Tars buried a knife in Eder's belly. Stegall, watching in horror, reached to his waist for his sidearm which was not there but down around his knees. Suddenly he felt a hand over his mouth and a sharp pain in his back. Erika twisted the dagger around in his kidney, then withdrew it and cut his throat. He was unconscious when his head thudded on the cobblestones and bled out in seconds. Tars let Eder live a few moments longer. She cut his vocal cords so he couldn't scream, careful to avoid his jugular, and castrated him before he died.

"You won't need your balls in hell," Tars told him, not caring that he couldn't understand. As Eder coughed in his death throes she finished him by plunging the knife through his left eye and into his brain.

Erika recognized the other man as the camp guard who told Eder about the party. She and Tars dragged the bodies to a large trash receptacle, lifted them in and covered them with trash. Erika took off the blood-soaked raincoat that protected her uniform and threw it into the same trash bin. Tars wiped her bloody hands with paper strewn in the alley.

It would be two days before the bodies of the two AWOL Auschwitz guards were found.

[eight hours later]

Two hours after dawn, the Storch lifted off and banked westward. Erika again sat behind Suse, Tars behind Erika. To protect Suse, Erika decided not to tell her about the horrors of the camp and told Tars her decision. Suse would be devastated, and if she spoke of the atrocities back home she would come under suspicion. Erika knew the German people would someday learn the truth.

Erika wasn't naïve enough to think eliminating two guards would slow the camp's gruesome business, but the opportunity presented itself and men like them needed to die and the sooner the better. Eder's comrade mentioning the gathering at the Krakow tavern in her presence and the delay in leaving the camp that prohibited them from flying out yesterday sealed the men's doom.

As the plane gained altitude the camp came into view off to their right. A train, apparently empty could be seen backing out of the main gate. Beyond, in the distance, gray smoke bellowed from the stacks.

Erika turned away and fought the urge to retch. She had not slept after returning to the hotel, lying awake all night with the picture of Eder's *display* seared into her brain: the sweet-faced child hanging from a noose looking for Heaven, her doll hanging next to her and her mother dead on the ground.

Part 6

Heinrich Himmler addressing an audience of Totenkopf-SS charged with administering the Final Solution.
Speech delivered in Posen, 6 October 1943

"Most of you know what it means when a hundred corpses are laying side by side, or five hundred, or a thousand. To have stuck it out and at the same time—apart from exceptions caused by human weakness—to have remained decent fellows, that is what made us hard. This is a page of glory in our history which has never been written and is never to be written. . . . We had the moral right, we had the duty to our people, to destroy this people which wanted to destroy us."

Chapter 81

AWOL

Berlin—Abwehr Headquarters
Friday, 26 May 1944

"Any word of her, Pfeiffer?"

Doktor Erich Pfeiffer had just walked into Walter Schellenberg's office.

"No, Herr Oberführer." Pfeiffer took a chair.

Lorelei had disappeared. Five days ago she called Schellenberg to request a leave, saying she planned to return in two or three days. Schellenberg would never have granted such a request with the SOE capture mission on hand, but a call from Martin Bormann informing him the Führer had personally promised Karl Lehmann's daughter a furlough whenever she wanted it put an end to any arguments Schellenberg could raise about the inopportune timing. Even so, wartime protocol demanded she furnish Abwehr information on where she could be reached, and it was her duty to check in by telephone every day. She had done neither.

"Has Stephanie Fischer come across any leads concerning the Irishwoman?" Schellenberg asked. Maeve O'Rourke was also missing.

"I spoke with Fischer this morning: nothing yet, Oberführer."

"I assume Fischer has moved into Lehmann's hotel room by now." Yesterday, Schellenberg ordered Stephanie to take over the SOE capture team in Erika's absence, including moving into Erika's hotel room so she could intercept any messages and telephone calls from Victor Knight.

"Yes. She stayed there last night."

[same time—Gestapo/SS headquarters, 8 Prinz Albrechtstrasse]
On Thursday, one of Himmler's fastidious paperwork clerks came across a concentration camp report that included a prisoner release. The report was sent up the ladder to Adolf Eichmann. Normally,

paperwork for a camp prisoner release crossed Eichmann's desk *before* it left Prinz Albrechtstrasse, so, concerned that something was amiss, Eichmann tagged the report and immediately sent it on to Heinrich Müller. After reading the name of the person who gained the prisoner's release, Müller made a beeline to Himmler's office.

Now, a day later, Müller sat in Himmler's office giving his latest report.

"Lehmann's plane refueled at the military airfield outside Krakow, Reichsführer."

"Do we know anything about the airplane?"

"The Luftwaffe sergeant in charge of the refueling crew remembers that the plane was a Fieseler Storch."

"That's all? What about the plane's identification number?"

"No, Reichsführer. Since the paperwork was in order, the ground crew saw no need for caution."

"Göring and his damned Luftwaffe and its sloppy protocols."

"Yes, Reichsführer. Now about the traitor in our midst. I've narrowed the list to thirty-eight officers in the building who could access the paperwork without suspicion. Shall we inform Schellenberg that someone here at headquarters supplied Lehmann with camp release papers?"

Both men now knew a mole worked inside their organization, someone inside the very building where they now sat. The papers authorizing the prisoner release from Auschwitz could have come from nowhere but 8 Prinz Albrechtstrasse.

"No, absolutely not. I'm certain the traitor was planted by Canaris before he was removed. This has his name all over it. If that's the case, Schellenberg will know nothing that can help us and I don't want him initiating an internal investigation at Abwehr and tipping our hand to the infiltrator. I spoke with Schellenberg yesterday after we learned of this. He's not aware of the incident at the camp. He knows only that Lehmann is missing. I want to keep it that way."

◊ ◊ ◊

[later that day—the forest near Falkensee]

Maeve heard the car pull up outside. She grabbed her gun, walked to the window and pulled back the shade enough to peep out. She had stayed at this cabin deep in the woods since Monday when Stephanie Fischer brought her here and told her to sit tight. The car stopped and two people got out. Maeve ran to the door and flung it open.

"Tars!" Maeve ran out and hugged her.

"Let's go inside," said Stephanie.

"Where's Erika?" Maeve asked as they stepped into the cabin.

"She's not coming," Stephanie answered as she set a box of groceries on the table.

"Why?"

"I don't know, Maeve," said Stephanie. She told the truth. Wednesday, Erika wired Stephanie a message to the Kempinski (correctly guessing Schellenberg would order Stephanie to move into Erika's room to await contact from Knight). The message contained the location of a public telephone booth not far from the hotel and gave the time for Stephanie to be there. Earlier today, Stephanie met Erika and Tars in Leipzig where Erika requested she take Tars to the cabin to watch over Maeve. As for Erika's immediate plans, Stephanie knew nothing. "All I know is you and Tars are to stay here. Erika will come for you when it's time. Remember what I told you: Don't wander away from the cabin. Stay inside unless you need the toilet." An outhouse sat thirty yards from the cabin. "Keep the blackout shades in place at night if you burn a light; a solitary cabin in the woods with light coming from a window will draw attention from any plane that might fly over at night. I need to get going. It will be dark soon and I don't want to drive away from here with headlights shining."

As Stephanie prepared to leave, she told them that if she didn't hear from Erika in the meantime, she would be back in two days to check on them and bring more supplies. "Do you remember what I told you to say to anyone who might stumble upon the cabin?"

Maeve nodded. "Mein Mann ist auf der Jagd. It means 'My husband is off hunting.'"

"Since there are now two of you, say: Unsere Männer sind auf der Jagd. It means 'Our husbands are off hunting.'" Repeat that. Maeve repeated it a couple of times. "Then just close the door before they say or ask you anything else. Closing the door on them won't look suspicious; any woman might react that way with her husband not around. And hunting in Germany is only afforded the privileged. They'll probably think your husbands are Party big shots and leave you alone."

Driving away, Stephanie questioned why she was doing this—why she was working with Erika and hiding things from Abwehr. She couldn't come to a satisfying conclusion other than perhaps she trusted Erika more than she trusted Walter Schellenberg. Maybe that was what it was, but she wasn't sure.

Inside the cabin, Tars began disassembling the handgun Erika gave her; she always cleaned any new gun before using it.

As Tars worked, Maeve asked, "What happened to your hair?"

"Bad salon," Tars quipped grimly.

"What's that number on your arm?"

"That's my new name. The SS at the concentration camp were kind enough to give it to me."

"What are those camps like? Are they as bad as the British say, or is that just propaganda?"

Tars did not answer.

When Stephanie returned to Erika's room at the Kempinski Hotel, she wasn't there more than ten minutes when a knock came. She opened the door and Kai Faust barged in.

"Where is Erika?" he asked impatiently as he looked around the room.

"Erika told me you'd show up."

"You didn't answer my question. Where is she?"

"I don't know."

"You don't know? What are you doing here in her room?"

"Erika will have to tell you that."

"She can't tell me if we don't have contact. Now where is she?"

"I told you I don't know."

Faust grabbed her arm and backed her against the wall. "You're lying!"

"Take your hands off me!" She jerked away. "Look, I know you want to find her, but I don't know where she is. I met Erika in Leipzig this morning but I don't know where she's staying or even if she's still in Leipzig."

"Leipzig? What did you talk about? What did she say? Why has she disappeared?"

"She didn't tell me much and I can't talk about what she did say. She trusts you but I gave her my word. She did tell me to warn you not to go to Schellenberg. He doesn't know where she is. Erika said she would contact you soon."

"Do you have a piece of paper?" Faust asked. He wasn't convinced Stephanie was telling him everything, but he realized arguing with her would get him nowhere.

"By the telephone."

He walked over, wrote down a phone number, ripped the page from the pad and handed it to her. "This is my apartment telephone number. Please call me if you hear from her. She's my wife."

Chapter 82

A Good Catch

Berlin
Two days later; Sunday, 28 May 1944

The first bomb fell shortly after midnight.

The target area for the American B-17 Flying Fortresses of the 398th Bombardment Group was Berlin's Siemensstadt district, home to not only a Siemens research facility but other firms that produced essential components for weaponry and radar. Unfortunately for the Americans, few bombs found their mark. Bright searchlights flashed cockpit windows and blinded pilots, and flak towers located around Berlin damaged or destroyed a number of bombers. Puzzled bombardiers mistakenly pushed their drop buttons over outlying areas succeeding only in landscaping farmland with craters or flattening a barn here or there. The few bombs that chanced to drop within Berlin city limits wrought their destruction in residential neighborhoods.

After dropping its payload, one B-17 with nose art of a naked woman wearing an Indian feather headdress turned north, reduced speed, and passed over a rural area east of Oranienburg, about 20 miles north of Berlin. A container dropped out its bomb bay doors and a man immediately followed. *Apache Doll* throttled up and banked for home.

[forest near Falkensee—11:00 a.m. that morning]
Twelve-year-old Wendel and his younger brother Fedde had a good catch. Early that morning, they had set out for their favorite spot on the lake, a spot that nearly always yielded a good string of carp.

"I wonder if Aunt Mina is alright," asked Fedde as they trudged through the forest on their way home. Aunt Mina lived in Berlin. Last night when their father saw searchlights in the distance he woke the family and took them into a homemade bomb shelter under the house.

Falkensee offered nothing the enemy would care to blow up, but Father was cautious. As they ducked into the shelter, the boys could hear the faint booms in the distance.

"Papa said he would try to call her this morning," said Wendel.

"I have to use the toilet," Fedde announced.

"Just pee in the woods like we always do," Wendel suggested.

"I don't have to pee. I have to go the other way."

"Okay. Head that way." Wendel directed his younger brother to the right. "The toilet shed by that old cabin isn't far." The boys had used the outhouse near the abandoned cabin on previous excursions to the lake.

After five minutes walking, the boys saw the outhouse through the trees. Fedde handed his fishing pole to Wendel and ran ahead to take care of his emergency. When he opened the outhouse door he screamed. A woman sat inside.

"Hey!" she blurted loudly. "Get lost ya little wanker!"

From a distance, Wendel heard his brother scream and saw him run away. Wendel dropped the poles and string of fish and broke into a sprint. As Wendel cut past the outhouse, he saw what startled Fedde—a woman emerged. Almost simultaneously a second woman, this one holding a knife, ran out of the nearby cabin and began chasing them.

"Keep running, Fedde!"

When Wendel caught up to his brother, they ran until Fedde tired and slowed down. The woman with the knife still pursued, but the boys had enough of a head start in the dense forest to allow them to dart behind one of many heavy thickets and out of their pursuer's sight. Wendel picked a spot and pulled Fedde into a large area of undergrowth. Hiding on the ground, the boys couldn't see through the heavy leaves and brambles, but they heard the woman stop just yards away. Wendel knew she was looking around and held his hand over his trembling brother's mouth.

[same day—1:30 p.m.]

Stephanie Fischer's KDF Volkswagen bumped over the rough forest path. Overgrown in many places, the path objected to the car's intrusion by placing small saplings and bushes as barriers that the car's bumper was forced to kowtow along the way.

Stephanie had brought Maeve to the cabin nearly a week ago. Friday she delivered Tars. As promised, today she returned to check on them and deliver more supplies. She had not heard from Erika.

When the path brought her to within a few yards of the cabin, Stephanie killed the engine, got out, and retrieved a box of food from the trunk. After two knocks she tried the door and found it unlocked, but Maeve and Tars were not inside. Stephanie walked outside and looked around. After scouring the immediate area, she called out but heard no reply.

[9:20 p.m.]

Despite it being Sunday, the Lili Marlene Café was in full swing. Prewar restrictions prohibiting cafes that served liquor from opening on Sundays had been lifted in 1942. Joseph Goebbels had suggested to Hitler that access to these modes of relaxation and diversion would serve a positive purpose during the demanding days of rationing and other sacrifices levied on citizens during wartime.

Kai Faust walked up to the bar, ordered a beer, and sipped it as he waited. He was not in uniform. In twenty minutes, Stephanie Fischer walked in.

"Shall we step outside?" she asked.

Faust left his beer and followed her out.

"So," Kai said, "what's this all about? Do you have something to tell me about Erika?" Stephanie had called him an hour ago and requested this meeting.

"No, I haven't heard from her." She had been shocked when on Friday Faust told her that he and Erika were married. Although he offered no proof, Stephanie had observed the close interplay between them, and knew something united them.

"Then why are we here?" he asked.

"The women you rescued in France and brought to Berlin are missing. Erika asked me to hide them, and when I went today to check on them they were gone."

"Where did you hide them?"

"A cabin in the woods."

Kai nodded. "The forest over by Falkensee. I've been to that cabin with Erika and her father. Why are you telling me this? You told me the other night you couldn't tell me anything."

"That other night the women weren't missing. Under these circumstances Erika will understand that I have to break my promise. Since I have no way to reach her, I'm asking for your help finding the women. Neither speaks German and they won't last long on their own."

"Why didn't they stay put as directed? Why would they chance running on their own?"

"Late this afternoon, a report came in to the Gestapo that this morning two boys stumbled across two women in the forest. When the boys got home, they told their father who reported it to the Kripo. One of the boys said one of the women said something in a strange language and the other chased them with a knife. The oddity of the strange language caused the Kripo to send the report to the Gestapo. The women must have realized it was too risky to remain at the cabin."

"How did you find out about the Gestapo report so quickly?"

"A contact."

"They might be in Gestapo hands already."

"As of thirty minutes ago, when I left to come here, they had not been caught."

"I agree they won't remain at large very long. If one of them spoke German she might manage to cover for the other, claiming the other was deaf and dumb, or had a throat cancer or injury. But if neither speaks German they'll be lucky to last a day or two. They can't stay in the forest forever."

"You might remember the Irishwoman's name—Maeve O'Rourke. I recall Erika mentioning it during the meeting in Schellenberg's office that you sat in on—the meeting about the capture team."

"Yes. I remember the name."

"Do you know the other one's name?

"The bodyguard? No."

"How do you know she's the bodyguard?"

"Quite obvious during the time I spent with them."

"She's called Tars. She's a Jew and was taken away to a concentration camp. Erika rescued her and hasn't been back to Berlin since—at least not that I know of."

"So where do you suggest we begin looking for these two needles in a haystack?"

"Maeve knows Erika has a room at the Kempinski; she stayed there with her after Schellenberg granted Erika custody. I'm afraid Maeve and Tars might show up there looking for Erika. Schellenberg also knows where Erika stays, of course, and he knows Maeve was there for a few days. If Schellenberg knows, Himmler knows. Himmler most likely already has people watching the hotel, hoping Erika will return."

Kai looked confused. "You mean Himmler hopes the foreign women might return to the hotel looking for Erika."

His response surprised Stephanie. *Was it possible he didn't know about how Erika's father really died and that she had returned to seek the men responsible?*

Her silence made him wonder. "What is this all about? It's time you level with me for Erika's sake."

He didn't know! Stephanie looked at him intently. She knew he was right. If there were any way to avoid disaster, Erika's husband had to know the whole story. Stephanie told him the things about Erika that had been briefed to the SOE team in Scotland: Erika's suspicions that Himmler ordered her father's murder, the Gestapo hit man Himmler sent to America to kill her, Erika's plan to avenge her father—everything.

When she finished, a stunned Kai Faust stood putting the pieces together. What had perplexed him earlier now became clear. *This is why Himmler sent the Gestapo team to Spain.*

Chapter 83

Death of *Lorelei*

Forest near Falkensee
Next day; Monday, 29 May 1944

Maeve and Tars sat on a hill in the forest fringe eating the bread and pickled eggs they brought along from the cabin. Below lay the small town of Falkensee.

"Luck was with us as far as weather last night, wasn't it, Tars?" Maeve referred to their dry night's sleep in the woods—no rain, and the late-spring temperatures kind. Tars studied the town below as she ate.

"I guess so," she replied. "But we might not have had to leave the cabin if you'd used those words in German the Abwehr broad told you and not yelled out in English."

"The lad startled me. I didn't have time to think. Would you have killed those boys?"

"That was my first thought. But as I chased them I realized it wouldn't do us any good. If they didn't return home, dozens of people would be stomping around in the forest looking for them. When a search party came across the cabin they would question us to find out if we had seen the boys. We wouldn't be able to communicate and that would cook our gooses. That's why I didn't waste a lot of time looking for them. I knew we had to get out of there."

"What do you say we do now? After Erika rescued you, did she tell you anything about where she was going?"

"Nope."

"Well, that town down there is too small to hide out in, and we can't stay in the wood. I say we go back to Berlin and look for Erika. A big city is better if you want to be ignored, and maybe Erika has gone back there by now. We don't know that she hasn't, and I know where she stays—the hotel and the room."

"The Gestapo is probably watching the hotel. Either that or that dumb-shit at Abwehr with the dickless monkeys has people watching. But you're right. We can't stay around here. People will be looking for us. You know those kids told their parents about your English."

"And about you chasing them with a knife."

"We can't hitch a ride without being able to speak German," Tars stated. "We'll have to steal a car. If we make it to Berlin, we'll call the hotel from a public telephone and see if Erika is there. We can't risk waltzing into the hotel and knocking on her door. If she's not there, I don't know what we'll do. We'll be up shit creek."

"If we can't find Erika, maybe we can make it to Switzerland."

"Do you know how many people have tried that? The Germans protect those cross points like trolls guard their bridge."

"We'll find a wild place and cross the border there; we're getting good at hightailing it through the wood."

"Maybe. We'll take one thing at a time."

[Hotel zum Türken on the Obersalzberg]

"Excuse me."

Absorbed in his paperwork and with his back to the registration desk, the hotel clerk looked up and spun around when the woman's voice surprised him.

"I'm sorry," he apologized. "I did not hear you walk up." She stood at the reception desk looking at him. "How may I help you, Madam?"

"I wish to speak with Karen Hinderliter if she's available."

"I believe Frau Hinderliter is in her office. May I tell her your name?"

"Erika Lehmann."

"Thank you." The clerk disappeared through a doorway. The Hotel zum Türken sat a short distance down the road from Adolf Hitler's chateau and was often used by important officials who had traveled to the mountainous area above Berchtesgaden to conduct business with the Führer, Martin Bormann, or another of Hitler's subordinates. The hotel also hosted various lower-ranking SS and Gestapo officers seeking relaxation while on leave.

A tall, raven-haired woman walked out, the clerk on her heels.

"Erika, so nice to see you," the woman said.

"Nice to see you, Karen."

"What can I do for you? Will you be staying with us?"

"No, I'm afraid not," answered Erika. "I would like to talk to you privately if I may."

"Of course. Let's go into my office."

After returning from Poland, Erika left Tars at the farm outside Ulm with Suse and traveled to Munich where she spent two days with Ada. So Tars could rejoin Maeve, on Friday Erika bought two rail tickets and took Tars to Leipzig where she handed Tars over to Stephanie Fischer. The weekend saw Erika in Oberschopfheim visiting her father's grave and talking to family about his death last summer. As expected, her family members believed he had been killed in a boating accident. Unlike Erika, they had no reason to doubt, and she told them nothing. To reveal the real circumstances of her father's death would put them in danger. Erika no longer cared about the business in Berlin: the capture of the SOE team, or her duty to keep Abwehr abreast of her whereabouts. After Auschwitz, she was finished with Abwehr. *Lorelei* died on the gallows at Auschwitz alongside the sweet little girl. The only thing that mattered now was finding the people responsible for her father's murder.

Karen sat down behind her desk and motioned for Erika to take a chair. "So, what is it you want to talk to me about, Erika?"

"I need a list."

Chapter 84

Car Thieves

Falkensee
Next day; Tuesday, 30 May 1944

"Don't try talking German to anybody," Tars whispered. "Just keep looking for keys. If any of these yokels says something to us, we just ignore them and keep walking."

For the past hour, Maeve and Tars had walked the streets of Falkensee, a town about 40 minutes west of Berlin, hoping to find a car with keys in the ignition.

"You'd think we'd have found one by now," Maeve commented softly. "These Germans don't trust their neighbors."

After 15 more fruitless minutes, they came upon a farm-supply store. Out front, a farmer loaded a bag of chickenfeed into the bed of his old truck, then went back into the store for another. The engine was running.

"We finally got a break," said Tars.

They sprinted to the truck and both ran up to the passenger side. "You're driving," Tars said. "I don't know how."

"I don't know how, either," said Maeve.

"What? Why didn't you tell me that?"

"It was your idea to steal a car. I thought you knew how to drive."

"Shit."

"I've watched how people do it," said Maeve. "I can try." She ran around to the driver's door. Once behind the wheel, Maeve found and released the emergency break, loudly ground the gears finding first, then let out the clutch pedal too abruptly. The truck jerked forward and the engine died.

"Come on! Get us out of here!" said Tars. "That dumb-ass farmer will be back any second!"

Maeve pushed in the clutch pedal and turned the key. The engine started and this time she let up on the pedal more slowly. The

418

truck started down the street but the engine screamed for need of second gear. Maeve jerked the gear stick back and forth but could not find second.

"Shift the damn thing!" Tars yelled.

"I'm trying! Hump off!"

Finally finding second, Maeve zig-zagged down the street, barely missing parked cars. When a bicyclist approached on the opposite side of the street, Maeve inadvertently forced the man off the road where he crashed into a light pole. He raised a fist and shouted something in German as he picked himself off the sidewalk.

When they came to an intersection, Tars pointed to the left. "I think we go that way. Turn there."

"I think we go the other way," said Maeve.

"No. I know the way . . . I think. Turn left."

Maeve tried but missed the turn and crashed into the side of a parked sedan. The crash killed the engine and water gushed from the radiator.

They jumped out and ran down an alley.

[Berlin—that evening]

Just after dark a black Volkswagen pulled over and stopped two blocks from the KaDeWe department store. The largest department store in Europe, Berlin's KaDeWe sat on the Ku'Damm, seven blocks from the Kempinski Hotel.

"Don't forget your vow," Maeve said from the back seat. Tars sat in front with her open switchblade held to the ribs of a very nervous old man. After the debacle of trying to steal the farmer's truck, Maeve and Tars hustled from the crash site until a safe distance away where they discussed Plan B. Since neither drove, Tars suggested a carjacking. Maeve refused to take part unless Tars vowed not to kill the driver once they reached Berlin. With little choice, Tars was forced to agree. Eventually they came across the old man getting into his car. Maeve communicated well enough to let him know Berlin was their destination; Tars' knife did the rest of the talking.

"You're making another big mistake," warned Tars. "If you would have let me kill those German pilots like I wanted to, the Gestapo in France would never have known about us. Plus, we've had to talk English in front of this guy. He'll report us and those shits looking for us will know we're in Berlin."

"We can't kill innocent people."

"Why not?"

"It's not right. And it's bad luck."

Tars had few superstitions and certainly no qualms about burying her knife in the old man, but she knew she had to release him. The code of the 'Ndrangheta demanded vows be kept. She had sworn to never break the code during the *Cerimonia di Sangue,* the "Ceremony of Blood," where a cut was made over her heart with the *Pugnale d'oro,* a centuries-old gold dagger. "Can you tell him to drive on and not look back?"

Maeve thought for a moment. I know *drive* but that's all."

"When we get out, tell him that. We'll need some money. How do you say *money* in German?"

"Geld," Maeve answered.

Tars turned to the old man and pressed the point of her knife more firmly to his side. "Geld!" The perspiring driver quickly handed over his Reichsmarks. Tars looked around the street and told Maeve, "Let's get out."

The women exited the car and Maeve told the man "Fahren" as she closed the door. He gladly put the car in gear and stepped on the gas. The women watched until the Volkswagen disappeared into traffic a block away.

"We'll make the phone call from that big department store down the street," said Tars. "Are you sure you can speak German good enough to not give yourself away to the hotel switchboard girl?"

Maeve nodded. "'Room' is *Zimmer* and Erika is registered under the name Anne Drexler. I'll just say: *Fräulein Anne Drexler Zimmer, bitte. Bitte* means *please.* I should think that would be enough."

When they reached the KaDeWe, they chose a phone booth from several just inside the main doors. Maeve entered and closed the booth door while Tars waited. It was several minutes before Maeve stuck her head out.

"Some man answered so I hung up," she whispered.

"Damn," Tars said, also softly. "You got through the switchboard okay?"

"Yes, and it's still Erika's room or she wouldn't have connected me."

"We'll have to try back later," said Tars.

[same time]

Stephanie Fischer walked into a dark alley four blocks from the Kempinski Hotel. Victor Knight had called an hour ago. As she stepped past a tall stack of discarded boxes and a series of trash cans, she made out two dark figures in the shadows.

"Hello, Fischer." The voice was John Mayne's. Knight stood beside him.

Chapter 85

Maeve Rings

Berlin
Same day; Tuesday, 30 May 1944

A siren could be heard growing louder on the Ku'Damm. Stephanie Fischer, Victor Knight and John Mayne retreated more deeply into the shadows even though they knew the siren was not for them—the Gestapo never announced its arrival. In a moment they watched a Kripo police car speed by the alley.

Forced to speak English for Mayne's sake, Stephanie spoke softly as the siren grew faint: "John, I assume you came in with the bombers Sunday night."

"That's right," said Mayne.

Victor Knight broke in. "If I might interrupt the jolly reunion, where's Lehmann? Why didn't she answer the telephone at the hotel?"

"She disappeared."

"Disappeared? What do you mean—*disappeared?*"

"Last week she rescued Tars from a concentration camp. On Friday, I met Erika in Leipzig where she turned Tars over to me. I haven't heard from her since, and she has not checked in with Abwehr. No one knows where she is."

"By god, she didn't have my permission to go after Tars. I specifically stated. . . ."

Stephanie interrupted, "You don't control things anymore, Knight. Operation Kriemhild is in shambles; it's over. The wise thing for both of you to do is get out of Germany immediately. Make your way to the Balkans—that's the safest escape route. I can help."

Knight was furious but kept his voice low. "We're not turning tail to save our hides, goddammit."

"You won't help your side by staying here and getting yourselves killed," Stephanie advised. "Escape won't be easy, but if you manage it you'll live to fight another day."

"As a Jew, I'd think you'd want to keep up the fight, Fischer," argued Knight. "Even without Lehmann, we can still eliminate some Gestapo and SS, even if they aren't on our list."

"I'm not a Jew. That was a cover Admiral Canaris devised in order to insert me in your SOE." With a hand in her jacket pocket, Stephanie was ready. When Mayne stepped toward her she pulled her pistol. "Back off, John. I can shoot you both right here and be a hero."

"You better aim well," the imposing Mayne said as he took another step forward.

Knight placed a hand on Mayne's shoulder to stop him.

Stephanie said, "Himmler and Schellenberg know everything about Kriemhild. A team has been assembled to capture you and I'm on it. I'm expected to inform my superiors as soon as John arrives. If you won't do the wise thing—forget about this blown mission and leave Germany—then I suggest you listen to me. I assume you brought the weapons and explosives, John."

Mayne only glared at her. Knight answered for him. "We have them in a safe place."

Stephanie lowered her gun.

At eleven o'clock, or perhaps a few minutes after, Stephanie returned to Erika's room at the Kempinski Hotel. Kai Faust had been there when she left, and was there now.

"The telephone rang twice after you left," Kai said as soon as she stepped in the door. "I answered, hoping it was Erika, but whoever it was hung up."

"They said nothing?"

"No. How did the meeting go?"

"John Mayne, the SOE agent we've been waiting for is here. He dropped in Sunday night during the attack."

"Good. Now we can capture them and get that out of the way so we can turn our attention to finding Erika. This time away from my squad that Obersturmbannführer Skorzeny granted me can't last much longer. Rumor among some of my comrades is there's a mission in the planning stages. When training begins, I'll be away full-time."

Before Stephanie could reply, the telephone rang.

"Hallo."

Silence.

"Hallo," Stephanie repeated.

After a delay, a voice finally said, *"Erika, bitte."*

Stephanie recognized the voice and replied in English. "Maeve! This is Stephanie." Kai walked over.

"I want to talk to Erika."

"She's not here."

"Who was the man who answered the phone earlier?"

"Kai Faust. You met him."

"Where's Erika?"

"We don't know, Maeve. Is Tars with you?"

"Yes, she's here." Maeve was calling from a phone booth in a cable-car station she and Tars came across while walking. Tars opened the booth door slightly and jerked on Maeve's arm to get her attention. *"Hold a minute,"* Maeve told Stephanie. She lowered the phone and placed her hand over the receiver.

"Is that Erika?" Tars asked excitedly.

"No, it's Stephanie, Erika's friend who took us to that cabin."

"Hang up."

"I'm not hanging up. Erika trusts her or she wouldn't have asked her to hide us." Maeve put the phone back to her ear. *"I'm back."*

"Listen carefully, Maeve. It's dangerous to be out late at night when you don't speak German. If the police see two unescorted women out late they will likely ask you what you're doing. You need to find someplace to hide yourselves away tonight. Can you do that?"

"We'll find someplace."

"Do you have any Reichsmarks?"

"Yes."

"Okay. Meet me tomorrow at noon at the zoo in the Tiergarten—that's the large park in the center of Berlin. Do you know numbers in German?"

"I do up to one hundred."

"Good. Since you know numbers you can pay a taxi driver. A cab will be the safest way to get there. I don't know where you're calling from, but a cab ride to the park from anywhere in Berlin shouldn't be more than four or five Reichsmarks. When you get in the taxi, all you have to say to the driver is: 'Fahrer, zum Tiergarten Zoo, bitte.' If he wants to chat as he drives, just ignore him. He'll think you're haughty and leave you alone. Got that?"

"'Fahrer, zum Tiergarten Zoo, bitte.' I got it."

"I'll meet you in front of the lion den at noon. Don't be late, but don't be standing there before that time. It's important that you walk up to the lion den at exactly noon."

"Is that all?"

"That's all. Be careful, Maeve."

As soon as Stephanie hung up, Kai started to speak but she placed a finger on his lips and then guided him to the bathroom where she turned on the bathtub faucet.

"Schellenberg will have ordered the phone tapped," she told him, "and maybe the room bugged."

"Why do you think that?"

"He ordered me to stay here in case Maeve returned looking for Erika. I'm sure he no longer trusts Erika since she went on leave and isn't following daily contact protocol. The phone is tapped, take my word for it."

"Why did you tell Maeve *tomorrow?* We should pick her up tonight."

"The Gestapo will be at the rendezvous. We need time to prepare."

"If the Gestapo knows of the rendezvous, the zoo sounds to me a poor choice of location. It's too wide open."

Stephanie shook her head. "My sister and I worked at the zoo when we were teenagers. I know the underground caverns that access many of the animal areas. Those tunnels will prove useful."

"Well, if the Gestapo will be there, daytime is wise," Kai acknowledged. "Night would only aid them." As a bodyguard, Kai knew it was easier to protect someone during the day. If Stephanie was right about the phone tap, the Gestapo would know the exact location—in front of the lion den. At night, the Gestapo could gain a position to see the women and use darkness to remain undetected. At least during daylight, he and Stephanie would have a chance to see the Gestapo coming. "So after we capture the women, then we turn our attention to the Engländer?"

"You and I aren't going to capture Maeve and Tars, and we're not going to capture the Engländer—not if you want to see Erika again. I didn't tell you, but every morning at five o'clock I walk to a phone booth three blocks away where Erika calls me. She doesn't tell me where she calls from, but when she calls tomorrow, I'll tell her about John Mayne and fill her in about the zoo."

Chapter 86

Nancy

Berlin
Next day; Wednesday, 31 May 1944

Last night, after Stephanie's advice to get off the streets and lie low, Tars jimmied the lock on an overhead door to a loading dock at the back of a grocery store closed for the night. The brick floor offered little comfort, but the sheltered, enclosed dock tendered security. They slept among crates and barrels, out of view of anyone who might walk down the alley. Tars woke first and shook Maeve.

"What time is it?" asked a bleary Maeve.

"Four-thirty."

"Four-thirty? It can't even be first light."

"We have to get out of here at daybreak. Whoever runs this store might show up early."

Maeve sat up and looked around. A ventilation gridiron in the store wall allowed the weak night lighting inside the store to filter into the dock.

Tars commented, "At least you didn't sleep naked. I knew you could do it."

"I can't sleep without me drawers on these bricks. I'd wake up with the brick hollows tattooed on me arse."

Tars handed Maeve an apple. "There's a crate of these behind your head."

They ate their apple breakfast in silence until Tars asked a question. "Why did you pray for me?"

Maeve stopped chomping. "What?"

"On the freighter when the Germans from that U-boat were about to come through our cabin door, you prayed for me. Why?"

"I don't understand the question," said Maeve. "Why shouldn't I have prayed? We thought we were going to die."

"You shouldn't pray for me."

"Why not?"

"I have no hope for Heaven; I've done too many bad things. God won't have me. You insult Him praying for me. You shouldn't do it."

"That's crazy. People don't insult God by praying for people, no matter what they've done." Silence for a moment, then Maeve asked, "Why did you knock the *L* pill out of me hand when the Gestapo caught us at that barn in France?"

This time a lengthy silence followed until Tars said quietly, "My first name is Nancy."

[8:00 a.m.—Abwehr headquarters, 72 Tirpitz Ufer]
Stephanie Fischer sat across from Walter Schellenberg.

"Well done last night, Fischer," praised Schellenberg. "It looks like you have the Irishwoman convinced you will help her." Schellenberg had read the transcript of Stephanie's telephone conversation with Maeve the previous evening. "What about Kai Faust?"

Stephanie had guessed right about the tap on the hotel room telephone, but the room itself had not been bugged. She answered, "He believes I arranged the zoo rendezvous in order to reacquire the women and help them escape Berlin."

"Still nothing from Lehmann?"

"No, sir. I haven't heard from her."

"Well, after we finish this business today we'll turn our attention to Lehmann. Last night I notified Reichsführer Himmler. He'll send a capture team to the zoo. I made it clear that you work with us so you won't be harmed."

"Thank you, Oberführer."

[same time—Gestapo Headquarters, 8 Prinz Albrechtstrasse]
When Heinrich Himmler entered the strategy room with Heinrich Müller on his heels, nine men and one woman stood. One of the men was Conrad Gerber.

"You may be seated," Himmler said while remaining on his feet. "Gruppenführer Müller assures me everyone here is well-versed in their duties." Himmler and Müller had huddled in Himmler's office all night devising the plan and deciding on the appropriate personnel to carry it out. At four o'clock, Müller summoned the team members to headquarters for briefings. "The two women must be stopped," Himmler continued, referring to Maeve and Tars. "This is an *arrest-or-kill* assignment. If arrest is possible, do so. But the women must not escape. If you think they might get away, you are authorized to kill them. If any bystanders are killed or harmed that will be unfortunate, but you will not be held responsible as long as the assignment is successful. You have been given a photograph of the Abwehr operative Fischer. She is working with us and will signal you as soon as she makes a positive identification of the two women."

Himmler focused on Conrad Gerber. "Gerber, I brought you in on this because you've seen the Irishwoman." He did not elaborate about where Gerber had seen Maeve. Himmler could have simply shown the team an Abwehr photo of Erika Lehmann so everyone in the room could identify Maeve, but in this company any mention of either of the Lehmanns was strictly avoided. "But I certainly can't trust you to be in charge for reasons we both are aware of. That's why Kriminalrat Rode heads this assignment. You'll do what he tells you."

"Yes, Herr Reichsführer," said Gerber, too loudly as always. He could not care less about being in charge; after Spain, Gerber was euphoric just to be breathing.

[11:45 a.m.—Tiergarten Zoo]

At 230 hectares, Berlin's Tiergarten measured twice the size of London's Hyde Park. The zoo, kept open on Hitler's orders despite Allied bombings, lay near the park's southwest corner. Two hours ago, Maeve and Tars had the taxi drop them at the Tiergarten's northeast edge and they meandered through the park checking their surroundings before entering the zoo. Now they stood in front of the hippo pond, the exhibit farthest from the lion den that still allowed a line of vision.

"I still haven't spotted her," said Tars, referring to Stephanie Fischer.

429

Maeve checked her watch. "She said it was important for us to be at the lion den at noon sharp and not before. She's probably waiting to do the same. I wonder if Erika will come with her."

"Erika won't know about this. Fischer doesn't know where she is. At least that's what Fischer told us at that cabin."

At five minutes before the hour, they began walking toward the lion exhibit. A weekday, the zoo was not crowded. As they neared the rendezvous point, they saw two boys with roller skates strapped to their shoes, two workers sweeping, a woman with two toddlers in tow, another woman pushing a baby carriage, a clown handing out balloons, and a man selling pretzels and apple juice from a cart. At exactly twelve o'clock, Maeve and Tars arrived at the rail in front of the lion den. In the den below, a male lion with a magnificent mane sat sleepy-eyed; one lioness watched the people and a second licked her cub. From out of nowhere, Stephanie Fischer appeared at the women's side holding a zoo map in her left hand.

"Listen carefully," Stephanie said, "and don't react to what I say. The Gestapo tapped Erika's telephone and they are here. It's likely the sweepers are Gestapo, and I know the woman with the baby carriage is; she's been in this area for nearly an hour and hasn't once checked on her baby. I'm not sure about the clown or the vendor, but more Gestapo will be hiding nearby. They think I'm working with them. They're watching me and waiting for my signal. When I move the paper I'm holding from my left hand to my right, that signals them that I'm sure you are the women they're after and they'll move in for the arrest. Your only escape is through the lion den."

"Jesus, Mary and Joseph!" Maeve exclaimed.

"Quiet, and listen—." Stephanie spoke quickly. "Keepers feed the lions at ten every morning; they will not be hungry, and the lions are used to keepers entering the den. If you walk, they should not bother you, but don't run. They react to running. Don't look the lions in the eye, and especially don't look at the cub—that will set the mother on edge. Ignore them but act confident, as if you belong there. Walk calmly through the den and into the cave in the den's far wall. That cave leads to the lion cages and the keeper's corridor that leads to a series of tunnels that run to other animal areas and end at the worker's entrance in the park at the other side of the zoo. Follow the signs with arrows and the word 'Ausgang' and they'll lead you out. It's your only chance to escape. The jump down to the den floor is fifteen feet but the ground near the wall is kept muddy and soft so the lions can't jump up the wall; roll when you hit and you'll be fine. Now, one of you hit me hard in the face and go over the rail. Do it now."

"Where do we go if we make it out?" asked Maeve.

"Do it now, dammit," Stephanie repeated quietly but sternly.

Tars did not hesitate. She punched Stephanie in the face as hard as she could and Stephanie made sure her collapse was convincing. Maeve and Tars hopped over the waist-high rail and jumped.

Chapter 87

Der Zoo

As soon as Maeve and Tars jumped into the lion den, the woman pushing the baby carriage pulled a Schmeisser machine pistol from it and ran to the rail. The sweepers dropped their brooms, pulled pistols and joined her. Seven other Gestapo agents ran from various buildings and sheds along the exhibit walkway. Stephanie, acting groggy, sat up and struggled to her feet.

Maeve and Tars, covered in mud after landing and rolling, drew their guns but did not point them at the lions. Holding the guns at their sides they began their walk through the den. The male, now fully awake and on his feet, watched the intruders. Both lionesses rose to a crouch but neither approached. The cub took notice as well and sat up on his haunches, then fell over.

Rode, the agent in charge, watched flabbergasted. The criminals jumping into the lion den was certainly not one of the escape contingencies discussed. Finally, he shouted to Maeve and Tars, "Stop! You're under arrest!" but then realized if the women did stop, who would go arrest them? "Take aim," he ordered, and the other agents pointed and cocked their weapons.

Tars understood the *Halt!,* and she understood the cocking of guns. Positioning her body between Maeve and the rail, she turned to Rode. "Why don't you come down here and get us, ass-hole! We'll wait for you!"

Rode said to the others, "What did she say? Does anyone speak English?"

Stephanie, also with her gun trained on the women, answered. "She invited us to go down there and arrest them. She gambles that we want them alive, and she's right if indeed that's possible. Where can they go? Surely that cave leads only to the cages. I suggest we see if the lions are hungry. I'm ready for some entertainment."

Rode and several of the other agents smiled. "Very well," he said. "Hold your fire."

Apparently the shouting set the king lion on edge and it slowly began approaching the women. Maeve froze. Tars said, "What are you doing? Keep moving."

Maeve was trembling. "That big one's coming over here."

"It's not roaring or acting pissed off. Get going—just keep walking slowly."

"I can't do it, Tars."

"It's kind of late to decide that when we're in the middle of them. If they attack, we have our guns. *Walk.*"

Maeve started walking. They progressed slowly toward the opening in the rock wall. As they got nearer and nearer to it, up at the rail Rode grew frantic. "Those lions are letting them pass!" he said, incredulous, then turned to Stephanie: "Are you sure that cave leads only to the cages?"

"Where else would it lead?" she answered. "I'm no expert on zoos, but that's my assumption."

Rode watched Maeve and Tars inch closer to the cave. "I'm not taking the chance."

Stephanie knew Rode was about to order fire and said quickly, "I'll arrest them." Not waiting for his okay, she hopped the rail and jumped into the den.

Rode wasn't satisfied, or about to entrust the arrest to one woman who wasn't even Gestapo. "Open fire!" Rode shouted. "Kill the two criminals!"

Maeve and Tars were within 10 feet of the cave when the Gestapo began firing. Except for the woman with the Schmeisser, all were armed with pistols, inaccurate at that distance. But the spray from the Schmeisser chopped the ground all around Maeve and Tars. As Tars used her body to shield Maeve, she was hit twice in the back and once in her right leg. As she collapsed, she shoved Maeve the remaining few feet into the darkness of the cave.

"Tars!" Maeve screamed and ran back out firing.

With the Schmeisser's clip spent, the female Gestapo agent began loading another. From the den floor, Stephanie turned and shot the woman.

"Kill them all!" Rode shouted. By now, any bystanders had found something to hide behind or had run away. The gunfire and spitting dirt confused the lions; they ran amuck and roared but were not threatening the women. Suddenly two Gestapo agents at the rail fell, struck by fire from the cave. Victor Knight and John Mayne ran out of the cave firing. Knight was hit in the arm as he attempted to drag Maeve back into the cave.

Maeve jerked from his grasp. "Tars is alive! I'm not leaving her here!"

Mayne and Fischer kept Knight and Maeve covered while they dragged Tars into the cave. Mayne held an American Thompson sub-machine gun in each hand and its deadly spray forced the Gestapo to hit the ground. When Knight and Maeve had Tars safely in the cave, Mayne and Fischer followed them in.

When the shooting from below stopped, Rode lifted his head and yelled, "Everyone get down there now! If the lions get near, shoot them!"

At the back of the cave, two belligerent, caged lions roared and shook their cages as Knight and Maeve carried Tars past. Knight opened the heavy steel door to the keeper's corridor and they laid Tars down. He ran back to the cave entrance to help Mayne and Fischer hold off the Gestapo who were now jumping over the rail into the den after moving to a place that kept out of the line of fire of anyone inside the cave.

"Tars!" Maeve said, tears flowing as she held her wounded friend. "You'll be okay! We'll find a doctor! I promise!"

Tars coughed blood. "I'm . . . not afraid," she struggled to say. "It's . . . my time now." She coughed more blood.

"No, it's not! You're going to be okay! You saved my life and I'll save yours. Sweet Virgin, please ask your Son to help Tars," Maeve prayed.

Tars smiled weakly. "That's the second time . . . you prayed for me." Tars coughed more blood and tightened her grip on Maeve's hand. "I . . . love . . . you, Maeve."

The light in Tars' eyes turned off.

"Tars! . . . *Tars!*" Maeve put her face to Tars' chest and wept bitterly. Then, suddenly enraged, Maeve picked up her gun, ran to the cave entrance and began firing, killing the closest Gestapo agent. Mayne and Knight, standing just inside the dark entrance, didn't see her until she passed them but Mayne, the closest to her, reacted quickly by reaching out and yanking her back inside as the Gestapo returned fire.

"Time to go!" Knight shouted.

They ran into the corridor where Maeve said, "I'm not leaving her here."

Mayne quickly checked Tars, "She's dead. Let's go."

"No!" Maeve shouted and knelt to pick up Tars.

"I'll take her," said Mayne. He picked up Tars' body and they fled down the corridor.

On the floor of the den, the six remaining Gestapo agents slowly worked their way toward the cave. The king lion wasn't close but his snarl apparently made Gerber nervous. He aimed his pistol and shot the king just before another shot rang out from above. Gerber screamed in pain, and all the agents turned. A blonde who looked just like the woman who fled through the cave stood at the rail, a pistol in each hand. When she started firing, the Gestapo ran toward the cave and two more were wounded. The Schmeisser-firing agent who Stephanie Fischer shot lay near Erika's feet. When the woman groaned, Erika shot her in the head. Once inside the cave, the agents expected to be fired on by those they chased, but no one was there. They took positions to return fire with the woman at the rail, but when they looked out she, too, was gone.

Rode and the two agents who could still walk found the door to the keeper's corridor and ran hoping to catch the group. As they entered the series of tunnels they heard an explosion up ahead. They continued on, following the exit signs and wending their way through the maze until they came to a smoke-and-dust-filled passageway blocked by a cave-in. Rode stopped, coughed twice from the dust, and cursed.

In the Tiergarten, a heavy iron door to an underground workers' entrance flung open and two men and two women ran up the steps and into the park. In a moment another man emerged from the exit. Too risky for one of Skorzeny's commandos to be seen and possibly recognized by the Gestapo, Stephanie Fischer had demanded Kai Faust stay out of sight. Faust had guarded the tunnel exit from inside, and set up and detonated the explosives that collapsed the tunnel after the others ran by.

Several park walkers stopped to stare at the massive man running by with a limp woman in his arms. "She fainted," Stephanie shouted to them. "Perhaps a heart seizure. We're taking her to the hospital." A dark-green cargo van sat parked on the closest street. Mayne loaded Tars' body into the van and everyone followed him in. Kathryn Fischer put the van into gear and drove off, at one point pulling over and stopping with the rest of traffic for passing Kripo police cars, their sirens blasting as they fishtailed around corners on their way to the zoo.

Chapter 88

Licking Wounds

Berlin
That night—Wednesday, 31 May 1944

Before Victor Knight left Scotland, Kathryn Fischer relayed to STS 23 three Berlin-area addresses she considered the safest places to hide the non-German-speaking John Mayne. After Knight arrived in Berlin, he surveilled the locations and chose this flea-bag hotel in Neukölln, a district in south Berlin. Now late evening, Knight sat with Mayne in the shabby hotel room along with Stephanie and Kathryn Fischer, Kai Faust, and a dispirited Maeve O'Rourke. They had just arrived. Two hours ago, after darkness fell, they drove a few miles out of the city and buried Tars in a hastily dug grave in the woods. The body could have been disposed of with less risk, but Maeve demanded that Tars receive proper burial.

"Well," Knight started with the obvious, "today didn't go exactly as planned." The wound to his upper left arm remained unattended, but when checked earlier it was found it to be a flesh wound and not serious.

No one commented. John Mayne and Kai Faust sat glaring at each other. Maeve sat away from the group in a corner, her face pallid and puffy from weeping.

Faust moved his eyes from Mayne to Stephanie. "I thought you said we could expect Erika at the zoo."

"I said Erika told me she would do her best to be there," Stephanie said impatiently, her clothes, like Maeve's, caked with dried mud from the jump into the lion den. "Erika didn't tell me where she called from, only that she was not in Berlin but would try to make it to the zoo by noon. And that's exactly what I told all of you this morning when we met to review the plan. Obviously she couldn't get there in time."

"So how are we going to get in touch with her?" Faust asked.

"Erika has called me every day so there's no reason to think she won't call tomorrow. I'll tell her about Tars, and that I have to go underground." Stephanie knew her career with Abwehr was over. Her cover might have held up after Tars struck her and jumped with Maeve into the den, but when Stephanie was forced to shoot the Schmeisser-wielding Gestapo agent to save Maeve she knew there was no going back.

Mayne sat on the trunk of weapons and explosives he brought with him. He broke in to ask Kai Faust, "Why are you so fucking interested in Lehmann?"

"None of your goddamn business." The super-elite SS commando and the fierce SOE operative distrusted each other and had quarreled in the van. Faust felt similar animosity towards Victor Knight. Faust had nothing but contempt for the Gestapo, whom he now knew had tried to kill Erika in America and again in Spain (believing she was on the freighter), but he blew the tunnel today because he thought he was helping Erika escape along with these people. Had Faust known his wife would not be at the zoo today, he would be the first to arrest or shoot these British agents. A nationalist, Faust was fully committed to Germany. He wanted his wife safe, however, and knew the horrors that would befall her if she fell into Gestapo hands. Obviously, Erika trusted her fellow Abwehr operative, and he reasoned Fischer would provide his best chance to find her. After that, he would deal with the Engländer.

"Let's not claw at each other's throats again," Stephanie interjected. "As for what we do now, we'll lie low until after I speak with Erika then we can gather again. I'll take Maeve with me tonight and we'll all meet back here tomorrow night at nine."

By default, Stephanie had assumed leadership. Knight was in charge of Mayne, but he had little choice but to defer to Stephanie on the zoo mission. And as he sat listening to her, he was okay with that—at least for now. Knight knew Stephanie burned her Abwehr bridges today and was now fully entangled with the SOE whether she liked it or not. And even though Operation Kriemhild as originally planned lay in ruins, the way Knight figured it, at least some Gestapo died today and that was why he had come to Germany. Knight was prepared to die in Berlin as long as he took some Nazi henchmen with him.

"I want to be present when you talk with Erika tomorrow morning," said Faust.

Normally, Stephanie would never consent to a third party standing over her shoulder for such a call, but this man was Erika's husband. She nodded, then said as she rose, "Then we'll all meet here tomorrow night at nine."

Knight said he would stay there overnight with Mayne, and the others walked out together. In the van, Stephanie told Faust the location of the public telephone where she would await Erika's call tomorrow morning. Faust told Kathryn where to drop him and after a 30-minute drive she pulled over.

"I'll be waiting near the telephone booth at five o'clock," Faust told Stephanie as he left the van. He started walking as Kathryn drove off.

"He must live here in Spandau," Kathryn commented. "He wouldn't have me drop him in front of his flat, of course, but it's probably close by." They rode in silence for a block. Maeve did not want to talk to anyone and hadn't uttered a word since they buried Tars; she now sat at the back of the van hanging her head. Kathryn and Stephanie spoke in German, free to talk without concern of Maeve understanding.

"You must get out of Germany, Steph," Kathryn advised. "Remaining here underground won't work for long with both the Gestapo and Abwehr hunting you."

"At least your cover is still solid," Stephanie responded.

"I'm living on borrowed time, too. It's only a matter of time before the Gestapo discovers I'm a plant. I knew that going in."

"A lot depends on how long the war lasts . . . for both of us."

Kathryn looked at her sister, who just told her she was not leaving Germany.

Chapter 89

High Price

Berlin—8 Prinz Albrechtstrasse
Next day; Thursday, 1 June 1944

A morose Heinrich Himmler stared out his office window at the late-morning traffic on Prinz Albrechtstrasse, thinking about the high price already paid in his effort to eliminate Karl Lehmann's daughter.

Himmler assumed Axel Ryker was dead. Nearly two years ago he sent Ryker to America to find and kill her. The Gestapo's most skilled and deadly assassin, Ryker was not one to abandon a mission and disappear. Yet no one had seen Ryker since, and *she* still lived.

Eight agents died in Spain and two more yesterday at the Tiergarten zoo, with three agents wounded. Two Totenkopf camp guards had been murdered in Poland and, after putting the pieces together, Himmler became convinced Lehmann was responsible. The guards, reported AWOL the morning after Lehmann arrived at Auschwitz, were last seen alive outside a tavern in Krakow where, according to a Heer driver, Lehmann spent the night in a hotel. After more investigating, Himmler discovered one of the dead guards had escorted Lehmann through the camp.

Thirteen dead and three wounded.

Himmler's only consolation now was that Lehmann had become a rogue Abwehr agent working with the enemy and, therefore, a traitor. She could no longer count on the Führer's loyalties to her father to help her. For his part, all Himmler could do was keep hunting her and her partners, though the others were secondary at this point. Himmler reasoned that when he found Erika Lehmann, they all would turn up.

Conrad Gerber surviving the zoo fiasco was the lone positive development. Wounded in the buttocks, Gerber had already left the hospital. Himmler felt confident Lehmann could not ferret out any information about the real way her father died: No records existed, so even the mole inside the Gestapo who had furnished her the camp release papers could not help her there. If by chance Gerber or any of the men assigned to eliminate Karl Lehmann suddenly turned up dead, Himmler would at least know for certain Lehmann's daughter suspected the Gestapo. The wondering would be over.

[Berlin—that afternoon]
Kai Faust had waited beside the boathouse for 30 minutes. The arrangements for this meeting had been made that morning during Erika's call to Stephanie Fischer. Suddenly, Erika appeared on the walkway in a navy blue sweat-suit, glasses, and a knit-woolen skull cap that covered her hair. He knew she wore the outfit to alter her appearance, but he wasn't concerned that either of them had been followed. No one had reason to follow him but he had taken precautions nevertheless, making many unnecessary turns and keeping a keen eye in the rearview mirror during his drive to the lake. And he doubted anyone alive could follow Erika if she were wary of a tail. Kai walked to meet her; they embraced and kissed.

"I rented a boat," Kai said. Erika smiled. After they had married, during their brief weeks together before duty pulled them apart, they often enjoyed an intimate boat ride on the Wannsee, a large lake on the southwest outskirts of Berlin. Kai led her to a rowboat tied to the pier.

They stepped into the boat without speaking; Kai shoved it from the pier and took the oars. Erika sat at the stern, Kai facing her as he rowed out into the lake.

"I thought you would be at the zoo yesterday," Kai finally said. "That's why I was there."

"When I talked to Stephanie yesterday, I called from Ingolstadt. I started out right away but a bomb-damaged railway outside Bayreuth caused a delay, so the train didn't arrive in Berlin until a quarter to noon. I rushed to the zoo, but by the time I reached the lion den, all of you were gone and the Gestapo agents were in the den."

"What took you to Ingolstadt?" Kai asked as he rowed.

"I'm looking for someone."

"Someone?"

Erika nodded.

"Someone involved with your father's death?"

Erika glanced away.

Kai stopped rowing. "Stephanie told me you suspect Himmler is behind your father's death, and Spain proves he's now after you. Let me take you to a safe place, Erika. In two days I report to Friedenthal to begin training for a mission and will be gone for weeks. We need to act now. Our squadron has a two-seat Focke-Wulf fighter we use for training. Tomorrow morning I can fly you and Ada to Sweden and you can stay with my cousin Emelie and her family in Stockholm. You remember meeting Emelie a few years ago when she visited my mother in Cologne. You two hit it off; you and Ada will have a pleasant time there."

Erika looked heartbroken when Kai mentioned their daughter. "I know Ilse loves Ada and takes wonderful care of her, but still, I hope one of us survives the war—for Ada's sake."

"Then we have the solution. Tomorrow morning I'll fly us to Munich, we'll pick up Ada, then I'll fly you two to Stockholm."

"Kai . . . I came to say goodbye."

Chapter 90

Let slip the dogs of war.
— William Shakespeare

English Channel
Five days later; Tuesday, 6 June 1944

Lieutenant Robert Brice gave the order and PFC Stephen Floyd and 33 other U.S. Army Rangers of the 2nd Ranger Battalion, B Company climbed over the rail of the HMS *Prince Charles.* Floyd and other B Company Rangers descended a rope ladder to a small Higgins boat barely visible from the high rail in the dense Channel fog. Other soldiers up and down the rail climbed down into others in a long line of Higgins boats that, like Floyd's, bobbed and banged against the hull of the ship. It was a well-practiced routine being duplicated by tens of thousands of men in the thousands of ships struggling to hold anchor in the rough Channel waters off the Normandy coast.

[same time—Dog Green Sector of Omaha Beach near the Vierville Draw]
Standing atop a machine gun pillbox, Oberschütze Gerhart Brenner adjusted the focus wheel of his binoculars but knew he would see nothing in the fog of first light. Channel fog rarely lifted until an hour after dawn.

Brenner considered his new duty an improvement. Just three weeks ago, he slept in Italian mud at the bottom of a foxhole near Anzio. At least the pillboxes and tobruks offered dry bunks shielded from what had become regular nighttime bombing attacks along the coast of France from the Brest peninsula all the way north to the border with Holland.

Everyone knew the invasion was coming and it would be led by the Americans. The American, Eisenhower, had been given control, and the Americans held, by far, the bulk of men and matériel an invasion would demand. But many thought the attack would not happen here in Normandy; most of the gamblers among Brenner's comrades put their money on the area near the Pas de Calais. The Pas made sense; that location to the north was much nearer to England than Normandy and required a much shorter voyage across the Channel. Brenner wasn't a gambler but he hoped they were right. In four years of fighting, he had been wounded twice and lost many friends; he was weary of war and wanted to go home.

Again Brenner lifted the binoculars and focused on the fog.

[in the Channel]

A wave came over the side of the overloaded Higgins boat, drenching soldiers already overburdened with weapons and heavy field-packs, the water adding even more weight each man would have to carry onto the beach. PFC Floyd gripped his Thompson sub-machine gun and prayed. Just 19 years old, he was facing his first battle. Lieutenant Brice, beside Floyd at the front of the boat, saw the young soldier's white knuckles.

"You'll be okay, Floyd," Brice shouted over the boat's powerful Chevrolet engine. "Just stay low and keep moving."

Floyd nodded. The soldier next to him vomited, covering one of Floyd's boots.

This boat would be among the first to land in Hitler's France. Being first in was not left to chance or happened by bad draw. Floyd knew someday it would come to this—fighting at the forefront of battles—when he volunteered for the grueling Ranger training. The Rangers were the elite ground troops of the United States Army, their motto: *Rangers Lead the Way.*

Floyd increased his grip on the Thompson and prayed harder.

[Dog Green]

Gerhart Brenner wished he could light a cigarette but smoking on duty was verboten. He looked to his right. Another lookout stood atop the concrete tobruk across the draw. The tobruks, large concrete and steel-reinforced emplacements where troops slept, were armed with flamethrowers and cannons of varied sizes ranging all the way up to the 88s, the massive artillery pieces the Germans had used so effectively to wreak destruction across Poland, Russia, and the Low Countries. When Brenner thought about what would greet the enemy if they attacked here, he felt even more confident the invasion would take place elsewhere. Not only were tobruks and machinegun and sniper pillboxes in positions to rain death on every square inch of the six-mile-long beach, but the offshore waters were mined; iron hedgehogs, buried in the low-tide sand, sat ready to rip open the keels of landing craft before they ever reached shore. Although no land mines lay hidden in the tidal sand, any invaders making it as far as the beach shingle or promenade would find them aplenty.

The Amis are no fools, Brenner thought. *The invaders will not come calling at Normandy.*

Brenner noticed the fog starting to lift and he raised the binoculars. Thinking he saw something, he dropped the glasses to squint. Suddenly the remaining fog lifted like a theater curtain, and Brenner snapped the binoculars back to his eyes to gaze upon the greatest armada in the history of the world. Stretching to the horizon, a galaxy of anchored ships crowded the ocean, so numerous it seemed a man could jump from the deck of one to another. Between the great ships and the beach a constellation of small boats bounced over the waves as they sped toward the beach. From dozens of American destroyers and battle cruisers behind the small boats, Gerhart saw puffs of smoke then heard the scream of incoming shells. He dove into his pillbox as a cacophony of pole-mounted sirens behind the installations began blaring.

"One minute till ramp down!" shouted the coxswain at the rear of the Higgins boat as it slapped up and down amid the waves.

"Weapons up and cocked!" yelled Lieutenant Brice. Private Floyd and the other men pulled the gun bolts of their Thompson machinegun or M-1 rifle. A loud explosion boomed nearby as another Higgins boat struck a mine. Although the Higgins boat hulls were plywood so as not to attract magnet mines, their steel ramps negated that engineering detail if a boat drove directly over one. "Keep your head down!" Brice shouted lest any of his soldiers were tempted to rise and check the fate of their buddies in the doomed boat. "As soon as the ramp goes down, let's get our asses off as fast as possible! The Krauts will zero in on the boat!" The words were barely out of Brice's mouth when the screeching pings of bullets striking the steel ramp began.

"Thirty seconds!" the coxswain yelled. Another soldier vomited.

Gerhart Brenner's assistant gunner had been asleep in the neighboring tobruk when the sirens sounded. He jumped into the pillbox and began helping Brenner with the MG42 machinegun. The American naval bombardment was brief and ended when the small troop boats neared the shore. Some of Brenner's comrades in other emplacements were already firing. "They waste their ammunition," Brenner told his loader. As he readied to fire, Brenner saw one of the boats blow up, killing all of the 35 soldiers on board, victims of an offshore mine. As the first boat was about to gain land, Brenner tightened his grip on the trigger. "We wait till the ramps go down."

The coxswain screamed, *"Ten seconds! Brace yourselves!"* Private Floyd sat back against the hull. Suddenly, the boat thudded to an abrupt stop as if it hit a high curb and the ramp dropped.

"Now!" Lieutenant Brice screamed and led his men onto the ramp. Floyd followed him out with everyone else close behind.

Boats began hitting the sand up and down the beach, many having been under fire while still in the water. But Brenner waited, and when he saw the ramp on the boat directly in front of his pillbox drop he squeezed the trigger.

◊ ◊ ◊

As soon as the ramp fell, several men on Floyd's boat were struck before they could stand, the machinegun bullets easily ripping through the plywood hull. Lieutenant Brice never made it off the ramp. The impact of three direct hits to his chest sent Brice back, first into Floyd, then off the ramp. Floyd was the first to reach sand where a bullet tore through his right leg just above the knee. He went down and other Rangers jumped over or ran around him, many not making it more than a few steps before being struck.

Floyd lay in the sand not knowing what to do except cry, but he was too scared for tears. He knew no medic would come to tend him and he watched helplessly as his buddies kept up the assault. About 25 yards ahead on the beach, Joe Gallo abruptly stopped running, halted in mid-stride by a hail of machinegun fire. Gallo appeared to do a gruesome dance of death before his body fell like lead to the sand. Not far from Gallo, Elmer Olander was shot in the arm, the bullet shattering bone and nearly tearing the limb from his body. The heavy barrage of machinegun fire spit up sand all around Floyd and he realized if he lay there another bullet would find him at any second.

About 100 yards up the beach, Floyd spotted a few mounds of wave-wash rock that might offer cover. From the hundreds of boats assailing the long beach, too many Americans stormed ashore for the Germans to focus on individual targets. Floyd noticed a pattern of bullets impacting sand as German machinegunners methodically swept back and forth trying to mow down as many men as possible. The terrified teenager began crawling, weaving his way through the dead spots of spitting sand, firing his Thompson and praying the pattern would hold.

Adrenaline masked the pain from his injury but blood loss began to weaken Floyd. Halfway to the rock mound, he was forced to stop and rest, using the body of a dead buddy for cover. The body lay face down and Floyd forced himself to not wonder who it was; he didn't want to know. Willing himself on, he saw Mike Vetovich reach the rock pile and look back. "Come on, Floyd!" Vetovich yelled, but he rose up a few inches too many and a sniper sent a round through Vetovich's helmet, killing him instantly.

Floyd finally reached the rock pile and looked back, careful to stay low and not make the same mistake that cost Vetovich his life. Bodies lay everywhere. Higgins boats that didn't make it off the beach lay shredded at the edge of a sea now red with blood. Floyd took off his pack and found a rubber tourniquet and placed it around his thigh to staunch the bleeding. Other men were trying to make it to the rock pile. Hoping to give them cover, Floyd shoved another clip into his Thompson and held it over the rocks, firing blindly at the enemy as sniper bullets glanced off the top of the pile.

Chapter 91

Niflheimr

Berlin—8 Prinz Albrechtstrasse
Four days later; Saturday, 10 June 1944

Heinrich Himmler's week had been a dreary blend of rain, ill tidings, and bad moods.

After the Allied invasion on Tuesday, Himmler, Göring, and a half dozen generals spent the next two days and much of both nights in Hitler's Reichschancellery office enduring the Führer's rants about the foothold in Normandy the Allies had established. On Thursday, the report came in from Ingolstadt that Bardulf Theiss, one of Conrad Gerber's men from the Karl Lehmann elimination team, had been found with a bullet hole between his eyes—killed on a crowded cable car in broad daylight. No one heard a gunshot. Theiss' death left no doubt that Erika Lehmann knew about the plot against her father and intended to settle the score. Himmler immediately dispatched Heinrich Müller to Ingolstadt to personally handle the investigation and coordinate the search for the woman. He could not arrest her openly; she knew too much and posed too great a risk. When found, she would have to be taken quietly or disposed of.

Then on Friday another report: Julius Querner, another of Gerber's men now stationed in Vienna, was found behind the wheel of his automobile, his throat slit. Himmler's father always told him to find the good in any situation, so he found a bit of consolation in the fact that witnesses to his plot against Karl Lehmann (the men of Gerber's team) were being eliminated. At least that was something positive.

The buzzer on Himmler's desk sounded. "Yes, Frau Ziegler."

"A letter addressed to you has been examined and sent up from security, Reichsführer." All mail addressed to Himmler was opened and checked for explosives or toxins before being delivered to his office.

"Who is it from?" Himmler snapped. He was tired and didn't want to be bothered.

"I don't know, Reichsführer. Shall I look?"

"Yes!"

In a moment Ursula Ziegler said, *"I still don't know, Reichsführer. It's not written in German . . . I think it's Latin, if I'm not mistaken."*

"Latin?" Many knew that Himmler had studied Latin and Greek during his university days. He left his office, walked out to Ziegler's desk and snatched the envelope and paper from her hand. His secretary was correct; the note was in Latin.

I know what you did to my father, and I know what the Reich is doing to the Jews and others. Your problems are all in front of you, but will end when I deny you Valhalla and send you to Niflheimr.

Karl's daughter

[Vienna—same day]

Erika sat in the Vienna train depot awaiting her train back to Germany. After finishing Bardulf Theiss in Ingolstadt on Tuesday, she visited her daughter in Munich on Wednesday. On Thursday, she caught the *Orient Express* to Vienna and visited Julius Querner, the next man on her list.

Erika had sent the list of names she had gotten from Karen Hinderliter at the Hotel zum Türken to Kathryn Fischer. Kathryn checked Gestapo records and confirmed that the men at the hotel on the date Karl Lehmann died were working together—their team officially designated as "investigative." Erika knew the men who killed her father would have to have tracked him closely for weeks if not months. The Hotel zum Türken was very near the Königsee, the lake where her father supposedly drowned in a boating accident. The men on Karen's list had stayed at the hotel for two days, checking in the same day her father arrived at the nearby Berghof, just a short walk up the road. These men had to be the ones. Kathryn could also access records on the men's current assignments and locations. This led Erika to Ingolstadt where she located Theiss and began following him. Wednesday evening, Erika donned a black wig and followed Theiss to a beer hall. Once inside, she approached him, flirted, and encouraged

450

him to drink. The liquor loosened his tongue enough that he bragged about once being assigned a high-level mission by Himmler himself to "take care of" an important man who had for years been a thorn in Himmler's side. Theiss' fate was sealed.

The next morning, Erika used the British Welrod and a hole in a purse big enough for the muzzle to send a silent round through Theiss' brain as he sat nursing his hangover on an Ingolstadt cable car—the handgun procured for her by Stephanie Fischer from John Mayne's cache of weapons.

Victor Knight and John Mayne remained in Berlin, having refused offers from both Stephanie and Erika to help them get out of Germany. Maeve, though, was safe. Four days ago, Suse flew Maeve and Stephanie Fischer to Switzerland where Stephanie handed Maeve over to the American OSS who maintained an office in Berne. It was risky, trying to leave Germany for Switzerland, but from Ulm the Swiss border was only a one-hour flight in the Storch. Suse pulled it off by landing in a meadow on the German side of Lake Constance then waiting until dark to take off and fly low over the lake into Switzerland where Allen Dulles and his men awaited them in St. Gallen. As far as Erika knew, Maeve, Stephanie, and Suse all slept safely in Switzerland under American protection.

The announcement came over the train station intercom that passengers could now board the *Orient Express* for Munich. Erika picked up her bag and rose from the bench.

Chapter 92

A Ranger Returns

Caen, France
Six weeks later; Friday, 21 July 1944

PFC Stephen Floyd took a last draw on his cigarette and dropped it to the ground.

It had been the evening of June 6th when he was finally evacuated from Omaha Beach and taken back to England on an American LST along with scores of other wounded. Floyd turned 20 years old in a Southampton hospital where he spent six weeks before rejoining his unit today near Caen. Caen had been liberated a week ago but was now rubble, so the B Company Rangers camped just outside town along with numerous other American infantry and armored outfits.

Floyd saw many new faces when he arrived this morning. Ninety percent of his Ranger buddies had been killed or wounded on D-Day, and many of those wounded had gotten it much worse than he. *Rangers Lead the Way* and high casualty rates came with the job.

But at least one of Floyd's closer buddies had made it through uninjured that day on the beach. PFC Don DeCapp, who had gone through Ranger training with Floyd at Camp Forest, Tennessee, stood beside him. Both men sipped a Hamms beer.

"Did you hear the news about Hitler?" DeCapp asked Floyd.

"What news?"

"Yesterday someone tried to blow him up. The BBC reports it was some of his commanders."

"Tried to blow him up? So I guess it didn't work?"

"Hell no," said DeCapp. "That sonuvabitch is the luckiest guy alive."

"I haven't seen Farrar or Revels," said Floyd, changing the subject.

DeCapp gave the bad news. "They didn't make it."

"Pop Lemin?" Floyd asked about the battalion sergeant-major.

DeCapp shook his head. "A machine gun got Pop."

"I saw Klaus, Zieke, and Rotthoff in the hospital in England," Floyd said.

"How they doin'?"

"Klaus took shrapnel in a thigh and shoulder; he should be back before too long. Zieke lost a foot, and Rotthoff lost his nose and part of a kidney; they're going home."

"Jesus," said DeCapp. "Tough ways to earn a ticket home. How's the knee?"

"Sore but okay. I got lucky. The bullet passed through—chipped the bone, that's all."

"Getting shot doesn't sound lucky to me."

"Where's the latrine around here?"

"At the other end of camp, a couple of football fields that way." DeCapp pointed. "If you just have to piss, go in the woods. That's what we all do."

Floyd's sore leg convinced him the suggestion was sound. "I'll be right back." He walked into the forest and took care of business. After he buttoned his pants and turned to walk back, he was startled to see a woman leaning against a tree a few feet away.

"Feel better now?" she asked.

"Who are you?"

"My name is Erika. What's your name?"

"PFC Floyd. Civilians aren't supposed to be this close to camp." He assumed she was a French local; this afternoon he accompanied a detail into Caen to deliver foodstuffs to bombed-out civilians and a few of the locals spoke English.

"I'm not from around here. Where are you from, soldier?"

"I'm from Colorado. What do you want, lady? I've got a girlfriend back home."

She smiled. "What's her name?"

"Bertha."

"I'm sure Bertha is a great girl. I'm not here for that."

"Then what do you want?" Floyd repeated.

"Pull your sidearm and take me to your commanding officer, please." She raised her arms and said, "Ich will mich ergeben. That's German for 'I want to surrender.'"

[two hours later—Baker Street, London]

Two months ago, Leroy Carr was in Washington when Amanda McBride relayed a message from France to SOE London that Victor Knight had scuttled Operation Kriemhild but he and John Mayne would remain in Germany and improvise as best they could. When another communiqué from McBride arrived the next day informing the SOE that Erika Lehmann had disappeared, Carr was notified and caught the first available flight to London. He had been here ever since. Carr slept at the Savoy, but spent nearly every waking minute at SOE headquarters. He was at Baker Street speaking on the telephone with Kay back home when the message came through from the Americans that Erika Lehmann was in the custody of the U.S. Army Rangers just outside Caen.

Chapter 93

Powwow in Caen

Caen, France
Next day; Saturday, 22 July 1944

"What's the latest on Maeve?" Erika asked. She and Leroy Carr had just sat down in a tent within the U.S. Army Ranger compound outside Caen.

"Allen Dulles has her safely stashed away in Berne. Stephanie Fischer is keeping an eye on her."

"So Stephanie stayed in Switzerland . . . good. How about Suse?"

"Suse . . .?"

"Susanna Hohner. She flew them across the border."

Carr nodded. "Dulles reported that she returned to Germany. He said she flew back across Lake Constance just before dawn that next night. She planned to land in a meadow just inside the German border and wait for daylight to fly back to Ulm—basically the reverse of how she took Maeve and Fischer to Switzerland. Dulles offered her refuge, but Hohner wasn't going to leave her mother alone in Germany."

Erika nodded. "Sounds like Suse. She's a tiny little thing with the heart of a lion."

"We could make plans to sneak Maeve out of Switzerland and return her to England, but it's an unnecessary risk," said Carr. "It should be only a matter of weeks—a couple of months at most—until all of France is liberated; then we can simply drive her through France and send her across the Channel on an LST evacuating wounded."

"Your General Donovan needs to ask the SOE to recall Victor Knight and John Mayne from Berlin," Erika said. "Knight and Mayne will accomplish little there now other than getting themselves killed."

"They were recalled over a month ago, and Bill—General Donovan—didn't need to get involved. After you disappeared and Tars was killed, *Intrepid* realized Operation Kriemhild had no chance. A week after the invasion, he sent word to Amanda McBride to relay to

Knight that he and Mayne are under orders to make their way to France and into Allied hands. Everyone realizes it might take some time for them to get out of Germany on their own, but they haven't been heard from since. Any opinion about that?"

"Would they ignore an order from the top?"

"The Brits doubt Knight would ignore an order from *Intrepid,*" Carr answered.

"Well . . . I doubt that they're captured. Knight told me they wouldn't be taken alive and I believe that. As you say, getting out of Germany could take time. They will have to be extremely cautious with every move." Erika moved to another topic. "Any idea when Paris might be liberated?"

Carr looked at her thoughtfully. "Why do you ask about Paris?"

"Paris is in my plans. I must go there."

Carr lit a cigarette and offered her one. "What's in Paris? Or should I ask, 'Who's in Paris?'"

Erika put the cigarette in her mouth and Carr held a match. "Some men I must see."

"Some men who should hold few plans for the future, I suspect." He knew she wasn't finished looking for the men who killed her father.

Erika drew on her cigarette. "I need to go to Paris before it's liberated. Once the Allies are poised to take Paris, these men will return to Germany."

"Erika, I know the agreement allows you to avenge your father. But now that we're in France and making progress, wouldn't it serve your purposes to wait? Some of our top generals are optimistic the war will be over by Christmas. After the war, it will be much safer to pursue those men. They will have no government apparatus backing them, but you will—the United States. Once the war is over, you'll officially work for the OSS. After Germany capitulates, you can go anywhere and will have the credentials to allow you access to whatever is necessary to help you find these men and we can bring them to justice under international law."

Erika exhaled smoke. "As you said, Leroy, the agreement is that I can seek the men who killed my father. Nothing was mentioned about waiting until the end of the war, and no one can predict when that might be. You say some Allied generals think the war will be over by Christmas, but here we are a month and a half after the invasion and you're only a few miles from the coast. And what you say about bringing my father's murderers to justice under international law applies only if Germany capitulates. I can't count on capitulation from Hitler; I know him and he'll never surrender. He'll die first. But he might offer peace terms; he's done that in the past. If the war drags on and Hitler succeeds in talking the Allies into a peace treaty, Germany remains a sovereign nation and the men I seek will, like all German citizens, have protections under German civilian law. And then there's politics. If a mutual treaty is signed instead of an all-out surrender, the British will do everything in their power to stop my mission in order to avoid the political embarrassment of having ties to an assassin operating during peacetime. So will the Americans. I'll then be a fugitive from not only the Germans, as I am now, but also the English and American authorities. I prefer we keep our original agreement. Will you answer my question about an estimate on when Paris might be liberated?"

"The scuttlebutt going around is that Patton could take Paris in a couple of weeks, but Supreme Command might hold him up and let de Gaulle and the French come from behind and be the first into the capital. De Gaulle requested it and many think Ike will go along because Churchill is pushing for it. If we wait for the French, we're probably looking at a month from now to enter Paris. That's only a rumor about holding up our troops, and strictly a wild guess about the time frame."

"Thank you." She flipped her cigarette butt out the open tent flap. "And by the way, I'd like Maeve and Stephanie Fischer to join me in Paris."

Carr stopped puffing on his cigarette, and it now dangled from his lips. "What?"

Erika repeated, "I'd like Maeve and Stephanie Fischer to join me in Paris."

"Before liberation?"

"Yes, right away."

"I can't guarantee that, Erika. The OSS has influence with the SOE where you're concerned; you work with the Brits at our discretion. But Maeve and Fischer are SOE operatives; we have no pull with the SOE when it comes to their agents."

"But they are in OSS hands in Berne. You'll find a way, Leroy. You always do."

Leroy Carr was starting to get a clearer picture on why she showed up in Caen and surrendered to the American private peeing in the woods.

Chapter 94

Promise to a Valkyrie

Bamberg, Germany
Two days later; Monday, 24 July 1944

A few days after the Normandy invasion, Knight received a transmission from Amanda McBride recalling him and John Mayne. *Intrepid* ordered them to leave Germany and find their way into Allied hands in France. Even though at the time of the message only a small corner of Normandy had been liberated, Knight would obey orders. Then again, those orders said nothing about refraining from engaging the enemy during their journey.

Knight decided to take a zig-zag route, avoiding a straight jaunt toward the French border to make it harder for the Germans to track them. After boarding a bus in Berlin, the two SOE agents traveled to Wolfsburg, lay low there for three days, then continued on to Hanover. In Hanover, a Gestapo agent asked to see their papers as they stepped off the bus. Mayne snapped the man's neck then they fled down the street and darted into an alley.

From Hanover, they rode a train south to Kassel. One night in that city they spotted a Heer major sauntering down the street. Knight and Mayne walked quickly to catch up, and Knight was drawing his knife when at the last moment the major turned and entered an apartment building through a door protected by a security guard.

Now, after another train ride, the two SOE agents were in Bamberg where, for the past two hours, they had waited in alley shadows across the street from a brewery. They had followed a man here after watching him emerge from a Gestapo substation a few blocks away. He wore the common black-leather Gestapo trench coat so Knight held little doubt the man was Gestapo. The brewery had a small tavern where customers could mingle and enjoy beer produced on site; Knight and Mayne could see the man sitting at a table just inside a window.

"He looks like a loner," Mayne said quietly. "No one has sat with him."

"Would you want to drink with a Gestapo crud?" asked Knight.

"I guess I would if I were a Gestapo crud, too."

"Then there must not be any more in there."

"I'm glad that army major in Hanover disappeared inside that building," Mayne commented as they continued to watch the Gestapo agent drink beer.

"Why?"

"We gave our word to the Valkyrie we wouldn't go after regular army—only Himmler's people."

"That was part of the deal with Operation Kriemhild," Knight reminded. "When Lehmann disappeared she broke her end of the bargain, so that means all bets are off on former agreements."

Mayne shrugged. "I'm still glad. I don't want to break my promise . . . not to a Valkyrie."

Knight looked at him. "You've gone bonkers."

"Hey, look," Mayne said and nodded toward the brewery window. The man had risen and was dropping money on the table. Knight drew the Welrod from under his shirt, pulled the bolt to chamber a round, and steadied the pistol on top of a trash receptacle.

"Are you sure you can get him from here?" asked Mayne. "When he comes out, I can cross the street and plug him with my knife."

"I'll get him," said Knight. The man disappeared from the window but did not come out of the building. "Where in hell is he?"

"Probably taking a piss after all that beer," Mayne deduced.

Finally, the man emerged from the brewery and began walking down the deserted street. Knight took careful aim and pulled the trigger of the near-silent handgun. The man dropped to the sidewalk, his face slamming on the stones. Knight slid the gun back under his shirt and the two SOE men walked calmly out of the dead-end alley and down the opposite side of the street.

◊ ◊ ◊

[near Berne, Switzerland—same evening]

For the past seven weeks, Maeve had spent her time at a chateau in the Swiss Alps 35 miles southeast of Berne, near Lake Thun. An OSS haven, the Alpine chateau offered safe refuge to those the American spy agency chose to hide away, and Maeve was just one of several persons there under American protection. Sometimes she ate dinner with a Jewish rocket scientist and his wife. Occasionally at the table was a Polish cryptographer who had been at the chateau for over a year. He had worked behind the lines for the Americans but was finally forced to flee Warsaw when the Nazis were tipped about his whereabouts. Neither the scientist nor the cryptographer seemed hesitant to talk about their work or their backgrounds, and doing so was apparently not prohibited by the OSS, a policy that surprised Maeve. Although others stayed at the chateau, Maeve had few dealings with them and knew little about them.

As for Stephanie Fischer, she was also at the chateau—some of the time. Unlike Maeve, Stephanie came and went, sometimes disappearing for days. When Stephanie would return, she told Maeve nothing about where she had been and after a while Maeve quit asking. Yesterday, a man showed up and whisked Stephanie away in an American embassy car telling Maeve that Stephanie would be back today and that Maeve should be prepared to leave the chateau.

Packing her few possessions took only a few minutes and Maeve had been ready since that morning. Now dinner time, neither Stephanie nor the embassy man had returned. Maeve finished eating and excused herself. She climbed the stairs to her small room and, when she opened the door, saw Stephanie Fischer gathering her things and a dark-haired woman standing at the window with her back to the door. When the woman heard Maeve enter, she turned.

"Hello, Maeve. It's nice to see you again. Are you ready to see Gay Paree?"

The woman was Eileen Nearne.

Chapter 95

Favorite Café

Paris
Two days later; Wednesday, 26 July 1944

Erika Lehmann sat at a table outside the Café Les Deux Neveux sipping cool tea. Situated in the Latin Quarter with the Sorbonne only two blocks away, this neighborhood was Erika's favorite in Paris and the Les Deux Neveux her favorite Parisian café. Now late afternoon, the 90° temperature was abnormally hot for Paris even in late July, so, like most café patrons, Erika sat outside where a slight breeze in the shade of the canvas table umbrellas offered some respite from the sweltering café interior.

Erika knew Paris well. She had visited Paris several times with her parents, and she spent nearly two months here in the summer of 1939 while on her first extended leave from Abwehr. During that visit she met a young man. Though involved with Kai at the time, Erika never felt guilty about her fling. At that time, she and Kai had no agreement between them; nevertheless, before they married, she told her future husband about her Paris romance. Erika still wondered what happened to Claude Vauzous and once had tried to locate him when she returned to Paris briefly after her first Abwehr mission in Lisbon. But Claude had disappeared after the Germans marched through the Arc in June 1940.

It had not been difficult for Erika to convince Leroy Carr to agree to her request that Maeve and Stephanie Fischer join her in Paris; likewise, Carr easily convinced Bill Donovan to call *Intrepid* with the request. During war, any operation that might deliver a blow to the enemy rarely encountered opposition, even if the mission appeared unorthodox. War meant eliminating the enemy, and if personal revenge, rather than patriotism or ideology stoked the fire to do so, in the end it still served the war effort.

Three Luftwaffe officers sat drinking coffee at the table next to Erika's. A major who had ogled her for some minutes took the opportunity to smile and speak when she glanced his way.

"Bonjour, mademoiselle."

"Bonjour," Erika said. She wore a thin orange and white summer dress of a type common among Parisian women her age, and a matching sun hat. The dress was very short and her sitting offered the men even more of her legs to enjoy.

The major asked if she spoke German. "Parlez-vous allemand?"

Erika smiled and told the German she was sorry but she didn't speak his language. "Non, désolée."

He produced a German-to-French dictionary from his tunic pocket and looked up words until a gray Citroën sedan stopped in front of the café. Eileen "Didi" Nearne got out of the car and approached. Didi glanced at the Germans and said, "Bonjour." The men returned her greeting as Erika rose, dropped money for her tea on the table, bade the Germans adieu, and walked with Didi to the car. Didi took the wheel beside Stephanie Fischer. Erika got in the backseat next to her twin.

[same time—Berlin, 8 Prinz Albrechtstrasse]

Heinrich Müller was a busy man. Within the past week, one Gestapo agent had been murdered in Hanover, and another in Bamberg. On the surface, both killings appeared random and not tied to Erika Lehmann, but investigations continued. As he did every day, Müller sat in Heinrich Himmler's office prepared to answer questions.

"What is the latest from your Munich investigation?" was Himmler's first.

"I am confident there is a possibility Lehmann has some tie to the child, Herr Reichsführer," Müller answered.

Himmler chuckled. "You are *confident* there is a *possibility*. That's really hedging your bet, Müller. I'm *confident* there is a *possibility* fat Göring might flap his arms and fly away, but I think it unlikely."

The Abwehr personnel photo of Erika Lehmann had been used to make a criminal mug shot poster. For the past month, the "Wanted for Murder" posters had hung on bulletin boards in every library, train and bus depot, and government office in Germany. On Monday, a Munich woman who saw the poster in a post office reported she had recently seen the woman whose face was on the poster visit the home of a neighbor who lived across the street. Müller sent investigators to question the neighbor and they reported that she lived alone with a child.

"What is the neighbor's name who cares for the child?"

Müller looked down at a paper. "Ilse Dorsch."

"Continue."

"When our men showed the Dorsch woman a photo of Lehmann, Dorsch denied knowing her but both detectives reported that she blushed and seemed nervous when shown Lehmann's photograph. They think she's lying."

"So she lies about knowing Lehmann, or a woman who looks like Lehmann. She protects a friend—nothing new about that Müller. Our investigators deal with that every day. Why is this child of interest?"

"At first, Dorsch claimed she had the child out of wedlock and the father died on the Russian Front. When the detectives asked for the father's name, Dorsch became uncooperative."

"Uncooperative?"

"Dorsch said she didn't want to cause the father's family embarrassment, but when pressed by our men for the father's name, she changed her story and told our investigators she met the soldier at a beer hall, had a one-night fling, knew him only as Hans, and never saw him again."

"Doesn't she know bastard children of soldiers must be reported so a decision can be made as to whether the child is sent to a Lebensborn?"

"Dorsch claims she was unaware of the law."

"So what leads you to think Lehmann may have some tie to the child?" Himmler looked at a photograph of Ada that Müller had ordered taken.

"The nosy neighbor who called in the original report also told our men that an SS officer calls on Dorsch. The neighbor reports she has watched the officer play with the child in the yard. This morning, I ordered our detectives to show the neighbor a photo of Kai Faust." Both Himmler and Müller had read Walter Schellenberg's report claiming Faust and Lehmann had had some sort of past relationship. "The neighbor recognized Faust's photograph right away."

Himmler stared at his Gestapo chief and then looked again at the photograph of the 3-year-old child. "What color is this Dorsch woman's hair?" Himmler asked.

"Brown."

"And Faust's hair?"

Müller again said "Brown" as Heinrich Himmler stared at the photo of the child with bright blonde hair.

[Paris—that evening]

After their reunion in the car, the four women quickly took care of finding dinner. Didi Nearne pulled over when she spotted a street vendor's cart and Erika got out and bought American-style hotdogs and potato chips for everyone. Erika gave Nearne directions to a one-room flat she had rented above a tailor's shop on the Rue du Banquier. Once inside, Erika opened the windows and turned on a pedestal fan to combat the oppressive heat.

"Do you have anything to drink?" Maeve asked as she wolfed down her first hot dog.

"Water," Erika said and nodded toward the sink. Formerly used for storage, the floor above the tailor shop had been divided into four tiny apartments that shared a common bathroom at the end of the hall. The room had a small sink, an ice box that currently contained neither ice nor food, and a hot plate. "You'll find a pitcher and cups in the cupboard, Maeve. If you don't mind, bring water for everyone."

Erika had bought two hot dogs for each of them; everyone was hungry and the food disappeared quickly.

"Anything else to eat?" Maeve asked Erika. "I'm still hungry."

"I'm afraid not; I should have bought more. We'll go out later and get something else. Let's have a seat, Maeve. I'm sure you're curious as to why you're here." Erika knew Didi and Stephanie had told Maeve nothing about why she had been brought to Paris.

"I figured it had something to do with you," Maeve said as she sat down on a scuffed wooden chair. Stephanie and Didi sat on a small sofa with several rips in the upholstery; Erika sat on the floor.

"First," Erika began, "I was sorry to hear about Tars. I know you and she went through a great deal of adversity together and I think you two had grown rather close." When Maeve said nothing, Erika continued. "Didi and Stephanie brought you here, Maeve, because I can use your help. The men who killed my father know by now that I pursue them. Three of those men are here in Paris and I know they'll be ready for me. I won't be able to sneak up on them, and I'm sure they'll have their own plans for me—a trap. I need a diversion. That's where you can help me, Maeve. It will be dangerous; you should know that from the start. You don't have to do it. Didi can get you behind Allied lines and you can return to Ireland."

"I don't care about the danger. Tars planned to help you after my part was finished. I'll do it for Tars."

Chapter 96

Late Night Call

Paris
Two days later; Friday, 28 July 1944

As they did at the start of every day, Christoph Unger, Andreas Biermann, and Egon Dreher huddled around a large conference table at 11 Rue des Saussaies—the Gestapo Region V Headquarters in Paris. Besides their current assignments in Paris, the three men had in common their participation in the Karl Lehmann elimination mission the previous summer. Six other men also sat around the table. Unger was in charge of the meeting.

"Anything to report from yesterday?" Unger asked, directing the question to no one in particular. The six additional men had been assigned as bodyguards to Unger, Biermann, and Dreher—two guards for each man.

"I have seen no sign of her, Unger," said Dreher.

"Nor I," Biermann added.

"The guards?" Unger looked around. The six bodyguards either shook their heads or said *"Nein."*

"Do we have any reason to believe she's even in Paris?" Biermann asked.

"No," answered Unger. "That's why we go about our other duties. Just stay on your guard."

Three weeks ago, Conrad Gerber came to Paris to tell them that Karl Lehmann's daughter had eliminated two of their former comrades from the Karl Lehmann mission: Bardulf Theiss had his brains blown out in Ingolstadt and Julius Querner had been found with his throat slit in Vienna. On Himmler's orders, Gerber assigned bodyguards to each man. At least Unger, Biermann, and Dreher were *told* the men were bodyguards. But unknown to the three Gestapo agents, these six men, all sent from Berlin, came not to protect them. If Erika Lehmann surfaced in Paris seeking her revenge, Unger, Biermann, and Dreher would be sacrificed. What mattered to

Himmler, and to Gerber, was having killers on hand when she showed her face, a face the six *bodyguards* had studied photographs of for weeks.

"The guards should be at our sides when we are out on our assignments, Unger," Dreher piped in as if the guards were not in the room. "Following us from a distance isn't going to protect us."

A man named Reichel, who usually served as de facto spokesman for the bodyguards, spoke up. "Our orders are to not interfere with your day-to-day duties. Kriminalsekretär Gerber explained that when he accompanied us here. We are to remain as inconspicuous as possible."

Dreher confronted Reichel. "How do you expect to protect us when you walk a block behind or follow in a car a block away?"

"Reichsführer Himmler has given us our orders," said Reichel. "It is not our duty, or yours, to question those orders."

Dreher grunted and threw up his hands.

[that afternoon]

Egon Dreher walked out of a butcher shop on the Avenue de Clichy after questioning the shop owner about anti-German graffiti on an alley wall behind the shop. The butcher convinced Dreher he knew nothing about the graffiti or who might have put it there, so Dreher turned to walk to the next business, a small art gallery. But before he reached the doorway, he froze in his tracks when the woman from Conrad Gerber's photographs—the woman Gerber identified as Karl Lehmann's daughter who had murdered Theiss and Querner—came around the corner, eyed Dreher, and began walking briskly toward him.

Dreher spun and ran in the other direction, toward his bodyguards who stood on the street corner of the next block. "She's here!" Dreher shouted. The guards were too far away to hear his shout over the noise of automobiles and buses, but when they saw Dreher running toward them they knew something was wrong. The guards quickly checked for traffic then sprinted across the street. After they crossed, they saw the blonde running to catch Dreher who was in an all-out, frantic sprint for his life. Drawing their guns, they passed Dreher and continued toward the woman who suddenly darted into the butcher shop. They followed her in and saw the old butcher with his hands in the air but no blonde. The butcher pointed and blurted out in French that the woman went out the back door. The Germans didn't understand the language but followed his pointing. They raced out into the alley where Maeve stood behind Eileen Nearne and Stephanie Fischer. Before the men could fire, Nearne and Fischer both pulled the triggers of their Welrods.

On the busy street, Egon Dreher slowed to a walk and felt relief. *My guards will deal with the woman.* The feeling lasted only a moment, replaced by a sharp pain as Erika Lehmann sank the blade of her dagger into the side of Dreher's neck.

[that night—Hagenstrasse 22, Berlin—home of Heinrich Himmler]
Heinrich Himmler picked up the ringing telephone beside his bed and looked at the clock—11:50 p.m.

"Yes," he said as quietly as possible hoping to not disturb his wife.

"Müller here, Reichsführer. Sorry to disturb you, but you left instructions that I should call when any report concerning Lehmann came in regardless of the hour."

"Yes, yes, Müller. Are you in your office?"

"Yes."

"I will hang up and call you back from another room so I don't wake Margarete."

"Yes, Reichsführer."

Himmler replaced the receiver, donned his robe, and left the bedroom for his study where he dialed Müller's number.

"I'm here," Müller answered after one ring. *"She's in Paris—I just received the report. She knifed Egon Dreher on a busy street in broad daylight. He's dead, as are the two trailers assigned to him."*

"She killed the trailers, too?"

"Details are sketchy, sir. The trailers were found in a different location. Citizens who might have witnessed the killings have been

questioned and the investigation continues, but it's the same old story with the French: No one saw anything."

"Goddamn French."

"Exactly, Reichsführer."

"What about the other two agents in Paris who worked with Gerber last summer?"

"Unger and Biermann. They have not been harmed . . . yet."

Himmler almost laughed at Müller's grim outlook.

Müller continued. *"Do you have any orders for Unger and Biermann?"*

"No. What kind of orders can there be, Müller? They are to continue with their daily duties and we have to continue to hope the trailers do their job and kill her, although I don't hold much optimism there. Anything out of Munich?"

"Yes. That was my other reason for calling. The woman Dorsch tried to escape tonight. The detectives who called on her must have frightened her and forced her hand. She waited until after dark and left the house with the child and a suitcase. We picked them up on your orders."

Himmler had ordered Ilse Dorsch's home watched. In Himmler's mind, any attempt to flee always revealed a great deal. "Where are the woman and child now?"

"They're being held at one of our Gestapo offices in Munich. Do you think the child could actually be Lehmann's?"

"We'll find out soon enough, Müller."

"How will Lehmann know we have the child?"

"Simple enough. We found out the hard way at the zoo that she works with the British. Have *Doppelkreuz* relay to his British contact that we have the Dorsch woman and the child and that we suspect the child belongs to Lehmann." *Doppelkreuz* was the code name of an SD agent the British thought they had turned and who now worked for them. Himmler used *Doppelkreuz* to feed the enemy misinformation. "We can use something that's true to give the British; we can't send them lies all the time."

"Very good, Reichsführer."

"If the child is not Lehmann's, nothing will change in Paris. If the child is hers, it will be Unger and Biermann's lucky day. She'll likely disappear immediately from Paris and try to rescue the child. Move the woman and child to our villa in Grünwald and place them under heavy guard. Order *Doppelkreuz* to send that information to the British immediately, and make sure he includes the villa's location. If we can't find Lehmann, we'll make her come to us."

"Right away, Reichsführer."

Chapter 97

For Your Eyes Only

London
Next day; Saturday, 29 July 1944

With Victor Knight and John Mayne unreachable, *Intrepid* knew nothing of the two SOE agents' fates behind enemy lines. He, therefore, agreed to William Donovan's request that Leroy Carr, Donovan's counter-intelligence chief, assume temporary command of what had once been the British SOE mission codenamed *Kriemhild*. Donovan convinced his friend and British counterpart that Carr was the logical choice to sit in for Knight; after all, Carr had worked on *Kriemhild* from the get-go, and it was Carr who had established a working relationship with the German, Erika Lehmann. Both Donovan and *Intrepid* knew that if anything were to be salvaged from the current mess the mission had become, it would be through Lehmann's thirst for revenge. So, after meeting with Erika in Caen, Carr returned to London where he now occupied a small office in the SOE headquarters on Baker Street.

Two hours of briefings had just ended. Carr learned that Victor Knight and John Mayne had made it out of Germany but were still far from safe. At 4 a.m. this morning, MI-9 (the SIS branch in charge of communications with the French Resistance) received a transmission from a Resistance cell near Grenoble stating it had the SOE agents squirreled away and requesting instructions. Grenoble lay in an area of Vichy France still under German occupation. During the briefings, Carr and the Baker Street Irregulars (the tongue-in-check nickname used by the SOE to avoid the acronym) discussed ideas on the safest way to extract the agents. As Carr returned to his office, a WAAF secretary ran up from behind and flagged him down.

"This is for you, Mr. Carr," said the young woman as she handed him a sealed envelope. "It just came in and I was told to deliver it to you immediately."

"Thank you." Carr stepped into his office and closed the door. On the yellow envelope above his name was the red **Top Secret – For Your Eyes Only** stamp. Carr opened the envelope and read the one page.

INTELLIGENCE INTERCEPT REPORT FOR EYES OF CD
AND MR. CARR AMERICAN OSS
/ GERMAN CITIZEN ILSE DORSCH FEMALE / AND THREE YEAR OLD CHILD FEMALE BELIEVED TO BE CHILD OF LORELEI / HELD IN CUSTODY OF GEHEIME STAATSPOLIZEI AT KNOWN LOCATION NEAR MUNICH
/ END

SOURCE: REDLEAF

ORDERS FOR MR. CARR: REPORT TO CD IMMEDIATELY

Since *Intrepid* operated out of New York, the London-based head of the SOE, referred to as *CD* for Command Director, was Major General Colin Gubbins. Gubbins exercised complete control in London and answered only to *Intrepid* or Churchill. Carr sprinted to Gubbins' office on the third floor where a military aide waited outside the general's door.

"Thank you for coming, Mr. Carr," the aide said as he opened the door, his comment polite but absurdly unnecessary.

When Carr entered the office, Gubbins sat behind his desk holding the phone to his ear. He motioned for Carr to sit. The only words Carr heard Gubbins mutter into the phone were, "That's correct," before he abruptly hung up.

Without pausing, Gubbins looked at Carr. "Do you know anything about the child?"

"Absolutely nothing, General." Carr had a question of his own. "Who is *Redleaf?*"

"He's a German operative we captured in Norway last year. He turned to avoid the noose."

"How reliable is his information?"

"Hit and miss. We take what he can give, with a grain of salt I might add. Sometimes his information pans out."

"Something smells here. The message says the location is known. It's all too easy. If it's true about the child, it's obviously a trap," said Carr. "If *Redleaf* isn't a double agent feeding you misinformation intentionally, then the Germans leaked this information knowing someone would pick it up and relay it to London."

"I would agree with that. But before we waste time debating how to handle this, I'll tell you that I've already decided to send the information on to your *Lorelei.* If the child is not hers, I assume nothing will change in Paris. If she *is* the child's mother, we lose nothing if she turns her attention to Munich. In either city, she'll be there to serve the Jerries a rotten fish. Would you agree, Mr. Carr?"

"Now the Germans know only that she's in Paris. She's too skilled to be caught when she can strike when and where it best suits her. If there's any truth to her relationship to this child and she redirects, the Gestapo will know exactly where she will surface. That changes everything—the Gestapo has the advantage."

"That's why I'm turning this situation over to you. I recommend you find out if there is any truth in *Redleaf's* report. Since the only way to do that is talk to *Lorelei,* I suggest you contact her through Amanda McBride and withdraw her from Paris so you can get to the bottom of this. And you might want to send that transmission promptly. The information in the communiqué you just read is being relayed to McBride as we speak, with orders for her to have it delivered to Eileen Nearne in Paris."

[that afternoon—villa in the Grünwald, near Munich]

A frightened Ilse Dorsch huddled with Ada in a small, windowless room. Ilse did her best not to convey her dread to Ada, and she seemed to be succeeding. So far, Ada appeared more curious than alarmed, as if they shared an adventure.

After the Gestapo picked them up, she and the child spent only three hours at the Gestapo Munich office before being hustled into a car and driven to this large compound in Grünwald, a district south of Munich known for its fine homes and rich, powerful residents.

Ilse realized her plan to escape with Ada had been a mistake. She had hoped to make her way to her aunt's home in Salzburg and lie low until she could find a way to reach Erika or Kai. How she would locate one of them she didn't know, but at the time considered disappearing her only course. She knew it was only a matter of time before the Gestapo again called at her home, so she packed lightly for her and Ada and left the house after dark, only to be picked up before they had walked a block.

During the three-hour interrogation at the Gestapo office, Ilse stuck to her story that Ada was hers, the product of a one-night fit of passion with a soldier she never saw again. She knew if she admitted that Ada was not hers, the Gestapo would take the child away.

Suddenly the door swung open and a uniformed woman stepped in. "The child is coming with me," she rudely barked.

"No!" Ilse shouted as she drew Ada close.

The Gestapo Frau grabbed Ilse's hair, viciously slapped her face, and wrenched Ada from her arms. Ada bit the woman's hand.

"Agh! You fucking little brat!" When the Gestapo Frau raised her hand to slap the child, Ilse sprang on her. Forced to turn her attention to Ilse, the husky Frau began swinging and caught Ilse in the jaw with a forceful punch. Stunned, Ilse reeled back. The Frau jerked Ada toward the door.

"Mutti!" Ada pleaded as she tried to reach for Ilse. Ilse sprang to her feet and tried to pry the child from the Frau's grasp, but the stout woman kicked Ilse in the chest and she buckled to the floor. Ada began crying as the Frau roughly dragged her out of the room then slammed and locked the door.

[that evening—Paris]

In the Paris flat, Erika sat with Maeve and Stephanie going over the plan for the next day—the plan to eliminate Christoph Unger, next on Erika's list of Gestapo agents complicit in her father's murder. Didi was absent, away on her daily visit to a laundry on the Rue de Roissys. Amanda McBride and her transmitter were now hidden away at a farmhouse just outside Versailles. When *Intrepid* found out from Leroy

Carr that Erika had requested Maeve and Stephanie join her in Paris, the British intelligence chief insisted that Nearne, the only true SOE agent among them, be included on the team. For a week in June, the SOE thought Nearne was dead after being captured by the Gestapo, but Didi escaped. Amanda McBride was relocated closer to Paris to handle communications. From the laundry on the Rue de Roissys, Didi sent a daily update to McBride for transmission to London. And it was at the laundry where Didi could pick up any SOE transmissions McBride received for her. The laundryman's teenage son served as courier, delivering messages to or from McBride on his bicycle—risky for both father and son, but not uncommon in the Resistance for families to join in the cause.

"So, where do we go after we send these other two wankers on their merry way to Hell?" asked Maeve as Erika finished the review.

"You will return to England to debrief and then go home to Belfast," Erika answered.

"I stay until the job is finished," Maeve insisted. Tars' death changed Maeve. Staring danger in the face as many times as she had since boarding the *Raven* in New York Harbor had toughened her resolve. She was determined to complete her friend's assignment.

"You've done enough, Maeve. And I don't know where I'll be next. I have to find the remaining men, and I don't know how long that will take. If you don't want to return home, I want Stephanie to get you into Allied hands in Caen. You don't speak French and can't stay in Paris by yourself."

"Didi taught me French."

"A few phrases," Erika countered, "like I taught you German."

"Then take me with you."

Erika stood and shook her head. "No."

Maeve continued to argue but was interrupted when Didi entered the flat. The door was always kept locked, but Erika had given each woman a key. Didi's face revealed to everyone that something was horribly wrong.

Stephanie asked first. "What is it? What's the problem?"

On orders from Baker Street, all SOE messages, even if meant for one of the other women, were to be read first by Nearne. Didi didn't answer Stephanie; instead, she handed the half-page memo to Erika.

Erika read the message, turned pale, and dropped heavily into her chair.

Chapter 98

Skorzeny Delivers a Message

London
Next day; Sunday, 30 July 1944

Albeit Sunday morning, no days off existed in the world of wartime cloak and dagger. Leroy Carr sat in his office reading reports when the call came to report to the CD.

"Good news," General Gubbins said when Carr entered his office. "Knight and Mayne had to shoot their way through the checkpoint but made it out and have been taken to our embassy in Geneva."

The plan to extract the two SOE agents from occupied France entailed a bumpy ride in a farmer's chicken truck to the Swiss border, luckily only 100 miles from Grenoble. After yesterday's decision, Carr called Bill Donovan in Washington to request he be allowed to fly to Geneva and monitor the situation, but Donovan nixed that idea before Carr finished the sentence. Donovan would never allow his counter-intelligence chief to fly over enemy territory.

"Any injuries suffered by Knight or Mayne?" Carr asked.

"No. There were only three Jerries at the border crossing. Our sniper hidden on the Swiss side took out one; Knight and Mayne killed the other two."

"Any answer yet from *Intrepid?*" Yesterday Carr made a second request, this one to Gubbins concerning Carr's idea of what to do with Knight and Mayne once they were back in the fold. Gubbins told Carr only *Intrepid* could authorize such an appeal.

"I saw little point in sending your request until Knight and Mayne made it out," said Gubbins. "But it's now on its way to New York. I expect to hear from *Intrepid* this morning. He's not one to dally."

◊ ◊ ◊

[same time—Himmler's office, 8 Prinz Albrechtstrasse, Berlin]
"Is everything at the Grünwald villa in place, Müller?"

"Yes, Reichsführer. We have doubled the number of men inside the villa, and guards with dogs patrol the compound day and night. All have been briefed and given photographs of Lehmann."

"So the Dorsch woman sticks to her story the child is hers?"

Müller nodded. "Yes, and she again attacked a Frau, so I ordered Dorsch restrained. Do we need her at the villa? Beck, our Kriminalkommissar in charge at Grünwald, suggests we return Dorsch to our Munich station where she can be placed in a cell."

"No. I want her left at the villa, but keep her and the child separated. If the child is Lehmann's, it's obvious the Dorsch woman is a friend of hers. If Lehmann intends to free her along with the child she'll have to search the villa for both."

"She will never get inside the villa, Reichsführer. I'm confident our security is adequate."

"But I want her to gain access to the villa. Sit down, Müller."

[one hour later—War Ministry building on the Bendlerstrasse, Berlin]
Otto Skorzeny felt ill at ease behind a desk. A man of action, Skorzeny felt more at home slogging through mud or falling from the sky under a parachute than pushing papers. But 10 days ago he was ordered to suspend preparations for his next mission and report to Berlin immediately to help put down the attempted coup. A bomb meant to kill the Führer had exploded in a conference room at the Wolfschanze, the Führer's Eastern Front headquarters in Prussia. Luckily, the assassination attempt failed. Although a few generals were killed, the Führer escaped with only minor injuries. Skorzeny arrived at the War Ministry building 30 minutes after the leader of the conspiracy, Colonel Claus von Stauffenberg, was executed in the courtyard by firing squad. Since then, Skorzeny had helped coordinate efforts to secure Berlin against any remnants of the failed uprising. Now, ten days later, Berlin rested secure. Skorzeny hoped to be relieved soon so he could return to training his commando unit he brought with him to Berlin.

A secretary opened his office door. Skorzeny had instructed the secretaries to quit using the intercom—the buzzing got on his nerves—and simply open the door and speak to him.

"Herr Obersturmbannführer, one of your men is here," she announced. "Hauptsturmführer Faust."

"Send him in."

In a moment, Kai Faust entered.

"You sent for me, sir?" Kai asked.

"Kai, I received a message from Erika. It says *urgent* and there's a Paris telephone number. She wants you to call."

"Paris?"

"That's what the message said. It came through the OKW teletype addressed to me."

"What else did it say?"

"Nothing else." Skorzeny handed Faust a piece of paper with the telephone number.

Chapter 99

Grünwald

Berlin—8 Prinz Albrechtstrasse
Three days later; Wednesday, 02 August 1944

Heinrich Himmler had ordered his dinner brought to his office so he could work late. The sausages and red cabbage grew cold as Himmler pored over the latest report about a minor situation in Romania. Yesterday, an uprising in the Transylvanian village of Viscri had become an annoyance when area Jews refused to report to the village square for deportation. But for Himmler, this latest report was positive: The Totenkopf restored order this morning by shooting all males over the age of 15; the women and children were now on their way to Auschwitz. At the bottom of the page, the Totenkopf squad commander on scene included a request that the Viscri women and children be gassed immediately upon arrival at the camp in order to send a clear message. With his left hand Himmler forked a bite of his Bockwürst and put it into his mouth, while with his right he signed off on the squad commander's request as his intercom buzzer sounded.

"What is it, Frau Ziegler?"

"Gruppenführer Müller is here, Herr Reichsführer. He says it is very important."

"Send him in."

"Yes, sir."

Müller entered quickly and closed the door. "We received a communication from Lehmann," Müller said as he walked toward Himmler's desk. "She's ready to surrender if we release the child and the Dorsch woman unharmed." He handed the message to Himmler, but didn't wait for him to read it. "She claims to be in Munich and demands we have the woman and child at the compound gate in one hour if we seek her surrender. She says if Dorsch and child are at the gate, she will appear and turn herself over to our guards."

Müller stopped talking when Himmler raised his hand, signaling quiet while he read the message. The Gestapo's Grünwald villa was actually a compound located on several heavily wooded acres on the southern outskirts of Munich. Inside the compound's high brick wall were a spacious home and several outbuildings. With hills all around, both Himmler and Müller knew that, with binoculars, she could easily position herself to observe the compound gate unseen.

"What are your orders, Reichsführer?" Müller asked when Himmler lowered the paper and looked at a wall clock. "Lehmann left us with no way to contact her."

"She specified nine o'clock sharp—that's fifty minutes from now, Müller. We don't have time to make any detailed contingency plan. Do not have the child brought to the gate. Have the Dorsch woman at the gate so Lehmann can see her. Lehmann will realize what we want and show herself; she has no choice. She is to be told that when the guards have her safely inside the villa—and only then—will the child be taken to the gate and given to Dorsch. Then Dorsch and the child can be on their way. We'll implement the plan we discussed three days ago after Dorsch and the child were taken into custody."

"So the child and Dorsch are to be released?"

"Yes, Müller. The child is Aryan and the offspring of SS and a pure-blood German woman. We are not talking about Jews or Slavs. Let the child and woman go. We'll pick up the child in a day or two and have her taken to a Lebensborn."

"Very well, Reichsführer."

"Lehmann knows this is a trap," Himmler stated. "But she has no choice but to sacrifice herself for the child. Put our personnel at the compound on full alert, Müller. Make sure Lehmann is thoroughly searched at the gate before moving her inside the villa. If any of her accomplices from the zoo incident are still with her and stupid enough to accompany Lehmann to the gate, order the guards to shoot them on sight."

◊ ◊ ◊

[Grünwald, just south of Munich]

Darkness had fallen when Ilse Dorsch was escorted to the compound gate and handcuffed to one of the wrought-iron bars. The gate was closed and Ilse stood alone outside the compound. Ten Gestapo guards armed with Schmeisser machine pistols or Mauser rifles stood atop boxes looking over the eight-foot-high brick wall. The searchlight shining in her face blinded Ilse to her surroundings but revealed her to the guards and anyone outside the compound hidden in the woods.

For the past four days Ilse slept little and when she awoke was convinced she awoke from a nightmare. A brief moment of relief evaporated quickly once her eyes focused on her surroundings and she felt the handcuffs. The Gestapo Frau had handcuffed her on Sunday after Ilse again resisted when Ada was taken from her after breakfast. The child refused to eat unless with Ilse so they were reunited for meals. When finished, Ada would again be whisked away to another room in the villa. Ilse had undergone several interrogations, always accompanied by threats of torture, but so far the grillings had not progressed to that phase. Now she stood handcuffed to a gate with a bright light in her face not knowing why. She had been told nothing.

Fifteen or twenty minutes passed before Ilse heard the German Shepherds bark and a guard shout, "Achtung!" and then issue the order, "Hands up!" Ilse squinted, trying to see through the blinding light. Suddenly she felt a hand on her shoulder.

"Ilse, it's Erika. Is Ada unharmed?"

Ilse turned to see her friend. "Erika!" A commotion sounded behind the gate as it swung open, forcing Ilse to move with it. "Yes, Erika, Ada is unharmed," Ilse said quickly as three guards wrestled Erika to the ground. Erika offered no resistance as the guards handcuffed her hands behind her back, then lifted her to her feet and led her away.

The searchlight beam left Ilse and began sweeping the surrounding woods. Ilse remained cuffed to the gate for a half hour, maybe longer, before the gate opened and she heard Ada call, "Mutti!" Ilse turned and Ada ran up and hugged her leg. One guard roughly freed Ilse from the gate while another threw her suitcase over the wall. It landed on the hard dirt of the drive and split open, the clothes spewing out.

"Go now!" barked the guard who unlocked the cuffs.

Ilse picked up Ada, left the suitcase and clothes and ran into the night.

Chapter 100

Brewing Storm

Berlin—8 Prinz Albrechtstrasse
Same day; Wednesday, 02 August 1944

Himmler picked up his desk telephone. "Yes, Müller."

"Lehmann is in custody at the villa." Müller was calling from the communications room two floors below Himmler's office. *"The search revealed she carried no weapons."*

"You're certain it's Lehmann and not her double?"

"Certain. Our men questioned her and she answered fluently. It's our understanding from Schellenberg that the double speaks little German."

"Any sign she has backup?"

"No sign yet, Reichsführer. I ordered the Kriminalkommissar to send a team of men to scour the woods outside the walls."

"Very well. I want Lehmann bound securely and no fewer than three guards standing over her at all times. If she uses the toilet, they don't take their eyes off her. I will call our Munich office and set the caravan on its way." Himmler slammed down the receiver and buzzed Ursula Ziegler.

"Yes, Herr Reichsführer."

"Frau Ziegler, Kriminalrat Sanger at Munich Station Eight awaits my call. Get him on the line right away."

"Connecting now." After a moment's pause, Zeigler announced Sanger was on the line.

"Sanger, Himmler here."

"Yes, Reichsführer."

"Get underway immediately."

"Yes, sir. Everything is prepared."

"I know you're a good man, Sanger. I have confidence in you, but stay on your guard. This is no ordinary prisoner. The woman is cunning and highly skilled. Do you understand, Sanger?"

"Perfectly, Reichsführer."

"Have the pilot notify me immediately once you have her on the aircraft."

"I will, Reichsführer."

Himmler hung up. Saturday, after Ilse and Ada had been taken to Grünwald, Himmler related his plan to Heinrich Müller and ordered his Gestapo chief to make the preparations. If Erika Lehmann offered herself up to save the child, Lehmann would be transported under heavy guard from Grünwald to a Munich airfield. Waiting pilots would fly her to Cesena, Italy, a town still under German control on the eastern coast. Of course, the pilots would know nothing of the bomb placed aboard by the ground crew timed to detonate while the plane flew over the Adriatic Sea. The loss of pilots and guards was regrettable but unavoidable. Too many men involved in Karl Lehmann's killing were left to become potential witnesses and that mistake would not be made again. Lehmann's daughter had already eliminated a few of those witnesses, and Himmler knew he would have to deal with the rest soon. Himmler disliked eliminating faithful agents and blamed Axel Ryker: *If goddamned Ryker had done his job she would have never returned from America!*

So Himmler made up his mind to handle the cancellation of Karl Lehmann's daughter more efficiently. If she were taken away from Grünwald, his people there would know only that she was taken away—*nothing of concern in that.* But if he had her killed at Grünwald, a Gestapo Frau and nearly two dozen men would have to be eliminated, instead of just two pilots and the half-dozen guards accompanying her on the airplane. And there would be no trace of bodies or the airplane except for pieces at the bottom of the Adriatic.

Yes, it was regrettable that loyal men would die. Himmler's only consolation was that, despite having so little time to come up with a plan, he had found a way in which fewer agents would have to die.

◊ ◊ ◊

[Munich]

Richard Sanger was not typical Gestapo. Unlike most of his colleagues who had served no time in the military, Sanger had served in the Heer during the North African and Greek campaigns before burning shrapnel took out half his spleen and shattered a kneecap in Crete. Knowing his army career was over but still wanting to serve his country, Sanger improved his limp enough to convince the secret police hiring board that he could effectively carry out his duties. His two years of university and merciless treatment of enemies of the state ensured he rose quickly through the Gestapo ranks. One year ago Sanger received promotion to Kriminalrat, a rank equivalent to an army major, and placed in charge of a Gestapo substation in Nuremberg. Saturday, he had been ordered to Munich to oversee an operation that he was told came from the highest level in Berlin. The initial telephone call from Heinrich Himmler surprised Sanger, and he wondered why Himmler involved himself with such painstaking plans concerning one prisoner—and a woman at that. But it was not his place to ask questions and, after all, it was an honor to be chosen for any duty by the Reichsführer personally.

A storm was forecast for that night and Sanger felt a few sprinkles of rain as he rode beside the driver in an open-top Kübelwagen entering the dark, black-green forest-encroached roads of Grünwald. In the backseat sat two men armed with machine pistols. A paddy wagon carrying four armed men followed Sanger's Kübelwagen, and behind the paddy wagon sped another Kübelwagen with three more men. Himmler had ordered Sanger to pick up a female prisoner at the Gestapo's Grünwald villa and transport her to a nearby airfield just outside the Munich district of Haidhausen. Sanger and five men of his choosing were to put the prisoner on a waiting airplane and fly with her to an airfield in Cesena. There, agents on the ground would be waiting to take her into custody.

[Grünwald forest]

When Ilse first started out from the compound gate with Ada, she carried the child down the dirt road but soon took to the cover of the woods in case the Gestapo changed its mind and decided to come after them. Even though she knew the dogs could still track her, at least in the woods the Gestapo could not simply drive up and pull over beside her and Ada.

Carrying the child through rough terrain soon exhausted her but she knew the little girl could not walk through the thick undergrowth. And visibility was now a concern. When they entered the woods, the moon broke through fast-moving clouds often enough to shine its blue-platinum light on pitfalls in the way, but now the leaden sky had distilled away the sporadic pleats of forest moonshine. Ilse had lost her bearings in the total darkness and she heard drops of rain pat leaves in upper branches. Forced to stop for a moment's rest, Ilse sat down on a fallen log, held Ada on her lap, and realized she was lost. It was then she heard the snapping twig.

[Grünwald compound gate]

The Kübelwagen and paddy wagon had just arrived at the gate. The Gestapo guard who released Ilse Dorsch checked the prisoner-transfer papers handed to him by the Kriminalrat. The Kriminalrat quickly lost patience as the guard used his flashlight to study every word.

"Schnell!" the Kriminalrat bellowed. "There is no problem with the papers! The orders come from Reichsführer Himmler! Open the gate!"

"Yes, Kriminalrat Sanger!" said the guard, quickly backing down. He ordered the gate opened and the two vehicles roared into the compound.

[forest]

"Who's there?" Ilse shouted in German. A flashlight came on and shone in Ilse's face.

"Keep your voice down." It was a woman's voice and she spoke English. The woman trotted up and knelt beside Ilse and Ada. "You can drive a car, right?" she asked.

Ilse could now see the woman's face in the diffused illumination of the flashlight and a wave of exhilaration flooded over her. "Erika! You escaped!"

"Shhh. Speak softly," the woman said sternly. "I'm not Erika. Erika sent me to help you and Ada. My name is Maeve O'Rourke."

"Was willst du damit sagen, Erika?" Even though the woman's voice differed from Erika's and she spoke English, Ilse still believed her to be Erika and asked her to clarify what she just said.

"Erika told me you learned some English from a Scotswoman trapped by the war in Munich and that you can drive. So speak English and answer my question: Is Erika right that you can drive a car?"

"Ja, ja. I drive autos," Ilse answered in fragile English with a Scottish accent.

The stop to rest told Maeve that Ilse was tired. Maeve picked up Ada. "Follow me."

Chapter 101

Asking for a Smoke

Gestapo Grünwald compound
Same time

"Berlin notified us to expect you, Kriminalrat Sanger, and your papers appear to be in order," announced Kriminalkommissar Beck, the officer in charge of the compound. Beck had taken a few moments to examine the orders. Of the two copies, he kept one and handed the other back to the superior officer there to collect the prisoner. Beck wanted to make a good impression; he had heard of but never met Richard Sanger, reputedly a rising star in the Gestapo. "I will take you to her, personally."

"Very well," said the Kriminalrat. A Gestapo Frau stood by the Kriminalrat's side; she had introduced herself to the compound commander as an agent from Station 8. The rest of the Gestapo officer's personnel remained outside with the vehicles.

Beck ordered the two foyer guards to accompany the entourage to the room holding the prisoner.

[in the forest]
Using her flashlight, Maeve wended her way through the forest with Ada and Ilse until they were back on the dirt road. "Hurry," Maeve whispered. Carrying Ada, Maeve jogged down the road, leading Ilse around a bend to where a Gestapo Kübelwagen sat abandoned.

[inside the compound villa]
Erika sat handcuffed and chained to a metal chair in a small, windowless room at the rear of the villa. Three guards stood inside the room, near the door. She had seen Ada for a painfully brief moment when the guards first brought her through the front door. Erika's heart broke when Ada recognized the woman who had occasionally

visited her and reached out to her unknown mother to be held. But the guards would not allow it and dragged Erika through the foyer without stopping. Seeing no sign of harm done to Ada, Erika had silently thanked God.

When the door started to open, the guards in the room pointed their weapons, ready to fire on anyone not authorized to enter. Before he stepped in, Beck announced his name and the guards relaxed. Erika watched Beck enter, followed by two compound guards and Kai Faust and Stephanie Fischer.

[on a forest road]
"Get in," Maeve ordered Ilse.

"This is your auto? This auto I drive never."

"It drives like any car." Maeve got into the passenger seat and placed Ada on her lap. "Hurry."

Ilse got behind the wheel and Maeve aimed her flashlight at the dashboard. Ilse quickly studied the controls, checked to make sure the transmission was in neutral, then pumped the accelerator pedal and pressed the ignition button. The Kübelwagen started immediately.

"Go!" Maeve ordered.

Ilse turned on the headlights and moved the gearstick. When she let out the clutch too quickly, the vehicle jerked violently but did not stall. Ilse compensated with the clutch pedal and in a moment the Kübelwagen was underway.

"Turn it around," instructed Maeve. "This way takes us back to the Gestapo."

"We must for Erika go back."

"Don't be an eejit. We have a plan. I'm not alone. My job is to make sure the little lass is safe. Turn around now!"

Ilse hit the brakes and struggled to turn around on the narrow road, but finally pointed the vehicle in the opposite direction and began speeding down the road. When they passed the ditch where rested the bodies of the caravan's Gestapo agents, Maeve kept Ada's face turned away so she could not see them in the headlights. And Ilse, with a death grip on the steering wheel and a keen focus on the road, did not notice the bodies off to the side.

Ilse had been thinking. "How did you know Ada and I to be released?"

"We didn't know. If you weren't released we would have been forced to go over the wall and shoot it out as we searched for you. We had that plan ready, but lucky for all of us it didn't come to that. This is Plan B."

Saturday, at Gestapo headquarters in Berlin, the ever-vigilant Kathryn Fischer came across the paperwork from Himmler ordering a Kriminalrat in Nuremberg to report to Munich Station 8 and prepare a caravan for prisoner pickup at the Grünwald villa. The caravan vehicles and men were to be ready to depart on a moment's notice and remain on standby until further orders. No additional details were included with Himmler's order, but after Kathryn learned from her sister that Erika's daughter was being held at the villa, Kathryn quickly put two and two together: The caravan was for Erika if she were captured trying to penetrate the villa's security, or surrendered to save her daughter. Kathryn sent a transmission to Amanda McBride.

[in the compound]

Victor Knight, wearing a uniform taken off one of the bodies, leaned against the hood of the Kübelwagen that had carried the now dead Richard Sanger. Also in dead man's clothes (although ill-fitting on his heavily-muscled frame), John Mayne sat behind the steering wheel of the Gestapo paddy wagon. The second Kübelwagen had been left behind for Maeve and Ilse in case the Gestapo released the child.

The grounds in front of the villa were well lit by floodlights mounted on tall poles, and a guard walked over to the paddy wagon to ask Mayne for a cigarette. Mayne could tell the man asked a question and guessed his meaning when he heard the word *Zigarette*. Mayne shook his head. The guard launched into a longer conversation, none of which Mayne understood. When he paused, he looked at Mayne, waiting for a response. Mayne gave him an indecisive look and shrugged as if to say he hadn't an opinion one way or another. Knight came to the rescue, using his German to tell the guard he should not be smoking on guard duty, and that they were there to pick up a prisoner and not there to chat. The guard looked displeased at the rebuke and walked away.

Chapter 102

Thor Delivers Odin's Daughter

Gestapo compound in Grünwald
Same time

"Unshackle the prisoner from the chair," ordered Beck, "but leave her hands bound." The ankle chains had been looped through the chair supports, effectively binding Erika to the metal chair.

"The prisoner is now your responsibility, Kriminalrat Sanger," said Beck, glad to be off the hook for guarding a prisoner of such high interest to 8 Prinz Albrechtstrasse. "My men will give you any help you need. Do you want extra men to accompany you during transport?"

Posing as Richard Sanger, Kai did his best to act the part. "No," Kai answered, "we have everything under control." He looked at the prisoner. "Stand up!"

Erika stood. She thought the suit fit her husband well. Too warm in August for the infamous black trench coat, Kai had guessed right that Sanger would be in a business suit. Only the small, round lapel pin of the Nazi Party that Kai took from Sanger's blazer signaled allegiance.

Erika felt great relief. Seeing Kai and Stephanie without first hearing gunshots told her Ada was free. Whatever happened now was less important.

Stephanie walked over and roughly grabbed Erika's arm to pull her along. "Come on, you!" she snapped. "We have plans for you back at headquarters." Stephanie wore the standard Gestapo Frau uniform stolen by her sister: a calf-length charcoal wool skirt with light-gray knee socks, white blouse with charcoal necktie, ankle-high boots and the familiar Gestapo Frau cap with its tightly wound brim.

One of the guards who had been stationed inside the room looked intently at Kai, then turned to the compound commander. "Kriminalkommissar Beck," said the guard, "did I hear you say 'Sanger'?"

"Yes." Beck answered impatiently. "Why do you ask?"

The guard again looked at Kai. "May I ask your given name, Kriminalrat?"

"No, you may not!" Kai acted irked, as an officer might when questioned by a low-ranking guard. But he had the sinking feeling their luck, which had so far held, was turning.

"I was stationed in Nuremberg for four months under Kriminalrat Richard Sanger," the guard announced as he turned to Beck. "Herr Kriminalkommissar, this man is not Kriminalrat Richard Sanger, if that is who he claims to be."

Kai didn't wait for Beck's response. He landed a vicious right cross to the questioning guard's jaw, knocking him unconscious before he slammed to the floor, then Kai attacked a second guard before the man could sling the rifle from his shoulder. Because a silent Welrod was too large and heavy to conceal without a coat, Stephanie Fischer pulled a Mauser from the back of her waistband and began shooting. Erika, still handcuffed, reached the cuffs over the head of the guard nearest her and strangled him.

When shots rang from inside the villa, five nearby guards ran toward the door. John Mayne jumped out of the paddy wagon and he and Victor Knight opened up, Mayne with a Thompson submachine gun and Knight with his pistol. They managed to mow down three of the guards while the other two disappeared inside. In a moment, more gunfire erupted from inside the villa. Other compound guards, stationed farther away, began shooting at Knight and Mayne. A bullet struck Mayne in the left arm. Both SOE agents ducked down in front of the paddy wagon for cover. While Knight and Mayne reloaded, the guards who had been sent to search the woods outside the wall ran back through the gate and sought cover. The gate swung closed behind them.

◊ ◊ ◊

Kai threw a downed guard's Schmeisser to Stephanie and she ran ahead to clear the way out. Kai freed Erika's hands and grabbed Schmeissers for the two of them.

495

Stephanie emerged from the corridor into the foyer at the same time the two outside guards came through the front door. She fired on them and one guard went down immediately. The other returned fire and dove behind a sofa as the compound Gestapo Frau appeared from a corridor and began shooting a pistol. All could hear the gun battle start up again outside.

Because the escape plan required a Gestapo hostage, Beck, the senior officer, had been spared. Kai jerked the downed compound commander to his feet and pushed him out of the room. When Kai, Beck, and Erika reached the foyer, two guards and Stephanie Fischer lay on the floor. Stephanie, shot through the thigh, bled profusely but tried to stand. Of the two guards, one was dead and the other lay face down behind the sofa severely wounded. The Gestapo Frau who had dealt so cruelly with Ilse and Ada lay dead in the hallway entrance, her dead eyes open and her mouth gaping grotesquely.

Knight and Mayne endured a fusillade of bullets from compound guards concealed by darkness and hiding behind trees at the edge of the compound clearing. The SOE agents returned fire when they could, aiming at the bright muzzle fires flashing from the trees at the clearing's fringe. Mayne suffered another hit, this time in the shoulder. Knight was struck in the side of his hip by a ricochet. Luckily the paddy wagon took most of the hits: its windshield now in fragments on the hood and ground, its side pockmarked with bullet holes from hood to rear bumper, and two tires flat. The Kübelwagen was also put out of commission when one of the compound guards opened up on it. Knight took aim and shot out the pole lights. Light from the villa windows still lit the clearing to a small degree, but shooting out the floodlights increased his and Mayne's cover significantly.

When the shooting abruptly stopped, Knight looked around. On the villa veranda, Kai Faust stood behind Beck, holding him firmly and with the muzzle of his Schmeisser placed to Beck's ear. Stephanie Fischer hobbled out of the doorway with her arm over Erika's shoulder.

"Tell them to drop their weapons!" Kai ordered Beck.

Beck knew if the high-priority prisoner escaped, his life would not be worth a Reichspfennig. "Fire!" Beck screamed. "Kill them all!"

The guards opened up. John Mayne, already twice wounded, yelled at Knight, "Get the Valkyrie out of here!" then stood and walked out into the clearing firing his Thompson.

When Knight stood and screamed, "John!" a bullet shattered his left ankle. A barrage of bullets shredded Mayne's body as he calmly walked toward the fire. Incredibly, the fierce Englishman remained on his feet and took out three guards before turning his machinegun on one of the compound's two Krupp army trucks, disabling it. Finally, Mayne fell.

Staying in the shadows, Kai led Erika and Stephanie toward the only vehicle still operational—the second army truck. They refrained from firing to avoid revealing their position. Stephanie's weakness from blood loss made it slow going. Mayne had succeeded in lessening the incoming fire to a great degree, but as the remaining camp guards swept the area with bullets, one struck Kai's Schmeisser and careened through the palm of his right hand. A bullet ripped the collar of Erika's shirt and grazed her neck, opening a gash.

"You'll never make it with me," Stephanie said weakly. "Go." With all her remaining strength, she shoved away from Erika and limped into the open toward where John Mayne lay fallen. When Erika started after her, Kai grabbed his wife and forced her toward the second truck. Stephanie, now fully exposed in the clearing, dropped to her knees near Mayne's body when her wounded leg gave out, but she continued to fire the Schmeisser.

Kai and Erika helped the disabled Knight to the truck. Only four guards remained alive or unwounded, and they were forced to concentrate on Stephanie, who still fired on them. After loading the wounded Knight in the bed of the truck, Erika leapt down to return for Stephanie. At that moment, Stephanie's clip emptied and her Schmeisser clicked silent. Seeing her defenseless, the remaining guards rose from their ducked positions and fired. Despite the weak light, Erika saw blood geyser from Stephanie's chest, not red but black in the incandescent lighting from the villa windows. The truck's engine started. "Erika, get in!" Kai shouted from behind the steering wheel.

497

Enraged when she saw Stephanie keel over, Erika lifted her Schmeisser and charged toward the hidden guards. Purple lightning cracked so near it stunned the ear, shattered trees in the nearby woods, and illuminated the grounds in an eerie, ethereal glow. Before they died, three guards saw running toward them a golden-haired angel of death shrouded by forks of the bolt that in reality struck in the forest beyond the compound gate but seemed to cloak the woman. The fourth man lost his nerve when he saw the apparition delivered to earth by a hammer strike from Thor. He turned and fled into the trees.

Kai jumped out of the truck to go after Erika, either to retrieve her or to help in the fight, but the gun battle ended so quickly she didn't need his help. When he reached her, he grabbed her arm. "Let's go!"

"I'm going for Stephanie!"

"She's dead, Erika! So is Mayne! Ada is out there!"

They ran back to the truck. Erika jumped into the open bed with Knight. Kai put the truck in gear and crashed through the compound gate.

After the truck drove away, the man who had fled into the woods walked into the clearing. Conrad Gerber had been sent by Himmler as an observer to ensure things were as planned. Gerber's orders were to kill Erika if any chance of her escape developed, but once again she eluded him. He had been outside the villa watching for any of Lehmann's comrades foolish enough to come over the wall when he heard the shooting start inside, and his cowardice caused him to flee at the end. With the gun battle over and the woman who was laying waste to the feared Gestapo gone, Gerber walked up to Kriminalkommissar Beck who lay wounded on the veranda, struck in the groin by a bullet meant for Kai. Beck knew why Gerber was there and he accepted his fate. Gerber pulled his Mauser and shot Beck in the back of the head.

Gerber then walked over to John Mayne and Stephanie Fischer. Mayne was dead, having been shot two dozen times. Somehow, Stephanie was alive. Gerber gazed down at her as the heavens opened and rain began pouring. Lying on her back, mortally wounded and gasping for breath, Stephanie had only a few seconds of life left when her eyes focused on Gerber.

"She . . . made it," Stephanie gasped.

Gerber aimed his pistol at her head. "Yes, I'm afraid so."

Stephanie now recognized Gerber from the photographs Kathryn supplied Erika of the men on Karen Hinderliter's Hotel zum Türken list: the men Erika knew had stalked and killed her father. She looked Gerber in the eyes and smiled weakly. "She . . . will . . . find you."

Gerber fired a round between Stephanie's eyes, then sprinted into the villa to escape the rain.

Chapter 103

Daughter of War

Berlin—8 Prinz Albrechtstrasse
One week later; Wednesday, 09 August 1944

As he had found himself doing often lately, Heinrich Himmler sat in his desk chair looking glumly out his office window. A week had passed since Grünwald, a week in which Himmler dreaded sleep. That first night after learning of the devastation at the compound, Himmler awoke perspiring from a nightmare in which Karl Lehmann's daughter descended on him dressed in Viking battle gear and riding a white war horse. The dream repeated itself every night, and every night Himmler awoke startled when she plunged a heavy broadsword into his chest and cut out his heart.

He didn't know why the dream, but suspected it had something to do with her message threatening to send him to Niflheimr, the Norse equivalent of Hell, and Conrad Gerber's report about the end of the Grünwald gun battle when he said Erika Lehmann rode in on a bolt of lightning. Himmler scoffed at Gerber's ridiculous tale, but conceded that Gerber might be right about one thing: *Providence does protect Lehmann.*

The first two times the buzzer sounded Himmler ignored it. Finally, he wheeled back around to his desk and pushed the answer button. "Yes, Frau Zeigler. What is it?"

"Gruppenführer Müller is here for his daily reports, Herr Reichsführer."

"Very well," Himmler said half-heartedly. "Send him in." Himmler had grown weary of Müller and his bad news to the point he hated to look at his face.

Müller walked in and took a seat across from Himmler.

"Did I tell you to sit, Müller?"

Müller rose. "I beg your pardon, Reichsführer."

"Müller, you never enter a room, you seep in like a cloud of toxic gas. What calamity will you contaminate my office with today? . . . and sit down, goddammit!"

Müller sat and cleared his throat. He had made up his mind not to start his report with the topic of Erika Lehmann. "Some good news today. We captured another British spy, a woman, who helped coordinate escape routes through France for downed Allied airmen. She's not cooperating but we have identified her because she was captured previously but escaped. The name is Eileen Nearne. She will be taken to Ravensbrück for interrogation then transferred to Dachau."

Müller paused to check his notes. "The next item is Treblinka. An updated report from the camp commandant confirms the camp has been successfully evacuated per your orders, Reichsführer." In late July, with the Soviet army approaching the death camp near the Polish town of Malkinia, Himmler ordered Treblinka shut down.

"And the remaining prisoners?" Himmler asked.

"All shot." Müller glanced at his paperwork. "There were not many left to deal with—just over five hundred."

"Continue. What about Paris?"

"The Americans are within fifty miles of the city but have stopped their advance. Reports tell us Eisenhower is holding them up to allow the French to enter the city first. Our High Command is confident the Wehrmacht can hold the city from any French advance, but not from the Americans who will come on their heels."

"Start the process of shutting down Gestapo substations and return our personnel to Germany, Müller. I have already spoken to the Führer."

"Yes, sir."

"Anything from Gerber?"

Müller shifted in his seat. He knew the topic of Erika Lehmann could not be avoided. "Gerber remains in Munich on your orders, Reichsführer. The Dorsch woman has not returned to her home."

"What a great surprise," Himmler said sarcastically. "Who would have imagined that Dorsch wouldn't be waiting for us at home?"

"Do you have any further orders for Gerber?" asked Müller.

"No. Leave him in Munich. What did he learn about Dorsch's family?" Himmler had ordered Gerber to stay in Munich and identify and locate Ilse Dorsch's close family members. Taking family members into custody often worked well when the Gestapo sought to force someone to the surface. That strategy had worked with Erika Lehmann; unfortunately for the Gestapo, the outcome was catastrophic.

"Dorsch's only immediate family is her parents who also live in Munich. Gerber has their address, but has not called on them; he awaits your orders."

"Take them into custody."

"Yes, sir. Do you think Lehmann is still in Germany?"

Himmler looked tired and spoke slowly. "Gerber is in Germany, the two men she lacked time to kill in Paris will return shortly, and others from the Karl Lehmann mission still live. Yes, Müller, she's in Germany."

[same day—Barcelona]

Given the cloudy weather, Barcelona did not appear until the Junkers was just a couple of miles from the Spanish coast. The pilot banked the plane to the right and left the Mediterranean behind when the city came into view.

◊ ◊ ◊

A Red Cross ambulance wagon with a three-man medical crew, a British FANY, and a translator waited near the edge of the tarmac at Barcelona's civilian airfield. Two British military policemen sat in an American Jeep parked beside the Red Cross wagon. As Spain was neutral, the MPs wore suits and carried their pistols out of sight, under their jackets. Standing beside the Jeep, Leroy Carr and Al Hodge watched the Junkers escape the clouds and descend rapidly (Hodge was in D.C. when Carr sent for him four days ago). They watched as the plane's tires squealed and smoked when they hit the asphalt, briefly lifted off as the pilot made an adjustment, then kissed back down. Carr and Hodge jumped into the Jeep and the driver sped toward the rolling plane.

At the end of the runway, the Junkers stopped briefly before the pilot revved the engines and spun the tail around for takeoff. He cut the engines just as the Jeep skidded to a stop near a wingtip. Carr and the others climbed out and in a moment the medical wagon caught up and stopped behind the Jeep.

When the plane's side hatch opened, two medics went aboard. In a moment one appeared at the hatch and yelled for the third medic to bring a stretcher. In a few minutes they carried out Victor Knight. A bullet was still lodged in his hip and his ankle was shattered. With no access to morphine over the past week as the group hid away awaiting their chance to escape, he had endured considerable pain. But Knight was tough. As the medics carried him toward the ambulance he saw Leroy Carr approach.

"Ah, Mr. Carr. It seems you and I finally made our way to Barcelona," Knight joked about the original Operation Kriemhild plan to switch Maeve and Erika there, a plan aborted when Gibraltar was chosen instead. An airfield in a neutral country was needed for today's rendezvous, and Barcelona had been chosen because of Bill Donovan's strict orders that his counter-intelligence chief was not to fly over enemy territory.

"Yeah, we finally made it," said Carr. "How are you?"

"Jolly good. Nothing a quack and a few stiff belts of Glenfiddich won't set straight, old boy." Knight made light of his injuries, though he knew it unlikely he would ever walk again without a limp.

"Any other wounded aboard?" Carr asked.

Knight's jovial mood turned glum. "No, John and Stephanie didn't make it."

"I'm very sorry to hear that."

Next out of the hatch came a young woman carrying a child, and behind her a middle-aged couple carrying suitcases. Carr recognized none of the adults but assumed the child must be Erika Lehmann's daughter. Then Maeve emerged, followed by a man wearing an SS officer's uniform, his right hand bandaged. (Kai would have preferred to dress as a civilian pilot, but he could not have commandeered the aircraft from the Salzburg airfield without wearing his uniform.)

Carr did a double-take when the SS officer stepped off the plane. The counter-intelligence chief rarely packed a gun, but as of late carried a small Smith & Wesson revolver in a shoulder holster under his suit jacket. For a brief instant the thought flashed to reach for it. The MPs pulled their pistols and Carr held up his hand. "Stand down," he ordered, realizing Erika Lehmann would not entrust her daughter to a pilot she did not trust completely.

Only two brief transmissions from Erika had come in over the past week, and Carr understood why. Brief air time made it difficult for the enemy to triangulate a transmission location. Her sketchy communications to Amanda McBride in France specified date and location of the plane's arrival and requested an ambulance be on hand, but little else. Hence Carr arrived in Barcelona on little else than his faith in Erika, not even knowing exactly who would be on the plane. He assumed the child would be on board—that's why he brought the FANY—and he hoped Erika would be with her, but the SS officer was the last person out.

"Erika didn't come with you?" Carr asked Maeve. He knew it was Maeve. Her hair was returning to its natural color, a shade of blonde darker than Erika's.

Maeve shook her head. "No."

"The SS officer has to be the pilot. What's the story on him?"

"He's Erika's husband and the child's father."

Carr shot his head around to look again at Kai who stood apart from the others and was in return checking out Carr, Hodge, and the MPs.

Al Hodge overheard Maeve. "Good Lord!" he exclaimed.

Carr had been waiting in Caen with Knight and Mayne when Erika showed up to discuss the Grünwald rescue mission. In Caen, Carr asked Erika about her child's father but she refused to answer so Carr assumed the father was out of the picture.

"Who are the other three people?" Carr asked Maeve. "I assume the woman holding the child is the friend Erika told me about in Caen."

"Yes. That's Ilse, Erika's friend who has been raising Ada—that's the little lass's name. The older couple is Ilse's parents. Erika didn't think it safe for them to stay in Germany."

"I see," said Carr. While the medics loaded Victor Knight into the ambulance, Carr asked everyone else to assemble. The group formed a fairly tight circle except for Kai, who kept his distance, standing about 20 yards from the others.

Carr addressed the Germans. "My name is Mr. Carr, and this is Mr. Hodge. We're from the United States and are here to ensure your safe journey to London." He paused and turned to the translator. "Speak loudly so the pilot over there hears." The translator, a woman who before the war worked in the British embassy in Berlin, loudly repeated Carr's words in German. When she finished, Carr introduced the people he brought along, starting with the MPs.

"These two gentlemen are aides to Mr. Hodge and me, and the medics at the ambulance attending to the injured man are with the Red Cross." Carr waited for the translator then looked at Ilse who still held Ada. "Ilse, this lady is Mrs. Morrow, a member of the First Aid Nursing Yeomanry. Mrs. Morrow is here to give you any help you might need with the little girl."

After the translation, Carr again addressed all of the Germans. "The British government has agreed to offer you safe refuge until after the war when you can return home. We have a plane waiting. The Red Cross wagon has room for everyone, so if you'll get in we'll get you to the plane and we can be on our way."

Ilse's parents looked frightened; they had watched neighbors being loaded into trucks—neighbors they never saw again. Ilse spent a moment reassuring them and they hesitantly followed their daughter toward the ambulance. That left Carr, Hodge, the translator, and the MPs standing on the tarmac staring at the SS officer who gazed back at them. Carr told the translator to come with him and ordered the MPs to stay where they were. Carr, Hodge, and the translator approached Kai and when close enough, Carr identified his rank of Hauptsturmführer and immediately noticed the Leibstandarte emblem. But the patch that really caught Carr's eye was the one identifying the man as a member of Otto Skorzeny's commando unit.

Dubbed by Dwight Eisenhower "the most dangerous man in Europe" for his daring and successful special operations raids, Skorzeny ranked number 1 on the Operation Kriemhild list of SS candidates to be eliminated. Al Hodge also noticed the Skorzeny patch.

"Could you hear the translator when I spoke to the group?" Carr began. He locked eyes with the German as the translator did her job.

Kai moved his eyes from Carr to Hodge and then back to Carr before answering in English. "Yes, I heard everything twice. I speak English."

Carr immediately dismissed the translator, asking her to join the others in the medical wagon. After she walked away, Carr asked, "I noticed you turned the plane around for takeoff. You're not coming with us, Captain?"

"Of course not. Do you think perhaps your *aides* over there can persuade me?"

"After noticing one of your patches, I think I would need more than two military policemen to capture you. Your wife was wise not to let the SOE know who would be piloting the plane. It would be quite a coup to capture a Skorzeny commando."

"And it would be a much bigger coup if I brought back to Germany the head of counter-intelligence for the United States. But you also need not worry, Herr Carr. My only interest today is that my daughter reach England."

That answered Carr's question about how much Erika had told her husband concerning him. Carr turned to Hodge. "Al, take one of the MPs, go along in the ambulance, and get everyone settled in the plane."

"Should I have the plane taxi over here?" Hodge asked. The C-47 waited at the far corner of the huge airfield.

"No. Leave the Jeep and the other MP here as my driver, but tell him to wait in the Jeep. I'll be along shortly."

Hodge gave the Skorzeny commando one last look then turned and walked away.

Kai asked Carr, "What do you know about me other than what you can identify from my uniform?"

"Nothing until a few minutes ago when Maeve O'Rourke told me you're Erika's husband. I confess I was surprised to see an SS officer step off the airplane—and a Skorzeny Leibstandarte commando, no less."

"I bring a request from my wife. It is my request, also."

"What is it?"

"We want our daughter taken to my wife's grandparents in London. Erika told me you know her grandfather."

"Yes. I met Sir Louis in the United States last fall—in Cincinnati."

Kai nodded, reached inside his tunic and pulled out an envelope. "This is a letter from Erika to her grandparents about Adelaide. That's our child's name. We call her Ada."

"Yes. Maeve told me about Ada."

"The letter contains all of our wishes concerning Ada. Do I have your word you will deliver our daughter to her great-grandparents and give them this letter?"

Carr took the letter. "You have my word."

Kai said nothing more and did not offer his hand. He turned and walked toward the Junkers hatch. Just before he entered, he stopped and turned back to Carr.

"My wife tells me you are a man of honor." Before Carr could reply, Kai disappeared into the plane. In less than a minute the engines coughed smoke and the propellers began slowly turning, as if they resisted being awakened from their rest. Leroy Carr backed away from the wing as the engine roar increased. The plane started moving, picked up speed, and grew smaller as it moved away. Halfway down the runway, the wheels left the pavement, the nose steeped, and the plane piloted by a Skorzeny commando disappeared into the clouds.

507

Chapter 104

Otto's Lair

Austrian Alps
Next day; Thursday, 10 August 1944

Heinrich Himmler had guessed wrong. Erika Lehmann was not in Germany. In the cool mountain air whispering through the porch of a cottage high in the Austrian Alps, she stood gazing through the spruces at a doe nudging her speckled fawn to get moving.

The cottage belonged to Otto Skorzeny. Born in Austria, Skorzeny purchased the cottage before the war for times when his demanding schedule allowed short escapes for rest and quiet. No one, including Kai and the other men in his unit, knew about Skorzeny's hidden lair (Skorzeny offered it only after Kai told him of the dangers to Ada). With the war, Skorzeny had not used his retreat in over two years, and when Kai brought the group here after Grünwald, it took a full day to clear away the cobwebs.

But Himmler was only wrong by 10 miles. The cottage stood just that short distance from the German border. It was the perfect hideout: remote, difficult to reach, and at 6000 feet, not above the Alpine treeline. Tall firs and spruces swathed the hideaway and made it impossible to see almost until the moment a visitor reached the porch. The only road was an overgrown trail no one else used, and it ended 400 yards from the bungalow—the rest of the way on foot. It had been a struggle to carry Victor Knight through the dense forest.

Kai stood beside his wife, leaning on the wooden rail. He had returned from his meeting with Leroy Carr just an hour ago. Not wanting to revisit the Salzburg airfield where he had commandeered the Junkers in case inquiries had been made, Kai landed and abandoned the plane in a farmer's field near Innsbruck, where he spent last night in a small, out-of-the-way hotel. Early this morning he hot-wired a Volkswagen and found his way back to the cottage. The Volkswagen now sat in the forest, camouflaged with foliage near the end of the trail.

"What were your impressions of the American OSS man Mr. Carr?" Erika asked.

"I didn't speak with him long enough to form an impression," answered Kai. "There was another man with him, also OSS I assume. Mr. Hodge."

"Yes, Hodge is OSS."

"You said before I left with Ada that the Americans can be trusted. That's enough for me. I know you wouldn't turn our daughter over to people you did not trust totally."

Erika nodded.

"How is your injury?" Kai asked. He looked at the abrasion on Erika's neck, sustained in the gun battle. In normal circumstances, a doctor would have stitched the cut, but she had simply applied iodine and a bandage. The bleeding had stopped and the bandage was now gone, revealing the gash.

"It's healing. And your hand?"

Ricochets, because they had previously struck something else and become distorted, always left ragged entry wounds. This ricochet had entered Kai's palm and exited the back of his hand, leaving two nasty-looking tears, but missing bone. "Fine."

Kai had tried to talk Erika into leaving with Ada and the others. He gently placed his hands on her shoulders and turned her toward him. "I'm worried about you," he said, looking into her eyes. "Nothing good will come of what you insist on doing. I agree that the men who killed your father must pay, but wait until the war ends, when I can help you. My unit has finished training and moves out on another mission in a few days; the time I can be away is running out. After the war, I will help you avenge your father."

Erika looked at him but said nothing.

"I love you, Erika," Kai said and paused. "But I know that love is not returned. I've always known that you married me for Ada's sake, so think of her now. Your grandparents are in their seventies. You must survive the war—for Ada."

His words about love surprised her. She never realized he knew she didn't love him as a wife should love her husband.

"Or *you* must survive the war for Ada," Erika said, then turned away. "Yes, Kai, I've sworn to avenge my father. But it's not just about my father now. You haven't seen what I saw in Poland. Until Himmler is dead, nothing can be over for me."

[same day—home of Louis and Marie Minton, London]
When the first knock came, Maggie stood at the kitchen sink washing cups and saucers from afternoon tea. As she took a moment to dry her hands, the brass door knocker banged again, more loudly.

"Yes, yes, I'm coming! Keep yer ants on!" Maggie shouted in her cockney slang, knowing the person at the door could not hear her. She threw down the towel and stepped lively out of the kitchen, through the dining room, and into the foyer of the upscale rowhouse on the outskirts of west London. When she opened the door, a man in a business suit who had just reached out to bang the knocker a third time drew back his hand.

"Hello, my name is Leroy Carr," he said in an American accent.

"And I'm Betty Grable," replied Maggie. "What can I do for you?"

"I'd like to speak with Sir Louis if he's available. He and I know each other; we met in the United States when he visited there last fall."

"Sorry, the guvnah's not at home. He's in charge of the ration board and they have their meeting today."

"May I ask when he might return?" Carr knew he should have called first, but he did not want to tell Sir Louis and his wife about Ada over the telephone.

"I don't know. On Thursdays after his meeting, the guvnah and some of his old mates gather at the Hurlingham Club for a pint or a whiskey—probably won't make his way back till dinner, I would gander."

"Is Lady Minton at home?"

"Yes."

"May I speak with her? It's important."

Maggie looked Carr over. "What did you say your name is?"

"Leroy Carr. I'm with the American embassy."

It was not uncommon for important persons to call on Louis Minton, who had served as both an attaché and chargé d'affaires in several British consulates, including Berlin. Maggie had been with the Mintons for 15 years, and VIPs showing up on the doorstep had long ago stopped impressing the feisty housekeeper. "Wait here." She closed the door in Carr's face.

As he waited, Carr turned and glanced at the black four-door Wolseley sedan parked at the curb. In a moment, the house door reopened.

"Get yourself inside," said Maggie.

Carr stepped in and removed his fedora.

"I'll take that. Lady Minton will be down shortly. You can wait in the drawing room. My name's Maggie, by the way."

Carr handed her his hat. "Thank you, Maggie." He followed her to a room off the foyer.

"Sit where you like."

Carr nodded, but remained standing after Maggie left and closed the door. The room was nicely appointed and fragrant with summer flowers; the plush furniture looked expensive. Shelves of books covered one wall, red damask and cherry-wood railing the others. Two paintings hung on adjacent walls, one of a man and one a woman; Carr assumed they were Minton ancestors. A coat of arms was mounted over the hearth and brass-framed photographs sat along the gray-veined marble mantel. Carr walked over to look at the photos.

He recognized Louis Minton in one black-and-white photograph. Minton looked at least 10 years younger than Carr remembered from last fall in Cincinnati. Also in the photo was a woman about Minton's age—doubtless Lady Minton—and a smiling girl who looked about 12. Carr stared at the young Erika for a long moment. Another photo caught his eye and he picked it up for a better look. The young, blonde woman was perhaps in her early 20s; Carr saw the resemblance to Erika immediately.

The drawing room door opened and an elderly woman wearing a light-blue, dotted-Swiss frock with a pearl brooch on her collar stepped in. She was attractive and her appearance immaculate. She saw Carr holding the photograph.

511

"That's our daughter, Louise. You're Mr. Carr?"

"Yes, ma'am." Carr returned the picture of Erika Lehmann's mother to the mantelpiece.

"I've heard your name from my husband. I'm Marie Minton. Please have a seat, Mr. Carr. We just had tea, but Maggie is preparing more." Carr knew that many English considered it bad manners for a guest to refuse tea and that some proper English ladies, especially ones Lady Minton's age, considered handshakes with strange men unsuitable so he refrained from offering his hand.

"Thank you." Carr waited until Marie Minton sat down on the settee. He chose the chair nearest to him, a Windsor. "It's nice to meet you, Lady Minton, and thank you for seeing me. Maggie told me Sir Louis is out."

"I'm afraid so. Since the war began, my husband spends much of his time in meetings of one sort or another. I'm sorry you missed him. May I ask what business the OSS has with my husband? Am I right in assuming your visit may have something to do with our granddaughter, Erika?"

When he learned from Maggie that Louis Minton was not at home, Carr opted to not identify himself to his wife as OSS, but clearly Sir Louis had told his wife everything about last fall in the States.

Carr cleared his throat. Calling on people to spring unknown great-granddaughters on them would create a new line on his resume. "Uh, yes, Lady Minton. I'm here about Erika. . . ."

She interrupted. "What has happened to her, Mr. Carr?" Marie Minton immediately expected the worst. All too frequently these days a stranger showed up on a doorstep with the worst news about a loved one.

"Your granddaughter is alive, Lady Minton. Unfortunately, I can't tell you any more about Erika's present situation. But I'm here at her request." Carr decided to leap in with both feet. "Erika has a three-year-old daughter."

Marie Minton's eyes widened and her mouth opened slightly.

Carr continued, "The father is German. They married in 1941, the year the baby was born." Erika had told Carr in Caen that her grandparents knew nothing about Ada, which Marie Minton's face now confirmed.

"A . . . child?" Lady Minton almost stuttered. "Where is this child?"

"She's outside in my car. Erika hopes you and your husband will care for her until a time when she or her husband can come for her."

Marie Minton felt her head swimming. "Are you sure about this, Mr. Carr? I mean . . . of course, you're sure. Erika entrusted the child to you to bring to us."

"Actually, the father delivered the child to me. Her name is Adelaide; she's called Ada. I have a letter from Erika to you and your husband I was asked to give you." Carr reached into his jacket pocket and pulled out the envelope. "I'm sorry, but because of certain wartime protocols demanded by my government I had to open it, Lady Minton."

"I understand." She accepted the letter. "What am I doing? I'm not thinking correctly. Bring the child in, *please.*"

Carr walked out of the room as Maggie entered with a platter of tea and cakes. "Is he leaving?" Maggie asked. "What about the tea? Those Yanks are a sorry lot of cavemen. The only thing they care about is their chewing gum and getting a woman's knickers down."

Normally, Marie Minton would admonish Maggie for her coarseness, but instead said only, "Erika has a daughter. He's brought her to us."

Maggie shrieked and almost dropped the tray, but controlled it and set it on the desk. "I'll raise a pint to Erika tonight with the lads in Hartwick's Pub! The only time we've ever had any life in this stodgy old flat was when Erika was here! If her daughter is at all a chip, we'll finally get some life in this funeral parlor!" Maggie ran out the drawing room door.

Marie Minton rose, still in shock, and walked to the front door. Maggie almost beat Leroy Carr to the Wolseley and stood there as Ilse got out holding Ada. The FANY, Mrs. Morrow, exited from the other backseat door. The British army driver stayed in the car.

Carr had once heard someone remark that small children can identify those worthy to hold their innocent souls, and he watched

Ada immediately reach for Maggie. Maggie embraced Ada, laughed and kissed her, and ran with her to Lady Minton.

Marie Minton gazed at the child with hair the same color as Louise's and saw her long-lost daughter in the child's face. Ada looked at the elderly woman as if waiting for the angels to tell her the stranger was okay, then reached for her great-grandmother.

Marie Minton broke into sobs and took Ada into her arms.

Chapter 105

Gerber Celebrates

Munich
Two months later; Friday, 13 October 1944

Conrad Gerber had a new lease on life and a spring in his step he had not had since the disastrous mission in Spain last spring. Of the men who participated in killing Karl Lehmann, only Gerber still lived. Christoph Unger and Andreas Biermann, Gestapo agents who escaped Erika Lehmann's wrath in Paris when she left to rescue her daughter, now lay among the dead.

In late August, Biermann had mysteriously fallen head-first out of his sixth-floor Hanover apartment window in the middle of the night, flattening the roof of a Horch sedan parked below. If it was suicide, Biermann chose to end his life in his boxer shorts.

No mystery swirled around Unger's death. Last month on a desolate stretch of tracks northeast of Chemnitz, Unger was chopped in two by a train speeding to Dresden. The engineer came around a curve and spotted the man lying on the tracks much too late to stop. A quick examination of the body parts revealed Unger's hands and feet were bound, and he had been tied to the tracks. Unger was screaming for the train to stop when it sliced him in half lengthwise, starting at his groin.

And the rest of the team was also now dead. Two had been found in their beds, killed by gunshots to the head that no neighbors heard. One was found behind the wheel of his car, his throat slit; another turned up in an alley with his head bashed in.

But Gerber could finally relax after two months of keeping his head on a swivel every minute of the day—Erika Lehmann was dead at last! Müller had forwarded him a copy of the report. A stroke of bad luck did her in. Last week Lehmann had been spotted in Berlin by one of the Gestapo agents sent to Paris to trail Unger, Biermann, and Dreher. The agent was well-acquainted with her face, having studied photographs, and he tailed her to her hotel. It was the lucky break they needed. That night, a team smashed through her door and opened up, killing her in her bed. Walter Schellenberg identified the body and no doubts remained. To Gerber, Lehmann's end seemed fitting since she killed members of his team in *their* beds. Gerber smiled as he walked through the door of the Staatliches Hofbräuhaus. Although the enormous beer hall had sustained some damage during an Allied bombing raid last spring, the injured area had been sealed off, leaving the main hall and beer garden open for business.

Gerber had celebration in mind, and even though he could not tell his friends the real reason for his festive mood, he would silently raise a liter or two to Erika Lehmann's demise. He spotted five friends who were already drinking: one was Gestapo, two worked at the BMW plant, and the other two were local firemen.

"Hey, there's Gerber!" shouted one of the firemen.

"You're late, Gerber," said the Gestapo agent as Gerber joined them. "What delayed you? Did some Jewish princess seduce you?" The others laughed.

Gerber laughed, too, and flagged a nearby waitress. "I'm buying a round for all of these worthless Untermenschen, Fräulein. I'll have an Oktoberfestbier." Although the war had temporarily halted the annual celebration, the beer hall still brewed the event's special beer during September and October. As the Bier Fräulein turned to leave, Gerber slapped her buttocks. She shot him an annoyed look and all the men laughed again.

"Ach! Conrad buys a round," commented a factory worker. "It must be quite the occasion. We must have won the war and they forgot to tell us."

Over the next two hours, Bier Fräuleins kept busy refilling steins at Gerber's table while trying to avoid his groping. The waitresses were glad when Gerber finally turned his attention from them to lead his friends in renditions of "Deutschland über Alles" and "Am Adolf Hitler Platz"—the singing off-key but enthusiastic. Finally, after a third song, the "Horst Wessel Lied," where some of the lyrics were butchered but sung loudly with steins held high, Gerber slammed his stein on the table. "I have to piss!" he announced loudly enough that several tables overheard. He rose and wobbled off through the crowd toward the toilets.

A long line stretched from the door of the men's lavatory. Since few women frequented the beer hall there was no line at the women's door. Women were not welcome at most beer halls unless in the company of their husbands, and few men chose to bring wives. Gerber, half-drunk and eager to return to his beer guzzling, turned and walked into the women's lavatory. Inside, a Bier Fräulein stood at a sink washing her hands. When she saw Gerber she shrieked. He laughed, and when he began unbuttoning his trousers she ran out the door.

Gerber decided he had to do more than just urinate so he dropped his pants and sat down on a toilet. Each stall had side panels but no door. He had nearly finished when he heard the door to the lavatory open. Assuming it to be another waitress, Geber laughed and shouted, "Bring me another Oktoberfestbier, Fräulein!"

Instead of the screech of surprise he expected to hear, Gerber heard the woman walk toward him. She stopped and stood in front of his stall. With a depraved smile, he scanned her body. The beer hall dirndl accented her bosom and his eyes stopped at her cleavage. Then he raised his eyes to look at her face.

"Oh, shit!" Gerber said, not knowing how fitting his last words would be.

Chapter 106

Useless Confession

Berlin—8 Prinz Albrechtstrasse
Next day; Saturday, 14 October 1944

Heinrich Müller reported to Himmler's office earlier than usual. Today he brought good news.

"I'm pleased to inform you of our success, Reichsführer. Gerber is dead."

"Details, Müller," said Himmler.

"Last night his body was found in a women's toilet at a Munich beer hall. His pants were down and excrement smeared his face. She apparently drowned Gerber in a toilet bowl full of his own waste."

Last week, Himmler ordered Müller to send Gerber a fabricated Gestapo report of Erika Lehmann's death. Over the past months, Himmler had received reports about the other members of Gerber's Karl Lehmann elimination team meeting their doom, one by one. When Gerber was the only man left, it was time to eliminate the final witness. Himmler knew the phony report would relieve Gerber of fear for his life and bring him out into the open where he would be easy prey for Erika Lehmann.

She was Himmler's curse, a demon he sought to exorcise, and Himmler reasoned that since he was untouchable—he was Reichsführer—that when Lehmann had eliminated all the men on the elimination team, her blood lust would finally be satisfied.

Then, perhaps, his nightmares of the white war horse and of her broadsword plunging into his chest would end.

[same day—Munich]
Erika leaned over the lavatory sink, a churning stomach demanding she stay close to a toilet.

She had been changing her location often, never staying anywhere more than a few days. For the past three days she had posed as a German-Czech refugee and stayed here, in a rundown hotel near the train station now serving as a hostel.

The hollow eyes in the cracked mirror stared back at her. Her skin pale, she looked and felt sick in body and at heart. The past months had taken a toll; she was physically and emotionally drained. For weeks, sleep had been fitful, and after returning from the beer hall last night, nausea forced her to spend most of the dark hours near the toilet. She had sworn to avenge her father and it was done, but the release she hoped for was denied. Erika had never given up her Catholic faith, and she thought of confession. But she knew it useless. One must feel remorse for one's acts, and she was not sorry she killed the men who murdered her father.

Her thirst for vengeance had exacted a terrible price. Tars had given her life to protect Maeve. Stephanie Fischer and John Mayne sacrificed themselves so she could escape Grünwald with Ada. Himmler would have never found out about Ada if Erika had not returned seeking revenge; she had endangered even her own daughter. And Erika thought often of Stephanie, and would never forget that Stephanie could have betrayed her to Walter Schellenberg and walked away a hero.

Leroy and Kai were right: I should have waited until the war's end.

She had not seen or had contact with her husband since they left Skorzeny's hideaway two days after Kai returned from Barcelona. He had to report back to his unit; she, against his wishes, began her search for the remaining murderers. Erika longed to hold Ada and missed Kai. Maybe she was wrong about her feelings for her husband. Maybe she did love him. She stood gazing into the mirror wondering if there was any chance they would someday be together—her, Kai, Ada. *Will we ever live as a family?*

One person remained, but she was used up and could not go on. She would follow her husband's advice and wait until after the war.

Let Heinrich Himmler stew.

Chapter 107

Our Lady

Paris
Three and a half weeks later; Tuesday, 07 November 1944

At exactly noon, Leroy Carr walked past a group of American G.I.s snapping photographs from the street, climbed the steps, and opened one of the massive doors to Notre Dame Cathedral. He walked inside expecting to be impressed, but not expecting vertigo when he lifted his eyes to the ceiling.

Carr received Amanda McBride's encoded message two days ago. Now stationed in liberated Paris, McBride no longer lived in constant danger. In fact, her message that Erika Lehmann was in Paris arrived in London on a Gooney Bird, one of the American C-47 transports that had made constant flights between the cities since the Germans were driven from Paris in late August.

Inside the cathedral, touring American and British military men outnumbered worshippers. As Carr walked toward the high altar, he spotted her kneeling in the fifth row, praying. He sat down beside her. When she noticed him, she crossed herself and sat back.

"Hello, Erika."

"Hello, Leroy. How's my daughter?"

"She's doing well. Your grandparents are nuts about her, and Ada has taken to them."

"Ilse is still with her, right?"

"Yes, Ilse stays with Ada at the Mintons' home. Your grandparents turned a bedroom into a nursery, and Ilse's room is across the hall."

"A nursery? Ada is three and a half."

"You know grandparents."

Erika smiled. "Yes, I know they will dote on her, and I'm glad Ilse is there. Ilse is the only mother Ada knows." In her letter to her grandparents, one of Erika's requests had been to allow Ilse to stay at their home with Ada, at least till war's end when Erika or Kai could

520

come for their daughter. That request also benefited Ilse, who dared not return to Germany until after the war. Erika did not want her friend spending the duration in an overcrowded refugee camp.

"Where are Ilse's parents?" Erika asked.

"I'm housing them on an American air base just outside London. They get to see Ilse and Ada regularly. They ate dinner at your grandparents' home Saturday."

"Thank you, Leroy. Shall we walk?"

On the street, she removed her white lace church scarf and placed it in a jacket pocket. She carried no purse. Carr instructed his French army driver to follow but at a distance.

"This is my first time in Paris," Carr said as they began walking. "I didn't realize Notre Dame was on an island in the Seine. When I first walked into the church, I looked for the hunchback but got dizzy looking up." Erika neither laughed nor commented. "Okay," he added, "bad joke."

"No, it's not bad, but everyone says it."

"So you're saying I better keep my day job and forget about replacing Burns and Allen."

For a few moments they walked in silence down the Rue du Cloître Notre Dame, then began crossing over the Pont Saint-Louis to the next island.

"I have some good news about Didi Nearne," Carr announced. "You probably didn't know this, but in August she was again captured by the Gestapo and again escaped. That's the second time she escaped the Gestapo."

"She's amazing," said Erika. "Of course, you can't tell me where she is now."

"That's right. I can't. Sorry."

A small flock of gray pigeons pecked corn dropped on the walkway by bird-feeding locals. As Carr and Erika approached, all but one flapped wings and whirled into the air. The one, appearing too fat to fly, clucked its neck and waddled away as they stepped from the bridge.

"I'm ready to walk in, Leroy."

Carr's eyebrows shot up in surprise. He assumed he was in Paris because Erika needed his help with a problem. *Walk in* was an intelligence community euphemism used when a spy considered a mission over, either because the mission goals were complete, or the mission blown beyond repair. "You found the men you were after?"

"I'd rather not talk about that if you don't mind."

Halfway over the bridge, Carr stopped. "If you walk in, Erika, you know what that means: It's over—both the mission and the agreement between my government and the British concerning you. Are you sure?"

"Yes, I'm sure."

"We promised you could avenge your father. If you don't want to talk about it now, that's fine, but you'll have to talk about it at your debriefing. We received intelligence reports telling of Gestapo agents coming up dead in Germany. Just so you and I are clear, your request to walk in tells me you feel we've kept our agreements concerning your father. That's important, Erika. When you work for us after the war, I don't want you having any doubts that Uncle Sam keeps his word."

"You Americans have kept your word to me, Leroy, and I think that's mostly your doing. I thank you. I assume you'll take me to London, and that I'll be allowed to see my daughter."

"London will be your first stop. Part of our agreement with the Brits is that they also can debrief you. And, yes, of course you can see Ada. After the British debriefing, you'll eventually be shipped back to the States, but right now I can't tell you when that might be. That depends on General Donovan. When he orders me back to Washington, you'll go with me."

"I'd like for you to arrange a way for me to occasionally contact my husband while I'm in London. I just want to know he's okay and keep him posted about Ada. Will you do that?"

"He's an enemy combatant, Erika. I'm not sure I will allow that. His brief collaboration with Knight and Mayne happened only because you and Ada needed his help. When I met your husband in Barcelona, I tagged him as a man of integrity, but also a staunch enemy. I got the distinct impression that if we crossed paths under different circumstances, Hauptsturmführer Faust would cheerfully put a bullet in my head."

"As I said, any contact will be for personal reasons only."

Carr paused. "I'll think it over, but that's a request that goes beyond prudent during wartime, Erika."

"I understand. When can we leave?"

"Immediately. I didn't know if I would be here for a few hours or a few days, so I told the pilots to wait with the plane until I found out and notified them. Do you have anything to take with you?"

"Only a bag at my hotel."

Carr turned and waved to his driver. "Let's get it and be on our way."

Chapter 108

Christmas Present for Maeve

London
Seven weeks later; Sunday, 24 December 1944

Victor Knight sat down and propped his cane against his desk. Nearly five months after Grünwald, walking remained painful, but he counted it a blessing that he walked at all. Early on, more than one doctor assured him a wheelchair, or at best crutches, would be his companion for the rest of his life. But Knight refused to stay in a wheelchair after the first three weeks, and last month threw the crutches out a window of the army barracks where he billeted. He would use the cane and endure the pain stoically.

Since the ruined ankle made it impossible to resume his SOE instructor duties, Knight was reassigned as an interrogator and posted at the POW camp at Tooting Bec in the south London borough of Wandsworth. It was to Tooting Bec that the Allies sent many of the captured German radio operators, along with those suspected of having any knowledge, however minor, of German clandestine operations. Knight longed to return to the field, but since Colin Gubbins refused to consider it he resigned himself to his new post. Here at least he could use his German and his cloak and dagger expertise to stay involved in the war.

A knock sounded at his office door (Knight wasn't allotted a secretary). "Come in," he shouted.

A warrant officer opened the door but did not step in. "She's here, Mr. Thomas. The driver just dropped her off."

"Send her in, then that will be all. Thank you."

The man turned and motioned the woman to enter. Maeve walked in.

"Hello, Maeve," said Knight. "Take a load off. How are things in Slough?" Maeve was housed at a British army encampment in Slough, west of London, that served mainly as a motor repair depot.

She sat down on a metal folding chair beside Knight's desk. "Grand. They won't let me leave the place without permission and an escort. I've been told my debriefing is over, so why can't I leave? I thought the Germans ran the concentration camps."

Knight chuckled. "It can't be that bad. You're not a prisoner, and you know why we billeted you there, Maeve. We simply need to keep tabs on you for now. You learned a few things considered sensitive information—things the Jerries would be keen to know. We can't have you running around London or Belfast unescorted just yet, now can we? And there remains that little matter of the bank in Belfast and your unexpected withdrawal. It might prove dicey for all of us if you were slogging about and got picked up on that warrant."

"So why did you send for me? Can you tell me about Erika or the little lass? Why is everything a secret?" Maeve got all her questions out at once.

"I can answer only your first question, Maeve. As for your other questions, Erika is no longer under our authority; the Yanks are in charge of her now. Her daughter is safe, and that's all I can say just now. But as far as why I sent for you, it's because I have some news that I know will be a jolly good Christmas present. Certainly your Christmas this year will be better than last year when you spent the holiday in the Camden Town jail."

"Good news? What is it?"

"Last week we captured your brother in Dublin. It seems he went south to lie low."

Maeve sprang to her feet. "That's your good news? Fook you, you British bastard!"

Knight laughed. "Now there's the old Maeve O'Rourke, Belfast bank robber, we know and love. Or is it the old Maeve Shanahan, Piccadilly Circus tart? I get them mixed up."

"I've always hated your guts! I bet your wife hates your guts!" Maeve picked up a heavy paperweight from Knight's desk and raised it to strike; Knight deftly whacked it out of her hand with his cane.

"I don't have a wife, but just because I have a sorry ankle doesn't mean I forgot my training." Knight used the cane to rap her hard on the side of her hip. She shouted in pain, then he whopped her on top of her head, but more gently.

"Ouch! You're a sonuvabitch! And you've always been one, Thomas. On your tombstone they'll carve, *Here lies the sonuvabitch. We're all glad he's dead.*" The news of her brother brought tears to Maeve's eyes. Now both her brother and father were in prison.

When Knight saw Maeve's tears, he felt badly for having fun at her expense. "Maeve, your father and brother received pardons and, as of yesterday, have been free men. I'm sure this will be quite the Christmas to remember for your mother. You've been pardoned as well."

Maeve was flabbergasted. The British government kept its promise despite nothing going according to plan in Operation Kriemhild: Maeve's planned switch with Erika never occurred, and the SOE kill team failed to eliminate any of the high-ranking SS or Gestapo officers on the Kriemhild list.

The bargain had been kept largely because of Victor Knight's persistent messages to *Intrepid* over the past months pleading on Maeve's behalf.

"Only one more thing, Maeve. I've been invited to a Christmas Eve dinner tonight and I'm allowed to bring a guest." The tough, former First Airlanding Brigade commando hesitated and appeared embarrassed. "And I was wondering if you would consider going with me."

Chapter 109

No Goose

London
Later that day; Christmas Eve 1944

"Thank you, Corporal," Victor Knight said to the driver. "I was told you're from London, so my orders to you are to go home and enjoy Christmas with your family. I'll summon a taxi for our return."

"Thank you, sir!" The corporal said enthusiastically. "I will. And thank you again."

Knight and Maeve got out and walked the flagstone path through the tiny front yard. Maeve thought of helping Knight when he struggled climbing the porch steps, but reconsidered knowing it would embarrass him. When they reached the door, Knight banged the knocker.

Maggie opened the door and started to speak, but spying Maeve dammed the flow of words in her throat.

"We're a bit early, but we're expected for dinner," Knight told Maggie. "I'm Victor Knight, and this is Maeve O'Rourke."

Maggie stood speechless, staring at Maeve. Suddenly Erika appeared by Maggie's side, and now it was Maeve's turn to gape.

"Victor, what's going on?" Maeve asked. She had not seen Erika since the day she and the others left the Alpine cottage for Barcelona.

"I couldn't tell you where we were going, Maeve. More Secret Service protocols, I'm afraid—discretion and all that."

Erika stepped out to hug Maeve, then said, "Come in."

Maggie finally emerged from her trance, and while she took Knight's coat and hat, Erika took Maeve's arm and walked her toward the parlor.

"*Victor?*" Erika whispered. "The only name I've ever heard you call him is 'Thomas the wanker.'"

"In the car he told me to call him Victor, but he's still a wanker. Where's Ada?"

"Napping."

"Erika, me brother and Da have received pardons. And me, too."

"Wonderful!" said Erika. "Leroy Carr told me Victor Knight has been working for months to ensure you and your family received the pardons, but I didn't know they came through. I'm so happy for you, Maeve—and for your family."

"Victor was behind the British keeping the bargain?" Maeve asked surprised.

"It looks that way. You deserve it, Maeve. How about a drink to celebrate?"

"Sounds grand. I'm ready for a wee bucket."

Leroy Carr touched his napkin to his lips and thanked his hostess. "A fine dinner, Your Ladyship. Everything was delicious. I want to thank you and Sir Louis for inviting me."

"Oh, I deserve little credit, Mr. Carr," Marie Minton admitted. "The only part of the dinner I prepared is the Christmas pudding—my mother's recipe. Maggie and her mother did the rest."

"So Maggie's mother works for you, too?"

"No, but she comes to help Maggie at dinners when we have guests."

"I see," said Carr. "Well, I'll have to also thank Maggie and her mother."

"Before the war we ate roasted goose every Christmas Eve," Louis Minton interjected. "Now duck is the only fowl other than chicken an honest household can come by, and one is lucky to find duck."

Opposite Carr at the long oak table sat Erika and Ilse Dorsch with Ada between them elevated by a thick pillow on her chair. Ilse's parents sat to their daughter's right. Victor Knight and Maeve sat on Carr's side of the table, with the host and hostess at either end. After Carr finished thanking the hosts, Ilse's father thanked them in German and Erika translated. With Ilse still learning English, and her parents' English nonexistent, Erika served as translator during dinner.

Erika was not free. Serious charges of wartime espionage hung over her in both England and the United States, and in America

528

murder charges in two states—Indiana and Ohio. Erika knew her future was very much in question, despite the offer from the Americans to drop the charges if she worked for them after the war. And even though the British would have to follow suit if the Americans requested it (that stipulation being part of their deal with the U.S. for Erika's wartime services), it had been made abundantly clear to her that these agreements would hold only if both countries were pleased with her work during the British mission. And as things turned out, both governments could assert fairly that she failed to uphold her part of the bargain when she abandoned the team and disappeared after her visit to Auschwitz.

But at least for now she was in London with Ada and not 4000 miles away in America. *Intrepid* had convinced William Donovan to allow Leroy Carr and the German spy to remain in England until victory was assured. Eisenhower had told FDR and Churchill that assurance would come only once the Western Allies crossed the Rhine and the Russians stood on the banks of the Elbe. Thus, Carr and Erika remained in London where he continued to coordinate intelligence efforts between the OSS and Baker Street; she answered questions in intelligence meetings concerning Himmler's Gestapo or Totenkopf-SS. Erika declined to answer questions about the Wehrmacht or other branches of the SS, much to the consternation of the British.

Although in the same city as her daughter, Erika was housed at the American Embassy and not allowed to leave unless picked up by Leroy Carr or someone he sent. She saw Ada only twice a week on average. As Christmas approached, it was Erika's wish to spend the holiday with Ada, an opportunity never before afforded her, and Carr granted it. Erika could spend tonight and tomorrow night at her grandparents' home. She would not be allowed to leave the house, and two-man shifts of American MPs sat in a car outside to ensure that she complied. Leroy Carr knew Erika Lehmann could easily outmaneuver the token guard, but he was not worried she would stray. She had given her word, and Carr knew Erika would not break her promise and thereby lose any chance of spending future time with her daughter.

Leroy Carr's family situation this Christmas ran opposite to Erika's. Despite his many travels, Carr had always managed to spend Christmas with his wife. This was his first one away and he missed Kay. Facing the prospect of Christmas dinner alone in his hotel, or among total strangers, Carr accepted the Mintons' invitation. Their pleasant dinner included Christmas memories from the diverse diners at the table, and interesting comparisons of Christmas traditions in their native lands. England's Father Christmas was compared to the American Santa Claus and the German Christkind. Maeve told a funny story from her childhood about Saint Stephen's Day, and as the meal progressed her conversation grew ever livelier. By the time Maggie served the pudding, Maeve was inebriated.

"Lordy," Maeve slurred, "I think I'm flootered." During the early years of the war, the stronger spirits became scarce in England, with ale the only alcoholic beverage readily available. But thanks to the Americans, England was now restocked with wine and hard liquor. Maeve had actively enjoyed an impressive sampling of the Mintons' replenished reserve during dinner, with special attention to the American whiskey. "I've shaken too many paws with the red dog."

Ada had been watching Maeve carefully. Ada spoke and understood only German, and merely to the extent typical of a child her tender age, an age much too young to understand alcohol or its effects. But for her own reasons, Ada giggled at Maeve, causing everyone else to laugh.

After her guests finished dessert, Marie Minton asked, "Shall we move to the parlor for a brandy and tea . . . or coffee? I know our American guest will rejoice to hear we have coffee." She looked at Carr and smiled.

"Make mine an Irish coffee," said Maeve.

"I'll excuse myself," said Erika. "I want to take Ada upstairs so we can play for a while before her bedtime. Frohe Weihnachten, everyone."

Everyone returned her *Merry Christmas,* and Erika gathered Ada into her arms and left for the stairs. As the others followed Marie to the parlor, Louis Minton turned to Carr and Knight. "Gentlemen, will you join me in my study for a whiskey and cigar?" Along with meeting

Carr in the States in fall 1943, Minton also met Knight, at the time known only as *Mr. Thomas.*

In the study, Minton closed the door and invited the two men to sit. He walked over to the hearth and with an iron poker pushed around in the glowing embers before adding another log. Satisfied with the fire, he crossed the room and opened a drawer of a roll-top desk. "Mr. Carr, I think Mr. Knight and I owe you Americans a good deal of thanks. Until just recently, whiskey was very hard to come by here in England." Minton took a bottle from the drawer and looked at the label. "I never knew why the Americans call their whiskey *Bourbon,* but I now know not all American whiskey goes by that name, only whiskey distilled in the Bourbon region of your state of Kentucky qualifies. Am I right?"

"Yes, that's right," Carr answered.

"I must admit I'm a fan of the horses—a pastime that fails to meet my wife's approval, I'm afraid. I know of your Kentucky Derby, of course." Minton smiled, "Bourbon and horses, your Kentucky sounds like a jolly good place to live."

Carr chuckled.

Three crystal highball glasses sat on the desktop, evidence that Minton's request for Carr and Knight to join him in the study had not been impromptu. Minton poured and handed out the Bourbon, then brought over a humidor and set it on the tea table. He took a cigar and said, "Help yourself, gentlemen."

Carr and Knight each chose a cigar from a variety. Minton snipped the end of his and lit it, then passed around the guillotine and matches.

Niceties completed, Louis Minton launched directly into serious discussion. "What can you gentlemen share with me about the current German offensive? Just last month Londoners were hearing Hitler is finished, and now we have this situation in Belgium. Mr. Carr, since it's mostly the Americans caught up in the fighting, what are your thoughts? I'm not asking for classified information, mind you, just your opinion."

"The press back in the States has started calling it the *Battle of the Bulge,"* said Carr. "My responsibilities don't include sitting in on

Supreme Command military strategy meetings; I work solely from the intelligence side. But the German offensive indicates to me Hitler isn't finished yet; he's got some fight left in him."

"Sadly, I agree," said Minton. "Every year the romantics among us claim the war will be over by Christmas. I remember hearing that in '40 during the Battle of Britain, and every year since. Now we're on the doorstep of '45 and still fighting. Damn discouraging sometimes when you think about it."

"Weather is helping the Jerries in Belgium," said Knight. "The heavy cloud cover is preventing our flyboys from coming to the rescue of the ground troops."

Minton puffed on his cigar and nodded. "Yes, let's hope the skies clear soon."

"Let's hope so," Carr agreed.

The three men continued to discuss the war, so far as discretion allowed, for nearly two hours. At ten o'clock, Marie Minton appeared at the study door.

"Louis, the army driver has arrived to take Ilse's parents back."

"Very well, my dear," said Minton. "I'll be there straightaway."

"And it's time I return Maeve," Knight said, using his cane to stand. "I planned to call a taxi, but I'll wager Maeve and I can fit in the car here for the Dorschs."

"Mr. Carr, what's your transportation situation?" Minton asked.

"I can call an embassy driver."

"Good. So there's no need to rush. Feel free to stay a while longer."

Everyone gathered in the foyer. Since Maggie had left to spend Christmas with her mother, Marie Minton brought the coats. Those departing again thanked their hosts. Ilse kissed her parents. Erika, with Ada in her arms, kissed the Dorschs and the unsteady Maeve.

Knight, Maeve, and Ilse's parents bade good-bye and stepped out into a freezing fog.

"Not quite a white Christmas would you say, Maeve?" Knight asked.

Instead of responding, Maeve asked, "When do I get to see me family?" Just then her feet slid on the iced porch. With the cane occupying his left hand, Knight shot his right arm around Maeve's waist to prevent her from falling.

Marie Minton closed the door on the fog and, with all but one guest gone, bade her husband and Leroy Carr goodnight. The two men returned to the study, where Minton poured Carr another whiskey.

Carr took the drink. "Thank you, Sir Louis."

"We've had enough of that 'Sir Louis' balderdash. My mates call me *Louie.* Shall I call you *Leroy?*"

"You bet. It sounds younger than *Mr. Carr.*"

Minton laughed.

The men had found they enjoyed each other's company. Louis Minton considered Carr a straight shooter—such directness he valued. Carr sized up Minton as a down-to-earth sort who, despite achieving lofty credentials and a title, remained an affable, modest man.

"Marie and I are amazed at Maeve's resemblance to our granddaughter," Minton commented. "Seeing her in the company of Mr. Thomas . . . Victor . . . leads me to assume Maeve played a role in my granddaughter's recent mission. I won't ask you about that mission, but can you tell me where you came across Maeve?"

Apparently Erika had told her grandfather nothing, which did not surprise Carr. Because Maeve's work was finished, Carr decided he could reveal how she entered the picture. "Last Christmas, after a fruitless search, people working with Victor stumbled across Maeve at a USO dance in Fortune Green—all by accident."

"Happened upon her by chance at a USO dance? Fascinating." Minton reached for another cigar then turned the humidor to Carr.

"No. Thank you, anyway."

"Where does my granddaughter now stand, Leroy?"

Carr had expected the question. Last year in the States, Victor Knight made Minton aware of the arrangement between the two allies concerning Erika. It was only natural for a grandfather to ask.

"I won't soft-soap the situation, Louie. Things can go either way for Erika. All I can say is that the mission, and her participation, didn't go according to the British plan. She's cooperating now, but only in areas of her own choosing. We'll all have to keep up our hopes for her.

In the end, the decision on Erika's future will lie with General Donovan."

Carr wished he could give Minton a better report, but he knew honesty best served everyone. Minton suddenly looked very tired and a long silence followed while his cigar, no longer of interest to him, died in the ashtray. Finally, Minton redirected the conversation to general topics of the war. At midnight, Carr asked to use the telephone to call for a car.

Minton nodded, and Carr used the telephone in the study. When he finished, Minton said, "I'll wait with you, Leroy."

"That's not necessary, Louie. You look tired. I can show myself out when my driver arrives. Will the door lock behind me?"

"Yes, it will. Well, if you're sure you don't want me to wait, I must admit you're right—I'm tired, indeed."

The men walked out into the foyer. Minton shook Carr's hand. "Leroy, thank you for all you've done for my granddaughter, and I know you'll continue to help in any way possible. It's good night, then. And Happy Christmas."

"I promise I'll do everything I can for Erika. Merry Christmas, Louie."

Minton slowly climbed the steps and disappeared down a hallway. Carr remained in the foyer, waiting for the embassy driver, who would knock. In the still nighttime silence of the house, Carr heard a faint lilt coming from the parlor and his curiosity demanded he investigate. The parlor door stood half open and Carr gazed in. With the rest of the house retired for the night, Erika Lehmann, dressed in a bathrobe, sat in a rocking chair beside a candle-lit Christmas tree, singing a German lullaby to the child in her arms.

Chapter 110

Cowboy Roy

London
Four days later; Thursday, 28 December 1944

"Ike remains under heavy guard in Versailles," said Colin Gubbins. Gubbins and five other men sat around a conference table at SOE headquarters on Baker Street, all of them British except Leroy Carr. "We have no choice but to take the report on Skorzeny and his gang seriously."

In early December, Eisenhower moved Supreme Allied Expeditionary Force headquarters from England to France. Shortly after the Battle of the Bulge began in mid-December, MI-6 received intelligence revealing a possible plot to assassinate Dwight Eisenhower and indicating that Hitler put Otto Skorzeny in charge of carrying it out. Although the plot had not been confirmed, no one wanted to take any chances. Eisenhower spent Christmas in Versailles under triple security.

"Major Wires," Gubbins continued, "what's the latest on Skorzeny?"

A Scot from Glasgow, Wires had last year been given the unenviable task of heading a section of MI-6 devoted solely to trying to keep tabs on the elusive German commando and his activities.

"Right now we have no evidence of Skorzeny or any of his men surfacing in France," Wires reported. "But you'll remember my report on Tuesday that we suspected Skorzeny's brigade was in Belgium; we've now confirmed that report. A contingent—we don't know how large—of Skorzeny's English-speaking commandos has been impersonating American officers and issuing false orders to American units, altering signposts, spreading rumors, cutting communication lines—that sort of mischief."

"How do we know they're Skorzeny's men?" a colonel asked Wires.

"Yesterday, three Germans wearing American Army uniforms were captured outside Bastogne. We suspected they might be Skorzeny's men, so we checked their photographs taken yesterday against pictures processed from German newsreels released just after the Mussolini rescue. They're Skorzeny's men, all right, and I sent that information to the Americans holding them in Bastogne. The prisoners refuse to cooperate but it doesn't really matter in the end; being captured wearing American uniforms cancels their POW protection under the Geneva Convention. They'll hang or be shot."

Wires passed the photos around. When they came to Leroy Carr, he immediately recognized one of the captured commandos as the man he met in Barcelona.

[same day—a police station in Bastogne, Belgium]
Yesterday, Kai and his two comrades had been taken under heavy guard to one of Bastogne's civilian police stations now being used as an interrogation center set up by the American 4th Armored Division after the relief of Bastogne two days ago. Their capture had been one of those flukes of war—an accident of combat that can occasionally occur in any war.

The three Skorzeny commandos, all fluent in English, had come across a convoy of seven Sherman tanks clanking their way down a road through frozen forest near Sainte-Ode, each tank covered with hitchhiking American infantryman so plentiful they looked like barnacles on the hulls of overturned ships. Kai, wearing a U.S. Army major's uniform, and his two comrades (also dressed as American officers) stopped the caravan, got out of their captured American Jeep, and convinced the lead tank commander that they had been sent with new orders: This convoy was to divert to the west and join up with Patton's 3rd Army (at the time, Patton was really due south). Kai spoke fluent English but not without a German accent so one of his comrades did the talking. The American lieutenant in charge of the tank patrol was in the midst of telling the other tank commanders about the change in course when the incredible fluke transpired.

An American war correspondent riding on the third tank became curious about the stop, came forward, and recognized the German commando doing the talking. The journalist had covered the 1936 Berlin Olympics. Kai's fellow commando had competed in the javelin competition, and the journalist remembered the man's face because they shared the same uncommon last name of *Kluga,* though not related. Skorzeny had ordered his men to not engage in combat with Americans while dressed as Americans, and armed only with holstered pistols and surrounded by dozens of soldiers holding rifles or carbines, the three Skorzeny commandos had no opening to shoot their way out even if they had not been under Skorzeny's "no combat" orders.

Upon arrival at the interrogation center, Kai and the other two Germans were separated, searched for the second time, photographed, and then spent the rest of the day being grilled under hot lights by shadowy forms. They spent the night in separate cells. Yesterday, Kai received no food or water during the nonstop questioning; this morning, he was given a cup of water, a bowl of oatmeal, one bread roll, and five minutes to eat while in handcuffs. Then, still wearing the American major uniform, he was taken from his cell to one of the interrogation rooms to start the grilling anew. The MPs cuffed him to the chair, turned on the bright light, and aimed it at his face. Kai heard the door open and someone walk in.

"Are you ready to cooperate today?"

The glaring light again made it impossible for Kai to see a face, yet he recognized the man's loud, gruff voice and Texas accent similar to those he had heard in American Western movies. Akin to the day before, Kai did not answer.

The Texan continued, "I know you're aware that prisoners of war are obligated to divulge name, rank, and serial number so the Red Cross can notify your country of your POW status. It's not an act of cowardice to reveal that information; you're supposed to do so under the accepted rules of war that even you Nazis have endorsed.

"We know you're SS; we saw your blood type tattoo when we searched you." All SS had their blood type tattooed inside their upper left arm. "Just being SS makes you likely to be shot, and wearing that uniform *guarantees* it. The protections of the Geneva Convention apply only to prisoners captured wearing their own country's uniform. Spies and saboteurs wearing civilian clothes, and combatants disguised in enemy uniforms have no rights under the Convention. Your side executes them and so do we."

The experienced interrogator paused for a moment hoping the reality of this German's future would cause him to open up.

"Your only chance is to cooperate. For starters, I want name, rank, and serial number. Then I want to know how many of Skorzeny's men are doing what you were doing."

Kai looked up, trying to focus on his inquisitor, but the Texan stood directly behind the bright light.

"I can see that was a surprise," said the Texan. "How do I know you and your buddies are Skorzeny men, you wonder? Because one of your buddies spilled his guts and told us everything."

"You're lying," said Kai. *Neither Kluga nor Hoffman would break,* thought Kai. He refused to believe any Skorzeny commando would break under interrogation, or even torture.

"Well, shit fire and save the matches, the Kraut speaks after all!" Earlier that morning, the Texan learned he held three Skorzeny commandos when he read a communiqué from the British SOE in London. And he now worked one of the oldest interrogation ruses in the book: trick A into thinking B had turned against him. "I say we get started before it's too late for you. What do you say?"

"First, I have a question," said Kai.

"Yeah? What's that?"

"What does Roy Rogers mean: '*Get along little doggies*'?"

[that afternoon—Savoy Hotel, London]

"What's up, Leroy?" Wild Bill Donovan was on the phone in Washington.

"We've got a situation here, Bill," said Carr. Not wanting to telephone from Baker Street, Carr had returned to his room at the Savoy to place the call to E Street.

"What?"

"You remember my report about meeting Erika Lehmann's husband in Barcelona—the Skorzeny commando?"

"Of course I remember."

"During a briefing at SOE headquarters this morning, I learned he was captured yesterday outside Bastogne."

"Bastogne. So he's in American custody?"

"Right."

"So what's the situation?"

"He was captured with two other Germans. The British know they're Skorzeny commandos but don't know their names. I didn't tell them I recognized the one—Erika's husband. His name is Faust."

"What kept you from telling SOE?"

"The last person I want to hear about this is Erika, and if the Brits find out one of the commandos is her husband they'll want to question her about him. She'll know that Faust will be shot for wearing an American uniform and she'll try to break him out. I know her pretty well by now, Bill. She'll disappear on us and the next we hear of her will be in a report from Bastogne that all hell has broken loose."

"Lock her up."

"Can't lock her up all the time, Bill. You've given your okay that she can attend briefings and answer questions when the Brits request her. If we lock her up they'll want to know why."

After a pause at the other end, Donovan asked, *"So what's your solution?"*

"For now, you and I keep it to ourselves that one of the men is Erika's husband, and we keep the news about the capture buried so Erika doesn't find out from a newspaper that some Skorzeny men have been captured. Normally, with such a high profile capture the Brits would release the news to the newspapers and BBC for propaganda. You'll need to send a request to *Intrepid* to hush things up. When I picked her up in Paris, she asked me to allow her to occasionally contact her husband for personal updates, which I haven't allowed. So even if names aren't published she'll be curious."

"Okay, Leroy. Intrepid is in New York. I'll call him when we get off the phone. What else?"

"We can keep a lid on this for only a short time. Since Skorzeny's men likely know some degree of sensitive information and they're in American custody, you can have them reclassified as 'intelligence-significant captives.' That places us—the OSS—in charge of them. We'll split them up: turn one over to the French and bring one here to England so MI-6 has a crack at him. That'll make everyone happy. England and France will consider it a fair gesture on our part."

"I see. And we keep Erika's husband. What do you want to do with him?"

"The whole idea is that each of the Western Allies gets a Skorzeny commando. You order Faust brought to the U.S.—"

Donovan finished Carr's sentence. *"And take away any motive Lehmann might have to head back to the Continent."*

"Right."

Chapter 111

Quick Removal

London—Savoy Hotel
One week later; Thursday, 04 January 1945

The morning after Leroy Carr spoke with William Donovan about his plan for the captured Germans, two American Army Air Corps Ford Tri-Motor aircraft landed at the Bastogne airfield. Skorzeny commando Richard Kluga was loaded aboard one and flown to London where he was turned over to the British. The other "Tin Goose" flew Kai Faust to Glasgow where he spent one night behind bars before a long-range C-47 took him to America. Faust was now in the Army War College stockade in Washington, D.C. Given that they were Skorzeny commandos, both men had traveled under heavy security and utmost secrecy. The tight security and quick removal of Kluga and Faust from Belgium proved a wise move by the Americans.

The French were not as wise with their level of security.

The third German commando, Gregor Hoffman, was turned over to the French and in short order found himself back with Otto Skorzeny. The French detail transporting Hoffman to Paris in a gendarme prison wagon with only one lead vehicle came across a downed tree blocking the forest road 25 miles west of Bastogne. When the French vehicles stopped, Otto Skorzeny and seven of his men suddenly appeared from nowhere and freed Hoffman without firing a shot. The French guards confirmed that the famous commando chief was among the Germans—his tall stature, pencil moustache, and long facial scar left no doubt about the identity of the man giving the orders.

Now, four days after Kai Faust's arrival in the United States, Leroy Carr sat in his London hotel room on the telephone with Al Hodge who was sitting behind his desk at OSS headquarters in D.C. Donovan had placed Hodge in charge of Faust's interrogation.

"I spent nearly the entire day with him yesterday, Leroy," said Hodge. *"Just like the day before and the day before that."*

"Any progress?"

"What do you think?"

"It must run in the family," Carr commented, comparing Faust's and Erika's similar lack of cooperation when under interrogation.

"I'll turn up the heat today. I've twice offered him the 'cooperate and avoid the hangman' deal but that's not working—just like it didn't work with his wife at Fort Knox. Do you think she told him about our deal with her—about dropping the charges if she works for us after the war?"

"Knowing her, I doubt it. How do you plan to turn up the heat?"

"I'll roll the dice and assume he doesn't know about our deal with Erika. I'll hit him with some crap that if he cooperates we'll drop the charges against her. If he won't save himself maybe that will light a fire under him."

"Good idea; nothing to lose by trying."

"Yeah, I'll give it a shot, but I have a feeling he's not going to tell us shit unless it's some bull he thinks will fuck us up. Any news about the Skorzeny man who got away?"

"No. He won't be found. Skorzeny's too good."

"I'm surprised any of those Frenchmen on the transport team are still breathing."

"I was, too, at first. Then I remembered no one was killed and only warning shots fired when Skorzeny rescued Mussolini from the mountaintop at Gran Sasso. Skorzeny, Faust, and the others used gliders to drop in silently, then announced to the guards holding Mussolini that they could live if they didn't resist, and they kept their word. The French guards in Belgium last week said Skorzeny offered them the same deal."

"When they saw Skorzeny, I bet those Frenchmen's hands shot skyward faster than a cat on a hot stove."

"Now, old buddy, let's not criticize our French allies."

"Bill told me to tell you his plane leaves at three this afternoon—our time."

"Okay. With the time change, that should put him in London around dinnertime tomorrow. Tell him I'll pick him up at the airfield."

After months of deliberation, Wild Bill Donovan and Leroy Carr had finally determined Erika Lehmann's future role in the OSS, and Donovan was heading to London to tell her personally.

Chapter 112

Plans for Erika

London—Savoy Hotel
Two days later; Saturday, 06 January 1945

"Don't open the wine, waiter," said William Donovan. "We'll handle that ourselves later." No alcohol would be consumed until the meeting ended.

"Very well, sir," the room service waiter replied, then finished placing meals on the table in front of Donovan, Leroy Carr, and Erika Lehmann. Carr had placed the ration-friendly orders: roasted chicken breast, a boiled potato, a grilled carrot, and a roll sans butter or margarine. Nearly all butter went to the fighting men on army bases or naval warships, and the fats in margarine ended up inside bombs.

Leroy Carr's small hotel room two floors below unbefitted a three-person dinner, so he reserved this suite. When not in the Washington area where top-secret meetings were, by order, held only at the OSS E Street Complex, protocol demanded such meetings take place inside an American embassy or in a hotel suite reserved under alias with specific knowledge of location withheld from anyone attending who lacked the proper security clearance. Those without such clearance were given the hotel's name only, met in the lobby, and escorted to the suite. In Erika's case, Carr need not divulge the hotel's name ahead of time: Carr and his driver simply picked her up at the American embassy where she stayed. Donovan, wishing to keep his London visit discreet, chose the hotel suite over the embassy.

Finally, after the waiter wheeled his cart out into the hallway and closed the door, the OSS chief began. "Leroy has told you why we're here today," Donovan said to Erika. "To brief you on what we consider the best way to use your skills to serve the interests of the United States after the war."

Erika nodded.

Donovan went on, "First, concerning your status with the British Admiralty. Before I left Washington, I received the First Lord's report.

I'll put it this way: The Admiralty is not exactly singing your praises. They consider you failed them when you abandoned the team in Germany and disappeared."

Erika responded with a poignant argument. "What I did was in the best interests of the team members and not the cause of any of their deaths. After the mission unraveled in Berlin—and that happened quickly because Operation Kriemhild was ill-conceived from the start—I tried to convince everyone to leave Germany and I offered my help. If they had followed my advice, everyone would be alive today. They died because they displayed too much courage during an operation rife with faulty parameters. It was doomed from the start. I stated my low opinion of the mission to Victor Knight as soon as he briefed me in Scotland. Despite that, except for the uncontrollable parachute accident that claimed James Granville, only at the Tiergarten zoo and at Grünwald did any field agents die. Both those actions were sanctioned by the SOE ahead of time. That said, no one can harbor any doubts that Tars, Jimmy Granville, John Mayne, and Stephanie Fischer died heroes and should be remembered for that heroism by their countrymen. They could have escaped but chose not to for their own noble reasons. Stephanie Fischer could have turned me in to Schellenberg and been decorated and likely promoted. I owe my life and the life of my daughter to those heroic fighters, and I really don't give a damn what the Admiralty thinks. I don't think you give a damn either, General. Now, may I hear what the OSS has in mind?"

Unblinking, Donovan launched right in, perhaps indicating she was right about his lack of concern over the negative Admiralty review. "We know the Russians are in dire need of battlefield interpreters. The lack of Russian military personnel who can translate German during interrogations is causing them a great deal of problems as their front moves closer to Germany. Before the war ends, we will insert you behind Russian lines where you'll become a field interrogation interpreter for the Russians. We'll give you a background history that will appeal to the Russians."

"What is that background?" asked Erika.

Donovan looked at Carr. "Leroy?"

"You'll be a German communist who escaped from a concentration camp," said Carr. "Your communist parents were murdered at the camp. Of course, for that you have a blood hate for the Nazis. We can make sure paperwork exists that backs up your story in case the Russians look into it. The Treblinka camp, Belzec, or Sobibor—any of those will work. I lean toward using Sobibor."

"Sobibor," Erika responded. "Because of the well-documented escape by . . . what was it? Five hundred prisoners about a year ago?"

"Six hundred," Carr answered. "October of '43. The Totenkopf kept detailed records and *we* hold those records, not the Russians. Besides Jews and Gypsies, many Polish and German communists or Red sympathizers were imprisoned at that camp. Sobibor works perfectly for our purpose. Whatever names we decide on for your fictional parents, we'll insert those names into the official SS records of those who died at the camp and list your name as one of the six hundred who escaped. If the Soviets request the records, as we assume they will, we'll cooperate with our ally and send them copies of the documents. Most of the escapees were rounded up and shot, but a few lucky ones found refuge among Polish resistance groups. You'll be one of the lucky ones."

"This seems to be a great deal of effort, and for what?" Erika asked. "A few bits and pieces of combat intelligence from the Eastern Front I might be privy to as a battlefield interrogation interpreter? I'm not quite sure how that information will aid the United States. Surely Russian and American generals coordinate battlefield intelligence."

"Yes, our generals work closely with the Russians on military strategy," said Donovan. "We don't care about the military information you might hear. That's not why we want you with the Russians. Inserting you now, before the war ends, offers you a way to earn their trust. No one in Washington is daft enough to believe that, after the war, Stalin will withdraw from lands he's conquered. That's not Uncle Joe. After the fighting stops, the Russians will need trusted, German-speaking agents who can function in their newly acquired German territory."

It took Erika only a moment to put the pieces together. "You want me to gain the Russians' trust by serving them as a battlefield interrogation translator now, with the goal of convincing them I have the makings of a spy. Then, after the war I will spy for the Soviets, but as a double-agent working for the OSS."

"That's the size of it," said Donovan. "Now dig in, your food is getting cold."

Chapter 113

On Board the Good Ship OSS

London—Embassy of the United States
Two days later; Monday, 08 January 1945

Just before noon, Erika Lehmann and Leroy Carr walked into a small, sound-proof consultation room on the second floor of the American Embassy. After Donovan and Carr revealed the OSS plans for Erika on Saturday, the three spent most of Sunday discussing ideas on implementation. Donovan's plane back to Washington departed three hours ago. The OSS chief had kept his London visit secret, but this morning on his way to the airfield Donovan made a brief, unannounced visit to Baker Street and reaffirmed with a surprised Colin Gubbins that news of the capture of three Skorzeny commandos must remain restricted and not released to the press.

"Why did you choose a hotel suite for our meetings with General Donovan?" Erika asked Carr after he closed and locked the door. "Why didn't we meet here?"

"It was the general's choice," Carr answered. "He wanted to stay below the radar while he was here so he could get in and get out without being dragged into endless meetings. He's got a lot on his plate in Washington and couldn't spare the time to be here longer than a weekend." They sat down across from each other at a small table. "Oh, before we start, I want to tell you about Maeve. She was given a four-day furlough starting today. Victor Knight is taking her to Belfast for a reunion with her family. Maeve isn't being released yet; Knight will bring her back. But I thought you'd be glad to hear she gets to visit her family."

"Knight is going with her to Belfast for four days?"

"That's right. He ordered a plane. It looks like Maeve has conquered her fear of flying."

"Intriguing."

"Why is Maeve conquering her fear of flying intriguing?"

"No, I'm referring to Knight leaving with Maeve for four days. A chaperon for a family visit hardly requires a man of Knight's station and responsibilities. But I noticed he was quite attentive to her at my grandparents' Christmas Eve dinner. Maeve O'Rourke and Victor Knight—wouldn't that be a shocking match? She had her knife to his throat in Berlin."

"A match—Maeve and Knight? What are you talking about?"

"Never mind. Men don't notice such things. But speaking of reunions, when will you get to see Kay? I remember you mentioning at the Christmas dinner that it was your first Christmas apart."

"As a matter of fact, Kay is coming over for a visit in a few days. But I don't want her staying here in London. I wouldn't get anything done worrying about a V-2 dropping in. I'll find a safe town."

"I'm glad you'll get to see each other. Okay, shall we get to business?"

"I want to take a step back and hear your thoughts about what we've discussed the past two days."

Erika shrugged. "It's a clever plan."

"But?"

"I'm tired Leroy. I've accepted the fact that lies and deceit will be my life, but I wish it wasn't so soon to get back in."

"I know, Erika. But to go forward we have to move quickly—now, before the war ends. The entire plan to insert you into Soviet intelligence after the war hinges on you getting a foot in the Russians' door now, during the war. In peacetime they won't need battlefield interrogation interpreters. Once the war ends, they can send prisoners to Moscow to wait their turn for interrogation. We have an opportunity now we won't have after the war ends. I know you agree."

"As I said, your 'foot in the door' scheme is clever. It shouldn't be difficult to gain a place as a battlefield interpreter. The hard part will come after the war. If Russian intelligence works anything like Abwehr, volunteers are not considered—they approach those they consider candidates. I'll need to come up with something that convinces them to recruit me."

"That's where the OSS steps in. After the war, when the time is right, we can create a scenario where it suits Russian interests to

549

include you in an espionage mission against the United States—perhaps using a situation from your fictional past that makes it logical for them to at least let you tag along with other Soviet agents. Whatever it is, we'll make sure you shine for the Russians, of course, and put them in a position where they'd be foolish not to recruit you into Intelligence. Your biggest challenge will come during your Russian spy training when you have to act the part of a novice and not reveal your skill level too quickly."

"So when do I start?" Erika was thinking of Ada, and how duty was about to separate them again.

"You have some time before you leave. I estimate we'll need at least a month to get our ducks in a row. We have to alter Sobibor records, gather intel to decide exactly where and how you'll fall into Russian hands, and handle a few other details."

"What about my daughter?" Erika knew her role as an interpreter carried minimal risk, but the life span of a double-agent often measured in months, not years.

"I thought about Ada, too, Erika. General Donovan gave me carte blanche to ensure your daughter's situation is whatever you deem best for her. We'll do everything in our power to support and help bring about your wishes."

"All right, Leroy. I told you last year at your Fort Knox I would gladly work against the Bolsheviks. I still feel that way."

"So, you accept."

Erika Lehmann nodded.

"Welcome aboard, Agent Lehmann. Any questions?"

"Just one. When were you going to tell me my husband had been captured?"

Leroy Carr's jaw had never dropped so fast. *"How in God's name did you know?"*

"Where is Kai? Is he here in England?"

"How did you know he had been captured, Erika? This is a serious breach!"

"Otto Skorzeny told me, and he asked me to tell you that the Allies have until midnight Wednesday to release his men. Since I'm now OSS, Leroy, I feel it's my duty to state I think it would be wise on our part to release Kai and Richard Kluga before Otto comes to get them."

Chapter 114

Al Returns

London
Next day; Tuesday, 09 January 1945

Leroy Carr and Al Hodge sat alone in a car parked on a dark SoHo street. Twenty-seven hours after Erika revealed her message from Otto Skorzeny, Carr picked up Hodge from the American airfield west of London. Wishing to talk confidentially as soon as possible, during the drive from the airfield Carr asked the driver to pull over and wait outside.

"You look beat," Hodge observed. "Didn't you get any sleep last night?"

"Nope, as a matter of fact, I didn't."

"Wild Bill is one pissed-off cowboy, Leroy. Thanks for pulling me out of Washington. Davis is taking over Faust's interrogation while I'm here." Since Carr could not talk freely on many matters with any assistant the British assigned him, he had asked Donovan to send his OSS partner to London. "Bill says our number one priority is finding out how Skorzeny established contact with Erika."

"Or," Carr said, "how *she* established contact with *Skorzeny.*"

"What do you mean?"

"How did Skorzeny know where she was?" Carr countered.

"Okay, I've been on a plane since eleven o'clock last night and I'm loopy, but how would she get in touch with Otto Skorzeny while she's under guard in London?"

"I don't know, Al. I can only guess. Her first Abwehr assignment took place in Lisbon where she broke into a safe at the American embassy. She's quartered now at another of our embassies and watched closely, but not every minute. She's unguarded while in her room and has free access to the bathroom down the hallway. Do you think Erika Lehmann could break into an embassy safe undetected, but not gain access to an embassy telephone with a direct line to the Continent?"

"She's a fucking pain in the ass!"

"You're telling me!" Carr was not about to disagree. "My job is to oversee all OSS counterintelligence, but for the past two years I've worked nearly full time either chasing that woman or dealing with her intrigues after I caught her—actually, after she allowed herself to be caught. She told me yesterday she's tired. If she wants to know about tired I can tell her a few things."

"And when she told you she was tired she probably had some scheme behind telling you *that.*"

Carr was too tired to laugh. "If Skorzeny has information on Faust's and Kluga's whereabouts, it's not Erika who leaked it. She didn't know Faust was captured until Skorzeny told her. What's Bill doing about a possible mole?"

"I don't know. But after your call yesterday, he spent a long time on the SIGSALY with *Intrepid.*" The SIGSALY was a terminal used for top-secret voice communications that used a random noise mask to encrypt voices. "They'll cook up something, you can bet your skivvies. So Erika revealed nothing about how she received Skorzeny's message?"

"I spent ten hours cooped up with her at the embassy today. She insists that because her contact with Skorzeny happened before she became OSS—which was yesterday—she's not obligated to tell us how that contact took place. Basically, she's telling us that anything she did before yesterday is none of our damn business."

"None of our damn business." Hodge shook his head. "I'll let you be the one to tell that to Wild Bill. What about the British plans for Kluga?"

"General Gubbins briefed me this morning before I went to the embassy. Late last night, MI-6 took Kluga to Liverpool and loaded him onto a Royal Navy gunboat to be taken to an unknown location—at least unknown to me. Gubbins clammed up after that. I'm sure the Brits blame us for this situation."

"How do you think all this will play out, Leroy?"

"I know we'll never release a Skorzeny commando because Skorzeny, or Hitler, or the Man in the Moon tells us we better. Neither will the Brits. I'm amazed Skorzeny tipped his hand. If you're planning a rescue mission, you don't announce you're coming. One thing we have going for us is Erika doesn't know Faust is in the States. I'm sure she assumes he's somewhere in England. If Erika doesn't know, Skorzeny doesn't know. But to answer your question: I don't know how it will play out."

Hodge stated confidently, "Skorzeny's never going to get to Faust where he's at now, that's for certain. Even if he found out Faust is in the States, a rescue is impossible."

Carr said, "But I keep asking myself what I mentioned earlier: Why tip us off ahead of time? Take Kluga. After Erika dropped the bombshell, Kluga goes from being held at Tooting Bec to an even more secret and secure location. From Liverpool, the Brits could take him to the Isle of Man, Northern Ireland, or one of those remote SOE camps in Scotland. Hell, Kluga could still be on a British gunboat and getting an extended fishing trip in the Irish Sea for all we know. Makes no sense for Skorzeny to give his enemy time to make things more difficult for him. There's got to be something else here, Al."

"How about some better news? Kay told me to tell you she's packed and ready to go. When will she get here?"

"Friday. She's flying into Bristol."

"Good for you. Kay told me you two missed your first Christmas together last month."

"That's right," said Carr. "She wanted to come to London last summer, after the invasion succeeded, but at the time I thought the Luftwaffe bombing threat still too high and I wouldn't chance it. Now the V-2 rockets are hitting London so I'm having her stay in Bath. It's over a two-hour drive from my hotel, but nothing is exploding in Bath."

Hodge asked, "Not that I'm gung-ho to get back to the messy business at hand, but how will this Skorzeny situation affect Lehmann's standing with Bill?"

"It will improve it."

"Improve it?"

Carr nodded. "When I first went to Bill with my idea to bring her over to our side after the war, it wasn't her ability to speak Russian that convinced him to invest all the time, trouble, and OSS resources in the project. We have other people who speak Russian. It was her skill level that convinced him, and what she's done now is just more proof that our investment is justified. Look what she's pulled off: After somehow learning of her husband's capture, she's set into motion a plan to free him—all from behind embassy walls where her movements are restricted and she's under watch."

Chapter 115

A Wife Comes to Bath

Bath, England
Three days later; Friday, 12 January 1945

A light snow and an Electra carrying Kay Carr descended onto the Bristol airfield runway. After disembarking the Pan Am Dixie Clipper in Foynes, Ireland, Kay boarded the Electra her husband had waiting to fly her to Bristol. Watching from inside the small terminal, Leroy Carr walked out onto the tarmac after the plane touched down, glad the snow was not sticking on the runway.

As he waited for the plane to taxi toward the terminal, he thought about Otto Skorzeny's midnight Wednesday deadline that had come and gone. Skorzeny's captured men had not been released, of course. Carr knew Skorzeny could not possibly expect the release, but he also knew the man Eisenhower called "the most dangerous man in Europe" was not prone to idle threats. Past Skorzeny ultimata had never been bluffs. Something would happen, Carr knew. The ball was now in Skorzeny's court.

The Electra rolled to a stop near the terminal and the pilot cut the engines. A tarmac worker rolled the passenger stairs to the hatch and in a moment it opened. An American lieutenant, perhaps the co-pilot Carr thought, descended first. When Kay appeared at the hatch, Carr felt energized and put thoughts of Otto Skorzeny out of his mind for the first time in four days.

Kay Carr divided another bun and handed half to her husband. After the drive from the Bristol airfield, they dropped Kay's luggage at her hotel in Bath, and now waited for their dinner at Sally Lunn's.

"How did you find this place, Leroy?"

"I asked the hotel clerk about places to eat when I called in your room reservation. He said this is a historic place—that some type of eating establishment has been on this spot since Roman times. And apparently these buns are famous—that's the skinny from the desk clerk, anyway."

"The buns are certainly delicious."

"Any problems on your flights?" Carr asked.

"No, everything went well. The fuel stop in Newfoundland took forever—nearly four hours—but the weather was fine coming over. The pilot flew below the clouds and the view was spectacular. One of the stewardesses told me the low altitude kept ice off the wings. I've never flown over water before but I wasn't nervous."

Carr smiled as he spread honey on his portion of the roll, "You've never had a problem with flying and I knew you'd be okay. I'm glad you're here."

"Do you think they'll still offer flights across the Atlantic after the war?"

"It depends. Now Uncle Sam subsidizes Pan Am to keep the Clippers in the air for the diplomats and high-ranking military personnel who need to go back and forth but don't have the time or inclination to spend eight days dodging U-boats on an ocean liner. After the war, it's hard to predict. If enough civilians are willing to pay the big bucks so Pan Am or some other airline can make a profit, I'm sure it'll go on. It's all about the money."

She placed her hand on one of his. "I missed you."

"I missed you," he said. "You don't know how much."

"I love you, Leroy."

He smiled and squeezed her hand. "I love you."

"Will my husband be my Bath tour guide tomorrow?"

"I have to drive back to London early tomorrow morning, Kay. And even if I could stay I don't know anything about this place other than it hasn't suffered any bombing attacks since 1942. You probably know more about it than I do; you're the literary expert in the family. Doesn't this town have some literary link—*The Wife of Bath?*"

"Chaucer, *The Canterbury Tales.* The wife with a gap in her front teeth. According to the story, women with a gap in their front teeth are lusty."

"See what I mean? You know more than I do. Tomorrow you can have a taxi take you around."

"I was joking, darling. I don't care about sightseeing. I want to go to London and stay with you. You told me you decided on Bath because it was safer than London. I don't want my safety considered when hundreds of thousands of children in London are at risk from the rockets. It's not right for me to hide away here as if I'm more important than they are."

Leroy Carr had long admired his wife's strength. "I knew you'd say that, Kay. Think of it this way: You'll do me a great favor staying here. With you here, I'm relieved of the worry I know I'd have if you were in London. Will you think of it that way, please?"

Kay sighed. "And I knew you'd say that."

Kay's room was in a quaint, red-brick inn near city center that furnished guests free transportation around Bath in a horse-drawn taxi. The night had grown colder, and since automobiles were not allowed to park on the historic cobblestone street fronting the inn, Carr dropped Kay off and drove off to look for a place to park.

Since guests left room keys at the desk when leaving the building, Kay approached the clerk and asked for hers—a heavy brass skeleton with a long, red tassel. After climbing a flight, she entered her pitch-black room. But before she could turn on a light, someone grabbed her from behind and put a hand over her mouth. As she tried to scream, the hand did its job, turning her scream into a muffled groan.

A table lamp across the room clicked on, shedding light on a man sitting in a wing chair next to the small, round lamp table. In addition to him and the man with his hand over her mouth, a third man stood near the door. The seated man rose. Tall and impeccably dressed in gentry clothes, he looked the proper English gentleman.

"Good evening, madam," he said in English. "You will not be harmed. Please allow me to introduce myself. My name is Skorzeny."

Chapter 116

When military historians are asked to comprise a list of the top ten special operation commando leaders of all time, the debate starts at number two. Number one is automatic—Otto Skorzeny.

— Patrick Hulin
U.S. Army Ranger, Airborne, and Air Assault Schools,
Veteran of Desert Storm and Operation Iraqi Freedom,
Currently instructor of Human Intelligence Gathering at the
U.S. Army Military Intelligence Headquarters, Fort Huachuca, Arizona

Bath
Same time; Friday, 12 January 1945

The Roman town planners who laid out Bath's street configuration two millennia ago failed to address the need for automobile parking. It took Leroy Carr 15 minutes to find a spot near an alley two blocks away before walking back to the inn. When he finally reached his wife's room, the door was closed and he heard loud boogie-woogie music. Carr turned the knob, walked in, and saw a tall man standing beside the radio, looking out the window with his back to the door. Immediately, Carr felt a gun at his temple and a muscular arm reach over his shoulder to grab him and keep him from moving.

"What the....?!?" Carr shouted.

"Shut up!" the gunman ordered, cocking the pistol. Another man opened Carr's coat, pulled the Smith & Wesson from his shoulder holster, and frisked him.

"Where's my wife?" Carr demanded loudly.

The tall man at the window turned, reached for the radio, and turned up the volume even higher. Skorzeny had anticipated Carr's reaction and used the radio to cover his shouts. "Your wife is unharmed, Mr. Carr. However, if you don't keep your voice down, we'll all be forced to continue listening to this infernal music, or my friend will have no choice but to knock you out. I will regret either choice."

"Skorzeny!" Carr recognized him immediately. The thin mustache and long, jagged facial scar that started at his left ear, ran to the corner of his mouth then angled down to the tip of his chin all

559

stood out in the facial photos of the famous commando chieftain Carr had studied.

"Again, too loud, Mr. Carr. Let me relieve you about your wife. Perhaps that will help." Skorzeny looked at the man who had frisked Carr, who then walked into the bathroom and brought out Kay, her hands fettered behind her back and a gag over her mouth.

"You sonuvabitch!" Carr said, enraged. "Untie her!"

"If I do so, do I have your word you will hold down your voice?"

"Yes."

Skorzeny turned to Kay. "Mrs. Carr, if I remove your bonds, do you promise you will not scream or yell for help?"

Kay nodded. Skorzeny motioned with his hand and the commando who brought Kay out untied her hands and removed the gag. "Thank you, Mani," Skorzeny said, then looked at the commando holding the gun to Carr's head.

"Rolf, would you help Mr. Carr to his seat, please?"

Still holding the gun to Carr's head, Rolf guided him to a chair and forcefully pushed him down into it. Until now Carr had felt only the barrel, but now saw the pistol and noticed the silencer. Both of Skorzeny's men wore civilian clothing common in England, and both appeared to be in their twenties. Rolf was blond; Mani's hair was brown. Like their comrade Kai Faust, either commando could pose for a propaganda poster of the perfect Aryan superman. Both were square-jawed and well-muscled, and also like Kai, both understood English.

"Please have a seat, Mrs. Carr," Skorzeny said as he turned off the radio.

"If you release my wife—let her walk out of here right now—I will cooperate. You'll get no problems from me," said Carr. He did not, of course, say he would reveal classified information; Carr was willing to die before revealing secrets to the enemy. But if Skorzeny let Kay go, he would not resist capture or try to escape.

Kay looked at Skorzeny. "I don't know who you are or what this is about, but I won't leave unless my husband goes with me."

Skorzeny smiled. "Your wife just proved you're a lucky man, Mr. Carr."

"Who are these men, Leroy?" Kay asked. "Nazis?"

"Let her go, Skorzeny," Carr restated. "If you do, I won't resist."

"I've already assured you we will not harm your wife, and, yes, we will release her. She'll take with her a message for your General Donovan."

"Ah, now all the pieces slide together," said Carr. "I knew Erika couldn't tell you where Faust and Kluga are being held. She didn't even know Faust was captured until you told her. Am I right?"

"Yes."

"And I doubted you had a mole inside the OSS or British intelligence. Your message through Erika implying you would mount a rescue mission was a ruse. You have no way to find out where your men are being held."

"You are correct in that, so far as I know, German intelligence has no informant within your organizations."

Carr thought for a moment. Skorzeny could be lying to throw him off track, but Carr had doubted the existence of an infiltrator from the start. "The reason behind your threat was to send us on a wild goose chase and occupy our time looking for a mole so you could have time to put this plan together and catch us off guard. Am I on the right track?"

"I can see why you are the OSS counterintelligence chief," Skorzeny replied.

"And your message through my wife will be about a trade: me for Faust and Kluga." Carr was stating, not asking.

"The OSS director of counter intelligence returned for the price of two humble fighting men. Quite a bargain for the Allies, wouldn't you say?"

"Berlin would never agree to that trade. You have to be doing this on your own."

"The Führer gave me permission to undertake a rescue mission. I did not go into details of how I would accomplish it."

A knock sounded at the door and Skorzeny motioned to his men. Rolf moved quickly and stationed himself where he would be behind the door when it opened. Mani holstered his pistol under his coat, walked to the door, and opened it slightly so he could see who knocked without allowing that person to see into the room.

"Sir, Kai's wife has arrived."

"Good," said Skorzeny. "Let her in, Mani."

Chapter 117

Laura Returns

Bath
Same time; Friday, 12 January 1945

Mani closed the door behind Erika.

"Hello, Kay . . . Leroy," she said.

Kay recognized her. "Laura?" Her husband had introduced Erika as the OSS secretary, Laura, at their dinner in Annapolis.

"My real name is Erika."

Kay looked at her husband, who glared at Erika. Kay remembered doubting at the dinner that *Laura* was really a secretary.

Erika approached Skorzeny. He was too tall for her to kiss his cheek without his bending, so she hugged him. "It's good to see you again, Otto." Then she turned and acknowledged the two young commandos. "Mani . . . Rolf. I certainly never thought our next get-together would be in England."

"Hello, Erika," said Mani.

"Erika." Rolf said with a nod.

"Touching," said Carr. "I won't ask how you sneaked out of the embassy and got here. You're easily capable of both. And I have a good idea how you and Skorzeny kept in touch—a secured embassy hotline to the Continent. My only question is how you learned about this inn."

"It wasn't difficult, Leroy. During our long meeting at the embassy the other day, you stepped out of the room to take a phone call, leaving your jacket draped on the back of your chair. I simply searched the pockets. As they say, old habits are hard to break. I knew you would never leave anything classified in a jacket pocket; if I found anything, it would be personal. There was a note with the words *Bath hotels* and three phone numbers. You had mentioned Kay's visit, and said you'd find a room for her outside London. I memorized the numbers and called them that night, identifying myself as Kay and telling the desk clerks I wanted to check my husband's reservation. That first night, none of the hotels had a reservation under the name

563

Carr so I knew you hadn't yet decided on a hotel. The next night I tried again and the clerk here confirmed your reservation starting tonight. That told me when Kay would arrive and where you would be this evening."

"I guess I have to admit none of this should surprise me," said Carr. "But I'm disappointed you involved my wife. I didn't think you would stoop that low."

"My husband was captured wearing an American uniform. Put yourself in my place, Leroy. If Kay were captured and in danger of being executed, would you not use me in an attempt to rescue her if it was your only chance to free her?"

Carr said nothing.

"This *is* my only chance, Leroy." She studied Kay. "And it looks to me that your wife is fine. Her face tells me she's more angry than distressed."

"Bitch," said Kay.

Erika turned back to Carr. "For the record, Kay was not in our original plan. I've maintained weekly contact with Otto since November when you picked me up in Paris. I'll remind you that in Paris I asked you to find a way for me to keep in touch with Kai for personal reasons. You refused so I took matters into my own hands. You guessed correctly about the secure embassy hotline—very handy. I contacted Kathryn Fischer at her apartment. She has access to the SS record section at Prinz Albrechtstrasse and it was an easy matter for her to track down Otto for me. When I established contact with Otto, he passed me personal messages from Kai, and I gave updates on Ada for Kai—Otto and I talked of nothing else until Kai's capture. Then we discussed ways to free him. That began two weeks ago. I didn't find out Kay was coming to England until you told me on Monday. By then, Otto and these men were en route and I had no way to reach him. No one knows better than you, Leroy, how much preparation goes into an operation like this. Originally, we planned to capture you in London as you and I drove to Baker Street—a drive we took every day. That Kay got caught up in our plan is unfortunate, but as you can see, unavoidable."

"Skorzeny said Kay will deliver a message," said Carr. "I want to know when she'll be released."

"Tonight. The message will contain instructions on how and where the exchange will occur. When I saw no way to avoid involving Kay, I decided this was the best course. Kay is freed quickly, and we know she'll make sure the message gets in the proper hands. It works out for both of us."

"So what's your next move?" Carr asked.

"We have a place to take you. We can't stay here, of course. I'm sure you left notice about where you can be reached in an emergency, and I see you insisted on a room with a telephone for that purpose. Frankly, I'm surprised no one has called to tell you I'm missing."

As if on cue, the telephone rang.

"You will say *hello* and nothing more," Skorzeny ordered Carr. The cord was long enough for Skorzeny to pick up the entire phone and take it to Carr. It rang a second time. "Keep your hands down, Mr. Carr. Erika will hold the receiver. We'll now see if your offer to cooperate for the release of your wife was sincere."

As the phone rang a third time, Rolf walked over and stood behind Kay, sending an unspoken but ominous message. Otto Skorzeny held the telephone as Erika lifted the receiver from the cradle and held it to Carr's right ear.

"Hello," said Carr. Erika quickly took the receiver and listened.

"Leroy!" said an excited Al Hodge. *"I'm at the embassy! Lehmann has flown the coop! At lunch she told a matron she felt ill and went to her room to lie down. The matron checked on her at suppertime and poof—no Lehmann. Guards searched the building and grounds twice before I arrived, then I searched with them a third time. The goddamn broad is nowhere to be found!"*

"Al, this is Erika. I'm so glad you're in England; Leroy didn't tell me. As you now know, I'm in Bath with Leroy and Kay. You know the hotel. You can send men to pick up Kay, and I'm sure Leroy will appreciate you coming along. Kay will have a message for you to give to General Donovan." Erika nodded to Skorzeny and he pressed down the cradle.

Chapter 118

Crafty Devil

London
Three days later; Monday, 15 January 1945

SOE head Colin Gubbins led William Donovan, William Stephenson, Al Hodge, and Victor Knight into the White Room at the Baker Street SOE headquarters. The room's name denoting not the color of wall paint, but what could be discussed inside the room. During congresses in the White Room, the most sensitive issues were addressed and only those with top-level security could sit in.

Donovan and Gubbins knew Stephenson was *Intrepid;* Hodge and Knight did not. On the day Skorzeny captured Leroy Carr, Donovan was in Washington and Stephenson in New York. They boarded separate airplanes for London the next morning.

After everyone sat, Stephenson, using his alias *Mr. Jones,* spoke first. "The prime minister informed us that Great Britain will cooperate with our friends in any way open to us, including the release of Richard Kluga if necessary. General Gubbins, you've now read the note Skorzeny sent the Americans, what are your thoughts?"

"I find the swap date somewhat curious," Gubbins said. "Why is Skorzeny waiting two weeks?"

The typed message Skorzeny had given Kay Carr demanded the OSS exchange team number no more than six men armed only with one-hand weapons, thereby excluding weapons such as rifles and submachine guns that took two hands to fire. The OSS team was to take Kai Faust and Richard Kluga to the Greek island of Kythira, arriving no later than noon on the 27th of January. The OSS contingent was to check into the Dadiotis Guesthouse in the town of Kythira for that night, and have at their disposal an airplane; an unarmed, seaworthy launch; and land vehicles. The typed note ended by stating further instructions would reach them at the guesthouse on the evening of the 27th. Erika Lehmann had added a handwritten postscript demanding that Al Hodge lead the OSS team.

Donovan tackled Gubbins' question. "He could be waiting for a couple reasons, General Gubbins. Skorzeny's mission history tells us he's meticulous about dotting every *i* and crossing every *t* and he hasn't had time to do that. And that night there's a half-moon. If it's not cloudy, a half-moon supplies enough light to operate but still take advantage of the dark."

"Your men will be at Skorzeny's mercy, General Donovan," said Stephenson. "Your six men are allowed handguns only. Skorzeny can bring as many men as he likes, armed to the teeth, and choose the setting to his advantage."

"We have no choice," Donovan replied. "Skorzeny has us by the balls. He very well might have in mind a double cross—get his men back and keep Leroy Carr. But the U.S. can't leave its head of counter intelligence in enemy hands if there's any chance to get him back. We have to risk it. We'll work on a contingency plan in case Skorzeny plans to double-shuffle us on the switch."

"Skorzeny is a crafty devil," said Victor Knight. "By demanding you Americans have a plane, a boat, and ground vehicles, he covers all the bases. After you arrive on the island, you won't know if you'll fly Faust and Kluga to the Greek mainland, Turkey, or Africa; sail them to another island; or drive them somewhere on Kythira for the exchange."

"And," Al Hodge added, "all that may be a diversion to lead us to believe we'll be taking them somewhere else when Skorzeny might be planning to make the swap right there in town. Here are the logistics, gentlemen. The northern coast of the island of Kythira lies 10 miles off the southern Peloponnesus. The island's land mass is 110 square miles—mostly hills and forest—but it has an airfield built by the Germans after they occupied the island in May '41. Last September we liberated the island and it's now out of the war—doubtless Skorzeny chose it because we can't land in occupied territory. The *town* of Kythira, population 500, lies on the island's southern seacoast. There are two small guesthouses in town: the Dadiotis is one of them. Intel indicates both guesthouses are used almost entirely by Greek fishermen from the mainland."

"We can't have ships in the area or plane flyovers," said Donovan. "Any surveillance and backup teams must remain covert. In addition to Al and the other five agents Skorzeny allows, we'll send agents into town to work undercover as Greek fishermen, but backup won't help unless the switch takes place in that town. We've gone over the maps. If the boat comes into play, there are dozens of other islands in that area, especially to the east. And as Mr. Knight mentioned, by plane we might be taking them anywhere. "

"Let me know if there is any aid Great Britain can supply. I'll relay any needs or requests to *Intrepid*," said *Intrepid.*

"Thank you, Mr. Jones," said Donovan.

Victor Knight itched to return to the field and now saw an opportunity. Not knowing *Intrepid* sat across the table, he turned to Donovan. "General Donovan, I volunteer as one of the five to assist Mr. Hodge on the exchange team. I assure you my gimp will not make me a liability. As you know, I worked two operations with Lehmann and Faust in Germany—the Berlin zoo and Grünwald. And I've worked with Mr. Carr several times: in America after Lehmann was captured, at Camp X, and in Spain. I feel I can be of service to the team."

[that evening]

No one could keep Kay Carr in Bath after Otto Skorzeny took her husband Friday night. Now staying in Leroy's room at the Savoy, she sat across a table from Al Hodge in the hotel lounge.

"Thanks for coming, Al. What can you tell me?" Kay asked. She knew a meeting took place that afternoon.

"Bill said to tell you he's sorry he hasn't yet had the chance to come see you, but he will in the next day or two. He promises we'll do everything we can to get Leroy back as soon as possible. But that's all I can say, Kay. I'm sorry."

"Fucking Nazis."

Hodge had never heard Kay Carr voice even a mild curse word, and that one caught him off guard. He would have been shocked under normal circumstances, but the state of affairs was anything but. He took a drink of his ale. "Sorry I couldn't be with you when you gave your statement to MI-6 Saturday. I understand they kept you a long time."

"I just hope I helped."

"You helped," Hodge assured her. "MI-6 identified Skorzeny's men from the first names and descriptions you supplied. Everything helps. I'm glad you suggested this meeting, Kay. With other men in the car on the drive back to London Friday, I didn't want to discuss details, and we haven't had much of a chance to talk since. Fill me in on exactly what happened after I called your hotel room in Bath."

"After *Erika* hung up on you, she took Skorzeny's note from the envelope and wrote something on it, then put it back and sealed the envelope. She told me not to open it. Skorzeny ordered the blond, Rolf, to stay behind with me until they had Leroy in the car. Leroy threw a fit and cursed Skorzeny—I'm sure Leroy thought they were going to kill me and leave the message beside my body for you to find. That's what I thought, too.

"Erika told Skorzeny she would stay instead of Rolf, and that calmed Leroy somewhat; he seemed to trust Erika not to harm me. Or at least he trusted her more than he did Rolf. Then Skorzeny and his men left with Leroy. I guess the reason they left someone with me for a few minutes was to allow them time to get Leroy out of the hotel before I created a clamor."

Hodge nodded. "You're sharp, Kay. Better watch out, we might recruit you." He knew she wouldn't laugh.

A glass of white wine sat untouched in front of her. "After a few minutes, Erika told me to stand at the window so Leroy could see I was safe. When I went to the window and pulled back the blackout shade, the sky had cleared and there was enough moon that I could see Skorzeny and Rolf standing with Leroy across the street. But Mani was not there. Erika yanked the telephone cord from the wall and left. In the hall, she did something to the door knob so it wouldn't turn and I couldn't get out.

"I went back to the window and watched Erika cross the street and join the others. When a car pulled up, I knew Mani had gone to bring the car. Before getting in, Leroy looked up at me and smiled. In the weak light, I don't know how I knew he smiled; maybe I just felt it because it would be like him to try and reassure me. They all got into the car and drove off. It was impossible to read the plate, but I recognized the car to be a Bentley. I've seen magazine pictures of Bentleys and I told the MI-6 men I was pretty sure that's what it was."

"That's great work," said Hodge. "Go on. How did you get out of the room?"

"After the car drove away, I yelled and pounded on the door for nearly ten minutes but no one responded. I went to the window to shout down to the street but the window was painted shut. I was ready to smash it out when someone finally knocked on the door asking if there was a problem. Eventually the janitor jimmied the door with a crowbar. I didn't tell the hotel people about Leroy being taken; I knew not to do that. I told them my door wouldn't open and left it at that."

"Thanks, Kay. That was the right thing to do."

"I didn't know how to reach you, but I was sure you were on your way so I waited in the lobby. That's when I opened the envelope and read the message."

"That has to stay our secret, Kay. No one can blame you for opening a message that concerns your husband, but if anyone handling Leroy's abduction finds out you read the message, they'll insist that you're taken back to the States immediately. I know you want to stay here until Leroy's back."

"Yes. Thanks, Al."

"As far as anyone knows, I opened the envelope."

"Got it."

"Tell me about Skorzeny. What impression did he leave with you?"

"Poised, educated, an impeccable dresser, dashing and well-mannered." She paused. "And he'd scare the fangs off Dracula."

Chapter 119

Coffee with Spice

Algiers
Two days later; Wednesday, 17 January 1945

Leroy Carr had not seen Erika Lehmann or Otto Skorzeny in three days.

After leaving Bath on Friday, the group drove to the coast of Wales and spent the rest of that night and the following day in a cliff-side cottage on the Irish Sea. Erika told Carr she had used the same cottage in 1942 when she kidnapped the MI-9 supervisor, Henry Wiltshire. Carr remembered the file—the case that originally stoked his interest in the Abwehr *femme fatale*. With Wiltshire still in German hands, Carr was now the first to know she had established a romantic relationship with Wiltshire in London, brought him here, drugged him, and slipped him away on a U-boat.

One hour after Saturday twilight, Skorzeny's Schnellboot picked up the group and raced over the dark sea to Brest. There, Erika and Skorzeny disappeared. Rolf, Mani, and two more Skorzeny commandos loaded Carr onto a Junkers and in a few hours he was in Africa. Carr had not been bound since arriving in Algiers, but neither had he been outside the windowless room with an exposed toilet and wash basin in one corner. Without a bathtub or shower, Carr washed as best he could in the tiny sink. His clothes, worn since Friday, were wrinkled and smelly. Carr knew he was in some sort of safehouse— probably Skorzeny's personal safehouse since he could not tell his superiors he held a high-ranking OSS supervisor. If he had, Carr would be in Berlin.

With his wristwatch taken from him, Carr speculated on the time of day. When he heard the steel door unlock, he guessed lunchtime. But instead of a commando opening the door and a Muslim woman in her black hijab headscarf bringing in his tray, Otto Skorzeny walked in.

"I'm sure you would welcome fresh air, Mr. Carr," said Skorzeny. "Let's walk."

Carr grabbed his jacket and for the first time walked out of his room. Skorzeny said something in German to two of his men standing in the anteroom. Carr recognized one who had been on the S-boot and guarded him on the plane; the other he had never seen before. Skorzeny led Carr down a flight of stairs and out to the street. No one else came along, which surprised Carr. Otto Skorzeny and Leroy Carr walked alone. Both wore business suits: Skorzeny's sharp, Carr's rumpled.

"There is a pleasant café on the bay, just four blocks," Skorzeny announced. When they stopped at a street corner, a Muslim woman begged for a coin. Instead, Skorzeny gave her several notes. Expecting a rebuff or at best a small coin from the European, the woman put her hands together and bowed, fervently thanking Skorzeny or Allah, Carr didn't know which. "The husbands send their wives and children to beg while they sit in the opium parlors—the swine. At the end of the day, if the women and children return with too little, they can expect a beating. How can anyone not give?"

The café sat at the western edge of the Bay of Algiers, removed from the bustling dock area of the harbor. Skorzeny suggested an outdoor table. Under a bright sky with a smattering of swollen white clouds, the Mediterranean sparkled before them. Although a sea breeze could be expected so near the water, with the Sahara only 200 miles to the south, a January afternoon in Algiers rarely required a jacket. Both men removed theirs and draped them over their chairs.

"I did not bring you here to match wits, Mr. Carr," Skorzeny said as they sat. "Only for coffee. Algerian coffee is quite good. The beans come from South America, of course, but here they blend with spices. Have you tried it?"

"Yes."

"Where was that? Perhaps on a previous trip to Algiers?"

"This is my first time here," said Carr. "In '42 I was in Fes, Rabat, and Casablanca. I think the coffee there is similar."

"Yes, it is." Skorzeny flagged a waiter and placed the order in the local language.

"I see you speak Arabic," said Carr.

"Not well. I can function as a tourist. Many here speak Berber; I know even less of that language."

"Our files report you speak German and Italian, but do not mention English. I need to update our files."

Skorzeny laughed. "Yes, you need to do that."

"Excellent location for a safehouse, Herr Skorzeny."

Skorzeny nodded. "I agree. And thank you for not addressing me by my SS rank while we are here."

"You're welcome. I can imagine that would set locals on edge after the Africa campaign."

"During its long history, Algiers has suffered from many outside forces, including recently the French, British, and Americans."

"I can't argue that."

The coffee was served in clear glasses set on a silver tray along with two tiny, blue pottery pitchers: one contained goat's milk, the other honey. Skorzeny poured a dab of honey into his coffee; Carr drank his straight.

"Frau Faust has told me a great deal about you, Mr. Carr."

It sounded odd to hear Skorzeny refer to Erika as *Frau Faust* since on Friday and Saturday Carr had heard him speak to her using her first name. "I don't think Frau Faust knows much about me."

"She is complimentary. She tells me you're a good man."

"I'm surprised she's not with us."

"She'll rejoin us in a few days."

In a few days. Now Carr knew the exchange was at least a few days away.

As if Skorzeny read minds, he said. "That's right, Mr. Carr. The exchange won't occur until next week."

"You're confident in this exchange?" Carr asked, purely for his reaction. Donovan would arrange the exchange and Skorzeny knew it.

He looked at Carr and smiled. "If I didn't think so highly of you, I would think you insulted my intelligence. Frau Faust knew whom to choose and her access to you was exceptional. I confess I'm surprised you allowed her to get that close—a German spy invited to dine with OSS hierarchy and their wives in Annapolis." Skorzeny rubbed it in.

573

Carr admitted to himself that Erika completely fooled him. Obviously she cooperated with the British solely to avenge her father; she never intended to work for the United States after the war. "Touché. Yes, that was a mistake—trusting her. So now she's back in German hands where she wants to be, but she abandoned Abwehr and Himmler wants her for murder. If she returns to Germany it will be to a life always on the run."

Skorzeny offered no comment as he stirred the honey in his coffee. It was then Carr noticed the Ring on Skorzeny's right hand.

Chapter 120

In the Belly of the Whale

Mediterranean Sea
Ten days later; Saturday, 27 January 1945

Erika had finally appeared at Skorzeny's Algiers safehouse on Thursday morning. That night, a group consisting of Skorzeny, Carr, Erika, Rolf, and Mani boarded a fishing boat and sailed from the Algiers harbor to a waiting U-boat five miles off the coast. After Carr descended the hatch ladder, he saw additional Skorzeny commandos already on board. He recognized the U-boat as a class XVIIB, a coastal submarine half as long as the Atlantic *Wolfpack* U-boats. These coastal boats lacked the firepower of the larger, open-sea U-boats, but were more maneuverable and could operate in shallower waters.

They had sailed for two days, during which time Carr was not allowed on deck even though much of the voyage had been on the surface, the U-boat diving only when a lookout spotted an enemy plane or ship.

Yesterday, while the submarine's captain manned the control room, Skorzeny invited Carr to dine with him in the captain's cabin. At sea less than a day, the meal included fresh ham, an entrée available only during the first few days of any voyage. The meal might have been enjoyable if not taken in an atmosphere reeking of diesel fuel and while trying to keep condensation ever plopping from overhead pipes and valves from drenching the food.

Last night, Carr slept in a crew quarters' bunk, but now again sat in the captain's tiny cabin awaiting dinner. A crewman delivered a large bowl of scrambled eggs made from powder and a loaf of hard-crust bread Carr would share with Erika Lehmann.

"When you signed up with the OSS," said Erika, "I bet you never expected to get a complimentary ride on a U-boat. How do you like it?"

"I feel like Jonah in the belly of a steel whale," answered Carr. "The U-boat surprised me. Not that Otto Skorzeny would have trouble getting one for a sanctioned mission, but this mission is rogue."

"He doesn't need permission to use this U-boat," she said. "Last year it was allotted to him for his use whenever he needs it for missions in the Mediterranean. The boat makes normal patrols, but if Otto contacts the captain, the captain's orders are to comply."

"I noticed some of the crew are Skorzeny's men, not Kriegsmarine."

"The complement on this U-boat is only nineteen men, but it can be operated with as few as nine. To make room for more of his men, Otto had a few trained to handle some of the duties so the boat can sail with a skeleton Kriegsmarine crew." She tore from the loaf and put a piece of bread in her mouth.

"So where are we going?" Carr asked. "You needn't worry about my letting the cat out of the bag while I'm in the bowels of a U-boat."

"We're heading to the area where Aphrodite was born."

"Where's that?"

"I see you didn't pay attention in your college humanities classes, Leroy."

"So you won't tell me?"

"I just told you. You should have paid attention to your Greek mythology professor."

Carr now knew the exchange would take place somewhere in or near Greece, but her cryptic answer left the specific location a mystery—at least for him. He bet Kay would know where Aphrodite was born. The constant drone of the submarine's engines made it impossible for anyone outside the cabin door to eavesdrop, and Carr knew he could bring up more subtle topics. "Erika, the United States would not have executed your husband. We knew we couldn't do that and expect you to work for us. He would have been kept in the States then sent home after the war. I know you had to realize that. And I'd be willing to bet many wives of German soldiers would be glad to find out their husbands were captured by American forces. At least they'd know their men would survive the war. Now your husband might not."

She stopped chewing, swallowed, and washed down the bread with a drink of water from a canteen, never taking her eyes off him. "I had no guarantee, Leroy—about the execution. You have to realize that. But even if I had assurances, in the end I couldn't leave my husband in prison if I had a way to free him. Kai fights for his country. He would do the same for me, and I would expect him to. I think it would be the same between you and Kay. By the way, I know you're angry with me for involving Kay, but I had no choice, and no apprehension that she might be harmed. Otto promised me Kay would be safe. He lives by a code of honor and his word means everything to him. He would die before breaking it."

"I saw his Ring; it's the same as yours. That's the code you're talking about?"

"That, and Otto's personal code. That scar on his face isn't a battle wound; he suffered it during a fencing duel of honor."

"What are your plans, Erika? After this trade, you can't return to Germany and the good old days with Abwehr. Schellenberg wants you for desertion, and Himmler wants your scalp for the killings. To say you've burnt your bridges is a laughable understatement. And you know we'll find you after the war."

"If you're implying I broke my bargain with you, Leroy, think again about our agreement. I made it absolutely clear from the start I would not betray Germany. My pact with the OSS was, if allowed to avenge my father, I would work for the United States after the war. I gave my word and I will keep it. So don't be silly, I'm going back with you." She scooped eggs onto her plate.

[7 hours later, 2:00 a.m. Sunday, 28 January]
The United States Navy launch skimmed full throttle over the dark Mediterranean on a heading south-southeast from Kythira. Unarmed launches of this type saw duty mostly as transfer vessels ferrying admirals and VIPs from a dock to a ship anchored in a bay, or from ship to ship. In addition to the Navy coxswain operating the launch, whom Al Hodge did not count against his six-man team, on deck were Hodge, Victor Knight, and two OSS agents pulled out of Rome. Below deck, two Army Rangers guarded Kai Faust and Richard Kluga, the Germans shackled together.

A large envelope containing Skorzeny's instructions for Al Hodge reached the Dadiotis Guesthouse in Kythira at 8:00 p.m.

delivered by a 15-year-old local Greek boy on his bicycle. When questioned, the boy told Hodge a man gave him a 20-drachma note—more money than the boy had ever seen—to deliver the sealed package. It contained detailed instructions and a map plotting the exact course to be sailed.

The clear night and half moon allowed Hodge to spot the two tiny islands marked on Skorzeny's map. "There, up ahead!" he shouted to the coxswain over the roaring engine. "Those have to be the islands we're supposed to sail between." As ocean spray rose up and slapped down on the bow, the Navy coxswain adjusted the wheel slightly.

"Why do we have to sail between those islands?" the coxswain shouted. "We'll get there faster heading due south!"

Standing next to Hodge, Knight yelled, "Just do as ordered, Coxswain!" After receiving Skorzeny's instructions a few hours ago, Knight and Hodge had discussed the likelihood that the German commando chief might have men with binoculars on the small outcroppings watching to ensure the boat carrying the captured commandos was unarmed as instructed.

Hodge spent four years in the Yachting Club during his university days at Brown and was at home on the sea. He used his flashlight to study the map and added, "Stay this course until we clear the landmarks, then adjust two degrees starboard. After that, Antikythira should be seven miles dead ahead." Skorzeny's message stated the exchange would take place on the island of Antikythira, 30 miles south of Kythira, at the fishing village of Potamos on its northern shore. Hodge was instructed to dock at the fishermen's pier and wait on board until contacted.

Skorzeny held all the cards as long as one of those cards was Leroy Carr. After the exchange, things would change. Three American P-51 Mustang fighters waited on a runway in nearby Sparta for takeoff orders and would be airborne as soon as Hodge sent word that Carr was safe. When Hodge learned that the small, hilly island of Antikythira had no runway, he thought chances of catching Skorzeny spiked. Only by boat could he and his men leave the island.

The launch sped between the moonlit landmarks but before the coxswain had time to make the course adjustment the sea ahead frothed and the bow of a submarine shot out of the water like a breaching whale. The sub's bow lowered as its conning tower and deck rose from the sea. The coxswain was forced to throttle back and frantically spin the wheel to avoid ramming the submarine.

"Holy shit!" shouted the coxswain as he recognized the conning tower's distinctive silhouette that made a German U-boat easily distinguishable from American or British submarines. "It's a Kraut sub!" He gunned the engine to full throttle to get away. A conning tower searchlight came on, yet wasn't aimed at the launch. Rather, it illuminated someone standing on the U-boat's deck.

"Wait a minute!" Hodge shouted. "Turn back!" The light shone on a waving Erika Lehmann.

"No way!" yelled the coxswain as the launch raced away.

Knight pulled his pistol and aimed it at the coxswain. "He said to turn back!"

The coxswain spied the pistol but still hesitated, debating if he'd rather take his chances with the pistol or the U-boat. If he took his chances with the pistol, even if the Englishman were bluffing he would still face court-martial. The sailor turned the wheel and spun the boat. "What's the blue plate special this week at the Stalag?" he asked Hodge and Knight as they motored back toward the submarine, where several men now stood on deck.

It was now apparent to Hodge why Skorzeny had insisted on the rigid course. There were no lookouts on the outcroppings; Skorzeny had planned the route so the launch would come right to him at sea. *Damn it,* Hodge cursed to himself. He should have known the Antikythira plan was a diversion. Skorzeny would never back himself into a corner on an island with only one obvious escape option. Hodge could not call in the Mustangs until Carr was on the launch. By the time the fighters arrived, the U-boat would be submerged.

The U-boat's spotlight was redirected to the launch, and Hodge ordered one of the OSS agents to train the launch's spotlight on the submarine. Hodge could see the U-boat's manned deck cannon pointing at them, and men aiming submachine guns. More men scrambled up from below and began inflating a large rubber dinghy.

A tall man on deck spoke English through a bullhorn. *"Stop your vessel thirty meters from the Unterseeboot, turn your bow to expose your port side then cut your engines. It does not matter if you drift. We will bring Mr. Carr to you. Have my men on deck and be prepared to make the exchange."*

"Do it," Hodge told the coxswain. He turned to the other OSS men. "Bring them up."

"The Rangers, too?" one agent asked.

Hodge lost patience. "Yes, goddammit! Tell them to keep grasp of the prisoners and leave them shackled together. You two help keep the prisoners covered."

With four men rowing over uncooperative waves, the dinghy took 20 minutes to reach the launch, which had by then drifted another 50 meters away. Finally, the raft bounced against the launch's portside hull. A Ranger dropped the sea ladder and Otto Skorzeny was the first man on deck. Hodge was surprised that Erika Lehmann was in the raft and that Skorzeny had come himself, but then remembered reading in the OSS Skorzeny file that the infamous commando chief ignored the accepted military strategy of safeguarding top leaders. Skorzeny always led his men. As the American team and captured commandos waited on deck, Rolf, Mani, and two more commandos came over the rail.

As the Rangers and two OSS agents pointed their handguns at Faust and Kluga, Rolf and another commando raised their machine pistols and trained them on the American team. Mani and his partner went below. Surprisingly, Skorzeny did not order any of Hodge's men to surrender their weapons. Shots were heard from below as Mani and the other man destroyed all communication equipment. Appearing back on deck, they searched for and found another radio and fired several shots into it. When satisfied the Americans could no longer radio for help, they joined the others and held guns on the team.

"Victor Knight," said Skorzeny. "I finally meet you. What a pleasure."

"It's the great Otto Skorzeny," said Knight. "I would ask for your autograph to show the boys back at Baker Street but I don't have a fountain pen."

Skorzeny laughed. "I'm aware of your many exploits in Sicily, of course, initially with the First Airlanding Brigade, then later with the SOE. Well done."

"Same to you, Obersturmbannführer. Everyone knows about Gran Sasso, but I particularly liked your flair on that job in Hungary—kidnapping Regent Horthy's son and forcing him to step down in favor of a pro-Nazi leader. I studied the reports. Very well done, old chap."

The rapport and mutual admiration between Knight and Skorzeny surprised Al Hodge. During mission planning with Bill Donovan, Hodge expressed his concern that Knight might try to shoot Skorzeny, blowing the trade and getting everyone killed. But Hodge knew a bond many times existed between men—even enemies—who shared similar trials. Obviously, Knight shared more with Skorzeny than just scars on their faces.

"Which one is Mr. Hodge?" Skorzeny asked.

"I'm Hodge."

"I think we can all relax our weapons now," said Skorzeny. He gave the command and his men turned their guns away, holding them across their chests.

"Lower your weapons," Hodge ordered his men.

"Now unchain my men, Mr. Hodge."

On Hodge's orders, the Rangers removed the restraints. Carr was still in the dinghy with Erika, and Hodge began to suspect a double cross, but when Faust's and Kluga's manacles were removed, Skorzeny nodded to Rolf who went to the rail and signaled Erika to bring Carr on deck. She followed Carr over the rail.

"Hello, Al . . . Victor," said Erika.

"What's the matter, Erika?" asked Hodge. "You couldn't wait till hubby got on the U-boat?"

Erika ignored Hodge's sarcasm. "Otto, may I have a minute with Kai?" Skorzeny nodded and she led Kai below.

When the two were alone below deck, Erika said, "Take care of yourself, darling. Promise me I'll see you after the war."

Kai knew she could not return to Germany and hope to survive. "Come with me, Erika," he pleaded. "I told you at Wannsee that I can take you to Sweden and you can stay with my cousin, Emelie, in

Stockholm. Ada will be safe with your grandparents, and after the war you and I together will go get her."

"Where would we raise Ada?"

"What do you mean? Germany, of course. After the war, the Führer will find out what Himmler did and not hold you responsible for avenging your father."

"There won't be a Germany after the war, Kai. Not like we know it, and I've seen why."

"I don't understand."

There was not time to explain Auschwitz. "If we survive the war, we must raise Ada in America." She had daydreamed of family life with Kai and Ada. "Cincinnati or Evansville would be good places."

Kai had only a vague idea where Cincinnati was and he had never heard of Evansville. "Erika, please. You can't go back with the Americans—you betrayed them. They will deal harshly with you."

"I betrayed no one, Kai. Not Germany, not America."

"Neither country will agree with you."

"I'm confident the Americans will see—at least I'm hoping."

"They will not see! Your war is over. Let me take you to Stockholm. If the worst happens, we can take Ada to South America and live there. Do the right thing, Erika. If not for me, for Ada."

"Are you glad I freed you?"

"Of course."

"So now you will return to the war and I will worry about you. Should things be different with my staying in the war? Is your worry for me different than mine for you because I am a woman?"

With a look of desperation, Kai had nothing more to add. Erika put her arms around his neck. "I love you, Kai." It was the first time she had voiced those words to him. They shared a long kiss. When they separated she wiped tears before returning to the deck.

When Kai and Erika emerged from below, Skorzeny ordered all his men to the dinghy then turned to Carr, "Mr. Carr, you may now join your comrades. The war will end someday. Perhaps we will once again talk over coffee at a pleasant café."

"Perhaps," said Carr as he crossed the deck to stand beside Hodge.

Kai was the last of Skorzeny's men to go over the rail, leaving Eisenhower's "most dangerous man in Europe" standing alone on deck among armed enemies. Knight or any of the Americans could have easily shot him, but the wily Skorzeny knew he need not be concerned. If his enemies fired on him, the U-boat's deck cannon would reduce the wood-hull of the launch to fireplace kindling with one shot, and the Americans would not pay that price with the head of U.S. counter intelligence on board. Skorzeny had all the angles covered.

"Best of luck to you gentlemen on surviving the war," Skorzeny said. He offered Knight an informal salute which Knight returned, then swung a leg over the rail and was gone.

Erika moved to the rail and locked eyes with Kai for as long as possible as the dinghy carrying Otto Skorzeny and his men rowed away on the waters of Kythira where Aphrodite was born.

Chapter 121

Education Camps

Schwerin, Germany
Three months later; Saturday, 28 April 1945

Heinrich Himmler knew he could never return to Berlin—not while Adolf Hitler still lived.

SS General Hermann Fegelein, a Himmler informant stationed in Hitler's Berlin bunker, sent Himmler a communiqué telling him that the Führer had become aware of his Reichsführer's attempts at peace negotiations with the Western Allies. Earlier that month, Himmler had sent a representative to Count Bernadotte of Sweden asking him to assume the role of mediator. Since then, Himmler had sent Bernadotte several messages for relay to Eisenhower. So far, there had been no replies.

When Hitler found out about Himmler's secret dealings, he stripped Himmler of all titles, fired him from all offices, and ordered him arrested. Luckily, Himmler had left Berlin the previous week. On April 20th, just after stopping in at the bunker to extend his well wishes to the Führer on his birthday, Himmler drove north: first to Hohenlychen where he stayed in a private nursing home owned by his physician; then to Schwerin, 60 miles east of Hamburg, and a villa owned by Felix Kersten, Himmler's friend and personal chiropractor and masseur. Last week it was here that Himmler met with Norbert Masur, a representative of the World Jewish Congress. In surely the most unlikely meeting of the war, Heinrich Himmler, architect of the Final Solution, spent most of the 2½-hour middle-of-the-night meeting explaining his ideology to a Jew.

Masur had agreed to the meeting in an attempt to secure release for the remaining concentration camp prisoners, or if not released, at least fed and given medical care during these final days of the war. Masur also requested the camps be surrendered without resistance when the Allies neared.

Now, Himmler and his chiropractor sat in the villa's library sipping sherry. Himmler looked tired and bleary-eyed, having not slept well in months.

"The Swedes and their Jews should see I'm going out of my way to offer concessions to try and gain peace with the Western Allies," Himmler said. "I gave the Jew everything he asked for, but the Jew-controlled world press will never acknowledge my overtures." Himmler had released 2700 Jews to the Red Cross and they were now in Switzerland. He ordered 1000 women released from the Ravensbrück concentration camp, and, before being stripped of his Reichsführer title, he instructed the Totenkopf-SS to surrender the camps without resistance when the Allies rolled up to the gates. "When I sent the Jews to Switzerland, the Jewish press claimed I did it only in an attempt to improve my standing here in the eleventh hour. No man in history has been the target of more Jewish lies than I, Felix, not even the Führer."

"We must keep up our hopes, Heinrich."

Himmler shook his head. "No, everything is lost. We couldn't prevent the Jews from destroying Germany. That has been their goal since the first war and now they have succeeded. I hoped my concessions would gain peace with the Americans. They should join us in the fight against the Bolsheviks now, while there is still time. Soon they'll see that the communists are their real enemy, not the National Socialists."

"It's mindboggling that Eisenhower has not yet responded to your overtures."

"No, it's not surprising. Because most Jews are communists or sympathizers, the Jews in control of the world press have worked their sly ways." Himmler took a sip of sherry. "It all started when we chose the wrong name for the camps. The Jew press had a heyday with *Concentration Camp*. We should have called them *Education Camps.*"

Chapter 122

**If Hitler invaded Hell, I would make at least a favorable
reference to the devil in the House of Commons.**
— Winston Churchill

The Führerbunker, Berlin
Next day; Sunday, 29 April 1945

Walther Wagner wished they had found someone else. When the SS knocked on his door, he was hastily packing a suitcase. He knew his chances of escaping Berlin were minimal—more likely to be blown to bits by Russian artillery—but his options were limited. It was either run the gauntlet of exploding cannon shells or surrender to the Russians and be shot on the spot or spend the rest of his life in a Siberian gulag.

When the SS appeared and told him why they had come, Wagner tried to argue his way out, telling them he was merely a low-ranking Propaganda Ministry official. But Goebbels had sent the SS because of Wagner's status as a court official, the only one available and he would have to do. Now Wagner stood in a bunker 30 feet below the Reichschancellery holding a civil marriage manual.

"Will the bride please state her full birth name and age?" asked Wagner. Goebbels had ordered him to perform the ceremony straight from the book, instructions Wagner welcomed.

"Eva Anna Paula Braun, age thirty-three." Eva wore a black silk dress with a white lace collar.

"Do you swear you are of pure Aryan descent?"

"Yes."

Wagner's hands trembled as he turned to the groom. He flipped the page, realized his mistake, then turned it back. "Will the groom please state his full birth name and age?"

"Adolfus Hitler, fifty-six." His face ashen and eyes hollow, Hitler looked 70.

"Do you swear you are of pure Aryan descent?"

"Yes."

Now it was time to flip the page. Wagner turned back to Eva. "Do you, Eva Anna Paula Braun, take this man as your lawful husband?"

"Yes."

"Do you, our Führer Adolf Hitler, take this woman to be your lawful wife?" Wagner immediately realized his mistake with the name and glanced at Goebbels expecting a displeased look, but Goebbels ignored the faux pas.

"Yes," said Hitler.

"I now pronounce you man and wife," Wagner said quickly, then closed the manual, never before so happy to finish a duty. Goebbels and his wife, Magda, applauded the newlyweds, as did Martin Bormann and the adjutants and secretaries in the room.

"Now," said Wagner to the couple, "if you will sign the certificate, please. And we will need two witnesses' signatures." Wagner handed the fountain pen to Eva. The happy bride signed her first name then started writing *Braun,* stopped, hastily crossed out the *B* and wrote *Hitler.* Hitler signed next, followed by witnesses Goebbels and Bormann.

[same day—10 Downing Street, London}

Victor Knight sat in the backseat of an unmarked police sedan wending its way through the streets of Westminster. In front sat the two Scotland Yard detectives who had shanghaied him from his office 20 minutes ago without any explanation of why they were there, or where they were taking him. Knight went with them only because Colin Gubbins telephoned earlier to tell Knight some men would come calling later that day, and he was to go with them and ask no questions. So when the car pulled over and stopped, the location caught Knight totally off guard.

"Number 10?" Knight asked. "You're joking."

"Just follow me, Mr. Knight," said the detective in the passenger seat as he opened his door. The driver stayed in the car.

Though Knight had reconciled himself to the reality that a cane would always be part of his life, his mobility had improved dramatically in the nine months since Grünwald. He got through the exchange mission in Greece without proving a liability to the team, and each month since had seen his walking and stair climbing improve.

"This way to the lift," said the detective. He led Knight to an elevator that carried them to the third floor. When the lift door opened, a man waiting in the hall introduced himself as Patrick Kinna and escorted Knight down a hallway and into an apartment. Kinna deposited Knight in the tea room and asked him to wait. In a couple of minutes, Kinna returned.

"Please follow me, Mr. Knight." He led Knight to a bathroom. "Here we are; go on in."

"In there?" Knight said, baffled. "I didn't ask for the loo."

"Please." Kinna held his arm out to the bathroom door, signaling Knight to enter.

Knight looked at Kinna again then walked into the bathroom. In the bathtub sat Winston Churchill with a glass of whiskey in one hand and a huge cigar in the other. Bubbles covered him up to his navel.

"Ah," said Churchill, "you must be Knight. They told me you walk with a cane." Knight stood staring. "Well, don't stand there, have a seat . . . over there on the throne."

The flabbergasted Knight sat down on the toilet—after he dropped the lid. Churchill puffed on his cigar and looked Knight over.

"The Baker Street Irregulars praise you highly, Knight. Do you have any interest in returning to the field?"

"To the field? Yes, Prime Minister, I do."

"The war is about over," said Churchill. "If Hitler is still in Berlin, as we suspect, he can't last much longer—only a matter of days now, I should think. There should be little shooting involved in what we have in mind for you, but you'll be on the move. How is your bad leg?"

"It's fine, sir. I mean, fine enough."

"Jolly well enough, then. Patrick will show you out and the men who delivered you will take you to Baker Street. They'll fill you in there. Give it a good go, Knight. It's important."

"I will sir, thank you." Knight turned and left the bathroom, his meeting with Winston Churchill lasting less than 5 minutes. He left with no clue to what Churchill was talking about, but if it got him out from behind a desk, he was more than ready to grasp the opportunity.

Chapter 123

Better to reign in Hell than serve in Heaven.
— Lucifer in Milton's *Paradise Lost*

[Translated in the Office of the United States Chief of Counsel for Prosecution of Axis Criminality, Nazi Conspiracy and Aggression, 8 vols. and 2 suppl. Vols. (Government Printing Office, Washington, 1946-1948), VI, 259-263, Doc. No. 3560-PS]

My Private Will and Testament

As I did not consider that I could take responsibility during the years of struggle of contracting a marriage, I have now decided, before the closing of my earthly career, to take as my wife that girl who, after many years of faithful friendship, entered, of her own free will, the practically besieged town in order to share her destiny with me. At her own desire she goes as my wife with me into death. It will compensate us both for what we lost through my work in the service of my people.

What I possess belongs—insofar as it has any value—to the Party. Should this no longer exist, to the State; should the State also be destroyed, no further decision of mine is necessary.

My pictures, in the collections which I have bought through the course of years, have never been collected for private purposes, but only for the extension of a gallery in my hometown of Linz on the Donau. It is my most sincere wish that this bequest may be duly executed.

I nominate as my Executor my most faithful Party comrade, Martin Bormann. He is given full legal authority to make all decisions. He is permitted to take out everything that has a sentimental value or is necessary for the maintenance of a modest, simple life for my brothers and sisters, and also for the mother of my wife and my faithful coworkers who are well known to him, principally my various secretaries, Frau Winter [housekeeper], etc., who have for many years aided me by their work.

I myself and my wife, in order to escape the disgrace of deposition or capitulation, choose death. It is our wish to be burnt immediately on the spot where I have carried out the greatest part of my daily work in the course of twelve years' service to my people.

[Signed] A. HITLER   {Given in Berlin, 29 April 1945, 4:00 a.m.}

[Witnesses – Signed] Dr. Josef Goebbels
                            Martin Bormann
                            Colonel Nicholas von Below

The Führerbunker, Berlin
Next day; Monday, 30 April 1945

At three o'clock in the afternoon, Adolf and Eva Hitler walked slowly down the line saying their good-byes.

Hitler first thanked Martin Bormann then took a step to stand in front of Goebbels. "Thank you, Joseph," said Hitler, stooped and worn, as he shook Goebbels' hand. "We shared glorious years together, you and I. All my generals and highest-ranking officials betrayed me; only you among my important leaders remained faithful to the end." Goebbels, with tears in his eyes, could not reply. Eva, walking behind Hitler, also shook the propaganda chief's hand. Hitler kissed Magda Goebbels' hand and Eva hugged her. Hitler shook hands with two staff adjutants then came to his personal adjutant, Otto Günsche.

Hitler took Günsche's hand in both of his. "Thank you for all your years of service to the Reich, Otto."

Günsche forced himself to stay composed. Hitler had never before used his first name when speaking to him. "It has been my honor to serve you, mein Führer."

"You know my wishes, Otto." When Hitler learned that the bodies of Mussolini's and his mistress had been kicked and spat upon, then hung upside down from meat hooks for public display at a gasoline station in Milan, he put Günsche in charge of ensuring that his and Eva's bodies were not treated in like fashion by the Russians. That morning, Hitler instructed Günsche to burn their bodies immediately upon death.

"Yes, mein Führer."

Next came Hitler's longtime personal pilot, Hans Baur. Baur did not wait for a good-bye. "Mein Führer, I beg you. I can still fly you to safety, I'm sure of it. There are places to go: Argentina, Japan, perhaps one of the Arab countries where you have staunch supporters."

"One must have the courage to face the consequences," Hitler replied. "I am ending it all here. I know by tomorrow millions of people will curse me—Fate wanted it that way. Thank you for your faithful service, Hans. I want you to take the painting of Frederick the

Great as a personal present from me. I want it to remain for the future. It has great historical value."

Finally the secretaries: Hitler and Eva thanked Gerda Christian, then came to Traudl Junge at the end of the line. For years, Hitler had enjoyed lunching with his personal secretaries, so much so that he rarely agreed to hold working lunches with generals or foreign diplomats. Junge had always been his favorite, treating the young woman more like a daughter than a secretary. Last year, when he was informed that Junge's husband was killed at Normandy, Hitler walked out of an important meeting with his generals to spend over an hour consoling her. Yesterday, shortly after his wedding, Hitler dictated both his private Will and his Political Testament to Junge. She stood in a grim trance as Hitler smiled weakly, kissed her hand, and mumbled something she did not understand.

Earlier, Eva had given Junge her silver fox coat. As Hitler moved away, Eva stepped to Junge and said, "Traudl, my darling, please try to get out of here. Then say hello to Munich for me." When she saw Junge's tears, Eva burst into sobs but composed herself quickly.

Neither Hitler nor Eva looked back as they left the room. The others stood silently for a long moment; none of them, including Bormann and Goebbels, knew what to do. The principal figure of the 20th century to whom they had devoted their lives simply vanished through a door.

In the bunker's study, Hitler and Eva sat down on the sofa. She reached for and held his hand without speaking. Hitler wore his uniform and Eva the black silk dress she married in the previous day. From his tunic pocket, Hitler took out two glass cyanide capsules and handed one to Eva. He had ordered a supply of the capsules from Himmler, but because he no longer trusted his former SS chief, Hitler had allowed his doctor to try one on his dog, Blondi. The poison worked. From another pocket Hitler took out his Walther PPK.

Eva told Hitler she loved him, placed the capsule in her mouth, and bit down quickly, fearing she might lose courage if she delayed. Hitler, who had already placed the capsule in his mouth, glanced at the photograph of his mother on the tea table, put the pistol to his head and then simultaneously bit down and pulled the trigger.

Otto Günsche heard the gunshot as he stood outside the study door. Hitler had ordered him to wait 10 minutes after hearing the shot before entering. Günsche waited 5 minutes then opened the door.

Adolf Hitler sat upright on the sofa looking as if he were deep in thought, a small stream of blood running from his right temple. His wife of 39 hours lay on the sofa with her head in her husband's lap.

Chapter 124

SMERSH

[translation: "Death to Spies" – the Soviet counterintelligence agency created by Joseph Stalin in 1943 to subvert attempts by German forces to infiltrate the Red Army]

Berlin
Three days later; Thursday, 03 May 1945

General Aleksandr Vadis stepped carefully through the rubble of the Reichschancellery. Like Adolf Hitler's Thousand Year Reich, the Reichschancellery and much of Berlin lay in ruins.

"Over here, General," said a SMERSH senior lieutenant.

Accompanied by three aides, a photographer, and four SMERSH agents, Vadis climbed over a fallen beam and stopped at another corpse the dogs sniffed in the rubble. This would be the third body in the past hour one of his search team lieutenants believed might be Adolf Hitler's. As the head of SMERSH, Vadis had been attached to Marshal Zhukov's 1st Byelorussian Front during the Battle of Berlin. When the German capital fell and German radio announced that the Führer was dead, Stalin felt certain the announcement was a trick and personally charged Vadis with finding Hitler's body. Yesterday, when Zhukov's Red Army reached the Reichschancellery and found the bunker, Zhukov ordered the chancellery and bunker off limits until inspected for booby traps. Not until this morning could SMERSH begin its search.

Vadis knelt to inspect the decomposing body of a man with a small moustache and hair combed to one side. After examining the remains for several minutes, Vadis rose and said, "This man has darned socks. Hitler would never wear darned socks." Nevertheless, he ordered photographs taken and the body moved to the truck holding other bodies tagged for examination.

Suddenly, the SMERSH captain Vadis had placed in charge of the bunker inspection team ran up to the general's entourage. "General Vadis, one of my squad leaders reports that his team found two Germans hiding in the bunker."

"I was told two hours ago that all Germans had been brought out," Vadis said with irritation.

"These two were hiding in a cupboard."

"A cupboard? Have they been identified?"

"No, sir," answered the captain. "None of my men speak German."

"Where are these Germans now?"

"I ordered them left in the bunker, General, until I received your instructions."

Vadis had not yet been inside the bunker and decided it was time. "Lead the way, Captain." As Vadis and his men began making their way back through the rubble, he said to an aide, "Bring an interpreter." As the aide started off in another direction, Vadis added, "And not the Rumanian. I want that German woman who escaped Sobibor."

"Yes, General," the aide called back.

The SMERSH captain led Vadis and the group down the long series of concrete steps into the dark, dank bowels of the Führerbunker. Without electricity to run the sump pumps, lights, and ventilation system, when they reached the bottom floor they were forced to slog through six inches of water while Vadis's aides held flashlights to light the way. The sour air caused several men to cough.

As they progressed through the bunker, they passed other Russians going in and out of rooms conducting searches. The captain stopped at the kitchen door and ordered one of the guards to bring out the Germans. The guard brought out a boy in his early teens wearing a Hitler Youth uniform, and a younger girl.

"These are the Germans?" Vadis asked as he shone his light on their frightened faces. "They're children!"

The captain was horrified. The general's time was not to be wasted and those who wasted it usually paid a price. "I apologize, General. I was not told they were children. I will deal with the squad leader who gave me an incomplete report, I assure you."

"Where is that interpreter?" Vadis was becoming more irked by the second. He looked at an aide. "You! Go find her!"

As the aide turned to leave, a SMERSH agent pointing his flashlight behind them announced, "There she is, General."

Down the corridor, the interpreter and the aide Vadis sent to fetch her waded toward the group. When they joined them, Vadis told her, "Find out who they are and why they are down here."

The woman spoke German to the terrified children for several minutes until Vadis thought she was taking too long and lost his patience.

"What is taking so long?" he asked loudly. "For now just find out their names and what they are doing here."

"The boy is 13," she reported in Russian. "His name is Arne Schiffer—Hitler Youth as you can see. The girl is his 9-year-old sister, Hedy. Their parents were killed and apartment destroyed in an artillery barrage four days ago. They hid in the rubble of their home for a day, then the boy took his sister to look for food. They found the bunker entrance, and a secretary who remained behind after most of the bunker staff fled allowed the children to enter and gave them bread."

"Take them away," Vadis ordered one the SMERSH agents. "Put them in the holding area with the others."

"They haven't eaten in nearly two days, General," said the interpreter. "I will take them and feed. . . ."

Another agent interrupted. "Keep your mouth shut! You dare *tell* General Vadis what you will do?"

Vadis ignored the agent's outburst. "Stay with me," he said to the interpreter. "I can't spare you right now." Then he turned to the agent he had ordered to take the children. "Make sure they receive something to eat."

From the far end of an intersecting corridor, a voice shouted, "I need an officer over here!"

Vadis and his group immediately headed toward the voice and found a sergeant pointing to a room. Vadis led the way, followed by two agents and the interpreter. Inside, six children in pajamas lay still in bunk beds, faces blue in death. Erika Lehmann recognized the children of Joseph and Magda Goebbels.

Part 7

1961

"I can't go back to yesterday, because I was a different person then."

— Lewis Carroll

Chapter 125

Vienna Summit

CIA Headquarters—Langley, Virginia
Tuesday, 16 May 1961

"I'll take you in now, Mr. Carr."

Leroy Carr rose and followed the assistant into the CIA director's office. She smiled and closed the door behind her. When the director saw Carr, he stood and walked around his desk.

"Leroy, it's great to see you!" Allen Dulles said enthusiastically. "It's been too long."

The men shook hands. "A couple of years," said Carr. They last met at William Donovan's funeral in 1959. "How are you Allen?"

"Still busy." In 1947, the OSS became the CIA. Dulles had served as the agency's director since 1953.

"I bet," said Carr.

"Have a seat, Leroy. How's retirement?" Dulles walked back around his desk and sat down. Behind his chair the Stars and Stripes hung limp from a floor stand near a wall photo of President Kennedy.

Dulles and Carr had an intertwined work history dating back two decades. During the war, Dulles had overseen OSS European operations from his office in Berne, Switzerland. In 1943, Bill Donovan brought Dulles to Fort Knox, Kentucky, to serve on the committee with Carr and others there to debate Erika Lehmann's future. In July 1944, Dulles personally handled Maeve O'Rourke's and Stephanie Fischer's protection after Suse Hohner flew the two women to Switzerland. When President Eisenhower appointed Dulles CIA director shortly after his inauguration in 1953, Dulles named Carr Director of Clandestine Services, the job Carr retired from four years ago.

"Retirement is terrific," Carr answered as he sat. "It's hard to beat the fishing down there." In 1957, the Carrs moved to a home on Hilton Head Island in South Carolina. Since then, he occasionally worked at law for a friend's legal firm in Charleston if a case interested him, but typically spent more of his time working with bait and lures.

"You're looking well, Leroy. Not much brown left up there but your hair is still hanging around. More than you can say for me. How's Kay?"

"She's fine. Retirement started boring her so she returned to paralegal work at the Charleston firm where I handle a case now and then."

"Doesn't surprise me," said Dulles. "She's younger than you—too young to retire—and I don't blame her for not wanting to clean your fish. Please tell her I send my best."

"I will."

"I appreciate your coming to Langley on such short notice. The transition from Ike to Jack Kennedy these past months has been hectic to say the least. Schedules can get changed hourly around here and in Washington, so we do a lot of things on short notice."

"It wasn't a problem. What's up, Allen?"

"The President and Khrushchev have a summit next month in Vienna to discuss Berlin. No one knows better than you that CIA support of Gehlen remains a major bone of contention with the Soviets."

During the war, General Reinhard Gehlen served as the German military's Eastern Front intelligence chief. After the war, the Soviets sought to try Gehlen for war crimes citing evidence he ordered executions of Red Army prisoners of war without just cause. But because of American backing, instead of being brought before a war crimes tribunal, Gehlen was now director of the BND, the West German counterpart of the CIA.

"So the White House thinks Khrushchev is going to take a tough stand, is that it?" asked Carr.

Dulles nodded. "Since the President is young and has been in office only four months, his advisors think Khrushchev may feel he can play the bully. There's a White House committee being formed to gather information about how the OSS and later the CIA handled the Gehlen matter. We'll also face questions about former Gestapo or SD agents now associated with the BND, as well as a few other former Nazis we backed or turned a blind eye to."

"And you want me to answer questions from the committee?"

"I'll be there answering questions, too. We have no choice."

"What if the committee hears an answer it doesn't like or wasn't expecting?" asked Carr.

"Hopefully it won't go that deep. The Russians can't be outraged about something they know nothing about, so we don't have to volunteer information at the White House briefing—only answer specific questions. The committee wants to see files on these names." Dulles handed Carr a folder with the presidential seal on the cover.

"Who's on the committee?" Carr asked as he opened the file.

"The Secretary of State sent the cover letter but doesn't name the committee members, which leads me to believe Rusk hasn't yet decided who will serve on it. But it's closed door and will not include any senators or congressmen."

Carr glanced at the cover letter from Dean Rusk then looked for the list of BND names.

"The BND names appear on page four," said Dulles. "Other individuals the committee seeks information on are listed on the next page."

Carr turned to page four. "A lot of names. Luckily for the boys and girls in the research department you already have files on most of these people." In alphabetical order, the two-column page listed 82 names, all former members of Himmler's SD or Gestapo including four men who were close associates of Adolf Eichmann. Just last week, Eichmann had been captured in Argentina by the Israeli Mossad. The SS paladin in charge of Himmler's Jewish Affairs Section, Eichmann had for years labored as an assembly line worker at the Mercedes-Benz plant in Buenos Aires.

Carr took a minute to look over the names. "They missed a few."

"Sixteen, to be exact," said Dulles.

"And who are Alwin Eisenberg and Gisela Wirtz? I never heard of them."

"Those names must be a mistake. We have no files on them."

Carr turned to the next page. This list was smaller—only 13 names. Among them were: Mr. Thomas, Tarsitano, Kathryn Fischer, Otto Skorzeny, and a name spelled *Erica Lehrer*.

"Good God," Carr said when he saw the last name.

"They spelled both her first and last name incorrectly," said Dulles. "That gives us an avenue of plausible denial."

"We can't tell them anything about her—zero," said Carr. "There hasn't been a White House since Taft that didn't have leaks."

"Obviously. But with her name spelled like that, we don't have to lie. Our answer is simply we know nothing about an *Erica Lehrer*. Since those two names you mentioned from the BND page are mistakes, we'll claim that name has to be an error, as well. We won't be lying."

"And how about *Mr. Thomas?* That name shouldn't be on here. Don't they know Knight is British and worked for the SOE?"

"Apparently they don't know who *Mr. Thomas* is. I'm sure Knight's codename is on the committee's list because *Mr. Thomas* was on some of the top-secret reports from Lüneburg before the British altered the reports. Himmler's death has always been another sticking point with Moscow, and the White House wants to make sure they have solid information for a response if Khrushchev brings up Himmler in Vienna. We'll tell the White House what we know, Leroy. I agree that we can't reveal information about Lehmann, but we want to help the President, of course. On all other matters except Lehmann we'll be forthright. In fact, I'm going to call the Attorney General and suggest he contact Whitehall and request Knight be made available to the committee. If the White House wants to know about Himmler's death, Knight is the horse's mouth. I'm confident the SIS would allow the White House access to Knight if the committee agrees that the questions will be limited to the war. Then the ball is in the Brits' court as far as what is revealed about Himmler's death."

"What's our timeline?" asked Carr. "I don't see a date on the cover letter. When is the White House briefing?"

"Thursday next week. Nine days from now. I'm requesting you stay in the area, Leroy, instead of going home and coming back next week. You and I need some face time for discussion between now and the briefing. I'll have my assistant book you a suite and Kay can come up if she wishes. I know Clover would love to see Kay. What do you say?"

Carr nodded.

"I miss the old days, Leroy. At least during the war things were black and white—us against the bad guys. Life was as simple as that. Now everything is gray."

Chapter 126

Situation Room

The White House
Nine days later; Thursday, 25 May 1961

"Thank you for coming, Director Dulles and Mr. Carr," said Dean Rusk.

The briefing was held in the White House Situation Room in the basement of the West Wing. Allen Dulles and Leroy Carr had just sat down at a long, gleaming mahogany table with an inlaid presidential seal. The room was currently being enlarged and renovated. A large section of oak paneling and the burgundy damask were missing, leaving metal studs and concrete exposed. Other than the conference table and chairs, all furnishings had been removed for the construction. Old Glory was present, however. The flag and stand were brought in during meetings then removed when adjourned, at which time the table and chairs would be covered with canvas tarps.

In addition to committee chairman Secretary of State Rusk, across the table from Dulles and Carr sat Secretary of Defense Robert S. McNamara, Attorney General Robert Kennedy, and three of the President's advisors the press had dubbed the *Kitchen Cabinet*— McGeorge Bundy, Maxwell Taylor, and Theodore Sorensen. Allen Dulles had met everyone during previous White House briefings; Leroy Carr received introductions in the Diplomatic Room where the group initially assembled.

"Colonel Knight appeared before this committee this morning, Director Dulles," said Rusk. "We want to thank you for suggesting he might be of some help. Colonel Knight revealed that during the war he was, in fact, the *Mr. Thomas* on our list. The President will send his thanks to Prime Minister Macmillan for his government's assistance."

Carr wondered how much Knight had revealed about what the men across the table really wanted to know. He imagined not much since the British government had sealed most of the records relating to Himmler's death while in British hands.

Rusk looked at Carr. "Mr. Carr, Director Dulles sent us a copy of the file detailing your service to our country both during and after the war. The committee thanks you for that service."

"It's been my honor to serve, Mr. Secretary."

"The committee has broken down the list of topics," said Rusk. "Secretary of Defense McNamara will address page four. Attorney General Kennedy will represent the committee concerning page five. Secretary McNamara will start us off."

McNamara wasted no time. "Director Dulles, are the eighty-two names listed on page four of the documents sent you accurate as far as former Nazis who currently work, or did work at one time, for the West German BND currently headed by Reinhard Gehlen?"

"Yes, Secretary McNamara," Dulles answered. "With the exception of two names we have no files on and believe to be errors, the list is accurate."

"So eighty agents of the post-war West German government's intelligence apparatus were members of the Gestapo or SD?"

"That's correct." Dulles didn't add that several names were missing.

"Including some who were accused of war crimes but protected by our CIA and the British SIS?"

"Yes. These individuals had important contacts we desperately needed, and using these people served our country's interests—there is no arguing that. The British decided on a similar course and were aided, as well. I will add that all the individuals on your list underwent extensive de-Nazification."

"Director Dulles, is Reinhard Gehlen, head of the BND, himself a war criminal?"

"I would say that there are charges that could be filed against Gehlen that would fit within the parameters set forth at the Nuremberg Trials, yes."

The men on the committee shared glances.

"Director, we request that you prepare a detailed report on Gehlen's wartime activities for this committee," Rusk added.

"It's already prepared, Mr. Secretary," Dulles said. "I'll send it over this afternoon. The CIA will help in any way possible to aid the

President with background information for the summit, but it's my duty to remind you that everything I send you and everything said here today is classified. Any actions taken could be detrimental to U.S. foreign policy. The information is for the President's preparation only, Committee."

Rusk responded quickly, "Both this committee and the President are quite aware that we're dealing with sensitive subject matter, Director. And I will remind you that the State Department answers only to the President in matters of foreign policy, not to the CIA. With that clear, I assure you we didn't ask you here today because we have plans to revamp foreign policy. Now, Attorney General Kennedy has some questions."

"Thank you, Secretary Rusk," said Robert Kennedy. "Director Dulles, did the OSS have any involvement in the death of Heinrich Himmler in May 1945?"

"General Donovan always stated emphatically *no,* Mr. Kennedy," Dulles answered forcefully. "As you know, Himmler died while in British hands."

Kennedy moved on. "I'd like to address certain individuals named on page five with possible CIA ties, and about an operation codenamed *Kriemhild.* I understand Mr. Carr is here to supply those answers so I will direct my questions to him. Director Dulles, please feel free to add additional information if you can elaborate." Kennedy glanced at paperwork in his hand. "Mr. Carr, about Operation Kriemhild, it's my understanding from the documents furnished by Director Dulles that you played a role in this mission. Please explain the operation and your part in it."

"*Kriemhild* was a British SOE mission to eliminate certain high-ranking members of the Gestapo, SS, and SD during the spring of 1944," said Carr. "The goal was to cause disorder in those organizations shortly before the Normandy invasion. As stated, it was a British operation run by the SOE. Colonel Knight was in charge. My role was limited. Basically, I served as an advisor. The mission failed. No one on the list was eliminated and several of the British agents were killed."

"Mr. Carr," Kennedy continued, "did you personally have a hand in Otto Skorzeny's escape from a German detention center shortly after the war?"

"Yes."

Members of the committee sat up straighter.

"Explain, Mr. Carr."

"Otto Skorzeny was acquitted of war crimes by an Allied tribunal in 1947 but was then arrested by the West Germans who detained him without cause. Skorzeny fought on the Russian Front before becoming a commando leader. Despite his fame and well-known commando exploits, we never uncovered any evidence that Skorzeny ever killed an American soldier, let alone committed war crimes. It was unfair to hold him after he was cleared by the tribunal."

"What did you do to help him escape the West Germans?"

"I had phony transfer documents created that ordered Skorzeny moved to a different detention center, and I used a few of Skorzeny's English-speaking former commandos posing as U.S. military policemen to carry out the plan."

"We all know Skorzeny has been granted asylum in Spain. Does Skorzeny now work for, or did he ever work for, the CIA?"

"Director Dulles can better answer that question, Mr. Kennedy."

"We occasionally contact Otto Skorzeny," said Dulles. "He does not work for the CIA."

"Elaborate on *occasionally contact,* please," said Kennedy.

"Skorzeny still maintains an impressive list of contacts," Dulles added, "and he is willing to supply the United States information regarding the Soviets that helps us in the Cold War."

"Is Otto Skorzeny active in a post-war organization known as ODESSA that lends aid to former SS officers escaping Europe for South America?"

Dulles answered, "Detailed information on Skorzeny's current level of involvement with ODESSA is sketchy at the present time, Mr. Kennedy, but we know he does have ties to that organization."

Kennedy again referred to his paperwork. "Another name on page five is *Tarsitano.* Who is he?"

"I'll turn that question over to Mr. Carr," said Dulles.

"Tarsitano was a woman," Carr answered. "An Italian citizen who worked for the SOE as a member of the Operation Kriemhild team. She was killed in Berlin during the mission."

Kennedy moved down the list. "Kathryn Fischer, listed as a Gestapo officer."

"Fischer was an Abwehr agent planted as a mole in the Gestapo by Wilhelm Canaris, the head of Abwehr before he was replaced by Walter Schellenberg," Carr replied. "Fischer provided the United States invaluable help during the war, especially after her sister—a member of the Kriemhild team—was killed by the Gestapo. After her sister's death, Fischer stepped up her efforts to undermine the Gestapo and succeeded in several ways. Specifics will be in the files Director Dulles will supply the committee. After Berlin fell, Fischer was captured by the Red Army but managed to escape." Carr did not go into details of Kathryn's escape, facilitated by Erika Lehmann who by then worked as an interpreter for SMERSH. "Kathryn Fischer worked as a CIA field operative until 1955 and is now an instructor in irregular warfare at the U.S. Naval War College." Kathryn Fischer now lived and taught in Newport, Rhode Island.

"So Fischer was never actual Gestapo?"

"She became a Gestapo officer, but only to fulfill her Abwehr assignment as an infiltrator."

"Erica Lehrer," Kennedy read from the list. "A notation from U.S. Army intelligence in West Germany states: *Possible wartime Abwehr connection, currently at the top of the Russian KGB's 'kill on sight' list.*"

Dulles answered first. "We scoured our files, Mr. Kennedy. The CIA has nothing on an Erica Lehrer. The names *Alwin Eisenberg* and *Gisela Wirtz* on the BND page are mistakes; that name must be a mistake, too."

"I concur," said Carr. "I never had any dealings with an *Erica Lehrer.*"

Chapter 127

Dinner with Old Friends

Alexandria, Virginia
That night; Thursday, 25 May 1961

Leroy and Kay Carr shared at least one thing with John and Abigail Adams: Gadsby's Tavern in Alexandria was both couples' favorite D.C. area restaurant. Established in 1749, Gadsby's was a favorite of many Founding Fathers who started a tradition of Presidents, Senators and Congressmen, top Pentagon brass and a wide array of other movers-and-shakers dining at Gadsby's and rubbing shoulders with the good citizens of Alexandria. Decisions that radically altered (or only tweaked) everything from foreign policy and military strategy to farm subsidies had been discussed over the prime rib and lump crab cakes at Gadsby's.

A hostess led the Carrs to a corner table near a window.

"I'm looking forward to meeting the Knights," said Kay as her husband held her chair.

"And I look forward to seeing them again," Leroy replied. "I haven't seen Victor in seven years and his wife not since the war."

"Do you think they'll have trouble finding this place?"

"I found them a driver who is from around here. He'll drop them off and visit family until they call him for the ride back to Washington."

"Where are the Knights staying?"

"The Churchill," Leroy answered. "The name certainly fits." The Churchill was a historic D.C. apartment building on Connecticut Avenue that kept a number of apartments vacant for guests on short stays. The Carrs had not yet ordered drinks when Leroy glanced out the window and saw a car pull up and the Knights get out.

"Fine timing," said Leroy. "They're here."

When Kay looked out and saw the Knights walking toward the restaurant door, her look of shock did not surprise her husband.

"Kay, that's not Erika," he said.

"The heck it isn't. Older, like us all, but she's not a woman I'll forget. Why didn't you tell me?"

"It's not her."

The Knights walked in, spotted Leroy, and pointed out the table to the hostess who led them over. Leroy stood, shook hands with Victor Knight, then turned to Mrs. Knight.

"Maeve! How wonderful to see you again. How are you?"

"I'm sleeping with the enemy, Leroy. Besides that I'm well." Maeve hugged him. "It's grand seeing you again. I finally made it back to America. When Tars and I sailed past the Statue of Liberty I told her I'd return some day."

"Well, America is happy you're back," said Leroy. "Victor and Maeve, this is my wife, Kay."

"Hello, Kay," said Victor.

Kay temporarily suspended her Maeve-staring to return his greeting. "I'm very happy to meet you both."

A waiter stood nearby ready to take drink orders as Leroy and the Knights sat. The Carrs ordered their usual: he a gin and tonic, she a glass of white wine, this time a Riesling. Victor ordered bourbon and Maeve a Guinness.

"I've acquired a taste for your Kentucky whiskey over the years, Leroy," said Victor, laying his cane on the floor beside his chair. "I remember the first time I tried it—at the Christmas Eve dinner in '44 you and I attended. Being a Scotsman, I feel a bit guilty not ordering Scotch. I might be banned from my country if word were to leak out."

"Your secret's safe with us," said Leroy.

"When you mentioned Gadsby's *Tavern*, I told Maeve I thought we were meeting in a pub," Victor commented as he took in the eloquent table setting. Sparkling Waterford glassware and Lenox china rested on the white-linen tablecloths. "We weren't expecting . . . what do you Yanks say? Swanky?"

"Kay and I dined here at least once a month during all those years I worked in Washington. Quite a history to this place. Of course, I imagine it looked a little different when George Washington and Thomas Jefferson ate here."

Maeve looked at Kay. "I see in your face that you knew her."

Kay blushed. "I'm sorry; please forgive my staring."

Maeve smiled and placed her hand on Kay's. "No. It's okay. It's nice to have a mutual acquaintance."

Leroy knew the subject of Erika would come up and tried a detour. "So, how is your son, Maeve? Victor once showed me a photo when he was a baby. He's how old now?"

"Patrick is eleven," Maeve replied. "Fallon, our daughter, is seven."

"You have a daughter now? That's great. Any plans for more?"

Maeve looked at Kay. "That's a man for you, isn't it, Kay?" Kay smiled, and Maeve looked at Leroy. "I'm forty-two, Leroy. How many more do you want me to have?"

"Sorry. I wasn't thinking," he said. She was not talking about Erika Lehmann so it worked. "Victor. Congratulations on the promotion. I didn't know about it until today when the committee referred to you as *Colonel.* Last I heard you were lieutenant colonel."

"The promotion came through a couple of years ago."

Leroy asked, "Are you still headquartered in Ulster?" Victor Knight applied for a post in Northern Ireland after he and Maeve married.

"We live in Belfast now. I'm attached to Regional Command. I was transferred from the Ulster Brigade when the promotion came through."

"Here's a belated toast to your promotion," said Leroy. They all raised and clinked glasses. "Maeve, how's your family?"

"No one's in the soil yet, but Ma and Da are feeble. Me brother moved to Dublin and married—three wee ones now running about, though I guess I should no longer call them *wee,* the oldest is nearly a teenager."

"I'm glad things worked out for your family," said Leroy. "They owe a great deal to you."

They placed food orders and time during the meal was used for more catching up. Kay filled in the Knights about life in South Carolina. At one point during dinner, Kay commented about the unusual ring Maeve wore on her right hand. Maeve replied it had been given to her during the war. Victor gave Leroy a rundown of his day-to-day duties with the British Army's Northern Ireland Regional Command. By the time her third Guinness was brought to her, Maeve was telling funny stories, some off color. One extremely explicit explanation of something she had suggested her husband try during their love-making turned Kay crimson and forced a laugh from Leroy. Maeve had not changed and he was glad. Victor could only sit silently with an "I gave up years ago" look.

"Good golly, Molly Maguire," Maeve blurted out. "That Guinness always goes through me faster than a bell clapper in a goose's arse. I have to take me pee. Oh, excuse me. Victor gets upset when I say that around company. I have to powder me nose. Will someone kindly point me to the loo?"

Kay couldn't figure out the goose simile, but still she liked the straightforward Irishwoman immensely. "I'll take you, Maeve."

As the women left the table, Leroy said, "Victor, this might surprise you but over the years I've thought often about John Mayne. He was a helluva man, and I know he was a good friend of yours."

"You're right on both, Leroy. As you know, it's not common for those in the secret services to receive the honors they deserve, but finally in 1949 John was awarded a posthumous Military Cross. Since he had no wife, his sister received it."

"Stephanie Fischer and Tars both received a posthumous Medal of Freedom from my country. Kathryn accepted Stephanie's. But we couldn't find anyone to accept Tars' medal." Leroy pulled a box from his jacket pocket. "It's been gathering dust in an archives warehouse for over a decade. Maeve should accept it on Tars' behalf. Tars would want that. I think Maeve was Tars' only friend." He handed the box to Victor.

"This will mean the world to Maeve, Leroy. She speaks of Tars often and still tears up on occasion." Victor opened the box and placed the heavy star attached to a blue-and-white ribbon on the table where Maeve would see it when she returned. "I was sorry to hear about Agent Hodge. I know he was your valued assistant for a long time."

"Al was a friend," said Carr. "I always thought of him more as my partner than my assistant." Al Hodge died of a heart attack in 1960.

"How is Skorzeny?" Knight asked. "Have you seen him since you retired?"

"Two years ago when Kay and I were in Paris on vacation he flew up from Madrid and the three of us attended the opera."

"I remember you telling me once that Otto sent your wife a bottle of champagne," said Knight.

"He still does. Every year on January 12th Kay receives a bottle of Spanish Cava with the note: *From an Admirer.*"

"January 12th?"

"That's the date he met Kay in Bath. I'm sure the wine carries double significance. He admires Kay, and he gets a kick out of reminding me of the date he captured me."

Knight laughed loudly.

A moment of silence followed before Carr asked, "Do you ever miss it, Victor?"

"Intelligence work?"

Carr nodded. Both men's careers in secrets had run a parallel course. Both the OSS and SOE were dissolved shortly after the war. Carr continued on in the CIA before retiring, while Victor moved to MI-6 for several years before resigning to return to where he started—the British Army.

"No, not really. I was in that game long enough, Leroy. How about you?"

"Same here. So, how was your visit to the White House this morning?"

"Nothing I wasn't expecting, old boy. Same questions I'll be asked till I go six-feet under. How did Himmler get another cyanide capsule after he was strip searched and his capsule found and taken from him? And there's always the query about the autopsy revealing he suffered a broken nose shortly before he died. All the questions leading to one: Did Churchill order me to Lüneburg to dispatch Himmler so the Reichsführer wouldn't reveal his peace negotiations with the British rumored to have begun long before he tried to contact Eisenhower near the end of the war?"

"And what was your answer?" This time both men laughed. Carr knew Knight would never reveal it if the rumor was true. "Of course you'll take it to your grave along with the other rumor that an unknown mystery woman joined you in Lüneburg shortly before Himmler died."

"Rumors abound, old friend," Knight said. "They always do with a death some consider puzzling, especially if the dead person is a well-known figure. But since we're speaking of rumors, I know Erika was forced to *walk in* to the CIA after the KGB discovered the damage she caused them. We knew about that at MI-6, of course. The Rooskies are still trying to recover from it. But none of us has heard a peep about what became of her since. For a time rumors swirled in certain circles that she was dead or living in Argentina. Then, according to later hearsay, our CIA friends gave her and the husband and daughter new names and shipped them out to someplace in America's heartland. I guess the daughter would be a young woman by now. There was even crazy gossip within MI-6 that the former Skorzeny commando is now a policeman somewhere here in America. Any truth to any of that?"

"Victor, I'm an attorney. If I answered with anything other than 'I don't know,' in a court of law it would serve as proof that I know of her whereabouts. As you said, *rumors swirl.*"

Leroy Carr smiled and raised his gin and tonic. "Here's to secrets and swirling rumors, Victor."

APPENDIX

Otto Skorzeny

Hard to find would be a list of the all-time greatest military commandos that does not have the name Otto Skorzeny at or very near the top. In fact, many military historians consider Skorzeny the father of modern-day "black ops" special forces, his daring exploits studied by military strategists to this day.

If Hollywood were to make a movie of Skorzeny's life, no embellishment would be required to add thrills; more likely, the screenwriters might feel pressured to remove or downplay some of his life's real adventures over concern audiences might scoff and shake their heads in disbelief.

Many books detail the wartime missions of Skorzeny and his band of elite commandos. Anyone interested in learning more need look no further than the Internet or their local library.

After the war, Skorzeny was tried for war crimes for masterminding Operation Greif, the Battle of the Bulge operation in which he sent a contingent of his English-speaking commandos behind the lines dressed in American Army officer uniforms to cause chaos in the American ranks. Skorzeny admitted to the charge. But during his trial, evidence was presented that Skorzeny's men did not engage in combat while dressed as Americans. When asked why, Skorzeny testified that doing so would have violated his own code of honor. Skorzeny's order that none of his men fire on Americans while dressed as Americans saved him. When a British SOE agent testified near the end of the trial that SOE agents had dressed in German uniforms while behind German lines, the American tribunal acquitted Skorzeny.

Upon his acquittal, the post-war German authorities promptly took Skorzeny into custody and held him without charges. In his memoirs, Skorzeny tells how the Americans helped him escape from the German detention camp. After his escape, Skorzeny began a lifetime of freedom and merrily traveling the world, eluding all attempts by German authorities to recapture him. Adopting disguises, he returned to Germany several times (seemingly whenever he felt like it) to visit old friends, some while they lay in hospital beds. He even attended funerals in Germany of former comrades.

Hitler's "personal commando" whom Eisenhower had dubbed "The Most Dangerous Man in Europe" finally settled in Spain. After being granted asylum by Franco, the former engineer from Vienna started his own engineering firm in Madrid and became a rich man.

For many, Otto Skorzeny will forever remain an enigma—on one hand admired for his courage in battle and keen sense of duty and honor; on the other hand reviled for never renouncing his Nazi past or severing ties to it. After the war, Skorzeny helped former SS men on the run escape to South America or other places around the globe through ODESSA, an organization he helped found. But then, in another ambiguity, while high on Simon Wiesenthal's list of wanted Nazis, Skorzeny helped the Israeli Mossad with intelligence concerning Iran and other Arab nations where he had conducted commando operations during the war and still maintained important contacts. And Skorzeny's collaboration with the CIA in its Cold War rivalry with the Russian KGB is no longer being denied.

Otto Skorzeny was reported to have died of cancer in 1975 at age 67. He received a Roman Catholic funeral but after his family declared the body had been cremated, at the time forbidden by the Church, eye brows rose. In the absence of a body to confirm his death, it has been impossible to discredit several Skorzeny sightings reported since 1975. Even death could not prevent Otto Skorzeny from offering the world one last puzzle.

Eileen Nearne

In September 2010, the body of a destitute 89-year-old woman was found in her apartment in Torquay, England. She had been dead for several days. Neighbors knew nothing about the recluse and authorities located no relatives. Given she had no personal wealth, certainly not enough to pay for a funeral, the woman's body was marked for the potter's field.